PENGUIN BOOKS

AUGUSTUS JOHN: A BIO

Michael Holroyd was born in 1935, studied science at Eton College and read literature at the Maidenhead Public Library. He has written biographies of Hugh Kingsmill, Lytton Strachey and Augustus John, and edited, with Robert Skidelsky, William Gerhardie's posthumous *God's Fifth Column*. From 1973 to 1974 he was Chairman of the Society of Authors, from 1976 to 1978 Chairman of the National Book League, and in 1985 became President of English P.E.N. Apart from his books, he has written scripts for radio and television, and lectured abroad for the British Council. He is married to the novelist Margaret Drabble and is at present working on the authorized biography of Bernard Shaw.

MICHAEL HOLROYD

Augustus John

A Biography

PENGUIN BOOKS

Penguin Books Ltd, Harmondsworth, Middlesex, England
Viking Penguin Inc., 40 West 23rd Street, New York, New York 10010, U.S.A.
Penguin Books Australia Ltd, Ringwood, Victoria, Australia
Penguin Books Canada Limited 2801 John Street, Markham, Ontario, Canada L3R 1B4
Penguin Books (N.Z.) Ltd, 182–190 Wairau Road, Auckland 10, New Zealand

—

First published in Great Britain in two volumes by William Heinemann 1974, 1975
First published in the United States of America
by Holt, Rinehart & Winston, Inc. 1975
Revised edition published in Penguin Books 1976
Reprinted 1987

—

—

Made and printed in Great Britain
by Richard Clay Ltd, Bungay, Suffolk
Set in Linotype Pilgrim

Poor soul, the centre of my sinful earth,
Fool'd by these rebel powers that thee array,
Why dost thou pine within and suffer dearth,
Painting thy outward walls so costly gay?

SHAKESPEARE, SONNET CXLVI

Contents

PART TWO:

THE YEARS OF EXPERIENCE

Note to the Revised Edition

Second editions are rarer than first and more valued by their authors. I have seized upon this edition to eliminate what blunders I could find from the original hardback publication and to incorporate some new information. I am indebted to those readers who have assisted me with this revision.

MICHAEL HOLROYD
DUBLIN 1976

PART ONE

The Years of Innocence

'the most innocent, wicked man I have ever met'
(W. B. YEATS TO JOHN QUINN, 4 OCTOBER 1907)

I

Little England beyond Wales

Who *am* I in the first place?   AUGUSTUS JOHN
Finishing Touches

1. 'MAMA'S DEAD!'

A regiment of women, monstrously feathered and furred, waited at Tenby railway station. The train that pulled in one autumn day in the year 1877 carried among its passengers a young solicitor and his wife, Edwin and Augusta John. With his upright figure, commanding nose, his brave whiskers and moustaches, he had more the bearing of a soldier than lawyer. She was a pale woman of twenty-nine, with small features, rather fragile-looking, her hair in ringlets. She was expecting their third child.

The train stopped, and the landladies of Tenby fell upon it, jostling over the new arrivals. But the Johns stood aloof. By prior arrangement the most regal of all the beldames swept across, escorted them to her carriage and drove them up the Esplanade to a large mauve building on the edge of South Cliffs: No. 50 Rope Walk Field.* From their windows they looked over the sea to Caldy Island and to a smaller island St Margarets, now a bird sanctuary, that at low tide seemed, like a long umbilical cord, to attach it to the mainland of Wales.

Augusta's other children were all born at home in Haverfordwest. But she and Edwin had decided that, for perfect safety, she should give birth to their third child in Tenby, Haverfordwest having recently been hit by an epidemic of scarlet fever. Soon after the New Year her labour pains began, and at 5.30 on the morning of 4 January 1878 the new baby was

---

* This lodging house was Corporation property owned by Ancient Grant. Its lease was assigned to William John on 23 October 1877. Two years later, on 27 December 1879, the lease was devised to William Williams.

born. It was a boy, and they named him after both of them: Augustus Edwin John.

Victoria Place, Haverfordwest, had been built in 1839 to commemorate the opening of the new toll bridge. The houses were narrow, and all had small square windows with wooden sides that sloped inwards, and windowsills you could sit on.

The John family lived at No. 7.* Almost immediately behind the front door rose a steep staircase. Small alcoves had been cut into the wall. From the second floor it was possible to see into Castle Square opposite, one side of which was formed by the Castle Inn with its ramparts and its archway down which coaches drove to the stables. Above this towered the ruined Norman castle, its stone windows gaping at the sky. All around the uneven slate roofs of the houses stretched, now high, now low, undulating away to the perimeter of the town. And beyond the town lay green hills that on summer evenings grew blue and hazy, and in winter, when there was frost, stood out hard.

In the eleven years of their marriage Edwin and Augusta John had two boys and two girls. Thornton was nearly three years older than Augustus; Gwen eighteen months older; and Winifred was born almost two years later.†

For all of them, Haverfordwest was a strangely exciting town in which to grow up. On market days the streets and square heaved with a pandemonium of country folk and animals – women from Langwm in short skirts, bright shawls and billy-

---

* After Augustus John's death in 1961 a plaque commemorating the place where he spent his early years was affixed by the Haverfordwest Council at No. 5 Victoria Place. On neither his brother's nor his sisters' birth certificates had any number been given. Winifred, who was still alive in America, could not remember the number; Thornton, nearing ninety and living in Canada, appears to have accurately copied down number 5 from the address (5, Tower Hill) of the solicitor who wrote to him asking after his birthplace.

No. 7 Victoria Place is now part of Lloyds Bank. The John family never bought the house, leasing it from a Mr Joseph Tombs. But the number is confirmed by several directories of the period in the National Library of Wales. No. 7 Victoria Place is also given on the birth certificate of Augustus's youngest uncle Frederick Charles John, born on 20 September 1856.

† The exact dates of their births were: Thornton, 10 May 1875; Gwendolen Mary, 22 June 1876; Winifred Maud, 3 November 1879.

cock hats carrying baskets of oysters on their backs; philo-
sophical-looking tramps wandering through with an air of
detachment and no obvious motive; and gypsies, mysterious
and aloof, shooting down sardonic glances as they rode by in
their ragged finery on horse and cart. And from this continuous
perambulation arose a cacophony – barking dogs, playing
children, the perpetual lowing of cattle, screaming of pigs and
the loud vociferation of the Welsh drovers.

For Augustus it presented a compelling spectacle to which
was added the irresistible lure of danger. For Papa had warned
them all against walking abroad on market days in case they
should be kidnapped by the gypsies and spirited away in their
caravans, no one knew where.* It was a warning Augustus
never forgot.

Regularly, on week-ends, Edwin John would lead out his
children on well-conducted expeditions in the outskirts of the
town. Augustus loved these walks. One of his favourites was
along a path known as 'the frolic' which ran south-east, parallel
to the river Cleddau where barges were pulled in over the
marshy ground to dilapidated wharves. There was a phenomenon here at which he never ceased to marvel. For, beyond
the tidal flats, in the middle distance, a railway train would
sometimes seem to issue, as if by magic, from the ruins of an
ancient priory and rumble industriously onwards under its
white banner till, with a despairing wail, it hurled itself into
the hillside: and vanished.

Another popular walk was along a right-of-way called 'the
scotch-wells'. Under a colonnade of trees this path followed
the millstream past the booming flour mill from which the
terrifying figure of its miller, white from head to toe, would
occasionally emerge. Sometimes, too, Papa would take them
along the Gyle, or the Parade, high above the Cleddau valley
and perilously close to the cottage of a known witch.

On all these walks Edwin John marched in front, preserving
a moderate speed – the pace, he believed, of a gentleman and
an officer – only halting, in primrose time, to pick a few of his
favourite flowers, to make a nosegay against the frightful

* Until 1850 the abominable crime of 'associating with gypsies' was
punishable by hanging.

exhalations of the tannery, or, when on the seashore, to gather shells for his collection. Behind him, heard but not seen, the children crocodiled out in an untidy line, darting here and there in a series of guerrilla raids.

On Sundays they were led or sent to Church. Augustus much preferred being sent with the servants to their humble Bethels, Zions and Bethesdas. The sonorous unintelligible language, the fervour of their singing, the obstinacy of their prayer, the surging and resurging crescendos of the orator who, like one possessed, worked himself up to that divine afflatus with which all good Welsh sermons must terminate, were awe-inspiring.

The religious atmosphere of Victoria Place was for several years fortified by two of the children's aunts, Rosina and Leah Smith.* They were younger sisters of Augusta, both in their twenties, and both ablaze with zeal for God. They had come to Haverfordwest from Brighton where they lived, when Augusta's health began to fail. After the birth of Winifred, Augusta seldom seems to have been well, and was often away for long periods. She suffered from chronic rheumatism which the damp climate of Haverfordwest was thought to aggravate, and she travelled much of the country in search of a cure. A photograph of her with the children, taken about the year 1882, shows that a surprising change had come over her. No longer is she the timid, withdrawn, delicate-looking girl at the time of her marriage. Perversely, she looks more alert and vigorous, her mouth hard-set, a brow like thunder, quick eyes. She has put on weight, and the severity of her expression is probably a sign of struggle against pain.

In her absence Rosina and Leah quickly took charge of the children's upbringing. One of their first demands was for the dismissal of their nurse, on the grounds that she had permitted the children to grow too fond of her. They had been allowed, for instance, to go to her cottage in the Prescelly mountains north of Haverfordwest, where they would sit wide-eyed over their bowls of *cawl*, stare at the dark-bearded woodmen with

---

* In *Chiaroscuro*, Augustus refers to these aunts as Rose and Lily. Whether in fact the children did call them by these names or whether he misremembered them many years later, one cannot be certain, but in the first draft of his autobiography he does name the elder aunt Rosina.

their clogs, thin-pointed and capped with brass, and argue on the way home whether their feet were the same shape. Few of these men knew a word of English. Old pagan festivals, long-forgotten elsewhere, still flourished, and on certain dates the children were given sprigs of box plant and mugs of water, and told to run along the stone flags of the streets asperging, with complete impunity, any stranger they met. These were habits of which Aunts Rosina and Leah could not approve.

The new regime under aunts was a bewildering experience for everyone. Both were Salvationists, held rank in General Booth's army, and abominated Roman Catholicism on account of its heretical worship of the Virgin Mary. These were the two fixed points on their religious horizon round which all else revolved. Aunt Leah, a lady of ruthless cheerfulness and an alarming eloquence, had once 'tried the spirits' but found them wanting. Also found wanting was a young man who had had the temerity once to propose marriage to her: she had rejected him, she explained, because of his *wickedness*. But she had been seduced by the Princess Adelaide's Circle, of which she soon became a prominent member.

Aunt Rosina was a more lugubrious character with a curious ferret-like face. Her choice of religion seemed to depend on her digestion, which was erratic. 'At one time it might be "The Countess of Huntingdon's Connexion", with raw beef and hot water, at another Joanna Southcote and grapes, or again, The Society of Friends plus charcoal biscuits washed down with Rowntree's Electric Cocoa.'[1]

In their quest for truth, and for the promotion of truth, the two aunts toured the neighbourhood of Haverfordwest in a wicker pony-trap known locally as 'the Hallelujah Chariot', bringing souls to Jesus. Their success was phenomenal. Strong men, it was said, pickled in sin, fell prostrate to the ground before them, weeping miserably. Edwin John, a man of violent moods rather than strong opinions, was certainly no match for them, and their presence dominated Victoria Place. Each day began with morning prayers, and continued with the aid of such improving tracts as *Jessica's First Prayer* and *The Lamplighter*.

Although, very naturally, the theatre was out of bounds, the

children were permitted without scruple to attend an entertainment called 'Poole's Diorama'. This was a precursor of the
cinema. It consisted of a vast historical picture, or series of
pictures which, to music and other sound effects, was gradually
unrolled on an apparently endless canvas across the stage. At
one corner a man with a wand pointed to features of interest
and shouted out his explanations to the audience, who could
thereby make these informed journeys through time and space
from the comfort of their seats. But when The Bombardment
of Alexandria was depicted the aunts judged matters had gone
far enough and, fearing that the infernal din would do permanent damage to the children's nerves, they bustled them
outside.

Even more exciting, though viewed with some family misgivings, was the children's first visit to the circus. Though later
in life Augustus used to object to 'that cruel and stupid convention of strapping the horses' noses down to their chests',
this circus, he claimed, corrupted him for life. It wasn't simply
a question of the animals, but the dazzling appearance of a
beautiful woman in tights, and of other superb creatures, got
up in full hunting kit and singing 'His moustache was down to
heah, Tiddy-foll-ol' and 'I've a penny in my pocket, La-de-dah'.

In summer the family used to go off to Broad Haven, twelve
miles away, where Edwin had had a one-storey house specially
built for him out of the local stone.* And the aunts came too.
But here the regime was less strict and the children happier.
Their house was on St Bride's Bay, had a large lawn and faced
the sea, in which the children spent much of their time. Yet
even in the waves they were not wholly beyond the religiosity
of the Welsh which extended offshore with their dangerous
ceremonies of Baptism by Total Immersion.

The Johns at this time were an isolated family. The uncompromising reputation of the aunts, the formidable respectability
of Edwin, and their rather dubious origins, limited their number
of friends while failing to win them entry into the upper
reaches of Haverfordwest society. The children were obscurely

---

* This house, though altered and now precariously named 'Rocks Drift', still
stands. It has a large entrance hall and stair well, drawing-room, dining-room
and six bedrooms. It was built using the stone from Settlands, the next bay.

aware of this insularity. They were at ease in the sea or roaming the wilds on their doorstep at Broad Haven, but in the company of other people they were abnormally nervous. 'Our invincible shyness,' Augustus later recorded, 'comparable only to that of the dwarf inhabitants of Equatorial Africa, resisted every advance on the part of strangers.' Their grandfather, William John, used to exhort them: 'Talk! If you can't think of anything to say tell a lie!' And: 'If you make a mistake, make it with authority!' But the children stayed speechless as before.

With his grandfather Augustus appears to have made no contact at all; while of his father, who was of remote and uncertain temper, he was much in awe and even afraid. Once, at the age of four, he was violently kicked upstairs by him – an incident of which he was to be poignantly reminded twenty-five years later. Between all the family the failure in communication seemed complete.

The only adults with whom Augustus appears to have formed any real contact were the servants. At Victoria Place the one room where he felt at home was the kitchen, and he passed many hours sitting on a 'skew' by the kitchen fire, listening to all the quick chatter and watching the comings and goings. Sometimes an intoxicated groom would stagger in, and the women would dance and sing to him till his eyes filled with tears of remorse. Unlike the upper storeys of the house, there was always warmth and laughter here, a sense of natural life going on.

Probably all the children needed the influence of their mother. But she was absent more and more. One day, in the second week of August 1884, the servants were lined up in the hall of Victoria Place, and Edwin John informed the household that his wife had died. The servants stood in their line, some of them crying quietly; but the children ran from room to room, chanting with senseless excitement: 'Mama's dead! Mama's dead!'

2. THE RESPONSIBLE PARTIES

'We come from a long line of professional people,' Edwin
John would tell Augustus when questioned by him about their
antecedents. Since he was then seeking to enter the freemasonry of fashionable Pembrokeshire society, Edwin, who
probably knew this to be untrue, had his reasons for not being
more explicit. But Augustus, who had little sense of belonging
to his parents' unknown families, feared it might be true and
was discouraged from probing further. They couldn't *all* have
been middle-class lawyers, he thought; then he would glance
at his father again and reflect that perhaps, after all, they had
been and it was better to remain in the dark. At least *he* would
be different.

In view of the many legends that were to camouflage
Augustus's origins – some of them amiably spread by himself
– it is important to establish the facts. Both his paternal great-
grandfathers, William John* and David Davies, were Welsh
labourers living in Haverfordwest; while on his mother's side
he came from a long line of Sussex plumbers, all bearing the
name Thomas Smith. William John's son, who was named after
him, was born in 1818. At the age of twenty-two he married
a local sempstress, Mary Davies, the same age as himself. On
the marriage certificate he described himself as a 'writer',
though whether this was a euphemism for clerk (as seems probable) or an indication of some literary aspirations is not now
known. That he had cultural interests, however, is certain. By
the end of his life he had collected a fair library including, most
prominently, leather-bound volumes of Dickens, Scott, Smollett
and an edition of Dante's *Inferno* with terrifying illustrations
by Gustave Doré; and he had done something rather unusual

---

* Besides being a labourer, William John had abilities as a violin player. 'I am
hoping that the musician will turn out to have been a wandering minstrel,'
Augustus wrote to H. W. Williams on discovering this fact (16 May 1952).
'. . . His musical gifts reappeared in one or two of my descendants.' Perhaps
the most celebrated musician among these descendants is the 'cello player
Amaryllis Fleming. Augustus's sister Winifred played the violin, and her
daughter Muriel Matthews is a respected 'cellist in America. Augustus's son
David was for many years an oboist in the Sadler's Wells orchestra, and
another son Edwin played the flute.

for a man of his class in the mid-nineteenth century: he had travelled through Italy, bringing back with him a fund of Italian stories and a counterfeit Van Dyck to hang in his dining-room.

If William John ever had ambitions to be an author, they were soon extinguished by his marriage, and on the birth certificate of their first child, Joanna, nine months later, his occupation is given unequivocally as 'attorney's clerk' – a job that was not to vary over the next fourteen years. They had begun their married life in a workman's cottage in Chapel Street, moved shortly afterwards to Prendergast Hill and in 1850 were living at 5 Gloster Terrace. Each move, though only a few hundred yards, denoted a rise in the world, and the climax was reached when, in 1855, they transferred to Victoria Place. On a modest scale, the career of William John was a considerable success story. His life appears to have been one of blameless diligence of a kind that would have horrified his grandson. In the Michaelmas Term of 1854 he was admitted as a solicitor and following this there was no holding back. He started his own legal firm in Quay Street, served for several years as town clerk of Haverfordwest, bought a number of properties and, on his death, left a capital sum of nearly eight thousand pounds. In politics he was a Liberal, and had acted as Lord Kensington's agent in all his contests up to the late 1870s. He had established himself as a much-respected figure in the district, well known for his speeches in Welsh at the Quarter Sessions. But although, in the various directories of the time, he is listed among the attorneys, he is not among the gentry.*

Between 1840 and 1856 William and Mary had six surviving children, three sons and three daughters. Edwin William John, the fourth child and second son, was born on 18 April 1847. No. 5 Gloster Terrace, where his earliest years were spent, was a tall thin house into which were crammed five children,†

* His obituary in the *Haverfordwest and Milford Haven Telegraph* (9 July 1884) notes that 'the remains of the deceased gentleman were interred this (Wednesday) morning in St Mary's Cemetery. The funeral was largely attended by the principal professional men, as well as the leading tradesmen of the town and neighbourhood.'

† Joanna (b. 1840), Emma (b. 1842), Alfred (b. 1884), Edwin, and Clara Sophia (b. 1849).

William and Mary, Mary's sister Martha Davies, fourteen years younger than herself, who helped to look after her nephews and nieces, and, rather confusingly, another Martha Davies of about the same age, who acted as a general servant.

In later years Edwin John let it be known that he was an old Cheltonian. In fact he was at Cheltenham only three terms and, according to his younger sister Clara, this single year produced a devastating effect upon him. His disposition, tolerable before he attended public school, was 'impossible' ever afterwards. He became victim to the cult of appearances. He forgot all he knew of the Welsh language and greatly exercised himself on the subject of his social reputation.

Edwin's main education, however, had been conducted locally in Haverfordwest. He knew Lloyd George's father, William George, a Unitarian schoolmaster who ran a private school in rooms he rented in Upper Market Street, and here Edwin went for several years. William George 'was a severe disciplinarian', he afterwards recalled, ' – rather passionate, sometimes having recourse to the old-fashioned punishment of caning'. His wife, whom he married while Edwin was at the school, was 'a sweet lady whom the boys liked very much'.

It was the eldest son Alfred, not Edwin, who had originally been intended for the law.* Alfred had married a Swansea girl and had had three children in three years, but after a period working in his father's law office his spirit suddenly revolted. While still in his twenties he ran away to London – and eventually to Paris – to play the flute, first in an orchestra, later on in bed. He was pursued, but to no avail. So, since he seemed determined to prove a black sheep,† the burden of family

---

* William John used to describe Alfred as a solicitor, though in fact he never passed the law exams, and probably acted as managing clerk, a position he could hold without legal qualifications.

† By reason of his dissimilarity to his younger brother Edwin, Alfred John came to fulfil Augustus's ideal of an English gentleman. His haggard good looks proclaimed an innocence, unconquered by lifelong poverty. Visiting his nephew one hot summer day, he accidentally revealed by a spontaneous gesture that, underneath his mackintosh, he wore no clothes at all. With equal innocence, he judiciously added to his family's name a 'St' and, as Alfred St John, was rewarded with a very fine funeral service, free of charge, by the clergy of St David's Cathedral.

responsibility was passed on to Edwin. He filled this role impeccably. Leaving Cheltenham at the age of sixteen, he was immediately articled to his father and, in the Easter term of 1870, admitted a solicitor. For a further two years he was employed as an assistant, after which, on his twenty-fifth birthday, William John made him a partner, and the practice became known as William John and Son. When William John retired seven years later, Edwin took it over entirely. He had done all that could have been expected of him, perhaps more.*

He had even married with his father's 'lawful consent'. The legal atmosphere appears to have been so thick that, on the marriage certificate, his wife accidentally gave her own profession as that of solicitor.† Her father Thomas Smith's profession she described as 'Lead Merchant', a delicate euphemism for plumber.

Thomas and Zadock Smith had been born at Chiddingly in Sussex, the sons of Thomas Smith, a village plumber. The elder son, who inherited his father's business, moved to Brighton and in 1831, at the age of twenty-two, married Augusta Phillips. They lived in Union Street, and between 1832 and 1840, produced three children, Sarah Ann, Emily and Thomas who was later to inherit the Smith plumbing business. That there may have been other children who did not survive seems probable. In any event, early in 1843, Augusta was again pregnant and her condition must have been serious. She was given an abortion, but afterwards was attacked by violent fevers. On 25 May, at the age of thirty-two, she died.

* Edwin was made the main beneficiary of William John's will, which is dated 14 June 1881. From this document it appears that his two eldest daughters Joanna and Emma had already died, and that his youngest son, Frederick Charles John (then aged twenty-four), had, like Alfred, turned out in his father's opinion a ne'er-do-well. Each of them was left a small annual income provided that, at the time of William John's death, he was not 'an uncertified bankrupt or through his own act or default or by operation or process of law or otherwise disentitled personally to receive or enjoy the same during his life or until he shall become bankrupt', etc. Frederick Charles John died on 9 April 1896, aged thirty-nine.

† It was not until the removal of the Sex Disqualification Act in 1919 that women were permitted to qualify as solicitors. The first woman was admitted in 1922.

A year later Thomas Smith married again. His second wife was a twenty-six-year-old girl, Mary Thornton, the daughter of William Vincent Thornton, a cupper from Cheltenham. Before her marriage she was living in Ship Street, Brighton, and it was here that Thomas Smith and his three children now moved. In the next fourteen years they had at least ten children,* but the mortality rate among the boys was high, four of them dying before their twelfth birthday. As befitted the grandfather of Augustus John, Thomas Smith was 'a person of full habit of body' and outlived nine of the seventeen children he had by his two wives.

In its way Thomas Smith's career was comparable to that of William John, and from humble beginnings he became a successful and much respected local figure. By the age of fifty he was a Master Plumber, glazier and painter, employing ten men and three boys in the painter's shop he had bought next door in Ship Street, and in the home a cook, housemaid and nursemaid. His will is a chauvinistic document that might well have drawn a word of approval from the Town Clerk of Haverfordwest. In one respect at least it is superior to William John's: he left a sum of almost fourteen thousand pounds.

Mary Smith's third child, born on 22 September 1848, was named Augusta after her father's first wife. From a comparatively early age she appears to have shown a talent for art. She was sent to 'Mrs Leleux's Establishment' at Eltham House in Foxley Road, North Brixton, and here, in December 1862, she was presented with a book, *Wayside Flowers*, as a 'Reward for Improvement in Drawing'.

She continued drawing and painting up to the time of her marriage, and to some extent afterwards. The few examples of her work that still remain show that her subjects were mostly pastoral scenes. A study of Grasmere Church, seen across a tree-lined river and delicately executed in soft cool colours, is

* Benjamin died on 12 January 1856 of hydrocephalus and convulsions, aged two months; William had died six days earlier from the same cause, aged one year and eleven months; Sydney died after fourteen days of diarrhoea on 13 August 1861, aged five weeks; and Thornton, on 15 May 1861, aged eleven years, died of congestion of the brain, fever and debility.

signed Augusta Smith and dated 1865*; a picture of cattle with friendly human faces, painted three years later when she was nineteen, is signed 'Gussie'. But a charming Landscape with Cows painted after her marriage and simply signed 'A. John' is part of the celebrated Dalton Collection in Charlotte, North Carolina, where, attributed to her son, it hangs happily in company with Constables, Rembrandts, Sickerts and Turners.

But for Augusta painting was only a pastime, and she had no thought of any professional career. Her father's taste for biblical christian names, and the fact that almost none of his daughters married before his death, suggests an Old Testament view of women's place in the scheme of things to which, while he lived, Augusta was obedient. But on the night of Thursday, 20 February 1873, Thomas Smith suffered a stroke. His intellect was unaffected, and for five days he lay paralysed on his bed, gradually sinking under the attack until, at four o'clock on the following Thursday afternoon, he died.

His relatives filled three mourning coaches at the cemetery. Such was his reputation as an honest plain-dealing tradesman that, despite appalling weather, a great concourse of people gathered at the grave, while in Brighton itself nearly every shop in his part of the town had one or two shutters up. 'In fact,' the *Brighton Evening News* (4 March 1873) commented, 'so general a display of shutters is seldom to be seen on the occasion of a funeral of a tradesman, only but honourably distinguished by his strict and uniform integrity during a long business career.'

Four months later, on 3 July, Augusta married Edwin John at St Peter's Church in Brighton. It was said to be a love match. One of the tastes they held in common was for music: she would play Chopin on the piano, while he preferred religious music and in later life wrote a number of 'chaste and tuneful compositions' for the organ, including a setting for the Te Deum and a Berceuse. The three eldest children, who were unmusical, were all encouraged to draw, and a large pencil

---

* Now in the Tenby Museum. It is believed to be a copy of a Cox. The picture of cattle is owned by Muriel Matthews, Augusta's American granddaughter.

drawing of a dog by Thornton John testifies to the fact that he too inherited his mother's ability.

But the strongest reaction Augusta produced on all her children came through her absence. She died, apparently among strangers, at Ferney Bottom, Hartington, in Derbyshire. The cause of her death was given as rheumatic gout and exhaustion. She was thirty-five years old;* and Augustus was six-and-a-half.

3. DEATH WITH FATHER

The year 1884 was for Edwin John a particularly unhappy one. Everything had gone wrong. His marriage, ruined latterly by his wife's ill-health, was at an end; and his father, who had been suffering from what the locals called 'water on the brain', had died the previous month.† He had four children, two fanatical sisters-in-law, few friends, but an army of voluble neighbours who, with eager pessimism, would point, particularly to Winifred, and exclaim: 'Is this the little motherless child? She doesn't know yet how terrible it is – *but she will later!*'

That autumn Edwin made a great decision, gave up his practice in Victoria Place, sold his house at Broad Haven and, taking with him two Welsh servants from Haverfordwest, moved to Tenby where, for a short spell, he had enjoyed unclouded happiness with Augusta. Leah and Rosina left too, transferring their proselytizing zeal to the wider horizons of the New World,‡ and leaving Edwin to lapse back into the

---

* The death certificate inaccurately gives her age as thirty-four.

† William John died of cerebral softerina on 6 July 1884.

‡ Aunt Leah went straight to America where she picked up a slight American accent and a large band of marching American disciples. Aunt Rosina's travels were more circuitous, and her destinations always preceded by a series of brown paper parcels. Sustained by a diet of over-ripe fruit and protected by a dense fur muff, she set off for Switzerland from where she wrote a number of indecipherable letters in purple ink testifying to her brief enthusiasm for Dr Coué, a gentleman who had propounded the theory that if everyone repeated 'Every day in every way I am getting better and better' many thousands of times, the world might become a more cheerful place. From here she went to Japan, where she collected a miniature Japanese maid, and later, improbably passing through Mason, Nevada, married Owen H. Bott, a druggist with two sons. Under the pitiless blue of the Californian skies, she caught up with Winifred, terrifying her children with her severe cotton-wool hair, her

Bosom of the Church-in-Wales.* He was thirty-seven years of age – not too late to start another life.

Victoria House, 32 Victoria Street, into which he and his young family now moved was a very ordinary mid-nineteenth-century terrace house, with three main floors, a basement for servants and an attic for children. It stood just round the corner from Belgrave House.

Augustus disliked his new home almost from the beginning. Dark and cube-like, with a peeling false façade, it was like a cage and he a bird caught within it, unable to use his wings. Set in a dreary little street off the Esplanade, from where you could hear but not see the Atlantic, it was furnished without taste or imagination, its dull mahogany tables and chairs, its heavy shelves of law tomes and devotional works, its appalling conglomeration of unauthentic Italian pottery, pseudo-ivory elephants and fake Old Masters – all tourist souvenirs from William John's European wanderings – contributing to the atmosphere of mediocrity and gloom. In the twelve years he lived here, Augustus came to feel that it was not a proper home nor was Edwin John a real father. Existence there was a sort of death. 'I felt at last that I was living in a kind of mortuary where everything was dead,' he records, 'like the stuffed doves in their glass dome in the drawing-room, and fleshless as the abominable "skeleton-clock" on the mantelpiece: this museum of rubbish, changing only in the imperceptible process of its decay, reflected the frozen immobility of its curator's mind.'[2]

The key to Edwin John's character was a form of acute anxiety. For what he had lost with the death of his wife, for all he had seemed prevented from attaining by his terrible reserve, he found solace in the contemplation of a stubbornly unspent bank balance.

The regime at Victoria House was a direct expression of this financial and emotional stringency. Sometimes, at night, the children were so cold that they would pile up furniture on

---

humped back and restless scuttling from place to place, and her pale grey eyes that seemed to glare at them with ceaseless displeasure.

* Gwen, Augustus and Winifred were baptized at St Mary's Church, Tenby, on 21 January 1886.

their beds. During the daytime, too, the atmosphere was scarcely warmer. Meals were particularly grim. Though timid in public, Edwin was something of an authoritarian at home and demanded of his children an unquestioning obedience. He was determined to do the right thing – and the right thing, it seemed, so often combined unpleasantness with parsimony. Gwen, who abhorred rice pudding, was required to swallow it to the last mouthful; Winifred, who was rather fragile when young, was specially fed on a diet of bread-and-butter pudding full of raisins which she was convinced were dead flies. The children's tastes were never consulted. Certain food was bought because it was cheap, and eaten because it was there.

But more awful than anything else were the silences. Whether because of his shyness or of some deep vein of melancholia, Edwin seemed shut off from his children, as from all other people, unable to mix or communicate with them. Breakfast, lunch and eventually dinner were eaten sometimes without a word spoken. Once, when Winifred hazarded some whispered remark, Edwin turned on her and asked sarcastically: 'Oh, so you've found it at last, have you?'

'Found what?'

'Your tongue.'

After which the silence plummeted deeper.

When they were very young Gwen and Winifred invented a touch and facial expression language, but were forbidden to use it in the house since it made them look so hideous. So they would go upstairs before each meal and try to decide in advance what each would say.

'I'm going to say ...'

'No. I want to say that.'

'I thought of it first.'

'Well, I'm the eldest.'

Augustus's method of non-communication was at the same time more simple and more sophisticated. On one occasion, at a fairground, he had seen a boy of about his own age fall off a roundabout and be led away bleeding at the mouth. This scene had so impressed him that he later transferred it to himself. When called upon to answer some question he would struggle gallantly with his partly amputated tongue but be quite unable to enunciate anything beyond a few grunts. This handicap left him at last when he became a self-elected son of the Antelope Comanche Indians, crying 'Ugh! Ugh!'

In this bleak atmosphere, small occasions assumed a grand importance. Games, birthday parties, Christmases gave rise to moods of almost unbearable excitement. Though excessively formal, Edwin John was not an unkindly man and, his parental prerogative once set aside, he could be humane and even playful. At night, the children would tell him what to play on the piano, and the sound of his scrupulous rendering would float up to their icy bedrooms. He also read to them in the evenings from *Jane Eyre* and Mme Blavatsky's *Isis Unveiled*, from bowdlerized versions of *The Arabian Nights* and, more haltingly, from the complete works of a Flemish writer, Hendrijk Conscience, translated into French – a language in which Edwin was being tutored by Monsieur de Berensburg, a Belgian exile in Tenby. All his children had a quick ear for languages, and Gwen and Winifred were for a time taught by a French governess who was so delighted by their progress that she told their father it must be due to some French ancestry. This intended compliment so shocked Edwin that he discontinued the lessons and substituted in their place instruction in German grammar – the declensions of which, Winifred later claimed, turned her against the whole nation for life.

As at Haverfordwest, it was the servants who enjoyed themselves most and they were much envied by the other servants in Tenby. Shrieks of laughter were often to be heard rising from the basement and invading the funereal stillness of Edwin John's rooms. Occasionally relatives called, and the children would be dragged out from behind furniture and under beds to deliver their cold kisses.

But it was not an unhappy life. Their emotions were chiefly directed to their animals, the sea, wild countryside and to the occasional best friend. Gwen had a cat, Mudge, who fought. Out walking, Edwin would meet him on the town wall, torn, bleeding and looking so disreputable that he refused to recognize him and would hasten his pace to shake him off. But when Winifred lost her spaniel Floss, Edwin arranged for the town crier to walk through Tenby ringing his bell and shouting out the news. And once Floss was found, he hurried round, accompanied by a maid, to interrupt her lessons and tell her.

Thornton grew into a small quiet boy, more at home in the sea than on land. Rather slow and very precise in his speech, with an air of unblinking naïvety, his calmness would provoke Augustus into all sorts of exasperating tricks to discover the limits of his endurance. Destined by his father to be an engineer, he cherished a romantic ambition to live the life of a gold prospector, and before the age of twenty left luggageless for Canada, sprouted a moustache and spent the next seventy years happily, though with complete unsuccess, digging.*

The two girls, Winnie with long fair hair down her back, and Gwen who was dark, used to walk about Tenby alone, which was regarded then as very peculiar. Both were intensely shy, but whereas Winnie was timid, with a self-deprecating sense of humour, Gwen's unobtrusiveness contained a far more intractable nature. Together they used to go for long bicycle rides along the green Pembrokeshire lanes, climbing on to the stone walls whenever they met a flock of sheep. Once they encountered a company of soldiers, whose officer gave a word of command as they approached so that the columns of men separated, allowing them just room to ride down the centre, at full speed, blushing furiously.

Winifred, who was to become an accomplished violinist in

---

* Either he would discover a good partner and no gold, or gold and a partner who ran off with it. But, except for a brief period when he dreamed of starting a tobacco factory in Ireland, he seemed to have found what he really loved — mountains, prairies, horses and empty spaces. Among the trappers, cowboys and prospectors he soon earned the honourable title of 'the rider from away back', and, in company with a band of these wild and woolly fellows, crossed Canada on horseback, fording rivers and bathing in hot springs till his skin turned orange. Above all he relished solitude and for some years before 1914 went to live beside an Indian encampment, whose inhabitants would suddenly appear outside his tent, sit for hours silently smoking their long pipes, then vanish. He also travelled through Montana 'and always on horseback'; he wrote: 'I used to make my bed on the ground without a tent, and the dawn was the most important part of the day.' He married late in life a woman who had had two previous husbands and whom he discovered after her death to have been twenty years older than he thought. He had no children, but one foster daughter. He died in British Columbia on 19 March 1968, aged ninety-two.

America,* and who also loved dancing, shared many of her sister's tastes, in particular her strange affinity for the sea and passion for flowers. But Gwen's need for these things, nurtured by greater solitude, was more obsessive. She used to dream of flowers as others dream of people, and she would spend the last halfpenny of her pocket money on them if she could not pick them. Out of sight of her father and the well-dressed persons of Tenby, she loved to throw off all her clothes and run along the beaches.

In this wildness, and the quick switchback of her emotions, Gwen resembled Augustus much more closely than Winifred or Thornton† who were both softer personalities. Gwen was naturally independent. She and Augustus would stage elaborate arguments as to who was the elder, neither of them appealing

* From Paris, where she stayed with Gwen, Winifred crossed the Atlantic while still in her early twenties. By the summer of 1905 she had reached Montana, living some months with Thornton surrounded by Indians, 'rattle-snakes and all sorts of wild animals'. The two of them planned to travel to Mexico, by boat, along the Mississippi. 'The idea of orange groves and sunlight is *enchanting*,' Augustus wrote to her, '– but too remote from *my* experience to be anything but a lovely dream. But depend on it, you have only to perjure yourselves to its reality to bring this family at any rate helter skelter on your tracks . . . I can just *see* you and Thornton installed on the top of some crumbling teocalli with the breath of the Pacific in your nostrils.' Eventually this plan was abandoned, and Winifred journeyed instead to Vancouver where 'the weather was perfect: it rained every day', and to San Francisco, 'a beastly town'. For a number of years she gave violin lessons in California, and on 30 January 1915 married one of her pupils, Victor Lauder Shute, a failed painter who had turned engineer and worked mostly for the railroads. They had three children, Dale, Betty and Muriel, a fourth child being still-born in 1924. Although she claimed to have developed 'such strong nerves I have played to a room full of people and forgot everybody', she always preserved her extreme shyness. When, during the First World War, she wanted to write to her friend Irene about the birth of one of her children, she felt it was so delicate a matter that she would have to use code – with the result that her friend was arrested by Scotland Yard.

She never returned to Wales or England, but died in Martinez on 12 April 1967, aged eighty-seven.

† But to some extent Thornton certainly shared the melancholia that affected Gwen and Augustus. Writing to Augustus on 18 March 1947 he refers to Gwen's 'moods of sadness' and adds: 'It is not for me to pry into this but I fully understand her for I have felt the same tendency myself – perhaps it is hereditary.'

for judgement to Papa because, they explained, they would then have to find something else to argue about.

More than half of Augustus's life at this time was fantasy. He would ransack his father's library for books and, poring over them, seem to leave his body and hover on the threshold of other worlds. When he read the story of Gerda and Little Kay, he was overcome by ungovernable tears, and had to shut himself away in his room. His favourite author was Gustave Aimard, whose tales of Red Indians absorbed him. So personal was his feeling for these books that he took to studying his father's features in the hope of discovering in them some trace of Antelope blood.

But it was outside Victoria House that Augustus came fully alive. Striding through the streets of Tenby on the tallest stilts, diving off rocks and swimming far out into the cold Atlantic, gathering wild strawberries that overhung the cliff tops, exploring hidden ways, gazing fearfully down disused coal pits or up through the terrifying blow-holes that bellowed out volumes of yellow sea-spume over the fields, or wandering alone across the salt-marshes up to the rock-pools in the hills where the snow outlasted the winter, listening to the larks in the long summer evenings, chasing the butterflies, building castles in the open air – Augustus was in his element.

Outdoors he seemed completely fearless. One day, coming across an untethered horse, without a word he jumped on it bareback. As it started to gallop along, he fastened his arms about its neck but slowly began sliding off until he was soon hanging down in front of it. So this odd pair hurtled towards the horizon. But in the end, when the horse had finally come to a halt, Augustus was still clasped to it. His climbing exploits were extraordinary. He would descend the dizzy perpendicular rock-cliffs between Giltar and Lydstep to wet shingle beaches and, like Gwen, fling off his clothes and perform wild antics in and out of the water while the tide advanced giving him that special thrill which came from not being quite sure of getting back again.

In particular he loved the harbour at Tenby with its fleet of luggers and fishing-smacks, and the russet sails of the trawlers in Tenby Bay; and he loved the long expanse of Tenby beach, its sand spongy like cake – a golden playground two miles long. Here, while still very young, Augustus would play all day with his brother and sisters, catch shrimps in the tidal pools where sea-urchins delicately flowered, paddle through the shallow waves that gently broke seething and criss-crossing the shore, dig, fill and elaborately haul buckets of sand up the blue, slate-coloured cliffs. Where the sea had worn these cliffs away tunnels and devious caves had been hollowed out, as if gnawed by giant sea-mice – dark, dangerous and exciting. Great slabs of slate rock lay bundled at the entrances, covered with barnacles and emerald sea-weed.

This beach was the fashionable meeting place for all Tenby. Under the cliffs a band played patriotic airs and nigger minstrels sang and danced; donkeys, led by donkey-boys and ridden by well-dressed infants, trotted obediently to and fro; gentlemen in boaters or top hats and ladies in long skirts with wasp waists carrying parasols promenaded the sands, inspecting from a safe distance the calm and superficial sea. Every week-day, bathing – a complicated procedure in voluminous serge costumes – was permitted before 8 a.m. and after 8 p.m. Between these hours horse-drawn bathing machines, strewn along the sands, had to be used – and bathing from boats was not lawful within two hundred yards of the shore. These bathing-machines were upright carriages on wheels, advertising the benefits of Beecham's pills and Pears soap. They were looked after by a company of boys, celebrated for their vulgarity, who shocked Augustus by whispering unheard-of obscenities – 'Bloody Bugger!' – into his ears. A frantic man, summoned by the shouts of these boys, would canter up and down the sands harnessing horses to the vehicles which were pulled out deep into the ocean. The occupants could then enter the water with the least possible hazard to modesty. Once they had completed their swimming, they would re-enter their horse-drawn dressing-room, regain their clothes, then raise a flag as a signal that they were ready to be towed back.

As he grew older, Augustus began to avoid this beach, roaming beyond North Cliff Point where he and his companions could bathe from the rocks and bask naked in the sun. He longed for a wider world than that symbolically enclosed by the town walls of Tenby and was happiest when he and his brother and sisters were invited to stay at Begelly, in a house on the hill overlooking an infertile common populated by geese, cattle and the caravans of romantic-looking gypsies. Here, and with the Mackenzie family at Manorbier, the rules and repressions of Tenby were forgotten, Papa was left behind, and the strangely brooding children of Victoria Street were transformed into a turbulent troupe of Johns, running wild.

One of Augustus's best friends at this time was a boy, eighteen months younger than he, called Arthur Morley. With their butterfly nets, the two boys spent much of their time wandering along the dunes. 'We used to go for walks together, sometimes to a place known as Hoyle's Mouth, a cave in a limestone cliff about 1½ miles from the town near a marsh where flew many orange-tip butterflies,' Morley later recalled. 'On the floor of the cave we used to dig pre-historic animals ... We found that leading out of this cave there was a second which we could reach by crawling along a very small passage with a lighted candle.'[3]

His greatest friend was Robert Prust, whose family occupied, with their parrot, a fine house on the south cliff. Robert Prust was keen on Red Indians, and for a long time Augustus hero-worshipped him. The two of them would lead out a pack of braves along the rough grass tracks, across the sand-dunes known as 'the Burrows' to advance upon the army encampment at Penally. No one took his Indian life more seriously than Augustus. 'Under the discipline of the Red Man's Code,' he wrote, 'I practised severe austerities, steeled myself against pain and danger, was careful not to betray any emotion and wasted few words.'[4] Such a Spartan regime was eventually too much for his companions who, one by one, abandoned the warpath to chase instead the paleface Tenby girls. At last only the two of them were left. The final betrayal came when, having helped Augustus set fire to a wood, Robert Prust revealed a most un-Indian lack of stoicism by breaking down. So Augustus was left to roam the Burrows alone, attended by a phantom tribe of Comanches.

The cult of the Red Indian was, for Augustus, more than a game: it gave him an alternative world to Tenby. Yet everywhere there were encroachments. His hunting-ground, the Burrows, was soon converted into a golf-links; the nigger minstrels under the cliffs were replaced by a refined troupe of Pierrots who could be invited with impunity to tea; even the annual fair, with its blaring cacophony of roundabouts spinning away late into the night, was removed from under the old town walls to a field on the outskirts.

Tenby, in the last two decades of the nineteenth century, had become a town much favoured by relatives of the county landowners of Pembrokeshire, by retired colonels and elderly sea-dogs. It was also a fashionable holiday resort for the upper-middle class who arrived each summer to play their golf, badminton and high-lobbing lawn tennis, to shoot, to hunt foxes and otters. There were regattas, much blowing of marine music, balls in the Royal Assembly Rooms and, in the evening, the twilight ritual of the slow promenade along the cliffs.

Everywhere the strictest rules of snobbery were observed. Edwin John much applauded this scheme of things. One of the first things he did was to throw away his professional brass plate – though he continued intermittently and on the quiet to practise law from his home as if it were a not quite reputable occupation or, at best, merely a gentleman's whim or hobby, like his amateur shell collecting. He associated himself with the church, and was appointed assistant organist at St Mary's. Every Sunday morning he would insist on lining up his children, like small soldiers, in the hall, to be inspected before they set off for the service. He himself, in a top hat and frock coat, led the way, and drew many curious glances. He did more: he took up photography; he played the harmonium; he entered cold baths in the early morning; above all he did – and was conspicuously seen to do – absolutely nothing whatsoever. He saw to it that his manner was never less than frigidly unapproachable: and no one approached him. It was very odd. He redoubled his efforts. His hair grew white, his cheeks turned pink, his collection of cowries multiplied, his walks became longer and longer, his collars, always of the stiffest, stiffened even further: everywhere throughout the district his gentility and rectitude were freely acknowledged. But with the elite of Tenby – the Prusts and Swinburnes, the Morleys and Massays and Hannays and de Burghs, whose children were Augustus's companions, Edwin was never on visiting terms. For although his propriety was unexampled, curious rumours persisted of some scandal back at Haverfordwest – rumours fanned into life by Augustus's lively imagination.

The conformist who sacrifices all for his conformity usually achieves the unconventional. Edwin John was an eccentric who detested eccentricity. He longed for the superior decorum of polite society, yet the drawing-rooms of Tenby remained closed to him, and he took his place, quite unaware, among the town's most bizarre characters – with the gentleman who tied a rope to his topmost window and, shunning stairs, swarmed up and down it; and with another who wore socks on his hands; with the lady who struggled to keep an airless house, stuffing paper into every crevice of window and door; with Cadwalladyr, the speechless shrimper, massive and hairy and never less than up to his waist in water; and with Mr Prydderch, bank manager and Captain of the Fire, who, 'swaggering fantastically, his buttocks strangely protuberant', paraded the town to the music of a brass band until captured and confined to Carmarthen Lunatic Asylum.

From the start, Edwin John made sure that his children were seen to be educated in the most proper manner. Nothing excessive was required; in particular the girls' education was so reticent as to be almost invisible. As soon as the family had settled into their house at Tenby, Gwen and Winifred were sent to what was referred to as a 'private school' a few yards away in Victoria Street. This school took its privacy almost to the point of secrecy. It consisted, *en masse*, of three pupils, the mother of the third one, a German lady married to a sequestering philosopher named Mackenzie, acting as teacher. This arrangement combined for Edwin the advantages of cheapness with those of social prestige in claiming for his daughters a foreign 'governess', optimistically described as 'Swiss'. Mrs Mackenzie was a kind and homely woman who, to a limited extent and more especially with Winifred, took the place of their mother. Her daughter Irene became a particular friend of Winifred's – the two of them laughed so much together that if one caught sight of the other even on the horizon she would be convulsed with giggles. Gwen, at this time, suffered from a type of back trouble that gave Mrs Mackenzie's lessons a drastic appearance. On doctor's advice Gwen would spend hours stretched out on the schoolroom floor, where both Irene and Winifred insisted on joining her.

When they were older both of them attended Miss Wilson's academy, a school that placed more emphasis on impeccable conduct than scholarship. Miss Wilson herself was an ice-cold woman of unguessable age, who wore an expression of un-relieved sternness and who later committed suicide by striding off into the sea. On one occasion she took Gwen, Winifred and some of their friends on an excursion to Manorbier Castle, and on the way home it was proposed they give three cheers for her. 'Hip, hip ...' they began, as Miss Wilson stood stonily facing them – but halfway through the cheer died out into a series of frantic whispers: 'Why didn't you go on?' – 'I was waiting for you ...'

Augustus's education was equally unusual. Late in 1884 he went to an infant school in Victoria Street, and at the age of ten was sent to join his brother at Greenhill, a rambling build-ing set on a plateau on the slopes of lower Tenby.* This school catered both for the sons of tradesmen and of the middle classes, and its pupils, faithfully mimicking the ways of their parents, segregated themselves into two classes: 'gentlemen' and 'cads'. It was run by Mr Goward, a tiny man with a large spectacled face topped by a flame of hair, and invariably dressed in mock-clerical neckwear and curiously short turned-down trousers. An ardent Liberal and Congregationalist, he began each day with a Gladstonian homily, followed, accord-ing to his mood, by hymns or, more secularly, a rendering of 'Scots, wha hae!'

Gussie, as everyone called him, was a mutinous pupil. He was always getting into trouble for breaking school rules, libellously caricaturing the masters and retaliating when cor-

---

* This building (the original house of which was built by Edmund Morgan in the 1830s) has now been converted into a public library. In the cemented grounds are two trees, an oak planted in memory of Augustus, and a birch in memory of Gwen. Greenhill School carries on, but has moved to the outskirts of Tenby.

rected. With the other boys he seems to have been popular. It was here that he won his first serious stand-up fight, collapsing into uncontrollable tears after his victory as if in sympathy with the loser.

It was here, too, that he received from the drill master a smashing blow on the ear that, for the rest of his life, made him partially deaf.

Regularly, every term, his misdeeds were reported to his father who meticulously committed them to paper. Then, one day, something shocking happened: Augustus struck the second master – instead of the other way about – and Edwin felt he could ignore these delinquencies no longer. Having entered this last enormity in his ledger, he summoned Augustus to his study, read out the full catalogue of his crimes stretching over the years and with an impassioned cry of 'Now, sir!' had, to use his own words, 'recourse to the old-fashioned punishment of caning'. The decline in Edwin's authority began from that day. Essentially a passive man, whose chief ambition for his children was that they should cause no trouble for him, he was unable to inject any conviction into his performance as irate pater-familias: he simply didn't care enough. And Augustus, sensing this, began to lose respect for him.

When, shortly after this incident, Mr Goward left Greenhill for British Columbia, Thornton and Augustus were sent to boarding school at Clifton, near Bristol. This choice is, at first sight, rather curious. Edwin had not planned for either of his sons to go to his own school; possibly he was not anxious for them to find out just how tenuous his connection with Chelten-ham had been. The new school, however, took a number of pupils from Pembrokeshire and was well thought of in Tenby. Edwin, at any rate, was glad to be released from the perpetual company of his sons, and may well have looked for a change in them similar to his own. If so, he was disappointed.

Augustus never fitted into this school. The top hat, Eton jacket and collar uniform made him feel uncomfortable and faintly ridiculous. At football, which he liked, he played centre forward and achieved some success. But cricket, by which his father set great store, left him cold – it was so elaborately unspontaneous: he could never bowl, the long drudgery of fielding bored him unutterably, and at batting, which seemed more promising, he was always being given out. It was while day-dreaming on the cricket field that a ball struck him on his ear and did for that one what the drill instructor's baton had successfully done for the other at Greenhill.

In the foreign atmosphere of the English preparatory school Augustus was strangely shy. Though strong for his age he seldom entered into the tribal games of the other boys and he made no lasting friendships. The only boy for whom he cared at all was, like himself, an outcast from the community, being a half-wit, but so sweet-natured that Augustus at once befriended him.

Everything that appealed to him at this time seemed to lead him away from Clifton – the river Avon flowing westwards under wooded cliffs towards the Golden Valley and the sea; the docks of Bristol where, for a few pence, it was possible to watch a platoon of rats being mauled to death by a dog or ferret; and, in the dark autumn evenings, while he was at prep., the distant wail of an itinerant street vendor, stirring in him a painful longing, like despair.

'Gloom, boredom and anguish of mind'[5] were his predominant moods at Clifton, but they did not last long. Early in 1891 he left to continue his schooling back at Tenby which, for all its disadvantages, was still the only home he knew.

St Catharine's, where he passed the next two-and-a-half years, was a brand new spick-and-span school which had recently opened on the north-east corner of Victoria Street.* It had just one classroom and only seven pupils – though this number doubled later on – and the atmosphere was like that of a family party, far happier than at Clifton.

'A lonely adolescent' was how Augustus later described himself up to the age of sixteen. Sometimes he was rebellious, at other times rather staid – but at all times conspicuous. There appeared to be two sides to his character that set up within him a curious tension. From time to time he claimed to be a descendant of Owen Glendower, and was readily believed. But when one boy, Peel minor, expressed scepticism, Augustus

---

* At the junction with South Cliff Street. Recently the property has become the Hallsville Hotel.

marched up to him glaring terrifically and waving his fists before his nose. This argument had a devastating effect, and the
doubter retired in confusion.

The school was so small it could not raise a full team for
any game, and they devised all sorts of ingenious miniature
variations – hockey on roller skates on a concrete rink; four-a-
side football; golf on the sand dunes with one club; and a
game with wooden sticks with which you endeavoured, without being hit yourself, to hit your opponent's elbow. Augustus
enjoyed all these sports without going out of his way to excel
in them. But there was one game at which he was in his
element. 'We each had to make a shield of some sort and were
given six tennis balls,' Arthur Morley remembered.

We were then divided into two sides ... The idea was to attack
the other side with the tennis balls. Anyone who was hit was out.
Gussie naturally was captain of one side, but instead of trying to
take his enemies by surprise he stood on the highest dune challenging them all loudly – he had, I think, been studying The Lady of the
Lake. He was a striking figure.[6]

With such small numbers and a wide diversity of ages, little
teaching in class was practical, and the boys worked on individual lines under the headmaster's supervision. Augustus
was almost completely innumerate, steadily maintaining his
place in arithmetic at the bottom of the school. But his reading
and writing improved greatly. He devoured almost every book
he could lay his hands on, especially any volume of poetry,
and his stories and essays were so vividly written that the headmaster, who thought he might become a novelist, often used
to read them out loud to the class.

It was not long before Augustus established himself as the
star pupil. With the headmaster, Allen Evans, a clever Welshman who had passed his written examination for the Indian
Civil Service but failed to pass the medical, he was an obvious
favourite. On one occasion Evans delivered to the class a
triumphal address in which he expatiated on the boldness and
idealism of Augustus's aspirations, picturing him with one foot
on Giltar Point and the other on Caldy Island, and in effect
comparing him to the Colossus of Rhodes.

To these encomiums, which might have embarrassed another boy, Augustus responded like a bud in the sun. He had longed for encouragement from his father, but Edwin's unyielding lack of interest affected him as a winter blight. The hero-worship he had wanted to fix upon his father he now transferred to Allen Evans. This halcyon period lasted for over a year. But their relationship later became the subject of speculation and was eventually terminated in the most painful way. 'One day when we were at work in the classroom the headmaster and Gussie stood together in a quiet but very bitter argument,' Arthur Morley recalled.

I think that the former was accusing the latter of some offence which Gussie was vehemently denying. In the end the headmaster no doubt feeling that the argument had gone beyond the bounds of reason turned towards me and said: 'Morley, did you hear what we were saying?' This was embarrassing, but I said: 'I could not help hearing, sir.' He then turned to Gussie and said: 'There is a boy who talks the truth.'

For Augustus, the effect of this scene was out of all proportion to the trifling incident from which it arose. He had been accused of dishonesty and his plea of absent-mindedness over a new school regulation, though exactly true, was brushed aside as a lie. Charged publicly with deceit by the man whom he idolized, he was unable to find words to defend himself and broke down before the school.

He had been badly bruised, and the marks never left him. Incidents – disappointments – in later life would press upon this point and unaccountably cause him pain, giving rise to blasts of anger, moods of sarcasm. He never forgot it and, fifty years later, when writing the first draft of an autobiography, he castigated this 'amateur pedagogue', long since dead, for his 'intellectual weakness' and 'appalling meanness of soul'.

Not long after this episode he left the school. He was just sixteen and about to start on a career that would take him far from Tenby and all its associations. Once his tears had dried, resentment purged all feelings of misery. A little later, while he was away, he heard that Allen Evans had committed suicide – and began to wonder, half-seriously, whether he possessed the evil eye. In his fragmentary autobiography, *Chiaroscuro*, he alludes briefly to the headmaster's 'unhappy end'.[7] But there is a sentence, not eventually included in that book, of terrible insensitivity, poignant in its parenthesis, that expresses his deep sense of retribution: 'Not long did my master (whom I had loved) enjoy his satisfaction and when he had punctiliously cut his throat, I grieved no more.'

4. A CRISIS OF IDENTITY

'I am visiting my father,' Augustus John wrote to William Rothenstein during a stay in Tenby over thirty years later, 'and suffering again from the same condition of frantic boredom and revolt from which I escaped so long ago. My antecedents are really terrifying.'

Yet he loved Pembrokeshire; and since he was never cruelly treated and the conditions of these first sixteen years were in many ways outwardly agreeable, some other factor must have accounted for this extreme sense of 'boredom and revolt'.

The presence of his father saturated the home and dominated these years. In *Chiaroscuro* Augustus gives a brilliantly amusing portrait of Edwin John:

Too shy to be sociable, he made few friends; and these few he often found an embarrassment. Walking at his side through the town, I would be surprised by a sudden quickening of pace on his part, while at the same time he would be observed to consult his watch anxiously as if late for an important appointment: after a few minutes' spurt he would slow down and allow me to catch up with him. This manoeuvre pointed to the presence of a friend in the vicinity ... he was delighted when a bemused soldier from Penally Barracks, mistaking him for a retired officer of high rank, saluted him. In reality he lacked every martial quality, except, of course, honour. Excessively squeamish, he would never have been able to accustom himself to the licence of the camp; even the grossness of popular speech shocked him as much as would have done the politer bawdry of the smoking-room.[8]

Perversely, Edwin John was the single most influential person in Augustus's life, and their relationship shaped the pattern of his adult behaviour. But to what extent is this picture of his father accurate? Winifred, who was probably Edwin's favourite but who saw less of him than any of the others, told her daughters she felt Augustus had been unfair; and some critics have suspected that he deliberately caricatured him in *Chiaroscuro*. But both Gwen and Thornton's attitude to their father exactly supports Augustus. In about 1910 Edwin John visited Gwen in Paris. 'My father is here,' she wrote to her friend Ursula Tyrwhitt,

– not because he has wished to see me or I to see him, but because other relations and people he knows think better of him if he has been to Paris to see me! And for that I have to be tired out and unable to paint for days. And he never helps me to live materially – or cares how I live. Enough of this. I think the Family has had its day ... We don't go to Heaven in families now – but one by one.

Edwin had two ambitions. The first and least likely of these was the revival of an old day-dream: to enter the church. All his life he entertained a great admiration for churchmen, and had once considered preparing himself for the priesthood. This dream was fractionally realized when, in his fifties, he became organist at Gumfreston, a tiny inaccessible church two miles from Tenby. Every Sunday morning, wet or fine, dressed in his best suit and tallest collar, he would walk there alone, play the hymns and psalms in a style curiously deliberate – loud and slow: then walk back. This he persisted in doing until he was almost ninety – a feat that can only be appreciated by those who have trodden the precipitous route in Welsh weather.

His other ambition was to remarry. For a short time he became engaged to Alice Jones-Lloyd, and on another occasion proposed marriage to Teresa George. Both girls were considerably younger than himself, very handsome and of good family. There is also evidence to show that in a rather diffident manner he kept company with a number of girls nearer in age to his own children than to himself. These matrimonial skirmishes were always most proper and discreet, but news of them eventually leaked out bringing down on him the combined rage of Gwen and Winifred. 'I was furious at this heartless and extravagant outburst, and took his part,' Augustus records, 'but my overheated intervention only earned me the disapproval of all three.'[9]

The ordinary people of Tenby liked Edwin – they liked the look of him. 'I am not clever,' he once boasted, 'but I am independent, and I believe in a good appearance all the time. With a good appearance I can accomplish much.' His chief accomplishment was to convert this good appearance into the appearance of goodness. His unflagging church-going, his cast-iron empty routine, above all this unrelenting loneliness and longevity excited much admiration. Stranded by his peculiar temperament from adult companionship, he was attended in later life by a succession of well-behaved cats in the home, while outside he made several friendly overtures, assisted by money, to children. He offered to pay for the education of his housekeeper's son; he taught a number of local children to play the organ; and when he wished to try out some new air he would call on a young chorister and present him afterwards with a shilling for his trouble. Another of the children in the neighbourhood, John Leach, remembers that

my own father in spring and summer often took my sister and me to evensong ... and usually we walked home with Edwin John through the woods and lanes. It came about through these walks that he asked my sister and me to go with him to the cinema, of which he appeared to be very fond. These were the days of the early Chaplins, the Keystone cops and the serial with its weekly threat to the life or virtue of the heroine. Perhaps Edwin John was fortified by the presence of children on these occasions ... Besides being generous, one recalls [him] as a quiet, gentle, soft-voiced courteous man, who talked to children without condescension.

But for his own children he could find no love. He was faced with the obstacle of their existence: an obstacle to re-marriage, to the church and to almost any ambition he may have had. Out of this stalemate there developed the cult of appearance, the parsimony, the solitude, all reinforced by his natural timidity. 'He became an object only,' commented Thornton (3 February 1959). 'Is it any wonder we felt the effects of this?'

The effect of this loveless climate on Augustus was like that of a poison remaining in the human system for life. It was more lethal to him than to the others because they extricated themselves early on from their father's influence and set up separate lives in foreign countries: Thornton in Canada; Gwen in France; Winifred in America. 'I hold no grudge against him [Edwin],' Thornton remarked towards the end of his life. But Augustus, who never wholly escaped, did hold a grudge. He had needed a hero, and the hope that his father might somehow reveal himself as this hero had died a slow death. Following the disillusion, his desire to become absolutely independent was to be effected by a traumatic experience at the age of seventeen that weakened his willpower, making it subject to upheavals of hysteria. He once described his father to Darsie Japp as 'a revolting personage',[10] and their many points of similarity made him over-anxious to destroy every particle of this involuntary attachment and develop into someone utterly different. To this refractory spirit must be attributed many of his shortcomings and much of the ill-fortune that was to befall him. 'I wanted to be my own unadulterated self, and no one else. And so, taking my father as a model, I watched him carefully, imitating his tricks as closely as I could, but in reverse. By this method I sought to protect myself from the intrusions of the uninvited dead.'[11]

Very many of his actions represented not simply a wish to be different from his father, but to be someone other than his father's son. His claim to be a descendant of Owen Glendower; his vivid fantasy life, nourished by books, which developed into the cult of the Red Indian; even the vicarious symptom of dumbness that afflicted him when he saw another boy bleeding from the mouth: all these were signs of his identification with non-John people. The great kinship he felt for the gypsies, too, and which later became so close that many people actually took him to be a gypsy, arose not just from the fact that Edwin John disapproved of them but from his having warned Augustus they might capture him and bring him up as one of their own children. This was a fate better than life as he knew it. At home he felt an outcast, and at school it was with the outcast he grew most sympathetic – the half-wit at Clifton, even the boy he beat in a fight at Greenhill.

This drive to be someone else did not cease after adolescence, but grew more complicated. To know Augustus John was to know not a single man, but a crowd of people, all different, none of them quite convincing. His reaction against the paternal environment of his early years was in perpetual conflict with the strongly marked characteristics he inherited from his father. Between the two opposing forces in this civil war there existed a barren No Man's Land where Augustus uncertainly drifted. At first he hovered very near the rebel camp, but the genetic pull of the Johns dragged him gradually away, ever nearer the forces of tradition. This battling against part of himself produced a state of crisis: a crisis of identity. In later years everyone else would recognize readily enough the manly and melodramatic form of Augustus John – but he himself did not know who he was. His lack of stylistic conviction as a painter, the frequent changes of handwriting and signature in his letters, his surprising passivity and lack of direction in everyday matters, the abrupt changes of mood, the sense of strain and vacancy, the acting: all these point to this central lack of identity. 'When I am in Ireland I'm an Irishman,' he told Reginald Pound, and it was partly true. He was Chameleon. He had half turned his back on Wales and, while continuing to revisit it, chose to live fifty years of his life amid the lushness of Hampshire and Dorset – a green-tree country he never painted and to whose beauty he was not particularly responsive. His wholesale dismissal of the past went even further. He claimed not to know the date of his birthday, and boasted that he never celebrated it. In 1946 he told a *Time* interviewer, Alfred Wright, that his mother's name was Augusta Petulengro; and six years later (14 May 1952) he wrote to John Rothenstein: 'As for Gypsies, I have not yet encountered a sounder "Gypsy" than myself. My mother's name was Petulengro, remember, and we descend from Tubal-Cain via Paracelsus.' What he did not tell Alfred Wright or John Rothenstein was that Petulengro was the Romany version of Smith.* It was a deliberate teasing, a fantasy that was irresistible to him but in which he did not actually believe. His real state of mind concerning who he was seems to have been a genuine bewilderment. 'I am in a curious state,' he

* The word Petulengro means horseshoe-maker or smith. It was T. W. Thompson who first identified Borrow's Jaspar Petulengro with a certain Ambrose Smith.

confessed to Lady Cynthia Asquith in 1918, '– wondering who I am. I watch myself closely without yet being able to classify myself. I evade definition – and that must mean I *have* no *character*. Do you understand yours?'

This void seems to have come about through the deliberate rejection of all Augustus knew of his background. He could not remember his mother; he knew nothing of his origins; he abominated his father and their home. The antipathy he felt for Victoria House was reinforced by an instinctive fear of the one indisputable genetic strain he had inherited from Edwin John: melancholia. It was a disease compounded of extreme shyness, anxiety and a feeling of 'alienation', of being irretrievably segregated from other people. This quality of soundless isolation persisted very strongly in many of the John family, especially the men, and affected their lives in one of two ways. Either they would stylize their companionless state by the most painstaking methodicity; or else be driven to extreme wildness by their impatience to touch and communicate with others. Gwen, who believed 'it isn't pious to suffer long'[12] and who made solitude part of her religion, was to adopt the first course; her uncles Alfred and Frederick seem to have fallen into the second. Edwin was a supreme example of the first type, and, partly in reaction to him, Augustus became the archetypal rebel, incapable of coming to terms with his legacy of melancholia, endeavouring always by sheer force of energy to hurl it from him, to escape from this spectre of boredom, depression and loneliness simply by outpacing it, like a boy running against his shadow. To many who, like William Rothenstein, believed that Augustus had been born 'with a whole series of silver spoons between his gums',[13] this stampeding through life seemed just a thoughtless squandering of his natural gifts. But Augustus, though seldom introspective, took a more sombre view of himself: 'I am not so perverse as unfortunate,' he told Mrs Meynell (15 September 1899). All the children had, of course, been unfortunate in losing their mother and in having to contend with the John melancholia. But Augustus was particularly unfortunate in having been afflicted while still at school by a partial deafness that magnified his sense of exile, raising up an invisible barrier between him and the rest of the world.

'If our mother had lived it would have been different,' Thornton wrote to Augustus over seventy years after her death (3 February 1959). From 'her the children had inherited their artistic talent, and while she was still alive she had encouraged them to draw. Afterwards, at Tenby, Gwen and Augustus had continued drawing and painting, using the attic at Victoria House as their studio. 'Wherever they went their sketch-books went with them,' their father liked to recall later on.

In their walks along the beach ... on excursions into the country, wherever they went the sketch-books went too, and were used. They sketched everything they saw – little scenes, people, animals ... I can remember when they were a little older, and I sometimes used to take them to the theatre in London, how, even here, the inevitable sketch-books turned up as well. Then in the few minutes interval between the acts they worked feverishly to draw some person who had interested them.[14]

Although he conceded that 'it was possible that I was a less keen observer of the boy's work than his mother would have been', Edwin later on (especially after Augustus was elected an R.A.) took pride in having failed to put a stop to all this sketching. He had 'left' his children's talent to 'develop freely and naturally'. He neither encouraged nor discouraged them until, one day on Tenby beach, Gwen, who 'was always picking up beautiful children to draw and adore',[15] came across Jimmy, a twelve-year-old boy with a pale, haunting face and corkscrew curls down to his shoulders, dressed in a costume of old green velvet. Having made friends with him, she would invite him back to her attic, and, in the hope of some payment for these sessions, his mother came too – much to Gwen's disgust. Edwin quickly grew alarmed. He disapproved of strollers, and the sight of this woman wandering into his house was open to misinterpretation. He therefore decided to put his foot down and forbid Gwen inviting such 'models' home. But already it was too late. He objected; Gwen insisted; and he gave way. It was the pattern of things to come.

From these earliest days there are – at least in retrospect – indications that Augustus saw life in terms of pictures. 'Once when we were walking together over the sand dunes and saw a piece of hard perpendicular sand,' Arthur Morley recalled,

'Gussie pulled out his penknife and very rapidly carved out an attractive hand and face. On another occasion when he was sitting on my right in class he seized my Latin Grammar book and on the first empty page drew in ink with amazing speed two comic faces very different from each other, face to face.'[16]

At Greenhill there had been special art classes in which the pupils, armed with coloured chalks, copied lithographs of Swiss scenery. But Augustus also practised drawing from life, discovering from among the masters some challenging models. Great caution was necessary. One day, for example, while hard at work, he was observed by his favourite subject, the headmaster, who called him up, examined some caricatures of himself and, after permitting himself a wry smile, viciously attacked the artist's hand with a ruler.

At Clifton he had been given no encouragement and no instruction. 'Philosophy was eschewed,' he afterwards wrote, 'Art apologized for, and Science summarized in a series of smelly parlour tricks.'[17]

But back at Tenby, while studying at St Catherine's, he endured a course of 'stumping' under the tuition of a Miss O'Sullivan. 'Stumping' was a substitute for drawing prescribed by the State Art Education Authorities. The stumps were spiral cones of paper, and the stumping powder a box of pulverized chalk. With these instruments and a sheet of cartridge paper, he would reproduce the objects placed before him by means of a prolonged smudging and stippling process that gave him a method of representing form without risking the use of line. At first he copied simple cones, pyramids and cylinders, then gradually advanced, via casts of fruit and flowers, to Graeco-Roman statuary until he finally arrived at the Life Room where he spent several months studying a fully clothed model almost as bored as himself. At this stage his work was submitted to the Central Authority, since each successful student received a certificate qualifying him to indoctrinate others in the Theory and Practice of Stumping, while the school received a grant from the Exchequer. Augustus was awarded such a certificate and at the age of sixteen became a Master Stumper, Third Class.

He was more than ever anxious by this time to escape from

Tenby. But what was he to do? He had relinquished his dreams
of becoming a trapper on the Red River, or of leading a revolt
of the Araucanian Indians, and his mind now explored the
exotic possibilities of China. He would join the Civil Service
perhaps, if that would carry him to such enchanted lands: he
would do *anything* to get far enough away from this stagnant
little backwater which was slowly suffocating him. He still
loved parts of Tenby and the wild sea-coast and rocky country
round it, but the meanness of his life at home constricted him
unbearably, and his hunger for a larger world was every day
growing more acute. His father, who would have preferred to
launch him on a barrister's career, had to acknowledge that he
was unfitted by nature to such a profession, and for a short
time it was agreed between them that he should join the army.
Augustus began his army training locally, and in the evenings
the respective merits of Sandhurst and Woolwich would be
weighed.

Then, all at once, he changed his mind. He had decided, he
told his father, not to join the army after all, but to study art.
Edwin had never, he later admitted, 'taken their drawing seriously'. But for some months Augustus had been going to an
art school in Tenby run by Edward J. Head, a Royal Academician, who had reported very favourably on his progress. Edwin
was impressed by these reports. As a lover of Nature, he was
an annual visitor to the Royal Academy. Fully alive to the
claims of culture when officially sponsored, he read with appreciation in *The Times* accounts of various sales and successes
in the art world. Landscape painting in particular recommended itself to him as a gentlemanly pursuit. Admittedly his own
choice of bedroom pictures testified to a strange susceptibility
to the lure of fleshly beauty, but then he knew how to restrict
his emotions to the academic field, while for others landscape
was undoubtedly safest. These days, it seemed, the artist's profession might be tolerably respectable, provided it was practised
with sufficient financial success. Mr Head himself, if not exactly a gentleman, hardly ever got drunk and managed to live
very comfortably. When a number of his pictures had first been
hung at the Academy, Edwin's civic pride had swelled notice-
ably – it was an example his son might well strive to emulate

some day. Naturally he would have preferred him to go for a soldier, but since Augustus seemed resolved to study art he had better do so – for the sake of peace and quiet as much as anything. After all he was such a temperamental fellow, so moody, so rebellious and with no head for serious business : it might be just the job for him. One thing bothered him : had he been sufficiently unenthusiastic? Certainly he had failed very ably to encourage his son, but was that by itself enough? He had no wish to appear dilatory in the way of putting up difficulties : that would be irresponsible. In his own account of this time, Edwin explained his sanction by means of paradox :

Obstacles put in his [Augustus's] way would only have strengthened his determination to become an artist ... He suggested being allowed to attend the Slade School in London. The earnestness he put into this request made me first think he might after all make an artist ... he could display plenty of determination when necessary, and his whole childhood had proved that he could give untiring application to either drawing or painting. This, combined with his obvious eagerness, made me give my consent quite willingly.[18]

It was Mr Head who had recommended the Slade. The fees, Edwin discovered, were pretty stiff, but a legacy of forty pounds from Augusta would see to his son's upkeep – and there was always the possibility of a scholarship. Besides, it would take them out of each other's sight for a while and put an end to the domestic ructions that were now breaking out more and more seriously. On the whole, things could have turned out worse.

So, in the autumn of 1894, Augustus left Tenby for London, with his father's cautionary advice ringing in his ears : 'Be a Michelangelo if you like, but first make your living.'

Also, landscape was safest.

2

'Slade School Ingenious'

What a brood I have raised!   HENRY TONKS

The Slade continues to produce geniuses, we turn them out
every year.

HENRY TONKS TO RONALD GRAY (NOVEMBER 1901)

1. NEW STUDENTS – OLD MASTERS

On his first day at the Slade, in October 1894, Augustus was led
into the Antique Room, presided over by Henry Tonks – and
almost at once a rumpus broke out. Some of the new students,
who had already worked for several months in Paris, were ob-
jecting at not being allowed straight into the Life Class. Professor Tonks however was adamant: the students' taste must
first be purified and elevated by Graeco-Roman sculpture before
it could be judged fit to deal with the raw materials of life. And
from this judgement there was no appeal.

Augustus was not one of those who objected. To him the
absence of stumping was in itself wonderful enough. Far from
having been to Paris, he had scarcely been to London before,
and he felt keenly his immense ignorance of everything. To the
others he appeared a very spruce and silent figure, white-
collared, clean-shaven and guarding his dignity with great care.
Tonks sat him down on one of the wooden 'donkeys', next to
another new student, Ethel Hatch. 'I found myself sitting next
to a boy about sixteen', she later recalled, 'with chestnut hair
and very brown eyes who had the name "John" written in large
letters on his paper. It was the young Augustus John. He was
very neatly dressed, and was very quiet and polite, and on the
following mornings he never failed to say good morning when
he came in.'[1]

He seemed an unremarkable personality, out of the ordinary
only in so far as he was quieter than the other students, and

perhaps more timid. But one of them, Michel Salaman, noticed
that, when he called for an india-rubber one day and someone
threw it to him, he caught it and began rubbing out all in a
single movement. He was superbly well-coordinated.

Every student had been instructed to provide himself with a
box of charcoals, some sheets of *papier Ingres*, and a chunk of
bread. Their first task was to make what they could of the Dis-
cobolus. Augustus fixed it with an intent stare, then using a few
sweeping strokes, polished it off, as he thought, in a couple of
minutes. Tonks, however, thought differently. It was bold, certainly, he admitted, but it was far too summary. Yet he was
obviously surprised by Augustus's sketch – and interested.

The atmosphere at the Slade was unlike anything Augustus
had encountered in Wales. He was dazzled by almost everything. The spirit of dedication by which he felt himself to be
surrounded, thrilled and abashed him. He hardly knew where
to look. The girls were so ornamental and the men apparently
so self-assured that whatever imperfections he observed in their
work he attributed to his own lack of understanding. He felt
humble, determined to succeed, yet willing for the moment to
be led.

The Slade, and in particular the teaching of Tonks, gave
Augustus the sense of direction he had so far lacked. In such an
environment he seemed to know who he was and the part he
had to play, so that, whatever successes he gained later in his
career, he remained to a certain extent a Slade student all his
life. In its strengths and limitations, this was the single most
complete influence on him as an artist.

When Augustus John came to London, the Slade School was
just twenty-three years old, and about to enter one of its most
brilliant phases. Its tradition, to which Augustus responded so
deeply, was founded upon the study of the Old Masters, and
laid special emphasis on draughtmanship – on the interpretation of line as the Old Masters understood line, of action and
anatomical construction. 'Drawing is an explanation of the
form,' he was told. This was the Slade motto, and he never forgot it.

The school had opened in its apparently unique form in 1871, at a time when British art was at a low ebb. Cut off by its indifference from the exciting new developments that were taking place on the Continent, the Royal Academy was all-powerful, steeped in the English literary tradition. In such a climate, art schools were at their nadir, and the time was ripe for some form of revolution.

The new school took its name from Felix Slade, a wealthy connoisseur of the arts, who, on his death in 1868, had left £35,000 to found professorships of art at Oxford, Cambridge and the University of London. The Oxford and Cambridge chairs – the former taken by Ruskin – were to be solely for lecturing. In London the executors were asked to found a 'Felix Slade Faculty of Fine Arts', and University College voted £5,000 for building the Slade School as part of the College quadrangle off Gower Street.

The first professor, Edward Poynter, was an unlikely choice. A fellow student in Paris of Du Maurier, he was portrayed in *Trilby* as Lorimer, the 'Industrious Apprentice'. In his inaugural address he attacked the system then almost universally taught in the schools with its months spent upon a single elaborate drawing, and recommended 'the "free and intelligent manner of drawing" ... of the French ateliers, of which he had considerable experience as a pupil of Gleyre ...'² There were other shocking novelties: students were not examined on admission, and all the teachers had to be practising artists.*

Poynter did not remain long at the Slade. The very essence of

* In his inaugural lecture, *Systems of Art Education*, Poynter had attacked the current methods of English art teaching in which 'a trivial minuteness of detail [was] considered of more importance than a sound and thorough grounding in the knowledge of form', and only at the end of the course was the student allowed to do what he should 'have been set to do the first day he entered the school, that is to make studies from the living model'. He himself intended to adopt the methods used in France. 'I shall impress but one lesson upon the students, that constant study from the life-model is the only means they have of arriving at a comprehension of the beauty in nature, and of avoiding its ugliness and deformity; which I take to be the whole aim and end of study.' In his later lectures, Poynter's academicism becomes increasingly evident. He concentrates on the problems of style, and recommends the student to study not any contemporary painter, but the Italians of the fifteenth century, Titian, Velasquez and Michelangelo. See *Lectures on Art* (1879) by Edward Poynter and also *The Slade 1871–1960* by Andrew Forge.

Victorianism, which he had first rejected so categorically, soon seeped into his blood stream: he subsided into success, consented to be knighted, was made President of the Royal Academy, and in 1876 handed over the Slade torch to Alphonse Legros. Much in the condition of British art over the next sixty years is symbolized by his career.

At a time when almost all English art students were fixed in the stippling of one drawing for months on end,[3] Legros taught his students to draw freely with the point, and to build up their drawings by observing the broad planes of the model. A friend of the great French artists of the period, he was himself a considerable draughtsman, a disciple of Raphael and Rembrandt, of Ingres and Delacroix. One of his pupils, William Rothenstein, has described his methods of teaching drawing:

As a rule we drew larger than sight-size, but Legros would insist that we studied the relations of light and shade and half-tone, at first indicating these lightly, starting as though from a cloud, and gradually coaxing the solid forms into being by superimposed hatching. This was a severe and logical method of constructive drawing – academic in the true sense of the word ... He urged us to train our memories, to put down in our sketch-books things seen in the streets. We were also encouraged to copy, during school hours, in the National Gallery and in the Print Room of the British Museum ... Legros, as a student of Lecoq, had no doubt of the wisdom of this. He used to say 'Si vous volez, il faut voler aux riches, et pas aux pauvres.'[4]

Neither Poynter nor Legros were revolutionaries: they were traditionalists rather than experimenters. But Legros took no trouble to hide his hostility to the Royal Academy which, he believed, represented neither tradition nor scholarship, and he invariably encouraged his students to be independent of Burlington House. He became an isolated figure; even to his wife he spoke not a syllable of English, and his instruction in painting came to be interpreted by Walter Sickert as 'almost a model of how not to do it.'

Legros retired from the Slade a year before Augustus John arrived there, but by this time the principles which he had helped to introduce were firmly established. The key to the school's independent character lay in the fact that none of its professors had been taken up by the École des Beaux Arts, or the Royal Academy schools, or the Royal College of those days. Poynter and Legros had been trained in the studio schools of Paris, and were links in a chain of studio teachers (as opposed to teachers of academics) stretching back to the Renaissance. This was the atmosphere in which Augustus found himself at the age of sixteen – that of a medieval-Renaissance workshop school, which launched him on his Renaissance life.

By the time Legros retired, the Royal Academy had apparently become aware of the Slade's growing strength, but despite its efforts to get one of its men appointed, the chair was offered to Frederick Brown. Brown was then forty-two, 'a gruff, hard-bitten man, of great feeling, with something of the Victorian military man about him, such as the colonel who had spent his life on the North-West Frontier, surrounded by savages, which indeed his life as a progressive artist and teacher during the 'seventies and 'eighties must have rather resembled'.[5] This rather grim figure, with his greying hair, moustache and chin-tuft, his prognathous jaw and grave bespectacled eyes, was invariably dressed in a black frock coat. His masseter muscles were especially prominent, as if his teeth were permanently clenched, giving him the appearance of a man who would stand no nonsense – nor would he. His physical energy was manifest – at an advanced age he still often walked home from Gower Street to Richmond. The son of an artist and teacher, he had studied in Paris under Robert-Fleury and Bouguereau, and for the past fifteen years had been head of the Westminster School of Art, which he expanded from evening classes and ran on the lines of the French school. Brown's ability as a teacher laid a hold on his pupils, many of whom followed him from Westminster to the Slade. His severe expression and high standards were complemented by a great, if rather obvious, patience. But he endeared himself to many of them by his wonderful memory – he would often refer to drawings they had done years before – and he became a great collector of their work.

One of these students who was to follow Brown to the Slade was a young Fellow of the Royal College of Surgeons, Henry Tonks. Tonks had become increasingly attracted to the artist's

life and very eloquent in persuading his patients to pose as
models, and, when obliged to fall back on the dead, seized
every opportunity to draw the corpses that were dissected in
his class. In about 1890, while Senior Resident Medical Officer
at the Royal Free Hospital, he had started to attend the Westminster School of Art as a part-time student, hurrying off to its
evening classes once his medical duties were over, smelling
strongly of carbolic.

Tonks was exactly the person Brown felt he needed to support him at the Slade. He was well-educated and businesslike,
had a gift for teaching and an expert knowledge of anatomy
that gave him an almost divine insight into the process of figure-
drawing. Like Brown, he was dissatisfied with the mechanical
methods of instruction employed in most art schools. If Brown
resembled a Victorian colonel, Tonks had the commanding
presence of a nineteenth-century cardinal – immensely tall and
gaunt, with a fierce expression, vehement tongue and opinions
most tenaciously held.

In the late autumn of 1893 Brown offered Tonks the post of
his assistant. Tonks was 'amazed, almost beside himself with
pleasure'. Without hesitation he forsook surgery and, a few
months before Augustus arrived there, took up his new career
at the Slade. So began the famous partnership of Brown and
Tonks, those two lean and rock-like bachelors, which was to
carry on the teaching reforms of Legros, establish the Slade
tradition of constructive drawing, of which Augustus would
shortly be the star, and produce a crucial effect on succeeding
generations of British Art.

From morning till late afternoon, day after day, Augustus
toiled over the casts of Greek, Roman and Renaissance heads.
Then, initially for short twenty-minute poses, he and the new
students were allowed down into the Life Class. Augustus
entered this studio for the first time with feelings of awe
which deepened into something like panic when he saw, seated
on the 'throne', a girl, Italian and completely naked. 'Perfect
beauty always intimidates,' he wrote. 'Overcome for a moment
by a strange sensation of weakness at the knees, I hastily seated
myself and with trembling hand began to draw, or pretend to

draw this dazzling apparition.'⁶ Looking round, he was astonished to observe that the other students appeared almost indifferent to the spectacle: and his respect for them mounted
even higher.

The regime at the Slade during this time was still austere. Men
and women worked together in the Antique Rooms only, were
carefully segregated elsewhere and rarely met in the evenings.
'This is not a matrimonial agency,' Brown told Alfred Hayward,
a student whom he had come across saying good morning to a
young girl in one of the corridors. Models and students were
forbidden to converse, communication being limited to short
barks of command.* Older students in the Life Rooms had little
to do with the new pupils, for the hierarchy was almost that of
the public school. There was no drinking – certainly no womanizing. Augustus seemed fixed in his work all day long and half
the night. Wherever he went he took his sketch-book, which
was filled with rapid drawings of his fellow students.

In criticizing their monthly compositions one day, Tonks had
said he wanted his students to study the National Gallery more,
and the *Yellow Book*, with its *avant-garde* drawings by Aubrey
Beardsley, less. 'I cannot teach you anything new,' he told
them; 'you must find that out for yourselves. But I can teach
you something of the methods of the Old Masters – if that will
be of any use to you.' Augustus took this lesson to heart, spending much of his free time at the National Gallery, the British
Museum and other permanent collections. What he saw in these
places awed and overwhelmed him. There was so much – he
could not sort out his ideas, could not decide what excited him
most, what suited his own talent best – the pickings of all
Europe were before him at the end of a bus ride to Trafalgar
Square. He flitted from picture to picture like a butterfly.
Should he be a Pre-Raphaelite or a latter-day disciple of Rembrandt? Or both – or something else again? Looking back at this

---

* Even so, as Randolph Schwabe later noted in *The Burlington Magazine* (No.
CDLXXXIII, June 1943, p. 142) 'we had progressed from the days when Sir
Edward Poynter could not be seen with students in the women's Life Room
while a nude female was posing. They had to file out when he came in, and
he wrote his criticisms, in their absence, around the margins of their drawings.'

period years later, he concluded: 'A student should devote himself to one Master only; or one at a time.'[7]

All London stimulated and confused him during these first
months. The pervading smell of chipped potatoes, horse-dung
and old leather; the leaping naphtha flames along the main
roads; the wood-blocks of the streets looking like squares from
some strange Battenberg cake; the glittering, multicoloured
music halls; the costermongers with their barrows of fruit and
flowers; the vendors of pickled eels, ices and meat pies; the
jugglers and conjurers who performed for pennies; the whole
crowded cosmopolitan atmosphere: it was all too foreign and
bewildering for him to absorb. He walked everywhere – from
Bermondsey to Belgravia, from the narrow streets of cobble-
stones where chickens scavenged and the shabby slum children
played to the fashionable promenading in Hyde Park where
men and women, glossily hatted, rode to and fro, their horses
gleaming with health, their drivers decked out in authoritative
livery. To Augustus it seemed that no encounter was impossible, and every adventure for the asking – if only he had the
courage to find his voice.

But he was boorishly shy and very poor. Most evenings he
would return after dark to a dreary little villa, 8 Milton Road,
in Acton where he lived with one of his 'Jesus Christ Aunts';
and every morning he left early on his long day's journey into
town. But occasionally his father would send him a small
cheque, and then he would hurry off to the music halls. This
was life! – or as close as he could get to it for the time being.
The Alhambra, the Old Mogul, the Metropolitan, the Bedford,
Collins', Old Sadler's Wells with their variety shows and their
Victorian melodramas held him in thrall.* They were more

* Some of John's Music Hall sketches at the Alhambra, of buskers, singers
and dancers (among them Cissy Loftus, Cadieux and Mary Belfont) were
exhibited at the Mercury Gallery, London (15 January–10 February 1968).
John also made a portrait of Arthur Roberts dated, almost certainly inaccurately, 1895, now in the National Portrait Gallery. 'I consider him [Arthur
Roberts] about the most important buffoon England has ever produced – a born
comedian and a most accomplished artist,' he wrote to the National Portrait
Gallery (14 May 1929). On 3 June 1929 he wrote again: 'Roberts I hear is
appearing on the Music Hall at East Grimsby at present – so there's life in the
old man yet. If I kept the drawing I might of course pre-decease him, so I think

real than reality. He went whenever he could afford it, and sometimes when he could not: and once or twice was ignominiously thrown out.

He was alone a lot to begin with, but it was a crowded loneliness. On Sundays he would often wander round Speakers' Corner, listen to the orators, watch the crowds, grow excited at all the outlandish sights – then, bursting with nervous energy, march all the way home. Often he travelled great distances, resolutely and in no fixed direction until late at night, staring into people's faces, carrying under his arm one or other of his two favourite books – Walt Whitman's *Leaves of Grass* and *Hamlet*.

Increasingly during this first year, he sought the company of two other Slade students, Ambrose McEvoy and Benjamin Evans. McEvoy was a fearfully short-sighted youth, with a low dark Phil May fringe, an oddly cracked voice and spare muscleless body supported by twin spindles tipped with patent leather. He was something of a dandy, and cultivated an arresting, rather sheep-like appearance – dancing pumps, a monocle, high collar of modulated white and a pitch-black suit. He was distinguished through knowing the legendary Whistler, in deference to whom he had converted himself into an almost perfect 'arrangement in black and white'. From under his extraordinary fringe and through the monocle with which, his eyes on pivots, he myopically peered out, the world too seemed a black-and-white place – a simple two-dimensional right-or-wrong arena where men and women acted out the mild melodrama of their enchanted lives. His natural amiability, his talent for quick design (which led to early employment as comic-strip draughtsman for a paper called *Nuts*), and his gift for comedy all endeared him to the solitary Augustus. For a time he believed his friend might marry Gwen, but instead he became secretly en-

---

it had better hang along with Kipling etc. in the Board Room en attendant.' In Henry Savage's autobiography, *The Receding Shore*, there is a brief mention of John doing a portrait of Arthur Roberts in about 1922, which was to have been the cover or frontispiece to a book of reminiscences which Henry Savage and Randall Charlton were going to ghost. But the authors fell out and the book was never written. Roberts was born in 1852, and so was nearly eighty when he appeared at East Grimsby.

gaged to another painter, Mary Edwards, eight years older than himself, to whom Augustus had introduced him in the National Gallery. In later years Augustus fell rather out of sympathy with him.* It wasn't simply that he was unspeculative or that his childlike curiosity about life was held in check by childish timidity: it was that, like Augustus, he was taken up by society as a fashionable portrait painter, but, unlike Augustus, seemed wholly content. His easy temperament bobbed happily within the circle of the *beau monde*; he longed for no wider seas. His ambition, it was said, was to paint every holder of the Victoria Cross and every leading debutante, and by the time he died at the age of forty-eight, he was well on the way to achieving this.

Benjamin Evans, who had been at the same 'frightful school' as Augustus at Clifton, was an altogether different character, an intelligent and witty draughtsman, deeply versed in Rembrandt. His disconcerting style of humour seemed to spring from some abysmal lack of self-confidence that, when not directed to amuse, enabled him to exceed in dullness anyone Augustus had met. Yet these stolid and facetious moods answered some alternating current of melancholy in Augustus and were a good counterfoil to his romanticism and to McEvoy's blandness.

The three of them went everywhere together. Sometimes they would start out in the small hours of the morning and walk to Hampton Court, or Dulwich; then, after breakfasting at some cabman's pull-up, spend the rest of the day at the picture gallery. At other times they would take their sketch-books to the anarchist clubs off the Tottenham Court Road. In the mild climate of England, the foreign desperadoes who gathered here seemed to have grown curiously genial. Augustus saw many of their most sinister celebrities including Louise Michel, 'the Red Virgin', who had once fought on the Barricades during the Commune in the uniform of a man, now a little old lady in black; and that doyen of revolutionaries, Peter Kropotkin, dressed in a frock coat and radiating goodwill to everyone. Most innocent of

---

* 'McEvoy has had great successes lately which has completely turned his head,' William Orpen wrote to a friend (undated), '– he now goes about abusing John and saying he's down – his day is over – etc. which is hardly nice of Mr Mc. and very untrue.'

all were the American anarchists – not a bomb, not an ounce of
nitro-glycerine between the lot of them. The leader of the
English group was David Nichols, founder of 'Freedom', whose
rashest act was to recite some passages from Swinburne in
cockney. Despite a vehement Spanish contingent, the general
atmosphere was one of sturdy handclasps, singing and dancing,
and voluble monologues in subdued voices and indecipherable
dialects.

Augustus's tendency still was to hero-worship those whom he
liked, but since few people are natural heroes, this idolatry was
often replaced by an aggressive disillusionment. Friendship
with him was a dangerous business. If McEvoy became the
wrong type of success, Evans turned out the wrong sort of
failure. Augustus had looked up to him as immensely gifted,
predicted for him a great future. But when Evans gave up art to
become, of all things, a sanitary engineer, Augustus felt personally betrayed. So far as he was concerned, his friend had
'gone down the drain'.

Almost the only person who seemed capable of sustaining
Augustus's adulation was Tonks himself. He looked forward to
his visits with some alarm, for Tonks was a scathing critic, his
drastic comments, like amputations, cutting off many an unpromising career. 'What is it?' he would ask after closely ex-
amining some student's drawing. '... *What is it?* ... Horrible!
... It is an *insect?*' Mere accuracy never satisfied him. 'Very
good,' he remarked of one competent drawing – then added
with a deep sigh: 'But can't you see the *beauty* in that boy's
arm?' Much to his own consternation, he would reduce many
of the girls to tears. But behind the Dantesque mask lay a benevolent nature. Sometimes he would have brief flirtations, even
love-affairs, with the girl students, but his lasting passion was
for the teaching of drawing and, as Augustus wrote, 'the Slade
was his mistress'.[8]

Augustus never felt discouraged by Tonks, and responded
well to his zeal. Since Tonks's personality was not one to welcome over-familiarity, Augustus did not lose his awe of him
and for several years was much influenced by Tonks's fondness
for the Pre-Raphaelites – 'the intense study of natural appear-

ances', as Evelyn Waugh has described that movement, 'devoted to the inculcation of a lofty theme'.

In Augustus's second term at the Slade two new teachers arrived. Both taught painting. Wilson Steer was already one of the most celebrated artists in the country, and one of the worst art teachers in the world. He was built upon a pattern very dear to his fellow Englishmen – a large, genial, small-headed, slow-moving man, thoroughly inarticulate, incurious and easygoing. People loved him for his modesty. When he was awarded the O.M. he took it along to show Tonks and asked: 'Have you received one of these?'* Although he was England's most distinguished living painter, there was no nonsense about him: you'd never guess he painted – or at least you hoped you wouldn't. He travelled the country with his painting materials locked up in a cricket bag, explaining: 'I get better service that way.' There was something reassuring about his bulky and obvious presence, with its bulwarks of English insularity. It was true that he had studied in Paris, but he'd never troubled to learn the language, simply repeating himself very slowly in English, as if there were something deficient in French ears. He was loved, too, for the untroubled paradox of his character and for his monumental calm. As England's most revolutionary artist, he was a deeply conservative man, opposed to all change; he had gained a reputation for immense wisdom yet scarcely ever spoke; of his own fame he seemed unaware and would refer to his job (if there were no avoiding it in front of strangers) as 'muddling along with paint'. Yet he could be unexpectedly witty and had a keen sense of character. 'Will Rothenstein paints pretty well like the rest of us,' he once murmured, '– but from higher motives, of course.' Asked one evening what was wrong with some artist who had recently been accused of an attempt upon the virtue of a servant girl, and who now entered his drawing-room leaning upon a stick, he replied briefly: 'Housemaid's knee, I suppose.' At the same time he disliked being startled by anything the least surprising in

* John was awarded the O.M. shortly after Steer's death. 'I was delighted his [Steer's] O.M. shd. have gone to John,' William Rothenstein wrote to his brother Albert Rutherston (13 June 1942); 'this is right and proper.'

his friends' conversation, and, sitting with his hands folded across his stomach, would enjoy nothing better than to hear some old jokes retold, mouthing them contentedly to himself like some silent echo. A complete conformist, he was beset by eccentricities. He was an avid collector of Greek coins and Chelsea china, an impassioned valetudinarian. His chief enemy was draughts, and to outwit them he would dress, at the height of summer, in a heavy overcoat, yachting cap and policeman's boots. So effective was this disguise that he evaded death until his eighty-third year. Cosy and lethargic, he was English to the core: triumphantly unromantic despite his eye for painting pretty girls; purposefully uncompetitive while acknowledged to be superior to all his contemporaries, his greatest ambition, to lead a quiet life.

To the young Augustus, Steer was largely a figure of fun. When Steer grew a beard, possibly to help with the draughts, Augustus's letters became filled with the vicissitudes of this growth which, by all accounts, was a remarkable object. In his correspondence with Ursula Tyrwhitt* he traces its history with a wealth of illustrative detail, leading up to a final caricature, 'The Shearing of Mr Steer' and a reflection: 'Mr Steer has no doubt made brushes from his ill-fated beard.'

In his teaching at the Slade, Steer gave full expression to his inertia. Students awaiting his criticism as he sat behind them would turn at last to find him fast asleep. The result of such methods, so far as Augustus was concerned, was that he was never taught to paint, only to draw, and he benefited from Steer's early impressionist work only very indirectly, some twelve years later, through his friend J. D. Innes.

This lack of instruction in painting was reinforced by the other new teacher, Walter Russell, a dry uninformative man, scrupulously dressed, and unique for his unmemorable qualities. Russell's career, however, which in a minor way ran parallel to that of Edward Poynter, gives an index to the condition of English painting and explains the peculiar predicament in which almost all British artists of Augustus's generation were soon to

* These letters are in the National Library of Wales, Aberystwyth, No. N.L.W. MS 1964–5. See also *The National Library of Wales Journal*, Vol. XV, No. 2, Winter 1967, p. 236.

find themselves, especially perhaps those trained at the Slade.

Only three years after joining Brown's team, Russell, a member of the New English Art Club, was exhibiting his work at the Royal Academy. Since the New English was the chief rallying ground for opposition to the Academy, and since the Slade of Brown and Tonks was a nursery for this opposition, Russell's career seems to embody an extraordinary contradiction.* Increasingly he became a link between the Royal Academy and the forces that had set themselves up violently to oppose it. In 1910, the year of Roger Fry's revolutionary exhibition 'Manet and the Post-Impressionists', Russell held his first one-man show at the Goupil Gallery. He remained at the Slade another seventeen years – totalling thirty-two years altogether – was knighted, dwindled into a senior academician, trustee of the Tate and National Galleries.

The close ties that Russell quietly formed between the Slade and the Royal Academy enabled an injection of new blood to be pumped into the academic tradition of art in Britain at a time when the rhythm and mood of the age were no longer behind that tradition. It was an artificial stimulus that helped to keep alive this form of art well beyond its normal life span. So when at last the 'Roger Fry rabble', as Tonks captioned them, advanced across the country with their rallying cry of 'Cézanna!' they were opposed not just by the diehards at the Royal Academy, but by alert and combative reformers such as Tonks, who had behind him some of the most brilliant young artists in the country and who, for the next twenty years, fought a vigorous defensive campaign against the invasion of post-impressionism, futurism and all abstract art.†

* By 1933, the connection between the N.E.A.C. and the Slade, for many years under stress, was soon to be broken. 'I am automatically cut off the N.E.A.C. Jury this year by the new rule,' wrote Randolph Schwabe (who succeeded Tonks as head of the Slade) to Albert Rutherston (7 October 1933). 'I would not have served anyhow, having had so much abuse for my efforts in the past, and having heard so much of the Club being "run by a lot of Art-Masters".'

† 'I think Manet from a very rapid glance at the exhibition comes out best among the moderns,' Tonks wrote to Albert Rutherston (5 January 1932). 'It is interesting to observe, and this is a fine lesson, how degradation sets in at

Those who, like Augustus, owed their loyalty to Tonks, soon found that the solid ground under their feet was no longer connected to the mainland of contemporary art. To the few individuals who were self-sufficient – J. D. Innes, Gwen John and Stanley Spencer – this isolation made no difference: they went their own way. But Augustus, who had little sense of what his style might be, was cut adrift and, disdaining the trades of fashion, steered a blind and desperate course, never reaching home. In his seventies, tired and deeply disappointed at not yet having fulfilled the inexhaustible promise with which so many had burdened him, he wrote in explanation: 'I was never apprenticed to a master whom I might follow humbly and perhaps overtake.' Tonks, remarkable man though he was, could only act as go-between, pointing his way back to the Old Masters. But the Old Masters were many, and all of them were dead. Because of his insupportable loneliness, Augustus needed a living master, someone moving and breathing near him. With patience, with calculation and foresight, he might then have attained some equilibrium between life and art, some method of discovering himself and expressing what he had discovered, even the search itself, in paint. But in the summer of 1895 he suffered a bad accident, the long-term effects of which, unappreciated at the time, were to remove beyond his reach those very qualities of patience, calculation and foresight.

2. WATER-LEGEND

Augustus was happy at the Slade,* but at home he was discontented. Never had Tenby seemed more provincial, Victoria

once with the coming in of contempt for Nature. We are no good without it, we are like children, without guardians. The last twenty years have been I believe the worst on record, speaking generally, and because of this Roger Fry has upset the applecart.'

* In his second year he won a certificate for figure drawing, a prize for advanced antique drawing and, much to his father's gratification, a Slade scholarship of thirty-five pounds per annum for two years. The next year (1896–7) he was awarded a £3 prize for a study of a nude male figure, standing; and a certificate for advanced antique drawing. In his final year he won a certificate for Head Painting, a £6 prize for figure painting, and another £10 for the figure composition prize ('Moses and the Brazen Serpent').

House more mean and squalid. Whenever possible he would
avoid staying there, and go off on expeditions, at first in Britain,
later to Belgium and Holland, with his two friends Ambrose
McEvoy and Benjamin Evans.

But sometimes it was not possible to escape, and then he
occasionally invited a friend down to share his exile. One
winter Michel Salaman came for a week. It was an alarming
holiday. Salaman was a Slade student of the same age as
Augustus and belonged to a large and distinguished red-
haired fox-hunting family that had made its fortune in ostrich
feathers. The atmosphere of Victoria House was unlike anything he had experienced. Edwin, very dry and upright, hardly
spoke at all, and made all conversation by the others, even
their whispers, sound a vulgarity. Thornton appeared to be a
sort of hobbledehoy, utterly miserable when not playing cards.
Winifred was at all times extraordinarily dull and musical
except in the presence of Gwen, when the two girls would
giggle continuously, much to Salaman's dismay. Gus, he
thought, was quite out of place in this strange environment.
Between dismal meals, the two boys would hurry off to the
caves where Gus leapt from rock to rock in the most agile and
death-welcoming way. They also penetrated deep into the
blackness of these caves, using up all their matches and un-
nerving Salaman with the thought that they'd be discovered,
two heaps of bones, fifty years later. On another occasion, seeing a navvy who was bullying a child in the street, Augustus
strode up without hesitation and, while Salaman looked on in
horror, put a stop to the affair by challenging the navvy to a
fight. By the end of his visit Salaman was exhausted. He never
returned.

At the beginning of the summer holidays of 1897 Augustus
set off on a camping trip round Pembrokeshire with McEvoy,
Evans and a donkey. It was a journey full of adventures, in
keeping with his zeal, culled from Whitman's *Leaves of Grass*,
for Freedom and the Open Road. At Haverfordwest they fell in
with a party of Irish tinkers 'rich in the wisdom of the road';
at Solva they were taught by a tramp how to snare rabbits;
they drank beer in wayside inns, made friends with villagers,
entered themselves unsuccessfully in regattas, joined with

more success in old-fashioned village games 'which included a good deal of singing and kissing',[9] and, in the intervals, painted 'the Rape of the Sabine Women'. It was an exhilarating time, perhaps more charming than heroic. 'My friends and myself are encamped in a place called Newgale with two cottages and one partially built and a stretch of sand two miles long,' Augustus wrote to Ursula Tyrwhitt.

The Atlantic continually plays music on the beach. Outside browses the Donkey, our hope and pride. On this animal we depend to draw our cart and baggage ... Outside the tent the odour of the fragrant onion arises on the summer air, it is McEvoy who cooks. One night we slept under the eternal stars, one of which alone was visible – Venus – and that I regret was placed exactly over my head.

When they arrived back in Tenby, McEvoy and Evans left for London. Augustus expected to join them again shortly at the Slade. Meanwhile he had to steel himself for a week or two of duty at Victoria House. The boredom was excruciating. He felt tempted to do all manner of wild things, but did nothing – there was nothing to do. One afternoon towards the end of his vacation he went to bathe on the South Sands with Gwen, Winifred and their friend Irene Mackenzie. The tide was far out but on the turn, and he decided to go off on his own and practise diving from Giltar Point. He climbed the rock and looked down. The surface of the water was strewn with seaweed but seemed deep enough for a dive. At any rate it was worth a try. He stripped off his clothes and plunged in. 'Instantly I was made aware of my folly,' he later recorded. 'The impact of my skull on a hidden rock was terrific. The universe seemed to explode!'[10] Possibly because of the cold water he did not lose consciousness and somehow managed to drag himself to the shore. Part of his scalp had been scissored away and lay flapping over one eye. The ebb and flow of his blood was everywhere. He did what first aid he could, dressed slowly, turbaned his towel round his head and set off back to the South Sands. 'Presently he came running back,' Irene Mackenzie recalled, 'with blood pouring from his forehead.'[11] Edwin, who had joined his daughters on the beach, was greatly alarmed. They must get him back to the privacy of the house as discreetly as possible. At all costs, short of death itself, publicity must be avoided. Augustus was already feeling very weak. Supported and camouflaged on all sides by his family, he was hurried back by a curious zig-zag route to the safety of his bed. Here he seems to have lost consciousness for a time. The next thing he knew was that he was being examined, rather to his gratification, not by the family's usual practitioner, but by Dr Lock, a far more eminent and romantic figure. Dr Lock stitched his wound, told him that he probably owed his life to his uncommonly thick skull, and left. There was no concussion, though some element of shock, and, since the stitches held, little more needed to be done. It was essential, however, that he rest and endure a long period of convalescence in Victoria House. Soon this 'durance vile'[12] grew almost insupportable. It was by far the worst part of his accident. 'As my brain clears I find my confinement here more galling,' he complained to Ursula Tyrwhitt.

But I'm healing like a dog – the doctor is amazed at the way I heal. The wound is the worst of its kind he has had to deal with. If I appear at all cracked at any time in the future, I trust you will put it down to my knock on the head and not to any original madness. The worst part of it is the beef tea, I think. I am not allowed to remain long in peace without the slavey bearing in an enormous cup of that beverage ... Man cannot live by beef tea alone.

The Slade students went back, but Augustus was not among them. Even Gwen had gone to London. He perspired with impatience. His wound healed, it seemed, by the sheer force of his willpower. Even so it was a slow business and the doctors were taking no chances. For a time Augustus tried working on his own. 'I have been doing sketches for a Poster for cocoa,' he told Ursula Tyrwhitt. '... It's great fun, but difficult – like everything else.' Then suddenly he tired of this: 'I'm sick of doing comic sketches ... I don't feel in a comic mood at all.' His feelings were of colossal tedium, colossal revolt. Once he was free from this appalling imprisonment he would do such things – what they were he was not yet sure, but they would be the wonders of the world. In the meantime: 'I am horribly dull. I was hoping for some signs that my brain was affected – a little madness is so enlivening. I do hope this dullness is not permanent.'

His handwriting in these letters to Ursula Tyrwhitt grows increasingly wild and is interrupted by drawings of himself, like a wounded soldier, with a bandage round his head and the beginnings of a beard. 'You must have lots of news to tell me, if only you would,' he pleads. 'I am insatiable.' And when Ursula does write to him he calls her 'an angel' and replies:

Your letter did more for my head than tons of that other stuff [beef tea]. In fact I got up this morning before the doctor came and he was quite annoyed ... they've cut away a great patch of my hair which will look funny I daresay. I'm longing to see a good picture again ... I'm going to paint next term. Hurrah! How exciting it is ... I feel sure *another* letter would complete the cure.

His own letters also contain a rather tentative declaration of romantic love. He recalls, with nostalgia, the last day of the summer term. 'How the strawberries sweetened one's sorrow! – how the roses made one's despair almost acceptable! How you extinguished everybody at the Soirée! Before you came it was night – a starry beautiful night, but you brought as it were the dawn which made the stars turn pale and flee, remaining alone with its own glorious roseate luminescence. Selah!'

At first he is merely in love with love, with the melody of the words themselves. But later he alters key to a more practical tone. He wants to hear from her precisely what she is doing, to extract from her 'like a tooth' the pledge that he may keep company with her once he returns. Is he to be allowed 'to take you home', he asks. 'I mean to accompany you?' In return he will lend her his Rembrandt book. They must have a definite understanding.

When he does go back to the Slade that autumn he is transformed. Upon his head he wears a defunct smoking-cap of black velvet and gold embroidery produced by his father to conceal his wound from public gaze; and round his cheeks and chin sprout small tufts of red hair, like fungus. He had become, Ethel Hatch noticed, very untidy – quite unlike the spruce, clean-shaven youth whom she had met three years ago.

In this way the Augustus John legend was conceived.

This legend, which stalked his life like a shadow, is a perfect example of how a remarkable man may be simplified into a myth by popular fancy acting through suggestible minds. In the public imagination he was to represent the Great Artist, the Great Lover, the Great Bohemian Enjoyer of Life. It was a cruelly ironic comment on his actual career, one which he did not accept himself but never effectively contradicted, and from the pressures of which he constantly suffered.

The story is perhaps most succinctly told on the back of a Brooke Bond Tea Card, as one of a series of fifty Famous People. Here Virginia Shankland writes that Augustus John

hit his head on a rock whilst diving, and emerged from the water a genius!* He became a magnificent draughtsman; this mastery later spread to painting. John was a fiery personality with a passion for independence and personal liberty, which he expressed in his paintings, especially those of gypsies. He felt great affinity with their roving lives and often lived among them.[13]

To this brief account must be added one further ingredient of the legend, perhaps not palatable to Brooke Bond tea drinkers. This was what a *Daily Telegraph* leader writer gallantly referred to as his 'prowess with the fair sex'.†

Like many fables, this picture does partake a little of the reality from which it grew, but the truth has been coated with accretions of popular sentiment. To judge from the facts, it seems clear that from 1897 onwards Augustus was a changed man. He was changed not just in appearance, but also in his work and behaviour. In his first two years at the Slade, Tonks had described his work as 'methodical'. Now the drawings he began to do were passed from hand to hand, everywhere exciting admiration. They were extraordinarily precocious, remarkable for their firm, fluent, lyrical line, executed with the point of the pencil and with astonishing vigour and spontaneity. They seemed to promise a new force in British art. Suddenly his genius was manifest. Even his rejected sketches were eagerly

* In 1930 Augustus's second son Caspar dived on to a rock and emerged from the water an Admiral!

† 'As a man he was larger than life-size. Even while still young his prowess with the fair sex was legendary and the stories about him legion. He attacked everything with vigour.' *Daily Telegraph*, 1 November 1961.

snatched up by other students from the waste-paper basket.

His personality, too, seemed different. As his beard grew, so his clothes grew shabbier, his manner more unpredictable. For long periods he was still very quiet: but suddenly there would be an outburst of high spirits, some outrageous exploit; then silence again. In his earlier years, according to Edwin, he had been 'a happy healthy child, not at all given to brooding or moodiness, who loved games and in every way was much the same as other children . . . a docile tractable child not subject to passionate outbursts'.[14] Edwin, very characteristically, was eager to present a picture of a family that was ordinary to an extraordinary degree, united and respectable to the extreme of banality. His son's docile manner may often have been a symptom of the moodiness he denies to have existed, but which Augustus had undeniably shared with him. From about the age of eighteen Augustus's energies were directed against those factors he held in common with his father – that is, almost all the first seventeen years of his upbringing – and much that he had inherited. He grew intermittently less docile and more to resemble what Wyndham Lewis was to call 'a great man of action into whose hands the fairies had stuck a brush instead of a sword'.

Augustus disliked this description, and for much the same reason that he disliked the magnificent portrait painted of him in 1900 by William Orpen.* Both, he felt, degraded him; neither showed any trace of the shy, uncertain, dreamy person he knew himself to be. But the outer man had already begun to eclipse that vague unrealized inner being: he was a moon that was paling to invisibility in the sunlight of the John legend. 'I am just a legend,' he once said. 'I'm not a real person at all.'

The essence of all such legends is the substitution of the

---

* This portrait is now in the National Portrait Gallery, London. Many years after it was painted John described it in *Finishing Touches* as 'most regrettable'. Orpen had painted it in frank, romantic imitation of Whistler's 'Carlyle', and at the time John wrote of it to Michel Salaman: 'Orpen's portrait of me extracts much critical admiration. It is described in one notice as a clever portrait of Mr John in the character of a French Romantic.

'One far-seeing gentleman hopes that I will emerge from my Rembrandtine chrysalis with a character of my own! I have just been to the Guildhall and return exalted with the profound beauty of Whistler's Carlyle.'

private by a public self. Very often this substitution is made as a deliberate act of will, an early resolve to detach oneself and rise superior to life. Of all Augustus's near-contemporaries, probably the example of Bernard Shaw illustrates this self-myth-making principle best. Much of his childhood and youth, before he had formed a protective covering, was spent in tears. But at the age of fifteen he had seen Gounod's *Faust*, been profoundly impressed, and begun to model his personality on Mephistopheles. He clothed himself in a detachment from human emotions, and by sheer willpower achieved a kind of Mephistophelian immortality on earth.

The John and Shaw myths were bubbles blown by the unsatisfied desires for power and pleasure. But Augustus, unlike Shaw, never 'decided' to become a legend, never modelled his life on anyone, neither planned nor carried through any fabled programme. He did not even grow a beard, he once told John Freeman; it just grew of its own accord.[15] But, like Shaw, he adopted a simple military slogan: the best method of defence is attack. It is a technique that accounts for many paradoxes: why it is the shy who make the most outrageous statements, the timid who are suddenly bold, the frightened who attack, the doubtful who act most decisively.

The clue to Augustus's performance at the Slade, which was to nourish his larger-than-life legend, was *impatience*. His bang on the head had not infected him with a genius for draughtsmanship. His sister Gwen, a no less remarkable artist, though certainly quite capable of cracking her head on any rock,* somehow completely failed to do so. Augustus himself described the theory of a rock releasing hidden springs of genius as 'nonsense', and he added: 'I was in no way changed, unless my fitful industry with its incessant setbacks, my wool-gathering and squandering of time, my emotional ups and downs and general inconsequence can be charitably imputed to that mishap.'[16]

* When staying at Pevril Tower, Swanage, in 1899, Gwen wrote to Michel Salaman: 'I bathe in a natural bath 3 miles away, the rocks are treacherous there, and the sea unfathomable. My bath is so deep I cannot dive to the bottom and I can swim in it – but there is no delicious danger about it, and yesterday I sat on the edge of the rock to see what would happen – and a great wave came and rolled me over – which was humiliating and *very* painful – and then it washed me out to sea – that was terrifying – but I was washed up again.'

This common-sense denial, however, does admit some change obscurely connected with the incident. Almost certainly, it seems, the claustrophobia of his convalescence was what most strongly affected him. Like alcohol, it did not confer on him any quality he did not already possess. But it greatly magnified certain traits, leaving him with an obsession against being confined, a terrible impatience, a sense of walled-in isolation from the human race, and a rising revolt against the surroundings of his imprisonment and all they represented. He was unable now to tolerate stress, but had simply to outpace his anxieties. The assurance of his early drawings testifies to the speed with which he did them rather than to any deep self-confidence. His natural doubts and hesitations had no time to crowd in on him: * he would not let them. By the time they had caught up, he had finished; he was somewhere else. It was a way of life that served him magnificently while he was still young. He actually raised the standard of work at the Slade, lifted other students to a level they might otherwise not have reached. But later on, as his lyrical inspiration faded, it was replaced by nothing, by emptiness, or sentimentality masquerading as lyricism. The anxieties, half-smothered with boredom, easily overtook him and reached the canvas while he was still at work on it.

It was his vitality and restlessness that gave Augustus such tremendous initial impetus. People worshipped him. Everything contributed to his God-like aspect: his very name, Augustus, suggested the deified Roman Emperor.† By his eighteenth birth-

---

* In a letter Charles Morgan wrote to D. S. MacColl, he recalls some words of Wilson Steer's: 'Do you remember that drawing by John? It was done at a time when he drew with many lines and many of those lines were superfluous or even wrong, but then at the last moment, he would select among them and emphasize those which were right, and so, by an act of genius, save a drawing which, in the hands of any other man, would have become a mess and a failure.'

> † 'Augustus Caesar,' so the poet said,
> 'Shall be regarded as a present god
> By Britain, made to kiss the Roman's rod.'
> Augustus Caesar long ago is dead,
> But still the good work's being carried on:
> We lick the brushes of Augustus John.

Punch, 27 February 1929

day he had already grown into an imposing figure: a picturesque giant nearly six feet tall, with a Christ-like beard, roving
eyes and beautiful hands with long nervous fingers that gave a
look of extreme intelligence to everything he did. He was not
talkative. But sometimes his eyes would light up, his whole
being come alive and he would speak eloquently in a deep,
rumbling, Welsh voice.

Physically he was the stuff from which heroes are made, and
the age was right for heroes. England was on the decline.
Over the next thirty years psychic forces that would earlier
have gone into politics or art seem to have turned inwards and
inflated the personality. From Oscar Wilde, who put his genius
into his life and only his talent into his work, to the Sitwells,
English civilization threw up a fantastic gallery of 'characters'
– dandies and eccentrics, prophets and impresarios of the arts.
The age was becoming more mechanical, personal liberty more
restricted, behaviour more uniform. The collective frustration
of Edwardian England was soon to focus upon Augustus and
elect him as the symbol of free man. Through him people
lived out their fantasies; for what they dared not do, it seemed
he did instinctively. There was nothing mechanical, nothing
restricted or uniform about him: there was *wildness*. Wyndham Lewis, who got to know him at an early age, caught this
reverence perfectly when he described Augustus as

the most notorious noncomformist England has known for a long
time. Following in the footsteps of Borrow, he was one of those
people who always set out to do the thing that 'is not done', according to the British canon. He swept aside the social conventions, which
was a great success, and he became a public lion practically on the
spot. There was another reason for this lionization (which is why he
has remained a lion): he happened to be an unusually fine artist.

Such a combination was rare. The fashionable public found as a
rule that it had been leo-hunting some pretentious jackal. Here was
one who had gigantic ear-rings, a ferocious red beard, a large angry
eye, and who barked beautifully at you from his proud six foot, and,
marvellously, was a great artist too. He was reported to like women
and wine and song and to be by birth a gypsy.[17]

3. FADED PRIMROSES AND STRAW

No one could have been more different from this exterior vision
of Augustus than his sister Gwen. If he seemed all circumference and no centre, she was all centre. Physically, she appeared fragile. Her figure was slender, with tiny hands and
feet; her oval face very pale; her soft Pembrokeshire voice
almost inaudible. She dressed carefully in dark colours, and
latterly in black. Her hair was brown, neatly arranged, with a
big bow on top. But this modest impression was corrected by a
look of extreme determination. The receding John chin, which
Augustus had camouflaged so redly, seemed to symbolize
Gwen's withdrawn nature. Socially ill at ease, she preserved an
air of aloofness.

At opposite poles both their personalities were elusive: hers,
in its stern reticence, manifestly so; his, more deceptively,
behind the smoke-screen of his 'reputation'. Despite appearances, they had much in common* – an essentially simple
attitude to life, a passionate response to beauty: the beauty of
nature and of people, especially women, sometimes the same
women. They had also inherited the same sense of isolation
from other people. But the isolation of Augustus had been intensified by his partial deafness and made hysterical by the
aftermath of his bathing accident. Unlike Gwen, he could not
bear to contain his emotions, could never absorb and sublimate
them on to his canvas. Instead, he had to disburden himself at
once, dissipate them into the thin air about him. So, although
they were confronted by many identical problems, their
methods of dealing with them were entirely different.

Before Augustus had been at the Slade many months, he was
urging Gwen to join him. She needed little encouragement

* In a letter to Sir John Rothenstein (14 May 1952) written after having read
Rothenstein's essay on Gwen John in *Modern English Painters*, Augustus sent
some notes on himself and his sister: 'With our common contempt for sentimentality, Gwen and I were not opposites but much the same really, but we
took a different attitude. I am rarely "exuberant". She was always so; latterly
in a tragic way. She wasn't chaste or subdued, but amorous and proud. She
didn't steal through life but preserved a haughty independence which people
mistook for humility. Her passions for both men and women were outrageous
and irrational. She was never "unnoticed" by those who had access to her.'

and, as he later implied, would have done so anyway: 'She wasn't going to be left out of it!'[18] Her need to escape from Victoria House was as urgent as his. She had no energy in Tenby, she once confided to Ursula Tyrwhitt (30 July 1908): 'So if you feel as I did in Tenby you cannot work much.' She wanted to work. She had only to travel three or four miles from home and she would feel marvellously revitalized. It was 'strange' – she attributed it to the local weather.

On coming to London, Gwen put up at first at 'Miss Philpot's Educational Establishment' at 10 Princes Square, Bayswater. But during the autumn of 1895, when she started to attend the Slade, she moved to 23 Euston Square,* very near University College. By this time Augustus had left Acton, his growing paganism having proved too much for his aunt, and was living at 20 Montague Place, a superior lodging house in a street of temperance hotels, private apartments and the occasional boot-maker or surgeon. In *Chiaroscuro* he described himself and Gwen sharing rooms together and, like monkeys, living off fruit and nuts. Very early in 1897 they did take the first floor flat of 21 Fitzroy Street, a house that had recently been bought by a Mrs Everett, mother of one of their friends at the Slade, who hurriedly converted it from a brothel† into a series of flats and studios. Here they seem to have lived intermittently for over a year, sharing it with Grace Westry, another Slade student, and with Winifred John who had come up to London to study music. Apart from this, and a flat over a tobacconist's in which they lived very briefly after leaving the Slade, the only rooms they shared were other people's. They were fond of each other, but incompatible, and it was not practicable for them to remain together very long. He felt that she danger-ously disregarded her health in a way that could not benefit her work. His objections to her policy of self-neglect were exactly those expressed a few years later on her behalf by Rodin, who was always insisting that she ate well and took proper exercise. But whereas Rodin sounded sympathetic, Augustus's sympathy was often mixed with irritation. Her

* On the University College, London, form she filled in, '10 Princes Square' has been crossed out and '23 Euston Square' substituted.

† The proprietress described herself as a 'feather dresser'.

indifference to physical conditions and to what people thought
of her seemed like a family parody of his own unconventionalism, and it was difficult for him to be detached.

Although Gwen never took Augustus's advice and sometimes ridiculed his opinions, she was worried by him, for she
was not strong enough to retain her single-mindedness while he
was near. He did not belong to that part of her heart and mind
– the same part where her love of art lay – which remained
undisturbed by the events and difficulties of life. This part,
perhaps, could only be shared by those, mostly women, whose
sensibility came directly from the soul, not the nerves.
Augustus, she felt, was hostile to her desire for a more interior
life. He could not share her solitude, was not part of her atmosphere. Until she removed herself beyond its influence, his
forceful character dominated her. His life, where so much
energy was squandered on *doing things*, dissipated her mind, led
into a whirlwind of impressions that tore chaotically through
her and away again before she had time to catch hold of them,
make them her own. In order to realize her feelings, express her
thoughts, she had to confine them to a small private area she
could control. In a crowded life this was impossible, and the
enervation and waste left her exhausted. 'I should like to go
and live somewhere,' she told Ursula Tyrwhitt (undated),
'where I met nobody I know till I am so strong that people
and things could not affect me beyond reason.'

People especially were always threatening to affect her beyond reason. Though chaste and even puritanical in her
attitude, her relationships were sometimes extraordinarily
passionate, and she did not get over them easily. While at the
Slade she formed a particularly intense attachment to another
girl* there. When this girl started a love-affair with a married
man, Gwen was appalled and decided that it must be stopped.
After failing to persuade her by argument she declared an

---

* Possibly Grace Westry, the Slade student who lived with Gwen for a year
or two and whom Gwen painted as 'Young Woman with a Violin' and
Augustus drew (the drawing is in the Fitzwilliam Museum, Cambridge. P.D.
942). Though attractive she appears not to have married, her various addresses
up to at least 1912 showing a startling similarity to those of Ambrose McEvoy
and his wife.

ultimatum: either the affair must cease – or she herself would commit suicide. There was no doubting her sincerity. 'The atmosphere of our group now became almost unbearable,' Augustus records, 'with its frightful tension, its terrifying excursions and alarms. Had my sister gone mad? At one moment Ambrose McEvoy thought so, and, distraught himself, rushed to tell me the dire news: but Gwen was only in a state of spiritual exaltation, and laughed at my distress.'[19] The girl's love for Gwen had now turned to hate, and she was quite obdurate. Something would have to be done. Augustus, very shocked, decided upon an athletic solution. He sought out the man and declared his own ultimatum: either the affair must cease – or he would fight him. Confronted in this way, the man retreated to his wife.

From dreadful involvements of this kind Gwen had to protect herself. Only then could she put all this energy of loving into her work. Once she had developed her ideas, begun to achieve something, then she could endure any misfortunes that might engulf her, not threaten suicide, but still go on in her search for 'the strange form'.[20]

To pursue this search without hindrance she forced herself to develop certain habits that counterbalanced what she considered to be her inherent weaknesses. 'One must be patient,' she counselled,[21] and this was the refrain to many of her letters. She had to fight a terrible tendency towards 'impatience and angoisse',[22] she had to make sure, in the face of all her instincts, that everything went slowly; she had to harness her extraordinary inner excitement to an equally extraordinary painstaking and methodicity. For a picture she would prepare endlessly – then paint it with great rapidity. 'I think a picture ought to be done in 1 sitting or at most 2,' she told Ursula Tyrwhitt (2 August 1916). 'For this one must paint a lot of canvases probably and waste them.' In this lifelong acquiring of patience, struggle for composure, lay her strength. 'I cannot imagine why my vision will have some value in the world – and yet I know it will,' she wrote. '. . . I think it will count because I am patient and recueillé in some degree.'[23]

She was not naturally sombre – Augustus testifies to her 'native gaiety and humour' – nor did solitude altogether suit

her. In time she developed a rather sickly obsession about
'God's little artist' as she liked to refer to herself. The detachment which she cultivated to modify her passion for beauty, to
transfer it from 'people and things' to paint, was never complete. Ruthless towards those who bothered her – 'I will not be
troubled by people'[24] – she remained poignantly vulnerable to
those whom she loved and admired. While, for example, she
was begging Vera Oumançoff, Jacques Maritain's sister-in-law,
for some answer to her letters, she would make use of her
father's poignantly unanswered correspondence simply for
pencilling out small prayers. 'Prayer is asking and receiving,'
she scrawled without any sense of irony or of the impartial
truth suggested by Coleridge's lines:

> O Lady! we receive but what we give,
> And in our life alone does Nature live.

Like a plant, Gwen was nourished by Nature and by those
few people, like Rodin, who were in spiritual communion with
Nature. From the rest she guarded herself with her Catholicism
(which she adopted in 1913) and her cats. Of her faith she tried
without complete success to make a substitute for relationships
with people; while her quarantine of cats provided the practical
excuse why she could never leave, for any extended period,
her solitary rooms. They were also the knife that kept so
painfully raw her dislike of that mass of human beings who
together made up what Augustus called 'life', by reminding
her constantly of their cruelty to animals. She was a weak
person ('I am ridiculous. I can't refuse anything that is asked
of me'[25]) magnificently armed.

About Augustus's pictures Gwen said very little – neither of
them talked painting. But in a letter to Ursula Tyrwhitt written
in the winter of 1914–15 she wrote: 'I think them rather good.
They want something which perhaps will come soon!' Of her
work Augustus was the staunchest admirer from the very
earliest days, believing her to be a more talented painter than
himself, though possibly less accomplished as a draughtsman.
In his last years, after Gwen had died, this admiration curdled
into a sentimentalized concoction – 'Fifty years after my death
I shall be remembered as Gwen John's brother.' – but his ap-

preciation was genuine, often expressed and acted upon during her lifetime. 'I have seen him peer fixedly, almost obsessively, at pictures by Gwen as though he could discern in them his own temperament in reverse,' John Rothenstein recalls; 'as though he could derive from the act satisfaction in his own wider range, greater natural endowment, tempestuous energy, and at the same time be reproached by her single-mindedness, her steadiness of focus, above all by the sureness with which she attained her simpler aims.'[26]

Round Gwen and Augustus there soon gathered a group of young artists whose talent appeared extraordinarily precocious. A new spirit of comradeship, unknown in Legros's time, invaded the school. Within its small pond these students created an enormous wave. There was Edna Waugh, very pretty and petite and with long hair down to her waist, who had gone there at the age of fifteen, won a scholarship and in 1897 scored a dramatic triumph with her beautiful watercolour 'The Rape of the Sabines'. She was proclaimed an infant prodigy, a Slade school 'genius'. The flexibility of her talent and the strange poetic imaginings with which she filled her notebooks particularly impressed Tonks, who informed her that she was going to be a second Burne-Jones, to which she immediately replied: 'No, the first Edna Waugh'. But to many people's dismay she did not remain Edna Waugh for long, and when only nineteen was married off to [Sir] William Clarke Hall. Even her best-known work, a series of haunting illustrations to *Wuthering Heights*, remained unfinished.

There was Gwen Salmond, who later married Matthew Smith,* a very self-possessed and outspoken girl, whose 'Descent

* In his obituary notice (*The Times*, 1 February 1958) of Lady Smith, Augustus wrote: 'The death of Lady (Matthew) Smith has removed one of the last survivors of what might be called the Grand Epoch of the Slade School. Gwen Salmond, as she then was, cut a commanding figure among a remarkably brilliant group of women students, consisting of such arresting personalities as Edna Waugh, Ursula Tyrwhitt, my sister Gwen John, and Ida Nettleship.

'Gwen Salmond's early compositions were distinguished by a force and temerity for which even her natural liveliness of temperament had not prepared us. I well remember a Deposition in our Sketch Club which would not have been out of place among the *ébauches* of, dare I say it, Tintoretto!

'. . . In what I have called the Grand Epoch of the Slade, the male students

from the Cross' was spoken of as a masterpiece. But already by the time she left the Slade she seemed to have lost any illusions about her future and that of most of her contemporaries: 'Of course, we've gone down in art,' she wrote to Michel Salaman,

– I wish we hadn't – and I shan't bring up the average anywhere near. My four years show me that – a sort of technicality is the wall I break myself against . . . I am really deeply ashamed of having done nothing for so long. I wish you'd try and do something you think beautiful and work it out – all you men go in for 'pleasant effect' or 'something good'.

Most brilliant of all was William Orpen. With his arrival at the Slade in 1897 from the Metropolitan School of Art in Dublin, a new force made itself felt in Gower Street. It was the force, primarily, of tireless industry and tireless material ambition. Orpen was a gnome-like and exuberant figure, very popular with the other students. Slim and active, he had high cheek-bones given prominence by sunken pale cheeks, light grey eyes, and thick brown hair, very unkempt. Invariably he wore a small blue serge jacket without lapels – of a type usually worn by engineers. In 1899, his last year at the Slade, he won the coveted Summer Composition Prize with his outstanding 'The Play Scene in *Hamlet*'. But his father, a rather stuffy solicitor, had by now had enough of his son's painting and gave him the alternative of taking up some serious business or being cut off with a hundred pounds. Orpen took the hundred pounds and never looked back. There seemed nothing he could not accomplish. He was already a devoted disciple of William Rothenstein and after a successful proposal of marriage was promoted to his brother-in-law. Stationed back in Ireland with the rank of art-teacher, he met a rich American patron, a specimen comparatively rare before the transatlantic jet. This American wanted his wife's portrait done, wearing a leopard skin topee and heavy pearls in the early morning. Orpen did it

---

cut a poor figure; in fact they can hardly be said to have existed. In talent, as well as in looks, the girls were supreme. But these advantages for the most part came to nought under the burdens of domesticity which . . . could be for some almost too heavy to bear . . . "Marriage and Death and Division make barren our lives". Gwen Smith had reason to know this but she also had the pluck to face it bravely, which is what made all the difference.'

with immense success and was paid a sum of money he had heard mentioned before but of which he had formed no accurate numerical notions, all figures beyond a hundred pounds being to him indistinct visions, clouds and darkness. From this moment onwards he was overwhelmed by lucrative commissions. The Rolls Royce had entered into his soul.

At first Augustus took to Orpen. He was an easy companion, very spontaneous, whimsical, high-spirited. But in due course, after Orpen had become what Augustus called 'the protégé of big business', their ways diverged. He succumbed very eagerly to those social and financial pressures that afflict the professional artist. These pressures Augustus also felt, but whereas in him there was always some struggle between the 'pull duchess' and 'pull painter' forces, Orpen seemed to experience no struggle, and organized his career with the very un-John-like efficiency of a tycoon. The result, which revolted Augustus by its vulgarity, was a degree of material success to rival Van Dyck and Reynolds and, in his own time, Sargent. Even in these early days at the Slade, people, it was said, came to praise John's pictures but went away with Orpen's.* He had cut his hair short as a soldier's, perched on its shaven dome a small bowler hat and encircled his neck with a stiff white collar. The artist was lost to sight. A sentimental Irishman in England, he was typically English when in Ireland, and though he claimed to have been brought up on 'the Irish Question', he confessed that he had never found out what it was.

Orpen cultivated ignorance, pursued superficiality with extreme zeal. There was not a single serious topic of which he could not claim to be unaware, not one good book he had not omitted to read. He had few prejudices, no opinions. His rapid-fire, staccato conversation had about it the suggestion of epigrams but was almost unintelligible and strenuously confined to subjects of microscopic triviality. If the talk threatened to turn to more adult topics, he grew scared and would fall

---

* Hence E. X. Kapp's masterly clerihew:
> When Augustus John
> Really does slap it on,
> His price is within 4d.
> Of Orpen's.

into the most extravagant feats of horseplay. It was not beyond him to get down on all fours at dinner and bark like a dog, or to produce from his pocket some new mechanical toy and set it spinning across the table. He also developed, his nephew John Rothenstein remembers, a 'habit of speaking of himself, in the third person, as "little Orps" or even as "Orpsie boy". It would be difficult to imagine a more effective protection against intimacy.'[27] There was to his life an inarticulate pathos. Money, fame, success – these were like delicious coloured sweets to him : he simply could not resist them.

Before Orpen had dwindled into success, he and Augustus were often together, and in 1898 they were joined by a third companion, Albert Rutherston.* 'Little Albert', as he was called, was the younger brother of William Rothenstein, very pink and small and regarded as rather a rake. 'Not content with working all day,' William Rothenstein recorded, 'they used to meet in some studio and draw at night. They picked up strange and unusual models; but I was shy, after seeing John's brilliant nudes, of drawing in his company.'[28]

Above the studio† in which they worked lived Mrs Everett, an improbable woman in her forties, fat and vigorous, her cheeks aflame, her eyes very blue, unevenly dressed in widow's weeds and men's boots. Her son Henry and niece Kathleen Herbert had recently gone to the Slade where she now attempted to join them, arriving there fully equipped with a Gladstone bag containing one large bible, a loaf of bread, a Spanish dagger, spirit lamp and saucepan, and a dilapidated eighteenth-century volume on art. She presented a phenomenon unique in Tonks's experience. In desperation he banished her to the skeleton room in the cellar of the Slade which, interpreting this as a privilege, she garishly transformed by introducing there various brass Buddhas, stuffed peacocks and a small organ, two grandfather armchairs loosely covered with gold-encrusted priests' vestments and a slowly-dying palm tree, like a monstrous spider, from which she suspended

---

* Albert Rothenstein changed his name to Rutherston during the First World War, and is generally now remembered by that name. To avoid unnecessary complication I have called him Rutherston throughout.

† 21 Fitzroy Street.

religious texts decorated on cardboard. Some nights she slept
there; some days she entertained her pack of dogs there; sometimes, night or day, her voice could be heard among the skele-
tons singing lustily: 'Oh, make those dry bones live again,
Great Lord of Hosts!' – to which the students above would add
their refrain, clapping wildly and chanting ribald choruses.

Excommunicated at last from the Slade, Mrs Everett started
what she called her 'Sunday School' in the converted brothel at
Fitzroy Street. Here, and later at 101 Charlotte Street, she encouraged the art students to gather for bread and jam, hot
sweet tea and intimate talk of the Almighty. These teas or
'bun-worries', as they were called, were lively affairs, especially
when Augustus and Orpen turned up, and would last late into
the night, culminating in the singing of 'Are you washed?'
with its confident refrain: 'Yes, I'm washed!' For Augustus the
atmosphere was uncomfortably like that of his Salvationist
aunts, but Mrs Everett was a fascinating subject to draw from
all angles and so he often came. 'One lovely day early in May,'
Ethel Hatch recalls,

Mrs Everett invited us all to a picnic in the country ... she met us
with a large yellow farm cart, she herself wearing a sun-bonnet, and
the driver a smock ... After lunch we wandered about in the lovely
park and grounds, and some of them ran races round the trees;
John was a very good runner, and most graceful. I can see him
now, chasing a red-haired girl through the trees at the bottom of
the lawn.
    ... afterwards a photograph was taken of the party in the wagon,
with John sitting astride a horse. I shall never forget the journey
home in the train, when John and Orpen entertained us by standing up in the carriage singing all the latest songs from Paris, with a
great deal of action.[29]

At another of her gatherings, Mrs Everett, drawing on the
full extent of her artistic knowledge, extolled John's great
talent, and informed him: 'God loves you.' But Augustus,
acutely embarrassed, mumbled: 'I don't think he has bestowed
any particular favours on me.' He was overwhelmed during
this period by an avalanche of flattery, but kept his head. When
Tonks on one occasion declared that he was the greatest
draughtsman since Michelangelo, he replied simply: 'I can't

agree with what you said.' It was this modesty that helped to endear him to his fellow students. One summer big baskets of roses were imported to decorate the gaunt walls of the Slade, and the students set about binding them into festoons. 'Several of us were standing about outside the Portrait Room with baskets of festoons,' Edna Clarke Hall remembered.* '... We were considering a pedestal, from which the statue for some unknown reason had been removed, when Professor Tonks came suddenly out of the Portrait Class. He stopped and from his height looked down on me, and with one of his sardonic smiles and indicating the empty pedestal asked "Is that for John?"'

Already, by 1897, it seemed clear to many that something of a phenomenon had come among them.† He excelled *au premier coup*. Sargent, the American portrait painter then at the height of his fame in London, exclaimed when he visited the Slade that Augustus's drawings were beyond anything that had been seen done since the Italian Renaissance. And William Rothenstein, in his memoirs, wrote: 'Not only were his drawings of heads and of the nude masterly; he poured out compositions with extraordinary ease; he had the copiousness which goes with genius, and he himself had the eager understanding, the imagination, the readiness for intellectual and physical adventure one associates with genius.'[30]

He was extremely industrious. After leaving the Slade in the late afternoon, he and his friends would go back to his rooms to continue drawing and painting and acting as one another's models. On one occasion Augustus lost his key. No amount of knocking fetched anyone and, becoming quickly impatient, he leapt on to the railings in front of the house and then, like a monkey, scaled up the outside of the building to the top floor, hanging on by his fingernails. Having got through an attic

---

* Unpublished reminiscences. But see 'Edna Clarke Hall: Drawings and Watercolours 1895–1947'. Slade Centenary Exhibition at the d'Offay Couper Gallery, October 1971.

† Gwen John was also successful at the Slade. In her second year (1896–7) she won a certificate for figure drawing, and the following year was awarded the Melvill Nettleship Prize for figure composition.

window, a minute later he was opening the door to the other students standing there terrified by his acrobatics.

In 1897, when Augustus was nineteen, Tonks offered his students a prize for copies after Rubens, Watteau, Michelangelo and Raphael. Augustus won it easily with a charcoal study after Watteau. His sheer manual dexterity was dazzling. Whatever style he adopted he did it supremely well and his work acted on the other students as a powerful catalyst. Before joining the Slade he had studied reproductions of Pre-Raphaelite paintings in magazines and been enormously impressed by them. Now this influence was passing. Gainsborough had become his favourite British artist; but he had also developed an admiration for Reynolds, in particular his power of combining fine design with psychological insight. The more he saw, the more he admired. He would, he told William Rothenstein, have given 'five years to watch Titian paint a picture'. But at the same time he claimed that 'J. F. Millet was a master I bowed before'. But by 1897 Watteau, probably, was the chief influence upon him, though he was about to be introduced by William Rothenstein to the work of Goya whom he later considered superior to all these. Rothenstein's book on Goya opened up for Augustus a world where, to the accompaniment of guitars, the artist lived dangerously. It was a life on which he would have liked to model his own career.

'We may say that the whole of the art which preceded it has influenced the work of John, in the sense that he has continued a universal tradition,' wrote T. W. Earp. But although he was an amalgam of so many Old Masters, he was beginning to produce unmistakable 'Johns'. After fifty years of painstaking Victorian pictures, his lightning facility was extraordinarily refreshing. There seemed no reservations in his attitude, and the immediacy of his drawings was marvellously invigorating. He wanted to register his first conception of beauty, his excitement, the mood of a passing moment. He wanted to fix all this with an almost spontaneous impact on the canvas. Draughtsmanship was in no way for him an intellectual exercise, but a matter of passionate observation involving the animal co-ordination of hand, eye and brain.[31] 'Does it not seem,' he once asked, 'as if the secret of the artist lies in the prolongation of the age of adolescence with whatever increase of technical skill and sophistication the lessons of the years may bring?'[32]

But while his drawings and pastels improved, his paintings remained uncertain. He found it difficult to control his palette. The Slade had taught him little of the relation of one colour to another and he had no natural sense of tone. Sometimes he would ruin a picture for the sake of a gesture, stamping down an attitude or splashing on some band of colour – a red scarf or green hat – because, on the spur of the moment, it took his fancy. But occasionally he gave promise of fine work.

In the autumn of 1898 he set off with Evans and McEvoy for Amsterdam, where a large Rembrandt exhibition was being held.* 'This was a great event,' he recorded. 'As I bathed myself in the light of the Dutchman's genius, the scales of aesthetic romanticism fell from my eyes, disclosing a new and far more wonderful world.'[33] They slept in a lodging house, wandered by the canals of old Amsterdam, lived off herrings and schnapps, and every day visited the museums. It was now that the last wraiths of Pre-Raphaelitism, the sorcery of Malory's dim and lovely world, faded in his imagination, to be replaced by the poetry of common humanity. Not long afterwards, he travelled through Belgium with the same companions, immersing himself in the Flemish masters for whom he now felt a deep and natural sympathy. 'Bruges, Anvers, Gand, Bruxelles have seen me and I have beheld them,' he wrote to Will Rothenstein. 'Rubens I have expostulated with, been chidden by, and loved. Jack Jordaens has been my boon companion and I have wept beside the Pump of Quinton Matzys.'

At other times he was condemned to Tenby. Edwin had recently moved from 32 Victoria Street to a house just round the corner in South Cliff Street. Southbourne, as it was called, was almost exactly identical to Victoria House: the same narrow, dark, cube-like prison. Augustus felt all the old sensations of claustrophobia, the panic and emptiness. 'An exile in my native place I greet you from afar and tearfully,' he wrote to Will Rothenstein.

* At the Stedelijk Museum from 8 September to 31 October 1898.

Rain has set in and I feel cooped up and useless. What we have seen of the country has been wonderful. But it is ten minutes walk to the rocky landscape with figures.*

Pembrokeshire has never appeared so fine to me before, nor the town so smugly insignificant, nor the paternal roof so tedious and compromising a shelter. Trinkets which in a lodging house would be amusing insult my eye here and the colloquy of the table compels in me a blank mask of attention only relieved now and then by hysterical and unreasonable laughter.

The great solace is to crouch in the gloom of a deserted brick kiln amongst the debris of gypsies and excrete under the inspiration of lush Nature without, to the accompaniment of a score of singing birds.

I hope to quit this place shortly and come home to London where I can paint off my humours.

In a letter to Michel Salaman of about the same date Augustus wrote: 'I intend coming up to London in a week or so when I shall start that Holy Moses treat.' He had chosen, from among the alternatives set for the Slade summer competition that year, Poussin's theme 'Moses and the Brazen Serpent'. The bustling bravura composition he now produced was by far his most ambitious painting as a student. Heavily influenced by the Italian Renaissance, the whole composition is very obviously an exercise – 'an anthology of influences' Andrew Forge described it – and, though far from being purely imitative, it lacks the true originality of, say, Stanley Spencer's prize paintings a few years later, 'The Apple Gatherers' and 'The Nativity'. This *tour de force* of eclecticism won Augustus the summer prize and he left the Slade in glory.

Two years before, while he was at work in the Life Class, he had seen Brown usher in a jaunty little man in black, wearing a monocle: James McNeill Whistler. 'It is difficult to imagine the excitement that name aroused in those days,' Augustus recalled.[34] They had all heard and read so much about this

* 'I have been blown upon by the wind, peppered with sand, moistened by spray – indeed borne all the rough handed caresses of the air, earth and water – not ungratefully,' he wrote from South Cliff Street to Michel Salaman this summer. 'To-day I had a glorious bathe in a little bay some distance away on the coast. The sun tho' far away shone hot and uninterrupted by clouds which however ranged themselves exquisitely in their right places.'

Mephistopheles in miniature; had spent so many hours in the Print Room of the British Museum studying his etchings of the Thames and of Venice; had seen in the galleries from time to time some reticent new stain from his brush – the image of a tired old gentleman sitting by a wall, or a young one obtruding no more than cuffs and a violin; or of a *jeune fille* poised in immobility, or some dim river in the dusk, washed with silver. No wonder a stir went through the students. 'An electric shock seemed to galvanize the class : there was a respectful demonstration : the Master bowed genially and retired.' By the end of the century Whistler's predominance had begun to wane, and Augustus himself was becoming the idol of the Slade. The students loved him for his bad drawings, for his willingness to destroy so much that he did, for his exhortation to them to take risks. There arose among them a veneration for the stylish, elegant vitality of his life – for his facility, spontaneous avoidance of profundity, his air of Greek classicism. For those in need of a hero, here was the obvious choice, and his entrance into the Life Class at the Slade in 1901 was at least as galvanizing as that of the formidable butterfly with the sting five years before. 'When I first saw this extraordinary individual was while I was a student at the Slade school,' Wyndham Lewis remembered.

... He had had the scholarship at the Slade, and the walls bore witness to the triumphs of this 'Michelangelo'. He was a legendary 'Slade School *ingenious*', to use Campion the door-keeper's word. A large charcoal drawing in the centre of the wall of the life-class of a hairy male nude, arms defiantly folded and a bristling moustache, commemorated his powers with almost a Gascon assertiveness : and fronting the stairs that lead upwards where the ladies were learning to be Michelangelos, hung a big painting of Moses and the Brazen Serpent ...

... One day the door of the life-class opened and a tall bearded figure, with an enormous black Paris hat, large gold ear-rings decorating his ears, with a carriage of the utmost arrogance, strode in and the whisper 'John' went round the class. He sat down on a donkey – the wooden chargers astride which we sat to draw – tore a page of banknote paper out of a sketch-book, pinned it upon a drawing-board, and with a ferocious glare at the model (a female) began to draw with an indelible pencil. I joined the group behind this redoubtable personage ... John left as abruptly as he had arrived. We watched in silence this mythological figure depart.[35]

4. FLAMMONDISM

And women, young and old, were fond
Of looking at the man Flammonde.
                              Edwin Arlington Robinson

Augustus's growing renown in the late 1890s and early 1900s was based not simply on his gifts as a draughtsman but upon his extreme visibility. The exhibitionism he seemed to cultivate – a kind of inverted Dandyism – made it impossible to overlook him. His shoes, created specially to his own design, were meticulously unpolished; the gold ear-rings he was soon to pin on were second-hand; he wore no tie or collar and was contemptuous of those who did – in their place he fastened a black silk scarf with a silver brooch; he did wear a hat but, far from being a respectable one, it was of gypsy design, patina'd with age; his eyes were restless, his hair alarmingly uncut.

He walked the streets with a terrific stride, bolstering himself up as if constantly to raise his own morale and to protect himself from other people. When he interrupted his silence he could be formidable. One day a gang of children fell in behind him and began shouting: 'Get ye 'air cut, mister.' Augustus halted, turned on them, and growled: 'Get your throats cut!'

Part of his reputation at this time depended on deliberate neglect. He neglected to shave; he neglected middle-class proprieties and conventional attitudes; he even neglected using very much common sense. By many he was regarded with a respect that was agreeably tinged with horror. There was no telling what he would say or do next – though very often he said and did nothing at all. He seemed a mass of inexplicably changing moods that might have appeared pretentious had they not been so awe-inspiring, so obviously authentic. The barometer of these moods shot up and down with extraordinary rapidity. Periods of great charm and tenderness would vanish suddenly before violent convulsions of temper; days of leaden gloom all at once dispersed, and he would glow with wonderful geniality. But often there seemed nothing to account for these alterations, or to connect them.

A vivid example of how others, who were themselves affected with romanticism, saw Augustus at the age of twenty-one is given by William Rothenstein:

He looked like a young fawn; he had beautiful eyes, almond-shaped and with lids defined like those Leonardo drew, a short nose, broad cheek-bones, while over a fine forehead fell thick brown hair, parted in the middle. He wore a light curling beard (he had never shaved) and his figure was lithe and elegant. I was at once attracted to John ... A dangerous breaker of hearts, he would be, I thought, with his looks and his ardour. He talked of leaving the Slade, and was full of plans for future work; but he was poor and needed money for models. [36]

Although not materialistic, Augustus was ambitious. He felt naturally eager to develop his talent, and he was anxious also for success partly as a vicarious means of fixing his own identity. Unable to exist within himself, he used an echo principle for defining his personality, seeing himself in other people's looks, hearing himself in their replies, recognizing himself in their attitudes to him. Many of his portraits are in this way strongly autobiographical.

Under the flamboyant exterior there was always much uncertainty. But his sense of ambition, and the impatience that had accumulated since his bathing accident, made him determined to outmanoeuvre his disadvantages and convert them into positive-looking qualities. To achieve this, he invented a part, complete with theatrical costume, that fitted only a fraction of the real Augustus John and, for the rest, acted as a form of concealment.

Hesitant, unsure of so much, he was dynamic in one thing: the pursuit of beauty, in particular of beautiful women. This was his inspiration as an artist, affording him what Wyndham Lewis called his epileptic 'fits of seeing'. A beautiful girl would act upon his eye like a lighted match upon a Catherine-wheel. Gone would be the fearful melancholy, the faltering indecision; banished the furred hesitation of speech, as there rang out the old commanding cry: *'Come on then, let's go!'*[37]

It is impossible to disconnect Augustus's work from his

passionate response to the beauty of women – 'these magnificent goddesses', as Lord David Cecil described the John girls, 'who, with kerchiefed heads and flowing, high-waisted dresses, stand gazing into the distance in reverie or look down pensively at the children who run and leap and wrestle round their feet. Wild and regal, at once lover, mother and priestess, woman dominates Mr John's scene.'

Like his maternal grandfather Thomas Smith, Augustus was a man 'of full habit of body'. But his view of women was idealistic rather than simply sensual, and had been formed by the early death of his mother. At first, back in Tenby, he had been drawn towards the full-bosomed majesty of maturer women, admiring from afar and usually while in church their rich proportions that seemed to offer all he most desired: warmth and consolation. Typical of these women had been the headmaster's wife at his unsympathetic school near Bristol, on whose generous bosom, he remembered, 'in great distress, I once laid my head and wept'.[38]

With the onset of adolescence his world had become invaded by disturbing forces. Whether upon the beach or in the streets of Tenby, by wood or field or mere, it seemed his fate to encounter at every turn the mocking glance of some fair girl, to gaze in wonder at her flashing limbs and flowing hair, catch some breath of fern-like fragrance as she passed. Under the eyes of such beauty his awkwardness was painful, the old-fashioned clothes his father made him wear an unspeakable insult. He would have felt less of an ass if, while wandering alone on the marshes, he had come across some faery's child lingering disconsolately amid the sedge. For she, like him, would have been silent, would not have laughed, but taken him perhaps into the cool ritual of her embrace. Such phantoms peopled his imagination in an atmosphere of hazy eroticism. Prevented by his abnormal timidity from making contact with actual girls, he consorted with imaginary creatures who had travelled from the languid reveries of Burne-Jones and Rossetti. Only with the governess who mainly looked after Winifred could he feel any assurance, and this because she was an alien, as he felt himself to be.

The conflict between the world of reality and his fastidiously

romantic dreamland gradually intensified. On Sunday afternoons in the early 1890s Geraldine de Burgh, her elder sister and
a friend of theirs used to walk from Tenby over the sand dunes
and rough grass tracks of the Burrows towards Penally and
Giltar. And almost every Sunday they were secretly met by
'Gussie', Thornton and their friend Robert Prust. Geraldine was
partnered by Gussie – the routine was invariable – though she
would have much preferred Robert Prust. Gussie, she thought,
was terribly backward: they did not even hold hands. But as
the youngest, it was not hers to choose. Over sixty-five years
later (1959), Augustus wrote to her:

You are one of the big landmarks of my early puberty. I was intensely shy then, besides you generally had your brother with you
to add to my confusion.* Perhaps your noble name intimidated me
too. But I was always afraid of girls then – girls and policemen ...
Yes, I have been honoured with the Freedom of the Burrough [sic]
– Freedom for what? We all had the Freedom of the Burrows long
ago and I greatly regret I made so little use of it as far as you were
concerned.

By this time Augustus had experienced what he called 'the
dawn of manhood'. The sexual facts of life, the biological
mysteries of reproduction were explained to him with much
raucous humour by the other boys in Tenby. He was horrified.
Gloom, terror and bewilderment mounted in him. So this was
how his father, in his salt hours, had amused himself with his
mother; to these wanton appetites and motions did he owe his
very existence! It seemed as if he would never be free from
it.

But, when all the exaggerations and dubious anecdotes of
Augustus John's life are set aside, he remains a man of astonishing virility. Therefore, inevitably, acclimatization to the real
world came with time. 'Further investigations both in Art and
Nature,' he wrote, 'completing the process of enlightenment

* It seems possible that John invented this extra obstacle to help account for
his extreme bashfulness. Mrs Violet Crowther, Geraldine de Burgh's daughter,
in a letter to the author (13 January 1969), wrote: 'He would have known my
mother's brothers, of course, even if only by sight, but he is, I feel sure, mistaken in saying one was present on the occasion of these meetings.'

thus begun, brought me down from cloud cuckooland to the
equally treacherous bed-rock of Mother Earth.'[39]

Having loosed this knot, he would never again be tied up
by sexual mores and taboos. Homosexuality did not shock him;
incest held no fears: both were part of village life, protected by
winter and bad roads. It was modern society, with its
sophisticated network of rules and regulations that complicated
what was a simple matter.

To Augustus, all women were mothers, with himself either
as child or God-the-father. Not long content to figure in the
public eye as doubtful or baffled, he produced himself, like
Meredith, as a robust pagan with a creed that personified
Nature as a mother. She was an object of desire, but also a
goddess of fertility, a symbolic yet physical being capable of
answering all the needs of man: a woman to be celebrated and
enjoyed. This pagan simplicity Augustus expressed most lyrically in the glowing figure-in-landscape panels he painted with
Innes in the years before the First World War. Here women and
children appear as part of the wild country – a connection
Augustus specifically makes in some of his letters. 'This landscape,' he wrote to Wyndham Lewis (October 1946) from
Provence, 'like some women I have heard of, takes a deal of
getting into. I am making the usual awkward approaches –
soon I hope to dispense with these manoeuvres and get down
to bed-rock, but the preliminaries are tiresome.'[40]

The Victorian preliminaries he found increasingly tiresome
after his third year at the Slade. Impetuosity – assisted by the
occasional glass of wine or whisky or, when in France, of
absinthe or calvados or even, at the Café Royal, hock-and-
seltzer or crême de menthe frappé – was always helping him
to accelerate past his awful shyness. His first serious girl friend
was Ursula Tyrwhitt, who allowed him to walk her home
every day after school. A bird-like, ecstatic creature, she soared
on flights of astronomical vagueness, being friendly one day and
cool the next, as if she could never recall what state their relationship had reached. When they were together they drew
and painted each other's portraits; and wrote love-letters to
each other when they were apart. 'How is it pray, that your
letters have the scent of violets? Violets that make my heart

beat,' Augustus asked her, '... Write again sans blague Ursula Ursula Ursula Ursula.' By mystifying him with her vagueness she continued to attract him, but any idea they may have had of marrying was scotched by her father, a crusty old gentleman, averse to Tyrwhittless* unconventionality. In one of his last letters to her, while they were both still students, Augustus enclosed a charming little self-portrait, pen and brush in black ink, inscribed 'Au Revoir, Gus'. Their love-affair had already come to an end, and Ursula was soon closer to Gwen, with whom she kept in touch for almost thirty years.

Before leaving the Slade, Augustus had taken up with another student, Ida Nettleship, one of Ursula's best friends. Ida was a very sexually attractive girl, with slanted Oriental eyes, a sensuous mouth, dark curly hair and a dark complexion. There seemed some untamed quality about her, yet for the time being these fires were damped down, smouldering. She was very quiet — 'tongueless' she called herself — her manner enigmatic; and when she did speak it was with a low, cultivated accent. She had been brought up in a strongly Pre-Raphaelite atmosphere and, at the age of four, was once snatched from the nursery floor to be kissed by Robert Browning — an experience she was instructed never to forget. By her mother, a martinet and dressmaker — an expert with the needle who made clothes for many of the smartest ladies connected with the theatre, from Ellen Terry to Oscar Wilde's wife Constance — Ida was worshipped and perhaps a little spoilt. Her father, Jack Nettleship, once the creator of imaginative Blake-like designs depicting lost spirits, had by now turned painter of melodramatic zoo-animals in conflict, mostly lions, leopards and polar bears, all lavishly reproduced in *Boy's Own Paper*. He had preferred painting to a career as writer† and became one of a group known as 'the Brotherhood' which included John Butler Yeats, Edwin Ellis and George Wilson.

* She later married a man named Tyrwhitt — a cousin.

† He wrote a biography of Browning. One of his brothers, Henry, was Corpus Professor of Latin at Oxford; another, Richard, was a Fellow and Tutor at Balliol, and a great friend of Benjamin Jowett; and the third, Edward, a prominent oculist. Jack always regretted not having done the lions in Trafalgar Square, of which, he believed, he could have made a far better job than Landseer.

'George Wilson was our born painter,' Yeats used to say, 'but Nettleship our genius.' As the Pre-Raphaelite spirit ebbed out of British art, he had lost confidence and painted only what Rossetti called 'his pot-boilers'.

He had sent Ida to the Slade in 1892; in 1895 she won a three-year scholarship and remained there altogether six years. From most of the students she held aloof, cultivating a small circle of devoted friends – Ursula Tyrwhitt, Gwen Salmond and Edna Waugh. These last two and Ida were known collectively as 'the nursery' because they were, or behaved as if they were, younger than the other students. The Kipling *Jungle Book* had recently come out, and Ida named each of her special friends after one of the animals, she herself being Mowgli, the man cub. Her early letters seem exaggeratedly fey, but have about them a certain intensity. She is frequently exchanging with 'Baloo' the big brown bear (Dorothy Salaman) tokens of 'friendship for always' which took the form of rosaries made from eucalyptus, pin cushions, ivy leaves and lavender and all manner of flowers and plants 'rich in purple bells, a joy to the eyes'. And she ends these letters on a high note of jungle euphoria: 'Bless you with jungle joy, Your bad little man cub, Mistress Mowgli Nettleship'. When 'Bagheera', the pantheress (Bessie Salaman) marries, Ida writes: 'I think you are a charmer – but oh you *are* married – never girl Bessie again. Do you know you are different? ... Mowgli will be so lonely in the jungle without the queen panthress. Oh you're worth a kiss sweet, tho' you are grown into a wife.'

Ida herself carefully avoided growing into a wife. All her most intimate friends were girls, and they lived together in a golden world of Victorian emotionalism, a timeless place with the prospect of being girls eternal. Their mood was that of Polixenes in *The Winter's Tale*:

> We were as twinn'd lambs that did frisk i' the sun
> And bleat the one at the other: what we chang'd
> Was innocence for innocence; we knew not
> The doctrine of ill-doing, no, nor dream'd
> That any did.

Men had no place in this sexless paradise, and about the

only creature to be credited with some degree of masculinity was Ida herself, the man cub. Her soft voluptuous beauty was of a kind that is at its finest in the late teens and early twenties. At the Slade she had many admirers, but she shrugged off all of them – except one. This was Clement Salaman, elder brother of Augustus's friend Michel Salaman, who became friendly with her through his sisters. It was not long before he fell passionately in love and, for a short time, they were engaged to be married. Ida seems to have consented to this partly for his sister's sake for, since she was not in love with him, she could not really believe he was in love with her. Love, surely, was a mutual experience – so he *must* be mistaken. Naturally she would like to be his friend always, as she was with Baloo. In February 1897 she formally broke off the engagement, explaining in a letter to the panthress Bagheera that this was 'a good and pleasant thing for both'. 'Don't you think a great friendship could come out of it?' she queried. 'The soft side surely can be conquered – indeed I think he has conquered it. It would be a life joy, a friendship between us. Think how splendid. No thought of marriage or softness to spoil.'

Shortly before the end of this engagement, Ida's sister Ethel 'happened to go into the room where they were spooning and I roared with laughter', she recalled, 'and afterwards Ida said to me: "You mustn't laugh at that, it's holy." '[41] From both parents she had inherited a strong vein of religiosity; Jack Nettleship had once confessed: 'My mother cannot endure the God of the Old Testament, but likes Jesus Christ; whereas I like the God of the Old Testament, and cannot endure Jesus Christ; and we have got into the way of quarrelling about it at lunch.'[42] Ida herself was very High Church when young. In vermilion and black inks she prepared an exquisite, tiny manual for use at Mass and Benediction, 'The Little Garden of the Soul', seventy-five pages long and done with scrupulous care: 'Ida Nettleship her book'. In everyday matters she was not above sermonizing to her friends. Girls still at school were earnestly warned to beware of 'affections', advised to walk a lot and play plenty of tennis. She herself had taken to practising the fiddle as a means of avoiding temptation. 'My dear, my sweet, go thro' life aiming for the highest you know,' she in-

structed Bessie Salaman who had just become engaged. '– Oh
don't fall from what is possible for you, keep a brave true
heart and be brave and kind to all other people – And think of
making happiness and not taking it . . . don't slip – strive high
for others – that is all.'

In March 1897, immediately following the break-up of her
engagement, Ida left England for Florence, moving among
various *pensions* and reassuring her 'dear sweet mother' that
she must not 'let the proprieties worry you – I do assure you
there's nothing to fear'. Superficially there did seem cause for
anxiety since here, as at the Slade, Ida quickly attracted about
her a swarm of young admirers, poets and Americans, who
brought her almond blossom, purple anemones and full-blown
roses; and a red-haired student, less romantic and with a funny
face, 'who began talking smart to me – and ended by being
melancholy and thirsty'. Most persistent of all was a musician
called Knight, 'very friendly and very boresome', who, she
explained to her sister Ethel, 'plays the piano, and reads Keats
and cribs other people's ideas on art. He looks desperately
miserable. . . . His complaints and sorrows weary my ears so
continually – and "oh, he is so constant and so kind". They all
are.' Her virtue vanquished all comers and broadcast much
disappointment.

Ida's letters from Italy reveal much about her character. On
the whole, the girls in the *pensions* took her fancy more than
the men – one very beautiful 'like a Botticelli with great grey
eyes'; and a pretty American one, 'dark eyed and languid in
appearance', who sat next to her at meals and 'says sharp
things in a subdued trickle of a voice'; even 'the little chambermaid here with little curls hanging about her face and great
tired dark eyes' who 'takes a great interest in me'. Almost the
only woman she did not find sympathetic was the fidgety
nervous little Signorina who gave her lessons in Italian and
self-control, and who 'says eh? in a harsh tone between every
sentence – I pinch myself black and blue to keep from dancing
round the table in an agony of exasperation'.

When she was not learning Italian she was drawing and
painting – 'dashing my head against an impenetrable picture
I am attempting to reproduce in the Pitti', as she described it.

'... I am so bold and unafraid in the way I work that all the keepers and all the visitors and all the copyists come and gape ... they think I am either a fool or a genius'. Every day she worked six or seven hours, copying Old Masters or sketching out-of-doors. But, she warned her mother, '*don't* expect great things – it's fatal ... it's no easier to do in Italy than in England'.

Yet Italy intoxicated her: bells on the mules passing below her window; chatter of carts and of people that carried along the stone streets on the evening air; sight of a dazzling green hill under olive trees; the river careering down by the *pension*, swollen and yellow with rain – all these sights and sounds stirred longings in her, she scarcely knew for what. 'I simply gasp things in now, in my effort to live as much as possible these last weeks,' she wrote towards the end of her time there. 'I can't believe I shall ever be here again in this life – anyway it's not to be counted on. And it's like madness to think how soon I shall be away, and it going on just the same ... I suppose Italy must have some intoxication for people – some remarkable fascination. She certainly has converted me to be one of her lovers.'

On her return to England, Ida felt flat. Even her drawing and painting left her dissatisfied. 'We have a model like a glorious southern sleek beauty, so hard it is to do anything but look,' she wrote to her friend Bessie Salaman. 'To put her in harsh black and white – ugh, it's dreadful.' Tonks had become rather discouraging. She grew uncertain in a way she had never experienced before. 'Some days I look and wonder and say "Why paint?"' she admitted to Dorothy Salaman. 'There are such beautiful things, are they not enough? It seems like fools' madness to ever desire to put them down.'

Before this she had always been swept upwards by gushes of enthusiasm. Now she felt herself being slowly enfolded by what she called an 'eternal ennui' that seemed to come between her and the actual experience her vigorous nature needed. Womankind cannot stand very much unreality. There must be more to life, Ida felt, than copying Old Masters and exchanging flowers. She began to feel sluggish. Her boredom – 'a giant who is difficult to cope with' – stood over her, overshadowing all.

It was about this time that she started to become involved with Augustus. His personality was so strong that it tore through her morbid self-consciousness, banishing the giant of boredom. He was made for open spaces. The least calculating of men, he strode capaciously through the streets, taking her arm with a sudden thrust of initiative, as one who might say: 'Come on now, we'll show them what we can do!' Never had she known such a companion – a great, sensitive, ebullient being, refreshing as a sea breeze. The stale familiarity of so much in London vanished when he was near; outward impressions intensified – even her faltering belief in art revived. He was, she thought, a wonderfully romantic creature with just that trace of feminine delicacy which made his invigorating influence so sympathetic. When they were together it was as if they were discovering life for the first time as no one else had ever done. Without him existence grew doubly tedious: she had to force herself into being occupied, doing and learning things, in order to lift herself over these dull parts of living. Her romanticism, tempered by practical experience, was beginning to recognize certain frontiers. 'There are myriads of things one can give oneself to,' she told Dorothy Salaman, '– one can make oneself a friend of the universe – but talking is no good. A want is a want – and when one is hungry it's no good – or not much – to hear someone singing a fine song.' Only Augustus, it seemed, could assuage her real hunger. Once, when she was playing with her sisters the game of 'What-do-you-like-doing-best-in-the-World', Ida gave her choice in a low whisper: 'Going to a picture gallery with Gus John.'

Among the many men who fell in love with her Augustus was now her obvious favourite, the first and only man with whom she was herself ever to fall in love. They did not become engaged. Their situation was awkward, for her parents disapproved of Augustus and of her friendship with him. His introduction into their Victorian household had been a disaster. It was Ada Nettleship,* Ida's mother, who chiefly objected to

* Her maiden name was Hinton, and she was the sister of James Hinton who wrote an enormous philosophical work in three volumes and then, according to David John, went off his head. 'I had an idea of "discovering" him,' Romilly John records (1 August 1972), 'but have always been completely baffled after

him: and her objections were not easily to be overcome. Since her husband's lions and tigers did not sell, she had become the 'business person' in the family. Her flourishing dressmaking trade provided for the lot of them and took up almost the whole of their house – a barrack-like building without bathrooms, No. 58 Wigmore Street. Her husband and daughters inhabited only the fourth floor, ill-lit by gas-jets, and her domestic life was likewise thinly sandwiched in between her business pursuits.

Ada Nettleship was fat and soft and contrived to look older than her age. For many years she had been careful to take no exercise and moved, when she had to, with extreme slowness. She seemed a formidable dumpling of a woman, with short grey hair, a round face, retroussé nose and plump, capable Queen Victoria hands. She encased herself in a uniform of heavy black brocade made in one piece from neck to hem, with a little jabot of lace and a collar of net drawn up and tied under her chin with a narrow black velvet ribbon. Her voice was high-pitched and rather flat; her expression full of 'character'; her temper certain, but bad – except towards her family for whose welfare she was solely responsible. She worked her staff of skirt-girls, pin-girls and the embroideresses whom she had imported from the Continent very hard and, before the hours were altered by Act of Parliament, very long. Her Spartan discipline was peppered with fines and instant dismissals. But though feared, she was respected by her girls for she was an imaginative dressmaker and competent business woman, her one peccadillo being a weakness for society people, who, however extravagantly titled, often postponed paying her bills.

Ada Nettleship was frankly horrified by Augustus. It is doubtful whether, in her opinion, anyone would have been good enough for her favourite daughter, but Augustus was too bad to be true. She had no use for him at all. The person she saw was no melodramatic Christ-like figure, simply a lanky, un-

---

reading two sentences and had to start again, and so on indefinitely. James Hinton's son was the author of a book on the fourth dimension, involving the construction by the reader of hundreds of cubes with differently coloured surfaces and edges.'

washed youth, shifty-eyed and uncouth to the point of rudeness, with a scraggy, reddish beard, long hair, and scruffy
clothes. She could not understand what Ida saw in him. Had
it been anyone else he came to call on, she would not have let
him in the house. She was confident, however, that her
daughter's peculiar affection for him could not last. He was
obviously not right for her in any way. Jack Nettleship was
more dismayed than horrified. 'I do wish he'd clean his shoes,'
he kept complaining, ' – it's so bad for the leather.' But he spoke
with little authority, generally going about the house himself
barefoot.

Augustus was at his worst in Wigmore Street. His developing and very painful love for Ida, combined with her mother's
unconcealed antagonism, made him increasingly ill-at-ease.
Max Beerbohm, who once saw him there, noted that he was
'pale – sitting in window seat – sense of something powerful –
slightly sinister – Lucifer'. Old Nettleship, though everyone
agreed he was the salt of the earth, only added to this
embarrassment. With bald head, heavily grey-bearded chin and
nose 'like an opera-glass',[43] he presented an eccentric spectacle
within this conventional setting. 'Years before he had been
thrown from his horse, while hunting, and broke his arm, and
because it had been badly set suffered great pain for a long
time,' wrote another visitor to the house, W. B. Yeats. 'A little
whisky would always stop the pain, and soon a little became a
great deal and he found himself a drunkard.'[44] Having put himself into an institution for some months, he emerged completely cured, though still with the need for some liquid to sip
constantly. This craving he assuaged by continual cocoa, hot or
cold, which he drank at all times from a gigantic jorum eight
inches in diameter and eight inches deep. An alarmingly modest
man, he would show Augustus his carnivorous pictures, begging for criticism. These pictures left Augustus cold, but if he
ventured the least remark Nettleship would rush for his
palette and brushes and begin at once the laborious business of
repainting. Although he had a way of accepting absolutely
other people's judgements, his admiration for Augustus's work
was, to use a masterly word of William Rothenstein's, 'hesitating'. Their appreciation of art was very different: it was like

blasphemy for Augustus to hear him describe Beardsley's creatures as 'damned ugly women'. Yet it was in this house that he first met many celebrities, from the old William Michael Rossetti to the young Walter Sickert, 'the latter just emerging from the anonymity of *élève de Whistler*'.[45]

In a rough synopsis* for his autobiography, scribbled on Eiffel Tower Restaurant paper some time during the 1920s, Augustus introduces Ida's name together with the word 'torture'. He was violently attracted to her. Her mature body, so chaste and erotic, the muted intensity, quiet deep manner, those strangely slanting eyes, that ingenuous mind: all this excited him frantically. His happiness seemed to depend upon the secret of her beauty, upon his possessing it, and he pursued her with a wild intermittent persistence. One day, for example, he turned up at St Albans, where she had gone to a party of Edna Clarke Hall's, who remembered what happened.

Ida and I had not seen each other for some time, so, to get away from the others, we climbed up a ladder to the top of a great haystack ... We had hardly settled there when up the ladder came Augustus John.

Ida told John very definitely that we wanted to be alone and he told us no less definitely that he wanted to be there, and to put an end to the matter he gave a great heave and it fell to the ground. And there we were! Ida was extremely vexed and told him so in no uncertain terms. John took umbrage and said that if we did not want him he would go. He flung himself on to the steep thatch and proceeded to slide down head first. We were horrified! The stack was a very high one, and the ground seemed a long way off. Securing ourselves as best we could, we both got hold of a foot – his shoes, then his socks came off, – we frantically seized his

---

* This synopsis was done for Hubert Alexander, whose family had been friendly with the McNeills, and who had got to know Augustus through Dorelia McNeill. In the 1920s Hubert Alexander had turned publisher and approached John for his memoirs. 'I've been thinking of the book and will send you shortly a provisional synopsis,' John wrote to him on 21 February 1923. Alexander believes he may have got the synopsis about 1927, but since there is a holograph synopsis among Augustus's papers, it seems likely that it was never sent. Certainly by 1932 negotiations were still continuing and Sir Charles Reilly remembered that year 'a publisher came down [to Fryern Court] and offered him great sums for his autobiography, finally reaching £13,000, the sum I heard him say Lady Oxford got for hers, but he nobly turned it down.'

trousers. He wriggled like an eel and his trousers began to come off. Then we cried aloud for help and some of the party came running, put up the ladder and rescued the crazy fellow!

But the peace of our solitude was completely shattered.[46]

Augustus was tortured not by unrequited love but unconsummated sex. Although Ida loved him, she refused to live with him, less perhaps for her own sake than for that of her parents who, she hoped, would come to like him. Meanwhile their love-affair, for all its passion, seemed to have reached a stalemate. Augustus was not faithful. Sight was mind, and out of sight was largely out of mind. On his journey through the Netherlands he grew excited as much by the surprising character and beauty of the people he saw as by the Flemish masters. The two were jumbled together in his letters as if there were no difference. He writes, for example, of Rembrandt's wife, Saskia van Uylenborch:

She was sweeter than honey, more desirable than beauty, more profound than the Cathedral. And in Brussels lives an old woman with faded eyes who made me blush for thinking so much of the young wenches.

But there was one in Antwerp I think Rembrandt would have cared for, Gabrielle Madeleine by name. She had azure under her eyes and her veins were blue and such a good stout mask withal, and she spoke French only as a Flamande can. Unfortunately she wore fashionable boots of a pale buff tint. (Besides which her room lay within that of her white haired bundle of a Mama.) You will shrug your shoulders hearing of my aberrations but I feel more competent for them, and that is the main thing.

Women continued to inspire Augustus only while they remained mysterious. As custodians of a happiness he could divine but never completely enjoy, they symbolized for him an ideal state of being that formed the subject of his painting. Yet his most immediate need was for a physical union that would dissolve momentarily the loneliness locked up within him. From external troubles and from his innate melancholy he sought release through multifarious love-affairs. These were affairs of the body, but while his body was comforted his spirit lost something. The penalty he paid for being unable to endure isolation was a theft from his artistic imagination of its essential stimulus. For his ideal concept of 'beauty', once divested of its symbolic majesty and enigmatic life, became empty, almost meaningless: beauty embalmed and unalive.

5. AMONG THE LIVING

'I am taking a studio with McEvoy,' Augustus had written to Michel Salaman in the summer of 1898. This was 76 Charlotte Street, once used by Constable, and now, over the next two years, to be shared intermittently with Orpen, Benjamin Evans and Albert Rutherston. All of them were desperately poor, but full of plans for future work. Most helpful to Augustus was Albert's elder brother William Rothenstein. His admiration for Augustus's work was tireless – 'a sight of some of John's drawings has taken any vanity I might have had out of me', he once wrote to his wife Alice. To his many friends, including Sargent, Conder and Charles Furse, Rothenstein began showing Augustus's drawings, and a number were sold in this way – though Furse was greatly taken aback at the price of two pounds apiece. It was mainly on this money, together with what he received each quarter through Thomas Smith's will, that Augustus subsisted.

'John – Orpen – McEvoy and myself are going to get up a class,' Albert Rutherston wrote to his father (20 January 1899), 'and have a model in John's studio once a week at night – it will come to about 7d each.' Augustus himself had found the model late one night in the Tottenham Court Road – a young girl with hair of flaming red and a pale mask of a face who, having no work, willingly agreed to sit. As the sittings progressed she and Augustus grew increasingly friendly, but one day when she dropped off to sleep on the divan he suddenly realized that her gleaming head of hair was curiously misplaced. Congenital baldness was no crime, neither was it contagious; yet so great was the disenchantment he felt incapable of finishing her portrait. He turned the picture to the wall, and soon she ceased to come.

Because the studio was small, Augustus spent a good deal of time roaming about the town with his sketch-book. He had been reading Heine's *Florentine Nights* and was particularly drawn to a tattered band of strolling players he met in Hyde Park who would give song-and-dance performànces full of Elizabethan charm and crudity. He often saw them and eventually succeeded in persuading the principal dancer to pose for him. 'Those flashing eyes, that swart mongolian face (the nose seemed to have been artificially flattened), framed in a halo of dark curls, made an impression not to be shaken off lightly.'[47]

His first commission in portraiture was to paint an old lady living in Eaton Square for a fee of forty pounds, half of which was paid in advance. 'As the work went on I began to tire of the old lady's personality,' he wrote; 'she too, I could see, was bored by mine, and getting restless. She even spoke rather sharply to me now and then. This didn't encourage me at all. One day, having made a date for the next sitting, I departed never to return. I had got her head done pretty well at any rate and the old lady got her picture at half price.'[48]* Looked at today, the picture seems very close in style and feeling to some of Gwen John's portraiture, and indicates that their development began on parallel lines. The colour has been toned down – monochrome with silvery-white flesh tones and slight touches of warm ochre. In the middle of an area of black dress, the old lady holds a red book. An orange frill on the cushion behind her head gives colour to her face and follows the line of her smile. Augustus's treatment conveys the impression of decaying beauty. Despite the atmosphere of sadness, the suffering is contained and the old lady's personality clearly comes through.

About the same time, through the mediation of a fashionable lady in Hampstead, Augustus was also commissioned to do two drawings in the West of England. His first destination was a large mausoleum of a house set in parklands that resembled

* In 1941 Sir John Rothenstein came across this picture in a dealer's gallery and brought it to John's studio for identification. At first John failed to recognize it, but later did acknowledge it to be his, and it was hung in the Tate Gallery. In his *Modern English Painters*, Rothenstein described it as a rather fumbling and pedestrian essay and, though probably a fair example of his painting at this time, very laboured, niggling in form, hardly modelled at all. But John himself, on reading this, objected: 'The "Old Lady's" head is very well modelled: the hands unfinished yet expressive. She couldn't move them easily.'

a cemetery – altogether a monument to boredom. On arriving there, he was struck by the beauty of his young hostess, which seemed, after a cocktail or two, very visibly to increase. They felt shy with each other and after the drawing was done she took him upstairs to show him her home-made chapel fitted into the attic. Her husband was away shooting, she explained – he often was – and during the dull days of his absence she would seek consolation here. Within the wall, Augustus spied a recess – perhaps a confessional, or a boudoir, or both ... But soon he had to be on his way for the next assignment. Here, too, there was much embalmed magnificence and beauty, though the atmosphere seemed less tense with melodrama. His new hostess, unencumbered with religiosity, was as amiable as the first. There seemed to be an epidemic of 'shooting' in the district, for her husband also had been carried off by it. When the drawing was done, Augustus returned to London with two cheques in his pocket, but richer in more ways than one.

Largely because of the emotional deprivation of his mother, Augustus had grown up without any inner source of self-esteem. But now, to his surprise and delight, other people were finding him to be a marvellous proper man. He began to sniff some of the power that his personality could exert, especially on women. So much that he had missed at Tenby, even at the Slade, seemed at last within his grasp. It was dangerous knowledge. In the heyday he was now entering, such was the devastating charm of his presence that old ladies on buses, it was said, would get up blushing to offer him their seats; and young girls in the Café Royal had to be led away fainting when he made his entrance there.

The letters that Augustus and his friends wrote at this time show them drawing and painting all day – self-portraits, portraits of one another or of some shared model – often in the hope of having their work accepted by the New English Art Club. In the evening they would hurry off to the Empire to listen to Yvette Guilbert, or go to the Hippodrome to see a splendid troupe of Japanese acrobats, tight-rope walkers, nightingale-clowns and swimmers. But best of all, Augustus loved the Sadler's Wells music hall in Islington, London's oldest theatre. He went almost every week, taking there for a shilling

a box from the very front of which he would fling his hat in
the air whenever he approved of a turn. The crowd in the
stalls, believing him to be a tremendous swell, nicknamed him
'Algy'. One night, when their teasing became too personal,
Augustus rose and delivered an abusive speech. The crowd,
after listening for a minute, went for him, but he emptied his
beer over them and, like the Scarlet Pimpernel, escaped.

After such breathless entertainments, whenever they could
afford it, Augustus and his friends would go to the Café Royal,
eat sandwiches, drink lager beer and sit up late gazing at the
celebrities. Orpen, Albert Rutherston and Augustus were together so much of the time that they became known as 'the
three musketeers'; but on less rowdy evenings they would be
joined by McEvoy and Gwen John, Ida Nettleship and some of
her special friends. Sometimes, too, by Mrs Everett, her hair
decorated with arum lilies, anxious to spirit them away to
Salvationist meetings where men with sturdy legs and women
with complexions shared a chorus of loud jokes.

On 14 September 1898 Ida and Gwen Salmond crossed over to
Paris, Gwen to stay there for six months, Ida for three. They
put up temporarily at what Ida called a 'very old lady style of
pension' at 226 Boulevard Raspail on the outskirts of the Latin
quarter: 'such a healthy part of Paris!' she exclaimed in a
letter to her mother (15 September 1898). They had invited
Gwen John to join them, but when she mentioned the plan to
her father, Edwin automatically opposed it. She was, however,
undeterred; went round the house singing 'To Paris! To Paris!';
and wrote to Ida in the third week of September announcing
that she was on the way. 'Gwen John is coming – hurrah,' Ida
told her mother (18 September 1898). '. . . We *are* so glad
Gwen is coming. It makes all the difference – a complete
trio.'

Gwen arrived punctually carrying a large marmalade cake,
and the three of them set off to look at flats – 'such lovely bare
places furnished only with looking-glasses'[49] – soon finding what
they wanted on the top floor of 12 Rue Froidveau, or 'Cold Veal
Street' as Ida called it. In a letter to her mother (20 September
1898) she described the moral architecture of the place, which
was

on the 5th floor – overlooking a large open space – right over the market roof. It had 3 good rooms, a kitchen and W.C. and water and gas – and a balcony. Good windows – very light and airy. Nothing opposite for miles – very high up. The woman (concierge) is very clean and exceedingly healthy looking. The proprietress is rather swell – an old lady – she lives this end of Paris and we went to see her. She asked questions, and especially that *we received nobody* – 'Les *dames* – oui. Mais les messieurs? Non! *Jamais!'* ... She wants to keep her apartments very high in character. All this is rather amusing, but it will show you it is a respectable place. It *is* over a café – but the entrance is right round the corner – quite separate ... We want all the paper scraped and the place whitewashed ... It is near the Louvre and Julian's – and is very open.

Gwen Salmond had sixty pounds and wanted to study at the *Académie Julian* under Benjamin Constant. Ida had thirty pounds and thought of going to either Delécluze or Colarossi, both of whom were less expensive. Gwen John had less money still and could afford to attend no school. But by a fortunate chance another studio was just opening in Paris that autumn – the extraordinary *Académie Carmen* in the Rue Stanislas. It was to be run by the luxuriant Italian beauty Carmen Rossi, a one-time model of Whistler who, it was announced, would himself attend twice a week to instruct the pupils. The price was the same as Julian's – too expensive for Ida: but Gwen Salmond, changing her mind at the last moment, decided to go there. 'Whistler has been twice to the studio – and Gwen finds him very beautiful and just right,' Ida wrote to her mother. '... [he] is going to paint a picture of Madame la Patronne of the studio, his model, and hang it in the studio for the students to learn from. Isn't it fine? He's a regular first rate Master and, according to Gwen, knows how to teach.' So enthusiastic was Gwen Salmond that she insisted that Gwen John accompany her, and by a benevolent act of intrigue smuggled her in as an afternoon pupil.

Whistler's name was enough to ensure the early success of the *Académie Carmen*, which was thronged when he first appeared there but which, by the beginning of 1901, had shrunk to a total of two ladies. The rules, which made it an unpopular institution with the men, were stricter than those of the Slade. Smoking was prohibited; singing and talking disallowed; charcoal drawings on the walls absolutely forbidden; studies from the nude in mixed classes banned – and the sexes quickly segregated into different *ateliers*. Whistler himself made a point of being received not as a companion in shirt-sleeves, but as the Master visiting his apprentices. Against all expectation he offered no magical short cuts : on the contrary he would have liked to teach his students from the very beginning, even the grinding and mixing of the colours. Tintoretto, he enjoyed reminding them, had never done anything for himself until he was forty, and that was the way he wished them to work for him. His high larks, which always contained some serious matter, very often bewildered them. The palette, not the canvas, was the field of experiment, he insisted, and he would frequently ignore their pictures altogether, earnestly studying their palettes to detect what progress was being made. His magisterial passions, monocled sarcasms, his old-fashioned romantic susceptibilities, and the need which his rootless nature felt for a band of dedicated disciples, antagonized the men, whose male competitiveness it aroused. But the women students adored him, understanding far better the poignancy and kindness of his character and responding to his courtesy and wit. 'Whistler is worth living for,' Gwen Salmond declared simply in a letter to Michel Salaman. At the least breath of criticism she and the others rushed to his defence. 'I hear there is a blasphemous letter about Whistler's teaching in one of the English papers,' Ida fulminated to her mother (December 1898). 'It is very stupid and unkind.'

In Augustus, too, Whistler inspired the prescriptive veneration due to one who has been a famous rebel victorious against the social conventions, and a great Master in his own right. With the thirty pounds he had won for 'Moses and the Brazen Serpent',* he followed the three girls to Paris that autumn, and in the Salon Carré of the Louvre the two painters met formally for the first time : Whistler a small, neat, erect old gentleman

---

* 'We have now the news of John's prize,' Ida wrote from 12 Rue Froidveau to Michel Salaman. 'He sent a delicious pen and ink sketch of himself with 1st Prize £30 stuck in his hat as sole intimation of what had befallen him. We were so awfully glad.'

in black, with crisp, curly hair containing one white lock, and a flashing monocle; Augustus a tall, dishevelled tramp. After some ceremony and a contest of compliments on behalf of Gwen, Augustus ventured to suggest that his sister's work showed a sense of character. 'Character? What's character?' Whistler demanded. 'It's *tone* that matters. Your sister shows a sense of tone.'

Augustus seems to have spent only a short time in Paris looking at Rembrandt, Leonardo, Raphael and Velasquez. His sister also took him to meet Carmen, and together they went to see Whistler in his studio, then at work on an immense self-portrait – a ghostly face set upon a body hardly discernible in the gloom. To explain her attendance at the *Académie Carmen*, Gwen had written home to announce that she had won a scholarship there. By this imaginary triumph she may have hoped to reconcile Edwin to the notion of giving her a small allowance. But Edwin decided to do better than this – that was, to come and see how she was getting along for himself. His arrival most likely accounted for Augustus's quick departure from Paris. To welcome him, Gwen arranged a small supper party, putting on a new dress designed by herself from one in a picture by Manet. 'You look like a prostitute in that dress,' Edwin greeted her. To which she haughtily replied: 'I could never accept anything from someone capable of thinking so.' Despite this setback, she continued going to Whistler's school and, in order to earn enough money, posed regularly as an artist's model.

Whistler's teaching was a perfect corrective to that of Brown and Tonks at the Slade. Painting, not drawing, came first. 'I do not teach art,' Whistler declared. 'I teach the scientific application of paint and brushes.' In this laboratory atmosphere, to which Augustus never subjected himself, where students could paint in the dark if need be, Gwen developed her methodical technique 'to a point of elaboration undreamt of by her Master'.[50] It was a short period of vital importance in her career, but, as always, much of her work was done independently. 'Gwen John is well and has not been lonely,' Ida reported to her mother. 'She has many more friends – one

Alsatian girl [Mlle Marthe] whom we are painting in the mornings. Such a beauty she is.'

Breakfast in Cold Veal Street was given over to reading *King Lear* and *King John*; while in the evenings the three of them sometimes ate at an anarchists' restaurant where beautiful, grubbily-dressed girls fetched their own food to avoid being waited upon. Between these times they painted. 'Gwen S. and J. are painting me,' Ida told her mother, 'and we are all 3 painting Gwen John.' Their life together, with all its excitements and difficulties, dedication and triviality, is charmingly described in a letter of Ida's to Michel Salaman:

We are having a very interesting time and working hard. I almost think I am beginning to paint – but I have not begun to really draw yet. We have a very excellent flat, and a charming studio room – so untidy – so unfurnished – and nice spots of drawings and photographs on the walls – half the wall is covered with brown paper, and when we have spare time and energy we are going to cover the other half ... Gwen John is sitting before a mirror carefully posing herself. She has been at it for half an hour. It is for an 'interior'. We all go suddenly daft with lovely pictures we can see or imagine, and want to do – as usual ... We want to call Gwen John 'Anne' – but have not the presence of mind or memory. And I should like to call Gwen Salmond Cynthia. These are merely ideals. As a matter of fact we are very unideal, and have most comically feminine rubs, at times; which make one feel like a washerwoman or something common. But as a whole it is a most interesting time ...

It came to an end early in 1899. Ida returned to Wigmore Street and Gwen John established herself in a little cellar below the dressmakers and decorators of Howland Street. Augustus, who disapproved of most places in which his sister chose to live, tried to include her in some of the invitations he was now receiving and the following spring the two of them went down to stay at Pevril Tower, a boarding house which Mrs Everett had opened at Swanage. Suffering from conjunctivitis, Augustus could do little work; and Gwen too was listless, wandering along the cliffs by moonlight, catching fire-flies and putting them in her hair and in Mrs Everett's. 'I have not done anything,' she confided to Michel Salaman, 'but have been tramp-

ing into the country – around by the sea. Yesterday I came to
an old wood – I walked on anemones and primroses – primroses
mean youth, did you know?

'... To-day the sky is low, everything is grey and covered
with mist – it is a good day to paint – but I think of people.'

Augustus, too, seemed much involved with people. Together
with Orpen, Albert Rutherston and others he had helped to
organize a revolutionary campaign against the desecration of St
Paul's by the mosaicist Sir William Richmond. During April
and May he was busy dragooning students from all the art
schools round London into meetings, trying to raise funds for
the printing of notices and arranging for a public petition to be
presented to the Dean and Chapter of the cathedral. 'Sir
William Richmond R.A. has for five years been decorating St
Paul's Cathedral and last year the mosaics were discovered to
the Public,' Albert Rutherston explained to his father. 'The place
has been utterly spoilt and looks now like a 2nd rate Café – it
is a mass of glittering gold etc. – he has also had the cheek to
cut away pieces of Wren's sculpture and replace it by his own
mosaics ... Even Sir Edward Poynter P.R.A. has asked Richmond to stop his decorations.'*

The other excitement of these months was Augustus's first
one-man show at the Carfax Gallery in Ryder Street off St
James's. This gallery had recently been opened by John Fother-
gill, a young painter, archaeologist and author, famous for his
dandified clothes and later as a pioneer amateur innkeeper.†
Arthur Clifton had been put in charge of the business side;
Robert Sickert, younger brother of Walter, acted as manager;
and the choice of artists was left to William Rothenstein.
Rodin, Conder, Orpen, Max Beerbohm all held exhibitions there
as well as Rothenstein himself. By the spring of 1899 it was
Augustus's turn. 'There is to be a show of my drawings at
Carfax and Co.,' he had written from Swanage to Michel Sala-
man. 'I hope to Gaud I shan't have all back on my hands. There

---

* See Appendix One, 'Desecration of Saint Paul's'.

† His inn was the Spread Eagle at Thame in which, for a time, Augustus's son
Romilly worked, and for which Carrington painted an inn sign (now gone). He
was the author of *Confessions of an Innkeeper*, *John Fothergill's Cookery Book*, *The Art
of James Dickson Innes*, *My Three Inns*, etc.

is however not much fear of that as Carfax himself would probably annex them in consideration of the considerable sum advanced to me in the young and generous days of his debut.' Singled out for praise by the didactic New English Art critic D. S. MacColl, the show was a success, earning Augustus thirty pounds.

With this sum in his pocket he set off to join a large painting party that had congregated at Vattetot-sur-Mer, a fishing village near Étretat on the Normandy coast. William Rothenstein and his new beautiful wife, the former actress Alice Kingsley; Albert Rutherston, now curiously nicknamed 'All but Rothenstein'; Orpen and his future wife (Alice Kingsley's sister)* Grace Knewstub, unfortunately known as 'Newslut'; Arthur Clifton and his red-haired wife: all these Augustus knew already. But in Charles Conder he was to meet, according to Will Rothenstein, a kind of bull-necked athlete of intimidating vitality. He was surprised to be introduced to a charming but in no way physically formidable person, a wistful, tentative, ailing man, his hair luxuriant but lifelessly hanging, a brown lock perpetually over one malicious blue eye, who admitted in an exhausted voice to being a little 'gone at the knees'.

Industry was the order of the day. Every morning they rose at half-past seven, drank a cup of chocolate, and worked until eleven. Conder did his fans; Rothenstein painted his 'The Doll's House';† Augustus did no painting, but drew, mostly land-

---

* 'Hugh Lane says Orpen has married a woman who looks about ninety, simply because Rothenstein, who[m] he admired immensely, married her sister. Now he doesn't admire Rothenstein so much as he did, but the wife remains.' Undated letter from Lady Gregory to W. B. Yeats (New York Public Library).

† Rothenstein had first heard of Ibsen through Conder, and in his *Men and Memories* (Vol. I, p. 56) writes: 'We were all mesmerised by Ibsen in those days.' The picture, now in the Tate Gallery, for which John and Alice Rothenstein posed, expresses the tension of Act III of *The Doll's House* when Mrs Linden and Krogstad are listening for the end of the dance upstairs. Subsequently it became famous as a 'problem picture' mainly perhaps on account of its dark colour. 'I am portrayed standing at the foot of a staircase upon which Alice has unaccountably seated herself,' John wrote in his Introduction to the catalogue of the Sir William Rothenstein Memorial Exhibition at the Tate Gallery (5 May– 4 June 1950). 'I appear to be ready for the road, for I am carrying a mackintosh on my arm and am shod and hatted. But Alice seems to hesitate. Can she have

scapes which Rothenstein described as remarkable. 'As for us,' Augustus wrote to Michel Salaman,

we grow more delighted with this place daily. The country is wonderfully fine in quality. In addition we have a charming model in the person of Mrs R's sister who serves to represent Man in relation to Nature. Orpen and I have been drawing with a certain industry, I think. Albert reads Balzac without cessation. Occasionally his brother drives him out into the fields with a stick but he returns in good time for the next meal with half a tree trunk gradated with straight lines to show.

Surrounded by farms and orchards, old barns and byres, enclosed by double and triple lines of trees to shield it from the cold winds, Vattetot was a quarter of a mile from the sea. At eleven o'clock on most mornings, the colony would lay down its brushes, make for the rocky white cliffs, and dive into the breakers. Augustus was a fearless swimmer and would crawl far out into the English Channel – a speck in the distance. 'Albert and I were seduced by that old succubus the Sea – the other day,' he wrote to Michel Salaman. 'The waves were tremendous and the shore being very sloping there was a very great backwash – it required all our virtue to prevail in the struggle.'

Everything Augustus did appealed to Rothenstein's romanticism. His drawings proclaimed an amazing genius, his actions a Byronic recklessness. One day, out of sheer exuberance, he jumped into a bucket at the top of a deep well and went crashing down to the bottom. It was all that the others could do –

---

changed her mind at the last moment? . . . Perhaps the weather had changed for the worse . . .'

For some 'The Doll's House' stands at the summit of William Rothenstein's art. It 'has impeccable form and a perfect contrast of light and shade', wrote his biographer Robert Speaight, '. . . *The Doll's House* suggest an anecdote and conceals a mystery; and the mystery is deeper than the anecdote – whatever the anecdote may have been. It was a strange picture to have come out of a honeymoon summer. The shadows of a native melancholy seem to have chequered the sunshine of personal happiness, and thrown out a hint of disillusionment. For one thing is clear about *The Doll's House* – this man and this woman, though they are so nearly touching, are each alone in the prison of their own thoughts.'

The picture, painted between June and October 1899, was finished at Kensington in January 1900. It was exhibited in the British section of the Paris Exhibition in 1900 where it won a silver medal.

Rothenstein perspiring with admiration among them – to haul
him back to the surface. And when he sprinted, stark-naked,
along the beach, it seemed to Rothenstein, paddling and prawn-
catching near by, that he had never seen so faun-like a figure.
The coastguards, too, ogled these antics through their envious
binoculars, and especially keenly when the girls undressed
in a cave under the Monet cliffs to race him. Once they
threatened court action – but the pagan goings-on went on.

After lunch at midday they worked until dinner. 'Under this
discipline we all ripened steadily,' Augustus recorded.[51] In the
evening they sat, Orpen, little Albert and himself, in the café
singing, smoking, drinking their calvados, and listening to
Conder, a bottle of Pernod at his elbow, telling his muffled
stories. But Orpen, who was now planning his ambitious
Summer Composition on *Hamlet*, would steal away early,
while Augustus was always last to leave. Conder's reliance on
Pernod, which he used both as a drink and as a medium for
his brush, filled Augustus with apprehension and he told the
Rothensteins that, in the event of his ever feeling tempted to
drink, Conder's example would act as a disincentive. As for
calvados, that was rather different: he felt bound to impregnate
himself with its quickening properties so as to draw nearer the
soil and, by a kind of chemical magic, grow fruitful. As a
counter measure, seeing the way things were going, Alice
Rothenstein began to import quantities of restorative tea from
England.

In August, Orpen returned to complete his 'Hamlet' and
Augustus spent a few days with him on the way in Paris. They
stayed close to Montparnasse station, spent their nights on the
town, their days half-asleep in the Louvre. 'It was so pleasant
there,' Augustus wrote to Ursula Tyrwhitt. 'I wish you had
been with us to wander in the Louvre, after the hot sun and
dazzling light outside to be in the cool sculpture galleries ... I
envy the sleeping Hermaphrodite its frozen passion, its marble
self-sufficiency, its eternal languor.'

Augustus's own passions were sleepless. 'Mr Augustus is very
well,' Orpen reported to Michel Salaman on his return from
France. 'I left him with a lady! He was to come to the station
to see me off (myself and Miss Knewstub) but did not turn up.'

Everything seemed to be going wrong for Orpen. 'My Hamlet would kill high morality,' he wrote in another letter to Salaman that September, ' – Hamlet ought to be treated like a "Day of Judgement". Miss John is settled in 122 Gower Street. She is a most beautiful lady! Miss Nettleship I have seen but she has not posed yet, to tell the truth I am afraid to ask her to take the pose as she has seen my Hamlet – I will wait till Gus comes back I think – Miss John says she would not take it.'

Any hopes Orpen may have had of Gwen John changing her mind were dashed when a day or two later she broke her nose. Ida, however, without waiting for Augustus's sanction, agreed to take the pose which involved a man and a girl leaning together, with their arms round each other. At last everything was ready – then Orpen fell ill. 'The wretched Orpen has got jaundice or verdigris or something horrible,' Augustus told Ursula Tyrwhitt. According to Orpen his complaint was more complicated still, and not unconnected with Augustus. 'My illness [jaundice] has been very severe. I was not able to eat for nearly ten days, but everything has started going down now! – I am still yellow – I have also got some nasty animals on a certain portion of my body – Gus's doing – Dog that he is – this is my judgement for Paris! Tell him not!'

Augustus himself seemed unaffected by these adventures. The laws of cause and effect appeared, in his case, to have become magically suspended. 'How he escaped getting the Ladies Fever we couldn't make out,' John Everett noted with irritation in his journal (1899). 'Tonks used to say it must be his natural dirt.'

He seemed protected, spiritually, by his natural innocence. 'The country here becomes still more beautiful with the arrival of autumn,' he told Salaman. With Rothensteins of various sorts he would go for long walks – to Fécamp, for the sake of the incomparable *pâtisserie*; to the little Casino at Vaucottes, Conder always leading; to Étretat,* a charming place full of

* 'A charming place, very small but immensely smart – none of the demiriche – but a great number of the French nobility stay there, also a good many Americans,' Albert Rutherston described Étretat (1 August 1899). 'It is delightfully amusing to watch the men and women bathe together – the women all wear black silk stockings with their bathing costumes.'

smart people and mixed bathing; and to Yport, four miles
away, where lived a tailor who decked Augustus out in a dazzling green corduroy suit with tight jacket and wide pegtop
trousers. 'He [John] looks spendid,' Orpen had reported to John
Everett, 'and is acting up to his clothes' – much to the terror of
Alice Rothenstein who, fearful that he or Conder would seduce
her sister, dispatched her back to London in what she supposed to be the more harmless company of Orpen. Late at
night, and chaperoned by the Rothensteins, they would
wander back from Yport along the beach, sometimes bathing
again by moonlight: 'wonderful days and wonderful nights
these were,' remembered Will Rothenstein,[52] who had begun his
honeymoon with hay fever and ended it with jaundice.

At the end of September, Augustus, Conder, Alice and the
convalescent Will left for Paris where, over the next ten days,
they passed a good deal of time in company with that 'distinguished reprobate' Oscar Wilde. Wilde had recently been
released from prison and was living in a small hotel on the
Left Bank. Though appreciative of him as 'a great man of
inaction' and a 'big and good-natured fellow with an enormous
sense of fun, impeccable bad taste, and a deeply religious
apprehension of the Devil',[53] Augustus felt embarrassed by his
elaborate performances of wit, not knowing how to respond. 'I
could think of nothing whatever to say. Even my laughter
sounded hollow.' The unnatural deference and trained astonishment put on by the rest of his audience, sickened him. Never
had the face of praise looked more foolish. Despite this, Wilde
seems to have been much taken with 'the charming Celtish poet
in colour'[54] as he described Augustus. Alice Rothenstein, noticing this friendliness, grew fearful for his reputation and
hurried him along to the hairdresser. Next day Oscar looked
grave. 'You should have consulted me,' he told Augustus, laying
a hand reproachfully on his shoulder, 'before taking this
important step.'

Augustus felt stifled by these long, unspontaneous lunches at
the Café de la Régence and the Café Procope, and was always
on the lookout to escape with Conder and find 'easier if less
distinguished company'. The two of them would go off 'whor-
ing', as Conder called it, visiting a succession of *boîtes de nuit*

in Montmartre until the first pale gleams of the Parisian dawn showed in the sky, and each with his companion went his own way. 'He [John] was drunk', Will Rothenstein gushed, 'with excitement.' Once again much of his waking and sleeping day was spent in the Louvre, of which he never seemed to tire. 'Imagine,' he wrote to Ursula Tyrwhitt, 'we were on the top of the Louvre yesterday! On the roof, and grapes and flowers are there. The prospect was wonderful – Paris at one's feet!'

Two painters in particular seem to have made a special impression on him. The first of these was Daumier who, John Rothenstein has written,* 'reinforced with immense authority the lesson he had begun to learn from Rembrandt, of seeing broadly and simply, and who taught him to interpret human personality boldly, without fearing to pass, if need be, the arbitrary line commonly held to divide objective representation from caricature'. The second was Puvis de Chavannes whose impressions of an idealized humanity and of the beauty of the relationship between figures and landscape was to be an inspiration to him.

Having spent all his money from the Carfax exhibition, Augustus now borrowed a further twenty from Michel Salaman. He had intended to travel back via Brussels and Antwerp, but the life in Montmartre held him enthralled until the last moment. 'I've had a fantastic time here,' he told Ursula Tyrwhitt (October 1899) ' – we spent all our money and can't go to Belgium so we're off home tonight.'

* *Modern English Painters*, Vol. I, 'Sickert to Grant' (Arrow Books), p. 200. Rothenstein instances 'The Rustic Idyll' of about 1903 as having been done under the immediate impact of Daumier. This work – possibly watercolour on dampened cartridge – is now in the Tate Gallery, and is called 'Rustic Scene'. It has an unusual texture – soft, blurred contours – and gives a more dramatic sense of atmosphere than is usual in John's work. ' "The Rustic Idyll" I remember well,' John wrote to the Tate Gallery (16 March 1956). 'It is one of several pastels I did soon after leaving the Slade. Though hardly an Idyll, it has dramatic character . . . I don't consider it has merit as a *pastel*.'

6. 'MORAL LIVING'

The legend that had been conceived when Augustus dived on to a rock at the age of seventeen was by now fully grown. Only after he left the Slade, and the exterior discipline of Tonks and Brown had been removed, did he, in Michel Salaman's words, 'kick over the traces'. The extent of this change in his personality has been vividly recorded by John Everett,* who had first met Augustus in October 1896, shared 21 Fitzroy Street with him during part of 1897, and who had left England for a year at sea in 1898. On his return to London in 1899 the first person he met was Orpen, who eagerly apprised him of all the scandalous things Augustus was up to: how he went pub-crawling and got gloriously drunk; how he kept a prostitute who would always go back to him if she could not pick up anyone in the streets; how he had careered all over the flower beds in Hyde Park with the police in hot pursuit – and so on. Remembering his friend of two years ago – 'a poor physical specimen [who] never played any games ... a very quiet boy, a great reader, a studious youth' who used 'to sit up late reading and get to the Slade about 11', when everyone else began at nine, who avoided all the organized rags and tugs-of-war and was thought by some to be 'a nonentity' – Everett was astonished. 'If you had told me that of any man at the Slade I'd have believed you,' he replied to Orpen. 'But not John.'

Shortly afterwards Everett met Augustus again and over the next year saw a lot of him. 'All the things Orpen had told me about John were true,' he recorded in his journal. 'His character had completely changed. It was not the John I'd known in the early days at the Slade.' In some ways he was very like the sailors Everett had rubbed shoulders with during his voyages. He was getting commissions for portraits and drawings and the

* Everett, who had been baptized Herbert, registered at the Slade as Henry Everett, but he always called himself John Everett. He added to the confusion by marrying his cousin – Mrs Everett's niece – Kathleen, who altered her Christian name fractionally to Katherine. A marine painter all his life, John Everett never sold a marine painting during his life, but bequeathed them all (1,700 oils and an even larger number of drawings and engravings) to the National Maritime Museum, which held a memorial exhibition of his work in 1964.

quality of his work had never been higher. He seemed however quite irresponsible. He would make an appointment with some sitter for the following morning, go off drinking half the night with his friends, then wake up grumpily next afternoon. Yet, Everett observed, he was not really a heavy drinker. Very little alcohol made him drunk and he could quickly become morose; unlike Conder, who drank far more, always remained cheerful, but had a tendency to see yellow-striped cats. Sometimes Augustus stayed out all night, and more than once he was arrested by the police and only released on bail next day. Despite his broken appointments, he was making a very reasonable income, though often obliged to borrow from his friends to get a meal. Money had only one significance for him: it meant freedom of action. To his friends he was spontaneously open-handed, and when in funds it was generally he who at restaurants demanded the bill, or was left with it. Other bills, such as the rent, he omitted to pay altogether. 'Gus says you need never pay Mrs Everett!' Orpen assured Michel Salaman. Some landladies were more exigent. 'I want to talk to you about this studio [76 Charlotte Street],' Orpen wrote in another letter to Salaman on his return from Vattetot. 'There is great trouble going on about Gus. I'm afraid he will not get back here.' Mrs Laurence, who kept the house, had grown increasingly alarmed by what she called 'Mr John's saturnalias'. One night, simply it appears in order to terrify her, he had danced with abandon on the roof of St John the Evangelist church next door. Other times he was apparently more conscientious, working late into the night with a nude model over his composition of 'Adam and Eve', and, in the heat of inspiration, stripping off his own clothes. Woken from her sleep by sounds of revelry, Mrs Laurence, chaperoned by her friend Mrs Young, went to investigate and, without benefit of art-training, was shocked by what she found. When Augustus had left suddenly for France with the Carfax money in his pocket, he had paid her nothing; and so, when he returned in October, she refused him entry. He retreated, therefore, to old territory: 21 Fitzroy Street – 'comfortless quarters', as Will Rothenstein described them, but economical.

Here was Will Rothenstein's cue, once more, to hurry to the

rescue. Having been invited to stay at Sale with his brother-in-law, he generously offered his house, No. 1 Pembroke Cottages,* to both Augustus and Gwen. Augustus used the house only spasmodically, preferring to sleep in Orpen's bed in the cellar of Fitzroy Street rather than make his way back to Kensington late at night. The springs of this bed had collapsed at the centre, so whoever reached it first and sank into the precipitous valley of the mattress was alone comfortable. Neither liked early nights, but Orpen was eventually driven by lack of sleep to extraordinary ingenuities, going to bed in the afternoon twilight, bolting doors, undressing in the dark, anything, to win a restful night. Augustus would then mount the stairs to John Everett's room, drink rum in front of his fire till half-past twelve, then jump up exclaiming: 'My God! I've missed the last train!' For weeks on end he slept on two of Everett's arm-chairs.

The following month Will Rothenstein returned from Sale. 'When I reached Kensington I found the house empty and no fire burning,' he wrote. 'In front of a cold grate choked with cinders lay a collection of muddy boots ... late in the evening John appeared, having climbed through a window; he rarely, he explained, remembered to take the house-key with him.'[55] This was testing Rothenstein's hero-worship to the full. 'There were none I loved more than Augustus and Gwen John,' he admitted, 'but they could scarcely be called "comfortable" friends.'[56] As for Alice she was adamant: the walls must be white-washed and the floors scrubbed before their little home would again be habitable.

Will Rothenstein had now finished, for the New English Art Club, a portrait of Augustus† that won the difficult approbation of Tonks and, more difficult still, avoided the disapprobation of Augustus himself. It shows a dreamy, soft person whose exterior efforts to roughen and toughen himself are visibly unconvincing – the beard fails even to cover the chin. Yet the life he was now leading was certainly rough. After making one last effort to recapture 76 Charlotte Street – from which he was repelled 'with a charming County Court summons beauti-

* Off Edwardes Square in Kensington.
† Now at the Walker Art Gallery, Liverpool.

fully printed'[57] – he took up a fresh position at 61 Albany
Street, by the side of Regent's Park. 'I've abandoned my kopje
in Charlotte Street,' he told Will Rothenstein, 'trekked and
laagered up at the above, strongly fortified but scantily supplied. Generals Laurence and Young hover at my rear ... the
garrison [is] in excellent spirits.'

He had briefly taken up with a new girl-friend, a Miss
Simpson who, dismissing him as hopelessly impoverished, now
decided to marry a bank clerk – and invited Augustus to her
wedding. Except for his green corduroys he had nothing to
wear. What happened was described by Orpen in a letter to
John Everett:

> I met John last night – he had been to Miss Simpson's wedding,
> drunk as a lord. Dressed out in Conder's clothes, check waistcoat,
> high collar, tail coat, striped trousers. He seemed to say he was play-
> ing a much more important part than the bridegroom at the wedding
> and spoke with commiseration at the thought of how bored they
> must be getting at each other's society ... He almost wept over this,
> gave long lectures on moral living, and left us.

Augustus's aversion to 'moral living' had strained his relationship with Ida almost to breaking point. He was painting a
portrait of her which 'has clothed itself in scarlet', she told
Michel Salaman (1 February 1900), adding: 'Gwen John has
gone back to 122 Gower Street.* John sleeps, apparently, anywhere.'

The break between them came after an eventful trip Augustus made with Conder that spring to Mrs Everett's boarding
house at Swanage. Augustus had had his hair cut short, trimmed
his beard and now went everywhere in part of Conder's wedding equipment – tail coat, high collar and cap. After the dis-
sipations of London, both painters tried hard to discipline

* Gwen John seems to have been living at 122 Gower Street illegally and
possibly even without furniture. The house was officially inhabited by a woman
called Annie Machew, who since October 1899 had paid no rates. The rating
authorities who attempted to collect the money owing to them throughout
1900 reported that there were 'no effects' there. For this reason the house
does not appear in Kelly's Post Office Directory until three years later, when it
had been taken over by the National Amalgamated Union of Shop Assistants,
Warehousemen and Clerks.

themselves.* Conder seemed to have perfected a technique for investing simultaneously in life and work. He would sit painting a watercolour of some Arcadian fan at the very centre of a rowdy group of friends. 'There would be a whole lot of us smoking, talking, telling good stories,' Everett optimistically recorded. 'Conder would join in the conversation, talk the whole time, yet his hand would go on doing the fan. At times it really seemed as if somebody else was doing the watercolour.'

'We drink milk and soda and tea in large quantities,' Augustus confided to Orpen. 'I must confess to a pint of beer occasionally on going into the town.' As at Vattetot, they worked hard. 'Conder is getting on with his decoration which becomes everyday more beautiful,' Augustus told Will Rothenstein. 'The country here is lovely beyond words. Corfe Castle and the neighbourhood would make you mad with painter's cupidity! ... I have started a colossal canvas whereon I depict Dr Faust on the Brocken. I sweat at it from morn till eve.' Not even an attack of German measles could interrupt such work. 'Conder had them some weeks ago,' he reported to Will Rothenstein.

I had quite forgotten about it when I woke up one morning horrified to find myself struck of a murrain – I have been kept in ever since, shut off from the world. In the daylight it isn't so bad, but I dread the night season which means little sleep and tragic horrors of dreams at that. I mean in the day I work desperately hard at my colossal task. I can say at any rate Faust has benefited by my malady. In fact it is getting near the finish. There are about 17 figures in it not to speak of a carrion-laden gibbet.†

* Conder, in a letter to Will Rothenstein from Swanage, wrote: 'I have nearly finished Harrison's decoration and John is working on a large decoration that promises very well – that seems to be his forte – a decoration 8 ft by 6 is no easy matter with a score of figures half life size, but he seems to work away with great ease. I found my decoration a great change and pleasure after smaller work and think it is quite equal to the latter.

'I am quite well now and had almost a providential attack of measles which left me undisturbed for some days to do my work.'

Not since his early days in France had Conder worked so consistently out of doors. He painted at least nine views of Swanage, all in a more robust style than hitherto. Three of these are now in the Tate Gallery.

† What became of the large decoration is not known, though a number of smaller versions of the subject exist, showing the influence of Goya and Delacroix. One is an oil belonging to Mr Humphrey Brooke; another, a wash draw-

If illness benefited their painting, the renewal of robust good health, seasoned by the salt air, imposed ever-increasing obstacles. Mrs Everett, protected from a knowledge of their world by her harmonium, had invited down two fine-looking Slade girls, Elie Monsell and Daisy Legge, to keep Conder and Augustus company. John Everett, who visited Pevril Tower during week-ends, watched the danger approaching with puritan *déjà-vu*. It seemed inevitable that a love-affair would develop, and before long Conder, to his dismay, found himself engaged to the Irish art-student Elie Monsell. Hauled up to London for a difficult interview with Mrs Monsell (who seems to have been considerably younger than himself), he shortly afterwards fled across the Channel to join Orpen and his mistress-model Amelia at Cany. The engagement then lapsed, fell into decay, and the following year Conder married Stella Belford.

Augustus, too, was experiencing what he called 'the compulsion of sea-air'[58] directed, not towards Daisy Legge, but to 'a superb woman of Vienna',[59] Maria Katerina, an aristocrat employed by Mrs Everett in the guise of parlourmaid. 'A beautiful Viennese lady here has had the misfortune to wrench away a considerable portion of my already much mutilated heart,' was how he broke the news to Orpen. 'Misfortune because such things cannot be brooked too complacently ... Conder is engaged on an even more beautiful fête galante.'

In a letter written nearly twenty years later (2 February 1918) to his friend Alick Schepeler, Augustus was to make a unique admission. 'The sort of paranoia or mental hail storm from which I suffer continually,' he told her, '... means that each impression I receive is immediately obliterated by the next girl's, irrespective of its importance. Other people have remarked upon my consistent omission to keep appointments but only to you have I ever confessed the real and dreadful reason.'

The mental hail storm that now sprang up within him ob-

---

ing in the Quinn Collection in New York, was sold by the Fine Art Society at the Slade Centenary Show (autumn 1971); a third, a pen and wash drawing, is in the Tate Gallery (reproduced in *Tate Gallery*, *Modern British Paintings*, *Drawings and Sculpture*, volume I, plate 51).

literated all feelings and thoughts of Ida. It was as if he had
never met her, as if he had been blinded by this Viennese girl
and could no longer see her. Possibly his confinement with
measles – 'German measles please!' he reminded Will Rothenstein. 'I did not catch them in Vienna.' – had helped to bring
about the dreadful impatience of his emotions; and this impatience was exacerbated by the girl's elusiveness. The letters
he wrote to his friends throb and reverberate with the echoes
of this new passion. 'It was without surprise I learnt she was
descended from the old nobility of Austria. Her uncle, the
familiar of Goethe, was Count von Astz,' he admitted to Michel
Salaman. 'This damnably aristocratic pedigree, you will understand, only goes to make her more fatally attractive to my perverse self ... She wears patent leather shoes with open work
stockings and –'

On, of all people, Conder's advice, he bought her a ring and
presented it to her one dark night at the top of a drainpipe
that led to her bedroom window. This overture had a magical
effect upon Maria Katerina's defences which, Augustus later
acknowledged, 'proved in the end to be not insurmountable'.[60]
She 'has sucked the soul out of my lips', he boasted to Will
Rothenstein. 'I polish up my German lore. I spend spare
moments trying to recall phrases from Ollendorf and am so
grateful for your lines of Schiller which are all that remain to
me of the Lied von der Glocke.' But with the very instant of
success, perhaps even fractionally preceding it, came the first
encroachment of boredom.

Sometimes when I surprise myself not quite happy tho' alone I
begin to fear I have lost that crown of youth, the art of loving
fanatically. I begin to suspect I have passed the virtues of juven-
escence and that its follies are all that remain to me. Write to me
dear Will and tell me ... those little intimacies which are the salt of
friendship and the pepper of love.

On his last night in Swanage Augustus and Maria met secretly
on the cliffs. She was wearing her ring and she promised to
meet him in France where he was shortly to go with Michel
Salaman. Back in London he felt desolate, and more than unusually un-self-sufficient. On 18 May, Mafeking Night, he

strolled down to Trafalgar Square to see the fun. London had gone mad with excitement. Bells rang, guns were fired, streamers waved; people danced in groups, clapping, shouting, kissing. The streets were filled with omnibuses, people, policemen without helmets. As if by magic, whistles had appeared in everyone's mouth, Union Jacks in their hands, and amid all the tumult of tears, laughter and singing complete strangers threw their arms about one another's necks: it was, as Churchill said, a most 'unseemly' spectacle. Many were shocked by this 'frantic and hysterical outburst of patriotic enthusiasm', as Arnold Bennett called it. 'The Square, the Strand and all the adjacent avenues were packed with a seething mass of patriots celebrating the great day in a style that would have made a "savage" blush,' Augustus wrote.

Mad with drink and tribal hysteria, the citizens formed themselves into solid phalanxes, and plunging at random this way and that, swept all before them. The women, foremost in this mêlée, danced like Maenads, their shrill cat-calls swelling the general din. Feeling out of place and rather scared, I extricated myself from this pandemonium with some difficulty, and crept home in a state of dejection.[61]

'You have evidently forgotten my address,' Augustus remarked with surprise to Michel Salaman. This was not difficult. By June, shortly before he was due to join Salaman in France, he had reached the same point of crisis at Albany Street as he had achieved the previous year in Charlotte Street, and by much the same methods.* 'I cannot come just yet,' he told his friend

– I have some old commissions to finish amongst other deterrents to immediate migration. Yet in a little while I have hopes of being able to join you. I have had notice to quit this place. I think I will take a room somewhere in Soho if I can find one – a real 'mansarde' I hope – I want to hide myself away for some time ... I shall have to see my Pa before I would come as it is now a long while since I

* For example, Everett in his unpublished journal writes: 'We all went back to John's place in Albany Street. On the way they picked up an old whore, made some hot whisky. The result was John fell on the floor paralytic, the old whore on top of him in the same condition ... Orpen and [Sidney] Starr tried to pull the old whore's drawers off, but she was too heavy to move.'

have seen him ... It would be nice if Gwen could come too and good for her too methinks.

Salaman had taken rooms at a house called Cité Titand in Le Puy-en-Velay, a medieval village in Languedoc built about a central rock and dominated by a colossal Virgin in cast iron. Augustus arrived here early in August. 'It is a wonderful country I assure you – unimaginably wonderful!' he wrote to Ursula Tyrwhitt (19 September 1900).

... There are most exquisite hills, little and big, Rembrandtesque, Titianesque, Giorgionesque, Turneresque, growing out from volcanic rocks, dominating the fat valleys watered by pleasant streams, tilled by robust peasants bowed by labour and age or upright with the pride of youth and carrying things on their heads. I have bathed in the waters of the Borne and have felt quite Hellenic! At first the country gave me indigestion; used to plainer fare it proved too rich, too high for my northern stomach; now I begin to recover and will find a lifetime too short to assimilate its menu of many courses ...

To the golden-haired Alice Rothenstein, who had recommended Le Puy, he wrote with equal enthusiasm:

Really, you have troubled my peace with your golden hills and fat valleys of Burgundy! ...
I work indoors mostly now. I am painting Michel's portrait. I hope to make a success of it. If when finished it will be as good as it is now I may count on that. I am also painting Polignac castle which ought to make a fine picture ...*
The very excellent military band plays in the park certain nights, and we have enjoyed sitting listening to it. It is very beautiful to watch the people under the trees. At intervals the attention of the populace is diverted from following the vigorous explanatory movements of the conductor by an appeal to patriotism, effected by illuminating the flag by Bengal lights at the window of the museum! It is dazzling and undeniable! The band plays very well. Rendered clairvoyant by the music one feels very intimate with humanity, only Michel's voice when he breaks in with a laborious attempt at describing how beautifully the band played 3 years ago at the

* John's drawing of the Chateau de Polignac is now in the Manchester Art Galleries. Very Flemish in its atmosphere, it provides an interesting demonstration of the diversity of his talent or, as detractors might claim, his ability to imitate.

Queen's Hall that time he took Edna Waugh – is rather disturbing – or is it that I am becoming ill-tempered?

Where Augustus went, could Will and Alice be far behind? They turned up early in September and stayed two weeks at the Grand Hôtel des Ambassadeurs. 'Every day we met at lunch in a vast kitchen, full of great copper vessels, a true rôtisserie de la Reine Pédauque,' remembered Will Rothenstein, 'presided over by a hostess who might have been mother to Pantagruel himself, so heroic in size she was, and of so genial and warm a nature.'[62]

On their bicycles, the four of them pedalled as far south as Notre-Dame-des-Neiges, where Stevenson had once stayed on his travels with a donkey. Augustus on wheels was a fabulous sight, and Will Rothenstein noticed that the girls minding their cattle in the fields crossed themselves as he passed, and that 'the men in horror would exclaim: 'Quel type de rapin!' At Arlempdes, a village of such devilish repute it went unmarked on any map, they were entertained by the curé, who commented ecstatically upon Augustus's fitness for the principal role in their Passion play. 'Who does he remind you of?' he asked his sister. 'Notre Seigneur, le bon Dieu,' she answered without hesitation. 'I take it as a compliment,' Augustus remarked, but refused the part – understandably, since the previous year, in the heat of the occasion, Christ had been stabbed in his side. On reaching Notre-Dame-des-Neiges, Alice took sanctuary at an inn while the three men spent the night in a Trappist monastery where Will Rothenstein anticipated he might encounter Huysmans, but did not. Rising early he involved himself in the monastic rituals, but Augustus and Salaman lay abed, each in his cell where he was served by the silent monks with a breakfast of wine and cheese.

After returning to Le Puy, Will and Alice wheeled their machines over the horizon and were gone. 'Is it that I am becoming ill-tempered?' Augustus had queried. By this time he had been made extremely so by the failure of Maria Katerina to come to him. He had written long letters urging her to meet him in Paris, but these were intercepted by Mrs Everett who, after Augustus left Swanage, had discovered hairpins in his bed.

With these instruments she had extracted from her servant a
full confession. Her duty now was clear. From reading
Augustus's letters it was a small step to writing Maria's, the
tone of which, Augustus noticed, suddenly changed. 'When
you will no longer have me – what will I do then?' she asked.
'What will become of me then? Repudiated by my husband
who loves me? Can you answer that?' Augustus did answer it
according to his lights, but at such a distance, and screened by
Mrs Everett, they were not strong enough to blind her doubts.
'Women always suspect me of fickleness,' he complained to
Alice Rothenstein, 'but will they never give me a chance of
vindicating myself? They are too modest, too cautious, for to
do that they would have to give their lives. I am not an exponent of the faithful dog business.'

Michel Salaman, who was financing their holiday, suffered
grievously from his disappointment. Augustus, he observed,
seemed to grow literally delirious about women. His temperature one evening shot up to 104, and almost every day he complained of numberless psychosomatic ailments from rheumatism
to at least one completely new disease. His womanizing brought
out in him a satyr-like quality. He would suddenly feel violently
attracted to some girl in a bar, and his whole nature changed.
Some women were alarmed, others hypnotized. Michel Salaman
was shocked.

Augustus did his best to pull himself together. He worked* –
'I am painting beyond Esplay,' he wrote to Will Rothenstein.
'... I want to travel again next year hitherwards and be a
painter. I am, dear Will, full of ideas for work.' He read – in
particular Balzac's Vie Conjugale which 'pains and makes me
laugh at the same time'. He travelled – to Paris for a few days
to see some Daumiers and Courbets and 'was profoundly
moved'.†

When Michel Salaman left Le Puy, Augustus was joined by

---

* Some pages from his sketch-book at this time were exhibited at the
Mercury Gallery, London, 15 June–10 February 1968.

† 'I asked a gend'arme where the paintings by Daumier were to be found and
he said "quelle puissance"!' John told Will Rothenstein. He had also been to
see the Paris Exhibition in which Rothenstein's 'A Doll's House' won its silver
medal, and reported: 'Your Maison des Poupées looked wonderful.'

'the Waif of Pimlico' as he now called his sister Gwen, and by 'the gentle Ambrose McEvoy'. 'I am conducted about by McEvoy and Gwen,' he told Salaman, 'who explain the beauties and show me new and ever more surprising spots.' Each evening they went for a long walk and would hurry back 'to cook a dinner which is often successful in some items'. Sometimes the two men – 'the absinthe friends' as Augustus dubbed them – would sit in a café where, he told Ursula Tyrwhitt, 'a young lady exquisitely beautiful, attired as a soldier, sings songs of dubious meaning'.

By October Augustus seems to have recovered from his disappointment and had become, according to McEvoy, a 'demon' for work, refusing to budge from his easel. He was quick to infatuation, as to anger: and quick to forget both. But for McEvoy and for Gwen it was a less happy time. McEvoy seemed in a dream, and could not settle down to work. 'After a strange period of mental and physical bewilderment I am beginning to regain some of my normal senses,' he eventually wrote to Salaman. '... At first I felt like some animal and incapable of expressing anything. Drawing was quite impossible. I should like to live here for years and then I might hope to paint pictures that would have something of the grand air of the Auvergne – but now! Gus seems to retain his self-control. Perhaps he has been through my stage. He constantly does the most wonderful drawings. Oh, it is most perplexing.'

During this month at Le Puy, McEvoy's relationship with Gwen appears to have reached some sort of crisis. For much of the time he was silent, drinking himself gently into oblivion; while Gwen, who spent many days in tears, seemed inconsolable. Unlike her brother, she could not externalize emotional disasters and bounce them away. They lived on inside her until she suffocated them.

'It will be a frightful job seeking for rooms in London,' Augustus wrote to Salaman shortly before his return. But by November he had found what he wanted at 39 Southampton Street above the Economic Cigar Company. This was no 'mansarde', but it would serve for a time. Many of the drawings he had done at Le Puy were now put on exhibition at the Carfax Gallery. 'Glad to hear of MacColl's enthusiasm,' he wrote to

Will Rothenstein. 'Tonks has bought 2 drawings. Brown thinks of doing so too. I have a great number if you like to come and amuse yourself.' It was again partly owing to Rothenstein's advocacy that the drawings sold so well. 'John is the great one at present,' Orpen assured Everett, 'making a lot of money and doing splendid drawing.' Augustus himself was delighted by this success – in a restrained way. 'The run on my drawings tho' confined to a narrow circle has been very pleasant,' he conceded in another letter to Will Rothenstein that autumn. 'People however seem better at bargaining than I am.'

People also seemed better, it occurred to him, at arranging their lives. He was growing increasingly dissatisfied by the quick rotation of pursuing landladies and girl-friends in retreat. Boredom and impatience constantly fretted him. Perhaps, after all, something a little more settled might suit him better, might even benefit his work.

He began to see Ida again. Although she had few illusions about the sort of life he had been leading, she still loved him. In one of the limericks he was fond of composing, he scribbled:

> There was a young woman named Ida
> Who had a porcelain heart inside her
> But she met a young card
> Who hugged her so hard
> He smashed up her crockery. Poor Ida!

It was more prophetic than he could have imagined. Soon the two of them were together again on the old basis. 'John is once more in the embrace of Miss Nettleship – the reunion is "Complet",' Orpen informed Everett. 'Marie (la Belle) has faded into the dark of winter, and disappeared in a dark back street.'

But the old basis was no longer enough for Augustus. Since the Nettleships would never agree to their 'living in sin', and since Ida would never consent to distressing them in this way, there was but one solution: 'moral living' as he had called it. Having, by devious routes, failed to avoid this conclusion, Augustus acted at once. He conceded the formality of a civil ceremony but, *en revanche*, insisted on an elopement, and set off with Ida early one Saturday morning for the Borough of St

Pancras where they celebrated the event in secret. 'I have news to tell you,' he wrote the following week to his sister Winifred. 'Ida Nettleship and I got spliced at the St Pancras Registry Office last Saturday! McEvoy and Evans and Gwen aided and abetted us. Everybody agreed it was a beautiful wedding – there was a wonderful fog which lent an air of mystery unexpectedly romantic.' This letter he illustrated with a drawing of himself standing on his head.

Jack Nettleship, when he discovered what had happened, took the news philosophically: his wife less so. 'It might have been worse,' Augustus noted.[63] But it was less simple than he implied. That evening Ida went up to the bedroom of one of her mother's employees, Elspeth Phelps. 'I want to tell you something, Elspeth,' she said, taking her friend's hands in both hers. 'I want to tell you –' and then burying her face in her hands she broke into uncontrollable sobs. After a few moments she continued: 'I want to tell you I've married Gussie – and I think I'm a little frightened.'[64]

She gave no sign of this fear in public. After the wedding they had gone round to tell Will and Alice Rothenstein the news. 'How pleased we were, and what mysterious things Ida and my wife had to talk over!' Will Rothenstein wrote in his memoirs.[65] That evening, to celebrate the wedding, the Rothensteins gave a small party. Ida looked 'exquisitely virginal in her simple white dress'. 'Mr and Mrs Nettleship, Mrs Beerbohm and Neville [Lytton], Miss Salmond, Misses John, Salaman, Messrs Steer, Tonks, McEvoy, Salaman and myself were there,' Albert Rutherston wrote to his parents. But Augustus himself was not. The last anyone had seen of him was on his way that afternoon to a bath. Then, late at night, he turned up wearing a bright check suit and ear-rings. 'We were very gay,' wrote Albert Rutherston. 'We had scherades [sic] towards the end of the evening which were great fun. Mr and Mrs John were radiant.' One of these charades represented Steer teaching at the Slade – a long silence, then: 'How's your sister?' This, Augustus swore, was a perfect example of Steer's methods.

'I pray the marriage may be a splendid thing for both parties,' Orpen wrote to Will Rothenstein. Augustus himself had no doubts. At last someone had given him the chance of vindicating himself. Though Ida and he had undergone a more or less conventional wedding, neither of them were conventional people: they simply loved each other. He felt perfectly confident.

For their honeymoon, he took his wife to Swanage, and they stayed at Pevril Tower.

3

Love for Art's Sake

An artist is at the mercy of his temperament and his pre-
ferences are apt to be purely personal, quite dispropor-
tionate and utterly unhistorical.

AUGUSTUS JOHN
(William Rothenstein Memorial Exhibition
Catalogue. Tate Gallery 1950)

What inconsiderate buggers we males are!

AUGUSTUS JOHN TO MARY DOWDALL

I. EVIL AT WORK

The New English Art Club, by the time Augustus John officially
became a member in 1903, was seventeen years old and, in its
influence, largely French.* It was founded, after some half-
dozen years of discussions, by a number of artists who had
worked in the Parisian schools and who wanted an exhibiting
society run on the lines of elective juries as against the closed
academic system of Burlington House. During the mid-nineteenth century the Royal Academy had been perfecting its
policy of caution. It had been slow to welcome the Pre-Raphaelites until Pre-Raphaelitism became diluted – by which time
it welcomed little else. To many of its forty immortals, Paris
was still a name of dread, to be associated with lubricity, blood-
shed and bad colour.

But to the mob of disgruntled outsiders Paris seemed an
elysium, and English Pre-Raphaelitism Gehenna. They found
their inspiration in the ennobling realism of Millet and Corot,
in the pleinairism of Bastien-Lepage and the school of Barbizon.
This movement had come to a head in 1886 when the New
English Art Club was founded and its first exhibitions held.

For perhaps a quarter of a century the club was to act as a

* One of the first names suggested for the club had been 'the Society of
Anglo-French Painters'.

salon des refusés. Its members numbered many hardened senti-
mentalists. Chief among them at the start was the 'Newlyn
Group', whose watchword was 'values'. They were not, in any
exaggerated way, revolutionaries. The pictures of Frank Bram-
ley, in the matter of domestic sentiment, could outdo those of
any academician; while George Clausen, Stanhope Forbes and
H. H. La Thangue's large-scale, open-air paintings of country
and fisher folk, which excited much popular acclaim, contained
nothing to vex the Academy of Millais. It was not long before
all these artists drifted off to Burlington House.

This dangerous contact with the open air, this accent upon
'realism' and concentration upon rustic themes seems at first
sight to have something in common with Augustus's landscapes. But these *plein air* Victorian painters were *theatrical*
realists, and their pictures were deliberately staged in an endlessly static way that was quite foreign to Augustus's work.
Sickert put his finger on the weakness of the 'Newlyn Group'
when he wrote:

> Your subject is a real peasant in his own natural surroundings,
> and not a model from Hatton Garden. But what is he doing? He is
> posing for a picture as best he can, and he looks it. That woman
> stooping to put potatoes into a sack will never rise again. The
> potatoes, portraits every one, will never drop into the sack, and
> never a breath of air circulates around that painful rendering in the
> flat of the authentic patches on the very gown of a real peasant.
> What are the truths you have gained, a handful of tiresome little
> facts, compared to the truths you have lost? To life and spirit, light
> and air?[1]

Life and spirit, light and air were what Augustus would seek.
He replaced social documentary with poetry, and abandoned
story-telling altogether. His subjects do not act out special
roles – the only parts they play are those they played in his life
and in the fantasy of his imagination.

By the early 1890s control of the N.E.A.C. had passed to
another group, sometimes called 'the London Impressionists',
the leading figures of which were Steer and Sickert. They, too,
looked to France for their inspiration – not to the humani-
tarian realism of Millet and Corot, but to Monet, Manet and

Degas. London Impressionism had not a great deal in common
with Monet's 1874 landscape entitled 'Une Impression', from
which the name strictly derived. It was impressionism without
colour, a puritan impressionism relying on line and tonality,
and dominated by the influence of Whistler. Whistler himself
had ceased to exhibit at the club in 1889, 'disapproving, perhaps, a society so less than republican in constitution as to have
no president'.[2] But Sickert was still a faithful disciple and,
moreover, a severe critic of Bastien-Lepage. Sentiment and invention were on the way out before a more impartial approach, an insistence upon 'the thing there'. When D. S. Mac-
Coll once praised Whistler on the aptness of a bit of wall-
skirting in a portrait, he retorted severely: 'But it's *there*.' And
Sickert, too, shared this principle. 'Supposing', he explained,
'that you paint a woman carrying a pail of water through the
door, and drops are spilt upon the planks. There is a natural
necessary rhythm about the pattern they make much better
than anything you could invent.'

Torn by cliques and divisions, hampered by difficulties over
galleries, the early exhibitions of the New English failed to
make any great impact. But then, in 1890, D. S. MacColl became art-critic of the *Spectator*, and shortly afterwards George
Moore was appointed to a similar post on the *Speaker*. Both
writers gave a leading place to the N.E.A.C. shows and incited
rising anger among the ranks of the reactionaries. In headmaster tones Sir William Richmond was heard to say of such
a dangerously *avant-garde* artist as John Singer Sargent: 'I
should like to set him copying Holbeins for a year.' The climax
came in 1893 over Degas's inaccurately named picture
'L'Absinthe', which was the occasion of one of the greatest
aesthetic battles in the history of modern art, MacColl, Degas
and the whole of the N.E.A.C. being abused 'from Budapest to
Aberdeen'. This controversy had the result of placing the club
at the forefront of non-academic painting, and its provoking
nature was preserved by the election to membership of such
unwholesome artists as Aubrey Beardsley. 'Degradation to suit
a decadent civilization,' thundered the *Westminster Gazette*.
'No longer does nobility of idea dictate subjects to authors; sex
is over-emphasized; the peak of abomination has been reached

by the *Yellow Book* ... All this relates to the evil at work as
expressed by the New English Art Club.'

By the turn of the century, when Augustus began to exhibit,
the club was about to enter a new phase in its history. Alphonse
Legros had disliked the aims of the N.E.A.C., but Brown was an
original member, a close associate of Sickert's, and the man
who had drafted the club's rules. Tonks, too, became a member
in 1895 and was elected to the jury, on which he represented
the revolutionary element in many an argument with Roger Fry
– roles that were later drastically to be reversed. It was not extraordinary, then, that the Slade should emerge as the chief
nursery of young talent, and that people should look to
Augustus, as the spoilt child of this crêche, to lead the way.

He and Gwen were soon regularly exhibiting there. 'Gwen
has had a portrait hung in the N.E.A.C.,' he wrote to Michel
Salaman from Swanage (spring 1900).

I don't know yet whether they have hung mine ... Orpen has sent
also and Everett so that there should be a healthy inoculation of
new and Celtic blood into the Aged New English at last. The jurors
have rejected both Mr Nettleship and Ida's works. I can't see why
the former should wish to seek laurels in this direction ...

I have returned now ... The New English has opened its doors on
the flabber gasted.*

From this time onward a change began to pass over the appearance of the N.E.A.C. exhibitions: more drawings and
watercolours were seen and the club became, in the words of
D. S. MacColl, 'a school of drawing'.[3] Then Roger Fry's appointment as art critic of the *Athenaeum* gained for the New
English another powerful platform. The Winter Exhibition of
1904, Fry wrote, was its most important one yet. 'Mr Sargent,
Mr Steer, Mr Rothenstein, Mr John, Mr Orpen, to mention only
the best known artists, are all seen here at their best.' But the
older members belonged to a group, he continued, 'whose tra-

* For the summer show of 1899 Augustus exhibited two drawings – one of
them a portrait of Miss Spencer Edwards – and a further two drawings in the
winter show. In the summer of the following year both he and Gwen submitted pictures – Gwen a self-portrait, and Augustus a Head of an Oriental and
a portrait of William Morgan.

ditions and methods are already being succeeded by a new set of ideas. They are no longer *le dernier cri* – that is given by a group of whom Mr John is the most remarkable member.'

There was nothing inimical in Augustus's work to Sickert's London Impressionists whose pursuit was 'life' and whose object was to draw it feverishly, Quentin Bell has explained, 'capturing at high speed the essentials of the situation'.[4] Between Sickert and himself there was respect tinged with irony. Sickert felt wryly amused by Augustus's moody character, boasting that 'I am proud to say that I once succeeded in bringing a smile to the somewhat difficult lips of Mr Augustus John.'[5] Yet he knew the value of his work, describing him as 'the first draughtsman that we have, ... the most sure and able of our portrait painters'.[6] And in the *New Age* he paid generous tribute to Augustus's 'intensity and virtuosity [which] have endued his peculiar world of women, half gypsy, half model, with a life of their own. But his whole make-up is personal to himself, and the last thing a wary young man had better do is to imitate John ... [he is] incessantly provisioning himself from the inexhaustible and comfortable cupboard of nature.'[7]

Perversely Augustus dismissed Sickert's writings as 'elegant drivel'.[8] Though he respected Sickert's work, he was often impatient of his aesthetic intrigues, for Augustus never interested himself in art politics. While other painters held stormy meetings about New Rules and Old Prejudices, the only record of Augustus invading their discussions is in the spring of 1903 when, so Orpen told Conder (2 May 1903), he 'demanded to know why after accepting Miss Gwendolen John's pictures – they [the N.E.A.C. committee] had not hung them. But alas this question was out of order ...'[9]

Gwen, however, was thankful to be free of the New English. 'I think I can paint better than I used – I know I can,' she told Ursula Tyrwhitt (8 July 1904); 'it has been such a help not to think of the N.E.A.C. – and not to hurry over something to get it in – I shall never do anything for an exhibition again – but when the exhibitions come round send anything I happen to have.'

Gwen finally ceased altogether showing her pictures at the

club in the winter of 1911,* while Augustus continued exhibiting
there regularly until the large Retrospective Exhibition of 1925
– and even intermittently after that. His attitude towards the
N.E.A.C. was exactly what his attitude to the R.A. would be:
nothing theoretical – it was simply a place to show his work
and a place to sell it. He deplored his sister's decision, largely
because he wanted her to be an acknowledged success. Yet hers
was an attitude that would ideally have suited his own temperament: only he could not afford to hold it. For she, in her
little prisons of homes, was free; while he, patrolling the whole
of Britain and the Continent, was to become more and more
tied down by the claims of a voluminous family and by multitudes of hangers-on whom he frequently invited, then resented.
The first knot was marriage, and he already needed more
money for that.

2. LIVERPOOL

I become more rebellious in Liverpool.
                    AUGUSTUS JOHN TO ALICE ROTHENSTEIN
                                        (DECEMBER 1905)

'We have taken the most convenient flat imaginable in Fitzroy
Street,' Augustus wrote to his sister Winifred a few days after
his marriage. 'It has an excellent studio. The whole most cheap.'

By the time he and Ida returned from their honeymoon, this
flat – three rooms and a huge studio in the top part of 18
Fitzroy Street – had been redecorated and was ready for them
to move into.† But no sooner had they got there than Ida fell

---

* After this last show, Gwen wrote to Mrs Sampson (5 December 1911): 'I
paint a good deal, but I don't often get a picture done – that requires, for me,
a very long time of a quiet mind, and never to think of exhibitions.'

† One of Mrs Nettleship's girls, Edith Phelps, remembered that 'Very little
was said in the house about Ida's marriage to Augustus John. The work girls
said: "It's a shame; he's not half good enough for her." Though I never discussed it with her sisters, I don't think they were very pleased, and Ursula was
disappointed there was no smart wedding, as Ida had several eligible admirers
who wanted to marry her.

'Ida's great friend Gwen Salmond helped her at this time and went round to
Fitzroy Street to tidy up the room, and Maginty the cook went too, and never
stopped crying for two days when she came back. "My poor lamb, it's heart-

ill with the Swanage complaint – measles – and returned to
Wigmore Street, leaving Augustus in their empty rooms. It was
not a good omen.

Money was now their chief worry. Augustus had recently
competed for a British Institute Scholarship, but failed to win
anything. Well though his work had sold in exhibitions, it was
not admired by everyone and could scarcely earn him enough
to keep a wife let alone any children for some time. But that
February, shortly after Ida had returned, a new opportunity for
making a living suddenly presented itself. Albert Rutherston,
staggering round to deliver his wedding present of a kitchen
table, reported that 'the Johns ... seem very comfortable in
their flat which is the most charming one. There is just a chance
of John going to Liverpool for a year to act as Professor in the
school of art there during the absence of the present one – it
would be very nice for him as he will get a studio free and at
least £300 or £400 for the year.'

What had happened was that Herbert Jackson, the art instructor at the art school affiliated to University College Liverpool, had run off to the Boer War. D. S. MacColl, when asked
to recommend someone temporarily to fill his place, had put
Augustus's name forward;* and, since there was no time to be
lost, his proposal was at once accepted.

Augustus arrived in Liverpool late that winter, 'a heartening
sight', one student recalled, '... striding across the drab quad
to the studios in his grey fisherman's jersey and with golden
rings in his ears'.[10]† The academics were greatly fluttered by
this spectacle, enhanced by the beard, long hair and large magnetic eyes, and by the sonorous voice with which he sang his
repertoire of ballads romantic and bawdy – rollicking songs
from the old troubadours and suggestive ones imported from

---

rending," she kept on repeating. "I'm quite sure she'll get an infectious disease
living in such a poor street".' *From Stomacher to Stomach: the Meanderings of a
Dressmaker*, an unpublished autobiography by Edith Fox Pitt.

  * Herbert Jackson was Professor Walter Raleigh's brother-in-law, while
D. S. MacColl was connected by marriage to Oliver Elton, who succeeded
Raleigh as Professor of English Literature at Liverpool.

  † Later on at Liverpool Augustus wore only one ear-ring, having, so the story
goes, gallantly presented the other one to a lady who admired their design.

Parisian cabarets, little verses from Villon and whining Cockney
limericks with the cringing refrain :

I'm a man as done wrong to my paryents.

Liverpool, which he had been warned was an ugly city, enthralled Augustus. 'The docks are wondrous,' he wrote to Will
Rothenstein. 'The college is quite young, so are its professors
and they are very anxious to make it an independent seat of
learning ... The town is full of Germans, Jews, Welsh and Irish
and Dutch.'[11] Everything seemed to delight him. Whatever was
new appeared exciting – and there was much that was new to
him, much that smelt of adventure here. He explored the
sombre district of the Merseyside with its migrant population
of Scandinavians on their way to the New World, and reported
to Alice Rothenstein, 'the Mersey is grand – vast – in a golden
haze – a mist of love in the great blue eye of heaven'. He
nosed around the Goree Piazza, still fainty reeking of the slave
trade, on the lookout for superannuated buccaneers day-dreaming over their rum; he reconnoitred the Chinese Quarter off
Pitt Street and Upper Frederick Street, with its whiff of opium,
penetrated the lodging-houses of the tinkers round Scotland
Road. Even the art school – a collection of wooden sheds on
Brownlow Hill – appealed to him. 'It is amusing teaching,' he
told Will Rothenstein.

Over the first few weeks he and Ida put up at 9 St James's
Street, and it was here that Augustus's only complaint lay. 'It
has been impossible to do much work yet – living as a guest in
somebody's house – a great bore.' He was hungry for work,
especially since there was soon to be another show of his
pictures at the Carfax Gallery. But already by April they had
found 'very good rooms', he reported, 'in the house of an
absent-minded and charming Professor, one Mackay'.

John MacDonald Mackay, Rathbone Professor of Ancient
History, was the most flamboyant personality at University
College – a wonderfully animating figure to whom Augustus
at once responded. 'Mackay – Professor of History is delightful
– the leading spirit of the College,' he wrote to Will Rothenstein shortly after moving into his house at 4 St James's Road.
'He avoids coming to the practical point most tenaciously –

when arranging about taking these rooms he refused to consider terms but referred us to the Swedish Consul – who was extremely surprised when Ida spoke to him on the subject.'

Mackay combined two qualities that appealed very strongly to Augustus's divided nature: comedy and idealism. With his right hand raised, half to his audience, half to the sky visible through the nearest window, a far-away look in his eyes, he would discourse in a weird moustached chant, interrupting himself with bursts of sing-song merriment or New Testament indignation, often abandoning the line of his argument, yet always struggling back to First Principles, always stressing those ideals he believed his colleagues should follow. Under the chemistry of his strange, broken-back eloquence, Liverpool was transformed into a new Athens destined to save the country from materialism by the clearness of its thought, the quality of its work, the beauty of its art and architecture. Through sheer force of character, whatever nominal positions others may have held, he was the father of the university while Augustus lived there.

Mackay was important to Augustus for two reasons. First, he became the subject of one of his most successful portraits. He had a magnificent head, with fair unkempt hair, a powerful jaw and square chin, and the broad shoulders and strength of torso of someone altogether larger. Augustus's 'official' portrait – a three-quarter view of him decked out in his red academic robes – catches in a remarkable way the spiritual energy of the man.*

Secondly, he introduced Augustus and Ida to many people whom, in their shyness, they might otherwise never have known. A number of these Augustus later drew and painted, and a few became close friends. 'We are to dine with the Dowdalls on Friday which I dread,' Ida wrote to her mother.

* This portrait, which now hangs in Liverpool University Dining Club, was later the cause of a historic decision. First exhibited at the N.E.A.C. in the Winter Show of 1903, it was to have been awarded the Gold Medal for painting at the great International Exhibition at St Louis in the following year. Learning that this prize was to go to so young and relatively obscure an artist, the President of the Royal Academy and the English members of the international jury took the astonishing step of withdrawing, without explanation, the entire British section.

'They are very nice, but I would rather hide.' A little later she is writing: 'We had a nice little dinner with the Dowdalls on Saturday. He is a lawyer, I think, with a taste for painting – and he has a little auburn-haired wife who spends most of her time being painted by different people. Gus is to draw Dowdall's mother.'

Harold Chaloner Dowdall, later to become a County Court Judge and, as Lord Mayor of Liverpool, the subject of one of Augustus's most controversial portraits, was a pompous good-natured barrister, very loyal to the Johns but with a tendency to dilate, perhaps for an entire day, on the extreme freshness of the eggs that morning for breakfast. His wife Mary, nicknamed 'the Rani', was 'the most charming and entertaining character in Liverpool', Augustus asserted. She soon became one of Ida's most devoted confidantes. 'The Rani has beautiful browny-red hair and is quite exceptional, and reminds me of the grass and the smell of the earth,' Ida noted. As always with those she admired, Ida likened her to nature, and to an animal in natural surroundings. 'Certainly you belong to the woods and where creatures start and hide away at any alien sound.'

The daughter of Lord Borthwick, Mary Dowdall was Liverpool's aristocrat; but she shocked Liverpool society dreadfully. It was shocked by her habit of walking barefoot through the mud – 'the gentle stimulant of cold mud welling between one's toes is a clarifier of thought,' she claimed, 'after a day's perfect irresponsibility'; it was shocked when, at the fashionable hour, she was to be seen seated, swinging her stockingless legs, at the back of a gypsy caravan trundling down Bold Street; it was shocked by her 'goings-on', her involvement with the Repertory Theatre which dared to give theatrical performances on Good Friday, her frequent modelling improperly clothed for artists such as Shannon, by her awful wit, sheer attractiveness, her unaccountable failure to take Liverpool society seriously. They did not think it nice for the Hon. Mrs Dowdall to be on such familiar terms with the unfamiliar. Above all, Liverpool was appalled by the books she wrote – novels, with such uncompromising titles as *Three Loving Ladies* and, most notoriously, *The Book of Martha*, which, embellished with a frontispiece by Augustus, dealt with tradesmen and servants. She was also the author of *Joking Apart*, and her jokes, delivered in the mock-magisterial tones of her husband, were introduced by: 'All virgins will kindly leave the Court.' No wonder she emptied the drawing-rooms of Edwardian Liverpool.

Augustus's contacts with the university staff were not pushed to extremes, but among the exceptions were Walter Raleigh, who abashed him with the early morning brilliance of his mind – 'he shone even at breakfast!'[12] – Charles Bonnier, the French professor, a victim to the theory and practice of *pointillisme*, who 'has been producing a most astoundingly horrible marmalade of spots yellow, purple, blue and green in my studio';* and Herbert MacNair, instructor in Design and Stained Glass, a dawn dipsomaniac and, of an afternoon, a lusty bicyclist who, in later life, became a postman. He and his wife Frances, working in perfect unison, involved themselves with a peculiar form of *art nouveau*, producing, to Augustus's dismay, friezes of quaint mermaids designed after the MacNair crest, staircases encrusted in sheet lead, lamps of fancifully twisted wrought iron, symbolic watercolours done with much delicate debility upon vellum, embroideries depicting bulbous gnomes and fairies prettily arranged, and as their *pièce de résistance* a burly door-knocker eighteen inches long, the delight of small boys.† 'We dined with two artistic people called Mac-Nair,' Augustus wrote to Will Rothenstein, 'who between them have produced one baby [Sylvan] and a multitude of spooks – their drawing-room is very creepy and the dinner-table was illuminated with two rows of nightlights in a lantern of the "MacNair" pattern . . .'

By far the most valuable new friend Augustus made was the university librarian, John Sampson.‡ A portly man, twice Augustus's age, ponderous in his speech and in his manner laboured, Sampson was at heart a poet, a romantic and a rebel. His influence on Augustus over the next two years changed his

---

* Augustus John to Will Rothenstein, 9 March 1902. He continues: 'I felt inclined to add my patch of home made sienna in reverence to the past.'

† 'The "MacNair" doorknocker is most popular with the children of the neighbourhood who by its means keep themselves in constant touch with the most advanced Art movement.' John to Rothenstein.

‡ Grandfather of (among others) Anthony Sampson the author.

life. The two men met in the late spring of 1901 and immediately struck up a close friendship. There was much in Sampson for Augustus to admire* – the monumental physique, the Johnsonian force of character and vast accumulation of strange knowledge, the sardonic humour – and his example contributed in time to Augustus's own *persona*.

'You are a learned man,' Walter Raleigh wrote to Sampson (16 July 1908), 'and a rogue, one of the sort of fellows who think they can conduct the business of life on inspirationist principles, and who run an office pretty much the same way as they make love to a woman.'[13] Both, by all accounts, he did pretty effectively. He was a commanding figure as he strode through the slums of Liverpool in his old velvet jacket, disgracefully baggy trousers, his muff, gin-bottle and battered old slouch hat set at an angle, his chest thrust out, legs moving powerfully. Despite much intimidating scholarship and overbearing ways, there was something extraordinarily lovable about him – a strange gentleness in his voice, a concealed but very vulnerable sensibility and much boyish ardour. He was followed everywhere by a battalion of devoted women who dedicated themselves to helping him with his work. 'The majestic Sampson,' Augustus once described him to the Rani, 'the large and rolling Rai – he reminds me of a magnificent ship on a swelling sea.' Their relationship was subject to several fiery quarrels and rivalries, but they made it up always and without difficulty.

Augustus was soon greatly in awe of Sampson. Here was a new kind of hero for him to admire. For Sampson was a mine of curious information. He had trained himself in Romany and Shelta, that mysterious jargon of the Tinkers, had mastered both Back and Rhyming Slang, cultivated Sanskrit, phonetics and philology, and would eventually produce a *magnum opus* in his *The Dialect of the Gypsies of Wales*. Already he was at work on an edition of William Blake that was to be acknowledged everywhere as a noble monument of British scholarship;

* In a letter to her father (24 December 1901), Ida wrote: 'Sampson came in last night and we talked till half past 12. He sits and says things in a heavy sort of way. He is rather like a huge and charming Redcliffe Salaman – but don't tell Gus that! he thinks Redcliffe is a mouse in comparison.'

his experimental translations of Heine into Romany were in their eccentric way perfect and, when in 1901 he finished his Romany version of Fitzgerald's Omar Khayyám, he invited Augustus to contribute a frontispiece.

Augustus had a quick ear for languages and under Sampson's tutelage he soon learned the English dialect of Romany and later the deep inflected Welsh dialect. But if he venerated the gypsy scholar, it was the 'Rai of Rais', as Sampson was known outside the university, who enchanted him. By the gypsies themselves, Sampson had been admitted as one of their own, and they revealed to him some of their most secret customs. Augustus had been attracted to gypsies since childhood, but always from a distance. Now, as the Rai's close friend, he was welcomed by them as a fellow vagrant – and indeed, in certain moods, actually appeared to believe he belonged to this 'outlandish and despised people'. They seemed to possess for him some consuming attraction. He could not keep away. Time and again Sampson would take him to Cabbage Hall, a strip of wasteland beyond Liverpool where there was no hall and no cabbages, only the tents and caravans of the gypsy tribes who congregated there throughout the winter; and their visits were rich in adventures.

There was something strangely satisfying in this life of singing and dancing and odd journeys. The tents, the wagons, the gaily painted carts, the great shining flanks of the horses, the wild beauty of the women with their children, fired Augustus's soul in a way he could not explain. He had always felt an affinity with outcast people, those who were powerless and oppressed. Then, too, they were so fine-looking, these open-air people, as they crowded round him and Sampson – their beauty somehow made more beautiful by a proud and enigmatic bearing. Carried away one evening at Cabbage Hall, he picked out an especially handsome Romany youth and, quoting Shakespeare – 'From fairest creatures we desire increase' – egged him on to choose the most beautiful *chai* (girl) he could find for his mate, so that they might produce the best-looking children in the world. The possibilities seemed endless. Noah, Kenza, Eros and Bohemia; Sinfai, Athaliah, Counseletta and Tihanna – their exotic names, and the mystery and antiquity of their origins conjured up a world that was remote yet oddly familiar, a world of which he should have been part.

And when he left them to return to the university and to Ida, he would try to reason out why he felt this fascination, what the true significance of it might be. As a race they seemed to have much in common with him; they were natural exhibitionists, yet deeply secretive; they were quick-witted, courteous, gay yet temperamental and with a dark suspicion of strangers; they were essentially honest, almost naïve, yet prevaricating; they loved children, yet without sentimentality. All this he knew, and yet it still left unaccounted that painful hammering of his heart whenever he approached their camps, caught sight of their young women, so provocative, aloof. His excitement came from obscure but vital needs, from desires damped down in childhood now magically re-kindled. In the sun and wind, like the trees and fields around them, they were truly alive. There was nothing confined, nothing claustrophobic here: they did what they wanted, went where they wished – over the next hill, far away – and they were answerable to no man.

He was exhilarated.

Very different was the atmosphere in 4 St James's Road where life had now begun to follow a steady pattern. 'We have callers pretty often,' Ida informed Alice Rothenstein, 'University men and their wives. Our room is always in disorder when they come as Gus is generally painting – but they survive it.' Generally he was painting Ida, but she too found time to continue with her painting and 'have an old man model, who goes to lectures on Dante, and takes part in play readings. He sits like a rock, occasionally wiping his old eyes when they get moist.' Her sister Ethel* bravely came to stay

* Ethel Nettleship was a 'cellist who, in the First World War, became an ambulance driver and nurse in Italy and Malta and who had such a bad time there that, on her return, she took to lace-making for her nerves. 'Untidy and gay,' Sir Caspar John remembers, 'always hard up – accessible and directly interested in all our lives.' Ursula, the third sister, was rather stern and aloof compared with Ethel. An adventurous mountaineer and skier, she became a singer and teacher of singing who, in an unobtrusive way, did an astonishing amount for music in England. She was for a long time closely connected with

for a week, and Ida contemplated going down to London for a few days, though 'I'm afraid Gussie won't come too. He works very hard.' It was an uneventful time, but not unhappy. 'I am afraid I haven't started a baby yet,' Ida apologized to Alice. 'I want one.'

The first disruptions in this gentle routine came that summer. Ida 'looks suspiciously pregnant', Augustus suddenly remarked to Will Rothenstein. The doctor soon confirmed her pregnancy, but in these early months there was a rumour of complications and, so this doctor warned her, the possible risk of a miscarriage. For this reason she passed the summer months very quietly, first at Wigmore Street, then with Edwin and Winifred John in Tenby.

Liberated from domesticity almost on doctor's orders, Augustus felt he had been let out from a narrow place. He could go where he liked, be what he liked. The effect was magical. One morning he set out intending to go for a short walk 'but instead went to Bruges and stood amazed before the works of Van Eyck and Memling', he explained to Will Rothenstein. 'The Belgians are as shoddy as they were formerly magnificent. Maeterlinck needs all his second sight.'

His truancy over, he then joined Ida in Tenby 'feeling rather metagrabolized', and carried her off for a month's rest-and-painting to New Quay in Cardiganshire. 'Now the child has quickened, I suppose there is very small fear of a miscarriage,' Ira reassured her mother that September. '... I have been very well here – no indigestion and very regular bowels. The baby moves from time to time – and I am growing very big and hard.' They were staying at 3 Prospect Place. Every morning Augustus would go bathing and, during the afternoons, he

the Aldeburgh Festival, at which Benjamin Britten dedicated his 'Ceremony of Carols' to her. 'Her energy, her eagerness, her determination to be satisfied with nothing less than the best, forced those she taught to give of their best, and produced remarkable results,' wrote Ann Bridge (*The Times*, 7 May 1968); 'if she could not inspire she drove, inexorable as a tank, over such human frailties as slackness, timidity or lack of perseverance. Moving about, gesticulating, her greying hair wild, Ursula Nettleship conducting her choir was in fact an inspiring sight – lost in the music, utterly unselfconscious, dragging the sounds she wanted out of, often, very unpromising material.'

admitted, 'have models in a disused school room'. Ida sat at home, letting out her skirts and creating new clothes for the baby, and these she would take up to the schoolroom at tea time, when the painting had to stop.

In the last week of September they returned to Liverpool – but not to St James's Road, since Ida could no longer manage the stairs there. For two weeks they put up with John Sampson and his sentimental mouse of a wife, Margaret – 'delightful people', Ida promised her mother – at 146 Chatham Street, a semi-slum. Then they moved off to rather grander accommodation, 66 Canning Street, a three-storeyed, red-brick house, complete with *art nouveau* metalwork on the doors and railings, and a black·projecting portico with Doric cornices.

So much, this autumn, augured well for Augustus. Ida's pregnancy had inflamed him with an intense excitement – a sense of power, massive tenderness and some curious feeling of fulfilment, almost as if it were he who was being born again. They had been fortunate in finding Canning Street, and Augustus himself had at last discovered a good studio* and was making it habitable.

The university, too, had 'raised my dole to a smug £200 and a day less in the week than last term'.[14] This increase reflected the excellent work he was doing at the Art Sheds. His predecessor, Herbert Jackson, had been an uninspiring teacher. He would slump down by a student's drawing board, sketch an ear or a foot, examine it, then remark : 'It's not much good, I suppose, but it'll do.' Augustus's methods, though not especially orthodox, marked a great improvement. 'Alas, how many brilliant drawings have I done on the boards of my pupils!' he once commented. It was as though he was learning from his own instruction. Above all he stressed the importance of observation. 'When you draw,' he told his class, 'don't look at the model for one second and five minutes at your drawing, but five minutes at the model and one second at your drawing.' He was immensely pleased when one of his pupils did well, and he was responsible for several gifted young artists later leaving the

---

* This building, which has now been destroyed, was between No. 2 Rodney Street and the hospital at the corner of Mount Pleasant.

School of Art and throwing in their lot with the Sandon
Studios Society.*

Despite the incursion which teaching made into his time, his
own work was also going well. Liverpool had stimulated him,
made him more keenly responsive to the visible world. 'For my
part a fine morning fills me with unspeakable joy,' he wrote to
Will Rothenstein, '– a tender sky tethers me to childhood, a
joyous countenance is an obstacle on the road to old age.'

His letters during this first year at Liverpool are congested
with joy, salted with the biological imagery he loved to use in
relation to his work. 'It has seemed to me of late I've been
passing through a transition stage,' he confided to Rothenstein
(4 May 1901),

taking my leave lingeringly and spasmodically, and with many runs
backward, of old traditions ... Something stirs within me which
makes me think so long and passionate company with so many
loves as I have kept has not left me barren. Hitherto I have been
Art's most devoted concubine, but now at length the seed takes
root. I *am*, O Will, about to become a *mother* – the question of
paternity must be left to the future. I suspect at least 4 old masters.

Between the winter exhibitions of 1900 and 1902, greatly to
Brown's disappointment, Augustus sent in nothing to the
New English. Instead he relied on the Carfax Gallery and in
particular on Rothenstein who seems to have set himself up
as, in some respects, Augustus's London agent. To him Augustus
would dispatch what he called his 'parcels of fancies' and
'pastels of sluts' – beggar girls, ballet girls and all manner of
remarkable-looking models he had collided with in the streets of
Liverpool. His purpose was to record the natural beauty he saw
in life, as directly as possible, without any message or moral,
any attitude or intervening glaze of intellectuality: simply the

* The Sandon Studios Society, of which John was elected an honorary member, was later set up in opposition to the University School of Art, to encourage freer and more vigorous draughtsmanship and a less restrictive attitude to
painting. It was officially opened at 9 Sandon Terrace on 5 December 1905, but
'any formality intended', records R. H. Bisson in his history of the society
(p. 28) 'was dissipated by Augustus John, who got very cheerful and fell
headlong down the stairs'.

thing itself – almost as Wordsworth had expressed it in *Peter Bell*.

> A primrose by a river's brim
> A yellow primrose was to him,
> And it was nothing more.

With these pastels Rothenstein was extremely successful, especially in selling them to other artists – Ricketts and Shannon, Brown and Tonks. Augustus's gratitude, both to Rothenstein and to his models, swelled to its most rhapsodic vein:

Beloved Will,

You know how nothing delights my soul more than your laudation! you have made me tickle and thrill, and gulp tears to eye and water to lip. And have my poor girls served me so well! Blessing on you Maggie and Ellen Jones!* Daughters of Cardigan I thank ye! And you Quean of the Brook whose lewd leer captured me in my dreams, may your lusty honest blood be never denied the embrace it tingles for!

... I pant to do a superb decoration ...

The most important development in Augustus's work during this Liverpool period was not in decoration but as an etcher. He had taken up etching at the suggestion of his friend Benjamin Evans, one of his first plates being a portrait of Evans.[15] Suddenly now he grew immensely enthusiastic over this new medium – 'I have been etching a good deal,' he informed Will Rothenstein. It was Rembrandt's example[16] that Evans had extolled and that now fired-off this burst of enthusiasm. Like Rembrandt, his first experiments included a number of portrait studies of himself in various poses and costumes – fur caps and wide-brimmed hats, bare-headed and in a black gown. But they also numbered several portraits of Ida, very plump and maternal, in a fur-tipped cape or with a special necklace, or simply as 'a brown study': and pictures of drapers, chandlers, old haberdashers, young serving maids, children and all the curious cosmopolitan population of Liverpool whom he encountered on the waste ground of Cabbage

---

* Two Liverpool models who later went 'to breed in the colonies. May they raise many a stalwart son to our Empire!' John wrote to the Rani.

Hall, within the university, at the working-men's dining-rooms and doss houses along Scotland Road – gypsies and mulattoes, the frock-coated bourgeois, the negresses, charwomen and old men with gnarled expressions, fierce and hopeless.

Augustus had made so close a study of Rembrandt's method, and assimilated it to such an extent, that a great many of his etchings have the appearance of being personal imitations. Yet however derivative his technique may be, these etchings do tell us a great deal about his aims as an artist, often by reason of their very imperfection. In his perceptive introduction to the Catalogue of Augustus's etchings, Campbell Dodgson wrote:

There are certain features in his work which make it unlike that of his contemporaries. His choice of figure subjects in preference to the landscape or architectural motives which are so much in vogue to-day is one of them. His consistency in restricting the size of his plates to small, or even tiny, dimensions is another. Both are significant traits which link his work to the great tradition of the painter-etchers of four centuries ... But a fault common to many of them is a fault that runs through Mr John's paintings and drawings as well, lack of concentration and acquiescence in an apparent finish, a facile substitute for true perfection. Or if we consider the subjects themselves, rather than the manner in which he treats them, is there not something unsatisfying, superficial, betraying lack of 'fundamental brainwork' in most of the compositions containing two or more figures? There is no apparent motive for bringing them together, and Mr John, with all his intense interest in single types, and his power, unequalled among etchers of to-day, of expressing individual character, lacks the imaginative, constructive, or dramatic gift of showing several characters in action. Though more than one of his groups possess a certain degree of idyllic charm, which is seen at its best in *The Valley of Time*, he has produced nothing that makes him notable as an etcher of action, and he is too easily content with inventing groups of aimless women who sit doing nothing particular, in a world of shadows, or stroll, leading children by the hand, through vague meadows of dreamland.

The fruit-sellers and philosophers, tramps and coster-girls who figure in so many of Augustus's visual lyrics were in fact very poor subjects – highly elusive, self-conscious, shy of being stared at. He had taught his students the value of observation – to look 'five minutes at the model and one second at your drawing' – but it was precisely this lesson he was unable to practise. He could catch them all right, these reluctant sitters, but well before the five minutes were up they were off. He was therefore thrown back on his memory and on his imagination, and to some extent these failed him. Everything made its impact on him at once, and seemed to last only so long as it remained physically in front of him. In his imaginative work, based on memory or invention, there is a lack of substance. Most of these studies of gypsies or fisher folk lack atmosphere, a feeling for place, often even accurate recollection of detail: the oxygen has gone out of their world, and they wilt. They have become propaganda pictures advertising a recommended way of life, from which the initial vitality has had time to seep away. This seepage is sometimes particularly noticeable in the case of his etchings because the medium was so slow. To fill the emptiness, he overworked them with a turmoil of feathery cross-hatching, suffocating them in lines.* Perhaps because he realized how far short they fell of all he wanted to communicate he could not reconcile himself to leaving off at the right moment. 'It is only that I feel ever inclined to add a few scratches on the plate that I husband them in this way,' he told Will Rothenstein.

Campbell Dodgson's other chief criticism Augustus would have refuted. It was not his desire artificially to inject action

* Undoubtedly some of the plates would have been better if they had been left in the pure etched state, without being carried to a finish by lavish use of dry-point, which sacrificed their original crispness, leaving them soft and veiled. Some of the very best ones are incomplete studies or sheets of studies, where the needle has been used like a pencil and the emphasis is on line; where, with a minimum of cross-hatching, the face has been left free from the rubberized pock-marks of dots and dashes intended to suggest variations of surface and of tone. These studies are often less self-conscious than the finished products, picked out more precisely in order to stress a curve or a fold, and they combine a more spontaneous execution with a regard for the personality of the model. Some of the series of heads form a natural design on the page, and some of the studies give the impression of a fine water-colour wash. But John is at his very best with single figures, and to his Liverpool period belong several extraordinary fine portraits including the Mulatto; the Old Haberdasher; the Jewess with her shrewd suspicious gaze; and 'Old Arthy' where the effect of strong light behind the head creates a silhouette which the dense cross-hatching emphasizes without negating the figure, since the lines become part of the creases of the face and the shadows cast by it.

or drama into these studies; it was not his wish to apply sophisticated 'brainwork' to these simple people. What action, what drama, what brainwork is there in a flower, a falling wave, the corner of a field, single tree, the look upon a half-averted face? What intellectual 'purpose' may be divined in such trivial shapes and ordinary sights? Augustus did not plot his pictures. His groups are deliberately motiveless. He etches them because they're there – and because he loves them. In a sense, the superficiality of which Campbell Dodgson accuses him is exactly what he sets out to achieve. His theme is the profundity of the superficial, an avowal that the look in an eye, a smile, a tone of voice – all these passing and unimportant things – have the power to move us beyond explanation or understanding, and become part of our lives. So far as the artist is concerned, the 'meaning' of his studies should be left, Augustus believed, to his unconscious. Augustus's intention, in so far as he may be saddled with one, was to fix the passing moment for eternity, to transport us to a timeless but earthly paradise, 'a romantic world composed in the image of his desire'.[17] But where the magic of timelessness fails, time hangs heavy; and where the passing moment will not pose for him, his mood in retrospect shifts so that idealism is mixed with caricature, and the physical presence from which he derived his inspiration is confused with disembodied day-dreaming.

So much this autumn augured well; so much seemed to trail, like a silhouette, its shadow of disappointment: and as the autumn changed to winter, these shadows began to lengthen.

The turning-point came in October. It was in the second week of this month that Augustus sustained a terrible bang on the head, reminiscent of his bathing accident at Tenby. Ida, in a letter to her mother (16 October 1901), explains what happened:

Gus has broken his nose and put his finger out of joint by falling from a ladder in the studio. The doctor came – a splendid big red-brown man – and sewed up the cut on the nose in two exquisite stitches. Poor Gus was very white, and bloody in parts. He is now a lovely sight, very much swollen and one red eye. His profile is like a lion. They say the scar will not show, and he will be well in a fortnight. The bone was a little damaged but it won't make any difference

– we think his nose may be straighter after! He goes about and has gone to the doctor now to have it dressed. His finger only needed pulling and bandaging. It was bent back! he thought it was broken.

After the first shock had passed, Augustus resolved not to be pinned down by his injury. 'My dear!' he wrote to Will Rothenstein,

a bang on the head has never and will never down me. Au contraire I feel double the *uebermensch* with a great patch on my nose! I have paraded it before my students with great effect. At the Sketch Club the other night it must have been grand to see me point a dislocated finger of scorn and turn up a broken nose at these purblind gropings in pictorial darkness.

Such was the devastating effect of this patch and bandage, he claimed, that students hurried over from other art schools, and his class overflowed. But what is evident from his letters is that this fall had resurrected his accident at Tenby, and that he was now, in a theatrical way, over-reacting to it, as if to break up some pattern formed on the earlier occasion. He wore his misfortune, humorously enough, like some sartorial accomplishment. But an extra wildness entered into his behaviour, as if he were pushing frantically against a door he feared might close on him.

In this mood the value of things altered. Up till now he had seemed to share the biological adventure of Ida's pregnancy, but suddenly it threatened him with confinement. The whole process was too long – a nine *days'* wonder was what he would have liked. He felt hemmed in. 'I really must come to town and see what my contemporaries are about,' he wrote in October to Will Rothenstein. But the following month he was writing: 'I fear I cannot come to London before our baby has squeezed its way through the narrow portals of life.'

London, now that he could not reach it, was marvellously desirable to him; while over Liverpool, so fresh and enthralling only that spring, a cuticle of boredom had begun to spread. London bought his pictures – sometimes the very pictures which Liverpool had rejected. But the Liverpool Academy refused him membership. He felt himself fallen among Philistines. 'I come now shattered from a visit to the Walker Art Gallery,' he wrote to Will Rothenstein. 'It contains the Ox Bovril of the R.A. shambles.'*

Because of Liverpool's antipathy to his work and because of his own spendthrift ways, he was often pressed for money and, on one occasion, obliged to settle a huge milk bill by handing over to the disgruntled milkman a number of masterpieces. 'I would paint any man a nice big picture for £50, if he paid down 25 first,' he complained to Rothenstein this winter. 'That's to say a good big nude.' But no one wanted his nudes. They were big, certainly; but they were not good, Liverpool decided: they were *ugly*.

His teaching, he increasingly felt, prevented him doing the work he panted after. 'What output can be expected of one who works at a school for 3 days!' he expostulated.[18] In such a climate of restriction, Mackay's lofty ideals seemed peculiarly irrelevant. 'Mackay talks grandiosely of a great art school with 300 a year for me and studio and my own will to follow – But I trust him not,' he confided to Will Rothenstein (16 April 1902). Blotting out Mackay's vision of a university palace with cloud-capped towers and a studio for every face of the day was Augustus's actual curriculum – a treadmill that grew more irksome to him each week. 'The three days I prostitute to foul faced commodity weigh on my soul terribly,' he confessed. 'My conscience is awakening and I see the evil of my ways.'[19] By the early spring of 1902 his university career had reached a point of crisis. 'I am now expected to examine *all* the work done by every student (50 to 60) during the past Session and choose an example of *each* to send to the National Competition S. Kensington,' he complained to Rothenstein (9 March 1902). 'You can imagine the brilliant result of such a rummage. I draw the line at that.' But if he drew the line too firmly he would be out of a job; and without a job he and his family would have no money. He was trapped.

---

* The Walker Gallery was soon to return this compliment. When, in 1902, a group of subscribers gave William Rothenstein's portrait of John to the gallery, it was catalogued anonymously as 'Portrait of a Young Man', under which title it can be seen there today. When offered John's official portrait of Chaloner Dowdall as Lord Mayor of Liverpool, the gallery refused it in 1918. The first example of his work it bought was 'Two Jamaican Girls', in 1938.

What particularly galled him was the way in which the most respectable, and therefore most despicable, elements of university life had begun to infiltrate his home. The wives of professors – some of whom he abominated – made it their duty to call regularly on Ida carrying with them pieces of black net, flannel nightgowns, wool socks or torn lace, disused blankets, second-hand pin-cushions, half the veil of a deceased nun, a miniature redundant stove for preparing baby's food, and all manner of ritual and nondescript items pulled out of old cupboards. Whenever Augustus returned from his studio, there they were, these affable vague females, tousled, dusty and bespectacled, parading their offerings and ceaselessly chattering about Ida's baby – when would it arrive? Would it be a boy? Would it be born before, after or even at the same time as the other College baby that winter, Mrs Boyce's? Under this pressure Ida began to entertain fantastic nightmares about her baby. 'I dreamt last night that the baby came – an immense girl, the size of a 2 year old child – with thick lips, the under one hanging – little black eyes near together and a big fine nose,' she wrote to her mother (16 October 1901). 'Altogether very like a savage – and most astonishing to us.'

Augustus's reaction to these Liverpool ladies was more realistic: he avoided them. Instead, he spent more and more time with his gypsies. That autumn there was a gypsy fair on Cabbage Hall. The place was crowded with carts and wagons, booths and cheap jacks; and everywhere the animal – both horse and man – was magnificently exhibited: turgid and strenuous. What utterly damnable things were towns and town-dwellers compared to all this! And how tawdry the tea-party wives who filled his home seemed when contrasted with the gypsy fortune-tellers, the very pictures of sin and supernatural knowledge, with their stately bearing and their unreadable eyes like black coals burning with concentrated hate – terrible to behold! Mesmerized, as if by some witch's spell, he would linger on there all day and half the night, till the fields and hills grew dark, a heavy mist enshrouded the tents, and the fiddlers one by one stopped their playing.

Like a gypsy himself, Augustus was growing ever more elusive. Ida seldom knew where he was. It was not only

Cabbage Hall that he preferred to his own home, but other people's homes – the Rani's at 28 Alexandra Drive which, according to Albert Rutherston,* 'is good for the moral tone of us all'; and the defunct Gothic school near Rodney Street where lived the 'Doonie', the artist Albert Lipczinski's generous blue-eyed wife to whom, in order to avoid trouble, Augustus wrote his letters in deepest Romany.

Ida took all this very calmly – though her dreams grew more fantastic.† 'Unless anything unusual happens the baby will not come till the beginning of January,' she had told her mother. With very un-John-like punctuality it was born, weighing six pounds exactly, on 6 January. 'My wife gave birth to a little boy yesterday,' Augustus wrote to Albert Rutherston (7 January 1902), 'and seems none the worse.' But his casual tone concealed a real sense of excitement.

For this event the household had been reinforced by the presence of Mrs Nettleship and a nurse. While Ida rested in bed and the nurse perambulated the infant out in the park, Augustus sat downstairs listening to Mrs Nettleship strumming out cheerful tunes on the piano. They reminded him of his father. After a fortnight Ida was allowed up. 'It was lovely,' she wrote to her sister Ursula. 'But I felt as if I were too light to keep down on the floor.' Her letters over the next few weeks were full of baby-news in which Augustus took as keen an interest as she did, noting each grunt, each ounce in weight. 'I cannot realise I have a little boy yet,' she told Ursula (21 January 1902). 'I *cannot* believe I am his mother. I love him very much. He has an intelligent little face – but looks, nearly always, perplexed, or contemplative. I do not think he has smiled yet. He is a wonderful mixture of Nettleship-John.'

---

* Albert Rutherston to Max Beerbohm (undated, Merton College, Oxford). 'The hospitality of Liverpool is truly wonderful,' he added by way of explanation, 'the women more so.'

† She dreamt of a tiny man, 'the size of the 1st joint of a finger', immensely charming, who drank milk out of a miniature saucer, like a cat, and who had a little boat in which he sailed off alone. He was very plucky, but eventually got lost and exhausted, frightened by the prickly larch trees, until he came across a tent in which lived Jack Nettleship, who took him up and carried him home, quite naked. 'Do you think the baby will be a lunatic, having such a mother?' she asked her father (24 December 1901).

What exercised Augustus's mind more than anything else was the choice of a name. It was another sign of his own lack of identity that, with all his children, this choice should be such a perplexing matter. By the time the child's birth had been registered, one name alone had been settled upon – and that was compulsory: Nettleship. As a preliminary Christian name, Augustus had given a good deal of consideration to Lewis. But no sooner had he firmly decided upon this than the baby would physiognomically alter so as to resemble an Anthony or a Peter. Then a new conviction would seize him: he would fix upon his son a good Welsh name – Llewelyn or maybe Owen or even Evan ... But which? Perhaps, since the child would after all be only one-quarter Welsh this too was wrong. Whichever way he looked at it, the problem appeared insoluble – yet it had to be solved correctly. He brought to bear upon it his utmost concentration. His eyes bulged, the veins stood out on his forehead, he strode off for long walks, he tried out names in the proximity of the baby as it slept, he read books. By March, Honoré was in the lead and seemed almost certain to win. But by May, Ida was writing to Alice Rothenstein: 'Really I cannot tell you the baby's name, as we can't decide. Gus has said Pharaoh for the last few days. But it changes every week. I don't mind what it is.' To meet the pressure of such inquiries, Augustus was eventually hurried into accepting David by the end of the year. But for much of his childhood David was called Tony, then reverted to David – with the occasional variant of Dafydd, being a quarter Welsh.

At the beginning of March, Augustus, Ida and 'Llewelyn De Wet Ravachol John' left Canning Street and moved to 138 Chatham Street, very near the Sampsons. Here, for five months, they endured the rigours of family life. 'I wish you would tell me something about your baby,' Ida asked Alice Rothenstein. 'Does he often cry? Ours *howls*. He is howling now. I have done all I can for him, and I know he is not hungry. I suppose the poor soul is simply unhappy.' Augustus too was not very happy. The birth of his son, with all its novelty and curiosity, had turned his attention back into their home, but now the noise began to drive him out again. He did little in the house and Ida sometimes felt that she had more to do than she could manage. But though the strain began to tell on her, she did not complain. 'Baby takes so much time – and the rooms we are in are not kept very clean, so I am always dusting and brushing. Also we have a puppy, who adds to the difficulties,' she told Alice. But, she went on : 'I think I enjoy working hard really.'

Augustus's pictures of Ida often show her encompassed by children. But she was far from being a conventional mother-figure whose *raison d'être* was child-bearing. In a sense she represented more of a mother to Augustus than to his sons. She did not feel about her first-born, she told the Rothensteins, as they did about theirs. 'I have not had any ecstasies over him,' she confessed. 'He is a comic little fellow, but he grumbles such a fearful lot. I think he would very much rather not have been created.' She never enjoyed that intense physical and possessive love of her children that the Rothensteins bathed in, and it is doubtful whether Augustus would have wished her to. 'How wonderful it seems to me how you and others love their children,' she wrote again to Alice about three years later. 'Somehow I don't, like you do. I love only my husband and the children as being a curious – most curious – result of part of that love.'

Augustus's attitude was different again. Though eminently unpractical in the home, he was one of those fathers who, while his children were infants with little developed character of their own, felt towards them a mother's jealous passion, primitive and possessive. Whereas Ida could not believe she was their mother, Augustus in certain moods almost seemed to believe it was he who had given birth to them; and at the start his relationship was more physical than Ida's, almost more female. 'Honoré is becoming a surprising bantling with muscles like an amorillo,' he wrote proudly to Will Rothenstein that spring. His new role as parent had greatly fortified his self-confidence. 'The arrival of Honoré gives me to see I cannot dally and temporize with Fate.'

One thing delayed him from severing at once his connection with the University Art School, and that was the fittest method of procedure. 'I am wondering,' he confided to Rothenstein, 'which is the best way to get out of this school, whether to be chucked out or resign ... the former I think would look best in the end.' He had made a number of friends in Liverpool, but they were all rebels in the university or individualists outside it. The very qualities that provoked hero-worship also stimulated aversion in people such as Charles Allen who taught sculpture at the university, and F. M. Simpson who held the Chair of Architecture. 'I become more rebellious in Liverpool,' he was to tell Alice Rothenstein – and it was true. He did dreadful things there. Mustering his courage at an important dinner party, he failed to rise to his feet when the King's health was drunk – 'it took some doing'. His name was a trigger for all manner of scandalous gossip. 'Mr [Wyndham] Lewis has been spreading very bad reports about everybody in London,' Orpen wrote a little later this year to Albert Rutherston, '... his last was that John had been kicked out of Liverpool and that he was going to leave his wife.'

Augustus was unrepentant. 'The school may go to hell,' he announced – and suddenly he felt much better. Even his work improved. 'I have started some startling pictures,' he claimed. 'Ah! if they would emerge triumphantly from the ordeal of completion.'

To make up for the loss of his salary, he had arranged to paint a series of portraits. 'I have some jobs on hand now, enfin, mon cher!' he told Rothenstein in May, 'les pommes de terre enterrées si longtemps commencent à pousser.' He had also made some rapid decisions about the art of portrait painting to fit in with these new commissions. 'Nowadays, I fancy, portraits should be painted in an hour or two,' he decided (16 April 1902). 'The brush cannot linger over shabby and ephemeral garments.' Of the intermittent series of Liverpool portraits he now began, three were to be outstanding – those of Mackay, completed in June this year, of Kuno Meyer and Chaloner Dowdall done several years later. Some of the other portraits* convey a feel-

* These included a rather military portrait of Oliver Elton, the English Literature don; a curious King Lear impression of Dr Muspratt, emerging from the shadows of a flat dark background; a sombre Victorian impression of Sir John Brunner, the radical plutocrat, whom John credits with mother-of-pearl flesh tones, a white beard and a moustache slightly ginger on one side; a likeness of Sir John Sherrington, the scientist and a special friend of Ida's, a timid, gauche figure, his eyes distrustfully peering through weak spectacles;

ing that he had made an effort to be interested in his subject, and failed. The significance of this Liverpool period however was that he experimented in several directions, searching out a personal form of beauty and celebrating some glimpse of it that was unique to himself.

But he was no longer painting Ida. 'I have not sat to Gus for ages,' she confessed to Alice. Although matters were far from being so bad as Wyndham Lewis reported, Ida felt very acutely the need of some sympathetic companionship. 'I long for Gwen [John],' she had written the previous summer. Now, at long last, Gwen arrived. Her life, too, had not been easy. During the summer of 1901 she had shared an address – 39 Southampton Street – with Ambrose McEvoy; but in December McEvoy became engaged to Mary Edwards, a damp-looking woman, nine years older than himself, who lived near the river. 'We were quite surprised,' Everett noted with relish in his journal, 'as he'd been running round before with Gwen John.' They did not marry immediately however, and an awkward period ensued with Gwen living at 41 Colville Terrace, the McEvoy family home in Bayswater, where, as if in mourning, the shutters were always closed to avoid paying the rates. It was from here that she had come to Chatham Street; and it was from Chatham Street that she wrote to Michel Salaman a letter that indicates the direction in which her life was to move.

As to being happy, you know, don't you, that when a picture is done – whatever it is, it might as well not be as far as the artist is concerned – and in all the time he has taken to do it, it has only given him a few 'seconds' pleasure. To me the writing of a letter is a very important event! I try to say what I mean exactly, it is the only chance I have – for in talking, shyness and timidity distort the very meaning of my words in people's ears – that I think is one

---

and a comfortable, spongy portrait of Charles Reilly, rather sadly wrapped in a black-and-white scarf.

The portrait of Chaloner Dowdall (1909) is now at the National Gallery of Victoria, Melbourne; of Kuno Meyer (1911), at the National Gallery, Dublin; those of Mackay, Elton, Muspratt, Brunner and Sherrington at the University College Dining Club, Liverpool; and that of Reilly at the School of Architecture in Abercrombie Square, Liverpool. John did not paint Sherrington till the mid 1920s, and Reilly till 1931.

reason I am such a waif ... I don't pretend to know anybody well. People are like shadows to me and I am like a shadow.

But with a few people, mostly women, Gwen was at ease – and one of them was Ida. She could trust Ida, she told Salaman, 'with all my thoughts and feelings and secrets'; and Ida felt the same way about her. Gwen had been hurt by McEvoy – 'Sister Gwen upset', Augustus noted.[20] An etching he did of her probably during this visit[21] shows her as a very upright figure, bristling, on her guard, the daughter of Edwin John. Her expression is impassive, giving nothing away. On her head sits a pancake hat with a hedgehog on top; her hair is pinned into a tight bun; her dress firmly tied at the neck; her lips buttoned. Yet there is a feeling of sadness in the eyes, an impression of loneliness, of reserve and the inability to share emotion. There is no gentleness, no hint of passion. The etching is almost suffocated in lines.

'I have been very busy with the baby,' Gwen wrote to Salaman. She would take him out for 'air', and, quite unawares, scandalize the neighbourhood by sitting unconcernedly on the nearest doorstep whenever she felt like a rest.

After Gwen left, Ida felt her own isolation with fresh sharpness. In the middle of April she went with the baby for a few days to London to see her father, who had not been well. 'I am left deserted,' Augustus exclaimed to Will Rothenstein (16 April 1902). 'As a consequence I lay abed last night with a moonlit sky in front of me and chased infinite thoughts. Decidedly it is inspiring to lie alone at times. I fear continued cosiness is risky ... I wish I had somebody to think with.'

He had never pretended to be an 'exponent of the faithful dog business' – it was not natural; certainly not natural for him. Ida knew this when she married him. She had made her bed, as it were, and sometimes she would have to lie in it alone. He trusted her to recognize that the overpowering attraction of other women which sometimes swept over him did not diminish his love for her. He loved her and would always love her – it was important she understood this – so long as they were not handcuffed together. He needed to play truant – she knew this – but he would always return to her, choosing the moment that best suited him. But if his freedom were curtailed, if he were criticized or prevented from acting as his energetic nature demanded, then a hot-and-cold madness would break out in him and instinctively he would say and do fearful things – things for which he was not responsible. It was as if another being had taken control and he was no longer 'himself'. The last thing he wanted to do was to hurt Ida, but too much 'moral living' might destroy them both.

At the end of July they left Liverpool* and returned to live in Fitzroy Street. Both of them, for rather different reasons, were happy to be back in London. But the 'cosiness' of their married life was almost at an end.

3. WHAT COMES NATURALLY

In the eighteen months since her marriage Ida had changed considerably. 'Ida with her shock of black hair, as wild as a Maenad in a wood pursued by Pan,' Arthur Symons had romantically pictured her.[22] 'Intractable, a creature of uncertain moods and passion. One never knew what she was going to say or do ... She had – to me – the almost terrible fascination of the Wild Beast. There was something almost Witch-like in her.' This had been her fascination for Augustus. But with the metamorphosis from Ida Nettleship to Mrs John she had developed into a more substantial figure – both physically, following the birth of David, but also in character. Gone was the feyness, the whimsicality of her early Mowgli letters; and gone too was much of her moralizing. Her intenseness had been the longing of a vigorous nature for those aspects of reality from which young Victorian ladies were hermetically protected. Now there was reality enough – she was glutted with it. Her character gained unexpected depths in grappling with new problems; she grew more resilient, more direct, at times more ironical. But, in Augustus's eyes, she lost something of her mystery. Her pre-

---

* 'I would subscribe to make Augustus John Director of a Public House Trust,' Walter Raleigh wrote to D. S. MacColl (27 May 1905). In fact John's time at Liverpool was later commemorated by a new public house, 'The Augustus John', which has been erected next to the postgraduate club.

sence was more obvious; she grew more tired, and she was forced to give up painting in order to become a mother. It was a full-time job to which she could not easily resign herself – 'I certainly was not made for a mother,' she admitted to Alice Rothenstein (1903). She was made, she felt, for Augustus. She loved him, wanted to be his mistress. But the roles of mistress and of mother were often in conflict, and in the nature of things – though not in her nature – the mother began to eclipse the mistress.

'Look what a grand life she had,' her sister Ethel later wrote, 'going full tilt.'[23] But really it was life that had gone full tilt into her. The first blow came shortly after her return from Liverpool. Her father had fallen seriously ill. Though having great difficulty in breathing, he would gasp out page after page of Browning day after day, until gradually he grew too weak. Ida and Augustus were with him during this final illness, though for much of the time he was barely conscious and could recognize no one. He liked the daylight and kept turning his head towards the window. After Browning was beyond him, he uttered very little. Once he called out: 'Are you there, Ethel?' and, after a silence, called back: 'Yes, I thought you might come and see us through this risk.' Every day Ida would go across to Wigmore Street to be near him. 'Old Nettleship is at his last,' Augustus told Will Rothenstein. 'He will die before the morning it is thought. Ida and I go round at midnight to see him. He has been in a high temperature ... and his mind has not been clear.'

Somehow he survived that night, and in a moment of consciousness assured Augustus that God was 'nearer to me than the door'. Next morning his arm went up like a semaphore and could not be kept down until, quite suddenly, he died. 'The dear old chap was quite unconscious,' Ida wrote afterwards to Will Rothenstein (1 September 1902), 'and did not suffer, except in the struggle for breath, and at the end he was quite peaceful. He was so grand and simple.'

Besides Augustus, her father had been the only man who meant anything to Ida. Now she would have to rely on Augustus alone. As if sensing this extra responsibility, he grew wilder.

He was meant to be hanging his pictures in the Carfax Gallery,* but this depressed him. To fling off his depression he drank more. 'I thank you sincerely for bearing me home in safety,' he wrote to Will Rothenstein after one night's entertainment. 'I was utterly incapable. I had been imbibing a quantity of bad rum. I knew it to be poison yet drank it with relish ... After having slept 3 hours I awoke perfectly well again.' His powers of recovery were truly remarkable – and he tested them to the full. 'John had the drinks,' L. A. G. Strong wryly noted in his diary, 'and his friends had the headache.'[24] One night Will Rothenstein received a telegram: 'Bail me out, Vine St, John.' Another night he came across him prostrate on the pavement – this while his father-in-law was dying.

The pattern that had established itself in Liverpool was now broadly repeated in London. By the autumn Ida was pregnant again. She was visited at Fitzroy Street by all her old jungle friends, and by her family, in particular her mother who brought along, brightly intact, all her old grievances against Augustus. It was as if the two of them were in a tug-of-war over the possession of Ida – but however deeply attached Ida was to her mother, she had given herself once and for all to Augustus. He tried to get on with Mrs Nettleship, but when she did not respond to him his temper would get the better of him and he would storm out of the house.

'Our life flows so evenly and regularly, I love it,' Ida wrote to the Rani soon after her return to London. 'But,' she added, 'I'm afraid Gus finds it rather a bore.' He had begun to find something of a home from home in the Café Royal. By the beginning of the century, the Café Royal had become the rendezvous of many artists and writers living in London. With its exuberant neo-classic ornament, its abundance of gilt, its ubiquitous flashing mirrors, its crimson velvet, it formed a cosily grandiose setting for such gatherings. It was unique in Britain, a café-restaurant on the French pattern where people could wander from table to table, sit drinking and talking with one group, move on to another. It was more popular with the

---

* 'The Carfax directors are not inspiring companions and numero s other people came in with whom I could not feel fortunate,' John explained in a letter to Will Rothenstein.

avant-garde than the academic, and to be *avant-garde* meant, in some degree, to be an exile from Paris. 'If you want to see English people at their most English, go to the Café Royal,' Beerbohm Tree advised Hesketh Pearson, 'where they are trying their hardest to be French.' The atmosphere owed something to the nineties – *crème de menthe frappée* drunk through straws; and drawings done on menus with napkins plunged into Grand Marnier. In the opinion of Max Beerbohm, the Café Royal was 'life', and in such a world Augustus loomed even larger than life.

He liked the place for its casualness, for the easy coming-and-going, the undemanding companionship. He liked it because, to a large extent, and by sheer force of personality, he dominated it. His Shakespearian domed forehead; his beautiful eyes, observant, outstanding in the literal sense that they stood far out, seeming to transfix his audience; his voice so soft and laconic, confiding, ruminating, rumbling; his noble manners, formal yet sympathetic; the hands which threw such a spell about his conversation; and that alarming residue of rage and outrage which could so innocently be stirred up : these ingredients contributed to a presence that could, almost physically, claw you into its orbit. 'Of all the men I have met,' wrote Frank Harris, who had a fine appreciation of such things and who claimed to have met everyone, 'Augustus John has the most striking personality.'

Though he tended to be morose at home and very silent, particularly when he was working hard, at the Café Royal he was a different person and, after a few drinks, wonderfully exuberant. Here, by popular acclaim, he was acknowledged a Bohemian king, with the waiters his courtiers, all his companions guests. In such a genial climate, his uncertainties dissolved, his morale shot up, and he inflated himself terrifically. He could be arrogant, childishly offensive to people, and he would grow sullen when others became too talkative. He liked to be at the centre of things, and because this suited him so well and he could exercise there such rare charm, people were generally happy for him to have the star role. He was unbelievably hospitable. Almost always he was left with the bill, and would pay it uncomplainingly with a huge fistful of notes that represented all the money he possessed. In a sense he paid friends to entertain him, and he valued them as entertainers rather than friends. His generosity contributed to the aura of his attraction, which was agreeably complicated by a vein of sardonic humour. One evening in the Domino Room, George Moore was denigrating him to Steer and Rothenstein – 'Why, the man can no more draw than I can!' – when Augustus himself walked in, apparently rather drunk, and sat down at their table. He took no notice of Moore, who tried to engage his attention, but in complete silence, Will Rothenstein recorded, 'he took out a sketch book, and made as if to draw, doing nothing, however, but scribble. Moore, flattered, imagining John to be sketching him, sat bolt upright not moving a muscle. When John, tired of scribbling, shut up his book, Moore asked to see it, and turning over the pages, said unctuously, "One can see the man can *draww*." '[25]

In the two most famous paintings of the Café Royal, those by Adrian Allinson and William Orpen, Augustus is prominently depicted. He liked best the company of other artists and of models – though he did not talk much about painting; of writers, preferably of the romantic school; and of eccentrics – magicians and bimetallists, Celtic gentlemen with a knowledge of archaeology, some philosophical or mathematical ambitions or perhaps a smattering of Sanskrit or Hindi, social creditors, practical jokers, picturesque anarchists of the Kropotkin school, Flamenco dancers, Buddhists – and all those who had been stranded in some shallow tributary away from the mainstream of twentieth-century progress.

With such companions he felt a natural affinity – for was he not also an exile from the modern world, however loudly, in fits and starts, it might applaud him? Was he not a revolutionary in almost everything except his painting? 'Be regular and ordinary in your life, like a bourgeois,' Flaubert had advised artists, 'so that you can be violent and original in your works.' But Augustus could not husband his energies. He was extraordinarily prolific, but he squandered his vitality in acts of nonconformity. 'Perfect conformity', he once remarked, 'is perhaps only possible in prison.'[26] His whole life was directed to avoiding, or escaping from, any form of imprisonment. In so far as he was revolutionary, it was not against the past but the fore-seeable future, with its threat of rigid standardization and more implacable rule of law. Like many Celts, he hung back from entering the twentieth century. Perhaps the last person to man-age this with complete success was W. B. Yeats, whom Augustus much admired. Both were untouched by industrialism and, being romantically involved in the mystery and poetry of life, shunned the arithmetical anonymity of our highly organ-ized society with its accent on the enlargement of the social conscience, the betterment of civic existence. But Augustus's romanticism became contaminated by the tame and tidy modernity he abhorred. 'The flower of art blooms only where the soil is deep,' Henry James once wrote. In England, especi-ally after the First World War, Augustus could find little depth of soil, could not achieve the full efflorescence of which he felt himself capable. 'The march of progress will leave the struggling artist behind,' he warned.

He is always an outsider, shunning the crowd, wandering off the beaten track and dodging the official guide and the policeman. Per-haps in a dream he has caught a glimpse of the Golden Age and is in search of it: everywhere he hits on mysterious clues to a lost world; sometimes he hears low music which seems to issue from the hills; the trees confabulate, the waters murmur of a secret which the sky has not forgotten.[27]

Yeats had not lost this secret – policemen and official guides were no obstacles to him. His dream was a vision seen in twi-light, a vision that held steady, not, as with Augustus, 'a passing light, a mere intangible, external effect . . . a dream that lingers a moment, retreating in the dawn, incomplete, aimless'.[28]

Augustus was seeing something of Yeats at this time at Will and Alice Rothenstein's house in Church Row, Hampstead. Alice was in the habit of entertaining a small elite of writers and artists that included, besides Yeats, Max Beerbohm, with his immaculately tailored human nature, so amusing at a distance, so invisible near to; W. H. Hudson, hopelessly and eternally in love with Alice; Cunninghame Graham, delivering a string of improper stories all decently clothed in his impenetrable layer of Scottish dialect; Walter Sickert, decked out, with his determination not to be seen as aesthetic, in a roaring check shirt and leggings, looking like some farmer from a comic opera; Epstein, as innocent and truculent as Augustus himself, smelling like a polecat; and William Nicholson and James Pryde, the dandified Castor and Pollux of poster art.

With Wyndham Lewis, to whom the Rothensteins also introduced him, Augustus now struck up a lifelong precarious friendship.* Lewis had come from Rugby to the Slade, a good-looking, shy, gloweringly ambitious young man, who drew with thick black contours resembling the lead in a stained glass window. He could be relied on to act unpredictably, yet in Tonks's opinion had the finest sense of line of any of his students. Rothenstein took him to Augustus's top-floor flat, which he himself would later occupy, probably in the summer of 1902 – 'there was a noise of children', Lewis afterwards recalled, 'for this patriarch had already started upon his Biblical courses'.

Augustus had by now attracted a great deal of steam to himself, and for a time Lewis, made heady by this atmosphere, became his most formidable disciple. 'I was with John a great deal in those early days in London,' he wrote in *Rude Assignment*. '... Unlike most painters, John was very intelligent. He read much and was of remarkable maturity.' They stimulated and exasperated each other in about equal measures. Lewis was much impressed by all that Augustus had so rapidly achieved. His success in art and with women appeared phenomenal, and by associating with him, Lewis seems to have felt, some of this success might rub off on him. Augustus, on his side, was flattered by Lewis's veneration. Here was someone mysterious and remarkable, a poet hesitating between literature and painting, whose good opinion of him served to increase Augustus's self-esteem. He seemed a valuable ally. For whatever else he felt, Augustus was never bored by Lewis, whose dynamic progress through life was conducted as if to outwit some invisible foe. This involved a series of improbable retreats – to Scandinavia

---

* In January 1903 John did two etchings of Lewis, and in the same year an excellent drawing and one of his very best oil portraits 'full of Castilian dignity', as John Russell described it, 'displayed in a moment of repose'.

Lewis did a drawing of John that is reproduced in his volume of memoirs, *Blasting and Bombardiering*.

even, where he would find a letter from Augustus demanding: 'Tell me Lewis what of Denmark?' or – 'Is Sweden safe?' Such places were not only safe, Lewis would hint in his replies, but the arenas of unimaginable conquests.

Very aware of his friend's superior education, Augustus strove to match Lewis's 'calligraphic obscurity' by what he called 'linguistic licence' – a fantastic prolixity that he thought the intellectual tenor of their relationship required. The result was an exchange of letters, part undiscoverable, part indecipherable, covering over fifty years, that is almost complete in its comic density. Both were flamboyantly secretive men with bombardier tempers, and their friendship, which somehow endured all its volcanic quarrels, kept being arrested by declarations that it was at an end – an event upon which they would with great warmth congratulate themselves and each other. Yet such was the good feeling generated by these separations and congratulations that they quickly came together again, when all the damning and blasting of their complicated liaison would start up once more.*

* 'I called you poltroon for not daring to let me know before in what contempt you held me – when I had admitted you – fondly – almost to my secret places, for not honouring me so far as to be frank in this,' John wrote (June 1907) in a letter that gives the flavour of their explosive friendship. 'I called you mesquin for jesting at my discomfiture, for playing with words over the stricken corpse of our friendship, ever sickly and now treacherously murdered at a blow from you, poor thing! And I called you bête for so estimating me as to treat me thus – cavalierly – for though my value as a friend has not proved great, it is neither nil nor negligible. And I say this from the very abysm of humility. Nor am I one to be dismissed with a comic wave of the hand . . .

'You may not believe me when I say that the "temper" you have remarked in me so often of late (too often) was the *best* part of the "friendliness (not perfect) I showed towards you". Must I too confess that on my side I have observed of late in you, *manners*, which would be more appropriate among strangers but which perfect friendship disallows. Will you be astonished to learn that a sensibility only less extravagant than your own has occasionally and inconsequently and involuntarily irked as at that subtle friction which subsists between two bodies that *are* not but which *have* been in contact? The wall you think fit to surround yourself with at times might be a good rampart against enemies, but its canvas bricks cannot be considered insurmountable to friends, and indeed (imagining them detachable) it would be an impertinence to level them in all seriousness at one's devoted head. I am as little inquisitive by habit as secretive by nature. I have never wished to, I have never committed the indecency of trespassing on the privacy of your consciousness, of which you are

Their correspondence, on both sides, is extremely generous with offensive advice which they attempt to make more palatable by adding the odd 'mon vieux' or 'old fellow'. Augustus frequently intends to return Lewis's letters by post in order to get him to 'admit [that] no more offensive statement could be penned'; but almost always he mislays the letter or, in his first fit of uncontrollable fury, flings it irrecoverably into some fire or sea. He is constantly being dumbfounded by Lewis's reminders to lend him money coupled with his forgetfulness in repaying it; and by his insistence that Augustus was influencing mutual friends to his discredit. His style grows more and more convoluted in grappling with these groundless charges until it becomes blameless of almost all meaning. Then, suddenly, the clouds clear and in a succinct moment of retaliation he announces that Lewis's drawings 'lack *charm*, my dear fellow'.*

---

rightly jealous. But in a *friendly* relationship I expect, yes, I expect, a frankness of word and deed as touching that relationship – an honest traffic – within its limits – a plainness of dealing, which is the politeness of friends. *That* we have never practised – you have never – it seems to me – given the Index of friendship a chance. It would appear that you live in fear of intrusion and can but dally with your fellows momentarily as Robinson Crusoe with his savages before running back to his castle . . .'

* 'Now, as for your recent drawings of which you sent me photostats, I must at once admit my inability to discover their merits, qua drawings,' John wrote to Lewis (undated). 'They lack *charm*, my dear fellow (from my point of view that is).' In *Blast*, No. 2 (1915), Lewis wrote an article called 'History of the Largest Independent Society in England', in which he called John 'a great artist', adding that he was lacking in control and prematurely exhausted – 'an institution like Madame Tussaud's'. He also credits John with bringing some exotic subject matter into English painting, before going on to describe his gypsy cult as hothouse and *fin de siècle*. Shortly after this article appeared the two painters met one night at a restaurant. John, all smiles at first and with a 'woman-companion', invited Lewis to join them, but later in the evening, when the talk turned to *Blast*, he lost his temper.

Next day John wrote to apologize. 'I must have been positively drunk to assume so ridiculously truculent an attitude upon such slender grounds. Your thrusts at me in "Blast" were salutary and well-deserved, as to the question of exact justice – any stick will do to rouse a lazy horse or whore and the heavier the better. I liked many of your observations in Blast if I don't feel the particular charm of those designs which last night I characterized as "pokey". Probably "charm" is quite the last thing you intend. I think pokiness is an excellent and necessary element of design and I understand and admire your insistence on

The whole relationship is bedevilled by ingenious misunderstanding. Each credits the other with Machiavellian cunning, while assuming for himself a superhuman naïvety. Lewis is amazed that Augustus never invites him for a drink; Augustus is perplexed that Lewis is never able to visit him – when he does so, Augustus is always out; while Lewis, on principle, never answers his doorbell. They make elaborate plans to meet on neutral territory, but then something goes wrong – the wrong time, the wrong place, the wrong mood. Lewis becomes increasingly irritated that Augustus so seldom writes. Augustus becomes irritated because when he does write his letters go astray, Lewis in the meantime having moved in darkest secrecy to some new unknown address – such as the Pall Mall Safe Deposit. The letters which do arrive express very adequately this irritation fanned, in Lewis's case, by eloquent invective, and in Augustus's by a circumlocution that marvellously avoids answering the most innocent of Lewis's inquiries. It is a most stimulating exchange.

Life itself – beyond Fitzroy Street – was constantly stimulating; but at home it was the old routine. On 22 March 1903 Ida's second child was born. Augustus had confidently predicted a

---

it. But I deplore your exclusion of all the other concomitants provided by an all too lavish creation – and with which I imagine none is better able to deal than you. But no doubt you have plans laid which, for all I know, may comprise a final emergence from a straight and disciplinary bondage to limitless caprices of Freedom.'

John concludes his painfully handsome apology by inviting Lewis to 'this bloody district [Chelsea]. I wish you'd call. I'ld much like to see you.' But Lewis, in his answer, writes: 'We will not meet again in any friendly way, if you do not mind.' As to John's work, Lewis 'resented your stage-gypsies emptying their properties over your splendid painter's gift'. Along with tilting at John's 'Borrovian cult of the Gitane', he praises his substantial talent – 'I consider you had, pour commencer, as much talent as a man may comfortably possess.' But he had shipwrecked himself on 'all sorts of romantic reefs'. His work had become stagnant after too much buccaneering, though he was sure, Lewis conceded, to enter the history books as 'a figure of controversy, nevertheless'.

As to their patched and splintered friendship, Lewis affirms that he is reluctant to go on scrapping and that John had better believe him 'unless you want your head broken'. Being active and strong, he explains, he would certainly 'try and injure your head' if they met. So they had better not meet – though John must not attribute this 'gentleness' to lack of spirit.

girl, but 'instead of Esther, a roaring boy has forced admittance to our household', he told Will Rothenstein. '... Ida welcomes him heartily.* But what will David say?' The boy, originally referred to as 'nice fat slug' or 'pig face' ('his face is like a pink pig's,' Ida boasted to Mrs Sampson), was eventually called Caspar – and nicknamed Capper – and a gate was fitted at the top of the stairs outside their flat to prevent the children from falling. Suddenly their home seemed very crowded.

In a highly oblique passage of *Finishing Touches*,[29] his posthumous and unfinished volume of memoirs, Augustus refers to himself under the pseudonym of George. George, a new recruit of Will Rothenstein's and said to be on the threshold of a brilliant career, is 'only just recovering from the nervous breakdown following his recent marriage'. At the informal parties in Will Rothenstein's house he found

an atmosphere no doubt very different from the climatic conditions of the home-life to which he was as yet uninured ... he began to expand and blossom forth himself, in a style combining scholarship with an attractive diffidence and humour. He felt perhaps that here was a mass of escape from the insidious encroachments of domesticity, and accordingly attached himself to Will Rothenstein with the desperate haste of a man caught in the quicksands.

If he expanded here and at the Café Royal, he at once contracted again when he got home. This concertina motion, to which Ida responded with a mixture of excitement and monotony, had by 1903 produced a strange fragmentation of himself. The pressures to which he felt himself increasingly subjected since marriage had made his condition more acute until it reached what he himself called 'a nervous breakdown'. His symptoms were several: maddening vagaries, fits of unexplained temper, sudden withdrawals from human contact, a lack of application or self-discipline, and perhaps most vital of all a tremendous difficulty in sustaining personal relationships. It seemed baffling that someone of such intelligence and strong physique could at times be so will-less. The only Will he had, apparently, was Rothenstein whose remedy was to send him off

* 'It was *much* nicer to have Gussie than the doctor, and a gamp twice a day than a hovering nurse in a starched cap,' Ida wrote to the Rani. 'Lorenzo Paganini is quite lovely and so quiet.'

on marathon walks round Hampstead Heath, to lend a sympathetic ear to his difficulties, and sermonize upon the rewarding virtue of hard work.

Yet Augustus was not indolent. He could work well if tactfully organized. But to organize him without provoking his temper was a full-time operation of ruthless diplomacy that Will Rothenstein, for all his energy and enthusiasm, could not begin to do, and even Ida, continually pregnant and encompassed by domestic duties, was unable to manage. It needed a team to organize Augustus, and a team was precisely what he was about to assemble round him: a team of patrons and art-dealers and of women. He did not know why he needed all this, only that he must have it. His first steps to achieve what he wanted were to cause great anguish, imperil his marriage and bring him to a state which, in his autobiographical synopsis, he described as 'madness'.

4. TEAM SPIRIT

To the winter exhibition of the New English Art Club, late in 1902, Augustus had sent two major pictures. The first of these, 'Merikli',[30] was a portrait of Ida holding a basket of flowers and fruit painted as if by an Old Master: Rembrandt, with a helping hand from Velasquez. Ida's figure, touched by warm light, emerges enthusiastically from the dark shadows of the background. The colouring is sombre, the tone low; the handling is conventional and the pose very fixed, making the cumulative effect rather artificial. But there is a possible *double entendre* in the fact that, although her basket is full of roses and cherries, she proffers – a daisy. As a portrait, it lacks the monumental force of, say, 'The Smiling Woman' of a few years later; but it was voted Picture of the Year at the exhibition, and although contemporary opinion differed as to its merits, it is generally regarded now as Augustus's first important portrait in oils.

The other portrait was of an Italian girl, Signorina Estella Cerutti. In the opinion of John Rothenstein, this picture 'proclaimed him a master in the art of painting'.[31] It 'is clearly stamped with that indefinable largeness of form characteristic of major painters'; it 'powerfully radiates a cool light'; it is modelled 'as plastically and as surely as a piece of sculpture'; it 'indefinitely holds the spectator's interest, without, however, yielding up the secret of the artist's power'. Estella Cerutti is a splendidly buxom creature. There is more than a hint of coquetry in her expression and the effect of foreignness has been well caught. Somehow one is given the sense of a figure, wonderfully pale, walking past a window – rather than held in a frame – and casting a backward glance.

It was a glance that Augustus followed. 'Esther' Cerutti, as he called her – the very name he was to have given his second child had it been a daughter – lived below them at Fitzroy Street. In the spring and summer of 1903 he made numerous drawings of her, at least one etching,[32] and painted 'several masterpieces'. Two or three times a week she would come up to their flat, and he would sometimes descend to hers. But this proximity put an additional strain on married life. Ida admired, envied and was irritated by Esther in the most confusing way. What style she had – how languid, large! She was an accomplished pianist, dressed superbly well on all occasions and suffered from such interesting illnesses which she gracefully set to music. It was almost impossible not to be provoked.

Augustus seemed held in tension between the two of them, as if between two magnets, motionlessly suspended within their opposing fields of attraction. 'For days I have been inert and dejected,' he confessed to the Rani.

I cannot account for the dejection except as the necessary complement of inanition, for my reasons to hope remain palpable and the same. Dearest Lady! how we married people need to cling and pull together and so make this holy state by union a force – for I begin now and then to suspect its weakening – or perhaps it is that I am a weak member, but then at least I am a link in the nuptial chain. But I think we ought to plan it so that we have the laugh of the others ... As to Miss Esther I don't know whether to be mühen again or not to be mühen, both courses being fraught with problems distant and immediate. At present I slumber in the studio surrounded by my works.

To side-step his problems he went that summer on a 'short but brilliant campaign in Wales with the admirable Sampson'. When he returned, the problems were still waiting for him, so he immediately set off again, this time for Liverpool with his sister Winifred, who was sailing to America. Once he had put her on board, he combed the town for old friends, finding none. 'The Town proved most inhospitable,' he complained to the Rani. '. . . I had hoped to see Sampson – but alas! his house proved nothing but a silent tomb of memories with those wonderful blinds drawn gloomily down.' The Rani herself was away in the country, though her elusiveness, he admitted, was stimulating in a disappointing sort of way. 'Curiously enough 'tis to a dream I owe my most vivid, most tender recollection of you. (And they call dreams vague . . . hazy . . .). It happened in Liverpool the last night I spent there. (Heaven knows how I spent the next!)' The following day he 'fled down Brownlow Hill to the station and so home again'.

A letter Ida sent Alice Rothenstein about this time indicates some of the changes that were taking place in the John household. From her mother Ida had got a few pieces of furniture, including their bed; on the walls of each room she had put plain white paper, and suspended baskets of roses from the ceiling. To do the cooking she had employed a rabbity young girl named Maggie – tempted, she maintained, by 'friendly lettuce' – and a maid called Alice whom David insisted on calling 'Aunt Alice'.

Her day began at 5.30 a.m. and ended at 7.30 p.m. Between day and night there were three delightful hours of idleness: then at 10.30 p.m. the night work began – 'it is the hardest part,' she told the Rani. 'I am breaking the baby of having a bottle at 3 a.m., and it entails a constant hushing off to sleep again – as he keeps waking expecting it. Also he has not yet begun to turn himself over in bed, and requires making comfortable 2 or 3 times before 3 a.m. This is not grumbling but bragging.' Nevertheless, it was a tremendous relief to her to get rid of the children for short spells. That summer they went down with Maggie to stay at Tenby, and Ida felt almost guilty at her sense of liberation. 'It is most delightful without them,' she admitted to Alice Rothenstein.

As soon as their flat was emptied of children, it filled up again with 'aunts' – models for Augustus. Esther, magnificently attired in expensive dresses almost bursting at their fastenings, came and posed, while Ida, who was not Mrs Nettleship's daughter for nothing, set to work creating clothes for herself so as 'to have at least one pretty feather to Esther's hundred lovely costumes. I shall have to come down naked in my fichu, for how can one wear grey linen by her silks and laces?'

But while Ida was anxious at being outshone by Esther, Esther was about to be eclipsed by another girl. In the same letter to Alice Rothenstein, Ida mentions that 'Gus and the beautiful Dorelia McNeill are here ... Gus is painting Dorelia'. He was, she adds, feeding Dorelia up for her portrait. This is the first mention of the legendary Dorelia, who was to remain at the very centre of both Ida and Augustus's lives until each died, and to play a short intense part in the life of Gwen John.

Who was Dorelia? To anyone acquainted with the work of Augustus John she is a very familiar figure. Over a period of sixty years, he drew and painted her obsessively, and her likeness can be seen in galleries all over the world. Yet what these pictures convey is not her identity but her mysteriousness. They never seek to analyse her character but to enshrine the aura of mystery that Augustus spun about her. The most celebrated portrait of all, 'The Smiling Woman',[33] has often been likened to the 'Mona Lisa', for in both cases the artist himself seems ignorant of the smile's genesis and meaning, is content to be its captive. Another picture,[34] at least as fine though in a quite different style, is more mellow and depicts her as a dream creature who, on our waking, continues to haunt and baffle us.

In this sense, Dorelia was a creation of Augustus's. He made her enigmatic; he made her his ideal woman. What he desired from women was at once very simple and very difficult to achieve: it was the unknown, timelessly preserved intact; it was fantasy blended with reality. Though he felt a romantic reverence for high birth – 'you darling little aristocratic love', he used to call the Rani – he disliked sophisticated women on the whole, and avoided women famous for their intellect. Great physical beauty and fragrant simplicity were what exercised his spirit to the utmost, for behind these qualities seemed to lurk the ultimate secret, the wonder of life. Cleverness he could find elsewhere, if he needed it: he could find it in men. But in some women he could behold the inscrutable moving in step with his moods, magically deceiving tedium. For some men, stupidity mixed with a powerful dose of beauty produces this paradox, this undying, spell-binding awe. For Augustus this was not so – stupid women, especially when good-looking, he had noticed, were inclined to talk too much. What he wanted was something rarer: silence.* Silence was freedom. Into silence, physically eloquent, he could read everything and nothing; like Nature herself, it defied explanations, soared above them, held him entranced.

All that Augustus aspired to is suggested by the fantasies he wove around Dorelia. In his pictures of her, we see Dorelia as tall, with a swan's neck and perfectly-proportioned head, often the mother-figure. In truth she was rather short, with a larger head and no more the conventional mother than Ida. He dressed her in broad-rimmed straw hats, their sweeping lines like those of the French peasants'; and in long skirts that reached the ground, with high waistlines and tight bodices, like the costumes of the peasant women of Connemara: but she was not a peasant, French or Celt. He laid a false trail across the life of a gypsy girl called Dorelia Boswell, so that many concluded that his Dorelia was probably a Boswell and certainly a gypsy: she was neither. He called her 'Ardor'; he called her 'Relia' and he called her Dorelia, and finally he called her 'Dodo': but none of these were her real names.

Dorothy McNeill had been born on 19 December 1881 at 97 Bellenden Road, Camberwell. Her father, William George McNeill, was a mercantile clerk, a position he held unwaveringly until promoted, through age, to the rank of retired mercantile clerk. Son of the stationmaster at Peckham, he had married a local girl, Kate Florence Neal, the daughter of a dairy farmer.† They were a forgettable couple. He cultivated a nondescript appearance and a presence largely unobservable: she

---

* 'Beauty is best silent, though the birds belie me,' John wrote in a copy of *Chiaroscuro* which he gave to Addyer-Scott. 'Speech may interrupt its spell: the eternal mother may smile indeed but hardly laughs aloud, and if it speaks it will surely be in a whisper . . .'

† They were married on 31 August 1870 at the Register Office in Camberwell when he was twenty-two and she eighteen.

made lace. Together they earned the collective nickname of 'Mr
and Mrs Brown'. But all their seven children (of whom Dorothy
was the fourth) were extraordinarily handsome – mostly small
with very dark complexions, prominent mouths curving downwards, and soft voices gentle and low, blue-black hair and large
eyes that were brown and brooding.

Each of the four daughters had been taught some profession.
Dorothy learnt to type. Her first job, at the age of sixteen, was
for the editor of a magazine called *The Idler*. Then, for a short
time, she worked for an author; but by 1902 she had become a
junior secretary copying legal documents, in the office of a
solicitor, G. Watson Brown, in Basinghall Street. She did not
appear discontented, but her personality was very passive and
she was not communicative, so it was difficult to know what
she really felt. Another young typist in the office, Muriel Alexander, remembers that Dora, as everyone there called her, al
ways dressed very 'artistically' in a style entirely of her own,
wearing long full-skirted dresses and having her hair parted in
the middle and drawn in a knot at the back of her head. Quiet
and unassuming, she was a mutely sympathetic presence in the
office. Everyone liked her; no one knew much about her. On
the surface, it seemed, she had accepted a secretarial career, to
be followed in the ordinary way by one as housewife. She was
not ambitious in the usual sense; but deep within her, unobserved by others, lay the utter certainty that she belonged to
the world of art. How this was she could not say; nor did she
ever speak about it. But instinctively she knew it to be true, and
accepted it as her destiny. However illogical, she would follow
this instinct wherever it led. It was her secret, her means of
emancipation. It was Dorothy who typed each day; but it was
Dorelia who dreamed.

And it was Dorelia who, in the evenings after the office
closed, went off to the late classes at the Westminster School of
Art. Here she got to know a number of artists and began to be
invited to their parties, at one of which she met Gwen John.
She had already seen Augustus once at an exhibition of Spanish
paintings at the Guildhall near her office, but they had not
spoken and he did not see her. Yet the sight of him riveted her
and she remembered this first glimpse till the end of her life. It

was almost as if, in that moment and without words or contact of any kind, she had chosen him as the vehicle of her destiny.

There are many stories of how they met. A popular one was that Augustus overtook her in a London street one day, looked back, and was unable to avert his eyes for almost the rest of his life.* However it really was, they must have met early in 1903 while she was living in a basement in Fitzroy Street. By the summer he was already writing her passionate love letters:

The smell of you is in my nostrils and it will never go and I am sick for love of you. What are the great beneficent influences I owe a million thanks to who have brought you in my way. Ardor my little girl, my love, my spouse whose smile opens infinite vistas to me, enlarges, intensifies existence like a strain of music. I want to look long and solemnly at you. I want to hear you laugh and sigh. My breath is upon your cheek do you feel it? I kiss you on the lips – do you kiss me back? Yes I possess you as you possess me and I will hear you laugh again and worship your eyes again and touch you again and again and again and again ... your love Gustavus ...

She was hypnotically beautiful – almost embarrassingly so, Will Rothenstein wrote: 'one could not take one's eyes off her'.[35] An early drawing[36] Augustus did gave her a sultry look, with high rounded cheek bones, slanting eyes and an air of devastating refinement. A painting entitled 'Ardor'[37] shows a full dimpled face, eyes that solicit, rouged cheeks and mouth. It is the portrait of a seductress, a comparable subject in some ways to 'Merikli', though by contrast Ida seems too wholesome for the part. In his portraiture, Augustus was like a stage director, assigning his subjects all sorts of short dramatic roles. Dorelia, it seemed, acquiesced in them, fitted each of them to perfection – mother, mistress, little girl, phantasm, goddess, seductress, wife. She became all things to him; she was every-woman.

---

* 'I had tea with him [Augustus], and then we went to all those Belgian Cafés in Fitzroy city,' Carrington wrote to Lytton Strachey (8 March 1917). 'He was most interesting, as he gave me a complete history of his life, and parents, the mysterious sister who lives in Paris, a brother, and yet another sister. You know it wasn't the Strand where he met Dorelia. I have ever since you told me (walking across N. Wales from the Dante Lake) thought when I was in the Strand, near Adelphi, of John looking back at Dorelia in a Black Hat and now it was all a false vision, as he met her in Holborn.'

It was not by her looks alone that she stimulated him. Beauty is not so scarce. What was uncommon about Dorelia was the enigmatic power and the magneticism that gave her beauty its depth. Rarer still, her serenity – something he so conspicuously lacked and the source of which, in her, baffled and attracted him. She was no intellectual; she was not particularly witty or articulate; and certainly not sentimental. It was her *presence* that was so powerful, above all her magical peace-giving qualities. People who were unhappy, agitated, could come to her, relax, share something of her extraordinary calm. Disasters, tragedies, crises appeared to shrivel up within the range of her strong personality. She seemed nourished by some distant source, and at all times guarded her secrets well, like a cat. Like a cat, too – a panther – she moved, with a smooth rhythmic action, intensely feminine.

Augustus did not conceal from Ida this sudden flare-up of love for Dorelia: concealment did not come easily to him – it was something he would learn, rather inadequately, later on. Besides, he might as well have tried to hide a forest fire – he simply could not do it. He presented Ida with the fact of his new love; he introduced her to Dorelia; and he left her to decide what should be done. Of the three of them, Ida was always the most likley to take a positive decision about the future. Augustus and Dorelia acted on impulse in a way that could appear decisive, but which was mainly a reflex.

The upheaval of Ida's feelings was deep and painful. Upon the decision she had to make depended the fate of their marriage. She knew Augustus better than anyone – 'our child-genius' as she was soon to call him with more than a shade of sarcasm – and she had to accept that alone she could not hope to confine his incendiary passions within the grate of married life. He maddened her, but she loved him. And she *liked* Dorelia. When the two women were together – it was strange – Ida's difficulties seemed less acute: she was almost happy. Reason therefore told her that, if Augustus's feelings persisted, some form of ménage-à-trois was the only practical solution. She must not object to his having a love-affair with Dorelia – that would drive him mad. Reason told her all this; but sometimes, like some tidal wave, a violent red jealousy would surge through her drowning reason, urging her on to pain and destruction. She felt useless, ugly. Marriage, which had imprisoned her, had left Augustus free, since her love for him excluded all other emotions, while his for her did not. But she steeled herself not to give in to the conviction that life was unfair. The quasi-religious advice she had poured forth in earlier days on her aunts and sisters she now turned upon herself. Her moral duty was to follow the sensible course of action and accept these awkward complications as a part of her love for Augustus. Whatever happened she must fight against jealousy, since that, like wounded vanity, was the very voice of the devil. So, for the time being, she appeared philosophical: 'Men must play,' she quoted, 'and women must weep.'

With Augustus infatuated and Ida raising no objections, Dorelia now moved into their married life. At first the part she played, though a vital one, was intermittent. She never lived in their flat, though she visited Augustus most weeks to be drawn and painted by him. He loved to dress her up, to buy her bright petticoats up to her knees, gay ribbons to tie in her hair, and curious costumes that took his fancy. And he relied on Ida to help him choose such stuffs. 'Don't forget to come on Sunday,' he reminded Dorelia. 'I want to get a new dress made for you, white stockings and little black boots and lots of silly little things for your hair ... Sleep well Relia and don't forget me when you go to sleep.' But sometimes, without warning, she did not turn up, and he would grow frantic with worry. 'In the devil's name! Why did you not come? Are you ill? ... or did you dance too much the night before, so you were [too] tired to come up here ... A true young wife and a lady you are ... Are your new clothes made [yet]? I should like to see you on the high road all dressed in fire-red. Are you coming next Sunday?' But already by Monday he found he could not wait till next Sunday.

I went last night down to Westminster to find you but you were not there. When are you going there again? as I would like to see your pretty eyes again. If you'll believe me my girl, I liked more than I can say sitting with you on the grass on the ferns. As you say, you are a young wild tree, my Relia. I love to kiss you just as I love to feel the warmth of the sun, just as I like to smell the good earth.

One gets used to the afterwards, my girl, and then they need not be
so very damned. My wife and I have been ransacking shops to find
a certain stuff for your picture ... I am getting excited over the picture. I will do it better now after I have kissed you several times.

He longed, also, to paint her in the nude, but she seemed unwilling. 'Why not sit for me in your soft skin, and no other
clothes – are you ashamed? Nonsense! It is not as if you were
very fat.' But still she would not.

At each point his excitement was matched by her imperturbability; his passion by her elusiveness; his doubts and speculations by her unastonished compliance. She had cast a spell
on him, and he began to weave one for her, a Romany spell.
'How would you like yourself as a Romany lady?' he asked. To
Dorelia, who was rather dismissive of her anonymous parents,
here was an intriguing question. Under Augustus's tuition she
began learning the language. All these early letters he sent her
were written in Romany,* mixed with odd English words, and
to them he attached careful word-lists. He was delighted how
swiftly she learnt, how eager she was to enter his make-believe
world. 'Sit and write down another letter for me,' he urged
her. 'Put in it all the Romany words you know, then a little
tale about yourself, and send it to me.' So she wrote and told
him about an old woman who drank whisky and had fallen in
love with her – and he was enchanted.

So his love grew. He could think of almost nothing else, could
scarcely endure being parted from her. 'Dear sweetheart
Dorelia,' he wrote to her early that summer on a short visit to
Littlehampton.

Now I am going to bed, now I am under the blankets, and I wish
that you were here too, you sweet girl-wife. I want to kiss you again
on the lips, and eyes, and neck and nose and all over your bare
fiery body. When our faces touch, my blood burns with a wild fire
of love, so much I love you my wild girl. I don't speak falsely. If
you laugh you cannot love. Now I see your white teeth. Why are

* They are written partly in the inflected Romany, like the so-called 'Welsh
Romany' which is really an older form of English Romany, partly in the broken
English Romany, and partly in English. The versions quoted here have been
done into English by the gypsy scholar Ferdinand G. Huth who writes that 'I
have made the translation as near as possible to the actual Romany words'.

you not here with me? I hear the sea that sings and cries in the old way, my own great sad mother. Send me word very soon – Tell me that you love me a bit. Yours Gustavus Janik.

It was not long before rumours of Augustus's love-affair began to be whispered among his friends – and among Ida's. 'I have come to the conclusion that it is very difficult to deceive anyone,' Ida wrote to Alice Rothenstein, 'and that people know one's own business almost as well as one knows it oneself. I suppose you know that, as you know most things (I am not sarcastic). In a certain way you are a very wise person.' This was Ida's difficulty : she had no one to whom she could confide. Alice was a loyal friend, but perhaps not a very understanding one. Her own life was so different, so safe. There was about her a suspicion of vicarious living, of looking with great relish and disapproval through keyholes at other people's goings-on. The smell of highly-principled gossip clung to her. Whatever one did, she already knew about it and knew one had done wrong. Nobody could doubt that she had Ida's interests sincerely at heart, but the two of them could seldom agree how those interests were best served; and Ida, who grew discouraged by Alice's conventionality, tried to avoid sharing with her too many of her problems. Besides, in all circumstances, Alice invariably counselled prudence, now that she had left the stage and married Will. 'I ask you why should a healthy young woman be particularly "prudent",' complained the Rani to Ida, '– or was Alice herself ever – such rot!' On the whole Ida preferred Will's counsel and companionship – they warmed her more. He too could lecture one, but when he addressed himself to young women his romanticism quite dissolved his moralizing. They were a strange couple, Alice and Will – she still beautiful, blooming, a faintly overblown pink rose 'large and fair and cushiony and sleepy', as Ida once described them; he 'a hideous little Jew with a wonderful mind – as quick as a sewing-machine, and with the quality of Bovril'.

Partly because of Alice, Ida was shy of disclosing many secrets to Will. To Augustus himself it was always difficult to speak of anything personal. One had to overcome the great silent well of his disapproval. When he did talk, it was usually to deliver some laconic sentence that effectively put an end to all further discussion. She was aware of becoming less attractive in his eyes when she tried to speak to him seriously. It was as if he believed that any talk about their problems could only exacerbate them, and that the only natural thing to do was to close one's eyes. This was one of the reasons he sometimes drank – to be rid of his problems : to be rid of himself.

Although she would have preferred a man to talk to, Ida probably confided most to the Rani. To her she felt she might occasionally 'grumple' without disloyalty. She could trust her, being closer to Ida than to Augustus – 'my heart's blood to you', she ended one of her letters, 'and my liver to Augustus'. Her vitality and humour were infectious, and the world was a brighter place after one of her letters. She never set herself up as a paragon mother – 'Yours is the proper way to have babies,' she told Ida, 'one after the other without fuss and let them roll around together and squabble and eat and be kissed and otherwise not bother.' She would write of the entertaining disasters that had befallen her, such as poisoning her family with mushrooms; she sent her appalling photographs of herself 'looking like the Virgin Mary with indigestion'; she told her how common and conventional her own children were becoming – born parents, every one of them; and she fulminated against the Liverpool middle-classes, 'all bandy-legged and floppy nosed and streaky haired', with their 'jocky caps and sham pearls and bangles and dogs and three-quarter coats' – they made her ache and roll and scream with anger, causing 'the glands behind my ears to swell'. And finally she would apologize for failing, despite everything, to be discontented. 'I am sorry I am so happy and you so much the reverse – I think I really am too stupid to be anything else. You must pay the penalty for having the intelligence, I suppose – The lady Dorelia is a strange creature.'

Dorelia's strangeness – 'her face is a mystery', Ida remarked, 'like everyone else's' – and the uneasy partnership to which she had been admitted was increasingly the subject of speculation. Almost the only people, it seemed, who were aware of nothing unusual were the participants themselves. Their friends were very alert to the situation, and many of them began

> to take each other unawares
> With moralizings manifold,

'I saw John last week and he doesn't seem to have been pulling himself together as he should have done,' lamented Will Rothenstein to his brother Albert (3 June 1903), '– he seems as restless as ever, and looks no better than he should do. Ida has gone off to Tenby for a month with her babes, so he is alive just now.'

A few weeks after Ida returned, Albert Rutherston went to dine with them at Fitzroy Street one evening and, unclouded by disapproval, was able to give a clearer picture of them all. 'They are well,' he told Michel Salaman (9 August 1903),

and John showed me some exceedingly good starts of paintings – they have bred at least a dozen canaries from the original twain which fly about the room – perch on the rafters and sit on one's head while one dines – it really was amusing ... Miss MacNeill came after dinner – she ... seems to be a great friend of all the Johns – I think John must have a secret agreement with that lady and Mrs J – but not a word to anyone of this – it is only my notion and a mad one at that.

Others who saw the crowded rough-and-tumble household, with its multiplying flocks of canaries, women and children, were sadder and more confident in their opinions. 'Really matrimony is not a happy subject to talk about at present,' Tonks wrote to Will Rothenstein (15 September 1903). 'The John establishment makes me feel very melancholy, and I do not see that the future shines much.'

But Augustus loved Fitzroy Street. Before Whistler died that summer, he would occasionally meet him there and they would have lunch together. He had always been amused by Whistler's panache, but in retrospect no longer had quite the same reverence for him as at the Slade. Whistler had been a man of cities; his curiosity 'stopped short at dockland to the east and Battersea to the west'.[38] He was almost the founder of the urban cult of English Decadence, against which Augustus had now started to rebel.

Augustus had loved Fitzroy Street, but the flat there was obviously too small for them all. He felt confined, unable to breathe in that bricked-in atmosphere. He dreamt of hills and fields, of 'the broad, open road, with the yellowhammer in the hedge and the blackthorn showing flower'.[39] As the summer wore on, this feeling grew more acute, reaching a peak while on

a visit to Charles McEvoy* at Westcot, near Wantage in Berkshire. 'I have fled the town and my studio; dreary shed void of
sunlight and the song of birds and the aspirant life of plants,' he
told Will Rothenstein.

Nor shall I soon consent to exchange the horizons that one can
never reach for four mournful walls and a suffocating roof – where
one's thoughts grow pale and poisonous as fungi in dark cellars, and
the Breath of the Almighty is banished, and shut off the vision of a
myriad world in flight. Little Egypt for me – the land without
bounds or Parliaments or Priests, the Primitive world of a people
without a History, the country of the Pre-Adamites!

The difference between town and country was like that between sleep and waking life. 'Don't get up so much,' he advised Dorelia from Fitzroy Street, 'it's better to sleep. What
beautiful weather we are having – it makes me dream of woods
and wind and running water. I would like to live in any wooded
place where the singing birds are heard, where you could
smoke and sleep and stop without being stared at.'

The best plan, he decided, was to find some house in the
country not far from London that would serve to accommodate as many as might reasonably find themselves there –
women, children, animals, friends, family, servants and, perhaps more intermittently, Augustus himself. Ida, who had
recently completed her decorations to Fitzroy Street, agreed. It
was a scheme that should advance all their interests: in any
event it seemed inevitable.

But Dorelia had other plans.

5. CANDID WHITE AND MATCHING GREEN

The Carfax Gallery, in the spring of 1903, had held a joint show
of Gwen and Augustus's pictures. 'I am devilish tired of putting
up my exhibits,' Augustus complained to Dorelia. 'I would like
to burn the bloody lot.' Of the forty-eight pictures – paintings,
pastels, drawings and etchings – forty-five were by Augustus.
Nevertheless, he told Rothenstein, 'Gwen has the honours or

---

* Charles McEvoy (1879–1929) was the brother of Ambrose McEvoy.
Described as a dramatic author, he was a village playwright and gifted clown.

should have – for alas our smug critics don't appear to have noticed the presence in the Gallery of two rare blossoms from the most delicate of trees. The little pictures to me are almost painfully charged with feeling; even as their neighbours are empty of it. And to think that Gwen so rarely brings herself to paint! We others are always in danger of becoming professional and to detect oneself red-handed in the very act of professional industry is a humiliating experience!'

The pain that Gwen had absorbed over Ambrose McEvoy was now disappearing. She had closed down her feelings for him, though keeping open an antipathy for Mary McEvoy. Until very recently she had continued living at the McEvoy family home in Colville Terrace, while Ambrose and Mary moved down to Shrivenham in Berkshire, an address used by Gwen's former friend Grace Westry. It was possibly at this time that Gwen transferred to a cellar in Howland Street – 'a kind of dungeon', as Augustus described it, '. . . into which no ray of sunlight could ever penetrate'. Indifferent to physical discomfort, she seemed filled with a strange elation. 'I have never seen her [Gwen John] so well or so gay,' Albert Rutherston told Michel Salaman (9 August 1903). 'She was fat in the face and merry to a degree.'

The source of Gwen's happiness may have been an adventure with Dorelia. On an impulse, she proposed that the two of them should leave London and walk to Rome – and Dorelia calmly agreed. There was nothing, no one, to hold Gwen in England. It was fitting that she should celebrate the opening of this curious new chapter in her life with such an odd pilgrimage, that she should want to cut off geographically, physically and emotionally her past. But for Dorelia the decision is less immediately understandable – after all, it meant abandoning Augustus, perhaps for months, at a critical stage of their relationship. With a man so volatile, what guarantee was there he would feel the same when she arrived back? Yet Dorelia's mind did not work like this. If Fate intended her to live with Augustus, then that was how it would be – and nothing on earth could alter this. There was therefore no risk in going away. However it might turn out, her future was certain if unknown; only the present could be shifting, complicated. Although she seldom revealed her thoughts, there can be little doubt that she was feeling the strain of being a visitor to Augustus's life, and not integrally part of it. Once Augustus and Ida had settled into their house in the country perhaps everything would be different. All she knew was that her life, whatever form it took, would be involved with art, and that there was nothing inconsistent with this in going off with Gwen.

The two girls were as excited as if it were an elopement. But Augustus found himself manoeuvred into a parental role, advising caution, good sense, second thoughts. Their plan was impossible,* he promised them: it was also mad. But Gwen brushed aside his objections, would not listen to his arguments – 'She never did'.[40] Finally, he came round, gave them a little money and some cakes, and they set off 'carrying a minimum of belongings and a great deal of painting equipment'.[41] Boarding a steamer in the Thames, they landed at Bordeaux and began trudging up the Garonne from village to village. 'I am sitting on the side of a road,' Gwen wrote to Ursula Tyrwhitt (2 September 1903); 'there are no hedges but great trees, on the side of the road there are fields of white grass with white flowers in it – it looks like spring. On the other side are vines we gather and grapes when we want them but they are not quite ripe yet.'

From this time onwards, though there were occasional good days, they found the going hard. Once they travelled in a motor car – 'till it broke down'; and more than once they were offered lifts in carts – 'every lift seems saving of time and therefore money too so we always take them', Gwen explained to Ursula Tyrwhitt. At each village they would try to earn some money by going to the inn and either singing or drawing portraits of those men who would pose. But their appearance provoked much astonishment, and their motives were sometimes misconstrued. At night they slept in the fields, under haystacks or, when they were lucky, in stables, lying on each other to feel a little warmer, covering themselves with their portfolios and waking up encircled by congregations of farmers,

---

* 'Miss McNeill came after dinner – she and Miss John were about to start for Boulogne from whence they intend walking to Rome!!!!!!!! it is true all roads lead to that city but methinks they have chosen a long one.' Albert Rutherston to Michel Salaman (9 August 1903).

gendarmes and stray animals. Between the villages, bowed beneath bundles of possessions that seemed larger than themselves, they would practise their singing. They lived mostly on
grapes and bread, a little beer, some lemonade. There were
many adventures; losing their tempers with the women, out-
witting the men, dying of fright, crying with laughter.

By the end of November they reached Toulouse where they
hired a room 'from a tiny little old woman dressed in black ...
she is very very wicked'. Here they stayed and worked. 'We
shall never get to Rome I'm afraid,' Gwen wrote to Ursula
Tyrwhitt,

it seems further away than it did in England ... the country round
is wonderful especially now – the trees are all colours – I paint my
picture on the top of a hill – Toulouse lies below and all round we
can see the country for many miles and in the distance the Pyrenees.
I cannot tell you how wonderful it is when the sun goes down, the
last two evenings we have had a red sun – lurid I think is the word,
the scene is sublime then, it looks like Hell or Heaven.

Augustus watched their progress with a mixture of amusement and irritation. 'I congratulate you both on having thus far
preserved body and soul intact,' he wrote to them when they
were about halfway to Toulouse. 'But with all my growing
sedulity I find it difficult to believe you are really growing fat
on a diet of wine and onions and under a burden of ½ a
hundredweight odd.' He also congratulated them on having
escaped the importunities of an old man in a barn 'with true
womanly ingenuity', and he enclosed five pounds for Dorelia –
'a modest instalment of my debt to you'. But already small
misunderstandings had begun to creep into their exchanges.
Perhaps Dorelia was affected by a vein, in Gwen's character, of
puritanism. In any event she decided she did not want random
gifts of money accompanied by jokes she did not care for – and
wrote to tell him so; at which Augustus excused himself indignantly.

But he was mainly concerned, at this stage, with Gwen's
pictures. He himself was contributing half-a-dozen works to the
Winter show of the N.E.A.C., including portraits of Mackay,
Rothenstein and Sampson : he was eager for Gwen to submit at

least one of her own so that she should not be forgotten. 'The day for the N.E.A.C. is Nov. 9,' he reminded both girls. 'I hope Gwen will do a good picture of you, and that it will contain all the Genius of Guienne and Languedoc. I hope it will be as wild as your travels and as unprecedented.' But Gwen refused to be rushed. 'The New English sending day is next Monday,' Augustus wrote again more urgently, 'and Gwen's picture doesn't seem to arrive.' When it did arrive – a wonderful glowing portrait of Dorelia entitled 'L'Etudiante' – it was almost six years late, and was shown at the N.E.A.C. Winter exhibition of 1909.

Augustus and Ida had taken a two-year lease on what seemed a perfect house, with a large garden, orchard and stables, at Matching Green in Essex. 'It is lovely here,' Ida wrote to the Rani, '. . . to go out into the quiet evenings and see the moon floating up above and feel the cold air.' They moved in with a lawnmower and a dog called Bobster during late November. Elm House, as it was called, stood next to a pub, had a studio but no telephone or electric light, and overlooked the village green. 'Several gypsies have been already,' Ida informed Mrs Sampson. 'Our house is one of the two ugly ones. Inside it is made bearable by our irreproachable taste.' Four-and-a-half miles from Harlow, their nearest town, and twenty from London, Matching Green stood in a tract of land, Augustus told Will Rothenstein, 'abundant in such things as trees, ponds, streams, hillocks, barns etc. . . . Pines amaze me growing stiff and lofty like Phallic symbols. I get dangerous classic tendencies out here I fear. London is perhaps on the whole a safer place for me.'

London meant money, and money was – or ought to be – security. Since leaving his Liverpool job, Augustus's income had been erratic, while his responsibilities steadily mounted. It was this state of affairs – 'living as I do in such insecurity' he described it[42] – that now persuaded him to collaborate in a scheme of Orpen's. 'I have committed myself to one day a week teaching at a school Orpen initiates with Knewstub as secretary,' he wrote to Will Rothenstein. 'We hope to make pocket-money out of it at least. It is a very respectable undertaking with none of the perfection you had insisted on. It is Knewstub who makes things feasible with his capacity for organising and letter writing.'

Jack Knewstub was the brother-in-law of both Orpen and Will Rothenstein. Nicknamed 'Curly' Knewstub, he had fair permanently wavy hair, very boyish good looks and a rather rough North Country manner. For a time he had acted as secretary to a Welsh Member of Parliament and it was presumably here that he learnt his skills as letter-writer. In his organizing capacity he was certainly superior to Augustus, but he was no business man: he was a romantic. His father had been both pupil and assistant to Rossetti – old Knewstub, it was said, could draw but not colour, and Rossetti, a superb colourist, could not draw: it was an ideal partnership. But Curly Knewstub, brought up in this Pre-Raphaelite world, could neither draw nor colour. He was an artist *manqué*, a dreamer with ambitious cultural fantasies to which this new school now acted as a focus. In the firmament of his imagination, Augustus shone like a star. He was infatuated with him and over the years schooled his own six children to draw precisely in the John manner, until they came to loathe John's very name.

If Knewstub worshipped Augustus, Augustus tolerated Knewstub. He was an agreeable drinking-companion, mercifully unintellectual and not arty, useful in countless little practical ways – the paper and sealing-wax of life. His dreams and inspirations effectively misted over any lack of business competence – of which, in any case, Augustus was no judge.

The Chelsea Art School, as it was called, opened in the autumn of 1903 at numbers 4 and 5 Rossetti Studios in Flood Street. On the prospectus, a higly respectable document,* Augustus and Orpen were named as its principals. Knewstub, who began by using 18 Fitzroy Street as his office, acted as secretary and general manager. The sexes were properly segregated, Gwen Salmond conscripted as 'lady superintendent' and various other 'Sladers' drafted to give occasional lectures. Everything began reasonably well. 'They have 35 students – but need to double that number to make it pay,' Ida wrote to Winifred John (January 1904). 'They have fine studios in Chelsea. Gwen

* See Appendix Two.

Salmond is the chief girl and looks after the women's affairs.
Isn't it mad?'

One person who thought the whole arrangement dangerously
mad was Alice Rothenstein. Did Ida, she wondered, know
nothing about men? It was inviting trouble, this burying herself
away in the country and permitting a man like Augustus to
roam the streets of London alone. Her head swam at the pure
folly of it. So strongly did she feel, that she might personally
have intervened – had she not been weightily pregnant at the
time. As it was, the very least she could do, from her bed of
confinement, was to pepper Ida with her warnings. Of course,
it was none of her business, but then what were friends for?
She owed it to Ida to volunteer the advice that everything she
was doing was fatal. Alice *knew* what Gus was like – had she
not been on the stage before she married Will? Ida had had so
sheltered an upbringing, was such a curiously innocent creature
– she must be protected by post. Ida endured her reprimands
stoically, then retaliated (12 December 1903):

> You are quite quite wrong, but I will not scold you now as you
> are just going to have a baby. In the first place I prefer being here.
> And healthy or no, Gus enjoys being in London alone.
>
> Think it pride if you will, but the truth is I would not come back
> if I had the chance. You do not understand, and you need not add
> my imaginary troubles to your worries. If I had not known it was
> alright I should not have come here. *I always know*. So there. Cease
> your regrets and all the rest of it. Yrs. Ida.

Alice was shocked. This was the last thing she had expected.
Was it not right for her to speak openly to a friend? She was
not hurt, she was *disappointed* by Ida. But the temptation to
appear more offended than she actually felt was almost irresistible. Ida, however, was having no nonsense. She refused to be
seen as forlorn, abandoned, irresponsible – it was simply
Alice's theatrical imagination. 'Dear Alice, I was not in the
least vexed,' she replied, 'and you know I was not. And please
always say exactly what you feel. Only I can't help doing the
same and disagreeing. And I know it is such a good thing we
came here, and you say it is a bad thing.'

Thereafter, whenever Alice's flurry of questions, counsels and
invitations grew too intensive, Ida turned a deaf ear. She would

counter this probing attention with observations of her own about the local weather; about the countryside – had Alice observed how lovely the trees were looking just now? – about the two piebald pigs she owned ('they grunt very nicely') – and about the terrific number of black-and-white cats* Gwen had left with them which by now, Alice would be interested to know, had had two sets of kittens and eaten all but one of them. Sometimes she would post her 'several pages of nothing'; at other times she would reveal that, with many disheartening interruptions, she was struggling to learn the piano or to make a hat. She sent flowers and embroidery and lists of 'scattered visitors – all very pale' to Elm House: her mother and sisters, Mrs Sampson, the Rani – 'we have giggled and been stupid and feminine all the time'. Alice must visit her too – it was so beautiful looking out of the window on to the elm trees, the green, the open skies: 'The geese still cackle and waddle on the green, and the bony horses graze. All the buds are coming out, and birds beginning to sing long songs.'

But by far the best method of deflecting Alice's formidable pity was to introduce the ever-interesting subject of children. Alice, who was extremely proud of her children, simply could not resist it. Ida's letters to her reveal something of her character, her family and their way of life at Matching Green. She is careful to establish that David and Caspar are in no way comparable to the magnificent Rothenstein boys. David, who 'is spoiled – or at any rate he is difficile', howls whenever the sun comes out, loves nursery rhymes with any mention of dying in them, says 'NO' a great many times each day and has taken to drawing, making their lives terrible with his ceaseless demands for pictures of hyenas, cows and 'taegers'. Caspar is enormous, struggles with a free style action on his tummy across the floor exclaiming 'Mama' as if it were some kind of joke, is perfectly toothless at ten months old, but has developed two fat and rosy cheeks from perpetually blowing a trumpet – 'his first and only accomplishment'. He is strong as a bull and has achieved a 'long dent in his forehead from a knock ... [which] really

---

* 'We now have 10 in all,' Ida wrote to Mrs Sampson, but 'only' 6 birds. She later bought 4 additional birds to even up the population. 'Domesticities amongst the birds are going on all around me.'

must have dented his skull as it still shows after several weeks'.

But sometimes her stream of entertaining trivia runs dry, and we catch sight of deeper aspects of Ida's life. 'Dear Alice, I have nothing to say – do forgive me. I am very tired.' The children dominated her night and day, sucked all energy out of her body. Never, it seemed, could she escape from them, from their noise, their eternal need for food and attention. 'I am getting a little restive sometimes,' she admitted (15 February 1904), 'but what I chiefly long for is 2 or 3 quiet nights. Not that they are restless in the night – but as you know they require attention several times.' She was a conscientious mother, determined to make the best of what, between the lines, merges as a pretty bad job. Motherhood was a medicine she had to swallow, and which must – to judge from its bitter taste – do her character much good. 'All my energies go to controlling my own children's passions,' she explained to Alice. 'I do get angry and irritable sometimes, but I am getting slowly better, and it is a discipline worth having. I have been so used to looking upon life as a means to get pleasure, but I am coming round to another view of it. And it is a limitless one.'

Intermittently this glow of moral optimism would fade and she envied Gwen her painting. There was no chance of returning to her own. 'I get very little time for contemplation now-a-days – and if I do get half-an-hour I am certain to tear my dress and have to mend it, or spill a box of pins, or something.' She enjoyed too little of Augustus's company and too much, much too much, of his children's. 'For the first time in my life Matching Green bores me – to extinction almost. I wish it did quite,' she confessed to the Rani after several months there. 'It would be quite a pleasant way of dying – to be bored away into nothing.' During the long days she prayed for the children to go to sleep, to be off their 'Mummy's hands and nerves'. Perhaps, she reflected, it was all due to her poor powers of organization, but 'I am beginning to wonder if my head will stand much more of the babies' society.'

From the nursery she began to escape into the kitchen. She was not alone at Matching Green. Though Alice, their maid at Fitzroy Street, had left them, Maggie their young cook, by now very 'fat and attractive' and nicknamed 'Minger', had come with them to Elm House. As the weeks went by, Ida did more cooking and Maggie more looking after the boys. 'I have begun to learn to cook,' she announced triumphantly (15 February 1904), 'and can make several puddings and most delicious pastry.' Cooking was so much quieter than children, so much more satisfactory, so much – despite what everyone said – more creative. 'I have been cooking and cooking and cooking – and have been so successful. I want to try and make Maggie nurse, and be cook and odd woman [myself] ... And cooking is so charming – and if Maggie will – However, it is not settled yet.' By the spring it was settled: 'Maggie is Nurse entirely now – and I am Cook General. It is so much less wearing.'

She also took up gardening, became a 'scientific laundress', grew 'mad on polishing furniture', involved herself in the manufacture of loud check coats. Guilt often stabbed at her. She was better off than many others. Besides Maggie, she employed from time to time 'a very large and conscientious child of 14' called Lucy Green to act as housemaid. Yet still she seemed to suffer from overwork. 'Matching Green is quite drunk to-day,' she wrote to Alice at Easter.

... soon the woman who lives on our other side will be helping herself home by our garden railings. It is remarkable the way they all make for the pub. Overwork. I know the necessity. I go to domestic novels – quite as unwholesome in another way. For my part I could not be really at leisure and able to follow my own desires with less than 4 servants. So what can these poor people do without one? And yet how gorgeous life is.

Then again this glow would darken and apathy sweep over her. 'I should like to have gone to Michel [Salaman]'s marriage feast but they will do well enough without me, and nothing matters.'

But one thing still mattered to her at all times: Gus. All winter he had been subject to dark moods, and when spring came these moods began to grow blacker and more frequent. His temper affected her as the weather affects a barometer, and her failure to pull him out of these depressions was a perpetual source of self-reproach. She lost confidence – perhaps she was the wrong person to help him; perhaps only Dorelia could do that – help both of them. Her exhaustion was added to his listlessness, and together they seemed oddly will-less, like two ships becalmed, waiting.

The Chelsea Art School absorbed much of Augustus's energy during its first two terms. For his own work he used a studio above the school, and would often spend a full week, or even a fortnight, in town. 'London is very beautiful,' he wrote to Dorelia, 'it becomes more like home every day.'

Orpen's chief contribution to the school was a series of lectures on anatomy. All pupils had to draw from the model, then 'skin him' and draw the muscles employed in his posture.

As at Liverpool, Augustus stressed the value of observation. He discouraged the use of red chalk because it tended to make a bad drawing look pretty. Every line should carry meaning, nothing be left vague. Students were taught to cultivate precision, to keep their drawings broad and simple avoiding too much detail, to use a hard piece of charcoal, to draw with the point and to perfect what he called 'the delicate line'.

Perhaps because it diverted his attention from personal worries, Augustus rather enjoyed his teaching.* 'He never despised nor discouraged a sincere, though unskilful, beginner,' one student remembered. 'But he was scathing about any kind of showing off.' On one occasion he called forth what Knewstub described as 'a flood of tears' by suggesting that some of the ladies would probably be better occupied at home with a little domestic work, such as nursing a baby. His most severe criticisms, however, were usually softened afterwards by an invitation to a drink or sometimes to a day trip up the river on a steamer from which, in his most rumbling bass, he would decant Romany verses: a sound very bold and incomprehensible.

The division of his life between town and country seemed to

* The draft of a rousing notice by John to the students of the Chelsea Art School with special reference to the Sketch Club compositions that were submitted for monthly criticism, reads: 'How is it there is so little work done for the Sketch Club? The neglect of composition makes drawing negligible, and is madness. How is it students are timid when they know Design demands Courage? How is it they are indifferent when they know that Art calls for Emotion? Why are they speechless while creation is a statement???'

suit him: he never quite had time to grow tired of either. In London he was meeting many people for the first time – Gordon Craig, Arthur Symons, Charles Ricketts, also Lady Gregory.* In March he dined at Hugh Lane's house, and Lady Gregory noted: 'John was there, and other artists. Martin Wood was there and kept saying "this is a very remarkable gathering". We went up-stairs after dinner to look at the Titian – Philip II, and I speaking to John for the first time said "How can the wonderful brilliancy of that colour keep its freshness so long?" And John said "Ah-h-h".'

From remarkable exchanges such as this, he would return with relief to the freshness of Essex. 'It has been wondrous fine in the country these last few days – a white frost over every-thing, our humble garden transformed; every leaf and twig rimed with crystal; in the moonlight things sparkled subtly and any old outhouse became the repository of unguessable secrets,' he wrote to Will Rothenstein. 'To-day all changed into the dreariness of mud – the green a morass – the sky all gone, and grey expressionless vapour instead ... I am bent on etching now and mark me Will I will have a new set out before it is time to think of potato planting. This bald little house is be-coming trim and homely and you will not find it inhospitable when you seek its shelter.'

Armchairs and green baize tables, a light oak bureau and a cottage piano had made their appearance in the house. Augustus's pipes and slippers littered the rooms; breeding cages for the canaries were raised upon the walls, each suspended by a single nail – 'they are charming and make an awful mess', the Rani wrote when she came to stay. The little brown book-

* In May 1904 Lady Gregory sent Augustus a copy of her *Poets and Dreamers*, an 'astonishing book', he called it. In a letter to Lady Gregory (25 May 1904) he wrote: 'Mr John Sampson of Liverpool know[s] more than any man about the Tinkers. He has collected a considerable vocabulary of their words besides tales and rhymes, and was the first to solve the mystery of their language and its origins. I have only known some English Tinkers whose language is but a debased and impoverished derivative of the Irish Tinkers'. Your book proves how much original feeling there is in the Irish peasant; he does not indeed take his impressions or pleasures at secondhand. If you would care I would willingly send you the hundred words or so I know of English Shelta but I feel it is the richer Irish dialect you ought to come across and Mr Sampson is its custodian.' (Berg Collection, New York Public Library.)

shelves in the chimney corners were filled with Turgenev and
Borrow, Darwin, Balzac and de Maupassant, elaborate works
on Italian painters, cookbooks, domestic novels and books about
Wales. The white-papered walls of the drawing-room were
covered with rows of Goya and Rembrandt etchings 'and part
of a Raphael cartoon in one corner'. But his own work was
subject to fitful delays. He saw everything in copper lines, but
when depressed he could not work, and there seemed no controlling these attacks of depression. 'Rumbling home in a bus in
a state of blank misery I found myself opposite a perfect queen
among women, a Beatrice, a Laura, a Blessed Virgin!' he wrote
to Will Rothenstein that winter. 'The sight of her loveliness,
the depth of her astonished eyes, her movements of a captured
nymph dispelled the turgid clouds from my mind, leaving an
exquisite calm which became by the time I got to bed a contradiction of almost religious exaltation. Would I could repay my
debt to the enchantress! Would that I too were a wizard!'

But he could summon up no spells to control his own emotions. New people, new visual experiences affected him as a
switch controls an electric light and he affected other people.
Alone, he was nothing. The clouds of his 'blank misery' rushed
in to fill the vacuum. They came and went again, forming and
dissolving according to no obvious laws, but each time massing
more densely, taking longer to evaporate. For Dorelia, like a
sun beyond the horizon, was out of sight: and he was cold and
miserable without her.

He had hoped she would return for their belated house-
warming party at Matching Green; and he longed to finish his
portrait of her. 'Your fat excites me enormously and I am
dying to inspect it,' he wrote to her.

I am itching to resume that glorious counterfeit of you which has
already cost me too many sighs. I have a feeling that the solitude of
Matching Green will do much towards its perfection. The thought of
this picture came upon me with an inward fluttering and I am fond
to believe that the problem will now find its final solution in your
newly acquired tissue. When are you two going to turn your backs
on Pyrenean vistas? How is it you are not going to assist at the
warming and consecration of Elm House? I imagine new papers in
the ladies smoking room with ribbons and roses on it and new chintz

on the chairs and sofa again with roses and ribbons. Ida has commissioned me to paint a silk panel for the piano, and the front door
is already a pure and candid white behind which no hypocrisy can
harbour.

He asked to be told of their exploits, but all he received was
a package of out-of-date Christmas presents – bonbons and
beautiful toys for the children, and elaborate cakes for him and
Ida. 'Gwen is still in Toulouse I believe,' Ida told Alice (January
1904), 'painting hard – and anxious as soon as her 5 pictures are
finished, to go to Paris.' 'They have a dog who is naughty *always*, Gwen says,' she wrote to Winifred the same month. And
that, it seems, was all they knew.

Even before the end of the year Augustus had been growing
impatient at their prolonged absence. The weeks went by; he
heard almost nothing, and what news did trickle through only
tantalized him. 'It was a bloody long time before I heard from
you,' he burst out in a letter from the Chelsea Art School.

Gwendolina says that you get prettier and prettier ... When are
you coming back again? You are tired of running about those
foreign places I know ... I have stayed up here now for many days,
laudably attempting to get things done, but these models, drat them,
don't give a man a chance with all this employment. However I am
getting into a weedy condition. My studio is grimey, my bed is un-
made, my hair uncombed, my nails unpared, my teeth uncleaned,
my boots unblacked, my socks unfresh, my collar unchanged, my
hose undarned, my tie unsafety pinned (I wish you'd send me some
safety pins, it's not too much to ask) – lastly, my purse unlined.

It was true that Gwen and Dorelia were by now growing
tired of Toulouse. Their room was bare; they bathed, when it
was not too frigid, in the river; and subsisted mainly on a diet
of old bread, new cheese and middle-aged figs – though there
were also some light-hearted evenings over a bottle of wine and
a bowl of soup. Gwen, Dorelia observed, was becoming very
puritan in some of her attitudes. She disapproved of the theatre
and spoke with disgust of the 'vulgar red lips' of a girl they
used as a model. Yet she was not unattractive to men, and
never careless of her appearance – 'in fact', Dorelia noted,
'rather vain'.[43] To maintain themselves the two girls made
portrait sketches in the cafés for three francs each. The rest of

the time Gwen worked at her five paintings, three of which
appear to have been portraits of Dorelia.⁴⁴ 'I look forward to a
little time in which I can try to express in some way my
thoughts,' she wrote to Ursula Tyrwhitt. 'I am hurrying so because we are so tired of Toulouse – we do not want to stay a
day longer than necessary – I do nothing but paint – but you
know how slowly that gets on – a week is nothing. One thinks
one can do so much in a week – if one can do a square inch
that pleases one – one ought to be happy – for after all to do
in a year something beautiful – "a joy for ever" would be
splendid! . . .'

By the end of February the five pictures were presumably,
for the time being, finished. Bundling their possessions on to
their backs again they made their way north, in the direction
of England.

Augustus was overjoyed: but a month later he had sunk
back into the most terrible lassitude. Gwen and Dorelia* had
got as far as Paris: and stopped. The Rani, who was staying at
Elm House in the last week of March, describes what the
atmosphere was like in a letter to her husband (24 March 1904):

Mr Augustus's habits are really remarkable. He came on Tuesday
with a bad cold and all Wednesday morning he stayed in bed and
played the concertina and we had to take turns to provide him with
gossip. All afternoon he read Balzac – never moved from his chair –
went out for a walk just before supper in piercing cold – read all
evening including meals – said 'I want to make some more sketches
of you' and dropped the subject. All Thursday (yesterday) he stayed
in bed and asked for no one – played the most melancholy tunes on
his concertina and got up at tea time – very silent, read his book but
as good as gold and ready to nail up bird cages or anything – after
tea went out – at tea he said 'Good God is it Thursday? – I thought
of doing that sketch to-day.' At 6.15 he appeared with a block and
some red chalk and began to draw me as I sat by the fire. I said 'I
hope you are not doing it unless you feel inclined' to which a growl
and 'I do feel inclined – that is I shan't know if I do until I've done.'
He drew furiously by firelight and the last glimmer from the window
and fetched a lamp and drew by that until supper – 7 o'clock – three

---

* 'I have ordered a mighty canvas against your coming,' Augustus wrote to
her. '. . . so better go in for Ju-Jitsu at once, dear, for you will have to fill it
spreadeagle wise.'

sketches – I didn't ask to see them knowing better – at supper we both took our life in our hands ... and asked to see the sketches he had done. He produced them ... each more charming than the other ... He worked with the tension and rapidity of ten Shannons rolled into one – scraped and tore away at it in the most marvellous way and did I should think fully six more of which I only saw one – too exquisitely squirrelly and funny for description but beautiful. They were mostly put in the coal scuttle as he did them but preserved all right. It must have been about 12 when he suddenly stopped, said 'thank you for sitting' and went off to bed.

The next day, 25 March, the Chelsea Art School officially ended its term. Augustus now began to spend more days at Matching Green; and time hung very heavy. The tension went out of his life; he languished. For a while he stayed mild and listless, only half-aware, it seemed, of the terrible cacophony of children, canaries, chickens and other cattle that reverberated through Elm House.

'Mrs John is beating the baby to sleep which always amuses me and appears to succeed very well – she is so in earnest over it that the baby seems to gather that she means business,' the Rani wrote to her husband a few days later (27 March 1904).

... The baby is simply roaring its head off and no one paying any attention – it is in another room ... You would hate to be here. Mr Augustus looks sometimes at the baby and says 'Well darling love – dirty little beast' at the same time. He is the sweetest natured person in the world. It is all indescribable and full of shades and contrasts and the whole is just like his pictures. He looks so beautiful and never takes a bath so far as I can make out. At least I know he is not three minutes dressing but always looks clean. He has cut his hair by the way a good deal – Ida likes it, I haven't made up my mind yet – I think she must have sat on the baby – it has suddenly stopped crying.

The sweetness slipped out of his nature soon afterwards on learning what Gwen and Dorelia were up to in Paris. At La Reole, on their way to Toulouse the previous autumn, they had met 'a young artist who gave us his address in Paris, so that we can be models if we like in Paris'. On reaching Paris in the early spring of 1904 they put up in a single room at 19 Boulevard Edgar Quinet. 'I am getting on with my painting, that makes me happy,' Gwen wrote to Alice Rothenstein. She had been followed from Toulouse by a married woman who, falling under her spell, had abandoned her husband to be with Gwen. But in Paris Gwen, happy now with her painting, would have nothing to do with the woman. 'She was extremely queer and hard,' Dorelia reflected,[45] always attracted to the wrong people, for their beauty alone. But her work was more important than anyone.

In their spare time the two girls made clothes. 'The room is full of pieces of dresses – we are making new dresses,' Gwen told Alice. 'Dorelia's is pink with a skirt of three flounces. She will look lovely in it. Our two painters will want her as a model I am sure when we go home.' But the news that enraged Augustus was that for one artist in Paris Dorelia was posing in the nude – something she had never consented to do for him. 'Why the devil don't I hear from you, you bad little fat girl?' he reprimanded her.

You sit in the nude for those devilish foreign people, but you do not want to sit for me when I asked you, wicked little bloody harlot ['lubni'] that you are. You exhibit your naked fat body for money, not for love. So much for you! How much do you show them for a franc? I am sorry that I never offered to give you a shilling or two for a look at your minj. That was all you were waiting for. The devil knows I might have bought the minj and love together. I am sorry that I was so foolish to love you. Well if you are not a whore, truly tell me why not. Gustavus.

Dorelia's reply, when it arrived, was little more than a scribble. In the heat of the moment, Augustus had forgotten to enclose his usual word-list, so much of his invective had gone astray. Certain phrases in his letter puzzled Dorelia. What, for example, did lubni mean? But Augustus already felt rather ashamed of his outburst and refused to answer. Instead he wrote to apologize. All this letter-writing was getting him nowhere. He needed to *see* Dorelia. It was over eight months since he had last seen her. What was he to do? Curiously, it was Ida who decided, suggesting that he spend ten days in Paris – he could see the show of primitives there at the same time. As soon as she had spoken, he acted. He was like a dynamo – one that needed someone else to turn the switch before it came to life.

What exactly happened during his stay in Paris is not now known, but something may be deduced from the developments that followed his visit. A week before he arrived, Gwen had written to Alice Rothenstein : 'We are getting homesick I think, we are always talking of beautiful places we know of beyond the suburbs of London and Fitzroy St and Howland St seem to me more than ever charming and interesting. We shall be going home in the Autumn I think or before.'

This, apparently, was their intention just before Augustus turned up in the second week of May. What they did afterwards was altogether different. That another man might take his place in Dorelia's life had not seriously occurred to Augustus. But this was what was happening in Paris while he lay lugubriously playing the concertina at Matching Green. His rival was a very young artist – half artist and half farmer – probably the man she and Gwen had met at La Reole. His name was Leonard, and from Dorelia's point of view he possessed certain advantages over Augustus : he was not married; life with him, while not contradicting her sense of destiny, might involve a farming background that appealed to her, and would certainly be calmer, more assured.

A contest now developed in Paris as a result of which Dorelia left Boulevard Edgar Quinet – not with Augustus back to England, but to Belgium with Leonard. She fled with him secretly, telling no one, leaving no address. She had gone, they discovered, to Bruges, was living with Leonard and for the time being could only be reached through a *poste restante* there. She would stay with him three months – or a lifetime : it depended how things worked out. It was, she afterwards remarked, 'one of my two discreditable episodes'.[46]

Exasperated, almost beside himself, Augustus hung on in Paris, doing nothing. He was completely deflated, reduced once more to writing letters – not mere prose ones this time, but page after page of poems, ballads and sonnets, odd rhymes running in his head which he stored up and subsequently sent her.

> But for the woman I hold in my heart,
> Whose body is a flame, whose soul a flower,
> Whose smile beguiled me in the wood, the smart

Of kisses of her red lips every hour
Branding me lover anew, is she to be,
Being my Mistress, my Fatality?

In the full stream of his romantic passion there are already
oddly shaped pebbles of pedantry that, in time, would grow
into veritable boulders. At one point, for example, he interrupts
one of his most anguished letters in order to instruct Dorelia
that 'the word "ardent" in the first sonnet I sent you should be
changed to "nodding". Kindly make that correction.'*

So prolific were these poems that there seems to have been
one left over for Ida who, he learnt, was now pregnant again.
Possibly on Gwen's advice, he does not appear for the time
being to have written anything except poetry for Dorelia; but
to Ida he explained very frankly all that was happening. Upon
Ida's reaction the whole course of their future hung. Since
Augustus's happiness depended on Dorelia, and Ida's on him,
she too longed for Dorelia to return. How happy the three of
them might be! The last months had been miserable. She felt
she had lost even the power of sitting to Augustus – and she
would rather have lost her child. Every day, it seemed to her,
she became more subordinate to him while he moved further
away from her. They could only come together again if Dorelia
were at the centre – of that she was now convinced. In a state
of almost religious exaltation she sent to Gwen and Augustus
two letters that were dramatically to alter the whole course of
events. To Dorelia herself she did not write, but Gwen at once
communicated the extraordinary developments:

Dorelia, something has happened which takes my breath away so
beautiful it is.

Ida wants you to go to Gussy – not only wants but desires it passionately. She has written to him and to me. She says 'She [Dorelia]
is ours and she knows it. By God I will haunt her till she comes
back.'

She said also to Gussy, 'I have discovered I love you and what you
want I want passionately. She, Dorelia, shall have pleasure with you
eh?' She said much more but you understand what she means.

Gus loves you in a much more noble way than you may think –
he will not ask you now because he says perhaps you are happy

* She did.

with your artist and because of your worldly welfare – but he only says that last – because he knows you – we know you too and we do ask.

You are necessary for his development and for Ida's, and he is necessary for yours – I have known that a long time – but I did not know how much. Dorelia you know I love you, you do not know how much. I should think it the greatest crime to take with intention anyone's happiness away even for a little time – it is to me the only thing that would matter.

I point out your happiness and the highest happiness. I know of course from one point of view you will have to be brave and unselfish – but I have faith in you. Ida's example makes me feel that some day I shall be unselfish too.

I would not write this if I knew you have no affection for Gussy. You are his aren't you?

You might say I write this because I love you all – if you were strangers to me, I would try to write in the same way so much I feel in my heart that it [is] right what I say, and good.

I am sorry for Leonard, but he has had his happiness for a time what more can he expect? We do not expect more. And all the future is yours to do what you like. Do not think these are my thoughts only – they are my instincts and inspired by whatever we have in us divine. I know what I write is for the best, more than I have ever known anything. If you are perplexed, trust me. But I know you know what I do. Gussy is going home to night. Come by the first train to me. I shall be at the gare to meet you. When you are here you will know what to do and Ida.

Do not put it off a minute simply because I shall then think you have not understood this letter – that it has not conveyed the truth to you. I fear that, because I know how weak words are sometimes – and yet it would be strange if the truth is not apparent here in every line.

You will get this to-morrow morning perhaps – I shall be in the evening at the gare du nord. I would not say goodbye to Leonard. Your Gwen.

It was not simply that Gwen wanted Dorelia to return to Augustus, but that she believed Dorelia belonged to the John tribe and that by running away she had contradicted her nature. Her letter, and the others she wrote over this period, are remarkable for their religious involvement with Dorelia's future. Only this is no ordinary religion, it is the religion of love for art's sake. Were not art and religious experience much the same thing? Was not Dorelia an idol in the temple of art?

But it is the tone as well as the content of what Gwen wrote that is so strange – that dogmatic certainty in her own rightness which, like a faith in some divinity shaping all their ends, shall not be denied. The other side of this moral conviction was a callousness that shows itself in her attitude to Leonard – 'what more can he expect?'

Just as remarkable was the subtle way in which Gwen took over and organized everything. It was, judged objectively, a most effective piece of practical politics that she, and not Augustus, should communicate with Dorelia. This avoided any hint of a sexual tug-of-war, of a man-versus-man situation. Nor was Gwen acting for herself – after all she would have no place in Augustus's home when Dorelia returned. What her letters do not reveal is that she had just begun her love affair with Rodin, that she was full of joie de vivre, happy and self-confident in a way that was unique for her. It was this that gave her such sureness, made Dorelia the counterpart in Augustus's life of Rodin.

If Dorelia was subject to anyone's will, it must have been Gwen's, whose hard queer company she had kept over the last eight months, who, alone of all the John tribe, knew Leonard, and who probably also knew Dorelia best. The timing and occasion of her first letter, too, was excellent: no appeal until Ida's sanction had been obtained. Finally, she called upon the one strain stronger than any other in Dorelia's character, one that Gwen understood well: her sense of destiny. There was only one weakness in Gwen's position, and that was inevitable: while she could only send 'weak words' on a piece of paper, Leonard was with Dorelia in person. It was her words against his physical presence. But what she could do to offset this disadvantage she did, recommending Dorelia to tell Leonard nothing, to leave him in the same furtive way as she had left Augustus. For this too was in Dorelia's character, and to have a weakness recommended as one's duty can be irresistible.

When Gwen went to the Gare du Nord the following evening, Dorelia was not there. She had written a letter. To go back, she claimed, would be for ever to curtail her freedom. With Leonard she was free. Therefore she must not act selfishly, but

think of Leonard's interests too, help him to develop his talent.
Gwen had written her letter in 'an ecstasy' : it was not cool
reason. Whatever happened Gwen must not come and seek her
out in Bruges.

If Gwen had not won as easily as she appears to have expected, she already sensed victory in Dorelia's reply. In her
answer she brushed aside all these objections. She understood
Dorelia's position, Dorelia did not understand hers. She returned to the attack, reiterating and elaborating her previous
arguments :

I must speak plainly for you to know everything before you
choose. Leonard cannot help you, he would have to know Gussie for
that and Ida and you a long, long time, he never could understand
unless he was our brother or a great genius.
Strength and weakness, selfishness and unselfishness are only
words – our work in life was to develop ourselves and so fulfil our
destiny. And when we do this we are of use in the world, then *only*
can we help our friends and develop them. I *know* that Gussie and
Ida are more parts of you than Leonard is for ever. When you leave
him you will perhaps make a great character of him – if he has faith
in you that you are acting according to your truest self – and what
good could you do him if he had no faith in you – by being always
with him? But faith or no faith he would know some day the truth
– and that is the highest good that can happen to us. To 'wholly develop' a man is nonsense – all events help to do that. I know as
certainly as the day follows the night that you would develop him
and all your friends as far as one human being can another by *being
yourself. That is what you have to think of,* Dorelia. To do this is
hard – that is what I meant by saying you must be brave and strong.
I am sorry for people who suffer but that is how we learn all we
know nearly – and that is the great happiness – knowledge of the
truth!
You know you are Gussy's as well as I do. Did you do wisely in
going away like that without telling him? Do you dare spend a
week with him or a day, or a few hours? Forgive me for speaking
like this darling Dorelia – I only want to help you to know yourself.
I love you so much that if I never saw you again and knew you
were happy I should be happy too. Oh don't be too proud to think
much of all these facts. You are unselfish but it makes it simple to
know all we have to do is to be true to the feelings that have been
ours longest and most consistently.

While Gwen was writing this to Dorelia, Leonard had posted
an answer to her first letter which, disobeying Gwen's instructions, Dorelia had shown him. Written in halting English, by
now partly indecipherable, combining pathos with dignity, it is
couched as a rebuke yet struggles to maintain a sense of fairness in grappling with the questions posed by Gwen's lofty
philosophy:

Dear Miss John,
Dorelia got your letter to-day and showed it to me. Your letter
forces me to explain to you several things you forgot, as well as I
can do.
Of course you don't know me neither do you know my sentiments to Dor; but this is the other side of the facts, at which you
did not like to look, anyway it exists and it is as true as your words,
if I allow myself to talk a little bit of myself.
You say L. has had his happiness for a time, what more can he
expect? Do you really think [— —] feelings are so [—] am constant [—] of happiness, do you really think that Dorelia's feelings
are small enough to love a man like this? People like me don't love
often and a woman like Dorelia will not pass my way again; you
would better understand, if you would know my life.
Your letter is full of love, the love of a woman for another one,
now imagine mine if you can. I am no ordinary man as you may
think, who loves a girl because she is beautiful or whatever. I tell
you and you are Dory's friend so you must understand it, I am an
artist and cannot live without her and I will not live without her –
I think this is clear. Very right if you say 'it is the greatest crime to
take with intention anyone's happiness'. You might say as you did
I had my happiness. Do you think happiness is a thing that you
take like café after dinner, a thing that you enjoy a few times and
something you can get sick of? Not my hapiness by God; I suffered enough before and I don't let escape something from me that
I created myself with all my love and all my strength. Well, all
those words are only an answer to yours, but something else that
you forgot.
We cannot force the fate to go our ways, fate forces us. This
[—] that. Dorelia is not free dis[—] then she was mine as [—]
with soul and body [—] understand.
That's all I have to tell you, compare now my fate with that of
John and his family perhaps you will see where it is heavier. My
words seem hard to you, but they are the expression of my feelings

as well as I can say it. I think it is not necessary to talk about Dorelias feelings and thoughts. I did *not* tell her what to do, I told her she might do what she thinks right and naturel, but remember your words of the crime and think that there are greater crimes which are against the rules of nature.

If you want wright to me your thoughts about everything and dont get mad against me, you must see that there is no world that [is] absolutely right.

L – – – ard   Bruges   kplaass 5.*

Wisely Gwen did not accept this invitation to write to Leonard. She was not interested in an academic discussion of 'thoughts about everything', but in outcomes; not in fairness, but rightness. Besides, it would have been a bad error of tactics to descend from her philosophic stratosphere to debate points of detail with him. His letter arrived in Paris before Gwen had posted her second letter to Dorelia, so she slipped into the envelope an extra pitiless page for Dorelia. In this, she neatly deflects his arguments to her own ends. His letter, she confesses, had disappointed her, had made her 'more certain if certainty can be more certain of everything I have told you'. Leonard's love was, after all, nothing better than possessiveness. She had supposed it to have been finer – perhaps he'd climb to better things in time, given the adversity. He loved her of course, no one denied that. But his love was selfish, like that of the Pebble of the brook in Blake's *The Clod and the Pebble*, while Augustus's, 'much more noble', resembled the little Clod of Clay's.† For, whatever his faults, Augustus was an artist; while Leonard, as yet, was a part of the bourgeoisie.

---

* It appears that Leonard unintentionally gave a clue here to their address. By a process of elimination (there is, for example, only one square or 'plaats' in Bruges that begins with the letter K), one can establish that they were probably living at Kraanplaats, 5, a large and beautiful dolls' house very near the Théâtre Royal Communal. This house belonged to a certain Lodewyk Van den Broucke and his wife Leonie (née Huys). He was evidently a man of some means, having 'no profession'. The records that might have confirmed Leonard to be his son were destroyed by fire in 1947. However, from other letters, we know that Leonard's surname began with a B, so it seems possible that he was (christened after his mother) Leonard Broucke.

† 'Love seeketh not itself to please,
    Nor for itself hath any care,

I have just read Leonard's letter. In self-justification I must answer a few things to you. I don't know what he thinks I mean – he does not understand certainly. I *never* thought he does not love you, I thought he loved you in a much finer way than his letter shows. When a person loves another they are only happy if the other one is – I don't see how they could be happy otherwise. He talks about his happiness and seems to think I want to take it away! He should be glad of everything I have said if it helps to show you how things stand and to be free, but he says 'you are not free anymore you are his, his body and soul'. He says there are greater crimes than breaking another's happiness that is to do things against the rules of nature.

He limits the laws of nature. You are bound to those whom you are in sympathy by laws much stronger than the most apparent ones. The laws of nature are infinite and some are so delicate they have no names but they are strong. We are more than intellectual and animal beings we are spiritual also. Men don't know this so well as women, and I am older than Leonard.

He said 'I *could* not live without her and *will* not live without her – this is clear.' Well a man who talks like that ought to be left to walk and stand and work alone – by every woman. Only when he can will he do good work.

Gwen's shock tactics exploded powerful doubts within Dorelia. And to Gwen's philosophy were now added Augustus's poetry, and letters of simple entreaty from Ida. This pressure by post built up steadily to a bombardment. Ida had already dispatched Augustus back to the front line of combat in Paris so that, when the critical moment came, he could advance upon Bruges with all haste. 'Aurevoir,' she wrote to him, 'and don't come here again alone. Mrs Dorel Harem must be with you.'

From Dorelia herself little or nothing was heard. Before the

But for another gives its ease,
And builds a Heaven in Hell's despair.'

So sang a little Clod of Clay,
Trodden with the cattle's feet,
But a Pebble of the brook
Warbled out these metres meet:

'Love seeketh only Self to please,
To bind another to its delight,
Joys in another's loss of ease,
And builds a Hell in Heaven's despite.'

west wind of passion that blew upon her, she was floundering,
quietly, hopelessly, without comment. Then, suddenly, she
seems to have capitulated. 'I have given in and am going back
with Gus soon,' she wrote to Gwen. How and when she was
going back was still left vague; hers was a conditional surrender of which no one quite knew the conditions. It was now
that Augustus, reinforcing his advantage, moved from France
into Belgium. And still, from further back, the John artillery
kept up its unremitting hail of letters. Ida was particularly insistent that Dorelia should return, not just to England or
London, but to Elm House itself. The three of them must live
together in Augustus's Essex harem – 'a wonderful concubin-
age'. This would be infinitely preferable to a dreary segregation,
with its periodic loneliness, dangers, dullness, incompleteness –
almost respectability. If Dorelia were elsewhere, Ida feared she
might never see Augustus, that he might actually leave her. She
could never be sure. This at least was part of her reason for
welcoming Dorelia into the home. But the prospect of it also
excited her curiously. She had begun to identify her feelings for
Dorelia with Gwen's, and to suspect that in some extraordinary way she loved her.

'Darling Dorel,' she wrote.

Please do not forget that you are coming back – or get spirited
away before – as I should certainly hang myself in an apple tree.
Whenever I write to you I think you will be annoyed or bored – I
seem to have written so often and said the same thing. But for the
last time O my honey let me say it – I *crave* for you to come here. I
don't expect you will and I don't want you to if – well if you don't.
But I do want you to understand it is all I want. I now feel incomplete and thirsty without you. I don't know why – and in all prob-
ability I shall have to continue so – as of course it will probably be
impractical or something and naturally there are your people – and
Gus will want you to be in town.

But I want you to know how it is Mrs Harem – only you needn't
come for 10 days as I am curing freckles on my face and shall be
hideous until I blossom out afresh.

I heard from Gwen 'Dorelia writes she has given in'. Were you
then holding out against Gus, you little bitch? You are a mystery,
but you are ours. I don't know if I love you for your own sake or
for his. Aurevoir – I wish I could help that Leonard. It is so sad.

It seems probable that Leonard still did not know what was happening. Dorelia kept everything secret – in a sense even from herself. She did not make an exact decision, she merely put herself in the path of the greatest current of energy, and let events take their course. By this time Augustus had reached Antwerp where he halted, expecting some news from Dorelia. 'I am getting to know every stone of Antwerp,' he wrote.

... The Devil keeps you away from me Ardor McNeill. Sometimes I talk to you while walking along and laugh so heartily all the people stare. All night I have strange dreams ... You have only written once and how many letters have I sent you. You make me feel like Jesus Christ sometimes. I sit and sip and call for paper and ink – I wonder if you call for my letters. Yes you must ... I think of the portrait I shall paint of you – there is a painting here by Rembrandt of little Saskia – a wondrous work – it is the repository of the inmost secret in the heart of a great artist. It is like the Cathedral here only more intimate more personal more subtle. In it is the principle of man's love of woman. You call me pirino – beloved, but do you love me enough to kiss me and laugh to me when I am dying? Beloved Beloved your hands are laid on my head and everything fades. Beloved do I not stand strong and stark upon the world with the wind of ages about my thin white body? Yes my feet clutch the rock of time and my arms are outstretched to the fingertips to polar stars – Target to the Firmament. I shall not quail. Butt of meteors I shall know how to smile. Ardor thou sylph with a secret for me let me hear you breathe. Gustavus.

By nature inarticulate, Dorelia found it more than usually difficult to reply to these romantic outpourings. They impressed her, but she was swamped* by them. They were music – and

---

* 'Miss Dorelia Ardor. Pirini, I must keep writing,' he wrote from Antwerp. 'I found this evening a letter to you I had not posted. I wrote it the day I came – I have sent you many letters. Have you taken the trouble to go to the Post Office for them? You have not written to me yet. Do you not believe you are precious to me, invaluable one! I am alone and what can I do but think, and thoughts of all sorts come to me. I know if I don't hear from you to-morrow I will come to find you again. I can always claim you; I will have you for myself. Why did you desert me before – why, I cannot think. Don't trouble to find an impossible answer. If anyone can understand you I can. Love I know you – Know me – Know me. I have tears of love for you and yet I am not drunk. Sweet I have met you on the high-way and I have recognised you and kissed you and you have fled into the woods and I have followed you at last and found you again. My girl, my sweet friend whom I love so much can you withhold your

how does one answer music? They were complete in themselves. During the whole of this dramatic episode on which their lives would pivot, while everyone else was discharging his very soul on to paper, she confined herself to the odd postcard – a time, a place, a piece of luggage, some weather, part of a dream, sometimes simply nothing at all but the picture on one side, her signature on the other. Augustus dashed from place to place – Antwerp, Brussels, Ghent – endeavouring to catch these cards, endeavouring to discover in them some clue as to what was going on. 'I hope you haven't sent word to Antwerp now that I have left,' he wrote from Ghent – but how would he ever know without travelling back again to Antwerp?

It appears that Dorelia had consented to see him, but only outside Bruges, presumably because Leonard still did not know she was going to leave him. Augustus himself hardly knew. 'I can come then on Tuesday morning?' he asked, perplexed, exasperated. 'Why come here, this isn't the way home, at least not the shortest. Beloved tell me where to find you – but if you can come here before *come in the name of all the Gods* – wait for me here opposite the station.' They met, almost by accident it seemed, certainly by good luck, but even now nothing was irretrievably fixed. Dorelia needed more time: a week. Allowing her to return was a torture to Augustus. It was not natural. 'What am I to do these last days?' he demanded. She did not reply. 'The time is nearly up – Ardor,' he wrote again. 'Gand is very near Bruges. I am to rejoin you on Tuesday morning. So be it.'

They set off on their return journey from Bruges station on 1 August 1904. They were to travel, not via Paris, but direct to London. Before leaving, Augustus wrote to Gwen arranging for Dorelia's belongings in the Boulevard Edgar Quinet to be sent to Flood Street. On the platform, waiting for their train, Dorelia also wrote to Gwen, finally breaking her long silence. Her postcard reads: 'How is the cat? Dorelia.'

---

lips your eyes and your heart and your mind from me your lover – he who will take no denial – no denial. No denial is valid with him henceforth. It is useless – my lady, sybil, Dryad, form without circumference, incomprehensible simplicity, earth and air –

Ardor McNeill, it is you I love – Gustavus.

Whether Leonard ever knew, until after she left, that Dorelia had 'given in' and chosen Augustus, is not certain; but it seems unlikely. He returned to Paris, imagining perhaps he was following Dorelia. But he only saw Gwen, who told him nothing. His name does not appear in their correspondence again: except once that autumn. 'Leonard came up to me a few days ago,' Gwen wrote to Dorelia. 'I should write him a nice letter if I were you. He will get very ill otherwise I think.' After this he vanishes, leaving just the echo of his letter to Gwen – 'I will not live without her.' The rest of Gwen's letter to Dorelia is about the complexities of making a skirt, about some 'earrings like Gussie's' she had mislaid. There is a mention of Rodin 'with some millionaires', and a description of four 'Toulousians' with umbrellas they knew. That was all.

Gwen had won the day – but thereafter she was to see little of Dorelia, Ida* or Augustus, and she moves out of the story of their lives. Deliberately. Despite the homesickness for England, even Wales, to which she had confessed less than three months ago, despite her intention to return 'in the Autumn I think or before', she never went back for any length of time. 'Stronger than a man, simpler than a child, her nature stood alone' – Charlotte Brontë's words about her sister Emily suggest a comparison with Gwen. Both of them were solitary and withdrawn, yet capable of passionate love; both of them deeply rooted in this life yet straining towards the perfection that implies another; both, after suffering, reconciling the will with the spirit. Gwen's certitude finds its parallel in Emily Brontë's 'Strange Power! I trust thy might: trust thou my constancy.' In a letter to Michel Salaman, Gwen was to write: 'I don't think we change, but we disappear sometimes.'[47] From the life she had known up till this time, she was about to disappear. She had renounced large ambitions of the kind towards which she felt Augustus was always tempting her; she had renounced her background and created another; she had renounced pleasure and risk and to some extent she had apparently renounced love. In Emily Brontë, too, there is the renunciation out of which certitude

* A letter Ida wrote to Alice Rothenstein reveals that Gwen did not get back to painting until December of this year.

grew, but it seems infinitely more tender – until one compares it to Gwen's portraits of solitary women.

> This summer wind with thee and me
> Roams in the dawn of day;
> But thou must be where it shall be,
> Ere evening – far away.

In the day-to-day world there was little left but triviality – those bits and pieces of wood by which we keep afloat. Gwen's letters are full of this. It was an art at which Dorelia, too, excelled – but it achieved epidemic proportions once Ida also succumbed. 'They are putting up a hen run in the garden here,' she wrote to welcome the returning couple. 'It will be much nicer – we shall be able to see them now. The hammock is up and there are some canvas chairs and we are becoming quite like a "country house" – and now the rain has come.'

From some correspondence he wrote to Charles Rutherston, it appears that early this autumn Augustus took a private studio on the other side of the King's Road from the Chelsea Art School – No. 4 Garden Studios, in Manresa Road. But Dorelia did not live with him there. Instead, as Ida had desired, she went down to Elm House.

Ida had desired it, but now that it was actually coming to pass she was beset by fears. After the great strain of the past months she felt exhausted, and for a time this summer came near to a nervous breakdown. Compared with Gwen who, she imagined, had no one at all now, she considered herself dreadfully feeble – she knew nothing of Gwen's new happiness with Rodin. She had planned to visit Gwen in Paris for a few days but was forced to abandon this 'for all sorts of reasons' – her pregnancy, a child's sickness, the portrait of her that Augustus promised urgently to do. Worried by the tone of her letters, Gwen came instead to Elm House for three days in September, and this fortified Ida.

But Augustus was happy. Everything would turn out for the best. Ida was 'ready to play up', he told Dorelia, and 'only wants rest'. Even if Paris was beyond her, she could still enjoy 'little journeys to London'. He looked, and saw that everything was good. 'Never have the beauties of the outer world moved me as of late,' he wrote to Will Rothenstein from Matching Green.

Our poultry run I conceive to be the most wonderful thing. So remote from human interestedness, so paradisiac, so unaccountable it seems under the slanting beams of the sun in the triumphant afflatus of a long day's chant of love. The hens moving about their simple concerns, ever with them a strange note from the East (subdued now, their wild flight forgotten on the way from India), dappled gold under gilded alders, moving among medicine bottles, the broken pots and pans, crockery, meat, cans, old boots and ancient dirt and indescribable debris – the uncatalogued tales of a human abode.

I have worked at my woman painfully, laboriously, with alterations of achievement and failure, impotence and power – you know the grinding see-saw – under a studio light, cold, informal, meaningless – a studio – what is it? a habitation – no – not even a *cowshed* – 'tis a box wherein miserable painters hide themselves and shut the door on nature. I have imprisoned myself in my particular dungeon all day to-day for example – on my sitters' faces naught but the shifting light of reminiscence and that narrowed and distorted by an atrocious 'sunlight' – let me not speak of the result – to work thus tho' manfully is to be foredoomed, 'tis to kick against the pricks. Now, mark you, this evening at sundown I escaped at last to the open, to the free air of space, where things have their proportion and place and are articulate – so by the roadside I came upon my women and my barking dog seated on the dark grass in the dusk, and sitting with them I was aware of spirits present – old spirits, ancient, memorable, familiar spirits, consulted in boyhood – insulted in manhood – bright, good, clear, beneficent spirits, ever-loving and loved spirits of Beauty and Truth and Mystery. And so we are going for a pic-nic to-morrow – and I will make sketches, God-willing. I wish we might never come back to dust-heap-making again. The call of the road is on me. Why do we load ourselves with the chains of commodities when the trees live rent free, and the river pays no toll?

There are gleams of beauty in this letter, though they are clouded by the convolutions of his style. Yet this was the man. The simple animal-and-vegetable world for which he longs is glimpsed from a distance – a vision of natural happiness, native to him, from which he has somehow been parted. But as each woman in her ideal landscape is seen as the custodian of this happiness, so he becomes more involved in the world of 'human interestedness' from which he is seeking to escape. All his life he would inhabit this purgatory, an in-between world where he was neither free nor sophisticated, but enveloped by an atmosphere that seems permanently transitional, and where he can never rest. So, with ominous foreboding of what was to come, he signs his letter: 'Yours with the Unrest of Ahasuerus in his bones, "John".'

4

Men Must Play and Women Weep

It was more circumstances than anyone's fault.
IDA JOHN TO ALICE ROTHENSTEIN (AUGUST 1905)

It is more difficult at first to be wise, but it is infinitely
harder afterwards *not* to be.
IDA JOHN TO MRS SAMPSON (MAY 1905)

1. DU COTE DE CHEZ ROTHENSTEIN

'My baby is getting so heavy I do not know how I shall bear
him (or them) by October,' Ida had written to Alice Rothenstein (August 1904). 'The two outside are splendid and well,' she
added, but 'I am such a size I think I am going to have a litter
instead of the usual.'

The usual, another boy of heroic proportions eventually
called Robin (or Robyn), was born at Elm House on 23 October.
He was so punctual that everyone was taken by surprise. 'I had
to race across the green for the wise woman,' Augustus told
Mrs Sampson. 'The doctor, with truly professional promptitude,
arrived in his express 16 horse motor car immediately after the
event was successfully accomplished.' Despite these emergencies
'there was less fuss than usually accompanies the advent of an
ordinary hen's egg,' he assured the Rani. '... Of course it's
staggering to be confronted with a boy after all our prayers for
a girl. Ida started the life of Frederick the Great last night which
I think must have determined the sex of the infant. It was very
rash ... Ida has just remarked "Tell her she can have it if she
likes." '

The new unconventionality of her married life cut Ida off
more than ever from her family and from a number of her
friends. What she called her 'blundering career' had left her
curiously isolated 'like a bird sitting on its eggs'.

'I have arrived at the point of eating toasted cheese and stout for supper,' she darkly confessed to the Rani. 'It is a horrible thing to do, but shows to what a pitch animal spirits can arrive in the country.' It was not especially for love, she explained, that 'I am hungry and thirsty, but for ethics and life and rainbows and colours – butterflies and shimmering seas and human intercourse'. She prized her friends very highly, even when they did not always approve of her Matching Green ménage. 'As you know,' she wrote to Will Rothenstein, 'the communicable part of my life is very narrow, and I have nothing to tell you about it. As to the other, you must understand that without telling or you would never count me one of your "dearest of friends" – a privilege of which I am only worthy in my most silent moments.'

The extent of what she felt able to communicate to her family is defined by a letter she wrote in the spring of 1905 to her aunt, Margaret Hinton:

Robin is quite a man! he crawls about and eats bread and butter, and this evening he sat on the grass in the front garden and interviewed several boys who stopped on their way from school to talk to him. He makes so many noises, and laughs and wags his head about. You say you wonder what we do all day. About 6.30 Robin wakes, and crawls about the floor, and grunts and says ah and eh and daddle and silly things like that. About 7 D[avid] and C[aspar] wake and say more silly things, and get dressed, and have a baked apple, or a pear or something, and play about with toys and run up and down. Breakfast about 8.30. Go out in the garden, Robin washed and put to bed about 9.30. D and C go out for a walk, or to the shop, and to post. Bring in letters at 11. We have dinner about 1. and they wake up about 2., have dinner, go out, and so on and so on till 7 when they're all in bed, sometimes dancing about and shouting, sometimes going to sleep. Robin now joins in the fray and shouts too.

It was an Allen and Hanbury world, with no time ever for anything else. But what Ida's letters also reveal is the increasing need she felt to share with others – other women, perhaps, especially – something more than this cooking-and-children routine. Triviality necessarily devours most of our lives – and in a civilized world triviality often comprises the mere business of keeping oneself and others alive. But, apart from this, there was also 'something that is behind the ordinary aspect of things,' Ida wrote. 'I think it is reality.' Triviality one could document; the reality which lay barricaded behind it one could only allude to with imprecision. For Ida, reality was coming to terms with the facts of her life as they now existed.

'Some days the curtain seems to lift a little for me,' she told her aunt,

and they are days of inspiration and clearer knowledge. Those days I seem to walk on a little way. The other days I simply fight to keep where I am ... I can understand the saints and martyrs and great men suffering everything for their idea of truth. It is more difficult, once you have given it some life – to go back on your idea than to stick to it. It torments you and worries you and tears you to pieces if you do not live up to it ...
... it must sound mad to you, especially talking of fighting.
It's wonderful what a different life one leads inside, to outside – at least how unknown the inside one is.

It was impossible, in England in 1905, for people to understand, or to admit they understood, her true life – as yet she hardly comprehended all its aspects herself. By admitting her husband's mistress into the home she had, in the popular view, either made the supreme sacrifice for love; or else acted with inexcusable weakness. And on the whole, in England in 1905, people would tend to believe the latter. Why, even in Paris, men and women were hardly so brazen! Her unknown life, therefore, had generally to stay unknown – especially to the Nettleships. In defiance of the social conventions, Ida believed – was determined to believe – that she lived a natural life: natural for her. But, as her reference to saints and martyrs implies, it was not easy and she embraced with some warmth the notion of self-sacrifice. Unfortunately, triviality would keep on breaking through in a way that drove her almost to distraction. Her days were full of problems about the children's tadpoles, the canaries' eggs. What infuriated her was her habit of growing infuriated – often over the most petty matters – when she had plainly settled for a manner of ruthless gentleness, of almost aggressive sympathy with everyone. 'What with babies, toothache and a visitation of *fleas* (where from we do not know) I am fast losing my reason,' she exclaimed to Alice.

Alice had grown curious again, but she was dismayed when eventually Ida, in a dignified, faintly exasperated letter, went some way to satisfying her curiosity. 'Gus and Dorelia are up in town,' she wrote this winter,

from which you may draw your own conclusions, and not bother me any more to know 'where Dorelia sleeps' – You know we are not a *conventional* family, you have heard Dorelia is beautiful and most charming, and you must learn that my only happiness is for him to be happy and complete, and that far from diminishing our love it appears to augment it. I have my bad times it is only honest to admit. She is *so* remarkably charming. But those times are the devil and not the truth of light. You are large minded enough to conceive the amazement [? arrangement] as beautiful and possible – and would not think more of it than you would of any other madness which is really sanity. You will not gossip I know as that implies something brought to light which one wants hidden. All this we do not wish to hide, though there is no need to publish it, as after all it is a private matter.

This letter is intended to be most discreet. It really expresses the actual state of affairs and you need not consider there is any bitterness or heartache behind, as, though there *is* occasionally, it is a weakness *not to be tolerated* and which is gradually growing less and will cease when my understanding is quite cleared of its many weeds...

The response from Alice was an unprecedented silence. 'Alice Rothenstein has at last shut up,' Ida reported triumphantly to Augustus. But to Alice herself she wrote: 'You and Will both ignore my letter but I suppose you don't know what to say – and really there is nothing. I hope you showed it to Will ... Write again and tell me about someone – anyone – and all the horrid gossip you can think of.'

But, of course, the only gossip Alice could think of was Ida's. How could it be otherwise? It took her breath away – she could think of nothing else. What Ida really needed from her friends were stories about their own lives, or other people's, so irresistible that they would draw her out of the shell of her own existence, focus her attention elsewhere. She wanted particular details to brood over; she wanted her friends' letters to be like chapters from a serialized novel, so absorbing, so full of suspense, that they supplied a wholly new fabric, uncontaminated by self, to the pattern of her life. What she got was something different; from the Rani a sweet exuberant amusement, eccentrically mistyped,* proclaiming that Ida's situation was far too interesting for her to leave for a second. This was some comfort – 'only one is apt to drown the interest in tears', Ida confided to her – 'how natural and how foolish this is you will know'.

The Rani's letters were an invitation to enjoyment – almost as if they were two spectators at the Matching Green theatre. But Ida could not see it that way – if only she *could* be a spectator instead of taking everything with such 'pudding-like gravity'. Yet the darling Rani was the best of her friends: 'Your letters make green places in my life,' she told her. It was only that, in moments of crisis, she plummeted beyond their reach 'like a stone falling down a well'.

From Alice she received advice, cautionary advice, reproachful advice, advice that ran contrary to everything she had already done. Such advice was stirred in with a curiosity so persistent that it sometimes drove Ida frantic. 'She [Alice] is so – oh I don't know – she wants to know *why* and *how* – as if Chinese Ladies had answers to their riddles,' Ida complained to the Rani. 'The only nuisance about a riddle is its answer. Riddles are most fascinating by themselves.' Yet although she was always *gênée* by Alice – and Alice by her – somehow they maintained a 'tremendous admiration of each other' so that, worse than all Alice's reproaches, were no letters at all. That was death. Alice's sudden silence seemed like an echoing wall, deafening Ida with her own doings – everything she wanted to escape from. 'Your silence is chilling,' she wrote to her. 'I do not think, if it is caused by displeasure, that it is fair . . . Please to write at once, and tell me you adore me and everything I do is right . . . Oh Alice Alice Alice why don't you write and tell me all your Nurse's faults and all about Johnnie – and how you hope I am well and are longing to see me – *Darling* don't be

---

* Most mistypings were of a single letter that drastically changed the meaning of a word – such as a reference to the 'diving room' in her house. But there were also delightful misspellings. 'The spelling of "tomorroe" is quite too sweet,' Ida told her, 'and I shall adopt it.'

cross – I can't help it. My heart is a well of deep [un]happiness and this makes me malicious.'

What bewildered Alice was Ida's attitude. Otherwise everything was as clear as a Victorian melodrama: Ida was the victim, noble but misguided; Dorelia the culprit who, if she had any decency, would take herself off; and Augustus was the man, an artist traditionally unconventional whom Ida must skilfully control as Alice controlled poor Will. She knew the plot well enough. Will, however, disagreed and blamed Augustus. 'Ida is simply an angel,' he wrote to Alice (19 October 1905), '– I think you are most unjust to Dorelia, who is looking after the children all the time and helping everything on, – Heaven knows she gets little for doing so.'

The friendship between the Johns and the Rothensteins was by this time developing symptoms of burlesque. Ida, being especially fond of Will, was besieged by Alice; Augustus, much attracted to Alice, was fêted by Will. It was as if each Rothenstein sought to protect the other from these explosive Johns. Ida's correspondence to 'darling Will' holds what are almost love-letters and these would be dutifully answered – by Alice. But when Alice herself sat to Augustus, Will strongly objected to her expression – the head flung back, the eyes closed – and would turn up at Augustus's studio to escort his wife home so punctually that on occasions Alice had not yet arrived there.

'You are a dear good friend to Gus,' Ida had written to Will – but Augustus, though he could not disagree, sometimes wished it were otherwise.

> Thy friendship oft has made my heart to ake:
> Do be my Enemy for Friendship's sake.

The trouble was that Augustus could not feel what he knew he was expected to feel. He could not even pretend to. Of course he appreciated very well that he should feel grateful – Will needed to be kept well-oiled with gratitude – but usually it was irritation that swarmed through him. His fate was to be helped, with extreme magnanimity, at every twist and crisis of his career, by someone whose personality he increasingly disliked. Whichever way he turned he seemed unable to avoid the rigours of Rothenstein's generosity, and his reaction, as he was only too well aware, seemed very mean. A number of times he tried to end their relationship – 'I have broken with Rothenstein by the bye which of course is base ingratitude,' he once wrote to Lady Ottoline Morrell (8 February 1909), '– in extenuation I must say the sensation so far has been quite tolerable' – but breaking with Rothenstein was no easy matter: he kept coming back for more. He was like a boxer for ever turning the other cheek to his assailant, yet never to be knocked out, a nightmare figure eventually wearing his opponent down with these blows of his chin.

'It is more difficult to receive than to give,' Augustus once wrote,[1] and this was the lesson so many of Rothenstein's beneficiaries had bitterly to learn. Epstein, for example, who once assured him: 'Your help so freely given me has been of the greatest service to me,' wrote later (20 June 1911):

Dear Rothenstein –
I want no more of your damned insincere invitations.
This pretence of friendship has gone on far enough.
Yours etc Jacob Epstein.
It is the comic element in your attitude that has prevented me writing the above before this. I did not believe till now you could have gone on with it.

Augustus's hostility was almost exactly parallel to Epstein's. 'I have had enough of him [Rothenstein], in spite of all his enthusiasm,' he wrote to Ottoline Morrell (23 March 1909). 'How I wish someone would record the diverting history of Rothenstein's career – it would be the most ludicrous, abject and scurrilous psychological document ever penned. He is I think ... Le Sale Juif par excellence de notre siècle. There is I think one man only who could write adequately about him and that's [Wyndham] Lewis ...'

According to his son, John Rothenstein, 'no-one among his contemporaries had shown such perceptive generosity towards his brother artists of succeeding generations from Augustus John and Epstein to Henry Moore and Ceri Richards'. This is completely true, yet except in the literary world he never became a popular figure. Many of the artists he helped turned on him and, in an uncharacteristic moment of exasperation, Max

Beerbohm once revealed to him that he had no friends at all.*
What, then, was the secret of this gift for unpopularity? It
seems to have depended upon several qualities. He had begun
his career as a promising artist, but as the years went on found
himself more and more enclouded by ethical art-politics. 'For
myself I want to paint my pictures and live within my means,'
he once wrote to Alice (4 September 1923). 'I am slow and un-
productive; but I am above all things an artist and I dread the
growing complexities of life.' Yet the loneliness of painting
never entirely suited him, and the complexities of public life
spread like a sea over his artistic career. Like so many British
painters of this period he apparently failed to fulfil his early
potential, and his dissatisfaction seems to have been contagious.
He grew into a figure somewhat similar, in the literary world,
to Hugh Walpole, increasingly the patron rather than the
creative painter, fixing his personal ambitions on the performance of his protégés. It was as if he sought to ride to immortality on their backs. His two prize rebellious steeds were
Augustus and Stanley Spencer, whom he entered against the
rival stables of Roger Fry. But of all his string, Augustus was
the greatest disappointment to him, winning in brilliant fashion
so many of the minor races, running under false colours, starting favourite for the classics, finishing last but one.

Already, by 1905, disillusionment had set in. 'I am sorry John
has no success,' Will wrote to Alice that year (19 October 1905).
'I slid some advice in on the subject before the Puvis decoration
at the Sorbonne, and I still think he may do great work – at
any rate he feels it, and can do it.'

Will's advice, like Alice's, was a formidable commodity. A
Max Beerbohm multiple caricature shows him advising poets
how to write poetry, playwrights how to stage their plays,
painters how to paint.† Augustus, unfortunately, was not sus-

---

* One of the guests at a dinner in honour of Will Rothenstein remarked: 'We
ought really to have been at a dinner composed of his enemies.' To which his
companion replied: 'They'd be precisely the same people.'

† At the centre Will is looking into a mirror, lecturing himself on modesty.
Upper left: lecturing Oscar Wilde on deportment, while Wilde casts his eyes
heavenwards. *Upper right corner*: lecturing Lord Coleridge on law, who looks
down benevolently at Will standing on tiptoe on a law book. *Upper right*:
skewering with a pen Pinero, who postures on its point like a ballet dancer

ceptible to advice. He needed Rothenstein, intermittently, for
one thing: money. 'I had a letter from John – not one I cared
for much, for there was a hint of further pecuniary needs,' Will
complained to his brother Albert (10 September 1908), '– he
writes as though he were entirely neglected, but this is scarcely
the case – one sees his drawings about everywhere, doesn't
one?' What Will traded in, what he purchased, was gratitude.
But Augustus had none to give – it was not a feeling he liked
to entertain. 'I have not found him [Augustus] the most grateful
of men in the days of his splendour,' Will sorrowfully confided
to the Rani years later (19 Augustus 1933). But then, who was
properly grateful? One was always being shortchanged. The
inverted gratitude he unerringly drew down upon himself was
partly due to the ill-will of the competitive art-world. But it
also came from peculiarities in his character. He felt he lacked
charm. 'The Gods who made me energetic & gave me a little
passion & a little faith did me an ill turn when they made
me ugly & charmless,' he confessed once (28 July 1915) to
Rabindranath Tagore.[2] He wanted above all things to be loved,
yet was fatally attracted to the wrong people – those who had
no love to give – and he was often thrown on the defensive.
The gratitude he squeezed out of people was a substitute for
the love he felt he could never command. He had been
brought up in the Whistlerian tradition where even the slightest
whisper of criticism was intolerable. To this sensitivity was
added an exceptional sanctimoniousness as he grew more and
more exercised over good causes. He became known as 'the
parson', and Augustus went out of his way to shock him: he
could not resist it. Will's tone, too, varied disconcertingly between the lofty and the obsequious; he was suspected of chasing celebrities; everything he seemed to view through a mist of

---

while Will lectures him on playwriting. *Middle right*: lecturing the Prince of
Wales on 'dress', Will very tiny in white tie and tails down to his heels.
Lower right: lecturing Aubrey Beardsley on decadence, and Mr Furse on 'folly'.
Lower middle: advising Lord Rosebery (simply a bald and faceless dome rising
out of a winged collar) on 'la partie politique'. *Lower left*: lecturing George
Moore on 'caution' – he looking very spindly and stunned. *Middle left*: lecturing
Mr Stratton on Art. The drawing is owned by Will Rothenstein's niece,
Mrs Powell.

high-mindedness. The discreet ebullience of his bachelor days gradually gave way before advancing austerity. In the racialist climate of Edwardian England, though he was not a practising Jew, he started off with disadvantages, and improved on them to fashion for himself a positive handicap. What Augustus objected to was his ugliness. Will was aesthetically reprehensible to him and the marriage of this erect monkey-like creature to the refulgent Alice, the pink rose, went against all his notions of propagating a masterfully beautiful race. If anything was immoral, that was.

Then there was the embarrassing problem of Rothenstein's praise. Augustus needed praise, as he needed drink, as he needed later on to associate with the aristocracy. But he was not so susceptible as to think more highly for any length of time of those who provided such props. Recognizing weakness in himself, in black moods he would assail those very people whom, in other states of mind, he had encouraged to indulge him. He would imbibe praise for a time: then suddenly it sickened him.*

It was partly because Will had placed an aesthetic investment

---

* An article Rothenstein wrote about the Slade celebrated Augustus for many of those buccaneering qualities that clustered round his weaker side and fed the John legend. But Augustus strongly objected to this. 'Your all too picturesque treatment of me, leaves me in any posture but that of the penitent. Tho' you have been good enough to clothe me in "Bravest green", I find myself much more comfortable in my own less operatic habiliments and much more likely to face with fortitude and detachment the kind of music you bring to bear on me; – I have heard such strains before – but never! oh never! did I expect to find you in the position of band master – you my dear Will, whose flair and vision have been among the conditions which make life tolerable in this island. Your picture of me hurling bombs at mankind is lurid but inaccurate; – had I bombs to throw, mankind would not be my objective . . . I am not enough of a business man ever to hope to become "an asset to our country"; "purely and divinely inspired" as I may be by "the beauty and grandeur of the world"; I trust however that "our country" will prove something of an asset to me – otherwise why should I stop in it? . . . Differing with you, I think that the artist may *not* without shame join with his fellow men. His isolation indeed grows more complete as his art becomes more pure, nor is it the "ultimate usefulness" of the art which ever inspires him. His goal lies within himself – nor in his audacity is he deterred or terrified or bewildered for more than one sickly moment by the clamour and bustle and siren voices that come to him from without.'

in Augustus's future that, unlike Alice, he welcomed the presence of Dorelia. The visual inspiration which Augustus originally found in Ida had begun to fail; but, in 'the matchless Dorelia', Rothenstein later rhapsodized, 'in her dazzling beauty, now lyrical, now dramatic, John found constant inspiration. Who, indeed, could approach John in the interpretation of a woman's sensuous charm? No wonder fair ladies besieged his studio, and his person, too; for John had other magic than that of his brush; no one so irresistible as he, nor with such looks, such brains, such romantic and reckless daring and indifference to public opinion.'[3]

The winter show of the New English Art Club at the end of 1904 included two paintings of Dorelia. 'This year for the first time Mr John gives promise of becoming a painter,' Roger Fry wrote in the *Athenaeum*.

... at last he has seen where the logic of his views as a draughtsman should lead him ... he has already arrived at a control of his medium which astonishes one by comparison with the work of a year or two back ... One must go back to Alfred Stevens or Etty or the youthful Watts to find its like ... People will no doubt ... complain of his love of low life, just as they complain of Rubens's fat blondes; but in the one case as in the other they will have to bow to the mastery of power ... In modern life a thousand accidents may intervene to defraud an artist's talents of fruition, but if only fate and his temperament are not adverse, we hardly dare confess how high are the hopes of Mr John's future which his paintings this year have led us to form ...[4]

With supporters like Fry and Sickert, 'an amusing and curious character – amiable withal',* who came down to Matching Green to look at his drawings; with his income from the Chelsea Art School and from occasional exhibitions at the Carfax Gallery, he could afford to dispense with Rothenstein's favours. He had further strengthened his position when, late in

* 'Sickert is certainly an amusing and curious character – amiable withal. But it offended me to hear him cast off his old master so lightly and perfunctorily the other day – after all, Whistler wasn't a bad artist. Sickert probably never saw his real merits, but he is singularly inept at times, for instance having once and for all disposed of poor Whistler he goes on to discover Robert Fowler Esq! But anybody who has served on a Jury with him must know he is quite futile ...'

1904, he was elected as one of the original members of the Society of Twelve, a small group of British draughtsmen, etchers, wood-engravers and lithographers. The Honorary Secretary of this group was Muirhead Bone, who organized its exhibitions at Obachs in New Bond Street. For Augustus this was another valuable outlet for his work; for Rothenstein, who was also an original member, it was a new arena in which to display, like an inverted Iago, his apparently motiveless generosity. His methods of alienating everyone were on this occasion particularly adroit. To the Society of Twelve he proposed electing a thirteenth member, Lucien Pissarro, who, not being British, was ineligible for membership. It was a masterstroke. Inevitably, when Pissarro failed to gain the necessary votes, Will resigned. Augustus, who hated being dragged into these affairs, was persuaded to use his influence to bring him back, and this, somewhat improbably, he achieved. But no sooner was Will re-elected than he was at it again, returning undaunted and unavailing for three years in succession to the same charge, resigning again, and throwing the whole group into confusion. 'I was tenacious,' he later owned, 'and many letters passed between Bone and myself, until Pissarro was admitted.' By which time the society was so shaken with squabbles it did not long survive Will's quixotic triumph.

Five years after Rothenstein died, Augustus wrote an Appreciation of him in the catalogue to the Tate Gallery Memorial Exhibition.* In this he paid tribute to him as a man 'always intransigent and sometimes truculent', subject to a rare disease, 'madness of self-sacrifice', and bound therefore to make enemies. But he also called him 'a generous, candid and perspicacious soul', and while walking round the exhibition the day before it opened his eyes filled with tears and he admitted that he had often been unjust to his old friend. Yet if Will had come tripping through the door just then, Augustus would soon have strode out, infuriated by his admirer. Both, to an unusual degree, were at the mercy of their temperaments, and however much they wished it otherwise their temperaments did not mix. One of the strongest features of Augustus's char-

* Sir William Rothenstein Memorial Exhibition. Tate Gallery, 5 May– 4 June 1950.

acter, arising from his antipathy to Edwin John, was an allergy
to anyone who assumed the role of father-figure. Rothenstein,
who came from a very authoritarian family, was infatuated
with the father-figure, feeling a need both to promote others*
in that part, and to leapfrog into it himself – especially in
relation to his brother Albert whom he smothered with admoni-
tions concerning the high seriousness of art until he stopped
him painting altogether. Augustus would neither play the
parent, nor swallow the well-meaning reprimands. In a word
they were incompatible. Yet each still felt he needed the other.
Despite his success, a new strain had been placed on Augustus's
financial resources by the birth of Robin that autumn. By the
New Year, he was even more susceptible to Rothenstein's help.
For Dorelia was now pregnant.

2. KEEPING UP THE GAME

For several months Dorelia seems to have kept her pregnancy a
secret – an index probably that things were not going well.
Already, by the end of 1904, scenes of unimaginable violence
had broken out between them. Shortly after Robin's birth, Ida
had made one of her 'little journeys' up to London for a few
days, avoiding her friends, feeling strangely hysterical. 'I
simply drifted – from one omnibus to another – without aim
or intention,' she admitted to Alice (December 1904). Yet the
sudden flow of freedom, release from duty appeared to have
'done me worlds of good'. She returned to Matching Green
shortly before Christmas, to find that a double portrait Augustus
was painting of her and Dorelia had gone wrong; that, in her
absence, Augustus had altered the design so that there was no
room on the canvas for Ida at all. Instantly she was plunged,
beyond anything this incident seemed to warrant, into misery.
Her unhappiness was so acute she could not contain it, and
'there was a black storm'. What bit into her was the *unfairness*.
It symbolized what was increasingly becoming her position in
the household. After the storm was over and, rather to their
surprise, they were still afloat, Ida felt easier and 'there was a

* Henry Woods was one, Herbert Fisher another, and to some extent
Robert Bridges a third.

fair amount of sunlight'. But the tension in the atmosphere had not been dissipated and over the rest of this winter, almost daily, there were bitter quarrels. To these there seemed no logical consistency. One morning Augustus and Ida would take sides against Dorelia, and Augustus would volunteer that she could leave whenever she liked; but the following morning it was Ida who was invited to leave – 'pack up your luggage and take your brats with you!' Next day Augustus would suddenly announce that *he* was leaving for 'the Blue Danube'; after which it was once more the turn of Ida (who threatened to leave for Amsterdam); then again Dorelia. Finally: 'We are all thinking of going to the tropics.'

But no one left. That winter shut him away in Elm House like some prison. It was unendurable, and largely of his own making. He went roaring from room to room driving the children before him, like cattle.

But Ida's pain went deeper. She had invited Dorelia to Matching Green, because the two of them had a better hold on Augustus than Ida by herself would have had. But then she was consumed by dreadful jealousy and doubt. For Augustus made no attempt to conceal his infatuation for Dorelia; while to Ida he seemed blind. 'Have I lost my beauty altogether?' she once asked Dorelia. Sometimes she felt ill with depression, and in fact was subject to a succession of minor ailments that conspired to make her look in her own eyes more ugly still. 'I have *an eye*,' she proclaimed in a letter to the Rani. 'Dr says due to general weakness! it has a white sort of spot in it and runs green matter in the evening – which during the night effectually gums down the eyelids so that they have to be melted open! Isn't it too loathesome?' The *eye* was followed by a *throat* – 'dear me what next? Varicose veins probably.'

Doubt and jealousy infected everything. Since Dorelia had come, Maggie had taken herself off, disapproving of their immoral ways. It was natural that, to some extent, Dorelia should take her place. But Ida seldom allowed her to do anything for the children or in the house, partly, it seems, because Augustus was quick to criticize her for treating Dorelia like a servant. Nor could she bring herself to speak about Dorelia's unborn baby; and she began to hate herself for this apparent meanness of spirit. Envy of Dorelia; sexual jealousy; self-hatred for harbouring such passions; frustration, anger, disenchantment so buffeted her during these dark months that she emerged from the winter a changed person, her love for Augustus impaired, her attitude to herself and to Dorelia altered.

It was to the Rani she confessed most. 'I feel simply desperate,' one of her letters begins; and another: 'My depression is so great as to be almost exhilaration.' As the days went by this depression deepened dangerously. 'I feel utterly – like this ☐ – square as a box and mad as a lemon squeezer. What is the remedy?' she asked her friend. '. . . Do you know what it is to sit down and be bounced up again by what you sat on, and for that to happen *continuously* so that you can't sit *any-where*? Of course you do – I am now taking phenacetin to keep the furniture still.' Up till this moment she had preserved the detachment and energy of humour. But the effect of her phenacetin tablets appears to have been to reduce this detachment. For the first time she contemplated suicide. From a distance the Rani sometimes knew more of what was happening than Augustus and Dorelia, from whom Ida camouflaged her emotions. She did not complain, but explained: 'I live the life of a lady slavey. But I wouldn't change – because of Augustus – c'est un homme pour qui mourir – and literally sometimes I am inclined to kill myself – I don't seem exactly necessary.' She still admired him – but was no longer intimate with him. Also he was 'impossible', and so life itself had become impossible. 'I long for an understanding face,' she told the Rani. 'I am surrounded by cows and vulgarity here. Isn't it awful when even the desire to live forsakes one? I *cannot* just now, see any reason why I should. Yet I feel if I tide over this bad time, I shall be glad later on. What do you think?'

The Rani thought Ida must not be left alone – and wired Augustus who was then in London with Dorelia, to return home at once. She also wrote to Ida urging her to shake off ill-thoughts of death. 'As to suicide,' Ida responded,

why not? What a fuss about one life which is really not valuable! . . . Am I not a fool to make such a fuss about a thing I accepted, nay invited, but I have lost all my sense of reason or right. All that seems far over the sea and I can only hear sounds which don't seem

to matter. It's so funny not to *want* to be good. I never remember
to have felt it before. It is such a nice free feeling – animals must
be like that.

But the crisis lifted, and she confessed:

You know *I was very near* the laudanum bottle – somehow it
seemed the next thing. Like when you're tired you see an armchair
and sit down in it. Now you 'know all' I feel a sort of support – it
is funny. Others know, but no one has given me support in the right
place as you have. One held up an arm, another a leg, one told me
I wasn't tired and there was nothing the matter ... With you I have
something to *sit on*!

Though she showed little, and said nothing, Dorelia too was
not happy. She felt responsible for the bickering, the guilt, the
deep dissatisfaction that pervaded the house. There were times,
she knew, when Ida must have wished her at the bottom of
the sea. She began to think it had been a mistake coming to
Matching Green. Then, early in 1905, while Augustus was
painting her portrait, she told him categorically that once this
picture was finished she would leave. There was nothing to stop
her; she had no wish to stay. Augustus was furious. Their life
together, of which he had had such clear and splendid dreams,
was failing. It should have been so natural.

The turmoil of emotions following Robin's birth had worn
Ida out, and she had gone to stay with the Salamans at Oxford
for a short holiday. But her imagination still stalked the rooms
of Elm House, remembering and reliving her reactions to so
many sights and sounds she had never wanted to witness. Unlike Augustus, she could not persuade herself that none of it
had happened; she lingered over everything, imprisoning the
details in her mind. No matter what her intelligence advised,
she was affected biologically by this poison. In a remarkable
letter she now sent privately to Dorelia, very long, but written
hurriedly in pencil, she set down the conclusions she had come
to over the winter they had endured together.

... I tried not to be horrid – I know I am – I never hardly feel
generous now like I did at first – I suppose you feel this through
everything – I tried to be jolly – it is easy to be superficially jolly –

I hate to think I made you miserable but I know I have – Gus
blames me entirely for *everything* now – I daresay he's right – but
when I think of some things I feel I suffered too much – it was like
physical suffering it was so intense – like being burnt or something
– I can't feel I am entirely responsible for this horrid ending – it
was nature that was the enemy to our scheme. I have often wondered you have not gone away before – it has always been open to
you to go, and if you have been as unhappy as Gus says you should
have told me. I do not think it likely Gus and I can live together
after this – I want to separate – I feel sick at heart. At present I
hate you generally but I don't know if I really do. It is all impossible now and we are simply living in a convention you know – a
way of talking to each other which has no depth or heart. I should
like to know if it gives you a feeling of relief and flying away to
freedom to think of going ... I don't care what Gus thinks of me
now, of course he'd be wild at this letter. He seems centuries away.
He puts himself away. I think he's a mean and childish creature
besides being the fine old chap he is.

I came here in order to have the rest cure, and I am, but it makes
things seem worse than if one is occupied – but of course it will all
come all right in the end. I know you and Gus think I ought to
think of you as the sufferer, but I can't. You are free – the man you
love at present, loves you – you don't care for convention or what
people think – of course your future is perilous, but you love it.
You are a wanderer – you would hate safety and cages – why are
you to be pitied? It is only the ones who are bound who are to be
pitied – the slaves. It seems to me utterly misjudging the case to pity
you. You are living your life – you chose it – you did it because you
wanted to – didn't you? Do you regret it? I thought you were a
wild free bird who loved life in its glorious hardships. If I am to
think of you as a sad female who needs protection I must indeed
change my ideas – and yet Gus seems to think it is all your sorrow.
I do not understand. It was for your freedom and all you represented I envied you so. Because you meant to Gus all that lay outside the dull home, the unspeakable fireside, the gruesome dinner
table – that I became so hopeless – I was the chain – you were the
key to unlock it. This is what I have been made to feel ever since
you came. Gus will deny it but he denies many facts which are daily
occurrences – apparently denies them because they are true and he
wants to pretend they aren't. One feels what is, doesn't one? Nothing can change this fact – that you are the one outside who calls a
man to *apparent* freedom and wild rocks and wind and air – and I
am the one inside who says come to dinner, and who to live with is

apparent slavery. Neither Gus nor I are strong enough to find freedom in domesticity – though I know it is there.

You are the wild bird – fly away – as Gus says our life does not suit you. He will follow, never fear. There was never a poet could stay at home. Do not think I consider myself to be pitied either. I shudder when I think of those times, simply because it was pain ... It has robbed me of the tenderness I felt for you – but you can do without that – and I would do anything for you if you would ever ask me to – you still seem to belong to us. I.

What Ida had overlooked was that, during the first few months of 1905, Augustus had grown rather less attentive towards Dorelia. The wild bird was caged and, no longer on the wing, looked less attractive. For Augustus love was like fire, and he was drawn to it for much the same reasons that society feared it. Confined within the grate of marriage, it could smoulder safely, drearily, giving out little heat or light, endangering no one. But its smoke sidled up and choked him and its dying ashes were cheerless. He wanted to spread it about, let it take light where it would, to burn it wastefully if need be, to make a splendid conflagration – rather than sit fixed before its sinking embers. And now Dorelia, whom he had once likened to a flame, was diminished by this domestic chill. His poems dried up, his gaze unlocked itself. What he needed from Dorelia, and even more from Ida, was less of them. He needed distance to get his romantic view in focus. Except in bursts he was not a demonstrative man and felt impatient over homely displays of affection, so that Dorelia, confused by this sudden heating-and-cooling of emotion, grew defensive. Ida had hardened towards her; Augustus, at moments, appeared indifferent; neither of them ever mentioned her unborn baby, and this, from Augustus, hurt her. She confessed as much to Ida who, contradicting her avowed loss of tenderness, her general hatred for Dorelia, wrote back to reassure her:

My dear, men always seem indifferent about babies – that is, men of our sort. You must not think Gus is more so over yours than he was over mine. He never said anything about David except 'don't spill it'. They take us and leave us you know – it is nature. I thought he was rather solicitous about yours considering. Don't you believe he came over to Belgium because he was sorry for you. He is a

mean skunk to let you imagine such a thing. If ever a man was in
love, he was – and is now, only of course it's sunk down to the bottom again – a man doesn't keep stirred up for long – and because
we can't see it we're afraid it's not there – but never you fear.

Such consolation was even more applicable to Ida herself,
and was soon to form the basis of a new bond between the two
women. The catalyst which would help to bring this about was
Dorelia's baby. But, for the time being, it was just one more
factor confusing everything. Like a lake, swollen by the rivers
of their mixed feelings that ran into it from every direction,
their bewilderment rose. At times, it was the only thing the
three of them shared. Augustus's pronouncements certainly
sounded unmixed, but then they were so quick, and so quickly
succeeded by other pronouncements equally strong and utterly
different. Ida, for all her disenchantment, still harboured a deep
affection for him – 'he's a mean and childish creature besides
being the fine old chap he is' – still exonerated him, as Dorelia
was to do, because of his talent. Admiration and anger,
jealousy and tenderness for Dorelia curdled within her. Amid
all this turbulent eddying of emotion, it was up to Dorelia to
steer a firm course. But for her pregnancy, it seems likely that,
as before in Paris and Bruges, she would have slipped away,
without a word. Words were not her *métier* – words, explanations, all this indulgence, this lavish outpouring of passion, was
not in her line. She was, so she always insisted, 'a very ordinary
person', blessed with the vicarious gift of inspiring an artist –
and that artist need not be Augustus. Yet she had little talent
for making independent decisions: she excelled at making the
best of other people's, and when, as now, no one made any
decisions, she drifted without a compass. Hoping that Ida might
decide for her – for the two of them had never been so intimate
as by post – she wrote expressing her confusion. But when Ida
replied, it was faithfully to mirror this confusion back:

About your going or not *you* must decide – I should not have suggested it, but I believe you'd be happier to go ... Yes, to stay together seems impossible, only we know it isn't – I don't know what
to say. Only I feel so sure you'd be happier away ... I know I
should be jolly glad now if we all lived apart – or anyway if I did

with the children. Don't you think we might as well? – if it can be arranged.

I don't feel the same confidence in Gus I did, nor in myself.

Yes I know I always asked you to stay on, but still I don't see why you should have – you knew it was pride made me ask you, and because I wouldn't be instrumental in your going, having invited you – also because I didn't see how I could live with Gus alone again. All, all selfish reasons.

... I have often felt a pig not to talk to you more about the* baby, but I couldn't manage it. Also I always feel you *are not* like ordinary people and don't care for the things other people do. Gus says what I think of you is vulgar and insensible – I don't know – I know I'm always fighting for you to people outside, but probably what I tell them is quite untrue – and vulgar. I know I admire you immensely as I do a great river or a sunny day – or anything else great and natural and inevitable. But perhaps this is not you. I don't feel friendly or tender to you because you seem aloof and like some calm independent animal – you don't seem to need anything from me, or from any woman – and it seems unnatural and a condescension for you to do things for me. Added to all this is my jealousy. This is a true statement of why I am like I am to you ...

As to Gus he's a poet, and knows no more about actual life than a poet does. This is sometimes everything, when he's struck a spark to illumine the darkness, and sometimes nothing when he's looking at the moon. As to me, we all know I'm nothing but a rubbish heap with a few buried treasures which will all be tarnished by the time they come to light.

This mistake I make is considering Gus as a man instead of an artist-creature. I am so sorry for you, poor little thing, bottling yourself up about the baby. Shall we laugh at all this when we're 50? Maybe – but at 50 the passions are burnt low. It makes no difference to now does it?

But so much of Ida's analysis, it seemed to Dorelia, made 'no difference to now'. Dorelia needed to simplify things in order to act, not to investigate them more minutely. So far as action was concerned, there was only one new simplifying factor in Ida's letter: she was no longer asking Dorelia to stay. Dorelia therefore wrote back briefly and cryptically, stating that she would 'treat it as an everyday occurrence' and, she implied, just wander off. But Ida, fearing that Dorelia would vanish before

---

* Ida crossed out the word 'your' and substituted 'the'.

she got back, and that she would have to return to Elm House
alone with Augustus, replied urgently:

'Do not go till we all go, it would be so horrid ... I want to
go out from Matching Green all together and part at a cross
roads – don't you go before I get back unless you *want* to ...
We shall have dinner all together – no slipping away.'

As an inducement for Dorelia to remain until she arrived
back, Ida promised 'a bottle of olives ... 2 natural coloured
ostrich feathers and some lace!'

Dorelia was persuaded to wait. Augustus had by this time
gone up to yet another new studio* in London, and the two
women joined him there in the last week of March. This was to
be the crossroads, the parting of the ways. He did not know
that they had been corresponding, and even seems to have
imagined that the crisis of Dorelia's departure had passed: after
all, no one had said anything. What then happened was unexpected to everyone.

'We had a *terrific* flare up,' Ida afterwards (27 March 1905)
told Alice Rothenstein.

... and the ménage was on the point of being broken up, as
D[orelia] said she would not come back, because the only sane and
sensible thing for us to do was to live apart. But I persuaded her to,
for many reasons – and we settled solemnly to keep up the game till
summer. Lord, it was a murky time – most sulphurous – it gave me
a queer sort of impersonal enjoyment. After it we all three dined in
a restaurant (which is now a rare joy) and drank wine, and then
rode miles on the top of a bus, very gay and light hearted. Gus has
been a sweet mild creature since.

The 'many reasons' for Ida's change of attitude are nowhere
specified. Certainly it must have taken Dorelia by surprise and,
so it appears, was not completely understood even by Ida herself. The 'queer sort of impersonal enjoyment' she felt may have
been the exercise of power. Where Ida led, Augustus and
Dorelia followed, overtook – and the knowledge of this must
have afforded her some satisfaction.

But one of the 'many reasons' was Ida's dread of living alone
with Augustus. If she remained with him, as she might have to,

* He moved from No. 4 to No. 9 Garden Studios in Manresa Road, Chelsea,
during the spring of 1905.

then he would take other mistresses, and none of them was likely to match Dorelia. It had been Ida's love for Augustus that had drawn all three of them under the same roof; but it was her affection for Dorelia that now held them together.

So far as the baby was concerned, Ida made an attempt to interrupt her own silence, to offer some diffident flourish of help and participation. 'If you would like me to help you over the baby's birth or if you'd rather I kept out of the way – I meant to of course, but probably you'd much rather not. I'd like to and I'd hate to. I would rather come, probably only because I don't like to be away from things.'

In the event Ida was not with Dorelia when the baby was born – and nor was anyone else. Apart from the fact that it was a boy, eventually to be called Pyramus, and that he was born on bleakest Dartmoor, what happened, and exactly when, is difficult now to ascertain. For the occasion Dorelia assumed the name of 'Mrs Archibald McNeill', wife of a naval officer long at sea, while Augustus on his arrival posed as her solicitous brother. Later on their identities changed. 'I'm quite certain there is no penalty attached to having a bastard in the family,' Augustus wrote to reassure her from a Liverpool pub called 'The Duke'. 'So better register him as my son – provided of course it isn't published next morning in the Daily Mail or Express – as your family and my father no doubt take in one of those journals and such advertisement would be very disturbing. Have you stuck to that list of names? A sensation takes possession of me that Pyramus may be omitted or Alastir ... The parish of Lydford wasn't it?'*

Pyramus was born during late April or early May, in a caravan that Augustus was buying from Michel Salaman.† Dorelia

---

* Dorelia was deeply allergic to certificates, and in the end the birth was never registered. In a letter that would make any biographer's heart sink, Augustus reassured her: 'There is no need to register Pyramus at all – or anybody else – you *may* register him for *nothing* within 6 weeks but after that you pay so much to do so. But you are not bound to register him. Sampson told me this. He has not registered Honor. So you can write to the registrar and tell him you have decided not to.'

† Michel Salaman had started off his honeymoon in this caravan, and sold it in the spring of 1905 to Augustus for thirty pounds, paid punctiliously over a period of thirty years.

was alone (except for a large herd of cows), though not far
from an inn owned by a friendly landlord and his wife, Mr and
Mrs Hext, who saw to it that a doctor and nurse visited her.
Both Augustus and Ida had planned to be there, but Augustus
'wearing my new suit so of course I cannot think very com-
posedly' was fastened in committee work at Liverpool where
Charles Reilly 'keeps at me about his scheme of a school of 10
picked pupils and walls and ceilings to decorate – and £500 a
year'. Ida, meanwhile, was held at Matching Green in polite talk
with her mother who had decided to stay with her over Whit-
sun. In their absence they both sent down money, advice
on diet ('don't live on potatoes'), and plenty of unanswered
inquiries – though most of these seem to have been about the
Hexts.

As soon as the telegram – in Romany – arrived at Elm House
saying Dorelia's baby was born, Ida abandoned her mother and
hurried down, travelling through the night by train and arriving
at the camp by eleven next morning. She found Dorelia lying
along the caravan shelf which served for a bed, with her infant
– 'a boy of course,' – beside her. Augustus, 'suave and innocent
as ever', turned up the following day 'to kiss the little woman
who is giving up much for love of him', Ida wrote to the Rani.
'The babe is fine, a tawny colour – very contented on the whole
– we have to use a breast pump thing as her nipples are flat on
the breast.'

A few days later the children flocked down, shepherded by
Minger who had returned for the emergency, and they all
settled down to graze upon the moor for two months, Augustus
coming and going at intervals. 'It is adorable and terrible here,'
Ida wrote. 'We work and work from 6 or 7 till 9 and then are
so tired we cannot keep awake – at least I can't. Dorelia is
more lively – owing perhaps to an empty belly.' All day they
were out of doors, wearing the same clothes, going about barefoot, growing very sunburnt – 'at least the women and children
are – the Solitary Stag does not show it much' – and eating
double quantities of everything.

Ida seemed transformed in this new climate. It was not
simply the setting that had transformed her, but a change in
Augustus's attitude. 'Gus is a horrid beast,' she eulogized in an-

other letter to the Rani, 'and a lazy wretch and a sky blue
angel and an eagle of the ranges. He is (or acts) in love with
me for a change, it is so delightful – only he *is* lazy seemingly,
and when not painting lies reading or playing with a toy boat.
Then I think well how could he paint if he has to be on duty in
between – duty is so wearing and tearing and wasting and
consuming – only somehow it seems to build something up as
well which is so clever.' Ida hardly knew how to interpret this
change. At the very moment one might have expected him to
give his fullest attention to Dorelia, he had turned back to her.
She had lost confidence in herself to such an extent that she
could not believe he really loved her. But then what was
Augustus's love? 'We had one flare up – nearly 2,' she confided
to the Rani. '... owing to Gus's *strange* lack of susceptibility –
or possibly by some human working, his being too susceptible.
It is a difficult position for him. He is so afraid of making me
jealous I believe – and he was not wildly in love with her – nor
with me, only quite mildly. With the result that he appeared indifferent to her, while really feeling quite nice and tender, had
I not been there. But Lord – it *is* impossible but interesting and
truth-excavating.'

Despite the difficulties, and odd flare-ups, these were marvellous months for Ida. She adored living in the van. Yet even in
her topmost hours with Augustus, she was assailed by doubts
– thoughts of Dorelia, lying near by. Was *she* happy? Could
they both be happy at once? She was painfully aware of
Dorelia's mute disappointment. They would have to work out
something better than this.

For Augustus too this was a good spring. He was free to
work, and work went well. May was productive of many
etchings – romantic pieces entitled 'Out on the moor' and
'Pyramus and Thisbe' and there is an excellent study of Dartmoor ponies. Close by their camp was a spring for washing and
drinking, which the women and children used; while in the
evenings Augustus would stride off out of sight to the Hexts, sit
in their plain flagged kitchen and warm himself before the peat
fire. Back at the camp he erected a tent of poles and blankets
after the gypsy fashion and, like the Hexts, lighted peat fires –
but they were 'usually all smoke'. At night they would retreat

into the tent to sleep 'and you can hear the stream always and always'.

The rest of this summer Ida and Dorelia passed together at Matching Green, while Augustus roamed the country between his school in London and his prospective school in Liverpool. In his absence the two women grew extraordinarily close. The whole basis of their friendship was shifting. They managed the house, looked after the children, made each other clothes and in the evening played long games of chess which Ida always won.* Towards Augustus, it appeared, they now occupied very similar positions. 'A woman is either a wife or a mistress,' Ida had written to Dorelia.

If a wife, she has (that is, her position implies) perfect confidence in her husband and peace of mind – not being concerned about any other woman in relation to her husband. But she has ties and responsibility and is, more or less, a fixture – and not free. If a mistress she has no right to expect faithfulness, and must allow a man to come and go as he will without question – and must in consequence, if she loves him jealously, suffer doubt and not have peace of mind – *but* she has her own freedom too. Well here are you and I – we have neither the peace of mind of the wife nor the freedom (at least I haven't) of the mistress. We have the evils of both states for the one good, which belongs to both – a man's company. Is it worth it? Isn't it paying twice over for our boon?

Our only remedy is to both become mistresses, and so at any rate have the privileges of the mistress.

Of course I have the children and perhaps, being able to avail myself of the name of wife, I ought to do so, and live with G[us]. But I shall never consider myself as a wife – it is a mockery.

The need to free herself from being Augustus's wife ran very strong in Ida. She relinquished for a time the name Ida, calling herself Anne (or Ann),† the third of her Christian names; and then, to escape further from her past self (and much to the initial confusion of this biographer) signed some letters Susan.‡

* 'Except once,' Dorelia positively remembered.

† A number of Augustus's etchings of Ida call her Anne; for example, 'Anne with a feathered Hat' (C.D. 59) and 'Anne with a lace shawl' (C.D. 46).

‡ She also began renaming her friends – the Rani, for example, who became Lady Polly. 'Lady Polly is such a much more suitable name for you than Rani,' she explained. 'You are quite like lots of Lady Pollies in cheap novels . . . of course you will think it atrocious.'

Her previous reaction against Augustus was invaded by a mounting attraction to Dorelia which, in a curious way, drew her closer to Augustus again. Like Gwen, she was fascinated by Dorelia romantically. 'I know it makes you mad to hear me rave on about her [Dorelia],' she teased Alice Rothenstein. 'Dear old darling pure English Alice – I can't help loving these fantastics however abnormally their bosoms stick out. As to Dorelia – she is a little water lily* – and, as Gus says, she has the gift of beauty.'

Alone with Dorelia, Ida was as happy as she had been for a long time. Envy and jealousy melted into love: she disliked their being apart even for a few days. 'Darling D,' she wrote while on a short visit to her mother, 'Love from Anna to the prettiest little bitch in the world ... I was bitter cold last night in bed without your burning hot, not to say scalding, body next me – ... Yours jealously enviously and adoringly Ida Margaret Anne JOHN.'

To establish their new regime on a more solid foundation, Ida now came out with the proposal that she and Dorelia should leave England and, with their children, set up house together in Paris. Their lease of Elm House was up that autumn, so that in any case they would have to move. She had loved Paris while living there with the two Gwens, and the Parisian atmosphere, she was convinced, would accommodate their ménage far better than anywhere in England. It was a new start. They would find an inexpensive studio for Augustus who could divide his time making little journeys between London and Paris. They would all see one another – not too much of one another. Money would certainly be a difficulty, but Ida would practise the severest economies and earn money from modelling again: for she was determined to go and to take Dorelia with her. She had already written a letter to Augustus, telling him she wanted to live apart – not because she didn't love him but because on a day-after-day basis they were incompatible. And he, still 'a sweet mild creature', had not sought to excuse himself, but blamed his 'nervous aberrations' for all their

* In a letter to the Rani, Ida described Dorelia as 'the queen of all the water-lilies'. Her correspondence with both the Dowdalls is in the Liverpool City Libraries.

troubles. Although, in his politeness, he did not say so, he wanted something new as much as she did.

'Dearest of Gs,' she had replied.

With people one loves one does not suffer from 'nervous aberrations'. And peace with Dorelia would never bring stagnation, as you know well. For a time that spiritual fountain, at which I have drunk and which has kept me hopeful and faithful so many years, seems dried up – I think lately I have taxed it. I think it would be a good thing, when it can be arranged, for us all to live quite apart, anyway for a time. You will not mind that – you know we never did intend to live together. I shall have to sit – there's no other means of making money – mais tout cela s'arrangera.

Yes, there is in those letters [to Dorelia] something you never did and never will write for me – I think it is because I love you that I see it. And I think if I had known it before I should not have wanted us all to live together. It has been a straining of the materials for you and I ever to live together – it is nature for you and her.

I am quite sure you will visit me and I will receive you, oh my love ... By rights Dorelia is the wife and I the mistress. *Is it not so?* Arranged thus there would be no distress ... Tu me comprends comme toujours parce que tu es bon et doux. Aurevoir – we will see later on what can be arranged –

Ever yours Sue.

What Ida now arranged was a variation of this plan. The 'two mistresses' scheme at first sounded less flatteringly in Augustus's ears, but suited his nature far better – 'You know you will be happy alone,' she told him. They would not detail things mathematically between them, but simply see how everything sorted itself out. 'Dodo says we can't trouble about "turns",' she told Augustus. The centre of this French plan, there can be no doubt, was Ida and Dorelia's closeness. 'I do not know rightly whether Ardor and I love one another,' Ida explained to Augustus. 'We seem to be bound together by sterner bonds than those of love. I do not understand our relationship, but I feel it is necessary for us to live [together].' Whether or not they loved each other, they both, in their fashion, loved Augustus who, at one time or another, loved one of them or the other. With so much love surging between them surely it must be possible, if only accidentally, to hit upon some system that satisfied everyone? 'We *must* go,' she insisted. And as always her decision, plunging through the general ocean of indecision, was conclusive.

As always, too, everyone began by trying to make the best of anything new. Dorelia's silence was enthusiastic; while from the north of England Augustus exuded amiability. Unless some ungovernable mood was on him, Augustus felt nervous of opposing Ida. He had been genuinely shocked by her contemplated suicide, and all the more alarmed at having to be told this by the Rani. The news had sobered him. 'My imagination is getting more reasonable and joyous now,' he wrote, 'I wish to God it would be one thing or the other and stay! I have longings to sculp – it's been coming on for years. Paris! ! ! ... I hope to paint two orange girls if I can get them. Before actual life at any rate moods and vapours vanish. Suppose I came back to the Green soon ... I look to you, Ardor, to restrain Ann's economical fury.'

But Ida would not allow him back just then. His moods were so strong, so destructive, so – as he admitted – unreasonable that the best-laid schemes might be exploded by them. She wanted to fix everything unalterably before meeting such risks. She wrote off to hostels, made detailed travel arrangements, gave the servants notice, contracted to sell all the furniture they could not take with them. She did more: she told the Rothensteins. 'I expect you'll think we're mad,' she assured Alice (July 1905).

We are going to live all together for a time again – it is pleasanter really and much more economical. We shall only need one servant. We shall do the kids ourselves – meaning Dorelia and me. Her baby is weakly, but a dear little thing – not much trouble. Gus of course will live mostly in London ... I feel this living [in] Paris is inevitable, and though there are 10000 reasons in its favour I will not trouble you with them. The reason really is that we're going.

Alice's reaction, predictably, was of extreme horror. She wondered whether Ida had taken leave of her senses. Paris! So it had come to that – shipwreck! She ought to return to London at once. It was not fair to do anything else: not fair on Augustus.*

* 'Alice Rothenstein is simply indescribable,' Ida complained to the Rani. '. . . She and I always feel quite opposite things. Lord! She wants us to take a

Will appears to have agreed with Alice. Indeed it may have been his opposition to the Paris scheme that helped to reconcile Augustus to it. 'It is mostly on your account that they [Will and Alice] are so against Paris,' Ida told Augustus. 'Alice says "you do not quite realise what it means to a man!" Does she mean in the nights? Anyway I cannot, dare not, allow her ideas of comfort etc to influence me at all . . . If anything would keep me it would be Mother.'

Unlike Augustus and Dorelia, Ida was encumbered by her family. 'It *is* selfish,' she admitted to the Rani, 'because of my Mother – but I can't help it.' Mrs Nettleship's strong sensible middle-class standards were like chains to Ida's freedom, and she had resolved to cut them. For, since they had once more settled to 'keep up the game', nothing could be concealed from Mrs Nettleship any longer – even that Dorelia had a baby of her own. Their departure called for drastic explanations, and as soon as everything was organized Ida broke the news.

The attitudes of Alice Rothenstein and Mrs Nettleship, representing those of society and the family, were very close. They harmonized their horror. But to all Mrs Nettleship's objections Ida returned one answer : that it was unreasonable to blame her for not placing her mother's welfare above that of her husband, or even, for that matter, above her own. Since her daughter's marriage Mrs Nettleship had begun to get on quite well with Augustus. At least he was not so *absolutely awful* as she had once feared. He amused her. 'They get on quite well in a queer way,' Ida had noted with surprise. '. . . What an instinct many – I suppose most – people have for keeping "on good terms". It necessitates such careful walking – and fighting would be so much more amusing – or perhaps not.' Now she had a real fight on her hands. Mrs Nettleship blamed Augustus for his lack of control; and she blamed Ida for countenancing it; and finally she blamed both of them for exposing this wretched state of affairs to the public gaze. Why couldn't Dorelia live a little way off, if such things must be? Why make themseves a subject for squalid gossip – had Ida given no thought how it would affect

"cheap flat" in London! – as if there were such a thing possible to live in . . . I can't think of the tight smiling life which London means for me now. Were I alone it would be different.'

her sisters and all the family? To which Ida could only reply that this was one of the reasons they were leaving the country. It was a good debating point, but no more. Exasperated, Mrs Nettleship declared that it was against the law to have two wives, and that she intended to institute legal proceedings. But no one took this seriously, and for Augustus ('my only husband' as Ida ironically called him) it added to the comedy.

The struggle continued with daily remonstrances and cajolings even after they had reached Paris, right up to the end of the year. The pull that Mrs Nettleship exerted on Ida was ingenious. She called on her other two daughters, Ethel and Ursula, who now joined in with their own appeals. To them Ida was obliged to justify herself all over again. Her letters, extraordinary for their tone of forbearance injected with small shots of scepticism, are a good index to her state of mind over this crucial period.

'Dearest angel,' she wrote to Ursula (6 December 1905).

It is quite unnecessary for you to feel miserable about us unless of course your sense of morality is such that this ménage really shocks you. But as you say you know nothing of actual right and wrong in such a case I suppose you feel bad because you think I am unhappy or that Gus does not love me. I think I've got over the jealousy from which I suffered at first, and I now take the situation more as it should be taken ... I don't know how they told you, but I suppose from your letter they made it pretty awful. As a matter of fact it is not awful – simply living a little more genuinely than would otherwise be possible – that is to say accepting and trying to digest a fact instead of hiding it away and always having the horrid consciousness of its being there hidden ... I know in the end what we are doing will prove to be the best thing to have done. It is not always wisest to see most. Do you understand. Oh do you understand? I think really if you were left to yourself you would understand better than almost anyone – instinctively. If you were to begin to think of the reasons against our arrangement I should be afraid ... It is a beautiful life we live now, and I never have been so happy – but that does not prove it is right. It seems right for us – but is it for the outside world? doesn't charity begin at home? and at most we only make people uncomfortable ... do believe I no longer grudge Gus his love for Dorelia – I never did, but he was so much 'in love' that no interested woman could have remained calm beholding them. But now that is over, and though he loves her and always must it is different – and we live in common charity, accepting the facts of the case – and she, mind you, is a very wonderful person – a child of nature – calm and beautiful and patient – no littleness – an animal if you will, but as wholesome as one – a lovely forest animal. It is a queer world.'

These patient, understanding letters called forth no sympathy from her sisters, since both of them were under their mother's control. Ursula even added a strange new ammunition to the moral bombardment. If their ménage persisted, she wrote, then she would never be able to come and see Ida again and never be able to give herself in marriage. Ida's immorality was like a blight, she declared, withering her own chances of fruitfulness – and those of Ethel.

Ida was stunned by this accusation. She could not believe it, did not know even whether Ursula herself believed it. In the past Dorelia had always left the house when any of Ida's family came to stay, but if they would not continue to come then Ida would simply have to go and visit them. 'As you can't accept her [Dorelia], I suppose it would be better,' she wrote. 'It *is* a queer world ... As to your prospects of marriage – that is the one unsurmountable and unmeltable object – till you are both happily married! Do write again after thinking about it a bit – I mean the whole affair.'

Ursula needed no prompting from overseas. She wrote again the same week announcing that, since Ida was unrepentant, she, Ursula, renounced marriage and resolved to live a spinster all her life.* Ida's reply (12 December 1905), the final letter in this exchange, blended irony and tenderness but contained none of the guilt that the Nettleships had sought to implant within her.

Darling Urla,
I was very glad to have your letter – I do think it was a little heroic. You have no business to feel so heroic as to be willing to give up marriage – or to say 'what would it matter'. Of course it might not matter – but dearest I understand you when you say that – it is like my painting – there are some things that seem so important which really don't matter in the least. It has cost me much pain to give it up – but it doesn't matter! It is a part of the artist's

* She did, and so did Ethel.

life to do away with things that don't matter – but, as you say, it
is unlikely you would love a man who couldn't at any rate be made
to bear with our ménage. He needn't know us. You do astonish me
with your idea of uncleanliness – I can't appreciate that – I am
differently constructed. It seems to me so natural – and therefore
not unclean ... To me your thinking it so appears absurd and almost
incredible – as if you'll grow out of it. A bit too 'heroic'. As to
'doing away with the whole thing' you might as well say you'd
like to do away with the sea because of wrecks and drowning.

The long struggle seemed at an end. But throughout all Ida's
difficulties of persuading Augustus and of resisting the Nettleships, there had been one factor which helped to blunt opposition, and gave added point to the new ménage: she was pregnant again.

3. FROM A VIEW TO A BIRTH

'Don't you too sometimes have glimpses so large and beautiful
that life becomes immediately a jewel to prize instead of a
burden to be borne or got rid of?' Ida had once asked the Rani.
Regularly the darkness of her life was shot through by these
lyrical searchlights. Painting had been one; marriage another.
'What great work is accomplished without a hundred sordid
details?' she demanded shortly after David's birth. 'To have a
large family is now one of my ambitions.' But already, by the
time Caspar was born, her ambition, still heroically proclaimed,
sounded more hesitant. 'I should say more than I meant if I
launched into explanations of why I want a large family,' she
wrote again to the Rani. 'I know I do, but it may only be because there's nothing else to do, now that painting is not practicable – and I must create something.'

Babies, as a substitute for art, had failed even before Robin's
birth,* and for a time the surrogates had become cooking, gardening, even hens. Yet still the babies kept on coming, and her
disenchantment deepened: 'We are all such imposters!' she exclaimed. Then, in a letter from Paris (April 1906) to the Rani,
Ida revealed that she had made 'violent efforts to dislodge' her

* 'As soon as I am up,' she wrote to Mrs Sampson after Robin's birth, 'I am
going to climb an apple tree – and *never* have another baby.'

fourth child during early pregnancy. Her ambition to have a large family had died completely, to be replaced by something different.

Even before Dorelia had arrived at Matching Green, Ida had written to the Rani: 'It suddenly strikes me how perfectly divine it would be if you and I were living in Paris together. I can imagine going to the Louvre and then back to a small room over a restaurant or something ... think of all the salads, and the sun, and blue dresses, and waiters. And the smell of butter and cheese in the small streets.' Conceived as fantasy, her romance had come to life as fact. It represented for Ida an entirely new attitude to the world, and to her proper place in it. 'I should like to live on a mountainside and never speak to anybody – or in a copse with one companion,' she wrote. 'I think to live with a girl friend and have lovers would be almost perfect. Whatever are we all training for that we have to shape ourselves and compromise with things all our lives? It's eternally fitting a square peg into a round hole and squeezing up one's eyes to make it look a better fit.'[5]

The girl friend was different, but the philosophy was the same. In her experience, men were of two conditions: the artists and poets, who were wild, beyond good or evil, and with whom one fell in love; and the others who were mostly fools and who bored her. Both, as husbands, were equally impossible. With girls, however, she could develop an enduring closeness, even an intimacy. 'I wish I'd been a man,' she confessed to the Rani. 'I should then have felt at home in this infinitely simple world.' To some extent, it was the man's part she intended to play in Paris.

Augustus, Ida and Dorelia, with David and Caspar, Robin and Pyramus and Bobster their dog, set sail for France at the end of September 1905. The sea was rough, the boat rolled and Caspar (who was violently sick) declared in some alarm: 'We'd better go back.' Ida had taken two rooms for them all at a small hotel near the School of Medicine where specially reduced prices were offered to adults accompanied by children. 'The hotel people are very kind and the food lovely,' she assured her mother. 'Children *perfectly* well and Tony [David] especially cheerful ... [he] asked last evening if all the people in Paris talked nonsense.' Robin, however, seemed to pick up the new language astonishingly fast, and very soon was calling everyone *fou, sot* and *nigaud* in the most threatening manner.

From the hotel they at once set out to find a flat or some studio with living rooms, and very soon came across what they wanted, near the Luxembourg Gardens. By the middle of October they had moved into 63, Rue Monsieur le Prince, and engaged a maid, a young girl called Clara, to look after them while they looked after the children. 'She [Clara] cleans a room thoroughly in the twinkling of an eye,' Ida informed Alice, 'cooks exquisitely, is clean to a fault, and can remember the exact mixture and amount and time of food for 3 babies under 1 year.' This beauty for work and competence was, moreover, not physically beautiful. She seemed ideally suited to them.

Ida's fourth child, confidently referred to as Suzannah since its conception, was born on 27 November. As usual it was 'another beastly boy – a great coarse looking bull necked unpoetical unmusical commercial snoring blockhead', she told Mrs Sampson. Yet he was the weakest of all her children and for over a year lived only on bread, milk and grapes. 'He is called Quart Pot – as being a beery fourth,' Ida wrote to the Rani. '... After my experience I have quite given up the belief in a good god who gives us what we want. To think I must make trousers to the end of my days instead of the dainty skirt I long to sew ... he is a difficult child like David was ... Poor little unwelcome man.' Later called Jim, he finally settled down, after gigantic difficulties in registering his birth, to the name of Edwin.

The world was fuller than ever of babies, but in these new surroundings, and fortified by her new outlook on life, Ida was not submerged by them. 'I almost think it worth while to live in this little world of children,' she confessed to the Rani. 'We are sometimes convulsed with laughter.' Laughter was the new ingredient in her life. 'Things mostly get worse in this world,' she had once written to Mrs Sampson from Matching Green. Now, from Paris, she wrote to her : 'I've come to the conclusion that laughter is the chief reason for living ... One is not bound to be too serious.' This was her new discovery, and with it rose 'those bubbles inside' that made her feel 'like a champagne bottle that wants to be opened'.

Dorelia was the centre of this happiness. She looked after Ida during her confinement and after Edwin's birth; she coped with crises ranging from burst hot-water bottles to outbreaks of measles. Difficulties dwindled in her presence like weeds starved of nourishment: it seemed ridiculous to get worked up over such trivial affairs. 'My dear, you have no idea of the merits of Dorelia,' Ida confided to the Rani. 'Imagine me in bed, and she looking after the 4 others – good as gold – cheerful – patient – beautiful to look upon – ready to laugh at everything and nothing. She wheels out 2 in the pram, David and Caspar walking, daily, morning and evening – baths and dresses them – feeds them – smacks them.'

Their new life contained many aspects of the old, but the two mothers were better able to deal with it all. Ida, in particular, had regained her self-confidence. 'This place is divine,' she wrote to Mrs Sampson, 'and one can do everything – one feels so strong.' Outside the flat, their routine achieved the air of almost bourgeois respectability. 'Time was spent taking the children out in a pram to the Luxembourg Gardens and in the evenings sitting in cafés or sometimes going to concerts, art shows, museums,' Dorelia remembered. 'How attractive Paris was in those days, separate tables outside the cafés and discreet lighting.'[6] On the surface, life was 'fairly ordinary'. But those who called upon these bourgeois-bohemians at Rue Monsieur le Prince saw something fairly extraordinary. There was only one bed between the lot of them – the children sleeping in boxes on rollers, the babies in baskets – and almost no furniture. 'Here is a picture of our life in one of its rarely peaceful moments,' Ida wrote to Alice early in 1906.

Imagine a long room with bare boards – one long window looking on to a large courtyard and through an opening in the houses round to the sky and a distant white house, very lovely and glowing in the sun, and trees. In the room an alcove with a big wooden bed in it. At a writing table David doing 'lessons' – on the floor two baskets – Pyramus intent on a small piece of biscuit in one – Edwin intent on his own hands in another. Robin in a baby chair with some odd toy – Caspar on the ground with another. The quiet lasts about ten minutes at the outside. Unless they are asleep or out there is nearly always a howling or a grumbling from one or more – unless a romp is going on when the row is terrific.

Will Rothenstein, who visited their flat on his way to Venice shortly after they moved in, was deeply shocked by what he witnessed. The Johns seemed like a slum family with Augustus, a fearful figure, stamping about at its head. 'He is very impatient with his children and they are terribly afraid of him – the whole picture is rather a dark one,' he reported to Alice (19 October 1905). '... I felt terribly sad when I saw how the kiddies were brought up, though anyone may be considered richly endowed who has such a mother as Ida. Ours seem so clean and bright compared with them just now.'

But in Augustus's eyes it was the children who terrorized him. They needed money, prevented work; wanted to be entertained, got on his nerves. One day, amid the uproar, losing his temper with David and Robin, he slapped both their faces very hard: and was suddenly consumed with remorse. 'They will never really forget my having clouted them in the face like that,' he told Dorelia. 'I have never forgotten my father (whom I would give you for 2d) kicking me upstairs once – when I was almost Tony's age. Tell Tony I want him to enjoy himself – but to be somewhat useful and intelligent at the same time.' Since it was impossible to work in such an atmosphere, he returned after a fortnight to England.

Ida was now free to construct the sort of life of which she had dreamed. Liberated from the man-dominated world, she struggled to free herself so far as was practicable from the domination of children by eventually employing, in addition to Clara, another servant – 'which is why we can saunter out, and spend money to an outrageous extent ... and we come in again, after an absence of 4 hours and find absolute tranquillity – babies everywhere asleep in cots (literally 3) and 2 virtuous little boys looking out of [the] window at the rain from a house built of chairs – too sweet for words. Life is pleasant and exciting.'[7]

At last Ida seemed to have won that great luxury, time: time in which to read Balzac, Dostoievsky, Emerson and the *Daily Mail*; time to buy straw hats and cashmere shawls, to make

clothes for pictures which Gus would some day paint; time for
music – Beethoven and Chopin – of which she and Dorelia were
especially fond; time to fill with talk and dreaming and sensuous laziness. They were not gregarious, the two of them: it
was a secret life they led. 'It is, for 2 or 3 reasons, impossible to
know people well here – so I keep out of it altogether,' Ida explained to the Rani. '. . . And it is just as nice in many ways not
knowing people.' Not knowing people was part of Ida's detachment, her freedom. 'How delightful not to care what the neighbours think!' she had once exclaimed to Mrs Sampson at Matching Green. 'My utmost is to tell myself and others that I do not
care – I do all the time.' In Paris she no longer cared so much.
She had escaped from her family and the neighbours. She could
be as free as Dorelia now: she felt sure she could.

   Almost the only person they saw at all regularly was Gwen
John – 'always the same strange reserved creature', as Ida described her.[8] They would dine with her on eggs and spinach and
charcuterie in her room in the Rue St Placide where she lived
with her 'horrid' cat and where they would meet Miss Hart, an
ex-pupil of Augustus's at Liverpool 'who has attached herself
uncomfortably to Gwen'.[9] Gwen gave them three beautiful
pictures for their bare flat: also, Ida wrote to Augustus, 'there
was a head of Gwen by Rodin in the Salon'.

   To be free, to be as irresponsible as she could allow herself,
'as gay as possible under the circumstances' – this was Ida's
ambition. Dorelia took to wearing bright jerseys and short
velvet skirts; Ida cut her hair short but did not look *very* 'new
womanish, because it curls rather'. Then David, presumably
pursuing this fashion, cut off for the second time all his own
and all Caspar's hair so that they were almost unrecognizable
when Ida and Dorelia returned home. Released from the awful
presence of their father – the eyes that stared, the voice that
roared – the children had never been more boisterous. David
imitated wild beasts, bears and baboons; Caspar, in a sealskin
cap, danced fantastic jigs, turned somersaults, and boasted that
he was a king; Robin was constantly teased by David and
Caspar, constantly teasing the beautiful Pyramus; while Edwin,
a long thin cross creature, howled independently in toothless
rage. But though the 'acrobats' as Ida called them had never

been more lawless, yet 'I lose my temper less than of yore –
Dorelia never did lose hers. We take it in turns to take them
out.'

Other people's tempers were less shock-proof. After three
months, the neighbours, unable to endure the continuous wet
tumult any longer, demanded their eviction. 'We shall probably take a small house,' Ida wrote (12 January 1906) to Alice
who, in the confusion of breeding, had sent a bonnet for Pyramus, mistaking him for Ida's baby. Not living on a mountainside or in a copse, it seemed impossible to avoid compromise.
In January they began house-hunting once again in the quarter
beyond Rue de la Gaieté. After exploring 'millions of studios'
and a number of houses, they provisionally decided on 77 Rue
Dareau, where Augustus had already booked a studio for the
spring. 'The concierge of your studio showed us his rez de
chaussée,' Ida wrote to Augustus (January 1906). 'Do you think
it would do?' There were many advantages: a garden, and the
studio to sit in during the evenings, besides three living-rooms, a
kitchen and scullery; the rent was low, they could take it on a
quarterly basis, and they would still be near the Luxembourg
Gardens. Best of all 'your concierge says there can be no objection to the kids – he says he understands "qu'ils crient – qu'ils
ne chantent pas!" He was incredulous when I said the neighbours would object – and if they do they can go and we'll take
their places.' Both Ida and Dorelia were convinced they would
not 'find anything so good in every way as the R de C'. Their
only doubt was Augustus's attitude. 'If you dread having the
kids and all at your place – if you think it will interfere with
your work – we will find something else.' Ida's letter reached
Augustus (who had just sold a number of his pictures) in a
jovial mood and he urged them to take the *rez-de-chaussée* at
once. The clamour of the children seemed no great impediment
now he could no longer hear it. 'I trust the family is well to the
last unit,' he replied (February 1906). 'I hope to get everything
done in a week and then back again my hearties! ... Feed up
well ... and circulate the money.'

The new apartment would not be ready till April. Meanwhile
Ida proposed taking the three eldest children to the South of
France. Mrs Nettleship had not been well and after a month's

rest in London was to descend to Mentone for three weeks' re-
cruitment. To accompany her she invited Ursula and Ida with
her children. 'I cannot refuse can I?' Ida asked Augustus.

They set off early in March and spent the rest of the month
at 'a highly respectable hotel' crowded with British gentle-
women of 'comfortable means' attended by their very correct
daughters – prim little moppets in muslin. To Ida these people
seemed violently dull; but the beauty of the country was intense, the change in atmosphere total. 'Shall I tell you of the
mountains?' she inquired of the Rani (29 March 1906),

– their grand grey forms right upon the clouds, the lower parts
covered with trees – fir trees – and the lowest with Olive trees –
and up at the top streaks of snow in the cracks (as seen from here)
in reality masses of snow in the ravines and crevasses. And the town
of Mentone all built up in piles against the hill and the sea – good
old sea, ordinary old sea – spreading out at the bottom, with the
steam yachts of the rich and the fishing boats of the poor and the
eternal waves – so stupid and so graceful. And the mongrel population – selling in silly sounding French. They're really all Italian or
half Italian.

In the hotel garden among the tulips and the wallflowers, the
pansies, stocks and daffodils, Ida would sit reflecting on how
strange it all was and how happy she ought to have been, but
wasn't. Instead she fretted impatiently, sucked back into that
awful sense of exclusion that had devoured her at Matching
Green. Augustus had returned to Paris not long after she had
left for Mentone: she longed yet dreaded to be back. These
blue and cushioned hotel days were a terrible waste of time.
She felt like some general witnessing a battle swinging away
from him, powerless to do anything about it. Good manners
and an English sense of duty – all she had endeavoured to
escape from by coming to France – held her in check. If only
she had been a different kind of person! 'I crave to go to
school,' she told the Rani.

Not quite literally, but to set about learning from the beginning –
Lord, how I long to. The 3 kids are here, and very brave and jolly.
Edwin is left in the care of the loveliest girl in the world God damn
her. And I believe Gus has gone back to Paris to-day; so they'll all
have a good time together, especially as his Poet Friend [Wyndham]

Lewis is there, and great friends with Dorelia, and Gus has found a new creation called Egmont Hake whom he names 'a jewel of a man'. So they'll be so happy and perfect, damn and I am here biting my nails with rage and jealousy and *impotence*. Because if I were there it would spoil the fun don't you see? Oh why was I not born otherwise?

This was Ida's first set-back since coming to France. Early in April she returned to Paris, and she, Dorelia and the children moved into the Rue Dareau.* Again hope rose in her, hope for her resurrection into a new person and a new life. With Dorelia she re-papered the walls of their new home, and covered them with sketches, pictures, photographs: it was a fresh start, but again, inevitably, it had many ingredients of the old life. Augustus came and went; the children ('it makes them all look very interesting') all caught colds; and Dorelia ('it's her turn') 'is decidedly enceinte', Ida informed Augustus. 'It is depressing.'

4. CHANNEL CROSSING

'About to embark shortly for England,' Augustus had written to Wyndham Lewis, 'I would be encouraged to the adventure by a word from you as to your welfare and whereabouts.' No sooner had he settled on a studio for his work in Paris than the work began to flow in – but from London. 'We had £255 in about ten days ago, to my amazement,' Ida wrote to him from Paris. 'You do make a lot.'

Augustus had hoped by this time to sell the Chelsea Art School to a Mrs Flower, a cousin of Ida's, so that he would be free to live in Paris, but the negotiations grew more and more

---

* In a letter to his mother, Wyndham Lewis primly reported John's move 'with his families' to this new home. 'He [John] has an apartment, garden and studio all together, parterre. The elder of his children, that I hadn't seen for some time, are becoming excessively interesting personalities: but their conversation, although sparkling, is slightly disgusting to a person of pure mind – which is the more distressing since it be so edifying, to the more urgent exigencies of the intellect. – They call me a ''smutty thing'' and a ''booby'' because I insisted that a lion could climb up a beanstalk, nay, *had* done so, in my presence! – and one of the first wife's children has contracted the indelicate habit of spitting at one of the second wife's children while having his bath: – by the way, Miss MacNeill is producing another infant.'

involved and it was not until the summer of 1907 that they staggered to some finality. This delay and the infinite complications it entailed exasperated Augustus. 'I am sick of the school and tired of Orpen,' he wrote to Dorelia (1906). 'The lady can't buy the school just yet. I think of chucking it – even if I have to pay off debts.'

That he did continue teaching at Rossetti Studios was partly due to an exciting new development that had grown out of the school early that winter. This was the acquisition of a gallery next to the Chelsea Town Hall in the King's Road. Orpen, who largely financed it at the start, persuaded Knewstub to open the Chenil Gallery, as it was called – a small town house ideally suited, Knewstub saw, for accommodating his cultural dreams. Downstairs were two small rooms: one he converted into a 'shop' selling canvases, paints and all manner of artists' equipment; the other he established as an etching press room for artists wishing to prove or print from their own plates. Upstairs there were two exhibition rooms, one of which held a permanent collection of work by the regular platoon of Chenil painters: Ambrose and Mary McEvoy, David Muirhead, William Nicholson, Orpen, James Pryde and Augustus himself. At the back was a large studio which Augustus was often to use in the years to come.

The first one-man show at the new gallery, in May 1906, was of Augustus's etchings, which acted as a stimulus to great productivity over the early months of this year. 'I have to spend days seeing to my etchings,' he explained to the pregnant Dorelia as the weeks passed and still he did not return to Paris, '– a man has ordered a complete set. I find to my astonishment I have done about 100.' This man was Campbell Dodgson who, on 20 February 1906, had written to Will Rothenstein asking him to approach Augustus and find out whether he would let the British Museum have a selection of his etchings and drawings. Rothenstein put Dodgson directly in touch with Augustus and a week later they met. 'I went to see John yesterday and looked through his etchings which interest me very much,' Dodgson reported to Rothenstein (28 February 1906). 'He is quite willing to give me specimens of his drawings hesitating only on the grounds that he hopes to do better, and would not like us to have things that he hopes to tear up some years hence; but there is not much fear of such a fate befalling certain things that I saw yesterday and would like to secure. But [Sidney] Colvin will go himself in a few days and settle the matter.'*

This interest from the British Museum had quickly spread to the Chenil Gallery, where Knewstub at once set about arranging this first large show of Augustus's etchings. It was not an easy exercise. Once his first interest in the plates had passed, Augustus was often careless about their preservation, allowing them to be scratched, battered and corroded by verdigris. So when Knewstub stepped forward to rescue these plates from further harm, and superintend their printing and publication in a methodical manner, he found himself confronted by a vast salvage operation. He cleaned, he scraped, he searched and, as many plates as he could find (whether in sufficiently good condition to yield editions, or so badly treated that they had to be destroyed) he took over and numbered, together with all such early proofs as he could discover in Augustus's studio.

The Chenil exhibition was a great success, and many came to see his etchings.† In a letter to Charles Rutherston, Augustus

* Campbell Dodgson (1867–1948) had entered the Print Room of the British Museum in 1893, and in 1912 he succeeded Sir Sidney Colvin as Keeper of Prints and Drawings. He became particularly well known as an expert on early German art and a collector of nineteenth-century prints and drawings. His catalogue of Augustus's etchings appeared in 1920. He married in 1913 the artist Frances Catharine Spooner, daughter of W. A. Spooner, of Spoonerism fame.

† The Chenil exhibition catalogue lists eighty-two etchings, the number of prints varying but never exceeding twenty-four. A significant quantity of these plates, Dodgson noted, mostly nudes, were etched 'somewhat hurriedly and in several cases without genuine inspiration', in order to be ready for the show. About fifteen were produced in the early months of this year, sometimes more than one plate being etched on the same day. It seems possible, too, that several numbers were added to the exhibition after the catalogue was printed: about seven are dated precisely (though possibly without accuracy) as having been done in the last week of May; while three excellent portraits of Stephen Grainger which Augustus appears to have completed that spring are not listed. Among those shown, some of the portraits, and a few of the groups in a landscape setting, are striking. Others in which the contorted forms are hastily drawn have little meaning to express. Many of the numbers in the exhibition were a frank act of homage to Rembrandt, and one of them was actually a translation on to copper of a Rembrandt pen-and-ink drawing.

wrote: 'I am of course very pleased with the results of the Chenil show, which far exceeded what I expected.' His enthusiasm, springing to some extent from an artificial stimulus, lasted another three years during which he continued to use needle and copper, though on a gradually diminishing scale. After 1910 he produced, over the rest of his career, only about half-a-dozen more etchings – a small group of portrait studies of a girl's head; a head of John Hope-Johnstone recovering from measles; and two self-portraits. His later work shows a real advance from the sometimes rather laboured earlier efforts, with their ample use of dry-point, to the pure etched line of his most successful plates. But the medium did not suit his temperament: it was too slow, too small. The paraphernalia of needles and plates, of nitric and sulphuric acid, which had captured his interest at first, finally bored him to extinction.

Augustus's treatment of his copperplates was similar to that of his friendships. He liked to keep an army of acquaintances in reserve, upon any number of which he could call when the mood was on him. He wanted fair-weather friends; he wanted them to be, like some fire brigade, in a permanent state of readiness for his calls; and he enjoyed summoning them fitfully. Among the etchings at the Chenil Gallery were several portraits of friends who had already sped out of his life: Benjamin Evans who had shot down the drain; Ursula Tyrwhitt and Esther Cerutti who had been outshone by later models. And there were others, too, of whom he saw only little now. Michel Salaman who had graduated from an art-student into a fox-hunting squire; 'little Albert' already partially eclipsed by little Will; the monkey-like Orpen who had grown attached to a gorilla in the Dublin zoo – 'perhaps the only serious love affair in his life';[10] and Conder who in June 1906 had become so seriously ill he was forced to relinquish painting.

There were two motives behind all Augustus's friendships: inspiration and entertainment. Either they stimulated him as an artist, or they induced self-forgetfulness. But none of them could live up to his veering idealism. He knew this himself, and mocked himself for it. 'I am in love with a new man,' he once (16 March 1906) told Dorelia, 'Egmont Hake – a bright gem!'

Such mysterious gems – and there were many of them – would glitter for a day, grow dull and be lost for ever. His most consistent relationships were, in some sense, the most tenuous – those which were held together by humour or, more simply, cemented by long periods of absence. He welcomed the retreating back, the cheerful goodbye, the disappearing companion whose tactful vanishing trick saved in the nick of time their comradeship from the cancerous contempt that grew with familiarity. He relished people such as John Sampson whom he could abandon 'in the Euston Road while he was immobilized under the hands of a shoe-black', and then meet again, their feelings charged with nostalgia; or even Will Rothenstein, oscillating violently between romanticism and austere morality, on whom, in spite of everything, Augustus still depended for financial support; and Gwen too, for whom, though she could not work under her brother's shadow, he continued to feel an admiration shot through with exasperated concern.

What Gwen had felt about Augustus, others, such as Wyndham Lewis, were beginning to discover for themselves. 'I want also to do some painting very badly, and can't do so near John,' Lewis complained to his mother (1906). '... near John I can never paint, since his artistic personality is just too strong, and he much more developed, naturally, and this frustrates any effort.'[11] Because of this frustration, Lewis turned to his writing, being known by Augustus as 'the Poet'. Now that Augustus was jostling between Paris and London, he was able to see far more of Lewis, then on the move between England, France and Germany while brewing up his Dostoyevsky cocktail, *Tarr*. Their relationship over-ripened rapidly. Augustus's romantic admiration for his disciple soon began to evaporate and what was left mingled curiously with lumps of more indigestible matter. They would go off to night-clubs together, or sit drinking and talking at a café in the Rue Dareau* recommended by Sickert for its excellent *sauerkraut*. 'Not that I find him absolutely indispensable,' Augustus conceded, 'but at times I love to talk with him about Shelley or somebody.'[12] Lewis himself preferred to talk about Apaches and 'to frighten young people' with tales of them. But what chiefly amused Augustus were Lewis's extra-

* Brasserie Dumesnil Frères, 32 Rue Dareau.

ordinarily ineffectual romances. These formed part of his
material for *Tarr* whose theme became sex and the artist, dis-
placing the stated one of the hero's spiritual progress. If the
artist, Lewis seems to argue, finds much in his work that other
men seek in women, then it follows that he must be particularly discriminating in his love-affairs, scrupulously avoid sentimentality and all other false trails that lead him away from
reality It was a theme nicely attuned to Augustus's own predicament, and almost certainly it formed part of their regular
conversations. Augustus understood very well the conflict between artistic integrity and appetite for life, knew that overlapping territory between inspiration and gratification. 'I am
like a noble, untaught and untainted savage who, embracing
with fearful enthusiasm the newly arrived Bottle, Bible and
Whore of civilization, contracts at once with horrible violence
their apoplectic corollary, the Paralysis, the Hypocrisy and the
Pox ... So far I have been marvellously immune.'

Lewis's immunity, however, appeared even stronger. Prudence, suspicion and an aggressive shyness ringed him about
like some fortress from which he seldom escaped. His love-
affairs seemed to be no more than word-affairs, though the
words themselves were bold enough. 'Lewis announced last
night that he was *loved*!' Augustus reported to Alick Schepeler.

At last! It seems he had observed a demoiselle in a restaurant
who whenever he regarded her sucked her cheeks in slightly and
looked embarrassed. The glorious fact was patent then – l'amour!
He means to follow this up like a bloodhound. In the meanwhile
however he has gone to Rouen for a week to see his mother, which
in my opinion is not good generalship. He has a delightful notion –
I am to get a set of young ladies during the summer as pupils and of
course he will figure in the company and possibly be able to make
love to one of them.

But when not in the vein to be amused by Lewis's eccentricities, Augustus would quickly get needled. It was almost as
if his own romanticism was being caricatured. 'The poet irri-
tates me,' he admitted, 'he is always asking for petits suisses
which are unheard of in this country and his prudence is
boundless. What a mistake it is to have a friend – or, having
one, ever to see him.'

Even so, Augustus could not be alone. Without an audience he lost confidence, began to disintegrate. This was why the luminous caverns of the pubs and cafés attracted him. One sauntered in as if on the spur of the moment, chose one's companion for an hour or two, a Juliet for a night: then it was over. Such encounters were marvellously invigorating. There was no long shadow of loyalty cast upon one, no tedious hangover of personal relationships to endure. If friends were God's apology for families, it followed they should be as unlike one's own family as possible. But perfection could not be found in a single man, for perfection must suit all weathers. 'I cannot find my man,' he told Alick Schepeler, '– hence I have to piece him together out of half a dozen – as best I can.'

Upon the construction of this composite friend Augustus spent much haphazard energy. A little less McEvoy, for example, was quickly balanced by more Epstein and the introduction of a new artist into his life, Henry Lamb. In his correspondence, Augustus sometimes makes fun of Epstein. 'Epstein called yesterday and I went back with him to see his figure which is nearly done,' Augustus wrote to Dorelia (1907). 'It is a monstrous thing – but of course it has its merits – he has now a baby to do. The scotch girl [Margaret Dunlop] was there – she is the one who poses for the mother – he might at least have got a real mother for his "Maternity". He is going about borrowing babies. He suggested sending the group to the N.E.A.C.! ! Imagine Tonks' horror and Steer's stupefaction!'

Augustus did a number of etchings of Epstein. Most revealing of all is a red pencil drawing which Epstein himself much liked. By using the point of a very hard pencil Augustus gives this portrait a taut quality, a tightness of face and mouth indicating both intellect and a sort of temperamental force. The rhetorical pose of the head bends a little to the romantic conception of genius, but the drawing[13] also emphasizes the 'closed to criticism' nature of Epstein's personality.

He had, of course, much criticism to close his mind to. The 'monstrous thing' Epstein was working on in his studio in Cheyne Walk early in 1907 was almost certainly one of the eighteen figures, representing man and woman in their various stages between birth and death, that were to embellish the new

Medical Association Building in the Strand. These figures, mostly nudes, caused a whirlwind of moral outrage when, in the spring of 1908, they began to be thrust upon the public gaze. 'They are a form of statuary which no careful father would wish his daughter, or no discriminating young man, his fiancée, to see,' one newsaper informed its readers.[14] Other experts, including clergymen, policemen, dustmen and the secretary of the Vigilance Society were soon adding their voices to this hymn of vituperation. The statues were called 'rude' and vulgar; they exerted a 'demoralizing tendency' and were said to constitute 'a gross offence'. They would 'convert London into a Fiji Island'. Who could doubt that these objects must surely become a focus for unwholesome talk, the meeting place for all the unchaste in the land? Many artists defended Epstein, but in his autobiography he does not mention Augustus who privately did much to assist him,* and who saw clearly that artistic support was irrele-

* For example, he wrote to the poet Arthur Symons: 'Perhaps you may not have seen or heard of the sculptured figures on a new building in the Strand by a man called Jacob Epstein, which are in imminent danger of being pulled down or mutilated at the instigation of the "National Vigilance Society" of sexual maniacs, supported by tradesmen in the vicinity – and the police. These decorations seem to me to be the *only* decent attempt at monumental sculpture of which the streets of London can boast. A few of the nude male figures however have been provided by the artist with the indispensable apparatus of generation, without any attempt having been made to disguise, conceal, or minimise the features in question. This flagrant indelicacy has naturally infuriated our susceptible citizens to such an extent that without the most sturdy exertions of the intelligent lovers of Art and truth, the figures will be demolished.

'So after having been *sweated* physically and morally outraged for some 14 months by commercial close fistedness and prurient timidity our artist is left now penniless and inarticulate to face the last ignominy. Being a foreigner Epstein is quite innocent of the parochial sentiment which is the breath of our metropolis, he has merely contrived to inform his figures with a World-Passion to which we are strangers over here. If you would view the works, or those which are visible, for the hoardings are not yet all down, I feel sure you will share some of my feelings and will do something in defence of Epstein and Art itself – Yrs Augustus E. John.'

To Dorelia, Augustus wrote: 'Epstein wrote to me in despair, his figures are being threatened by the police! It is a monstrous thing . . . I sent him a fiver on account of Rom[illy]'s portrait and have written to a few people. On comparing his figures standing in their austere nakedness above with the squalid horde that pullulate beneath, leering and vituperative, one is in no doubt *which* merit condemnation, sequestration and dismemberment. I stand much in need of air air air – and you you you!'

vant to moral indignation and would never impress the public. 'Epstein's work must be defended by recognised moral experts,' he wrote to Robert Ross.

The Art question is not raised. Of course they would stand the *moral* test as triumphantly as the artistic, or even more if possible. Do you know of an intelligent *Bishop* for example? To-morrow there is a meeting to decide whether the figures are to be destroyed or not. Much the best figures are behind the hoarding which they *refuse* to take down. Meanwhile Epstein is in debt and unable to pay the workmen.

Augustus's advice was quickly taken up, and the Bishop of Stepney, Cosmo Gordon Lang, later Archbishop of Canterbury, was persuaded to mount the ladders to the scaffolding, from where he inspected the figures very intimately and, on descending, declared himself positively unshocked. His imperturbability did much to reassure the British public and soothe the Council of the British Medical Association which instructed the work to proceed.

Though he admired Epstein's sculpture, Augustus was impatient with his personality. This milk-drinker from America excelled in blowing his own trumpet.* 'I hope Epstein will find his wife a powerful reinforcement in his studio,' Augustus wrote to Will Rothenstein (19 September 1906) on learning of his engagement to Margaret Dunlop. 'Perhaps she will coax him out of some of his unduly democratic habits.' As proud and touchy as Augustus was truculent, Epstein appeared determined to attract hostility. Augustus was well able to accommodate him here, and their friendship was often on the rocks.

But in these early days they got on well. Epstein needed encouragement; Augustus could afford to give it. Often they

* But he was always a good subject for anecdotes. 'I don't believe in the modern ideal of living in a cow-shed and puddling clay with somebody else's wife concealed in a soap-box, like our friend Epstein,' Augustus wrote to Alick Schepeler (summer 1906). A few days later he amended this in an explanatory passage: 'The soap-box or packing-can is well known in Bohemia as a substitute for a bed – and if turned over might very well be used to conceal somebody else's wife, provided she were not too fat – I was wrong however to provide Epstein with this piece of furniture. I forgot that he used to keep somebody else's wife in his *dustbin* – I hear recently that he has married her – so it's all right.'

would be joined by McEvoy in whose gentle company neither felt disposed to quarrel. Epstein used to drop round to the Chelsea Art School occasionally, and there would be black periods of silence as he and Augustus leant against one of its walls: then a remark from Epstein – 'At least you will admit that Wagner was a heaven-storming genius.' And from Augustus an ambivalent grunt.

A witness to these exchanges, and much impressed by them, was Henry Lamb. Lamb had recently thrown up his medical studies in Manchester and, in a desperate bid to become an artist, turned up in London. Here he at once started at the Chelsea Art School, and, having nowhere to live, used to sleep there on the model's throne. On coming in each night he would discover a fresh cartoon done by Augustus during the evening – large works of many almost life-size figures, which dazzled him. Sometimes Augustus would discuss one of them with him. 'I think of taking out that figure and introducing a waterfall,' he would say. Lamb felt himself to be in the heavy atmosphere of genius. The very silence was saturated with this property, and Lamb soon began to affect it himself as part of the artist's equipment – a sort of cloak. As a draughtsman he modelled himself on Augustus's work, and in his style and manner of life, his very looks, he schooled himself to emulate Augustus's example. Inevitably, Augustus was flattered by this handsome, gifted follower. What could be more proper than a young man wishing to act apprentice to him? It was a concept he had always understood and wanted to benefit by himself. He responded generously. 'I hope you are doing designs lightheartedly,' he wrote (24 October 1906) '– What is so becoming as cheerfulness and a light heart? I think the old masters are apt to presume upon our reverence sometimes – one is always at a disadvantage in the society of the illustrious dead – perhaps it would be high time to bid them a reverent but cheerful adieu! since we have invented umbrellas let us use them – as ornaments at least.'

Lamb was not slow to respond to this message and at once elected Augustus as a new master among the illustrious living. Augustus was delighted. Confidence swelled within him – confidence, but not conceit. If people believed in him, he believed in

himself. He needed other people's faith to fortify his own will.
'Your letter thrills me somewhat,' he replied to Lamb (5
November 1906).

I am not quite a Master – yet. I keep forgetting myself often. But
I am learning loyalty. We must have no rivals – and no fickleness. I
feel ashamed to go to sleep sometimes. I am learning to value my
own loves and fancies and thought above all others. But Life has
an infernal narcotic side to it – and one is caught napping and
philandering – – – alas! alas! if one had some demon to whip one!
I hardly believed you had faith in my possibilities – in my will. I
am so glad.

No friendship yet had begun on such a lofty note – none
would lead to such complications or remain so long and with
such embarrassment a thorn in the flesh of both artists.

'I think I shall be a supernaturalist in Paris, and in London a
naturalist,' Augustus wrote to Alick Schepeler. In London he
had found work and a few people to inspire him; in Paris entertainment and the promise of inspiration to come. Something of
the awe and wonder that had possessed him when he first went
up to the Slade now re-entered his life. Paris he described as 'a
queen of cities' and 'so beautiful – London can't possibly be so
nice'.[15] No atmosphere, surely, was ever more favourable to the
artist. On the terraces of the Nouvelle Athènes or the Rat Mort
it was not difficult to conjure up the ghosts of Manet, Camille
Pissarro, Renoir, Cézanne, Degas – figures from the last enchanted epoch, laughing and arguing across the marble tables.
But the real heart of Paris lay further back : it belonged to the
Middle Ages. Malodorous, loud with bells, its architecture full
of passion, of the cruelty and splendour of ancient superstition,
Paris seemed more dangerous than the carbolic climate of
London. It was closer to Nature, to the earth itself and man's
strange evolution from that earth. The murmur of the boule-
vards, deep and vibrant; the view of the city seen at dusk from
Sacré Cœur as the light began to pinpoint between the emana-
tions of a thousand chimneys; the landscape of the Île de
France with its opulent green as if depicted through medieval
windows : such beauty seized him with a kind of anguish, confronted him with unanswerable questions : 'What will become
of us? What could all this mean?'

For hours he would sit in the Rue de la Gaieté, watching, talking, drinking, listening to the infernal din of a mechanical orchestra, and not wishing to go home – not going home. There was more dreaming of painting than pictures painted.

'They are playing in this café just now – so I expect I shall get rhetorical presently,' he declared in a letter to Alick Schepeler. 'Yes, I shall paint yet; it is more like fighting than anything else for me now – it will be triumphant though ... Civilization getting in my way and making a dreary hash of things – and wasting time. I'd like to be kept by a prince. It's not safe to let me loose about the place in this way – and then send me bills to pay.'

The heady cosmopolitan world of Montparnasse intoxicated him – yet it was a literary world he had very largely entered. The talk was of Huysmans and Baudelaire, of Turgenev and Nietzsche and the newest Dostoievsky in bad French. Almost the only painter, living or dead, who is mentioned in his correspondence is Puvis de Chavannes. His Parisian friends were mostly writers, in particular the circle that gathered round the monocled, top-hatted figure of Jean Moréas at the Closerie des Lilas and which included Apollinaire, Colette, Paul Fort the wandering poet who, with his brother Robert, ran the journal *Vers et Prose*, and André Salmon the literary spokesman of *Les Jeunes*.

Of all this group his most valued friend was Maurice Cremnitz. Late at night, after the group had dispersed from the Closerie des Lilas, Cremnitz would lead Augustus off to louche, out-of-the-way areas of Paris. He introduced him to a Swedish lady famous for her exercises – 'yes, she was not to be sneezed at, as vulgar people say', Augustus conceded, 'her crystallization would take the form of the purest amour physique I thought with no corrupting element of physical passion'.[16] At other times they would explore the old quarters of the city, 'visiting the wine shops where the *vin blanc* was good – and cheap';[17] and they would go to the little Place du Tertre, to the Moulin de la Galette and the Bal Tabarin where such delightful songs as 'Petite Miette' and 'Viens pou-poule' were all the rage and where Cremnitz would sing, in amazing Cockney English, 'Last night down our alley came a toff.' 'I observed the true gaieté française last night,' Augustus wrote after his first visit there with Cremnitz, 'a little femme de mauvaise vie had a new song she kept singing and teaching everybody else – no one could have been more innocently happy – and the song – ! !'[18]

Innocent, too, at least in name,* was an obscure subterranean *bouge* near Les Halles into which they descended one night, 'and, I must admit, drank great quantities of white wine. A drunken poet joined us there and declaimed Verlaine and his own verses at great length. As he had the impudence to take exception to my style of Beauty I said "Voulez vous venez battre avec moi, Monsieur l'Antichrist?" He got up and, having put himself into a pugnacious attitude, sat down again. Afterwards he was very affectionate, informing me that he and I had fought side by side in the Crimea – frères d'armes!' This robust shadow-boxing was marvellously congenial to Augustus. Paris seemed to unite those two aspects of his personality that could, in his work and his attitude to people, so easily diminish each other : a romanticism that was idealistic, nostalgic; and his wry, rather satirical humour.

So, for a while, Paris diverted him. 'I've been damnably lazy this summer,' he admitted to Will Rothenstein (19 September 1906), 'but am happily unrepentant. I fancy idleness ends by bearing [more] rare fruit than industry. I started by being industrious and lost all self-respect – but by now have recovered some dignity and comfort by dint of listening to the most private intimations of the Soul and contemning all busy-body thoughts that come buzzing and fussing and messing in one's brain.'

All his life Augustus lived under the influence of an impossible ideal. What he sought in men – inspiration and entertainment – he also looked for in women, though in a different form. Men inspired him by reason of the poetry in them, by what they achieved, and many of his finest portraits are of writers and artists : Hardy, Wyndham Lewis, William Nicholson, Shaw, Matthew Smith, Dylan Thomas, Yeats. Other men – Trelawney Dayrell Reed and Chaloner Dowdall – entertained him by their eccentricities. The inspiration of women sprang

* Caveau des Innocents.

from the belief that they were closer to Nature and to the mystery of birth; and this he celebrated most lyrically in a number of small glowing panels depicting young mothers and children as part of a bare landscape. But women also entertained him simply and obviously by their sexuality; for sex, which had so worried him while he was an adolescent, had now become 'the greatest joke in the world':[19] and Augustus loved a joke.

His ideal was impossible because it was unrealizable in any permanent or material condition into which he tried to transform it. As symbols of the miracle of life, women must be seen and not heard, must be inviolate: they must guard their secret well, convey it by the slow rhythm of their movements, their quiet. Yet the miracle of life, of which women were the custodians, depended upon the joke of sex. Inspiration and entertainment were oddly harnessed, often pulling in different directions, sometimes failing to drag him past sentimentality.

No one, perhaps, catches his attitude to women so well as a new woman he had recently met in London. Her name was Alick Schepeler and, next to Dorelia herself, she became for a few years his finest model. But as the embodiment of Augustus's romantic ideal, she was almost a parody. No one, it seemed, knew who she was. 'Are you a Pole?' Augustus demanded – but in reply she could only smile secretly, without meaning. In *Chiaroscuro* he refers to her – 'Alick Schepeler, to whose strange charm I had bowed' – only once, and declares her to have been 'of Slavonic origin', adding that she 'illustrated in herself the paradox of Polish pride united to Russian abandon'. By naturalization she was in fact British, her mother Sarah Briggs being Irish and her father, John Daniel Schepeler, German. The facts of her life were unusual, though not extraordinary. Her real name was Alexandra, she was an only child and had been born on 10 March 1882 at Skrygalof, near Minsk in Russia, where John Schepeler worked as an industrialist. Her father died when she was five and she was taken by her mother to live in Poland. Here Sarah Schepeler found employment with a Polish family as 'English' governess, while Alexandra was boarded near by with a Mrs Bloch and her daughter Frieda. After some ten years in Poland Sarah Schepeler died, and not long afterwards Alexandra, who had by now become part of the Bloch family, travelled to London with Frieda. The two girls, who were about the same age and had become great friends, lived together at 29 Stanley Gardens in Chelsea. Frieda attended the Slade but Alexandra, who appeared to have no promise of talent in any direction whatever, took a course in typing and went to work as a secretary for the *Illustrated London News*. In her letters to Augustus she hints at leaving this paper and taking on grander work. In fact she never left, nor sought promotion. Her unsettled upbringing seemed to have implanted within her an allergy to change, even change for the better. She lived in Chelsea and typed at the *Illustrated London News* for over fifty years.

In the extent of her ordinariness lay her single extraordinary quality. Her mind was a polished vacuum where the imagination of the artist was free to roam unimpeded. She had nothing to hide, but from the presence of this nothing arose a mystery none could penetrate. In her relationships with men, this was her asset. She had no cards to play, yet her hand seemed full of trumps which she trembled on the verge of revealing. Her talk was of her cat, her clothes and her office. She was unbelievably uninteresting – and no man could quite believe it. Augustus, in his anxiety to avoid *intellectual* passion, could scarcely have chosen anyone with finer qualifications.

Yet she lived for passion. Love – physical and romantic love – was her escape from a destiny of unimaginable dullness, and in this she was very intense. Rootless, she had nevertheless come in contact with a kind of reality that Victorian and Edwardian young ladies never knew. She had avoided the hockey-and-inhibition of a British education, and unlike many young girls in London then she was eager for love-affairs. So her life took on a strange dichotomy. She gained something of a reputation as a coquette, abandoning herself anxiously to every sort of pleasure, and staying out at parties till late at night. Day came, and she was translated once more into a pale, contented secretary.

What she lacked in confidence she made up for with tedium. Yet she was not unattractive, and it is easy to understand why Augustus found her so striking. Five feet five inches tall, she had sumptuous brown hair and pensive blue eyes. She was highly strung, easily pleased, equally easily offended, and at both extremes intensely feminine. She walked in beauty like a mist impregnated by all those notions English people associate with Poles and Russians. But to many, her most bewitching quality was her gurgling voice, rich and soupy and full of flattering inflections when speaking to those she liked.

It was through Frieda Bloch and her Slade friends that Alick, as everyone called her, got to know Augustus and subsequently many other writers and artists from Wyndham Lewis to W. B. Yeats. Some of them treated her badly, though she never complained or explained. When questioned, for instance, about Yeats, she simply gurgled, her voice like hot air bubbling through lemonade: 'Ah Yeats – he was a won-derful man!' And Lewis? 'Yes – won-derful!' And Augustus? 'Won-derful!'

For all eminent artists and manly men her admiration was unfettered. Spontaneously, without premeditation, while Ida and Dorelia were tucked up together in Paris, Augustus and Alick had begun to see a great deal of each other. For once, inspiration and entertainment were well married.

'You are one of the people who inhabit my world,' Augustus wrote to her, '– a denizen of my country, a daughter of my tribe – one of those on whom I must depend – for life and beyond life. I am subjected to you – be loyal to your subject.' Almost nothing became Alick so well as her absence, and since Augustus had to spend much of his time in Paris, his infatuation for this 'jeune fille mystérieuse et gaie' deepened. Their relationship developed partly through a correspondence that was voluminous, purple, and of astonishing tedium. It is not that their love letters achieved this pitch of tedium gradually: they bored both of them at once. Augustus even owned that he had to have a constant supply of brandy in order 'to continue this correspondence which bores me so much'. Boredom was, indeed, one of the gifts they shared. They were experts in the subject, scholars, connoisseurs; they were competitors. In almost every letter he asks her urgently: 'Let me know if you are badly bored?' And in almost every answer she is able to boast of some new territory conquered by ennui. This ennui was an object of fascination to Augustus, who measures it wonderingly against his own so that it spreads into their most significant shared quality, becomes part of the very fabric of their love-affair, reaches pathos. 'Do you know I long to see you again,' he writes from France. 'You are such a love – your smile is so wonderful and nobody cries so beautifully as you. How bored are you Alick? I get quite desperate at times – really yesterday I caught myself in the act of beating my brow! All alone and quite theatrically – I tell you I was angry!' To paper up these areas of boredom, he begs her to 'cover six sheets with an embroidery of pretty thoughts and interesting information', and send them to him at once. 'Wrap yourself in the sheets, so to say, and leave the imprint of your adorable self behind for me.' But such an accomplishment is quite beyond Alick; she has nothing to say. To escape from himself, and assume another character part, Augustus then begs her: 'Do re-christen me!' But this feat too is beyond her; she can think of no names, her head is empty – and so Augustus remains inescapably Augustus, bored and bewildered.* Nevertheless, by a fraction, she was more bored than he, if only because he wrote more letters than she did. 'Ah, Alick – writing so often as I do how can one avoid being a bore?' he demanded.

I know what risks I run but still persist – it means talking to you vaguely, unsatisfactorily and blindly, but still some attenuated converse with you. I can't see the expression on your face nor hear the sound of your voice – it is worse than the telephone – and more open to misunderstandings. It is a kind of muffled dumbshow with hands tied.

How is it you mean so much to me – you are like a woman found on an island by one happily shipwrecked, who shows him the cave where she sleeps and the berries she eats and the pool in which she bathes herself – and in kissing her his soul flies to the moon henceforth his God as it is hers.

Boredom was to be outwitted by the most extreme romantics. As hypochondriacs of the soul, their search for new and extraordinary sensations with which to drive off the dreaded accidie must be unremitting. With great zeal, with inventiveness, they quarried after the purely superficial, and

---

* He called her 'Undine', meaning female water-sprite or elemental spirit of the water in Paracelsus' system.

from time to time, as remedy against tedium, they would add some *nouveau frisson* to their medicine chest. 'I can tell you how to procure a new sensation,' Augustus prescribed in one of his letters. 'First of all get hot – undo your waistband – indeed it is better to remove your outer dress, then, seated on your bed, pour white wine very slowly down your neck, breathing regularly the while. But you must be at the proper temperature to commence with. If this doesn't please you I will tell you another method.'

Alick's letters almost always disappointed Augustus; but the posts that brought no letters from her stirred him up very wonderfully.

'Alick – why don't I hear from you – won't you write even if you don't love me? Do not wait till you love me – it might take days to come on. What else can I say – nothing till I hear ·from you, my moon, my tender dove, rose of my soul. – John.'

Their correspondence was enclosed, at Alick's insistence, within a paraphernalia of espionage secrecy that artificially flavoured the masquerade between them. Augustus never kept letters, he merely failed to lose them. Alick, who sensed this, is always rousing him to the point of destruction. 'Yes I burn your letters,' Augustus assured her. 'Even the last, than which noth-ing less compromising could have been written, I took away to a lonely spot and consumed. I hope you dispose of mine with equal thoroughness. In case you are still without a cigarette I send you one – to be smoked with this letter.' But still Alick was not satisfied. She seemed to detect a bantering tone in this assurance, and on at least one occasion asked for her own letters to be returned to her through the post.

Here are your letters – you see I have destroyed many. My habit (an evil one of course) is to put them in my pocket where they re-main safely till it gets too crowded – when I weed out a few ... There is nobody here who would read *your* letters or understand them ... Yes – you may trust to my honour to *burn* all letters I get from you in future *instantly* and if you like I will eat all the ashes as a further precaution. You don't realise what depths of discretion I am capable of, and I am improving in this respect – under your tuition.

Alick distrusted flippancy. If Augustus had a fault, it was this disconcerting humour of his – for she was desperately anxious to conceal that she had nothing to hide. Unasked, she swore most earnestly and without any trace of humour that she consigned each item of his correspondence to the flames. It may now be read in its entirety at the library of the University of Michigan.

In his strangely muted world, isolated, swept by melancholia, Augustus welcomed Alick Schepeler as a fellow being. His instinct was not wrong. She mitigated his bouts of loneliness by being inexplicably lonely herself. She was, he told her, 'Keltic' like himself. Besides social shyness and physical passion, they had in common a background from which their adult life was divorced. With their quick perceptions they combined a curious amalgam of boldness and timidity; both were polyglots and read widely, though mainly as a refuge from solitude; both took their mental colouring from their friends. As revealed by their correspondence, the one taste they had in common absolutely was a sartorial obsession. Their intense excitement over clothes was often the only stimulus to quicken the movement of their blood. When Alick commanded him to write and tell her all he was doing in France, he replied : 'I would rather talk about you and your beautiful underclothing.' At other times he would question her : 'Tell me, Undine, how are your shoes wearing? It seems so *fitting*, that you – a soulless, naked, immortal creature, come straight out of the water, should take to *shoes* with such passion !' She would fill the page with detailed descriptions of her dresses, and he, in his answers, would ponder over which had demoralized him the most, the blue, the pink or the black-and-white.

Clothes are the clue to the two most significant aspects of this correspondence. 'I have bought a new hat and an alpaca coat,' Augustus announced, 'to give me confidence.' His clothes were like those in an actor's wardrobe, for he changed his personality with them. It has been said that he modelled his appearance on Courbet, but in fact he had no single model in mind, and many transitory moods and influences claimed him. Parental disapproval was always a strong recommendation. One morning about this time old Edwin John read in a newspaper a description of his son's appearance as being 'not at all that of a Welshman, but rather a Hungarian or a Gypsy', and at once sent a letter of reproof which Augustus had no difficulty in treating as Alick Schepeler was always imploring him to treat hers. But the reproof did not go unheeded and, to caricature his father's wishes, he secured a complete Welsh outfit with which to flabbergast Montparnasse. Edwin John's real wish was for gentlemanly inconspicuousness, and this perhaps was the starting point of his son's melodramatic uniforms. Especially in these early days, Augustus's clothes, like his handwriting and the style of his pictures, were always changing in the search for his real self – or the successful avoidance of it. 'I am so mercurial,' he confessed. 'Really I must cultivate a pose. It is so necessary so often.' It was necessary to steady him, to bring consistency to his attitudes and direction to his rudderless progress. So he experimented.

'Méfiez-vous des hommes pittoresques,' warned Nietzsche. Augustus quotes this in *Chiaroscuro*, but adds that, though weary of his extreme visibility, he was unable to achieve unobtrusiveness. At times he despised himself for this failure. 'I have half a mind to get shaved and assume a bowler,' he told Alick. 'My life seems more amazing everyday.' So he trimmed his beard and for a short time did wear a bowler – with the result that he grew more noticeable than ever: a victim of his own appearance, as Princess Bibesco later described him.

The correspondent who sent Alick Schepeler so many letters during 1906 is every inch a costume actor – but detachment and humour kept pulling the mask a little from his face. 'The thought haunts me that in a gross state of satisfaction I have allowed myself to utter the most abominable sincerity,' he tells her. 'I ask you in your turn to make allowances.' But these letters are not insincere; they are elaborately undeceiving. They expose, perhaps more clearly than anything else he wrote, the fluidity of his character, with its hectic cross-currents of whim and temper. They show the urge to cover up his uncertain inner being with the hats and coats and hand-made shoes of the confident outer man. But they also illustrate the unhappy paradox by which he dressed to attract the sort of attention that, once he commanded it, disgusted him.* What he intended to be a means of self-escape often made for agonized self-consciousness. He was embarrassed by his past self which, in a new mood, would seem to him false, full of sickening sentimentality. In just such a mood he later destroyed most of his letters to Ida, telling the Rani that 'they made me almost wither up in disgust'.

Clothes also form a natural part of this correspondence because they are essential to Augustus's pictures. His infatuation with Alick Schepeler had at its source the certain knowledge that, for whatever reason, her face and figure could summon from him great art. For this paragon of boredom was Lady Enigma to him: and that was enough – no need to question further. In the years 1906 and 1907 he drew and painted her numerous times. By all accounts his finest portrait in oils, entitled 'La Seraphita', he accidentally set alight in the 1930s during one of his cigarette fires. But there are at least half a dozen remarkable drawings in galleries and private collections.† Almost all of them have in common the suggestion that he had caught sight of depths in her not visible to others. Alick herself is said to have remarked that she had never noticed she was

* For example: 'An English fool, whom I had observed eyeing me in Rouen Cathedral to-day, rushed up to me outside, and started addressing me with extreme nervousness in lamentable French. He asked me if I were a Russian. I said "Mais non monsieur". He then began excusing himself so painfully that I invited him to speak English. He was thunderstruck and asked if I were a socialist. "No, are you?" "Er, no, I'm a Christian – first of all etc." He explained he was so struck by my appearance, the ass! He was a pitiable sight. His deplorable condition when I left him made me almost *feel* Christlike. Indeed I was about to make him the repository of the newest Beatitude. "Blessed are the ridiculous, for they shall entertain the Lord," when he oscillated confusedly and disappeared in a pink mist.' John to Alick Schepeler, undated.

† At the Fitzwilliam Museum, Cambridge, there is 'Study of an Undine' (P.D. 155), dated 1907, and 'Portrait of Alexandra', 1906 (P.D. 154–1961). At the Manchester City Art Gallery there is 'Study for Undine' (1182) and 'Miss Schepeler'. 'Alick Schepeler', a black-pencil portrait on grey paper owned by Mrs H. Alexander, is reproduced as No. 18 in *Augustus John: Fifty-two Drawings*. A full-length drawing (5⅜″ × 13½″) described as 'A lady with left hand raised to her cheek' – a very deliberately enigmatic pose – is probably a study for the burnt oil painting 'La Seraphita'. It was owned by Mrs Charles Hunter and later bought by Vita Sackville-West. It is now in the collection of her son Benedict Nicolson. 'I have a certain tenderness for this drawing,' Augustus wrote on 9 June 1938. 'It is of Miss Alick Schepeler.'

beautiful until Augustus drew her. Yet the drawings are in no
way prettified. They show a face which, though it may have
some characteristic John features – a slight slanting of the
eyes or high prominence of the cheek bones – is unique. It is a
face that haunts one. The eyes drill through the spectator with
a peculiar insistence; the hair, like great flying fingers, has a
curious wildness about it; the expression varies between ani-
mation, mischief and serene secrecy. Always enormous strength
is conveyed – a reflection of the force of Augustus's feelings –
without the cosiness occasionally present in his portraits of Ida
and even Dorelia. Sometimes, as in a drawing entitled 'Study of
an Undine', there is a hint of insanity. The face emerges out of
soft contours and shadow, with its wispy strands of hair, like
the head of Medusa. She is a cross between a witch and a nymph.

The letters he wrote to Alick Schepeler form a perfect commentary on these portraits. In the spring of 1906 he writes
from Paris: 'Am I painting? – why yes – and I have burst certain bonds too that bound my brain with iron and now my bewildered eye mixes dream with reality – and weeps with joy
and pain.'

To mix dream with reality was his ambition. He saw in Alick
Schepeler a perfect focus for this ambition since she lived most
intensely in his imagination. He observed her and painted her in
England; but it was in France that his portraits were conceived.

'I see you standing on the summit of a sea-hill and, turning
towards the sea with a gesture divinely nonchalant, project me
a surreptitious yawn which, carried by the waves is at length
deposited moistly yet merrily on my shore,' he wrote to her
from across the Channel. 'I picture you extended, partly in and
partly out of the water like an Undine hesitating between
immortality and love, or like some sweet reptile of old discovering the first dry land or like some formerly aquatic species
at the moment of differentiation. And how brown you are –
O pray – retain the bloom till I come. Do not wash till I see you.'

On land he saw her, thought of her, as a witch:

'It is regrettable that I have not persevered with my occult
studies, otherwise I might appear to you personally which
would be a much better plan than writing a dull letter,' he
wrote in the summer of 1906. 'I used to wonder whether you

were a young witch ... given to broom-stick riding and Sabbats of a Saturday. Perhaps if I surprised you astrally at this moment I should detect you in the act of performing some diabolical incantation or brewing a hellish potion or suchlike. Sweet one! More probably I should find you sleeping soundly and I would be able to see how many kisses one required to wake you up.'

Dream and reality, the very mainspring of his art, seemed by June 1906 to have moved to the Sleeping Beauty of Stanhope Gardens. Paris, which was to have given him the impetus for so much new work, had already begun to lose its glow.

5. A SEASIDE CHANGE

'A sojourn at Ste Honorine-sur-Mer, near Bayeux, was memorable for little save the birth of my son Romilly,' Augustus recorded over thirty-five years later.[20] In his voluminous correspondence at the time, and in that of Ida, there is much that is memorable, though no mention of Romilly's birth.*

Within two months of moving to the Rue Dareau, though living there only intermittently, Augustus was grumbling to Alick Schepeler (June 1906): 'So far rather gloomy here – I am decidedly sleepy and feel the dullest of all the devils.' His depression worsened until he resolved to reconnoitre a long holiday by the sea for himself and for what Wyndham Lewis had called 'a numerous retinue, or a formidable staff – or a not inconsiderable suite, – or any polite phrase that occurs to you[21] that might include his patriarchical ménage.'

'I am off to-night,' Augustus wrote to Alick Schepeler one June evening, 'to find a place by the sea, somewhere in Normandy I think. First of all I mean to go to Caen. The poet [Wyndham Lewis] is coming with me ... I shall be moving about ... Cher ange – why don't you come over too, as you thought of doing? I will find a place. I will arrange everything ... I have had a spell of complete sterility lasting several days, but now I see nothing but beauty. I refuse to see anything else.'

Rather irritably he roved the Normandy coast until he came to Ste Honorine des Pertes where, falling in with a band of

* Romilly John was never informed of his exact birthday. His birth, like that of his brother Pyramus, was not registered.

Piedmontese Gypsies* – about a hundred vans packed with
grand men and women and some beautiful children – his
spirits suddenly veered upwards. 'They spoke very good
Romany,' he told Alick Schepeler, 'and played very badly, alas.
At Port-en-bessin, near Ste Honorine, there are wonderful sea-
women who collect shellfish – they are very tall and quite
pre-historic – just the sort you'd hate. I suppose I want to do a
painting of them all the same.' His mind was now made up.
He would lead his families to Ste Honorine, and station Alick
Schepeler just off the coast on Jersey. She could wear her beret
and her spendid new pink dress – and she could bring her friend
Frieda Bloch too. It would be a terrific summer. A 'glorious
bathe in the sea' at Ste Honorine confirmed that this was the
correct decision, and he hurried back to Paris to fetch everyone.

'Gus has just come back from finding a little house by the
sea for all of us to go to,' Ida wrote to Mrs Sampson. 'The kids
ought to enjoy it.' Her implication that the adults might not
enjoy it was to prove drastically right. From July to the end of
September they lived 'chez Madame Beck' at Ste Honorine. 'It is
a tiny village,' Ida told Alice Rothenstein. '. . . We are between
Cherbourg and Caen. Bayeux is the nearest town, and we only
get there by cart and steam tram.'

Since flight was so difficult, Ida had to rest content brooding
over the 'patriarchical ménage'. As Dorelia had looked after her
during Edwin's birth, so now she looked after Dorelia. But the
children, with whom Dorelia had dealt so calmly, rasped on her
nerves. She was imprisoned: the place of her captivity was
fuller than ever of these children, and 'I don't care for them
much.'[22] David, who was 'very silly and not very interesting',
seemed in the last year to have advanced not at all: either he
would make cheeky jokes or noises like an engine. Caspar,
'very fat and solid', spent his time dashing in and out of the
water – up to his ankles; Robin did nothing but climb and
jump; Edwin, who now looked like a huge swollen doll – 'very
ugly with tiny blue eyes' – had developed so red a face that 'we

---

* A large charcoal drawing he did of these gypsies, 'Wandering Sinnte', is
now in the Manchester City Art Gallery. Though the figures are unrelated
psychologically, they have a compositional unity and a community of feeling
that makes it one of the best of Augustus's groups.

bathe him in sea weed';[23] Pyramus appeared more Words-
worthian than ever and, as ever, did nothing; and so on.

As at Matching Green, Ida's 'formidable staff' comprised two
girls – Clara, who had joined them when they originally came
to Paris, and Félice, a very ladylike woman who made disagreeable noises in her nose and suffered from palpitations. She
screamed at mice, had fearful starts when failing to spot people
approaching her, and yawned all day – huge, lionlike yawns.
Yet she worked very well, though no one liked her, least of all
Clara who could not endure the least shade of interference. The
two of them were seldom on speaking terms – either it was ear-
splitting peals of abuse rivalling the children's, or a disdainful
silence. Their bad humour contributed much to the tenseness
of this holiday.

The confidence, the strength, even the humour of Paris were
ebbing. 'We are in a village miles from the railway and by the
sea,' Ida wrote to the Rani (August 1906). 'It is very relaxing
and we all, except the children, feel awful.' What had gone
wrong? Everything, it appeared – and for all of them. At first it
had promised so well. The sun shone, and Augustus would lead
off his troop on bathing parties, on long walks to pick black-
berries for jam and 'English puddings', and on picnics – 'there
is a lovely place on the cliffs where we slide down. Gus goes
head first.' They encountered several battalions of gypsies –
'glorious chaps' – and Augustus bought Ida a guitar which she
promised she would 'learn to play well'. Gwen John came for
five days with her cat and surprised everyone by bathing twice
a day. And then there was the poet Wyndham Lewis – 'a nice
beautiful young man', Ida called him – who stayed for five
weeks, grew a beard, let off cheap fireworks and made everyone
cry with laughter* over his plans.

* 'The poet astonished the beach by appearing in a Rugby blazer and a
cholera belt,' Augustus reported to Alick Schepeler. '. . . He came back full
of the beauties of sea-bathing – that is to say: he had been viewing the girls
frolicking in the water from a prominent position on the beach. He assures me
there were at least 10 exquisite young creatures with fat legs, and insists on my
accompanying him tomorrow . . . He wants me to go to Munich in January
for the Carnival – he assures me I will dance with the Crown Princess.'
     Lewis's more laconic description of this long vacation was simply: 'I wrote
verse, when not asleep in the sun.' See *Rude Assignment*, p. 120.

Then, abruptly, the sun went in; the gypsies vanished; Gwen
John left; Wyndham Lewis, after sitting for his portrait, failed
to amuse any longer; and Augustus was 'plunged into gloom
by a thousand tragedies'.[24] These thousand tragedies sprang
from one central disappointment. Instead of turning up in
Jersey, Alick Schepeler had drifted north to, of all places,
Cumberland, giving as her reason the need to sketch for two
months; and she had taken with her Frieda Bloch. Augustus's
reaction was extreme. He shut himself away, refused to paint
out of doors, refused even to bathe except after dark. 'I have
had most horrible spells of ennui,' he wrote. 'I sat in a garden
the other day and wondered what there was in the world at all
tolerable. I examined a tree attentively to discover any beauty
in it – without success. The sky seemed an awful bore and I
wondered why it should be blue. If it had been dark indigo and
the trees gold perhaps I should have been rather pleased.' The
beauty which he had refused not to see at the beginning of this
holiday was extinguished. He could not paint, he could not stop
trying to paint; he could not rest, he had no energy. His
melancholia was not just the absence of high spirits : it was a
positive disease, a cancer that consumed his very talent. The
one cure was a stimulus for his work, and the one stimulus just
then was Alick Schepeler. Now that she was further off than
ever, her attraction redoubled. She began to obsess him.

'I have awful fits of boredom – *awful*,' he confided to her.

I dreamt such a dream of you last night – and you had at last
actually consented to take off your clothes – at any rate you were
quite naked and quite beautiful. Why are you so – "nice"? ... I
would love to lie about with you – no, I mean walk long walks with
you – and perhaps have a bathe now and then. The people I see on
the beach don't please me ... I am horribly restless – I wonder why
the Devil I came here now. I curse myself – and calculate the maximum of years I have to live ... Kiss me Alick – if you love me still
a bit – darling you strange one. It is time I went on with that portrait. I believe I shall do nothing before – almost. I am expecting a
letter from you – Alick – I kiss your knees and eyes and mouth.

He lived for her disappointing letters, wrote to her almost
nightly, and composed poems to her including a sonnet which

discovers (with apologies) her Christian name rhymes with 'phallic'.

Maddened by frustration – and insect bites – he could not wait to be out of 'this sea-side hole', and begin to paint 'Whitmanic' pictures. 'Just write, beloved,' he urged Alick, 'and keep my spirits up. I foresee dismal things if you don't. The sea is beautiful all the same – I would like to lie in the sun with you and let the water dry on us.'

The other side of these generous love-letters was a meanness to those around him. He could not help himself. For day after day Ida and the others were subjected to his highly charged apathy, a death ray of pessimism. Deprivation – if only as a conjecture – always affected Augustus violently because it restored the chief condition of his childhood: deprivation of a mother; deprivation of love. He reacted in a 'spoilt' manner, grew surly, then aggressive. So now, after many dangerous days of simmering, he could hold himself back no longer. 'I have been dissecting myself assiduously here,' he informed Alick, 'and as a consequence have thrown overboard all self-respect and feel infinitely more comfortable and free and on excellent terms with the Devil.'

This allusiveness concealed a crisis that split apart the love molecule Ida, with Dorelia's collaboration, had so carefully prepared. Augustus had no wish to hurt either of them, but misfortune moved in his blood like a poison, and he had to expel it or die. 'How I hate causing worry!' he exclaimed to Alick. And how much he caused! For he hated even more being 'unnatural', and he was allergic to secrets, which were claustrophobia to him. But his melancholy made him 'careless of other people's feelings'. What he now did was bluntly to tell Ida and Dorelia the truth – the unstable truth of the moment. He told them that domestic life, even of the unorthodox variety with which they had experimented, smothered him; he told them of his feelings for Alick, that his painting could not advance without her, that he needed her. There was nothing too personal in all this – but he could not be restricted; he would explode. Boredom, guilt, frustration, sterility: to such morbid sensations had their ménage led him. They stifled his work, and he could countenance them no longer. At the same time he wrote to

Alick : 'I think I have about done with family life or perhaps I should say it has done for me – so there is nothing to prevent us getting married now.'

But marriage to Alick was only another fantasy he indulged largely because 'I wish to remain as respectable as possible in your eyes.' What in fact he proposed was something less original: to duplicate the arrangement he had with Ida and Dorelia in Paris, with a similar arrangement, also in Paris, with Alick and Frieda Bloch. His letters to Alick are full of plans for her to join him. 'If I had a wish for the fairies to fulfil it would be that you would come to Paris with Miss Bloch before long and collaborate with me,' he begins; and later : 'I begin to see very plainly that Miss Blocky will never get on unless she comes to Paris and brings you with her. I will find her a studio – and I will show her things I'm pretty sure she never suspected.'

Only now, for the first time, did Ida and Dorelia acknowledge that they could not contain Augustus. He was not proposing to leave them, simply to add to their number. He made no secret of it. 'John is taking a studio in Montmartre, where he thinks of installing two women he has found in England,' Wyndham Lewis confided to his mother; 'and I think John will end by building a city, and being worshipped as sole man therein, – the deity of Masculinity.'[25]

It was Dorelia who first resolved that she wanted no place in this city. She secretly decided that once Romilly was three or four months old, she would quietly 'buzz off'.[26] Ida too would have liked to leave. Her predicament is set out poignantly in a letter she wrote from Ste Honorine to the Rani :

Dearest, daily and many times a day I think I *must* leave Augustus. Isn't it awful? I feel so stiffed and oppressed. If I had the money I think I really should do it – but I can't leave him and take his money – and I can't keep the kids on what I have – and if I left the kids I should not find peace – you must not mind these confidences, angel. It is nothing much – I haven't the money so I must stay, as many another woman does. It isn't that Aug is different or unkind. He is the same as ever and rather more considerate in many ways. It's the mental state – I don't understand it and probably I should be equally slavish – *No* – I know I am freer alone. However one has lucid moments anywhere. Don't think me miserable. All this is a sign of health. But it's a pity one's got to live with a man. I shall have to get back home sooner or later – not meaning 28 Wigmore Street – and it doesn't matter as long as I don't arrive a lunatic. It's awful to be lodged in a place where one can't understand the language and where the jokes aren't funny. Why did I ever go there? Because I did – because there lives a King I had to meet and love. And now I am bound hand and foot – darling how will it end? By death or escape? And wouldn't escape be as bad as bondage? Would one find one's way – ...

At the end of September they left Ste Honorine all together and returned to the Rue Dareau. The atmosphere between them was black. 'I am very maladif I regret to say – that is I get fits of depression about every two hours – alternately intervals of malign joy,' Augustus confessed to Alick. He felt it was time to fly off to new places, remote and unknown. 'Paris is a queen of cities but I think Smyrna would suit me better.' Next moment he hankered after Italy – the Italians were surely the finest people in the world, and besides, he would be able to see in Italy 'my darling Piero della Francesca'. Genoa might suit him best, or 'Shall we go to Padua?' he asked Alick. But even before his invitation had arrived, another brainwave was upon him: 'I am inclined to take refuge in Bucharest at the nearest, to seek serenity in some Balkan insurrection, or danger in a Gypsy tent, or inevitable activity in Turkistan ... I am horribly aware of the power of Fate to-night.' This self-destructive urge quickly passed and, in a more hibernating mood, he suddenly inquired: 'Perhaps I may depend on you for warmth this winter ... I feel that once back in London I shall never leave it.' By now Alick was thoroughly confused. What *was* happening? Augustus was astonished at her question. Surely everything was perfectly clear! 'As to my coming to London, is it not already definitely arranged?' he demanded. 'Haven't I said jusqu'à l'automne a dozen times? And is not my word unimpeachable – am I not integrity itself?'

He did return to London, and to Alick, that October, while Dorelia prepared to move off elsewhere the following month. Only Ida was to stay on at the Rue Dareau – with her pack of boys, and two quarrelling women. Her bondage there was tighter than ever now for, to add to the complications, Clara had become pregnant.

And, as if that were not enough, Ida herself was again pregnant.

6. 'HERE'S TO LOVE!'

For the next six months, between October 1906 and the spring of the following year, Augustus, Ida and Dorelia struggled to establish lives which, though inevitably they overlapped, would be essentially separate.

For Augustus the first taste of this new regime was sweet. His depression lifted like a cloud at evening, and a bewildered exhilaration blazed through. The world was one marvellously mixed metaphor and he stood, in superb uncertainty, at its centre. 'I feel recurrent as the ocean waves,' he boasted on arriving in London, 'blue as the sky, ceaseless as the winds, multitudinous as a bee-hive, ardent as flames, cold as an exquisite hollow cave, generous and as pliant as a tree, aloof and pensive as an angel, tumultuous as the obscenest of demons . . .'[27]

It remained to be seen how long this combination of feelings would persist. Augustus himself was as confident as a boy. 'I no longer suffer from the blues,' he told Alick, 'and my soul seems to have returned to its habitation. I think you are more adorable than ever.' All that summer he had been damnably lazy but, as he explained to Alick, 'it is when I am not at work enough that I get bored'. Once again the uncontrollable volatility of his temperament had swung him above gloomy vapours, and the will to work throbbed through him. Seldom had he felt so vigorous.

But first there were some small practical matters to attend to. For while his soul had found its true habitation, there was still no proper place to house his body. He required a new studio in London – a fine new studio to match his mood – and, while he was about it, another new studio in Paris. Then he would be free at last to paint. 'I am going to take a new studio in Paris,' he proclaimed (September 1906) '– remote and alone – in some teeming street – where I can pounce on people as they pass, hob-nob with Apaches and maquereaux and paint as I can. Then of course the studio in London – the new one – in your neighbourhood.'[28] He had found nothing in Paris before leaving, so he now took up the search in London. 'I hope the Gods will provide me with a good studio in London,' he wrote to Alick, 'a studio I can live in and where you can come and sit without being spied on.' But the Gods, and estate agents, led him a merry dance – to Paddington, Bermondsey and the East End: all without success. For the time being he still used Rossetti Studios which Knewstub offered to lease to him for a further year. But independence meant freedom from the Knewstubs, Orpens and Rothensteins, and so he refused it – while continuing to use it *faute de mieux*. For a short period he rented another studio in Manresa Road from the Australian painter George Coates. It seemed a splendid place – Holman Hunt had painted his 'Innocents' there – but Augustus did not stay long. Dora Coates noted with disapproval that he had 'a compelling stare when he looked at a woman that I much resented'. She also resented his treatment of the studio – soiled socks and odd clothes lay thick upon the floor amid the dust of weeks, and by the time he left it was as 'dirty as a rag and bone shop' and had to be scrubbed with carbolic soap. He found no other place so good as this, and by February 1907 was reduced to a 'beastly lodging' at 55 Paulton's Square, owned by Madame Herminie Considerant, corset maker.

The only virtue of such a place was that it was near Alick. They saw a lot of each other that winter, and a lot of the mystery began to leak out of their relationship. Quite regularly their meetings ended rowdily : she is always striking him in the face with her 'formidable fist', he apologizing too late for being 'so damnably careless'. Sitting, she soon discovered, like almost everything else, bored her excessively. Yet he had to paint her. 'You have not come to-day – but, dear, come to-morrow – You know I am not stable – my moods follow, but they repeat themselves – alas – sometimes – I must paint you dear – to-day – probably you don't quite like me – but do come to-morrow. Who knows? – You may find me less intolerable to-morrow ... à demain, n'est-ce-pas bien chère, petite Ondine souriante. Soyons intimes – franches – connaissants – alors amants.' By the end of the year, feeling 'I want to wash myself in the Ocean', Augustus returned to Paris.

It was desperate work looking for studios, but in Paris he was luckier, finding a vast room off the Boulevard St-Germain, in an old hotel belonging to the famous Rohan family. 'I have taken a studio – with a noble address. Cour de Rohan [3], Rue du Jardinet,' he told Alick. By February the workmen were busy converting it – 'my studio commences to be magnificent' – and by March he had moved in – 'I will be about doing things in it soon'. But by March it was too late.

As soon as Augustus had returned to London, Dorelia made her move. Ida sub-let the studio at Rue Dareau, and the two women set off to find a *logement* for Dorelia. By the beginning of November they had found what she wanted at 48 Rue du Château. 'It has 2 rooms and a kitchen and an alcove – one of the rooms is a good size,' Ida informed Augustus (10 November 1906).

It is in a lovely disreputable looking building – very light and airy, the view is a few lilac trees, some washing hanging up and a railway – very pleasant – and to our taste ... The logement is 300frs (£12) a year. It is rather dear in comparison with ours, but we couldn't find anything better or cheaper, and there will be room to store all your things in it ... Dodo and I had an amusing interview with the landlord and his wife of the logement last night at 9. We had to go down to his apartment near the Madeleine – a real French drawing-room with real French people – Very suspicious and anxious about their rent and Dodo's future behaviour – D. was mute and smiling. I did my best to reassure them that she was très sage and her man (they asked me at once if she was married or not and didn't mind a bit her not being) was 'solvent'. We said she was a model (she's going to sit again) and the wife wanted to know if the artists came to her or she went to the artists! The husband kept squashing the wife all the time though he had called her in for her opinion of us. He was small and concise and sensible, and she was big and sweet and stupid.

French opinion being favourable, Dorelia moved in with Pyramus and Romilly almost at once. But Augustus was not pleased. It had all happened so fast and while he was away. He did not want Dorelia disappearing again to Belgium. After all, it was not impossible that he had exaggerated Alick Schepeler's importance to him. There was nothing exclusive about it. Besides, it was easy to overvalue the significance of what he called his 'physical limitations'. At Matching Green when Ida had been suicidal over Dorelia, Augustus had explained his behaviour in a letter to the Rani – and in essence nothing had changed now that Dorelia was angry about Alick.

One [i.e. Ida] must grow accustomed to the recurrence of these perhaps congenital weaknesses – which you must remember have not appeared with Dorelia's arrival only but date in my experience from the first moment of meeting Ida – which are indeed included in her system as a mark of mortality in one otherwise divinely rational. Don't please ever think of me as a playful eccentric who thinks it necessary to épater les bourgeois; things take place quite naturally and inevitably – one cannot however arrest the invisible hand – with all the best intentions – to attempt that is pure folly.

But Dorelia was less tractable than Ida – she had entered the web less deeply. She saw no folly in his attempting to 'arrest the invisible hand'; she doubted his best intentions; she doubted even his motives in writing to her now. Augustus was quick to protest. 'My beloved Relia, I don't write to you without loving you or wanting to write. Believe this and don't suspect me of constant humbuggery. Who the Devil do you think I'm in love with? If you think I'm a mere liar, out goes the sun. I've been thinking strongly sometimes of clearing back over the Channel to get at you, you won't believe how strongly or how often.'

And it was true: she didn't. But at Christmas he arrived and there was a great party in the Rue Dareau. Gwen John turned up and Wyndham Lewis and Dorelia with her children. They ate 'dinde aux marrons', plum pudding and 'wonderful little cakes'; and they drank quantities of 'punch au kirsch'. For the six children, instead of a plodding white-bearded Father Christmas, they had 'le petit noël' who, though he descended the chimney, had 'a delicacy of his own entirely French'.[29] It was the last happy time they would spend together. 'The shops are *full* of dolls dolls dolls – it is so French and ridiculous and *painted*, and yet it doesn't lie heavy on the chest like English "good cheer",' Ida wrote to the Rani (December 1906). 'One can look at it through the window quite pleasantly instead of having to mix in or be a misanthrope as at home. Perhaps because one is foreign. It is delightful to be foreign – unless one is in the country of one's birth – when it becomes gênant.'

The holiday was delightful, but it solved no problems, brought no reconciliations: it was simply a holiday. After it was over, Augustus returned to finish his portrait of Alick Schepeler; and Dorelia went back to her *logement*. Gradually she was growing more independent. Her sister Jessie came for a few weeks to help with the children; she began dressmaking; got a cat of her own from Gwen John; started to model again. 'Dodo has just been to déjeuner, washed herself (1st time in 3 days) and gone off to sit at "Trinity Lodge",' Ida wrote to Augustus. 'I'm afraid she's forgotten to take her prayer book. She says for her last pose she didn't have to wash – it was such a comfort. But for Trinity Lodge the outside of the platter must be clean.' Soon Dorelia had established a routine of life very largely separate from Ida and Augustus. 'Dodo has only been once to déjeuner since she left,' Ida sadly observed. 'She is quite 20 minutes away. She poses in the afternoons and has a woman to mind the kids. Gwen gave her 100 francs for the black velvet coat she made. I think she is enjoying herself a bit in leaving the babies. Romilly is getting on.'

By March it seemed as if Dorelia had succeeded in achieving her independence.

'I am alone again – and alone – and alone.' From Augustus, with his permission, Ida was content to live apart – 'it is so easy to love at a distance,' she reminded him. And from a distance she still worshipped him. 'I say Mackay is 2nd rate,' she had written to the Rani.

... I have always known it, but the other day it flashed on me. So is Sampson. There is no harm in being 2nd rate any more than being a postman. It is just a creation ... Augustus has not that quality – he is essentially 1st rate ... As to a woman, I know only one first and that is Gwen John. You and I, dear, are puddings – with plums in perhaps – and good suet – but puddings. Well you perhaps are a butterfly or an ice cream – yes, that *is* more suitable – but we are

scarcely human ... This sounds tragic, but I have been living with
exhausting emotions lately and am – queer – Yours in a garden Ida.

In all aspects of her life, it now seemed to her, she had failed.
She had failed as an artist – even as a musician; she had failed
as a friend – she never saw her friends now; that she had failed
with Augustus was obvious; and, what was more painful still,
her relationship with Dorelia had failed – they were still
friendly, but that first sweet intimacy had gone. She had
failed too – was in the very process of failing – as a mother.

If Augustus's world that winter was a huge mixed metaphor,
for Ida it had become a mixed bowl of cough mixture, dill
water, cod-liver oil, milk of magnesia. The eldest children were
getting to an age when they demanded more attention but she
had no more to give them. Their future seemed bleak with such
a mother. David, she told Mrs Sampson, was 'such a queer
twisted many-sided kid. Horrid an[d] lovely – plucky and
cowardly – cruel and kind – thoughtful and stupid, many times
a day. He needs a firm wise hand to guide him, instead of a
bad tempered lump like me.' She had begun to arrange their
education, sending David and Caspar to the Ecole Maternelle of
the Communal School – 'there are about 300 all under 6', she
told Augustus, 'and they do nothing but shriek little ditties with
their earless voices, and march about in double file'. But both
boys were so unhappy she had to remove them: another
failure.

She was imprisoned during the children's pleasure, for so long
as the mind could tell, the eye could see. 'Life here is so curious
– not interesting as you might imagine,' she wrote to the Rani.

I crave for a time when the children are grown up and I can
ride about on the tops of omnibuses as of yore in a luxury of
vague observation. Never now do I have time for any luxury, and
at times I feel a stubborn head on me – wooden – resentful – slowly
being petrified. And another extraordinary thing that has happened
to me is that my spirit – my lady, my light and help – has gone –
not tragically – just in the order of things – and now I am not sure
if I am making an entrance into the world – or an exit from it! ...
As a matter of plain fact I believe my raison d'être has ended, and
I am no more the inspired one I was. It seems so strange to write all
this quite calmly. Tell me what you can make of it when you have

time. My life has been so mysterious. I long for someone to talk to. I can't write now – another strange symptom!

It was a sickness of living from which she suffered – quite different from the suicidal troughs of Matching Green. Then there had been dreadful jealousy; now, though she often dreamed of Augustus and Alick Schepeler, they were absurd dreams, never tortured. 'Last night you were teaching her [Alick] french in the little dining-room here while I kept passing through to David who had toothache and putting stuff on his tooth.' It was as if she was too tired to feel anything positive now. On hearing that Augustus was coming over at Christmas, she had remarked to the Rani: 'Funny – I haven't been alone with him for 2½ years – wonder what it will be like – boring probably.'

In Ida's letters, especially to the Rani, there is a fatalistic flirting with the idea of death: 'Oh Rani – Are you in a state when the future seems hopeless? I suppose things are never hopeless really are they? There is always death isn't there?' There was nothing new, except death, under the sun. She lived in a kind of pale stupor. 'The only way to be happy is to be ignorant and lie under the trees in the evening,' she had told the Rani. Never again could she recapture such green ignorance.

But she had not counted on Augustus. Now that he had finished his portrait of Alick, and now that Dorelia had coldly moved away, he suddenly proposed returning to live with Ida. What else was there for him? Ida was dismayed. She knew of course that he was temporarily feeling dissatisfied with the present arrangement, but he would not 'regret it later on I swear'. Had he considered the implications? What about the children, for instance – 'Can you really want to see them again?' she asked him. 'You know they worry you to death.' But Augustus complained he had no home. He could find nowhere to live in London, and he could not work. Was his request really so extraordinary? After all, they loved each other still; they'd come through a lot together – why should they not settle down in London and be happy? Without a proper home he seemed lost. Besides, he had given her scheme a long trial. It did not sound unreasonable. 'It may be I should come

back to London,' ·Ida reluctantly agreed. 'You must tell me. I
will come – only we get on so much better apart. But I understand you need a home. Dis moi et j'y cours. As to the love old
chap we all have our hearts full of love for someone at sometime
or other and if it isn't this one it's the other one over there.'

Her real feeling at the prospect of returning to live with
Augustus is explicitly stated in a letter she sent to the Rani:
'Gus seems to hanker after a home in London, and I feel duties
beating little hammers about me, and probably shall find myself padding about London in another ½ year – Damn it all.'

What still tied her to Augustus, as she had explained at Ste
Honorine des Pertes, was financial dependence. Throughout the
autumn and winter she had saved exorbitantly. To Augustus
she represented such thrift as an art, parodying his own: 'Am
still trying to take care of the pence with great pleasure in the
feeling of beauty it gives – like simplifying an already beautiful,
but careless and clumsy, work of art.' The real impetus behind
this economic fury was her desire to shore up some possibility
of independence against the future. But the little hammers of
duty were banging nails into the coffin of this last dream. She
had complained in the past of her own selfishness, but she was
not selfish enough.

In a letter to Alice Rothenstein, she wrote: 'It chills my
marrow to think of living back in England.' The Rothensteins
had become increasingly concerned about her life with, and
without, Augustus; and wrote to inquire, complain, praise and
comfort her.

'My only treasure is myself,' Ida insisted to Will,

and that I give you, as I give it to all men who need it, every time
I really live ... as to Gussie, he is our great child artist: let him
snap his jaws. What does he matter? It is *you* who matters, and you
dare not be frightened except at your own self.

I am glad to have your letter: it is such a comfort to hear a
voice. Life is a bit solemn and silent in the forest where I live, and
the world outside a bit grotesque and difficult. Certainly there are
always the gay ribbons you talk of but they are only sewn on and
are there to break the intolerable monotony, for which purpose,
darling Will, they are *quite inadequate* ...

Such gloomy letters greatly worried the Rothensteins, who

blamed Augustus for her depression. But Ida would not allow
this. 'I must write to say it is not so,' she firmly answered Will.
The devil, she explained, was in herself – 'and as soon as you
wound it, it heals up and you have to keep on always trying
to find its heart.' This devil had so many names: first it was
jealousy; then a vanity which masqueraded as duty; finally
sloth. Would she ever kill it? 'When one fights a devil does one
not fight it for the whole world? It is the most enchanting
creature, it is everywhere. God, it seems to spread itself out
every minute. Sometimes I do find its miserable fat heart and I
give it a good stab. But it is chained to me. I cannot run away.'

The three of them were in Paris during February: Augustus
moving into his new studio; Dorelia in her *logement*; Ida still at
the Rue Dareau. 'Let's go up the Volga in the sun,' Augustus
entreated Alick. But it was no more than a gesture: he could
not run away any more than Ida. He would have liked to. Paris
nauseated him. In letter after letter he complains that 'I find the
bourgeoisie here quite hateful'. As always when depressed he
petulantly externalized the cause: 'I am much depressed to-day
by the aspect of civilization – never was human society so
foully ugly, so abysmally ignoble,' he declares '– and I have
also had a cold which doesn't improve matters.' He revisited all
the places which had so delighted him less than a year ago – the
Louvre, the Luxembourg Gardens, the Panthéon ('to encourage
myself with a view of Puvis's decorations') – but everywhere
was filled with ugly crowds which 'brought my nausea to a
climax'. The whole French nation oppressed him. 'A good deed,
I think, shines with great difficulty in a naughty world,' he
wrote to Alick. 'I went into the morgue and saw 4 dead men;
they looked *awfully well* really – the only thing impressive I
found today ... These four unknown dead men, all different,
seemed enlarged by death to monumental size, and lacking life
seemed divested only of its trivialities.'

To be reborn was what he longed for – not through death,
but in the birth of Ida's fifth child. 'Oh for a girl!' she had
written to him – but she confidently expected a boy. The contemplation of another baby, which could still excite Augustus,
caused her heartache. 'In 3 weeks – si on peut juger – a new

face will be amongst us – a new pilgrim, God help it,' she wrote
to the Rani. 'What right have we, knowing the difficulties of the
way, to start any others along it? The baby seems so strong
and large I am dreading its birth. How pleasant it *seems* that it
would be to die.'

Wyndham Lewis – whom Augustus now accused of 'the
worst taste', but whom Ida claimed 'I love' – had spent much
of his time recently at the Rue Dareau. 'Mrs John and the
bonne will have their babies about the same time I expect,' he
wrote to his mother, '– I suppose beneath John's roof is the
highest average of procreation in France.'

As it turned out neither of these babies – nor yet a third one
that Wyndham Lewis had so far failed to spot – were born
under Augustus's many roofs. After some hesitation Ida decided to have her child in hospital. 'It is much simpler and I
don't pay anything,' she explained to Mrs Nettleship. 'I just go
when it comes on without anything but what I'm wearing!'

Clara and Félice had by now both left,* and Ida engaged a
new nanny called Delphine for the children. 'Gawd knows if
she's the right sort,' she reported to Augustus, '– one can but
try. She's fairly handsome 22 years old.' Under these circumstances Ida was obliged to ask Dorelia whether she would return to the Rue Dareau while she was in hospital; and Dorelia,
in agreeing, walked back into the web.

'Augustus is well in his studio now and a beauty it is – and
he has plenty of models just at present ... Dorelia – and all the
kids – to say nothing of me in spreading poses,' Ida wrote to the
Rani late that February. Although the writing of letters made
her feel 'pale green', she continued her correspondence right up
to the time of her confinement. To lighten the black humour of
some of these letters, she had told the Rothensteins: 'we shall
come up again next spring you know'. And then, she promised,
all their worries 'would melt away like the mist when the sun

---

* 'Clara is enceinte and will have to leave end of January,' Ida had written to
Augustus. 'It is so disappointing. She is such a good nurse. Félice is going to
snort over needles and thread and be a dressmaker – I bravely gave her notice
and had to bear a scene of tearful reproach – but within the week she found a
genteel place as mender to a school ... Poor old Clara is cheerful over her
affair but she would much rather not have it, and says had she been in Paris when
she found out she would have gone and had it destroyed.'

comes out'. But to the Rani, with whom she felt less need to dissemble, she confessed that it was not to the spring she was looking forward, but 'to the winter for some inexplicable reason'. She was suffering from an 'egg-shape[d] pessimism' and, in her last letter to the Rani, she writes: 'I am dreadfully off babies just now ... Awful nuisance considering in a fortnight or so the silent weight I now carry will be yelling its head off out in the cold.'

There was one further item of recurring news after Christmas that seemed to promise, for all their hectic efforts over the last months, that the entangled pattern of their lives would go on as before. Dorelia was again pregnant. 'Dorelia is decidedly enceinte,' Ida noted, '– it is depressing. Aurevoir.'

In the first week of March, Ida walked round to the room she had engaged at the Hôpital de la Maternité, ten minutes away in the Boulevard du Port Royal. Nothing, as she had written, could have been simpler. The baby was born in the early morning of 9 March: it was a boy.

The complications began immediately afterwards. Mrs Nettleship, who had gone over to Paris partly for business and partly to see Ida, explained to Ethel and Ursula what had happened:

My dears, Ida is to have a slight operation. It is serious but not very dangerous. In 48 hrs she will be quite out of danger. It will be to-night – I can't come home for a few days ... They think a little abscess has formed somewhere and causes the pain and the fever. She has to go to a Maison de Santé and one of the best men in Paris will do it. I am glad I was here as I could help ... I have been running about all day after doctors and people.

Augustus seemed paralysed by these events. The waiting, the suspense, above all the stupefying sense of powerlessness unmanned him. It was a nightmare, and he like someone half-asleep within its circumference. 'Apart from my natural anxieties,' he wrote, 'I was oppressed by the futility of my visits, by my impotence, and insignificance.'[30] Every decision was taken by Mrs Nettleship from her headquarters at the Hotel Regina. It was she who selected a specialist and arranged to pay him sixty pounds – 'I would have paid him £600 if he had asked it'; it was she who organized Ida's move to the new hospital and paid sixteen shillings a day for her room there (each sum scrupulously noted); it was she who wrote each day to family and friends keeping them informed of the latest developments. She was particularly reassured that the specialist, besides being 'the best man in Paris', was well-connected and had attended several diplomats at the embassy. When not busy at the hospital she would inspect the children at the Rue Dareau, interview Delphine and Dorelia, replant the entire garden there, and conduct David to his new school. 'He talks about "the boys in my school" just like an Eton boy might,' she noted with approval. Between times she managed to keep her business affairs going, sending off satisfactory messages to various titled clients. Her energy was prodigious, and in complete contrast to Augustus's stupor. 'Gus looks quite done up,' she confided to Ursula. 'He has the grippe and he is terribly upset about Ida. He does everything I suggest about Doctors and things, but has not much initiative – he has no experience.'

The Maison de Santé to which Ida had been removed was a light, spacious building in the Boulevard Arago. Somehow the atmosphere here engendered more hope. 'The place is the very best in Paris,' Mrs Nettleship reported. '. . . The nuns who nurse her are the most experienced and so quiet and pleasant. If it is possible for her to recover she will do it here.'

The crisis, which so galvanized Mrs Nettleship and demoralized Augustus, was observed by them at each stage differently. Where she is hopeful, he is pessimistic. 'Ida has got over her operation better than we expected,' she writes to her daughters, while Augustus the same day tells John Sampson that Ida 'is most seriously ill after an operation'. While Mrs Nettleship busied herself with complicated plans for Ida's convalescence, Augustus would scribble out wan messages to the Rani: 'She is a little worse to-day.'

But on one subject they were agreed: the baby. Augustus indeed was the more enthusiastic: 'The new baby is most flourishing so far. I really admire him,' he told Mrs Sampson. '. . . He has a distinct profile. We called him Henry as it was the wish of Mother Nettleship to memorialize thus her great friendship with Irving.' But on Dorelia and on Mrs Nettleship

Henry imposed an additional strain. 'He sleeps all day and cries all night,' Mrs Nettleship wrote to Ursula. 'Someone has to be awake with him every night.' He was, she added, 'a great beauty'; but 'I hope he will turn out worth all this trouble and anxiety.' This pious hope was to echo down his life, like a curse.

Ida was suffering not from 'a little abscess' but puerperal fever and peritonitis. 'It all depends on her not giving way,' Mrs Nettleship explained. 'She is no worse to-night than she was this morning and every hour counts to the good – but she might suddenly get worse any minute.' The main hope of her pulling through lay with what Mrs Nettleship called her 'natural vitality', but this had been worn away through the years to a degree that her mother could not appreciate, and it was Augustus who saw what was happening more clearly. To Mrs Nettleship her daughter's recovery was, once the doctors had done their best, a matter of simple determination. It did not occur to her that Ida might not want to live, that she could consent to die.

She was in pain and fever for much of the time. Except while under the anaesthetic, she did not sleep at all, night or day, following Henry's birth. Mrs Nettleship insisted that a whirl of cheerfulness be kept revolving round her bedside, almost a party spirit, so that she should not realize the full gravity of her illness. But Augustus had little heart for this charade. 'I do everything that is possible,' Mrs Nettleship assured Ursula. 'She is very unreasonable as usual and wants all sorts of things that are not good for her. I have to keep away a good deal as she always begs me to give her something she must not have and I can't be always refusing.' Augustus could refuse her nothing. She made him ransack Paris for a particular beef lozenge; she demanded violets; asked for a bottle of peppermint, a flask of eau de mélisse: he got them all. She seemed to understand that any definite activity, however improbable, came as a relief to him, and when she could invent nothing else for him to be doing she made him go and have a bath. To Mrs Nettleship it sometimes seemed as if he were acting quite irresponsibly, but she made no move to stop him. Perhaps Ida sensed some friction between them. 'Either you're all mad or I am,' she told them.

But on the morning of 13 March she demanded something
that even Augustus could not act upon. Sitting up in bed, she
declared her determination to leave the hospital and return to
Dorelia in the Rue du Château. Here she was going to cure herself, she said, 'with a bottle of tonic wine, Condy's, and an
enema'. Augustus, in a panic, 'got the doctor up in his motor
car' and at last he managed to dissuade her. But this was a bad
day for Ida, and having relinquished the hope of joining Dorelia,
her spirit seemed to give up the struggle.

'I adore stormy weather,' she had once written to the Rani.
On the night of 13 March there was a violent storm, with
thunder and lightning, lasting till the early morning. Lying in
her hospital bed, Ida longed to be out in it, imagined at certain
moments she was. 'She wanted to be a bit of the wind,' Augustus wrote to the Rani. 'She saw a star out of the window, and
she said "advertissement of humility". As I seemed puzzled she
said after a bit "Joke".'

The hospital staff tried to remove him, but Augustus stayed
with her the whole of that night. At times she was very
feverish, 'her spirit making preparatory flights into delectable
regions',[31] but there were periods of contact between them. He
rubbed her neck with Elliman's Embrocation and, at her special
request, tickled her feet. She pulled his beard about. To the
sisters she remarked: 'C'est drôle, mais je vais perdre mon
sommeil encore une nuit, voyez-vous.' In a delirium she spoke
of a land of miraculous caves, then, with some impatience, demanded that Augustus hand over his new suit to Henry Lamb.
Despite the fever, her pain had vanished and she felt strangely
euphoric. 'How can I speak of her glittering smiles and moving
hands?' Augustus afterwards told the Rani. And to Mrs
Sampson he wrote of that night: 'Ida felt lovely – she was so
gay and spiritual. She had such charming visions and made such
amazing jokes.'

In the morning, after the storm was over, she roused herself
and gave Augustus a toast: 'Here's to Love!' And they both
drank to it in Vichy water. It was a fitting salute to a life that
had steered such a brave ambiguous course between irony and
romance. Mrs Nettleship arrived shortly afterwards with Ethel
her daughter, just come from England. 'We are just waiting for

the end,' Ethel wrote to her sister Ursula. 'Ida is not really conscious, but she talks in snatches – quite disconnected sentences. Mother just sits by her side – and Gus stands the other side and sometimes holds her hand – she has some violets on her bed. I am just going to take the children for a walk – they are not going to see her as they would not understand, and she cannot recognize them.'

She died, without regaining consciousness, at half-past three that afternoon. 'Ah well, she has gone very far away now, I think,' Augustus wrote to Mrs Sampson. 'She has rejoined that spiritual lover who was my most serious rival in the old days. Or perhaps she is having a good rest before resuming her activities.'

The relief was extraordinary. As he rushed out of the hospital on to the Boulevard Arago, Augustus was seized with uncontrollable elation. 'I could have embraced any passer-by,' he confessed.[32] He had had enough of despair. It was a beautiful spring day, the sun was shining, the Seine looking 'unbelievable – fantastic – like a Chinese painting'.[33] He wanted to divest himself of the immediate past, escape the domination of death; he wanted to paint, but first to get drunk. 'Strange after leaving her poor body dead and beaten I had nothing but a kind of bank holiday feeling and had to hold myself in,' he told the Rani.

Many of his friends were mystified, shocked. 'John has been drunk for the last three days, so I can't tell you if he's glad or sorry,' Wyndham Lewis reported to his mother. 'I think he's sorry, though.'[34] Not everyone was so charitable as this. They blamed Ida's death on Augustus, hinted at suicide, and attributed his 'Roman programme' to justifiable guilt. Guilt there must often be with death – guilt and aggression. Augustus's drinking was a desperate bid for the sort of optimism he needed to keep him from the descent into paralysing melancholia. When John Fothergill wrote to express sympathy, adding that one had only to scratch life and underneath there was sorrow, Augustus replied: 'Just one correction – It is *Beauty* that is underneath – *not* misery, which is only circumstantial.' This he *had* to believe; it was his lifebelt. What particularly confused him about Ida's death, in addition to his natural grief, was that

it had come through childbirth, and that his children had been
deprived of a mother just as he had been. It seemed he was no
better than his father. He tried to keep the tide of melancholia
from advancing. But as the days passed the spirit of elation was
more difficult to sustain, and he drank more.

Ida was cremated on the Saturday following her death at the
crematorium of Père Lachaise. Almost no one was there – certainly not Augustus. A number of people had written from
England offering to come, but Augustus, who disliked formal
exhibitions of sentiment, refused them all. What was the use?
Friends, with their long faces, irritated him at a time when it
was crucial he did not succumb to depression. 'People keep
sending me silly sentimental lamentations,' he complained to
the Rani. 'I really begin to long to outrage everybody.' By far
the worst offender was poor Will Rothenstein who 'never for-
gave'[35] himself for not having gone out to Paris, and in meti-
culous expiation wrote long letters which Augustus found
'unintelligible'.[36] To the Rani he confided: 'That Will Rothenstein is an unhappy mortal – he's given to Uriah Heep-like
manifestations. He implored me not to give way to remorse
which was very Biblical of him, I'm sure.'

One man defied Augustus's instructions and, much to his
surprise, arrived in Paris on the morning of the cremation. This
was Ambrose McEvoy who 'had the delicacy to keep drunk all
the time and was perfectly charming'.[37] He had come for the
day, intending to go back to London the same night, but got so
drunk he was incapable of going anywhere for a week. 'He will
lose his return ticket if he doesn't pull himself up within a day
or so,' Wyndham Lewis predicted.[38]

Henry Lamb, who was now living in Paris and who had
taken Ida to a music hall the night before she entered hospital,
also attended the cremation. When the coffin and the body
were consumed, and the skeleton drawn out on a slab through
the open doors of the furnace, Lamb and McEvoy were still
able to recognize the strong bone structure of the girl they had
known. An attendant tapped the slab with a crowbar, and the
skeleton crumbled into ashes. The ashes were then placed in a
box and taken back to Augustus. Later a memorial service was
held in Lamb's rooms.[39]

One of the few people who understood Augustus's feelings
after Ida's death, partly because she shared some of the same
manic-depressive tendencies, was Gwen John. For a short time
she came to look after him at his new studio in the Cour de
Rohan. 'She was one of those who *knew* Ida,' Augustus explained to Mrs Sampson; one who understood that 'Ida was the
most utterly truthful soul in the world.'

It had been to Gwen that Ida had once admitted: 'Our
marriage was, on the whole, not a success.'[40]

5

Buffeted by Fate

God knows, I am buffeted mightily by fate.
AUGUSTUS JOHN TO ALICE ROTHENSTEIN

I. THE BATTLE OF THE BABIES

Ida was dead: but in many ways her influence was still alive. 'Ida keeps teaching me things,' Augustus told Alice Rothenstein. It seemed to him that she was teaching him at last who he was, solving the everlasting problem of his identity. 'I don't know that I feel really *wiser* through my sorrows, perhaps, yes: but at any rate I feel more "knowing" – I also feel curiously more myself,' he wrote to Alick Schepeler. '... I also feel still greater admiration for my view of things as an artist and at the same time my modesty is redoubled.'

His artistic aims had not altered, but he saw them more clearly and was to pursue them with more determination. 'I still feel extremely confident that given the right woman in the right corner I shall acquit myself honourably,' he had written to Will Rothenstein. '... I went to see Puvis's drawings in Paris. He seems to be the finest modern – while I admire immensely Rodin's later drawings – full of Greek lightness. Longings devour me to decorate a vast space with nudes and – and trees and waters. I am getting clearer about colour tho' still very ignorant, with a little more knowledge I shall at least begin ...'

Ida's death acted upon him as a catalyst, and very many of his finest paintings were done in the following eight years. 'It is so difficult to realize that Ida has gone so far away,' he told Mrs Nettleship. '... If she could only just come and sit for me sometimes. I've never painted her – I thought I had so much time, and began by getting at sidelights of her only, counting on doing the real thing in the end – she was such a big subject.'

It was this sense of time lost that accelerated his urge to paint, to seize every opportunity of doing so, to simplify life in

order to do so. But there was the difficulty. With seven children to support, almost as many studios and perhaps Dorelia (at
least while she was pregnant), how was he to start? His predicament was complicated by a new belief in his children.
While Ida was alive, he had tended to look at them as deafening interruptions to his work. But because of what he had lost,
and perhaps too because they were older, he began to see them
as the very subject-matter of his work. In order to paint them
he must have them around him; but to have them around him
he needed money; and to get money he would have to paint
commissioned portraits which were in any case a very hit-or-
miss business. However this conundrum was to be worked out,
he did recognize in what direction his painting must advance. 'I
must tell you how happy thoughts fill me just now,' he confided
to Alice Rothenstein. 'I begin to see how it is all going to come
about – all the children and mothers and me. In my former
impatience and unwisdom I *used* to think of them sometimes as
accidental or perhaps a little in the way of my art, what a
mistake – now it dawns on me they are, must be the real
material and soul of it.'

The sort of gossip from which Ida had partly shielded him
now reached him with lapidary intensity. He heard it everywhere – ill-informed, sentimental, full of malicious well-
meaning.

Lady M. F. Prothero to Alice Rothenstein:

I have been so much grieved to hear of Ida John's death. It sounds
terribly sad, – and all those babies left behind! I hear that Mrs
Nettleship was with Ida, so I feel she must have had care in her illness. But I wonder if she had been worn out lately in one way or
another. The thought of her quite haunts me, – and her heroic conduct all through – I should so much have liked to hear something
about her from you, and what is likely to become of those infants. –
I suppose John is quite irresponsible and it will fall to Mrs Nettleship to mother them. She, poor soul, has already had a hard struggle,
and this responsibility is a heavy one for her to bear . . .

It was nevertheless a responsibility Mrs Nettleship had resolved to shoulder. The fight between her and Augustus opened
up the very moment Ida had died. On the following day (15
March 1907) she reported the outcome to her daughter Ursula:

'Gus is quite willing for me to take them [the children] for the present but we have not made any plans for the future. I think he wants to get away to the country. I want to get a Swiss nurse for the children ... They are very pleased to be coming with us.'

Three days later she returned to Wigmore Street, carrying off the three eldest children. She was warm with plans for them – what they should precisely wear, what eat. The two babies, Edwin and Henry, she left in Paris, on the misunderstanding that they were to be looked after not by Dorelia but Delphine, who 'is a very good nurse'.

Augustus had not been 'quite willing' for his mother-in-law to take the children even on this temporary basis. He had no alternative. 'I am nearly bankrupt at the moment,' he confessed to Will Rothenstein. It was out of the question to saddle Dorelia with more squatters just as her own, Pyramus and Romilly, were 'beginning to get wise'; and so he was grudgingly forced to concede this first round in the child contest. 'Mrs Nettleship and Ethel N. took David and Caspar and Robin back to London,' he announced to Mrs Sampson, '– leaving us the incapables.'

He was determined to 'get them away again'.[1] To the Rani he confided: 'I have tried to make it clear that I shall kidnap them some day.' His plans were legion. His friends, none of whom lived so bourgeois an existence as his mother-in-law, could each take a kid or two and Augustus would then rent some small studio or flat in their houses throughout the country. It was not ideal, perhaps; but as a temporary solution it was, he flattered himself, pretty good. 'It is a pity to scatter them so,' he agreed with his outraged mother-in-law, '– one will know what to do a little later.'

At first this notion was greeted with acclaim. 'Everybody is asking for a baby and really there aren't enough,' he calculated, '– but I should like Mrs Chowne to have a little one *if I can find one* ... I wonder if Mrs Chowne can make Allenbury's and whether she understands the gravity of dill-water.'

The Chownes chiefly recommended themselves as prospective foster parents – probably for Henry – because she was good-looking and he, besides being 'a nice chap', had 'painted some charming flower pieces'.[2] They had no children, lived in Liverpool where Augustus would enjoy occupying a studio, and had known (if only slightly) Ida. It was a pilot scheme for the whole exercise of adoption. But it failed, and for the most inconsequential of reasons. Both the Chownes welcomed the idea – *but never at the same time.* As an example of political diplomacy it was expert. 'I should hate to disappoint Mrs Chowne,' Augustus admitted to the Rani who was acting as a sort of broker in the arrangements. Goodwill, like an unending stream, flowed between them without interruption or consequence: but afterwards there was no more talk of adoption.

The other practical matter that engulfed Augustus was the future of the Chelsea Art School. The business negotiations had been prolonged and for the most part unintelligible to all parties. This had been due to Knewstub's business methods, which involved muddling the money from the school with that of the gallery in such a way that at both places his cheques were returned to him. 'It is a great pity that Knewstub is such a tactless idiot,' Augustus had acknowledged to Trevor Haddon (4 February 1907). But he still aimed at using the school as a makeweight in the complicated balance between art and finance. He wanted from it the maximum dividend of money for the minimum investment of time. He proposed giving it the use, for advertisement purposes, of his name and, if it provided him with a studio, he guaranteed to be on the spot – from time to time. As his understudy, elevated with the name of Principal, he recommended Will Rothenstein. The goodwill of the school had apparently been purchased for two hundred pounds by Mrs Flower, who intended removing it to Hampstead Heath and paying Augustus one guinea for each of his appearances there – provided his understudy turned up when he did not. The trouble was that Will would ask such damned pedagogic questions: What was the exact constitution of the school? Could he have more details of his personal status there? Was it 'honourable', of the first rank, and established on a proper footing? Augustus would meet such inquiries at a more personal level: Mrs Flower was 'a very nice woman – rather remarkable. I think one of those naked souls, full of

faith and fortitude'; she therefore merited Will's collaboration.
'Knowing her pretty well,' Augustus added, 'I have not thought
it necessary to treat her too formally – she would be perfectly
ready to fall in with any views you or I held ... she would
give no trouble and understand she takes financial responsibility.' This responsibility embraced a fine new studio 'she will
erect for me, which will be an immense boon'; plus another, in
a neighbouring pine grove, where select young ladies could
pursue their studies under his tuition. Here too he would invite
his friends, Lamb, Epstein, even Lewis 'to roost among my
trees'. Mrs Flower, he concluded, 'should consider herself
lucky'.

Yet it was not to be. 'The school we might make of it is too
good to let slip too hastily,' he urged Will Rothenstein (28 July
1907) as it began to fade. But truthfully he was not interested
in teaching; only painting. It was a School in Spain, and as such
floated gracefully out of their lives.

Without money from the school he had to rely more than
ever on 'the asphyxiating atmosphere of the New English Art
Club ... Its corrupting amenities – its traitorous esprit de
corps – its mediocre excellencies even –!' he complained. 'I
always want to slough my skin after the bi-annual celebrations
and go into the wilderness to bewail my virginity for another
reason than that which prompted Jephthah's daughter.'

Over these next years there would seldom be a time when
his work was not being exhibited in London: at the Carfax
and the Chenil, the Goupil and Society of Twelve shows, at
groups, academies, clubs. Any new movement or gathering –
the Camden Town, the Allied Artists – any mixed show of
modern work automatically invited him, however foreign its
aesthetic programme might be. He was untouched by these
movements and counter-movements – their interest for him
was, like art-teaching, financial. But he was not hostile to them
and they welcomed his co-operation. Fry and Tonks, Rothenstein and Rutter – these and other painter-critic-politicians
wooed him. He bowed to their solicitations to exhibit, to sit on
hanging committees, to become president of societies: but he
was above art-politics, or at least to one side of them. They
were a means to an end when other means failed. 'I am longing

to borrow money so as to work till my show* comes, undisturbed by Clubs and Societies,' he hinted to Will Rothenstein
(22 June 1907). It was the uncertainty of his life that forced
him to rely so much on these institutions:

> Pendulous Fate sounds many a varied note on my poor tympanum
> – my darkness and lights succeed one another with almost as much
> regularity as if the sun and the Planetary system controlled them;
> and the hours of *moonless* nights are long dismal unhallowed hours.
> My life is completely unsettled; I mean to say the circumstances of
> my existence are problematic; but my art, I believe I can say, does
> not cease to develop ... I shall set about a composition soon – with
> a motive of action in it, controlling all – as in a Greek play.[3]

If the means were more than ever complicated, the ends were
simpler. Art historians sometimes write of painters who fail to
be swept up by the newest movements of their day as having
lacked 'courage'. This was not true of Augustus: he was an
authentic throw-back. Nothing could have been easier for him,
with his dexterity, than to copy with trivial variations the post-
impressionists in Paris. But to have done so would have involved a real loss of integrity. He was not blind to their merits.
'I want to start something fresh and new,' he told Will Rothenstein (April 1907). 'I feel inclined to paint a nude in cadmium
and indigo and orange. The "Indépendants" is effroyable – and
yet one feels sometimes these chaps have blundered on something alive without being able to master it.'

From the way in which he writes of pictures he wants to
paint, of subjects that excite him, there seems little to connect
him with his near-contemporaries in France or England –
Gauguin alone would seem to be within hailing distance.

> I should like to work for a few years entirely 'out of my head',
> perhaps for ever. To paint women till their faces become enlarged
> to an idiotic inanimity – till they stand impassively, unquestionably,
> terrifyingly fecund – fetiches of brass with Polynesian eyes and dry
> imperative teeth and fitful craving bowels that surge and smoke for
> sacrifice – of flesh and flowers. How delightful that sounds! Can

---

* 'Drawings by Augustus E. John' at the Carfax Gallery, December 1907.
'Knewstub's peculiarities have ended by tiring me out,' he had written to
Trevor Haddon (11 February 1907), 'and I have arranged for my next show to
be elsewhere.'

you* imagine the viridian vistas, can you hear the chanting in the flushing palm tree groves and the thumping of the great flat feet of ecstatic multitudes shining with the sacred oil. The 'Ah Ah Ah' of the wild infant world?

Primitive inspiration was not to be found in Paris. Parisian women were what Delacroix once described as 'on stage'.⁴ There are those who say that, by leaving Paris, Augustus turned his back on everything exciting that was happening in modern painting; that had he stayed he would have painted good pictures as did Derain, who had something of the same panache. But his instinct was sure. He wanted to find a place, untouched by the twentieth century, where the inhabitants still lived the life of their ancestors. His instinct was sure – but his thinking was weak: he did not plan to live in such a place, but to spend a holiday there.

He set off in April, patrolling the north coast – 'I have been right across the top of France,' he reported to Will Rothenstein. Finally he came across what he was looking for: Equihen, a village of primitive fisher-folk not far from Boulogne. 'The fish women are simply magnificent,' he wrote to Dorelia. 'I must get a studio or shed here soon and paint 'em – there's money in it!' It was good to get away from the 'steam music, literary society, bugs and other embêtements' of Paris. At Equihen one could see the marins getting the fish out of the sea and the matelots selling them – 'and the women go about in wonderful groups. Just the stuff for me. They resemble a community that live on the river by Haverfordwest distinct from their neighbours – in a village called Langum. The women go all over Pembrokeshire selling oysters in a peculiar costume and the men are supposed to mind the babies. When I think of them I burn to go and see them. It seems to me more wonderful than Spain and Italy, this little colony whom nobody knows anything about . . .'

In this 'desolate little place'⁵ he found a studio and summoned Dorelia and the four babies Pyramus and Romilly, Edwin and Henry. Since there were 'nice soft sand dunes' for the children to crawl on, he proposed, after they had settled in, sending for Ida's other sons. 'I am working pretty hard,' he

* i.e. Will Rothenstein.

assured Will Rothenstein, 'now and then. Having a little studio
here is a boon. I like the wenches here and the clothes they
wear and I wish I had more money to spend on them ...
Pyramus grows more lyrically beautiful every day. He is like a
little divine phrase from Shelley or Wordsworth. He is more
flower-like and "meaningless" than any child I know. He is the
incarnation of the daisy. I think I must try to do a "Mother and
Child" of him and Dorelia.'

But there were obstacles. The Mother was now trying to
bring about a miscarriage and for much of the time feeling too
ill to sit to Augustus. Once more he experienced 'those sub-
marine days when one begins to wonder what manner of
beings live above the air'.[6] The frustration that had consumed
him at Ste Honorine began again to smoulder. 'Meet me at
Boulogne next Saturday will you?' he suddenly invited Alick
Schepeler. But she, unchanged, absconded to Cumberland. 'As
to my work, I haven't got at it really,' he admitted to Henry
Lamb (13 June 1907). 'But my "head" still yields enchanting
suggestions. In fact call it what you will it is my best friend,
tho' I have other loyal parts. Sometimes I feel myself as if
slowly and surely settling down on some scrap heap.'

At this critical moment when, set in his viridian paradise,
inspiration failed to ignite, an invitation arrived from Lady
Gregory. She asked him to come over to Ireland, to stay with
her at Coole, and to do a portrait of her other guest that
summer, W. B. Yeats. Augustus hesitated – then accepted. 'It
may be that I shall draw Yeats' portrait,' he wrote to Alick
Schepeler, '– I am so hard up.'

2. IMAGES OF YEATS

The invitation to Coole Park had emanated from Lady Gregory's
son, the artist Robert Gregory, at whose marriage Augustus was
invited to be best man. He had helped Gregory with his work
in London, and this invitation was in the nature of a repayment
for his kindness. Appropriately, it was a business proposition.
Yeats was then revising his collected works in preparation for
A. H. Bullen's edition of the following year. The edition was to
contain a portrait by some contemporary artist. Yeats had

wanted Charles Shannon to do an etching for the frontispiece, but 'Shannon was busy when I was in London,' he explained to John Quinn (4 October 1907), 'and the collected edition was being pushed on so quickly that I found I couldn't wait for him.' It was then that Robert Gregory had put forward Augustus's name, to which Yeats rather nervously agreed: 'I don't know what John will make of me,' he faltered.

Augustus, too, was nervous – financially, 'I should like very much to visit you – and perhaps Yeats's drawing would make it possible,' he wrote from Equihen to Robert Gregory, 'but just now it is difficult for me. How much will the publishers pay, do you think? I would be glad to do the drawing. But as you see I am a long way off . . .' In reply, Lady Gregory sent him a fee of eighteen pounds in advance, plus a suggestion that should he wish to draw some of the family, then they might well wish to buy some of his drawings. The deal thus tentatively struck, Augustus sailed for Galway and the beginning of an illuminating new chapter in his career.

He arrived at Lady Gregory's big plain house in September. He had met Yeats before at the Nettleships' and at the Rothensteins', but never studied him as a subject. 'Yeats, slightly bowed and with his air of abstraction, walked in the garden every morning with Augusta Gregory, discussing literary matters,' he later remembered. 'With his lank forelock falling over his russet brow, his myopic eyes and hieratic gestures, he was every inch a twilight poet.'[7] It is as this not altogether youthful embodiment of Celtic poetry that Augustus portrays Yeats. The flat, dense colour areas of the oil portrait* suggest some comparison with Gauguin; and the design and colour are strong. Yeats, dressed in a white shirt and black smock, wears a loose cravat tied in a bow at the neck. The flesh-tones are wonderfully pale – a whitish-yellow; and this poetically consumptive complexion is enhanced by a backcloth of green meridian that isolates and freezes the poet by its density and airlessness. It is every inch a romantic portrait: this is what inspired Augustus; this is what he did best. For a moment Yeats fulfilled Augustus's ideal of a poet, and this ideal has been

* Now in the Manchester City Art Gallery. An unfinished study, one of several, is in the Tate Gallery (5298).

beautifully caught. Apart from the oil portrait, Augustus did numerous other studies* from which to work up his etching. But this final etching seems rather spoilt by the slowness of the medium. It has a pudding quality, the facial muscles solidified by laboured cross-hatching.

'I felt rather a martyr going to him [Augustus],' Yeats had reported to Quinn (4 October 1907). 'The students consider him the greatest living draughtsman, the only modern who draws like an old master. But he makes everybody perfectly hideous, beautiful according to his own standard. He exaggerates every little hill and hollow of the face till one looks a gipsy, grown old in wickedness and hardship. If one looked like any of his pictures the country women would take clean clothes off the hedges when one passed as they do at the sight of a tinker.'

Having glimpsed his studies with pen and brush, Yeats was certain at this stage that Augustus's 'best work is etching, he is certainly a great etcher with a savage imagination'. Shortly afterwards, to his horror, the etching arrived. It made him, he complained to Quinn, 'a sheer tinker, drunken, unpleasant and disreputable, but full of wisdom, a melancholy English Bohemian, capable of anything, except living joyously on the surface'.

Part of the trouble lay with Lady Gregory's reaction. 'John has done a terrible etching of Yeats,' she had written to Quinn (22 December 1907). 'It won't do for the book but he may do another, he promised to do two or three. Meanwhile I am trying to get Shannon to draw him. It is rather heartbreaking about John's for he did so many studies of him here, and took so much of his time ... But if they are not like Yeats, and are like a tinker in the dock, or a charwoman at a prayer meeting they and the plate shall go into the fire.'

About her reaction Augustus seems to have remained philosophical – at any rate his confidence was unshaken. 'Lady Gregory, much as I love and admire her, has her eye still clouded a little by the visual enthusiasms of her youth and cannot be expected to *see* the merits of my point of view,' he explained to Alick Schepeler, ,

* One of these, in pencil and wash on tinted paper, is at the National Portrait Gallery, London. It has what appear to be spots of Beaujolais on it. Yeats is wearing a macintosh.

tho' her intelligence assures her of their existence. Painting Yeats is becoming quite a habit. He has a natural and sentimental prejudice in favour of the W. B. Yeats he and other people have been accustomed to see and imagine for so many years. He is now 44 and a robust, virile and humorous personality (while still the poet of course). I cannot see in him any definite resemblance to the youthful Shelley in a lace collar. To my mind he is far more interesting as he is, as maturity is more interesting than immaturity. But my unprejudiced vision must seem brutal and unsympathetic to those in whom direct vision is supplanted by a vague and sentimental memory. It is difficult also to assure people that my point of view is not that of a particularly ill-natured camera – but on the contrary that of a profoundly sympathetic and clairvoyant intelligence. Another thing is I never paint without admiring.

It was almost impossible for any artist to see Yeats as Lady Gregory saw him. If Augustus had portrayed him in her eyes as an ugly ruffian, Shannon, by an unlucky chance, made him look damnably like Keats; Jack Yeats, of course, could only see him through a mist of domestic emotion; Mancini turned him into an Italian bandit; Sargent into a dream-creature. And so on. Yeats flirted with the idea of introducing the lot of them into his collected works, one after the other, 'and I shall write an essay on them and describe them as all the different personages that I have dreamt of being but never had the time for. I shall head it with this quotation from the conversation of Wordsworth: – "No, that is not Mr Wordsworth, the poet, that is Mr Wordsworth, the Chancellor of the Exchequer." '

Such flights of fancy were firmly censored by Lady Gregory, and in Bullen's edition a Sargent drawing took the place of Augustus's etching. But in subsequent editions it is almost always one or other of Augustus's portraits that have been chosen as the frontispiece.* Yeats himself had never really been so opposed to Augustus's interpretation of him as Lady

---

* 'The portrait was painted in 1907 at Coole by Augustus John,' Yeats wrote to Olivia Shakespeare on 13 November 1933, the year after Lady Gregory died. 'I am using it as a frontispiece for my collected volume of lyrics which you will get in a day or two.' When the etching was rejected, Yeats had written privately to his publisher A. H. Bullen (March 1908): 'The Augustus John is a wonderful etching but fanciful as a portrait. But remember that all fine artistic work is received with an outcry, with hatred even. Suspect all work that is not.'

Gregory. On leaving Ireland, he wrote to John Quinn (7 January 1908): 'I would like to show you Augustus John's portrait of me. A beautiful etching, and I understand what he means in it, and admire the meaning, but it is useless for my social purpose.' It took time before he appreciated the portrait. Years later he wrote: 'Always particular about my clothes, never dissipated, never unshaven except during illness, I saw myself there an unshaven, drunken bar-tender. And then I began to feel John had found something that he liked in me, something closer than character, and by that very transformation made it visible. He found Anglo-Irish solitude, a solitude I have made for myself, an outlawed solitude.'

Though fearing his 'savage imagination', Yeats was greatly taken with Augustus. His attitude, like Augustus's towards him, mingled romance with an amusing perception of character.

'He is himself a delight,' Yeats wrote to John Quinn (4 October 1907),

the most innocent, wicked man I have ever met. He wears earrings, his hair down to his shoulders, a green velvet collar and had two wives who lived together in perfect harmony and nursed each other's children on their knees till about six months ago when one of them bolted and the other died. Since then he has followed the lady who bolted and he and she are gathering the scattered families. Of course, nobody round Coole knew anything of these facts. I lived in daily terror of some benevolent gossip carrying on conversation with him like this,

'Married, Mr John? Children?'

'Yes.' 'How many?' 'Seven.' 'You married young?'

'Five years ago.' 'Twins doubtless?' – after that frank horrifying discourse on the part of Augustus John, who considers himself a particularly good well-behaved man. The only difference is in code. He told me how he tried to reform an old reprobate professor [John Sampson] who is an authority on gipsy lore. The old professor had a series of flirtations unknown to his wife, but one day when he was in a half-intoxicated state in a Welsh tavern where he had been studying gipsies he was plunged into deep depression because a gipsy told him he was getting bald at the top of his head. 'What shall I do?' he said to John. John replied sternly 'Return to your innocence', by which he meant sin openly and scandalise the world. He is the strangest creature I have ever met, a kind of fawn ... a magnificent-looking person, and looks the wild creature he is.

Dressed impeccably, according to his own standards, in an old Victorian coat, Augustus was on his very best behaviour. He was as charmed by Yeats as Yeats was by him, and the two of them would sit up late in intimate talk. 'He is most delightful,' Augustus told Alick Schepeler, 'nobody seems to know him but me – unless it is the Gregorys, but that is my conceit no doubt.' Except for these late-night conversations, Augustus spoke little, worked hard and would wander off for long solitary walks in the wooded park round Coole where he had located 'a region which is obviously holy ground'. Often he needed to escape out-of-doors and spent many evenings rowing idly on the lake, with only the swans, which Yeats had celebrated, for company. Then, to the apprehensive admiration of Robert Gregory and the astonishment of everyone else, he would surge indoors, do wonderful athletic things on the drawing-room floor, stride out again and climb to the top of the tallest tree in Coole garden, where he carved a mysterious symbol. Poets, playwrights and patrons struggled among its lower branches, but 'nobody else has been able to get up there to know what it is, even Robert stuck halfway'.[8]

By the time he left, Augustus had seen enough of Ireland to know that it was rich in motifs for him as a painter. Already he had vague vast schemes to paint all Galway. He would return, several times; and at the last he would again paint Yeats.

3. ALL BOYS BRAVE AND BEAUTIFUL

At Equihen Augustus had left a situation full of passionate uncertainties.

Attended by one of her sisters – 'voluptuous Jessie'[9] – Dorelia had enjoyed a successful illness culminating, to the satisfaction of all, in a miscarriage. Nothing could be wrong with this unless it was the timing, which coincided with the arrival of Mrs Nettleship, bringing with her Ida's three eldest boys.

Augustus had wanted to encircle himself with all his children this summer, and to spend his time happily at work over them and the admirable sea-girls. He had not reckoned on

Mrs Nettleship's presence, nor on the unpaintable school clothes
with which she had decked out her grandchildren. It was a
shock – but he was determined to prove the optimist. 'This is a
jolly place,' he wrote to Ursula Tyrwhitt. 'My numberless kids
are all here now. I have a dilapidated studio to work in. The
fish people here are very amusing. The girls look fine in their
old costumes. Multitudes of children teem in the gutters together with the debris of centuries.'

Such cheerfulness died hard. He was resolved not to put up
with the children's noise, but to *enjoy* it. After all, it was
natural: did he therefore not have a moral duty to enjoy it?
Enjoyment was necessary to work – it accelerated his perceptions: but it was elusive. Everything seemed to rub away at
this quality of enjoyment at Equihen and, because of the company of Mrs Nettleship, in the most abrasive manner. Before her
commanding presence, the very beauty of Nature seemed to
hesitate and retreat; even alcohol could no longer 'stimulate
those delightful sensations old Debaucheries used to procure
me ... angelic glimpses secreted like pearls in piggeries.'[10]

In a letter to Henry Lamb (5 August 1907) he wrote: 'I wish
this house were on wheels.' Wherever he was he wanted a
place of escape – like the magic lake or *Turlough* at Coole,
islanded, and mysteriously rising and subsiding. What he desired now was an encampment that contained all possibilities,
that moved yet rested, that congregated the right people –
artists and comedians, women and children – but that had
hidden places into which he could retire. In such a community
he saw the solution to that war between involvement and
solitude which confronts most artists.

'I understand that solitude is not always and ever good for a
man,' he wrote to Henry Lamb.

Are we not much too solitary? It's only those who live much
among men and women who can preserve and develop that internal
independence which belongs to a warrior. We are not made to do
battle with spirits and demons of the desert. I think company is
better medicine than loneliness. Let us see new faces, lest the old
ones grow old under our tiring eyes, and damn it we are artists not
misanthropists. Anthropology is our business. Solitude be damned.
One seeks solitude – with one's woman only.

These were brave-sounding words, but they trumpeted a virtue of what, for Augustus, was becoming a necessity. He needed more solitude, if possible, not less; more opportunity to train his memory in recapturing the fleeting moment; more emphasis on sustained imagination. But this gypsy way to artistic fulfilment was new and needed to be worked out.

Henry Lamb was by this time his new star. 'He is no ordinary personage,' Augustus was to assure Ottoline Morrell (20 September 1908), 'and has the divine mark on his brow.' Lamb had taken his apprenticeship to Augustus very seriously. His drawings, though more clinical, resembled Augustus's, and so did his clothes. He let his hair grow long; he failed to shave; he fastened on gold ear-rings. He was spectacularly handsome. With his hypnotic deep-blue eyes he fascinated men and women alike, and his entrance into any gathering was almost as striking as that of his master. Like his master, too, he had married a Slade girl, Euphemia, the very model of a John model. When the Chelsea Art School went into a decline – or rather when Augustus's attendances there declined – Lamb quitted it and followed him to Paris. By the beginning of 1907 he was living in the Rue Cels and studying at La Palette under Jacques-Emile Blanche.

Ida had liked Lamb; they used to discuss the French translations of Dostoyevsky. Dorelia liked him too: they played the piano together. After Ida's death, Dorelia and Lamb drew closer. 'Dorelia will I hope buck up under your sunny influence,' Augustus wrote to Lamb (13 June 1907), '– yours is evidently the touch. My person is like a blight on the household.' Meanwhile Augustus was doing countless studies of Euphemia. The mercurial presence of this girl, with her pale oval face and heavy honey-coloured hair, had already provoked rather a sharp inquiry from Alick Schepeler. 'I have never had time or inclination to consider her very seriously,' Augustus airily defended himself. 'I have simply taken her for granted. It is true I have thought her rather eccentric . . .' Then, in Paris, immediately following Ida's death, time and the inclination had been amply provided. She was comedian and model to him: he admired her body, was amused by her exploits. So the two households, the Lambs and the Johns, mingled, amoeba-like, revolved and came together again as in some complicated dance. But one partner was hurt – Euphemia, who fell into the arms of another British painter then studying at La Palette, Duncan Grant. 'That Lamb family sickens me,' he complained to Lytton Strachey (7 April 1907),

and that man John. I'm convinced now he's a bad lot. His mistress, Dorelia, fell in love with Henry and invited him to copulate and as far as I can make out John encouraged the liaison and arranged or at any rate winked at the arrangements for keeping Nina [Euphemia] out of the way, although Henry didn't in the least want to have any dealings with Dorelia. However it was apparently all fixed up that they should 'go on the roads' together when Nina was (according to her own story) found with a loaded revolver ready to shoot herself (and Henry as far as I could gather). So Henry was left by himself ... Dorelia and John seem to be the devils and the others merely absurd ...

This account, which suffers from being tied to Euphemia's version of the truth, nevertheless indicates how Augustus, and such artists as Innes and Derwent Lees, were always separated from Fry's group of Bloomsbury painters. It was not that they failed to admire one another's talent: they did. But Augustus was ill-at-ease in their tidy, educated presence, and he mistrusted their bloodless theories. And they were disconcerted by his deliberate thoughtlessness, his irrationality. There was no common ground between his pursuit of 'meaningless' beauty, and their imposition of 'significant form'. To Bloomsbury, Augustus was a meteor, dazzling and self-destructive, a phenomenon that attracted their alarmed gaze but from which, after a covert glance, all wise men must, they judged, avert their eyes. 'Oh John! Oh ... what a "warning"! as the Clergy say,' Lytton Strachey exclaimed to Duncan Grant (12 April 1907). 'When I think of him, I often feel that the only thing to do is to chuck up everything and make a dash for some such safe secluded office-stool as is pressed by dear Maynard's [Keynes'] happy bottom. The dangers of freedom are appalling! In the meantime it seems to me that one had better immediately buy up every drawing by him that's on the market. For surely he's bound to fizzle out; and then the prices!'

The entanglements in which Augustus wrapped himself,

while inviting all sorts of damage, were fundamentally un-
serious. That was how it appeared to Bloomsbury, and this was
the burden of their complaint. He lived a life (could there be
anything more shocking?) based upon the casual whim! Their
judgement was precisely logical, unpsychological. For Bloomsbury could not know the annihilating force of solitude upon
him, did not sense the panic.

Of course Augustus never subscribed to any theoretical rules
of behaviour and, since he did not trade in words, never defended or explained his philosophy. It was based, however,
upon a natural law of self-interest that did not necessarily
exclude the interests of others, but did not put them first. The
ideal collective sphere where 'each man shift for all the rest,
and let no man take care of himself' he considered absurd and
against human nature. If some desire swept through you, then
you must give expression to it with all your being – physically,
vocally, at once and until it was exhausted and you were left
empty or filled by another desire. Those who acted upon their
emotions lived longer because they lived by a biological reality
not just social convention. However admirable your motives
for bottling up feelings might be, this was wrong because the
contents of the bottle turned to a poison that seeped into your
unconscious – hence the fact that those with the most exquisite
consciences and elevating philosophies could spread the most
unhappiness. There was a danger in modern society of the
animal in man being neglected. But, however polished by tea-
time veneer, the principle of the survival of the fittest still
ruled our existence. Therefore give expression to it openly –
not in a thin trickle of financial self-interest, but as a nourishment and expansion of the soul-and-body. Lock antlers with
the men; copulate with the women; scatter your image through
the land. There will be wounds given and received; but there
will be no deception or the sour sediment of regrets and frustra-
tions taken to the grave. The wounds will be honourable and
will heal, not fester. This was how life should be lived.

Yet it was surprisingly difficult to achieve the simple life.
What could be more simple, for example, than to invite Henry
Lamb to Equihen? And what, in the society of Mrs Nettleship,
could be more unwise? 'I hope you will come and bathe here,'

had run his innocent invitation. But instead of Henry, Euphemia came, dressed rather improbably as a young man and followed by an enthusiastic, but bankrupt, Swede. Having relieved Augustus of some of his Irish money, the Swede hurried off to Paris, while Euphemia, falling ill with a mysterious disease, was condemned for a week to bed. 'She makes an irresistible boy,' Augustus admitted to her husband, '– I feel, myself, better after assisting at her recovery.'

Although she was not to allow him a divorce until the late 1920s, Euphemia had already walked out on Lamb and, amid much determined talk of divorce, embarked on an extra-ordinary career that was to be much caught up with other artists. Describing her in his mammoth *Confessions* under the pseudonym of 'Dorothy', Aleister Crowley, the Great Beast 666, wrote that she 'would have been a *grande* passion had it not been that my instinct warned me that she was incapable of true love. She was incomparably beautiful ... She was capable of stimulating the greatest extravagancies of passion.' For Augustus, who gave her the name 'Lobelia', these extrava-gancies were wonderfully comic. 'She has made the acquaint-ance of a number of nations,' he assured Lamb (5 August 1907); and he told Dorelia (April 1908) that 'Lobelia had 6 men in her room last night, representing the six European powers, and all silent as the grave.'

Dorelia had not seduced Lamb; he had fallen in love with her. For him it was almost inevitable, fulfilling his role as Augustus's *alter ego*. Since he was an artist, it also made destiny-sense to Dorelia. Already they had begun a love-affair – the second of Dorelia's two 'discreditable episodes' – that was to continue, with intervals, for twenty years.

For the time being their affair had no unpleasant repercus-sions: except with Mrs Nettleship. Mrs Nettleship had never liked Dorelia, and everything she learnt this summer confirmed her in this dislike. Obviously she was quite the wrong person to whom to entrust Ida's boys. It was not simply a matter of immorality: it was incompetence – an incompetence so super-lative it made Mrs Nettleship perfectly dizzy. It was out of the question for the children to be brought up in this lunatic way. They were decked out in fanciful rags, never washed, brushed or combed, and never properly superintended. Their bedrooms were full of unchecked frogs, absurd grasshoppers and other atrocities: it was bedlam. Even Augustus was forced to own that 'this crêche-like establishment is a little too heroic – in the long run'.[11] Within a week of arriving at Equihen, the boys had almost been drowned *en masse*, being uniquely rescued in the last second by a local fisherman who 'was getting food for his rabbits on the cliff when he heard their screaming,' Mrs Nettleship explained to Ursula (19 July 1907). 'He has never saved anyone before and he hopes to get a medal.'

So different was the atmosphere from Wigmore Street, she felt as if she had landed on some distant world where no one knew what was right or wrong, and no normal standards applied. The amoral beauty of it all drove her frantic. 'There never seems time for anything here,' she complained to Ursula, '– the weather is so lovely, we are out all day and in the evening we are too sleepy to do anything. It is almost irritating that this place is so lovely – I hate it all for being so placid and "only man is vile" . . . Something must come to relieve this tension.'

What came tightened the tension to breaking-point. Dorelia had succeeded in not telling anyone that her children this summer had suffered from ophthalmia, a painful eye disease. She had even forgotten it herself and, by arranging for all the children to share a single sponge and towel, had successfully spread the infection first to Edwin, then to Robin. Mrs Nettleship was appalled. Here was actual proof that Dorelia could not be trusted. She at once herded Ida's untainted sons together and drove them out of the infected area. 'I should like to bring them back right away,' she told Ursula, 'but Gus does not think it matters! . . . He says the village children get over it all right and so will ours! He is nearly driving me mad . . . I have never known anyone so impossible to deal with.' At the same time, for fear of losing the boys altogether, she had to remain outwardly friendly. Nor could she leave while the ophthalmia persisted, since no one did anything to cure the disease unless she personally insisted on its being done – Dorelia preferring what she called 'natural methods'. At first, Mrs Nettleship's monumental diplomacy seemed to be effective, especially when Augustus, responding to the strain of the holiday, remarked that the two families could never be brought up together. 'If either of our boys [David or Caspar] get ophthalmia I shall use it as a weapon,' Mrs Nettleship promised.

Twelve days later, diplomacy had disappeared for ever. 'It is war to the knife,' declared Mrs Nettleship. Each side had marshalled a team of doctors with strongly opposing advice. 'Gus is hopeless – just one mass of selfishness – not thinking of anyone, but his own desires – and so surly and cross,' Mrs Nettleship explained to Ursula. 'How Ida can have endured it I can't imagine – he has no heart at all.'

Another twelve days and Mrs Nettleship had returned to Wigmore Street, triumphantly taking with her David, Caspar, Robin and, if that were not enough, the urn containing Ida's ashes. It was less her victory than Augustus's defeat. For the time being he had nowhere for them to live, and it affected him keenly.

'I am saddened to realise that I have allowed an immoral and bourgeois society of women to capture my 3 eldest boys,' he acknowledged to Henry Lamb (27 July 1907). 'It will be the devil to get them back again but it must be done when opportunity offers. Perhaps I may ask you to assist me one day in recovering them. Can you shoot? I cannot stand finding those chaps in the hands of people among whom I shall always be a stranger, and no longer in the brave and beautiful attire their mother gave them to wear. I cannot leave them with people who although they are Ida's mother and sisters did not even know her.'

Mrs Nettleship was used to getting her own way and, once back in Wigmore Street, she set about consolidating her advantage. She knew that Augustus did not want to prolong the present arrangement, yet sensed he was somehow in two minds. His uncertainty was contagious and, untypically, she could not make up her own mind as to what her best tactics should be. If she wanted to mollify him she would approach him via her daughter Ursula; if she wanted to frighten him she would appeal to Edward Nettleship – 'Uncle Ned of Nutcombe Hill', said to be a dragon of a man. Finally she did both, in addition to canvassing opinion among various aunts and cousins. Ursula acted at once, writing to assure Augustus that, if the children were left with the Nettleship family, she would see to it that their education was not old-fashioned and would look after them herself. In his reply, Augustus set down his feelings with unusual explicitness:

Be sure that if any consideration could induce me to part with the children it would be the fact that *you* alone would have them. The *immediate* future has an unsettled aspect for me. Homeless, penniless and lawless I present a pretty spectacle of a paterfamilias!' But thanks to you things begin to look much more tractable. I want badly to retain the children as Ida's and mine – to keep them in the atmosphere they were born in – a delightful atmosphere and not at all dreadful you know – and to think of them being educated into ordinary little early Victorian bourgeois prigs is a horrid thought! You have eased me of that apprehension at least. I'm sure you would do your best to train them into men brave, intelligent, gay – like heroes: and you would have some of Ida's sublime gigantic composure in dealing with them – I really was beginning to fear I shouldn't recognise them in a year or so, or they me. I was preparing myself for the moment when they would approach me and earnestly implore me to get my hair cut! In addition to these perhaps morbid fancies the spirit of opposition was kindled somewhat on finding my section of the family treated to a kind of superdiscreet aloofness – and the three kids in question hardly to be viewed and that only under formidable escort: indeed one had the sensation of extraordinary and almost painful privilege that malefactors must experience when permitted to interview for a few brief moments their more fortunate relatives on the other side of the bars, attired, one seems to see them, in their Sunday best! Now I know that prejudice alas! is the most natural thing in the world, and meanness the commonest, and error the most universal. Yet it is natural enough too to seek to remove these weeds, at any rate when they come your way; and I must have a try at getting people to know that Dorelia is a Person and a very rare and respectable being, to wit full of sense and sensibility, having no shams in her being, indeed a kind of feminine genius I fancy. I would like to mention that had she been only my 'mistress' we would not be together now. Had she not been a worthy soul, do you think I could have stood it so long? I say this as no superior person, believe me – I might say like Hamlet 'I am myself indifferent honest, but yet I could accuse myself of things it were better my mother had not borne me. I am proud, revengeful, ambitious, with more offences at my back than I had thought to put them in, imagination to give them shape, or time to act them in. What should such a fellow as I do, crawling between heaven and earth!' But Dorelia was loved of Ida and her very good friend in spite of appearances and all great mistakes not withstanding. Barring their mother she had more to do with the children than anyone else; and because Ida happened to die it doesn't strike me as indispensable to hurry D. out by the back stairs. In a word she has been and so far remains part of my family and I should like her always to continue to give the children the benefit of her honesty and simplicity and affection, and help to dress them bravely too – as she knows how to. For without brave attire I can't put up with them. It would be a frightfully difficult thing to take them away from you even now: but I don't want to. They can always pay you visits, especially as you have an anti-Wigmorian plan – and heaven knows I may have a house in London – but wait till after my show when I hope to see my way better. Perhaps you will say you must have them altogether or not at all – Alas! But I suppose it's not impossible that you may have babies of your own some time, and you might think that better than having other people's babies ... since my proposal to reassume the parental responsibilities sooner or later – friendliness and Patience have become established ...

While Augustus was writing this letter to Ursula, Uncle Ned was sharpening his pen at Nutcombe. With long-drawn-out relish he was preparing himself 'a good slapping letter' for Augustus. It was congenial labour. He lingered lovingly over the vituperative phrases, savouring them, hardly liking to let them go. He was still remorselessly chewing over all this when he received from Ursula Augustus's letter and, as he read through it, it occurred to him that his carefully-charged time bomb fell 'rather flat'. It was a sad waste, but at least a little of his invective could be discharged vicariously. The letter he now (28 September 1907) wrote to Ursula shows between what bewildering changes of background some of Ida's sons were to pass their formative years. At first, Uncle Ned allowed, he had thought the fellow must have been mad drunk when he wrote, 'but on re-reading, there is too much essential coherence for that. He [Augustus] whines that he is penniless and homeless and lawless (the last evidently, like the other two, from his misfortune doubtless, not from any preventable fault!). He wants to keep the children for himself and Dorelia, but he

wants you with your gigantic composure to carry on their
Bohemian Education when in the intervals of their home life
they pay you visits in some place where the atmosphere is
"anti-Wigmorian".' Such a response, Uncle Ned urged, called in
question the whole policy of conciliation. Instead, he would
like to hear that Augustus was being instructed 'in quite simple
words that it is his business to put his back into his work to
maintain his children', that no Nettleship worth the name
would be a party to brave attire – if ' "brave" means (as I am
told it does) squalid or dirty or gutter-snipe attire'; and that to
talk of the inhabitants of Wigmore Street as bourgeois prigs
was 'impudent nonsense' for which an instantaneous apology
was required. This, like music, was what Uncle Ned would
like to hear – but it would have to come now from Ursula,
since she had opened the negotiations. She must change the
tune – but he, if called upon, would conduct her playing. It
must, however, be a solo programme – they couldn't have
every aunt and cousin chiming in. So the dragon roared his
last paragraph of flame:

'I think that subtle, absolutely selfish and introspective as he
is, and morose and bad tempered to boot, he is a coward at any
rate when dealing with women; and that hard hitting, at any
rate now, is at least as likely to succeed with him and Dorelia
(who of course is doing her best as wire-puller) as any other
plan ... Dorelia wants to keep him; she does not really want
Ida's children.'

So with both sides convinced of the other's immorality as
parents, the autumn passed; and, for their winter quarters,
they took up entrenched positions in this war to the knife. 'We
are rather harassed by babies,' Augustus admitted to Henry
Lamb (5 August 1907). 'We ought to have a few vigorous old
women to attend to them.'

4. OR SOMETHING

In one respect at least Uncle Ned had misunderstood the situation. He had attributed logic, even calculation, jointly to
Augustus and Dorelia, and in so doing had, from the very start,
mixed in with his reasoning an untruth that reliably falsified

almost any deduction he cared to make. His generalship behind the Nettleship lines was therefore of incalculable value to Augustus. 'Wire-pulling' or any other species of long-term cunning had no part in Dorelia's make-up. Her gift was for taking things as they came – and when they didn't come, but hung around some distance off, she had no talent for advancing on them by a subtle route. The present suspended state of affairs did not stimulate her best qualities. To a degree, her desires were the very opposite of what Uncle Ned had represented: she did not inevitably want to keep Augustus, but she did want one or two of Ida's children. Her point of view was beyond the comprehension of the Nettleships.

Over the summer, over the autumn, Dorelia and Augustus debated the situation as fully as two inarticulate people could. They evolved all manner of schemes for taking care of the future, but without Ida they were strangely undecided and, despite much activity, made little progress. There were two plans: first that they should continue living together; and secondly that they should not. The first plan came in many forms. One night, for example, Dorelia dreamt of 'a lovely country ... terrific mountains and forests and rivers – the people were Russians but I think it must have been Spain';[12] and next day they were hot for setting off to discover this place. Then, changing their minds, they thought of settling for a house in England. 'We must have an aquarium in the country,' Dorelia affirmed. 'We might get one in exchange for a baby or something.'[13] It was that continual 'or something' that foxed them.

Dorelia's difficulty was Henry Lamb, whose influence was like that of a magnet upon a compass. Her sense of destiny could no longer guide her, and she did not know what to do. At times she was almost passionately indifferent. 'I haven't the faintest wish to get married,' she informed Augustus (September 1907). 'I think it would be best if I went on the road and left you in peace which I should be only too glad to do if you would let me have one of the children – Caspar or Robin – he would be better with me than in that virginal atmosphere [Wigmore Street].'

Lamb, who was to walk through Brittany from inn to inn the

following summer with Caspar on his shoulders, had already been approached by Augustus in connection with the children. The argument was simple. Since Lamb was apprenticed to Augustus, what could be better than apprenticing one of Augustus's sons to Lamb? It was a merry scheme. 'I found Robin overwhelming!' he recommended. 'When one sings or even whistles to him, he lies back and closes his eyes luxuriously. It is he who should be your pupil ...'

During the next three years, the relationship between Augustus and Dorelia was to be more fluid and circumstantial than at any other time. Sometimes they lived on wheels together; sometimes the Channel flowed between them. Sometimes they were close; sometimes they seemed to float apart, carried this way and that by currents they could not control. 'Don't worry,' Dorelia reassured him this autumn, 'as I think either plan extremely desirable.' There were indeed times when *any* plan seemed desirable – but still they could not decide. Yet whenever Dorelia drifted too far away, Augustus would grow resolute: 'Beloved, of course it's *you* I want.'

One thing at least had been agreed: they could no longer afford, scattered through two countries, quite such a multitude of unsuitable flats and studios. On returning to London, Augustus wrote to Lamb ('mon cher Agneau') asking him to sell the lease of his studio in the Cour de Rohan. Though he would make other parts of France his second home in the future, he was never again to live in Paris. Ironically, perhaps, this parting was to coincide with his meeting with Picasso. 'I saw a young artist called Picasso whose work is wonderful in Paris,' he had written that summer (5 August 1907) to Lamb. And two months later, once his studio was let and all connections with Paris severed (4 November 1907), he had become convinced that 'Picasso is a wonder'. The two painters had visited each other at their studios, and Augustus was greatly impressed by Picasso's work, chiefly because, like his own, it was steeped in the past, drew part of its inspiration from Puvis de Chavannes and revealed 'elements derived from remote antiquity or the art-forms of primitive peoples'.[14] Some of Augustus's paintings done at this time, and perhaps even earlier, show a striking resemblance to Picasso's Blue Period, and indicate the direction his work might have gone had the geography of his life been different.

But only in London could he sell his work. Lack of money was the Nettleships' best weapon and he was determined to disarm them. However, for the first few days, having nowhere else to go, he was obliged to put up in, of all places, Wigmore Street.* Shortly afterwards he moved to Whistler's old studio at 8 Fitzroy Street where he stayed, intermittently, for almost a year. It was his sole foothold in London, from where, at the prompting of his spirit, he would wander off to pubs and music halls, to the Café Royal or, in some painted wagon, to remoter spots.

'I'm thinking of raising a little money with a preliminary show of drawings alone,' he wrote to Lamb on 11 November 1907. The results of this exhibition at the Carfax Gallery that December were encouraging. 'The show opened most successfully,' he told Dorelia. 'I sold about £225 worth the first morning. 'Twas a scene of great brilliance. Epstein and his wife looked grand.' After it was over he wrote to Lamb: 'I hope now to paint pictures for the rest of my life.' But he had other plans too. 'I *must* have a press,' he told Dorelia. 'I long to bring out a book of etchings. It might be called "etchings of Innocence" or "Phantasmagoria" or "The Simple Way" . . .'

Over the next months there were plenty of opportunities to sell his work: etchings and drawings at the Society of Twelve into which he was planning to elect Lamb; drawings and paintings at the N.E.A.C., which had opened that winter with the 'paltriest of shows'. He was arranging a one-man summer show at the Chenil Gallery and hoped to send in something big to the celebrated 'Exhibition of Fair Women' to be held early in 1909 at the New Gallery.† It was the field work for this last affair, at which he would exhibit one of his acknowledged

---

* 'I took a small studio here (28 Wigmore Street) which I now see is quite impossible,' he wrote to Henry Lamb (25 September 1907). After a short period of 'perfect hell' he went to stay with Charles McEvoy at 132 Cheyne Walk before settling into 8 Fitzroy Street – 'it is a fine place' he told Dorelia.

† The exhibition was held by the International Society of Sculptors, Painters and 'Gravers, at the New Gallery during February and March 1909.

masterpieces, that gave him the most trouble. He had been presented with a huge canvas by William Nicholson: the problem was how to fill it. 'I have a scheme for a picture of fair women in which Lobelia ought to figure,'* he instructed Lamb (24 December 1907). But Euphemia had temporarily vanished and he had to look elsewhere. 'I just passed Bertha in the street (the girl in black tights),' he wrote hopefully to Dorelia. But she, unlike Ida, was determined to be absolutely firm with him. 'That barmaid has disappeared from my ken,' he reassured her. Next he unearthed 'La Seraphita', his still unfinished (as he now thought of it) portrait of Alick Schepeler, named after Balzac's ambiguous novel. 'Having changed the background it now looks rather remarkable,' he wrote to Lamb (10 January 1908), '– her face embodies all that is corrupt, but the thing has a monumental character and the pose is perfect I think.' The picture showed Alick in a tight black dress, standing on a mountain top with strange ice-floes growing at her feet. It needed only a few more sittings. 'Seraphita still stands upon her crest and smiles her smile of specious profundity to a nervous and half-credulous world,' Augustus assured Alick. 'I hope you will come and see me here ... when I will show you some things.' But again Dorelia, who particularly disliked Alick for her public demonstrations of emotion, put her foot down; and again Augustus yielded: 'I have written to the Schepeler and said goodbye so now you cheer up and get well, there's an angel.' Finally it was a superb picture of Dorelia herself, 'The Smiling Woman', which he submitted to the Exhibition of Fair Women.†

Though he himself was doing good work, the English art world depressed him. Of many of his fellow artists, such as Bone and Dodd, he held no high opinion. In his letters over this period he seems to have been most excited by some drawings of Alfred Stevens, and some 'reproductions of wonderful

* The virgins of Damascus suing Tamburlaine for mercy.

† Originally called 'Woman Smiling', it reversed its title in 1910 when it was shown at the Manchester City Art Gallery in a loan exhibition of John's work. It was the first picture bought (for £225 at Manchester) by the Contemporary Art Society, founded that year to acquire works by living artists for loan or gift to public galleries. It was also the first picture presented by the Society to the Tate Gallery (3171).

pictures by Gauguin'. Of his contemporaries, Gwen was still the best. He had persuaded her to exhibit two pictures at the N.E.A.C. show in the spring of 1908: her portrait of Chloë Boughton-Leigh and 'La Chambre sur la Cour'. 'Gwen's pictures are simply staggering,' he told Dorelia. 'I have put up the prices to £50. They will surely sell.'

As for his own work, 'I seem to make millions as usual,' he told Lamb (10 January 1908) to whom, out of the blue, he sent a present of five pounds. But although no one exhibited more than he, no one in certain moods disliked it more. 'Would that I could leave exhibiting alone for years and years,' he confided to Lady Ottoline Morrell (20 September 1908). 'Perhaps some day I may be able to buy back the rubbish I have sold and have a grand auto-da-fé.'

The English art scene was dim, but there were some bright stars. 'It is surprising to find men in England apparently alive to the tendency of modern art to symbolism,' he wrote (17 January 1908) to Lamb, who had recently been telling him about the work of van Gogh.

I met [Roger] Fry the other night and he is quite a lively person – on the other hand 'Impressionism' is still lectured on as the new gospel by certain persons of importance. I feel utterly incompetent to cope with problems outside art – without my wife, whom I want. Terrible glooms and ennuis visit me in the evenings when I can think of no one I want to see and am yet tormented in solitude. Sometimes I have tried seeing how much I can drink in one night but it's a dismal experiment. At any rate I have nearly done a large painting which I think is lovely – a nude virgin by a lake. I am thinking of giving up models altogether.

His letters during this winter resound with vigorous complaints. 'My hypochondria comes and goes – and comes again,' he reported to Lamb (6 February 1908). 'It is a beshitten society. I know no man in London.' He suffered very energetically from the great malaise of the times: Edwardian neurasthenia – and treated it with complex diagnoses. 'I am myself a prey to chronic pulmonary bronchial and stomach catarrh but occasional spells of country air keep me going.' His symptoms were often valiant; he was the very battleground for giant contests between his phagocytes and every marauding macrophage. 'My macrophags are having a fight for it,' he cabled back from the front line of this war. But the real culprit was that malign monster, London. 'The London people are sickening,' he informed Ottoline Morrell (20 September 1908). On fine days he was suffocated in his dingy studio as in some dark hull of a ship; and gloomy days depressed him unutterably wherever he was. He had taken up riding, and this stirred his blood about a bit. 'You must come and ride over the downs with me,' he invited Lamb (14 December 1907). But then he got so hot riding, and afterwards so cold – it could not be good for his 'corpuscles'.

After the banishment of Alick Schepeler he felt more hemmed in than ever. He was seeing Dorelia only intermittently : it was an impossible situation. So he turned to, of all people, Ida's friend the Rani : 'La plus chère de toutes les dames ! !' he greeted her in his wildest handwriting. 'Let me have a word, please – I live here [8 Fitzroy Street] now. They tell me you are coming to London for the Slade dance – if that's true – mightn't I see you – yourself. I have heard with incredible joy how much better you are for Canary carryings-on. Let me then assure myself – formally – visually – tangibly of your well-being . . . After the ball come and rest under my lofty roof – there's a little angel.'

Like a Colossus chained, he seemed incapable of independent action except under the impulse of tremendous forces; while by others, for a while, he could be led as simply as a child. Only at present he had no one to lead him, no one opposite whom to play a new Augustus. Self-escape, by one means or another, was like a drug. 'For the moment dreadful glooms blot out the glittering vistas of life – even debauch would afford me no illusion,' he confessed to Lamb (14 December 1907), '. . . nor bring back a sense of triumphant reality. In a word I am in a sorry state. Perhaps the fog will lift before to-morrow. But meanwhile this hideous envelopment of dullness . . .'

He was about to meet, however, a woman quite different from any he had known before who would dispel this fog, and to whom, for special reasons, Dorelia could not object.

5. ETHICS AND RAINBOWS

Lady Ottoline Morrell had already encountered Augustus at
Conder's studio in Chelsea three years before. Tall and
mysterious-looking, intensely silent and with an air that was
somehow *méfiant*, he seemed to her a strangely memorable
person. Gold ear-rings he wore, and a sweater polo-necked and
very black; his hair was shaped like that of some figure in a
Renaissance picture, and he watched everyone with a curious
intentness. It was the eyes that first mesmerized her – his eyes,
then his voice, then his hands.

'They were remarkably beautifully-shaped eyes,' she recalled,
'and were of that mysterious pale grey-green colour, expanding
like a sea-anemone, and more liquid, more aesthetically and
poetically perceptive, than any of the darker and more definite
shades. His voice, when he did speak, was not very unlike
Conder's, only rather deeper and more melodious, but like
Conder's hesitating – and he also had the same trick of pushing
his hair back with one of his hands – hands that were more
beautiful almost than any man's hands I have ever seen.'[15]

Lady Ottoline was every inch as terrible a figure as Augustus.
When they met again early in 1908 at a smart dinner party in
Lowndes Place, he felt very self-conscious in his uncomfortable
dinner-jacket, shy and rather aggressive, until he caught sight of
Ottoline : then he forgot himself. Tall, with deep mahogany red
hair, a prognathous jaw, swan's neck and bold baronial nose, she
had the external force to command his self-forgetfulness. In
a magnificent portrait, painted nearly a dozen years later,
he depicts her as some splendid galleon in full sail, triumphantly breasting the high seas. Her head, under its flamboyant topsail of a hat, is held at a proud angle and she wears,
like rigging, string upon string of slightly moulting pearls
(painted with the aid of tooth powder) above a bottle-green
velvet dress. Her eyes are rolled sideways in their sockets like
those of a runaway horse and her mouth bared in a soundless
scream – almost as if the prototype of Bacon's portrait of Pope
Innocent X. This portrait when first exhibited produced a
furore, and people asked themselves how Lady Ottoline could
possibly have allowed the artist to paint such a freakish likeness

of her. Even Augustus grew rather nervous about her reaction to all this Press comment. 'I would like you to have that portrait but I don't think it's one you would like to hand down to posterity as a *complete* representation of you,' he told her (10 February 1922). He need not have worried.* She brushed aside the paper storm, went on to buy another portrait of Augustus's and hung it for all to see over the mantelpiece in her drawing-room. 'Whatever she may have lacked it wasn't courage,' Augustus acknowledged in *Chiaroscuro*; 'in spite of a dull and conventional upbringing, this fine woman was always prepared to do battle for Culture, Freedom and the People.'

Lady Ottoline was a unique personality and she inspired Augustus as vividly as she did many other artists and writers: Aldous Huxley and D. H. Lawrence; Simon Bussy and Duncan Grant. To stimulate the imaginations of such men was her talent – almost her genius. She had crossed over from her aristocratic homeland to this country of art and letters, and she offered those painters and authors whom she admired excursions to her native country. At her house in Bedford Square – a symphony of pale

---

* 'I am delighted you snubbed those stupid and impertinent journalists,' Augustus wrote to her (14 March 1920). 'I have kept them at bay as far as possible but they are very persistent. Even if one is induced to express an opinion it is sure to appear in a distorted form and minus the points.' Two years later, on 1 February 1922, he wrote in answer to a letter from Ottoline about the picture: 'I still have your portrait. People don't often buy other people's portraits. It's rather a cruel predicament as you know and yet I like it. I think I had priced it at £500 at the show but you can have it for much less. Would £200 be too much?' Ten days later he is hedging: 'In the meanwhile I have collected some pictures for a show at Pittsburgh U.S.A. and I thought of including your portrait among them as I think with all its deficiencies (and tooth-powder) it is one of my best in some ways. Would you mind letting it go for the show, and then we could decide later if you really wanted it, or try another.' On 9 January 1925 he informs her: 'The price I have put on your portrait is £400. Is that too much?' Eight months later (2 September 1925) he writes: 'I am delighted that on seeing the portrait again you still think well of it. It isn't good enough but I think it has distinction. I am sorry the price I put on it is too much – but I would not part with it to anyone else for less than twice that sum – and I know I shall be able to get it or more one day.' The following month, some seventeen years after he had begun this portrait, their transactions were at an end – and at once he suggested beginning another picture. 'Oh yes – your portrait is full of faults and I know I should love to do another.' By now Ottoline was middle-aged, and feeling perhaps that there was not enough time left for another portrait, she did not accept this offer.

grey walls and yellow taffeta curtains – Augustus first came into contact with the smart world, for which, in years to come, he would develop a gourmet's taste. It was like some extraordinarily rich food that melted in the imagination but, in large quantities, sickened the stomach. Yet in 1908 this drawing-room world was brilliantly new to him. Fashionable society appealed to him for much the same reasons as did the society of gypsies and anarchists: it offered him an attractive theatre where he could assume a different role. To avoid claustrophobia he needed to move from one self to another, to play many parts in succession like a travelling mummer. But just as some actors can only give fine performances when the lines they deliver are good, so Augustus needed to come under the strong influence of someone he could admire.

Ottoline provided just such a potent theatrical influence. Sitting next to each other at dinner in Lowndes Square they talked of troubadours and Romanies; and then, abruptly, Augustus demanded: 'Will you sit to me? Come and see me tomorrow in my studio.' This signalled the beginning of a friendship, important to each of them, that was to last until Ottoline's death in the 1930s. The very next morning she went round to Fitzroy Street chaperoned by her husband, the member of Parliament for South Oxfordshire. 'We knock, and John himself appeared – in his usual clothes: a greyish suit, the coat long and full in the skirts, and with a bright green velvet collar, a large silk handkerchief round his neck. He waved us in.'[16] After inspecting his pictures and making arrangements for sittings, they were introduced to Clive and Vanessa Bell. 'Vanessa had the beauty of an early Watts portrait,' Ottoline recorded, 'melancholy and dreamy. They stood in front of the picture of the lake, Clive Bell gesticulating in an excited way, showering speechless admiration, Vanessa, head bent, approving.'[17]

Augustus fulfilled Ottoline's pictorial notion of genius, and she was soon in love with him. The impression she gives of his appearance speaks eloquently of her romantic attraction:

'His dark auburn hair was long and cut across the front like a fringe, and with a square beard, his curious pale face and sea-anemone eyes, he might have been a Macedonian king or a

Renaissance poet. He had a power of drawing out all one's sympathy.'[18]

Over these first months he did many watercolours and drawings of her; and she grew more deeply hypnotized by him. Each visit to Fitzroy Street sent her into a turmoil of emotions. With every step along the short walk from Bedford Square what tension there was, what fear and pain! Before advancing, she would bombard him with a heavy artillery of gifts – fine editions of Wordsworth and Goethe, Browning and Plato, even Euripides, the works of Synge and eventually of Strachey. Augustus fell back. 'You keep giving me things,' he remonstrated (8 June 1908). But she could not stop, and the first trickle of presents became a downpour. There was about their relationship a curious reversal of roles : it is Ottoline who plays the masculine part, bold and despairing, almost aggressive at times. Augustus is shy, rather coyly flattered by all these attentions, sometimes embarrassed, always cautious. She invites him to concerts of love music, and to tragic melodramas. She sends him a little watch which keeps breaking – a kind of stop-watch; she sends him rings for his fingers and assorted jewellery including a magnificent opal. By every post the presents pour in – lilies (which Romilly ate) for his studio, and lotions for his hair; various scarves and cloaks for his hypochondria, a green shawl and a capacious wool cover for his bed which, he claims, will keep his whole family warm. If Augustus created the John-girl with her characteristic tight bodice, long-waisted full skirt and broad-brimmed peasant hat, Ottoline must have contributed generously to Augustus's own appearance. Her most triumphant adornment was a large replica of Carlyle's hat which 'is stupendous', he proclaimed (24 May 1909). 'It reduces even the rudest street gamin to speechlessness. But it is not a hat for every day of the week.'

Nor was their love-affair for every day of the week. His intense mobility and hibernating illnesses ('acute compound neurasthenic hypochondria – at least that's my diagnosis')[19] made him an elusive lover. Yet this elusiveness only scalded her imagination the more. Wherever she went she was haunted by thoughts of him : his poverty, his vagabond freedom, the simplicity of his life, the poetry in his paintings; those mesmerizing eyes, long fine sensitive hands, and his deep resonant voice echoing in her mind. At parties she would introduce his name into the conversation for the pleasure of hearing, like distant music, people talking about him. But so often what they said distressed her. Most conventional Englishwomen looked on her as affected or even amoral for knowing such a raffish creature. Even other artists and writers failed to hit the right note – Henry James, for example, who produced an off-key *mot*: 'John paints human beings as if they were animals, and dogs as if they were human beings'; or Lytton Strachey, who likened him to the cruel and sophisticated Byron.

But Ottoline knew him better. Despite her intoxication, there is a shrewdness in her observations about him. Her heart might beat for the legendary Augustus, but her intelligence comprehended the man.

'Engagements were intolerable to him. Luxuries, possessions, responsibilities were alien to him. When I mixed in an ordinary London life, the figure of this man, so unquestionably remarkable, living a life so completely different from anything I saw around me, haunted and disturbed me. He would appear to me in my imagination as if he passed through the room, suddenly making the conventional scene appear absurd.'[20]

Mysteriousness, which he so highly prized in women, she had discovered in him. It was like a grain of love-powder that itched and irritated, that stimulated and would not leave her in peace. Above all, it was his melancholia that affected her, the silence that alternated with his flashing high spirits, the sudden boldness that interrupted his old-fashioned courtly manner with women – so abominated by the new breed of feminists.

Perhaps the most astonishing aspect of their relationship was that they never quarrelled. His moodiness and her possessiveness made for difficulties, and many of their other friendships were split by bitter arguments. Their stamina lay perhaps in their awareness of this incompatibility. She could not get past his melancholy and her possessiveness had little to feed on. Often he would speak of her with reverence, call her 'an angel' – yet with the knowledge he could not walk in step with an angel very far. They remained on friendly but still quite formal terms until 30 May 1908. That day Ottoline sailed across to his studio alone, and suddenly confessed her painful love for him. The same night, after she had left, he wrote to her:

When you were in my studio to-day I wished I could cry – I should have felt more intelligent – perhaps – with the delicatest and noblest woman loving me so infinitely beyond my deserts. Do you know what a horror I have of hurting a hair of your head and bringing a shadow into your thoughts ... and you are trying to assure me you are just like others are!

Is it not something to realise that change and development is possible still – that one is not yet altogether finished and one is still young! still adolescent! still living ...

Four pages he wrote that night, and he ended with a sentiment that might have drawn a rueful smile from Ida: 'Since my wife's death there have been few opportunities of excitement or intoxication that I have let pass ...' Nevertheless, he concludes: 'We *can't* go on thus, darling that you are ... Good-night, angel.'

But, in a mood of reluctant passion, the affair did go on. Like the little watch she gave him, it was always stopping: then starting again. So far as was possible, Augustus acted honourably. He discouraged her quite gently, and from reasonable motives. 'You must know that I do care for you,' he told her (17 June 1908), '... and how I hate to pain you ... but I see the inevitable ... Forgive me Ottoline.' It is possible, of course, that he was not attracted to her, but some of his letters suggest the contrary. It is also possible that, seeing her as a patron for his work and as someone who would introduce him to prospective purchasers, he was at pains to avoid a situation that, by promising too much, might alienate her. But again his correspondence does not corroborate this. It is true he did benefit a little through Ottoline's friendship,* but those letters in which he writes of pictures invariably petition help for his friends, particularly Epstein and Lamb.† As his later dealings with the

---

* 'How good of you to get the Duke of Portland to buy my drawings,' Augustus to Ottoline Morrell (7 July 1908). The 6th Duke of Portland was Ottoline's half-brother.

† 'My friend Lamb has just 40 francs left to carry him through the summer ... Epstein is slowly being killed in London. It seems to be a general superstition that artists can live on air – whereas the truth is their appetites, like their other capacities, are exceptionally good,' Augustus wrote to Ottoline (20 September 1908). Later that month he wrote: 'You were good sending that

American collector John Quinn would confirm, he was secretly a generous man but, rather in the style of Bernard Shaw, tried to avoid a reputation for generosity.

Like money, love-affairs were a means to an end. They were explorations within himself of new continents, symbolized by his request to each woman to re-christen him.* They discovered aspects of himself he had never imagined before; they taught him to get away from the dull old stamping grounds, to become another person. But when the new continent had been thoroughly explored, the new self mapped and assimilated into the central empire of the self, there was no more mystery : and interest died.

Love-affairs gave Augustus energy – without them he was passive. They involved his vanity, compensated for his lack of conceit. But once the passion had flown and the husk of the relationship remained, it would depress him dreadfully. It is this he sees so clearly as the inevitable outcome of his affair with Ottoline – unless, that is, they could end it while it was yet unfinished. It is a contest between the fleeting present and the long waste of the future, with its quagmires of guilt, responsibility and unevenness of feeling. It was this hangover of love that sapped his energy.

He warns her as clearly as he can that contact between them can only lead to disenchantment. He needs her – as a model. 'I am aware of my brutalities – and all my agonies and joys, and will continue as God made me,' he writes (28 July 1908), '. . . and will do yet the work that no one else can do *quand même*.' For any unhappiness his character is to blame. 'I should be called Legion and you know only one or two of me yet.' Some of these selves were not attractive : they were melancholic-aggressive or inert – and he had no control over their comings and goings. 'I felt I was *fated* to cause you in the long run more pain than

----

cheque to my friend Lamb . . . Epstein is I think still very hard put to it . . . It would be grand if Portland or anyone else gave him a commission.' With characteristic generosity Ottoline gave Epstein an order for a garden statue and took likely clients to visit him, including W. B. Yeats and Lady Gregory, who commissioned him to do a bust of herself.

* Ottoline called him Elffin. When he no longer signs himself Elffin their love-affair (but not their friendship) is at an end.

happiness – and that I could not acquiesce in,' he writes in another letter (21 December 1908). 'I dislike sailing under colours none of my hoisting ...

'With every wish to be honest I suppose I cannot escape those notorious disabilities which I must share with all true Welshmen ...'

Truth gradually gives way before a curious rigmarole of romantic assumptions tenaciously held by each of them on behalf of the other. 'You are the most generous soul in the world and I the mouldiest,' he asserts (June 1908). But Ottoline maintains that it is *she* who is worthless – worthless without him. He is a genius: what do her petty pains and cares matter beside his needs? She will come to him tomorrow. Her letter awaits him when he gets back very late to Fitzroy Street, and at four in the morning (4 June 1908), in some panic, he replies: 'Ottoline. Don't come to-morrow. I'm not able – yes you are too great for me, vulgarly tragical or unhappy.' But Ottoline only wants to serve him. She feels humbled before his goodness, his concern and tenderness for her. If only she had *more* to offer him. The postman hurries back and forth with their bits of paper, delivering questions, answers, counter questions, often whole conversations on a single day. Even so, in their haste, they cannot always wait for him but must dash out to convey some vital postscript by hand. 'It is you who crush me with your goodness – no, exalt me!' Augustus contradicts her (3.45 p.m. 4 June 1908). 'Never will I cease to love and honour you, dear Ottoline. It is you have genius ... Elffin.'

Truth gives way: but it never disappears altogether beneath the haze of protective romanticism, for other people are involved. One of these is Ottoline's husband, Philip Morrell. Augustus's attitude to him had commenced jocular: 'Keep Philip happy,' he counsels her (9 June 1908), 'and make him blow up the houses of Parliament.' But Ottoline, who by now is infatuated with Augustus, cannot conceal her feelings and soon the situation grows awkward. 'I think it evident that your husband don't like me,' Augustus protests (8 January 1909). The possibility of a scandal that, since it involved a member of Parliament, would hit the headlines alarms him to the point of pomposity. 'I was not really surprised that Morrell should have

been out of humour,' he informs Ottoline (18 December 1908).
'I felt I was cutting rather an offensive figure in your house. I
should be very sorry to disturb so admirable a personage as your
husband. I have nothing but respect for him and would never
question his right to object to me ...'

The other person involved was Dorelia, whom Augustus was
very anxious to avoid offending. Whenever he sees Dorelia, he
reassures Ottoline: 'Do *not* harbour the thought that I am going
to forget you'; or 'I hope you will never suspect me of indifference'. But there is never any doubt that Dorelia comes first –
about this he is specific: 'I love no one living more than
Dorelia, and in loving her I am loyal to my wife and not else,'
he explains to Ottoline – then adds: 'You are certainly wonderful – Ottoline ... There *will always* be that infinitely precious
cord between us – so fine, so fragile that to strain it would
break it. And you will not continue to suffer too much, you will
have the fortitude of great hearts and unconquerable souls – and
the sweetness of the music of heaven will teach you to smile at
last with the sweetest smile of all, and the profoundest. Bless
you, Ottoline. Elffin.'

Although Dorelia was very strict at this time, and very suspicious, there were several reasons why she did not object to
Ottoline. There could be no doubt that their relationship was
partly a business one. Besides which, Lady Ottoline Morrell was
utterly unlike the barmaids, actresses and models Dorelia had
so far come up against. Then, until March 1909, she had never
met Ottoline.

They met for the first time in Augustus's studio one day while
Ottoline was sitting for her portrait. Dorelia seemed to take little
notice of Ottoline; but Ottoline studied Dorelia very keenly.
'She had the dignity and repose of a peasant from a foreign land,'
Ottoline noted in her diary. '... nonchalance and domination towards the children, a slightly mocking attitude to John, and shyness, *méfiance*, towards me, which melted by degrees. Between
my sittings we sat round the large table for tea, the children
eating slices of bread and jam, John looking a magnificent patriarch of a Nomad tribe, watching but talking very little. I saw
that in every movement Dorelia made there was such grace and

rhythm that she was indeed a stimulating model for any painter.'[21]

From this day Ottoline set out to make a friend of Dorelia. It was uphill work. The two women were utterly different – Ottoline sophisticated and histrionic; Dorelia simple and laconic. To complement Augustus's Carlyle, Ottoline bought Dorelia a large Leghorn hat. She put it on without a word, but with her special smile, looking secretly beautiful. Yet despite all Ottoline's overtures of friendship, Dorelia remained unforthcoming, and when Ottoline invited her with Augustus to a dinner party to meet the stars of Bloomsbury, Virginia Stephen,* Roger Fry, Clive and Vanessa Bell, she received a disconcerting refusal:

'Dear Lady Ottoline, Thank you very much for your invitation but I cannot come as I think it rather ridiculous to be introduced to people as Mrs John. I do not know the Bells.

'John asks me to say that he will be pleased to come. I'm afraid you'll think I'm rather ungracious.'

But, being simple, Dorelia saw clearly what so many clever men of Ottoline's acquaintance obscured: that she was essentially a generous woman. To this generosity Dorelia naturally responded, adding to the letter: 'I wonder if you would care to come here? I should be very pleased to see you. Yours sincerely Dorelia McNeill.'

In any solution between the four of them, there were several differences that could never be dissolved. But by a sudden unthinking act of genius, Dorelia averted trouble. She took Ottoline one day to meet Henry Lamb. He was the perfect understudy to Augustus. By the summer of 1909 he even occupied his studio in Fitzroy Street, Augustus having moved back into Chelsea. Arrayed in tobacco-coloured frock-coat and breeches, looking like some marvellous lackey, Lamb had flowered into an astonishing figure. Ottoline could not take her eyes off his slim

---

* 'The age of Augustus John was dawning,' Virginia Woolf had written. When she met him and Dorelia – 'figures as beautiful and almost as improbable as' Ottoline – she and her friends 'were all swept into that extraordinary world where such odd sticks and straws were brought momentarily together. There was Augustus John very sinister [?] in a black stock and a velvet coat . . .' See Quentin Bell's biography of Virginia Woolf, Vol. I, pp. 124, 144–5.

visionary silhouette, tinged with khaki, and by the end of the year he had very largely replaced Augustus as an emotional figure in her life. 'Elffin' was no more; but to Augustus and Dorelia, Ottoline remained a loyal friend. Not the least of her uses – and the one that first melted Dorelia – was to the children. And with these they needed all the help available.

6. FIGHTING THE PHILISTINES

Like a pair of skilled jugglers, Augustus and Dorelia had kept revolving in the air every one of the schemes they had first introduced into their act at Equihen. To be or not to be married; to live together, or apart, or both – and where or anywhere: the range of alternatives spun before their faces ever more fantastically.

For much of the winter of 1907–8 Dorelia had stayed on in France. There were many matters for her to attend to: sorting out 'clothes, curtains, cushions etc.' from the studios – 'and then there is the accordion and various musical instruments' including the gypsy guitar Ida had never learnt to play. She gave up her apartment and, with Pyramus and Romilly, moved through a series of hotels. She was seeing much of Lamb. Much time was spent 'making clothes for the kids' of the most anti-Wigmorian cut. She wrote to Augustus for supplies of wool, money and tobacco: and she waited.

He could not, however, get unstuck from his work long enough to investigate very much of the country, and this was the reason, he explained to Dorelia, why he began to 'look for a house about London'. To Lamb he wrote (10 January 1908): 'I'm trying to get a house in Hampstead on the heath – which is better than most country I seem to find in England – in fact the heath is incomparably lovely.' What his method relied on for success was a coincidence between what he happened to find and what his dreams of the perfect life happened to be. But coincidence was made difficult by his dreams flashing past so swiftly – no house seemed able to catch them. While exploring Hampstead, for example, he dreamed fervently of Toulouse. Wyndham Lewis thought of going there, and anything Lewis could do ... But then a brilliant new notion seized him. Spain!

A young friend, the celebrated practical joker Horace de Vere Cole who, in the guise of Sultan of Zanzibar had ceremonially inspected Cambridge, now (with a perfectly straight face) recommended a castle in Spain. 'I met the Sultan of Zanzibar in Bond Street yesterday,' Augustus reported to Dorelia. 'He said he was going to Spain with Tyler.' Royall Tyler,* he added, was 'my latest friend', a Bostonian and a profound student of Spanish matters. 'He is going to go mad one day,' Augustus predicted, '– I saw it in his hand and he knows it.' The more he thought of Spain, the less attractive Hampstead or even Wantage (which he had previously scrutinized) appeared. Despite rumours, there seemed nothing specially improbable about the Spanish scheme. After all, 'I am, by nature, clearly intended for the bull-ring.' Wyndham Lewis further kindled his imagination by declaiming pages of Spanish poetry to him. 'I found myself in a perfectly dangerous state of health ... I wrestled with [John] Fothergill and nearly killed him.'

By April 1908, inflamed by poetry, he set off in pursuit of some Spanish gypsies, picking up Dorelia in Paris on the way. From the Hôtel du Mont Blanc in the Boulevard Edgar Quinet, he wrote to Ottoline (28 April 1908):

'Spain is cruel – but I have blood-thirsty moments myself ... Have you ever found it necessary to strangle anybody – in imagination? There is indescribable satisfaction in it. At other times I feel more like bringing people to life. My Variability is rather disconcerting and hardly makes life easier. I must learn discipline and consistency.'

Spain, which had seemed for a few moments a likely winner among his many schemes, now began to fall back. He got no nearer the Spanish border on this occasion than Paris itself, and it took him almost another fifteen years to complete the journey. 'I am perturbed by the spectacle of Spring and the green leaves seem to cover the branches all too guiltily,' he told Ottoline (4 May 1908). He was staying at the same hotel as Euphemia, and

---

* Royall Tyler was the author of *Spain: A Study of her Life and Arts*, 'a capital straightforward business-like book ... My only objection is to the title, as I think Spain is a neuter noun,' A. E. Housman wrote to the publisher Grant Richards (6 July 1909). Richards himself had more to object to, since Tyler then ran off with his wife, a woman in the high Spanish style.

wondering whether he shouldn't after all 'shut myself up in my studio – and do something – not merely contemplate'.

His indecision was helped by Dorelia who had now determined to 'wander about' France with some of the children, in preference to settling down with Augustus. 'It would I think be out of the question to allow her to take Edwin for the reason that her own two boys are quite enough to keep her busy,' Augustus appealed to Mrs Nettleship, 'although she could cheerfully take charge of the whole lot ... I know no princess with maternal instincts unsatisfied, unfortunately, who would open her gates to my poor boys. Perhaps I may meet one ...'

Where Dorelia would wander and for how long was, like most other things, unsettled. Once again, and with several later entries, it was neck-and-neck between all their schemes. But some final decision was becoming urgent. 'Travel as we may,' Augustus wrote to Dorelia, 'we want a pied-à-terre *somewhere*.' In the interval there was nothing for Augustus to do but turn his back on Spain and go back to Fitzroy Street. 'I haven't taken the house yet – it seems to me sometimes quite unpractical without Ida,' he wrote to Mrs Nettleship. 'Just now I really don't know what to do – apart from painting. The house I looked at is lovely and the heath of course.'

So far as the children were concerned, Augustus was considering farms. He bundled them along to stay with various friends in the country, in particular to Westcot in Berkshire where Charles McEvoy lived,* and where they all went a number of times before deciding against it. 'There are grand backgrounds in Berkshire for noble decoration,' he reported to

---

* 'Charlie McEvoy nearly killed me in the evening by his drolleries,' Augustus wrote to Lamb (24 August 1907) after an early visit to Westcot. 'He has recently had a play put on by the Stage Society which was a great success, the most enlightened critics combining in a chorus of praise. He sketched me the plot of his next play which also endangered my life. It is regrettable I am at the mercy of these comedians.' In 1907, McEvoy had written 'David Ballard' and he was also the author of 'The Village Wedding', which was performed by the village players at Aldbourne. In 1908 Augustus had done an etching of him (C.D. 20) described by Campbell Dodgson as 'a wonderful example of direct and unprejudiced portraiture, a perfect likeness and a masterly, though by no means beautiful, etching, which ranks by general consent as one of the best of Mr John's plates'. It was first shown at the fourth exhibition of the Society of Twelve in 1908.

Lamb. 'It is unfortunate that the peasants have taken to motor caps and bicycle shirts.' Then, on his way back, he fell in with a man who told 'me about the country near Naples [where] he used to live,' Augustus wrote to Dorelia. 'I asked him how much one could live there with a family – he said £250. I have ordered a pass-port. It will be ready the day after to-morrow ...'

A real decision could only be wrung out of Augustus by some crisis, and it was Dorelia who now presented him with one, as he began to suspect she might never return from her wanderings.

'You know very well I want to live with you and no one else,' he wrote to her after she had left, 'but it seemed pretty clear you were too dissatisfied with me – and even found me repugnant at times. You were often enough talking about going off – as to making a beast of myself you alone can stop that. I wish you were here – if you want to be absolutely independent I don't want to be dependent ... Will you come over? or will I come back? Doing nothing is killing me. I wish you would come south with me. I can't stand the thought of separating – only if you *want* to I can do nothing.'

The danger of losing Dorelia concentrated Augustus's mind wonderfully. It was a kind of death. 'C'est bien que toi que je désire – mon ange,' he declared, '– c'est bien que toi.' When Augustus was decisive, Dorelia fell in step with him. Between their various schemes it was now a photo finish, which revealed – a dead heat! For they agreed to marry, and yet not to marry: to marry, so far as the Nettleships were concerned, almost at once; but not to translate this policy very urgently into fact. Augustus promised 'to raise the wind' in Wigmore Street 'which is quite willing to blow just now', and added: 'I'm beginning to feel myself – ten times as efficient as anybody else.'

This policy of marriage was partly to make it clear to the Nettleships that they proposed taking away the children and making a home for them. Believing that his life was falling apart, Mrs Nettleship had recently swung into the attack, apprising Augustus that 'a woman who kills an unborn child is not fit to have the care of children'. In a heated exchange between the two of them Augustus felt able to answer that, in accusing Dorelia of bringing about a miscarriage, she was condemning Ida,

'who had tried the same thing'. He himself took the other view –
that by 'annihilating a mass of inchoate blubber without identity at the risk of her life to spare me further burdens', Dorelia
had proved 'her unusual fitness for the bringing up of children'.
Was it not Mrs Nettleship herself who had first 'instructed Ida
in the mysteries of child-prevention? – mysteries which she was
evidently not quite equal to mastering, thank God! ... I would
have killed many an unborn child to keep her [Ida] alive – and
even have felt myself perfectly fit to take charge of children.'
The outcome of this row was that both of them lost their
tempers and Augustus finally notified Mrs Nettleship he 'was
taking all the children away and was at last happy at the
thought of resuming our ménage where it left off – with Ida
there in spirit and in the blood of her kids.'[22]

Realizing that by treating Augustus in the way Uncle Ned
had prescribed she had committed a bad error of tactics, Mrs
Nettleship now sent him a conciliatory letter in which she
allowed that to marry Dorelia was 'obviously the correct thing
to do'. But Augustus was only exacerbated further:

> It is by no means from a desire to be 'correct' that I am going to
> marry Dorelia. It is precisely because she is the only possible mother
> to Ida's children now Ida has gone, since I love her, knowing her
> to be such. And for no less reason would she consent to marry me,
> or I her. She is entirely and absolutely unselfish as Ida was and as
> their life together proved, with such proofs as stagger the in-
> telligence. She is besides the only woman who does not stifle one
> in domesticity and who is on my own plane of intelligence (or
> above it) in a word the one woman with whom I can live, work and
> still be a father to all my children. Without her I would have to
> say good-bye to the children, for I cannot recognize them or my-
> self in a house and an atmosphere which will ever be strange and
> antipathetic to me as it was to their mother ...
> If I were not supremely confident that Dorelia and I are able to
> bring up the children immeasurably better than you or anybody
> else, I would not hesitate to leave them where they are. But as I dis-
> tinctly object to the way they are being brought up with you, as I
> see quite clearly it is *not* a good way, nor their mother's, Dorelia's
> or my way, I am going to take them away at once ...

Privately, to Dorelia, he confessed some doubts 'as we can't
hamper ourselves too much'. But by now events seemed to have

gained a momentum of their own, pulling in Dorelia, who 'suddenly turned up here [8 Fitzroy Street] to help with the children', Augustus told Ottoline (26 June 1908). Together they would roam France with four kids, two of Ida's and Dorelia's two, he explained. 'They are not going to be brought up by Philistines any longer. I tell you I had to fight to come to the point.'

From Mrs Nettleship, however, he received literally more than he bargained for. At the end of June he had written to her outlining his plans: 'I am off to France in a few days and want to take David and Caspar with me – I would *like* to take them all of course – but am not quite ready for that. I think we may go to Brittany for the summer ... I hate the thought of leaving Robin behind – and Edwin – and Henry!' Events now followed each other with what he called 'admirable briskness'.[23] Mrs Nettleship at once replied that she was holding on to the children, and that if Augustus attempted to abduct them she would have him committed to prison. As for Dorelia, she would prefer to see her dead than in charge of Ida's sons. To this, Augustus sent back an ultimatum: '*Take your proceedings at once, but deliver up all my children in your charge by tomorrow morning.*'

Next morning no children arrived at his studio, and Augustus marched round to Wigmore Street. What then happened he described in a letter to Wyndham Lewis (28 June 1908). Mrs Nettleship, he narrated, tried 'to take refuge in the zoo with my 3 eldest boys and only after a heated chase through the monkey house did I succeed in coming upon the guilty party immediately behind the pelicans' enclosure. Seizing two children as hostages I bore them off in a cab and left them in a remote village for a few days in charge of an elderly but devoted woman. The coup d'Etat was completely successful of course. Dorelia appears on the scene with almost miraculous promptitude and we take off the bunch of 4 to-morrow morning ...'

Henry, who was only fifteen months old, missed this escapade and was exempted from the bargaining. For all of them, the results of that morning's manoeuvres round the zoo were to be lasting. Though they visited Wigmore Street in their holidays, Ida's four eldest boys were brought up by Augustus and

Dorelia; while Henry, the odd one out, remained with the Nettleships, with tragic consequences.

7. IN THE ROVING LINE

'Paris is amazingly beautiful and brilliant ... Was it not mad of me to abduct my children in this way?' Augustus asked Ottoline (1 July 1908). 'But I was provoked to the point of action.' Even so, too many children and too little money was a worrying predicament – to be relieved slightly by landing Caspar on Lamb's shoulders and extracting money owed to him in England via the ever-faithful Will Rothenstein. 'The evil worm of distrust had begun to tickle me with the cold sweat,' he wrote to Rothenstein (July 1908), 'including suspicion that I had bitten off more than I could chew. But a few days en plein air renewed my courage ...'

After a week in Paris, Augustus led his troupe off to Rouen, and from there they sailed to Cherbourg, the appearance of which 'pleased me well'.[24] He had money to last them all three months, but confidence enough to take them anywhere. Leaving Dorelia and the six boys in Cherbourg, he set off on foot. 'If my stars prove favourable I shall, I hope, start some beasts and vehicles and what not,' he announced to Wyndham Lewis.

From the first his stars shone dully. At Les Pieux he was seized by the police and interrogated on suspicion of loitering with intent, though he had been plainly walking without any intent whatever. Later he was robbed of his money in a restaurant and, without funds, refused a bed – 'so I stole into the country by bye-ways and slept under a hedge,' he told Lamb (July 1908), '– got down to a place called La Royel in the early morning, bathed my poor sore feet and ... was refused milk and coffee'. It was not before he reached Flamanville that his luck began to turn. Here he caught up with a fête, 'a modest circus and a number of revellers keeping it up, was recognised by a charming circus man I met at Bayeux 2 years ago ... There was also a little Gypsy girl black as night who did the fil de fer. An intoxicated man conducted me down to Dielette where I finished him off with a bottle of wine. In the evening the crazy band drove round in a kind of box emitting gusty strains from various base

instruments, the aged philosopher still capering and kissing his
hand to the girls – a very wonderful company this – a very
·wonderful meeting.'

Next day he was again stopped by the police, and it became
clear that any crime committed in the neighbourhood would
quickly be credited to him. For the rest of his journey he 'took
tortuous ways to avoid the police', he told Dorelia, sleeping in
ditches and fields, under bridges and hedges, and often walking
through the night. In a most revealing letter to Dorelia, written
from Dielette (to which, in his efforts to throw off the police,
he had secretly doubled back) he confessed :

My love of my kind had already vanished and I was becoming a
rooted pessimist – as for J. F. Millet, he seemed to me a damned
blagueur – a bloody romanticist and liar – as he was in fact. But
Dielette renews me – it is astonishing – it is even better than my
native town where I ought to have stopped ... The place is lovely –
so varied – sandy beaches, rocks, harbours and prehistoric landscapes behind. I wish to God I had the sense of figures. My *watch*
has stopped even, out of sympathy I suppose.

I shall probably be about here all to-morrow, so send me some
calculations, I pray you, to guide me a little ... You have only to
lose your temper to gain everything you want with people.

To Will Rothenstein he had written : 'I don't want to fix myself long in hired rooms.' Yet his designs to gather beasts and
vehicles together and follow a vagabond life through Europe
had been hit hard by the police hostility, and he reluctantly
decided to settle down in seaside apartments.

They moved into the Maison Delort late that July and
stayed there until the end of September. 'The boys are exceedingly well,' Augustus reassured Mrs Nettleship, 'so don't be
anxious.' They looked, so he boasted to Ottoline (September
1908), 'like healthy vagabonds'. He himself was anxious about
Henry. 'I trust he is not over-clothed,' he warned Mrs Nettleship.
'It is wonderful how children can stand cold if they wear few
things.'

The sun shone and he worked hard and happily. 'The days
are wonderful here,' he wrote to Ottoline (20 September 1908),
'and I am working up to colour at last. Do you know Cézanne's
work ? His colours are more powerful than Titian's and searched

for with more intensity.' His own colours he was now restricting to the three primary ones represented by ultramarine, crimson lake and cadmium, with green oxide of chromium. It was with these that he painted 'Girl on the Cliff', better known by its Buddhist title 'Nirvana'* – a state of perfect beatitude where all passions are dissolved and individual existence absorbed into the Supreme Being.

He profited much by his season at Dielette – 'I have got, it seems to me, much further,' he told Ottoline – but the prospect of a dingy London studio and dingy London streets was not alluring. 'I wanted to get to the Pyrenees or further instead of lingering in the chilly north, but I lack the necessary millions. So back again to the horrors of a Cockney winter. Are there no millionaires of spirit?' he asked Will Rothenstein.

He returned to London with Dorelia and his six sons early in October, and within a month he had found a house[25] 'in Chelsea with a big studio'. This was 153 Church Street, off the King's Road – 'a good house', Dorelia described it.[26] They took a two-and-a-half year lease and, after various delays, moved in shortly before Christmas. 'There is plenty of room and a piano,' Augustus invited Lamb (23 December 1908). '. . . I hope you will come at once. You'll have a room to yourself.'

London that winter seemed 'very hostile and the English sillier than usual'.[27] Unemployment was rife, jobless men roamed the towns in their thousands, and members of Parliament warned one another that blood would soon be flowing in the streets. 'I hope blood will flow as nothing good can happen without,' Augustus declared.[28] Meanwhile, despite his mood of anarchy and the usual number of conflicting plans – for another studio in Liverpool, a flight to Naples, and a country house on the north coast of Wales – he settled into the shell of his new home as if for protection against storms to come. 'Perhaps the Epsteins may come to dinner to-day,' he wrote to Ottoline (26 December 1908), '– now that we are bourgeois folk with carpets and front doors and dining-rooms.'

> Wanderers, you have the sunrise and the stars;
> And we, beneath our comfortable roofs,

* A pencil and watercolour study of this, which served as a sketch for the oil painting, is in the Tate Gallery (3198).

Lamplight and daily fires upon the hearth,
And four walls of a prison, and sure food.
But God has given you freedom, wanderers![29]

A broken collar bone partly accounted for Augustus having consented to turn bourgeois for the winter. But, with the coming of spring, mended and eager, he resolved to abandon his carpets and comfortable roof, and break out into Gypsydom. For three months he chafed within his prison walls, but found some relief in reading Dostoyevsky's *Les Possédés*, 'a wonderful book', and in submitting himself to be 'overhauled' by a new doctor. 'I am tired of nerves and glooms,' he told Ottoline* (13 January 1909), 'and one could certainly surmount them, unhandicapped physically.' By February he was already feeling 'dangerously healthy', the proper condition in which to take the road.

During this gloomy period of waiting, while he dreamt only of the freedom into which he would soon plunge, he threw off a wonderfully dandified and belligerent portrait of the painter William Nicholson. 'I have started Nicholson,' he wrote to Ottoline on 8 January 1909, '– as a set off to his rare beauty I am putting in a huge nude girl at his side. This will add to his interest, I feel . . .' But eventually he put in one of his own paintings – a girl, fully-clothed, against a mountainous landscape at the right-hand corner of the composition, where his signature would have been. 'William, overcoated, yellow-gloved, the picture of a Georgian buck, glares from the corner of an overdark eye at the beholder,' wrote Marguerite Steen : 'a superb piece of coloratura painting, ranking with the Suggia as one of the finest of John's portraits, though not quite convincing as a likeness of the sitter. Still, perhaps in those days William did look like a gentleman pugilist, or perhaps this aspect of his personality was called out by their mutual fondness for the ring.' For several years Augustus himself believed this to be his best portrait. He had recognized in Nicholson a superb subject, but unless commissioned he could not afford to paint him. So Nicholson himself commissioned the painting for a small fee which he nevertheless forgot to pay and for which Augustus forgot to ask.†

* Ottoline had recommended one of her own doctors who, Augustus told her (6 February 1909), 'was evidently a celestial emissary in disguise'.

† But which was nevertheless paid eventually. Probably one hundred pounds.

When, some years later, the Fitzwilliam Museum at Cambridge bought the portrait for a thousand pounds, the two painters happily pocketed five hundred each.

Even before this portrait was finished, there came over him the absolute necessity to travel. Ever since the birth of Pyramus, the caravan which Augustus was buying from Salaman had lain gently disintegrating on Dartmoor. But recently he had moved it up and anchored it at Wantage, where it was given a lick of fresh paint. A brilliant blue, it stood ready for adventurings. On his first expedition, he took along John Fothergill, architect and innkeeper, as companion. They trundled off on the first of April. 'I called on [Roger] Fry at Guildford and found him in a state of great anxiety about his wife who had just had another attack,'* Augustus reported to Ottoline (8 April 1909).

He sent off his children that day. I was sorry as I wanted to take them on the road a little. Fry came down and we sat in the caravan awhile. Next day I hired a big horse and proceeded on through Dorking and up to a divine Region called Ranmore Common ... I called at the big house to ask for permission to stop on the common and was treated with scant courtesy by the menials who told me their man was out. So on again through miles of wild country to Effingham where, after several attempts to overcome the suspicion attaching to a traveller with long hair and a van, I got a farmer to let me draw into one of his fields. At this time the horse was done up and my money at its last.

So he left his van in the field, along with the sleeping horse and the sleeping Fothergill, and caught the milk train up to London. He had covered eighty miles on the road and it had all been highly satisfactory. But this was a mere beginning, a mere flexing of muscles. The summer would be spent with all his family away from front doors and dining-rooms; with the wind in the night outside and the stars in the wind; with the sun and the rain on his cheek.

Ever since the market days in Haverfordwest, since his first visits to the circus and his sight, on the wasteland outside Tenby, of the raggle-taggle gypsy encampment with its wagons and wild children, its population of hard, high-cheekboned men and

* Helen Fry suffered from an incurable thickening of the bone of her skull and in 1910 was consigned to a mental home until her death in 1937.

women, their faces dark as the earth, he had felt attracted to
travellers and show people. Destiny had drawn him closer to
them after meeting John Sampson when he had begun to learn
their language. Since leaving the art sheds at Liverpool, he had
often revisited Cabbage Hall on 'affairs of Egypt'; and elsewhere, encounters with such people as W. B. Yeats, with his addiction to tinkers as well as countesses, and Lady Gregory, with
her studies of local myth and dialect, had helped to widen his
knowledge. But it was not until 1908 that he began to dream of
living as one of them. Two things that summer had contributed
to his dream. While in Paris he had met several new friends
in the luxurious apartment of Royall Tyler. Among these was
the gypsy guitarist Fabian de Castro. The two of them entered
into a deal where Augustus taught the guitarist to paint, while
de Castro passed on to Augustus some of the songs from his voluminous repertoire. During these reciprocal classes, de Castro
told Augustus something of his background. Now forty, he had
been born at Linares in the Province of Andalusia. While still a
lad he was seized with the *Wanderlust*, forsaking his respectable
family to take up with *gâjos* and other gypsies, like himself, in
the roving line. His conviction that he was of noble descent
from the Pharaohs was fierce and unalterable. He had travelled
alone and in strange company, on foot and otherwise, through
many lands plying many trades and practising many arts, to
which he now intended to add the art of painting. Augustus was
enchanted by his stories told with that serious self-mocking
gypsy humour which found fun in the most unexpected places
and was seasoned with a philosophy of which these wandering
Bohemians, it seemed to him, alone possessed the secret. After
a day spent in talk, song, paint and laughter, towards evening
they would be joined by other cronies, 'Dummer' Howard,
Tudor Castle, Horace de Vere Cole, and together they would set
off to see La Macarona and El Faico, the Flamenco artists. This
was Augustus's introduction to the Flamenco tradition of music
and dancing, and it moved him extraordinarily deeply. The intricate rhythms seemed to stir up under-currents of anguish and
regret that astonished him by their force. The harsh outcry of
the singers, rising convulsively from the very bowels, merged
with the insistent humming of strings into a heart-breaking

ululation, suggesting the lamentations of beings thrust out of heaven and debarred from all tenderness and hope: all but the hunger, the irony and bitter passion of the damned. While the dancers themselves illustrated, with superb precision, the pride and glory of the flesh.

After this week was up, Fabian de Castro left for Toledo, where, having painted after Augustus's prescription a huge and unorthodox Crucifixion, he was rewarded with imprisonment in the *Estaripel* for committing an act subversive of law and order. Augustus took something of a vicarious pride in his pupil's accomplishment, though imprisonment in Spain, he admitted, (even for *lèse-majesté*) was a thing that might happen to anyone, like lunching in England.

By this time Augustus had reached Cherbourg, where he had fallen in with a raucous band of Russian coppersmiths from Baku. 'I was thrilled this morning – and my hand still trembles – by the spectacle of a company of Russian Gypsies coming down the street,' he had illegibly written to Will Rothenstein. 'We spoke together in their language – wonderful people with everyone's hand against them – like artists in a world of petits bourgeois.' At once he set about compiling word lists of their beautiful, fragmentary vocabulary, and taking down their songs. This data he sent back to Liverpool. 'It was a difficult job getting the songs down,' he reported to Scott Macfie (11 August 1908), '– everybody shouting them out, with numerous variations – but they showed the greatest satisfaction on my reading them out ... I don't like extracting words by force from Gypsies – it is too much like dentistry. I prefer to pick them up tout douce-ment.'

Back at Liverpool, the gypsy scholars had dug up an international plot legally to expel the gypsies from Europe. This hideous news, reaching Augustus, lodged in his imagination. The very quality that the police feared and prosecuted, Augustus exulted in: it was the *unexplained* – to them merely the misunderstood – to him the mystical. His attempt to become a part of their wandering community, to be admitted as a *rai* (a non-blood brother) stemmed from his preoccupation with the lost, primitive world from which we all derive. In taking to the road he was not just following an isolated whim. He was reacting, as others were beginning to, against the advance of industrialized society, with its inevitable shrinking of personal liberty, its frontiers barbed-wired by a rigmarole of passports and identity cards, rules, regulations and Thou-Shalt-Nots, by the paraphernalia of permits, licences, censuses, forms in triplicate. This urge to escape from the city was the obverse of his longing to re-awaken an intuitive response to the natural world. Since he dared not be alone, a gypsy community seemed the best method of achieving this. By consorting with these people, by mastering their ancient tongues, by penetrating behind the false glamour and living, like them, round bonfires in the night, Augustus was searching for a way of holding in equilibrium all the contradictory impulses in his temperament. He was not alone. His obsession recalls that of Jacques Callot, but it was also finding a parallel in contemporary literature from Arthur Ransome's *Bohemia in London* (1907) to the pastoralism of the Georgian poets and the chunky anthologies in paper-boards produced by the Poetry Society.[30] No wonder the chief ornament of the Georgians, Eddie Marsh, lost sleep wondering whether he could afford a second John for his collection; and Rupert Brooke, beholding a John picture at the New English (1909) felt 'quite sick and faint with passion'.[31] To such poets and impresarios, no less than to student painters, Augustus, 'with his long red beard, ear-rings, jersey, check-suit and standing six feet high, so that a cabman was once too nervous to drive him', as Edward Thomas reported[32] to Gordon Bottomley, seemed a natural leader. But where could they expect him to lead, except backwards? Their movement, which was to be shattered by the First World War, sought as if by some gypsy spell to freeze the tread of industry across the country. But the best they could hope to win was a little extra time:

> Time, you old gipsy man,
> Will you not stay,
> Put up your caravan
> Just for one day?

Already, with his comings and goings, Augustus had grown 'so damned Gypsy like,' in the words of Scott Macfie, 'that unless one writes at once one runs the risk of missing you'. On his return to London in the autumn of 1908, harried by the French police, an event occurred which persuaded him that he had penetrated, if not to the heart, at least to the body of the gypsy world. In fact it was a sign of the one aspect that most gypsies, however great their liking for him, resented: his freedom with their women.

'This morning I find a parcel which opened – lo! the ear of a man with a ring in it and hair sprouting around lying in a box of throat pastilles,' he wrote to Wyndham Lewis, '– nothing to indicate its provenance but a scrawl in a mixture of thieves' cant and bad Romany saying how it is the ear of a man murdered on the highroad and inviting me to take care of my Kâri=penis, but to beware of the dangers that lurk beneath a petticoat. So you see even in England I cannot feel secure and in France the Police are waiting for me, not to speak of armed civilians of my acquaintance.'

His broken collar bone that winter and removal to Church Street had enabled him to pursue his gypsy studies at a more bookish level. The *Journal of the Gypsy Lore Society*, first born in 1888, though issuing songs transcribed by John Sampson 'on the highroad between Knotty Ash and Prescot', had ceased to sing only three years later. But now, like some sleeping beauty, she was being re-awakened by the kiss of scholarship, enthusiasm and, what she had so lacked before, the oxygen of money. They were, as the Devil is said to have remarked when he looked down the Ten Commandments, 'a rum lot', these Edwardian gentlemen who in company implanted this kiss of life: a cosmopolitan band of rogues and idealists led by the portly and pontificating Sampson and assisted by various willing girls indispensable, in Sampson's view, to serious gypsy studies. Folklorists, philologists and phoneticians, professors both Celtic and Scotch, zealous bibliographers from Columbia drew together to investigate the gypsy question. Under such learned attentions, the arms of the society stretched out to reach anthropologists in Switzerland and linguists in India, embracing on the way such odd bards as Arthur Symons, that living entombment of 'English Decadence', and (still at No. 2 The Pines) Theodore Watts-Dunton, author of the sultry best-seller *Aylwin*, now, in his middle seventies, about to be released from tending the sexually blighted Swinburne and – a final brilliant touch – married to a girl of thirty. Most prominent among these scholars and comedians whom Augustus discovered to be his colleagues was an intimidating vegetarian, 'Old Mother' Winstedt, John Myers, the finest scientific authority on gypsies' poisons, and, from Lincolnshire, the Very Reverend George Hall, expert poacher and approver of plural marriages, whose sport was collecting pedigrees. Sampson had hoped that the presence of a parson might give a collar of respectability, so far absent, to the gang's Borrovian adventurings – instead of which, his general appearance, tattered clerical coat, huge bandage over one eye (he having fallen head first off a cart) and habit of smoking a short pipe while drinking beer, produced quite the reverse effect.

All this was made possible by the new honorary secretary of the Gypsy Lore Society, Robert Andrew Scott Macfie, in truth the most endearing of men : and rich. Now in the prime of life, tall, dark and modest, of rueful and compassionate charm, he displayed a chivalry counted upon by the others – and not in vain – to bring in more lady members. He possessed the talent for getting on with absolutely everyone, the gift (much exercised by Augustus) of tact. His interests were wide and his abilities various. A skilful musician, expert in typography and well-known bibliographical scholar, he was also a fluent linguist and had soon learnt the Romany tongue. He also claimed authorship of an authoritative and absolutely unobtainable work on Golden Syrup and, after the First World War (during which he served as regimental quartermaster-sergeant), a military cookbook, everywhere lit up by flashes of his quaint humour.*

Macfie had been the head of a firm of sugar refiners in Liverpool before being seduced by Sampson into his gypsy career. Boarding up his large house near the cathedral, he moved to 6 Hope Place, which now became the headquarters of the society. Augustus, on his many trips to Liverpool, would often call on him there and was usually relieved of some frontispiece or article for the journal.[33] Fired by Macfie's tact and enthusiasm,

---

* For example: 'It is well known that putting jam or sugar on porridge, like wearing braces with a kilt, is one of the few crimes that definitely exclude a man from the Scottish suburb of Heaven.'

he was soon transformed into a vigorous recruiting officer in the ranks of the society. Patrons, dealers, private collectors, Café Royalists and society hostesses who wished to preserve diplomatic relations with him were obliged, as an earnest of their goodwill, to keep up their gypsy subscriptions. All manner of Quinns and Rothensteins found themselves enrolled, and some, for extraordinary feats, were decorated on the field.*

By April, Augustus was ready to penetrate beyond this screen of scholars into the fastnesses of Surrey, Cambridge and East Anglia. He had made what passed for the most elaborate preparations, obtaining letters of introduction 'from puissant personages to reassure timid and supercilious landowners, over-awe tyrannous and corrupt policemen and non-plus hostile and ignorant county people in general'.³⁴ He had done more. To the sky-blue van still stationed at Effingham he added another of canary yellow and a light cart, a team of sturdy omnibus horses, a tent or two and eventually Arthur, a disastrous groom. They mustered at Effingham – a full complement of six horses, two vans, one cart, six children, Arthur, a stray boy 'for washing up', a broken-down wagon, Dorelia and her younger sister Edie. 'We are really getting a step nearer my dream of the Nomadic life,' Augustus told Ottoline. 'The tent we have made is a perfect thing and the horses I bought are a very good bargain. The children are naturally all the better for so much fresh air. I would like all the same a few little girls running about. Will you lend me Julian³⁵ for one?' Their camp was like a mumper's, only, he boasted, more untidy. Undeterred by the scorn of the local gypsy, the convoy moved off to Epsom, where Augustus hit the headlines by protesting against the exclusion of gypsies from the racecourse on Derby Day. Then, the race lost, he set his black hunter's head towards Harpenden, which

---

* 'I have recently taken it upon myself (with what share of justification I know not) to confer the title Rai upon a friend of mine – one Percy Wyndham Lewis – whose qualifications – rather historical or anthropological than linguistic viz. – the having coupled and lived in a state of copulation with a wandering Spanish romi in Brittany – seemed to me upon reflection to merit the honourable and distinctive title of our confraternity,' he informed Scott Macfie (6 November 1908). '. . . I may add that my friend appears fully to appreciate the value of his new dignity. He remarks: "Henceforth, my brother, my seed is implicated with that of Egypt".'

they reached on 9 July. Augustus was exhilarated by their progress. 'It's splendid ... I ride sometimes by the side of the procession, but for the last two days I've been drawing the big van with two horses. It's always a question of where to pull in for the night. Respectable people become indignant at the sight of us – and disrespectable ones behave charmingly ... I'm acquiring still stronger views regarding landlords.'[36]

His next stop was Cambridge, where he had secured a commission to paint a portrait of the classical anthropologist Jane Harrison, 'a very charming person tho' a puzzle to paint'.[37] He had been offered this job on the recommendation of D. S. Mac-Coll who described him as 'the likeliest man to do a really good portrait at present', and who gave him preference over Wilson Steer 'whose tastes lie in the direction of young girls'. With this opinion Jane Harrison appears to have agreed, writing to Ruth Darwin, the promoter of the portrait: 'I personally should take his advice ... he [Augustus John] seems to me to have a real vision of "the beauty of ugliness" ... What I mean is that he gets a curious beauty of line: character, I suppose it would ordinarily be called, that comes into all faces however "plain" that belong to people that have lived hard; and that in the nature of things is found in scarcely any young face. Now this interests some people – I don't think it ever did interest Steer. If I were a beautiful young girl I should say Steer ...'

Augustus's painting, 'the only existing humane portrait of a Lady Don' as David Piper described it,[38] pleased its sitter, in particular because Augustus used Steer's 'Yachts', which Jane Harrison owned, as part of the background. To D. S. MacColl she wrote (15 August 1909) in praise both of the picture and the artist:

'Thank you for finding Mr John. He was delightful. I felt spiritually at home with him from the first moment he came into the room: he was so quiet and real and sympathetic too ... He was perfect to sit to; he never fussed or posed me, but did me just as I lay on the chair where I have mostly lain for months. I look like a fine distinguished prize-fighter who has had a vision and collapsed under it ... it seems to me beautiful, but probably as usual I am wrong!'[39]

Augustus and his retinue had encamped in a field by the river at Grantchester, and every day he would drive to Newnham, 'working away in utter oblivion',[40] while Jane Harrison smoked cigarettes and chatted with Gilbert Murray. 'Although a complete dunce,' he recalled, 'I enjoyed their learned conversation while I was painting, for in no way did it conceal the beautiful humanity of both.'[41] Even so, he felt little need to advance further into Cambridge and, apart from a visit to James Strachey at King's to spread the word of Dostoyevsky, he made almost no contact with the university. 'The atmosphere of those venerable halls standing in such peaceful and dignified seclusion seemed to me likely to induce a state of languor and reverie,' he wrote in *Chiaroscuro*, 'excluding both the rude shocks and the joyous revelations of the rough world without.'[42]

His presence, however, had already provided in itself a rude shock to Cambridge life. 'John is encamped with two wives and ten naked children,' Maynard Keynes inaccurately reported from King's College (23 July 1909). 'I saw him in the street today – an extraordinary spectacle for these parts.' Two days later he was writing to Duncan Grant: 'All the talk here is about John ...* Rupert [Brooke] seems to look after him and conveys him and Dorelia and Pyramus and David and the rest of them about the river ... According to Rupert he spends most of his time in Cambridge public houses, and has had a drunken brawl in the streets smashing in the face of his opponent.'

The talk reverberated round the colleges to such an extent that special parties of Raverats, Verralls and the like would arrange expeditions to the field to catch a glimpse of them, watching Dorelia make a pair of Turkish trousers, or the children gnawing bones for their supper then falling asleep on straw round the camp fire – and other marvels. 'We cause a good deal of astonishment in this well-bred town,' Augustus observed.[43]

The resurrection of the 'two wives' legend seems to have arisen not only because of Edie McNeill, but the more improbable presence of Ottoline Morrell who, dressed in her finer

---

* 'He [John] seems to have painted Jane Harrison at a great rate – 7 sittings of 1½ hours each. She is lying on a sofa in a black dress with a green scarf and a grey face on cushions of various colours with a red book on her lap' (Maynard Keynes to Duncan Grant, 23 July 1909).

muslins, had gaily accepted an invitation to their field. 'Come any day,' Augustus had wired. '. . . In case of any mistake our field is at Grantchester . . .' Her experiences there over twenty-four hours were a demonstration of the curious fact that the pleasures of the natural life are not naturally accessible to everyone. Augustus met her at the station with a horse and high gig.

'Directly I climbed up into the cart the horse, which was a huge ungainly half-trained animal, began to back, slipped and fell down,' Ottoline recalled.

John rapidly descended from our high perch; he stood calmly smoking a cigarette, looking at the great brute kicking and struggling, but made no attempt to help. However, station loafers came to the rescue, and we adjusted the horse and harness. Up we got again, and slowly trotted through Cambridge to a meadow . . . How damp and cold and cheerless and dull it seemed. John was morose, with a black eye, the result of a fight . . . Dorelia and her sister, absorbed in cooking and washing, treated me with indifference and taciturnity, and made no friendly effort to make me feel at home. But after all it would have perhaps been a difficult task to be at home in a melancholy, sodden meadow outside a caravan.[44]

For her dinner, Ottoline was thrown a crust of bread and some fruit, while the children munched bread and jam. Next day she hurried back to London 'chilled and damp and appreciative of my own home and Philip'.

Augustus's famous fight had been against Arthur, the groom, who, the previous evening, had been flung into a pugnacious attitude by the notion of leaving Cambridge. It fell therefore to Augustus to correct him, and between pub and trap they rained blows on each other, Augustus eventually carrying the day. Once recovered from their wounds they set off and gained a piece of waste ground near Norwich, where Augustus suddenly abandoned the lot of them. His next port of call was Liverpool and he had originally thought of travelling there in the vans. But 'it'll take me 3 weeks to get to you by road,' he told the Rani (July 1909), 'so I fear I must give up the plan and come by train'. So, leaving his women and children with instructions 'to come on steadily' or not at all, he walked into Norwich and caught a train on his way to paint one of the most notorious portraits of his career.

It was the custom in Liverpool for members of the city council to raise a private subscription of one hundred guineas and to present the retiring lord mayor with a ceremonial portrait. The mayor in 1908–9 had been Augustus's friend Chaloner Dowdall. Usually the chairman of the Walker Gallery was invited to choose the artist, but Dowdall, as whip of the Conservative party in the council, had so often collected the money for previous incumbents and knew so much about it all that when the deputation came to see him he at once asked it to let him handle the matter 'and you will have the biggest gate the Autumn Exhibition has ever had – and I shall have a picture worth five hundred guineas within five years time'. He then offered the commission to Augustus, who willingly consented: 'I'ld like very much to stay with you,' he wrote to the Rani. 'I believe Chowne has a studio for me if I want it. Don't let Silky [Chaloner Dowdall] worry any more. Tell him I'm coming ...'

Augustus was full of ideas for this portrait, and proposed to Dowdall, as they went together to buy the canvas, painting not only the Lord Mayor but his whole retinue of attendants which went with him on State occasions. Dowdall, slightly alarmed, demurred on the grounds that his house, though large, could hardly contain so monumental a work of art. Augustus, while nodding his head in agreement, nevertheless bought the biggest canvas available. 'I was an ass not to agree,' Dowdall afterwards claimed.[45]

That afternoon Augustus made a rapid watercolour sketch, about 24 inches by 18, and next morning when the canvas had arrived he set to work, beginning with the two lines – the wand and the sword – on which the design was based. By lunch it was all drawn in. 'He worked like a hawk on the wing,' Dowdall observed, 'and was white, sweating and exhausted.'[46] The two of them repaired for 'a good lunch' which was served by Smith, the Lord Mayor's footman. Noticing that Smith and Dowdall got along very well, Augustus suggested that the footman should be included in the picture, and to this Dowdall and Smith agreed. 'The whole thing was drawn in on the canvas at a single sitting,' Dowdall recalled, 'and painted with extraordinary rapidity.'

What struck Dowdall as being so remarkably rapid lasted an eternity for Augustus.* At first it went 'without a hitch', he wrote to Dorelia, 'and it'll be done in a few days. It's great sport painting jewels and sword hilts etc. My Lord sits every day and all day and I've been working like a steam engine.' The town hall itself made 'a devilish fine studio', and he predicted that the portrait would be 'a shade better than Miss Harrison's'.⁴⁷ His only trouble was the background, 'which I didn't have the foresight to arrange first'. After a week this trouble had advanced to the foreground, mainly because Dowdall would assume 'such an idiotic expression when posing'. This spirit of idiocy seemed to fill the town hall during his second week. 'It was frightful there,' he complained to Ottoline (9 September 1909), 'made all the more impossible by his lordship's inability to stand at ease. No more Lord Mayors for me. I used to be so glad to get out of the town hall that I roamed about the whole evening not returning till very late. I had but one desire: to submerge myself in crude unceremonious life.' Augustus had found he was expected to spend every evening and night with the Dowdalls, and to voyage back and forth with his subject in an official carriage and pair. The Liverpool police had appealed to Dowdall never to let Augustus out of his sight lest his excursions after dark be made a 'subject of comment in the town, and, ... be held to prejudice in some way the dignity of his Office'.⁴⁸ After tasting the freedom of the road, Augustus found this atmosphere intolerable. He was seized with impatience, the result of which, in terms of paint, was an inspiration: the portrayal of Dowdall as a civic Don Quixote attended by his doubtfully obsequious Sancho Panza, Smith.

Near the end of the portrait, feeling he could endure the municipal strain no longer, Augustus absconded to Wales. His friend Sampson had recently rediscovered the celebrated gypsy story-teller and great-great-grandson of Abraham Wood, King of the Gypsies: one Matthew Wood who, since 1896, had vanished from the face of the earth. To Sampson he was invaluable as the last of his race to preserve the ancient Welsh Romany dialect in

* In objective terms, about a fortnight.

its purity. Like some hedgehog, he had been quietly grubbing along in a remote village 'at the end of nowhere'[49] and seven miles from Corwen, called Bettws-Gwerfil-Goch. Having triumphantly tracked him there, like an 'old grey badger to his lair', Sampson resolved not to lose such a valuable creature again till he had got to know him 'as well as his own boots'. He therefore rented two semi-detached cottages on the spur of Bron Banog, overlooking the village, knocked them into one, and now moved in with two imposing pantechnicons of goods and chattels, with Margaret his wife, a dwarf maid named Nellie, their sheepdog Ashypelt, and their three children, Michael, Amyas and Honor in the charge of two young 'secretaries', the fair Kish and the dark Dora. And Augustus.

He arrived one evening 'in the best of spirits', determined to profit by his freedom from Liverpool town hall.

'Matthew Wood with his fiddle and I with my voice entertained the company till late – and there was great hilarity,' he wrote to John Quinn (September 1909).

There were two young ladies present, secretaries of the Rai. After going to bed I became possessed of the mad idea of seeking one of them – it seemed to me only just that they* should do something in the way of entertaining *me*. I sallied forth in my socks and entered several rooms before I found one containing a bed in which it seemed to me I discerned the forms of the two girls. I lay down at their sides and caressed them. It was very dark. Suddenly a voice started shrieking like a banshee – it might have been heard all over Wales. I thought then I had stumbled upon Sampson's boys instead of them I sought. I told the voice not to be silly and went away. On the landing appeared the two girls with a candle and terror in their eyes. I scowled at them and returned to bed.

Next morning at breakfast, the maid Nellie entered and demanded an explanation for his presence in her bed that night. Augustus, who had not seen her before, was horrified to observe that she was some four feet tall. He explained that it had been a mistake due to the peculiar pitch of Welsh darkness and the odd character of the house which together had left him entirely dependent on his sense of touch. But Nellie, very dignified,

* The words 'one of them' have been crossed out, and 'they' more accurately substituted.

remarked that this hardly explained the nature of the caresses he had lavished upon her – and the little girl with whom she slept, Miss Honor. Each revelation seemed to make the business worse, and Augustus could only fall back on the claim that he must have been dreaming. By lunch, the atmosphere in the house had grown so constrained that he decided to slip away. His exertions to make a joke of the matter by suggesting it might have been worse – after all, supposing it had been Sampson's arms he had blundered into! – were met with silence.

He left after lunch without a word, walking down to the village to see about a horse and trap. Here Sampson overtook him to volunteer the advice that he should not return to the house, and upon Augustus assuring him that 'nothing could have been further from my thoughts'[50] and that he was even then on his way, Sampson relented and proposed a drink. 'We passed several hours with drinks and gypsies,' Augustus told the Rani. The inn resounded to the melodious din of richly inflected Romany, but after a while a discord was introduced by Matthew Wood's half-brother Howell, a hefty degenerate brute who began provoking Sampson, trying to pick a quarrel with him. 'We got outside the Inn and Sampson was shouting that he'ld have this dog turned out of the village.' Feeling he might owe his friend a good deed, Augustus offered to turn him out of the pub. 'This I did and shot him into the road. Then ensued a bloody combat.' Within the sunlit square each stripped to the waist and, in the style of the old-fashioned prize fight, began battle. After two long rounds Augustus had him on the ground 'but he was biting my legs. Up came the others, Sampson vociferating blood and death! And the poor Gypsy was led off streaming with gore, howling maledictions in three languages.'

It was well past midnight when Augustus arrived back in Liverpool to find the Dowdalls' house, out of which he had been so eager to escape, impossible to enter. 'I climbed over the fence and tried all the windows at the back. I tried to pull down one of those damn lamps,' he told the Rani. 'Your house is like a fortress. So I went into Sefton Park and lay under a laurel bush till dawn ... about 6 [I] went and washed my gore and grime in the Central Station.'

Though much revived by experiences that would have half-killed another man, Augustus was in no frame of mind to do justice to his model, the Lord Mayor, and despite the head not being quite all there to his satisfaction,* he got off that same day back to Norfolk.

The reception given to the portrait when it was first shown that autumn was as extreme in its way as that shortly to be accorded Roger Fry's show : 'Manet and the Post-Impressionists'. The press called it 'detestable', 'crude', 'unhealthy', 'an insult', 'a travesty in paint' and the 'greatest exhibition of bad and in-artistic taste we have ever seen'. The art critic of the *Liverpool Daily Post* (18 September 1909) felt able to describe it as 'a work worse painted and worse drawn than any modern picture we can remember', and suggested that it was 'an artistic practical joke' which gave Smith grounds for legal action. Another critic (19 September 1909) detected moral danger on the canvas. It was, he declared,

an attenuated specimen of what Mr John chooses to call a man, over 20 heads in length, all legs, the pimple of a head being placed on very narrow shoulders and by his side, in a ridiculous attitude, a figure that I fancy I have seen before in a Punch and Judy show. All painted in rank, bad colour and shockingly badly drawn ... The public have none too great knowledge of art as it is; to publicly exhibit the work is calculated to do immense amount of harm to the public generally and the young art students who go to galleries and museums for guidance and help.

'You are being pounded and expounded (which is worse) in the *Liverpool Post* just now,' Scott Macfie informed Augustus (21 September 1909). To combat the public objection a strong body of supporters had quickly assembled, calling up phrases such as 'crystallized rhythm' to the defence. *The Liverpool Courier* (25 September 1909) interpreted it as a 'topical allegory' which had a 'symbolic value as representing the characteristic relationships of the Labour-Socialist Party and the Liberal Government'. While in the *Western Daily Press* T. Martin Wood, who described Augustus as 'the most revolutionary' of

* He later reversed this opinion. In 1911, when he had an opportunity to add to the head, he decided against doing so. 'I sent your portrait to the N[ew] E[nglish],' he wrote to Dowdall. 'I couldn't decide to touch it, merely gave it a thin coat of varnish. I think it looks well.'

'all the revolutionaries who are now alive', reflected upon the 'expression of countenance, in which a soul is to be seen'.

Liverpool was sent into an extraordinary hubbub by this controversy, echoes of which were to last many years. Day after day the Walker Art Gallery was packed with people coming to ridicule or admire this 'Portrait of Smith' as it was now called. Letters of anonymous indignation were everywhere posted in haste, and feelings of fury, adulation and merriment were kept at a high level by all manners of Tweedledum cartoons, satirical verses and stories to the effect that Dowdall had commissioned a gang of burglars to make off with it, only to find they had taken the valuable frame and left the canvas. Augustus himself did not immediately help his symbolic supporters by stating that he had introduced Smith into the picture 'for fun'[51] – and at no extra cost! But he was obviously taken aback by the venom of some attacks which he described as 'stupid, disgusting and unnecessary'.

After leaving Liverpool, the picture toured the country, always followed by a wake of argument, and was shown at the winter exhibition of the N.E.A.C. in 1911. 'There is nothing to justify the indignation expressed by the Liverpool worthies,' one paper proclaimed. But the *Athenaeum* (2 December 1911), as at some new Bonnard, could still 'marvel somewhat at Mr John's innocence of the science of perspective', while other critics invoked the names of Gainsborough, Sargent, Velasquez and Whistler.

One man who had stood up for the portrait from the beginning was Dowdall himself. On all public occasions he announced that it was splendid, and went so far as to supplement Augustus's honorarium out of his own pocket. 'I consider it a great picture, and for what my opinion is worth, I am prepared to go nap on it,' he was reported as saying.[52] Nevertheless it was to prove something of a white elephant to the Dowdall family, following them from house to house in its atrocious golden frame and dominating their lives. 'You will have to build a special room to hold it,' advised a friend.[53] Such friends had to enter through the back door at Liverpool because the portrait blocked the entire entrance hall. It also cost a fortune to insure, the hiring of a special railway truck to move and, when stationary, attracted crowds of Augustus's devotees who would call round and demand to view it, making the Dowdalls' lives a torment. Eventually, in 1918, Chaloner Dowdall decided to sell it. Liverpool, despite its hostility, still felt a proprietary right in the picture and was critical of Dowdall. But Augustus took a different line: 'I'm glad to hear you found the old picture useful at last,' he wrote to him (14 October 1918), 'and that it fetched a decent price. It was really too big for a private possession of course, failing the possession of a palace to hold it. I don't forget how well you acted by me at the time.'

The National Gallery had offered Dowdall six hundred and fifty pounds, but E. P. Warren, a private collector who lived with John Fothergill at Lewes House in Sussex, topped this with an offer of one thousand four hundred and fifty pounds. Dowdall asked the Rani whether their son (then aged ten) would prefer to see his father enshrined in the National Gallery at a fairly nominal price or enjoy the proceeds of the full market price – to which she simply replied. 'Don't be a fool!' So the portrait went to Warren's beautiful eighteenth-century house where it joined a Lucas Cranach, a Filippino Lippi and, in the garden, Rodin's 'Baiser'. With his money Dowdall then bought a house, Melfort Cottage, in Oxfordshire with three acres of land where he lived for the next thirty-five years. But the picture still had not come to rest. When Warren died, his heir Asa Thomas lent it back to the Walker Gallery. It was exhibited there in 1932, but Liverpool was still dead set against it, and the director refused to buy it. Not for another six years was it bought. 'I have now to make a confession,' Sydney Cockerell then wrote to Dowdall (2 June 1938). 'As London Adviser to the Felton Trustees of the National Gallery of Victoria I am guilty of having caused the banishment to Melbourne of your magnificent portrait by Augustus John. It is really too bad as it is perhaps his masterpiece and it certainly should have remained in England. How mad your fellow citizens of Liverpool were to allow it to go out of their hands!'

The price this time had risen to two thousand four hundred pounds – twenty-four times the original fee. It was shown at the Tate Gallery for a month, then left for Australia. Another sixteen years later it returned to Liverpool, and to the Walker Art

Gallery where, for six weeks in 1954, it was the centrepiece of an Augustus John show having Liverpool connections. 'It may well be that something of this conflict, aligned in the same way, will divide Liverpool again now,' wrote Hugh Scrutton with a nostalgia for the aggressive past. '... At all events visitors to the Walker Art Gallery can now see this stormy petrel of a picture returned to its original place of showing. And it may be their last chance. For the picture will return to the National Gallery of Victoria, Melbourne, in September and it is anybody's guess whether it will return again within their lifetime from Australia.'*

Returning, via London, to camp, Augustus found that everything was not well. Arthur had again misbehaved, and in a

---

* In July 1911 Augustus painted another Liverpool portrait that, amid much controversy, was exiled overseas. This was of the Celtic scholar Kuno Meyer. It shows him lolling in a chair, his waistcoat thrown open (and part of his trousers) to display a large expanse of shirt and a claret-coloured tie. It is a strong and weighty piece of portraiture, very robust and effective in style. Presented, through subscription, by some two hundred Liverpool friends, and shown at the N.E.A.C. (winter 1911) and the National Portrait Society (spring 1915), it was much admired by Sir Hugh Lane who, Lady Gregory told Quinn (16 March 1912), 'hopes to buy John's picture of Kuno Meyer for the Gallery [Irish National Gallery]. The Liverpool people don't like it, and he could sit to someone else for them. It is a fine thing.' But once again, though Liverpool did not like it, it did not especially want others to enjoy it elsewhere. Then, at the beginning of the First World War, Kuno Meyer came out on the side of the Germans, and left Britain for America. The portrait continued to hang at the Liverpool University Club, greatly to the embarrassment of the authorities who, by way of compromise, turned its face to the wall. Though it still belonged to the absent professor, Liverpool in its anxiety now to be rid of the traitorous object tried to remove it to the care of the public trustee as the property of an alien enemy. As the war continued, Ireland, England, America and even Germany fought for the right not to have it, and it remained in a state of suspended ownership. 'I have been thinking that I ought to sell John's portrait of me,' Kuno Meyer innocently wrote to Quinn on 3 November 1915, 'although this is not the best time to do so. Besides, John wouldn't like it, and I should be very sorry to hurt his feelings. For, unlike most of my English friends, he is one who will not put politics – and such dirty politics – above friendship ... the portrait (which my English friends no longer care for) is unsuited to my small flat and – entre nous – not liked by my family as a portrait, while it is one of John's masterpieces, as everybody admits.'

The portrait which Augustus had begun at Dingle Bank a 'Rotten' place and finished in two sittings at 4 Colquitt Street, went after the war to where Lane had originally wanted to send it: the National Gallery of Ireland in Dublin.

sudden fury Augustus fired him on the spot. They were now,
with their various caravans, carts, animals and boys, immovable.
In desperation, Augustus wired his friend Charles Slade,* who
lived not far off at Thurning. The muddled wording of his S.O.S.
admirably conveyed the emergency: '*Have fired Arthur can
you come help love conveniently at once John*'. Slade quickly
rode over and shepherded the convoy back to his farm. But the
romantic life had already taken a heavy toll of them. A number
of photographs which Slade took during September show in
detail the brave equipment with which they had encumbered
themselves. The vans, still bright, were in the 'cottage' style,
with ornate chip-carved porch brackets projecting at the front
and rear, and steps which, when the horses had been unhar-
nessed and put out to graze, fitted between the dipped shafts.
The tents, to judge from Augustus's drawings, were of the traditional gypsy construction – a single stout ridge-pole carrying
five pairs of hazel-rods shaped into a cartwheel, over which
framework blankets could be fastened by skewers or pinhorns.[54]
There are no horses in the photographs, possibly because they
had, at an alarming rate, begun to die off. One stumbled and
fell *en voyage*, projecting Augustus over its head; another fell
while standing in the shafts 'and I sold it to a knacker for a
sovereign'. Photographs of Dorelia and Edie suggest that they
too were almost on the point of death, worn out by the rigours
of road-life. The boys, while at Thurning, all caught whooping-
cough, which they communicated to the Slade children; and
gradually the general discomforts of their camp penetrated as

* Charlie Slade, whose brother Loben had married Dorelia's sister Jessie,
was known as 'the half-a-potato man' on account of his fantastic mystical
experiences which, Romilly John explains, 'originated in an experience of his
own nothingness in the ruins of Pompeii, and the revelation that came to him
that the cut surfaces of a potato sliced in half, however asymmetrical in shape
the potato, were exactly similar. He was subsequently promoted to station
master at Cambridge, when I became deeply involved in his ideas and was
urged (in vain) to produce a book on the subject.' Romilly John to the author,
28 July 1972. Felix Slade, Charles Slade's son, objects that 'the half-a-potato
man exists only in Romilly's imagination. My father did, however, often propound informal theories, which were put to us for study and topics of conversation . . . I remember the potato theory but was only slightly intrigued by it . . .
My father was the District Engineer, Cambridge (1924–27), and not the
Station Master.'

far as Augustus himself. 'I shall be damn glad to get on with my own work,' he wrote to John Quinn (September 1909). He had agreed to decorate the Chelsea house of Lady Gregory's nephew, Hugh Lane, and he returned thankfully to Church Street. He would not repeat such a rough-and-tumble journey, but it was not long before he began wondering about agreeable variants. 'I don't suppose we shall return this summer,' he admitted to Slade, with whom he had left a number of his vans and sons. 'I wish I had the vans in France. Do you know how much it would cost to heave them over the Channel?'

8. FATAL INITIATIONS

'I have been seeing a lot of Arthur Symons lately,' Augustus wrote to Ottoline (1 October 1909). 'I'm afraid he's about to break down again and that will be the end. He reads me poems that get more and more lurid.'

They were an ill-assorted pair. The son of a puritanical Wesleyan minister, Arthur Symons had been brought up along nervously conventional lines and indoctrinated with a vast dose of the Knowledge of Evil. Against the effects of this upbringing he had later received a partial vaccination at the hands of Dr Havelock Ellis who, during a week's visit to Paris, introduced him to the debauchery of cigarettes and wine. Upon such weeds and fruit was Symons's celebrated *Knowledge of French Decadence* brought to birth. He was a man, in George Moore's words, 'of somewhat yellowish temperament', who, according to Will Rothenstein, 'began every day with bad intentions ... [and] broke them every night'. His spirit was eager enough, but his body, undermined by those chronic illnesses which afflict men who will outlive all their contemporaries, was weak. Though much obsessed with notions of sex, he was not a passionate man but something different: a passionate believer in passion. The rhyme was preferable to the deed, and he would dizzy himself, in verse, with visions of belly-dancers, serpent-charmers and other exotic temptresses. More prosaically, he had married Rhoda Browser, a strong-willed scatterbrain who seems to have been a better performer off stage than in the various theatres where she occasionally acted. But he needed about him people who were strong, people who had an appearance of strength greater than his father's had been: it was this quality that had first attracted him to Augustus.

They had met in Gordon Craig's studio in Chelsea in 1902 – 'one of the most fortunate events of my life', as Symons described the meeting. The following spring, when Augustus held his show at the Carfax Gallery, Symons wrote a long appreciation of it in the Anglo-French paper, *Weekly Critical Review* (2 April 1903):

'I have just been to the Carfax Gallery, in Ryder Street, to see some of the work of a young man who, if he does not become a notable painter, will owe it entirely to his own fault. Mr Augustus E. John is, pictorially speaking, a man of substance; grave people say he is squandering his substance in riotous painting; but I contend he is living within his means, he need have no fear of using up his capital.'

Many years later, in an article entitled 'The Greatness of Augustus John', in which he selected Augustus as 'the greatest living artist', Symons recalled his first reaction to the Carfax exhibition. Two sentences from Baudelaire had occurred to him: '*Je connais pas de sentiment plus embarrassant que l'admiration*'; and '*L'énergie c'est la grâce suprême*'. These two sentences sum up very well the commerce of their relationship. Symons traded his admiration in exchange for Augustus's generous encouragement. He set out to please Augustus, sitting for him, dedicating books to him, deferring to his literary taste, assailing him with congratulatory poems; and he set out to take from him something he badly needed: energy. Wilde had once described him as 'an egoist without an ego'. It was Augustus whom he now elected to supply this ego from the dynamo of his overcharged personality. It was not difficult for Symons to identify himself with Augustus. In his article he had written that John's pictures 'revealed to me at once his primitive genius and his startling originality, and I knew that he, like myself, was a Vagabond, and that he knew the gypsies and their language better than anyone else.' In his letters and diaries he sometimes makes this identification between them quite explicit: 'I was born at Milford Haven in Wales,' he once wrote to John Quinn (30 January 1914) '– oddly nine miles along the

coast from where Augustus was born.' Were they not blessed
then, or afflicted, with the same Celtic blood? Had they not endured similar upbringings? In his diary he noted:

John's fascination is almost infamous; the man, so full of lust and
life and animality, so exorbitant in his desires and in his vision that
rises in his eyes.

His mother, who died young, was artistic, did some lovely paintings his father still keeps in Tenby. There he got some of his gift –
as I did from mine. I for verse, he for painting. Our fathers never
really understood us ... John's father hated art and artists; the
mother, imaginative. So was mine: both imaginative: one derives
enormously from one's mother.

They seldom saw each other before 1909, but Augustus lived
vividly in Symons's imagination. 'Arthur Symons has sent me a
poem he had dedicated to me – all about bones and muscles and
blatant nakedness,' Augustus wrote to Alick Schepeler. 'I ask
myself what I have done to merit this?' The poem, 'Prologue
for a Modern Painter: To A. E. John' is a hymn to vitality, a declaration of his faith in the kind of life he could never make his
own, except through someone else:

> Hear the hymn of the body of man:
> This is how the world began;
> In these tangles of mighty flesh
> The stuff of the earth is moulded afresh ...
>
> Here nature is, alive and untamed,
> Unafraid and unashamed;
> Here man knows woman with the greed
> Of Adam's wonder, the primal need.
>
> The spirit cries out and hymns
> In all the muscles of these limbs;
> And the holy spirit of appetite
> Wakes the browsing body with morning light.[55]

The rather embarrassed question which this poem prompted
from Augustus was valid. What, after all, *had* he done to merit
such rhapsodic rhymes? For one of the paradoxes of their
friendship was that where Augustus dreamed, Symons, in his
tireless search for 'impressions', had often acted. He had
breathed in the fantastical air of Dieppe far deeper than

Augustus, stopping impatiently for a night while in pursuit of some fish-women, could ever have done. And he had actually gone to many of the places, especially in Italy, that had been the destinations at the end of Augustus's rainbow plans. Yet because Symons dreaded action 'more than anything in the world',[56] he was determined to see Augustus as a great man of action. What mesmerized him was the apparent lack of that guilt which so weighed down his own actions wherever he went.

The flow of poems persisted and was for some years their main line of communication. It formed, for Symons, a kind of umbilical cord attaching him to a creative source of life. 'Dear Symons,' Augustus wrote from Church Street, 'To-day I've just come back to find another beautiful poem for me! I would have written columns of gratitude for the others you sent, only the words, not the will, failed me.'*

Then, in 1908, a terrible disaster had overtaken Symons: he had gone mad in Italy. From Venice, urged on by a sense of extreme exasperation, he fled to a hotel in Bologna where Rhoda, dressed like a dragonfly, hurried to his side. She found him racked by terrible imaginations, but her concern seemed only to sharpen his torment. For repeatedly she would demand, as if in pursuit of medical symptoms: 'Do you *really* love me, Arthur?' One night he disappeared: he had given his answer. 'So it has come at last!' she soliloquized. 'He no longer loves me!' Next morning, however, Symons returned and created some dismay by failing to recognize his wife, and then, with foul curses filling his mouth, rushing off chased by horrible shapes and shadows. The hotel manager then explained to Rhoda: 'Madam, your husband is mad. He has bought three daggers.' In hysterics she ran back to England to be arraigned by a herd of Browsers for having deserted her husband. Symons, meanwhile, had lost himself, drifting day after day in ever-increasing fatigue from one ominous spot to another. 'I walked and walked and walked – always in the wrong direction.' At last he was arrested in Ferrara, manacled hand and foot, and thrown into a medieval gaol. It was only with great difficulty

---

* Yet the words, so failing in gratitude, were more forthcoming in parody, and John wrote a number of verses in the Symons style. See Appendix Three.

that his friends and family got him released and dispatched back
to England where, in November 1908, he was confined to Brooke
House, a private mental home.

The doctors there were confident they could not cure him.
They had diagnosed 'general paralysis of the insane', which
could proceed, they confirmed, through hopeless idiocy to death.
They spoke matter-of-factly. They were kind, but firm: all hopes,
they promised, were ignorant and vain. Symons (who lived
thirty-six more years in perfect sanity) had, they declared, a life-
expectancy of between two months and two years – it could
not be more. His manner of life at Brooke House, though described by the specialists as 'quiet', seems to have been unusually
active. He assumed the title of Duke of Cornwall, and took off
all his clothes; he frequently dined with the King and kept forty
pianofortes upstairs on which he composed a prodigious quantity of music. He rose each morning at 4 a.m., and worked hard
on a map of the world divided into small sections; he also
wrote plays with the greatest frenzy and illegibility, devoted
endless time to the uplifting of the gypsy, and, when not occupied as Pope of Rome, involved himself in speculations worth
many thousands of pounds. But his main duty as a lunatic was
to arrange for Swinburne's reception in Paradise, and when
Swinburne died a month later the pressure of these delusions
began to ease. 'Had it not been for John,' he wrote later, 'whose
formidable genius is combined with a warmth of heart, an
ardent passion and will, at times deep, almost profound affection, which is one of those rare gifts of a genius such as his, I
doubt if I could have survived these tortures that had been
inflicted upon me.'

Already, by the summer of 1909, Symons was being allowed
out from Brooke House in convoy, followed by a Miss Agnes
Tobin, a West Coast American lady bitten with a passion for
meeting real artists, and, at some further distance, a hated
'keeper' from the asylum. This procession would make its ser-
pentine way to the home of Augustus who, after losing the
keeper 'without compunction or difficulty', would set them
high-stepping to the Café Royal, where he prescribed for Symons
medicines more potent than any administered at Brooke House.
'At the Café Royal, between five and eight, we each drank seven

absinthes, with cigarettes and conversation,' Symons wrote excitedly to John Quinn (20 June 1914). 'In spite of that we got a
few sensations.' There were many of these splendid occasions :
visits to the Alhambra and to the Russian ballets; glorious
luncheons at the Carlton and sumptuous suppers with young
models in Soho: all for the sake of what Symons called *'la
débauche et l'intoxication'*. Augustus had become the Sun in
Symons's life, whose absence betokened a dismal day: 'Alas I
never saw John. Worse luck for me then.'[57]

Augustus was extremely good to Symons. Under the impression that the poor man was very shortly to die, he set out
lavishly to entertain him and make his last few weeks enjoyable. 'I have seen Symons a good deal,' he told Quinn (25
October 1909) '– he keeps apparently well but one can see all
the same that he is far from being so. The doctors give him 2 or
3 more months. He is entirely engrossed in himself, his only
other preoccupation being to get me to listen to him while he
reads out his latest poems – which are all hell, damnation and
lust.'

What Augustus had not calculated was that, a dozen years
later, he would still be entertaining Symons 'a good deal', and
that Symons would still be counting on him to be (14 April
1921) 'as wonderful as ever'.

Egocentricity is a condition of all illnesses, and what Augustus
did for Symons, almost literally, was to dissipate his egocentricity. He blew into his life and kept blowing, ventilating it
with humour, filling it with people, elbowing out Symons's in-
trospection. The delusions melted into nothing before the heat
of actual events. But part of Symons's recovery was due,
Augustus maintained, 'to the kindness and devotion of Miss
Tobin'.[58] The presence of Miss Tobin, like that of a jester at
Court, was entirely appropriate to their meetings. She was forty-
five with the light behind her, hailed from San Francisco, had
translated Petrarch, and now lived in the Curzon Hotel. She was
a woman of the right instincts but the wrong clothes, and had
been observed to be 'a little bit flighty'.[59] Conrad (who dedicated
Under Western Eyes to her) called her Inez; Francis Meynell,
however, called her Lily 'because of the golden and austere
delicacy of her head and neck'; and she called Augustus 'my

poor butterfly'. He stood up to it well. Something of his attitude
to their tripartite meetings is conveyed by a nautical description he gave to John Quinn (18 December 1909):

> I've been seeing Symons and Miss Tobin now and then. Symons is
> still held up in Brooke House nor will he be released in a hurry I
> think. He keeps pouring out verses. He has developed a tremendous
> affection for me which I find as embarrassing as it is undeserved. He
> never suspects that there can be no complete understanding be-
> tween us, and one can't be frank with an invalid.
>
> The other night occurred a row as we came out of a restaurant.
> In order to cope more successfully with the exigencies of Symons'
> society, I had before meeting him, taken on board a considerable
> ballast in the way of drink and was thus, although the more sea-
> worthy in respect to plain sailing on an even keel, rendered less
> competent to oppose the squall that followed ... when we got
> outside, some man started buffooning me, holding out his hat and
> asking for alms. I regarded him for about a minute then gravely and
> neatly knocked his hat halfway down the street upon which I was
> set upon by his companions, a man and a woman armed with an
> umbrella, and the first man returning I was in the thick of an igno-
> minious struggle in which I stumbled and knocked myself, or was
> knocked, senseless on the curb. Miss Tobin was holding in Symons
> and she got some of the assembled multitude to put my limp body
> into a four-wheeler. She drove me home. I had regained conscious-
> ness very soon and my first words were 'Has anybody got a cigar-
> ette?' I still have an aching jaw from that encounter. I think Miss
> Tobin enjoyed the affair on the whole.

The three of them had been brought together, while Augustus
was briefly in London following his escape from Liverpool's
Lord Mayor, by John Quinn, the New York lawyer, who has
been called 'the twentieth century's most important patron of
living literature and art'.[60] Quinn had arrived in England this
summer to buy some pictures by Charles Shannon, Nathaniel
Hone and 'Augustus John, the artist who is much discussed in
London now'.[61] He had heard tell of both Symons and Augustus
from W. B. Yeats and, with American enthusiasm, had not
been content to see each of them separately, but seen to it that
they saw one another too. There appeared to be advantages in
this for everyone. Miss Tobin, who was coming into contact
with more artists and authors than once she could have dreamed

possible, made the suggestion, full of consequences, that Quinn
acquire manuscripts by Symons and her friend Conrad. 'Your
bringing A.S. and Mr John together was a miraculous success
and will, I think, be an immense solace to A.S.', she informed
Quinn (16 September 1909). 'Mr John told me he would keep up
the friendship – and wants A.S. to sit for him.' Augustus's
portrait of Symons was delayed until the autumn of 1917 when,
though advertised by Frank Harris* as showing 'a terrible face –
ravaged like a battlefield', it was warmly welcomed by the
Symons family. 'John has done a fine portrait of A[rthur],'
Rhoda confided to Quinn (29 October 1917), '. . . What an odd
fish he is; but he has great personal qualities. He has been true
to A[rthur] all thro' these years, and it's few who have . . . he's a
great artist, isn't he? . . . A[rthur]'s portrait is very El Grecoish!'

Of Quinn Augustus did a number of drawings (one of them
described by a friend as 'the portrait of a hanging judge') and a
large formal portrait in oils – all during a single week in August.
On the fifth and final sitting, just as Augustus was about to take
up his brushes, Miss Tobin stepped forward and exclaimed that
the canvas was perfect – 'at the razor's edge'. Augustus at once
laid down his brushes and began drinking – so the picture was
perforce finished.†

* '[Augustus John] has painted Symons with the relentless truth we all desire
in a portrait,' Harris wrote: 'the sparse grey hair, the high bony forehead, the
sharp ridge of Roman nose. The fleshless cheeks; the triangular wedge of thin
face shocks one like the stringy turkey neck and the dreadful claw-like fingers
of the outstretched hand. A terrible face – ravaged like a battlefield; the eyes
dark pools, mysterious, enigmatic; the lid hangs across the left eyeball like a
broken curtain. I see the likeness, and yet, staring at this picture, I can hardly
recall my friend of twenty-six years ago.'

† In a letter to his wife (25 August 1909) Symons gives rather a different
account of this afternoon. 'We went to John's studio at 3. The Quinn was
finished: a very fine living portrait: 5 days! Then I turned over heaps and heaps
of designs, and he gave me a delightfully sensual nude, with a sketch of a head
on the back. Then – in half an hour (I sitting as still as a statue) he did a magnificent drawing of me – almost more living than myself – the eyes marvellous! –
and what fat cheeks! – mouth! etc. It is full face. I crossed my knees and put my
left hand around my chin. His eyes went up and down every minute – his hand
went and went with a precision that I never believed any human being could do.
He sat on a stool in shirt and trousers, the sleeves turned up, holding the block
between his knees with his left hand. I sat on the edge of the platform. Then, a
few minutes after, I sat on the chair, upon it half-sideways with my eyes turned

At the end of their week, everyone was thoroughly delighted with one another. Miss Tobin wrote ecstatically to thank Quinn for his 'wonderful and royal kindness ... 7 taxis in a day ... Your visit remains with us something glorious – in the atmosphere of the Decameron. Really – *everything* we did with you came off.' And Quinn wrote to Miss Tobin (21 December 1909): 'I don't know when I have been so taken with a man as I was with John. He is a splendid fellow: nothing morbid, or introspective or posing about him ... a man of action, as I am fated to be, gets close to a man like John.'

Yet even now, in the very honeymoon of their friendship, there was a sign of what was to come: Quinn's portrait. Although he affected to think well of it – 'I liked the portrait John made of me,' he assured Lady Gregory (21 December 1909). 'And I liked John himself immensely' – it was not an encouraging likeness. When it was exhibited that autumn at the N.E.A.C. under the title 'The Man from New York', the critic of the *English Review* (January 1910) wrote:

'The peculiar note of hardness which Mr A. E. John has could not have found a better subject than "The Man from New York". It shows exactly that hardness which we look for and find in this type of American.'

Quinn insisted that, on reading this, 'I howled out loud with glee'.[62] There are few more doleful sounds than the hearty laughter of a man without humour. Quinn's lack of humour was a very positive quality. Uninhibited by any sense of the ludicrous, he enjoyed drawing attention to it by cracking jokes.*

---

to his. He sat on a high stool. Another half-hour – another totally different – but both magnificent – the latter gave, in a few strokes, my left hand with the rings on it. Then John said: "I am going away for three weeks or so, and when I come back I will do a portrait of you" ... Then Hugh Lane's, then Carlton for dinner, then the Empire where Lydia Lopokova, a Polish dancer, was ... Then we went back to the Carlton and had a few drinks (I mean the three of us). Then I put on a red silk tie and John said: "I must do another drawing." He seized Quinn's bill and dashed off a diabolical half face of me!!!'

* A fair example may be taken from a letter Quinn wrote to James Huneker, the American art critic (4 February 1913): 'In my cable to Fry I expressly said that I bought the picture on your recommendation only so that if you have any fish to fry or bones to pick with Roger of the same name, then why not fry Fry. Personally, I never take fries; I always go in for roasts or broils...'

His response to Augustus's portrait* was indeed partly the result of its being a very funny picture. It presents him at three-quarter length, seated with his left hand on his hip and his right hand extended, resting on a cane. The shape of his figure is, unmistakably, that of a tent and upon a face of pimple proportions at the apex of this design there sits an expression of the sternest vacancy. Quinn, his biographer B. L. Reid tells us, 'felt baffled and unhappy about it',[63] though Symons, Pissarro and others considered it 'extremely good'.[64] Bravely, he hung it over his mantelpiece for as long as he lived, but would indignantly protest that Augustus 'painted me as though I were a referee or umpire at a baseball game or the president of a street railway company with a head as round and unexpressive and under-developed as a billard ball. Thirty or forty years of life in school, college, university and the world has I hope put a little intelligence into my face. Intelligence is not predominant in the John painting of me, but force, self-assertion and a seeming lack of sensitiveness which is not mine!'[65]

Quinn's interpretation of the portrait was accurate: Augustus had depicted his hopes of intelligence, so aggressively held, as vain. 'Do not expect any subtle intelligence from him [Quinn] or any other Yankee,' he warned Will Rothenstein (20 September 1911). 'They are a disconcerting people ... I fear you will find New York a terrible place: money has literally taken the place of brains and character, and the American mind is a metallic jungle of platitude and bluff.'

In an earlier letter to Rothenstein Augustus had lamented the dearth of 'millionaires of spirit'. In Quinn he had found a millionaire of the purse. He would have liked to like him, and he described him, after their first few meetings, as 'a pleasant, jocular and open-handed Irish-American', adding hopefully: 'We became very friendly'.[66] But this is precisely what they never became: they valued each other for qualities other than friendship. 'He's a treasure,' Augustus told Dorelia (August 1909). 'He's offered me £250 a year for life and I can send him what I like. He's a daisy and will do much more than that.' It seemed to Augustus that so liberal a patron, and one tactful enough not to inconvenience him by living in the same country,

* The portrait is now in the New York Public Library.

was the ideal solution to his problems. This extra money would enable him to live where he wished, travel where he liked; it would release him from a lot of commissioned work and allow him to paint imaginative pictures. He believed too that Quinn's interest would encourage self-discipline: 'I can tell you honestly you did me a lot of good that week in London,' he wrote in his first letter to Quinn (September 1909), 'and that quite apart from pecuniary considerations. You will help me to keep up to the scratch.'[67].

The figure of Quinn, hopelessly beckoning, stood at the end of a long straight road lavishly paved with good intentions. When, for example, he asks for a complete set of his etchings, Augustus willingly consents, adding (4 January 1910): 'I mean to methodize my work more and put aside say one or two months every year to etching – it can't be done every day or any day.' In another letter (25 October 1909) he tells Quinn: 'I am extremely anxious to study Italian frescos as I am fired with the desire to revive that art ... I am quite ready to say goodbye to oil painting after seeing the infinitely finer qualities of fresco and tempera.' But when Quinn replies with dismay, Augustus hurriedly gives way (18 December 1909):

What you say about my remarks on fresco and oil-painting are words of wisdom – I wrote under the enthusiasm of the moment. But I have had time to realise that oil-painting has its own virtues and have given up despising my own past – a thing one is too apt to do, when struck with a fresh idea. I suffer from being unduly impressionable – and often forget the essential continuity of my own life: the result being I am as often put back on my beam's ends rather foolishly. What you say is true that one is apt to desire one's own facility – whereas one should recognise it as the road to mastery itself. I shall keep your letter and read it over whenever I feel off the track – *my own track*. It will be medicine for me who am occasionally afflicted with intellectual vapours.

To appreciate the full flavour of a relationship that was crucially unsatisfactory to both of them, it is necessary to understand Quinn's psychology as patron and collector. One of the contradictions of his character was that, while being financially generous, he was a triumphantly mean man. His letters to Augustus and other artists and writers are always business letters, and almost always interchangeable – except for the odd quirk that what is quoted in one has been the main body of another. Essentially this correspondence is a form of memoranda for his files; it is endless, pitted with headings and sub-headings, listings and elaborate recapitulations of earlier correspondence. He is not afraid of recounting events out of which he comes extremely favourably and everyone else greatly to their disadvantage. He confesses being partial to (like cheese) 'juicy girls', but at the same time he is a sexual Puritan much given to amatory philosophizing, for which Augustus seemed an obvious target. He is a loud believer in 'guts'. And finally, he is full of yarns that always open with the rhetorical challenge: 'Have you heard the latest story?'

To lack of humour he prudently added lack of charm, and equipped with such powerful machinery he perfected the art of boredom. Dullness by itself was not enough. He ensnared his victims in the web of his money and inflicted on them his terrible jokes, appalling lectures, his deathly political harangues. Many of his 'friendships' disintegrated under this treatment and always, on Quinn's part, with a sense of moral relish. There were many precedents for his eventual break-up with Augustus – his split, for example, with W. B. Yeats. 'I think he [Yeats] needed a lesson,' Quinn told T. W. Rolleston (5 August 1910), 'and he got a good one.'

He fed greedily on malicious gossip, extracting confidences and, 'in confidence', passing them on. It continually amazed him how extraordinarily stupid everyone else was – and sometimes he wrote to tell them so; though more often he preferred telling their friends. His personal dislike of people extended to those he did not personally know: 'If there is one man I loathe it is [Ford Madox] Hueffer,' he once told James Huneker (2 July 1914). 'I do not know him from Adam, but if I were an artist I would draw him with a hare lip.'

It is difficult to resist the diagnosis that Symons's 'fatal initiation of madness' had been swiftly cured at some mental expense to his companions. It was not long before Miss Tobin was seeking to employ Quinn for legal advice about her nightmares. 'I had a frightful dream which told me efforts were being made to make me out mentally unbalanced at some time or other,' she informed him (24 July 1911). 'This is a dreadful stigma. But at last I have come to feel that no credence can be given to it by anyone who knows me – and the only side of it that is of importance is the legal side. Can you find out for me if I have been found "incapable" at any time for any cause – that is the legal term ("incapable") isn't it? Irresponsible, I mean.' This was a subject upon which Quinn found some difficulty in taking instructions. Miss Tobin was at once sympathetic. Of course it was awkward commenting legally across salt water. She would therefore cross the Atlantic and call at his office. She would travel with an English nanny who would be seasick. So would he please 'have a man sent out on a pilot-boat'. There is real pathos when Quinn suddenly cries out: 'I am a dreadfully driven man!' But in his legal opinion to Miss Tobin can be detected the seeds of his own lunacy: 'My conviction [is] that the origin of most dreams is in the stomach or intestines.'

Quinn had rapidly diagnosed Symons's complaint as venereal disease. Symons might 'fool them all yet', he guessed, but Quinn himself would not be fooled. His duty was clear and indirect: CABLE FIFTY POUNDS PLEASE WARN FRIEND AGAINST DANGER VENEREAL INFECTION ITALY.

Such cables, which were intended specifically for Augustus and no 'friend', reached him wherever he travelled – the sweet smell of money rising from a nauseous draught of cautionary advice. However far he went, however fast or uncertainly, by van or train or simply on foot, the venomous torrent of Quinn's goodwill, choked with the massive boulders of punning and unintentional *double-entendres*, overtook him. At Arles, for instance, Augustus read (February 1910):

For God's sake look out and protect yourself against venereal disease in Italy. Remember the Italians aren't white people. They are a rotten race. They are especially rotten with syphilis. They don't take care of themselves. They are unclean. They are filthy. Whatever their art may have been in the past, to-day they are a degenerate, filthy, diseased race. They are professional counterfeiters, professional forgers, habitual perjurers, blackmailers, black-handers, high-binders, hired assassins, and depraved and degenerate in every way. I know two men who got syphilis in Naples and who, as a result of syphilis and drink, both got paresis and died horrible deaths ... I know another man who got syphilis in Rome. Therefore for God's sake take no chances. Better import a white concubine than take chances with an Italian. The white woman would be cheaper in the end ... Your future is in your own hands, my dear friend. I am convinced you have the intellect to keep the rudder true.*

In time, Quinn's medical lunacy took a deeper hold on him, spreading from venereal disease to diseases of the feet and teeth. He became a specialist in sciatica ('sciatica is a term of ignorance and a disease arising from ignorance'); in lumbago ('lumbago is a term of ignorance and a disease arising from ignorance'); and in the relationship between fornication and eye-strain. The cure for such distempers was soup, eight glasses of water a day and, of course, plenty of X-rays. In dentistry, which he proclaimed as a new American science 'like chiropody', lay the secret of 'healthful' life. To all writers and artists he was generous with his medico-legal expertise – and particularly on teeth, which were his first love. Whether they had bad eyesight or bad feet, he would urge them to visit their dentist. 'I think I wrote to you two years ago I told [James] Joyce that the trouble with his eyes was due to his teeth,' he reminded Symons (15 November 1923). 'I could see it.'

What was common to both Symons's and Quinn's relationship with Augustus was the quality he extracted from many people and from which derived the substance of his legend: a form of vicarious living. In Symons this vicariousness is plain: 'What I am certain of is that John – of all living men – has lived his life *almost* entirely as he wanted to live it,' he once (21 October 1915) wrote to Quinn. 'So – he is the most enviable creature on earth.' Symons sincerely believed the truth of this, and would have felt almost a loss of religion had he been persuaded otherwise.

* In a letter sent the previous day (31 January 1910) Quinn had written: 'Syphilis is the national disease of Italy. Before a white man has intercourse with an Italian woman or a white woman with a "dago" (our word for an Italian) male or female should be examined by a physician, a non-Italian of course, to see there is no gonorrhoea or syphilis and an affidavit by the dago of no connection since the medical examination, and even *then* there is danger. For Heaven's sake, if you do go to the rotten place look out for this. Whisky and syphilis are two of the greatest enemies of the human race and the latter often follows indulgence in the former ... Youth is a precious thing.'

The vicarious quality in Quinn is more complicated. He led two lives which were separate and simultaneous. In the present he worked hard as a lawyer and amassed a considerable fortune; and with this fortune he bought his paintings for the future. He had a good eye for pictures, but he neither enjoyed them aesthetically as credit in some spiritual bank, nor treated them primarily as financial investments. He collected them in order to shore up a kind of second-hand immortality; this was his motive. It was right, he believed, to enjoy hell for the present to undergo heaven in the future. But the unshrinking distance between his parallel lives is measured by a sentence of angry pathos he once (25 March 1912) wrote to Will Rothenstein: 'All my life, or rather for twenty years, it seems to me I have been doing things for others.' The thought gave him no pleasure.

Augustus was one of those for whom, he later came to believe, he had done too much – for he had hoped Augustus would do much for him. In his attitude to money and art there was a pagan fanaticism, defying logic, that cast Augustus as an angel on whose back he would ride heavenwards – only to discover that this was not Augustus's destination. By 1910 he had arranged to pay him three hundred pounds a year for the pick of his own work, and a further two hundred pounds to select, on Quinn's behalf, work by other British artists. In short, Augustus was to act as his patron's agent. Quinn's delusion, almost as fundamental as Symons's, was that Augustus possessed the sort of character which responded well under such an arrangement, that a man who, by his own admission, was inconsistent, temperamental and whose tastes were not the same as Quinn's, would be his top choice as representative. Nevertheless, held together by mutual advantage, the plan worked reasonably well for a few years, and it was the lunacy of Augustus, amply aided by such improbable characters as Mrs Strindberg, which killed it.

Augustus's lunacy was compounded of two ingredients. Of these the first was lack of common sense. Between his promise and the fulfilment of that promise fell an almost endless pause. His practical incompetence over small matters tuned Quinn up to a marvellous pitch of exasperation. What should have been simple was, again and again, made complicated with radiant ingenuity : paintings were sold twice, or painted over, set fire to, sunk, never begun, or lost for ever. But there was a second reason, a motive, for all this purposeless perversity. Augustus was allergic to patron-and-artist dealings : they reminded him horribly of father-and-son arrangements, and he felt an incurable itch to behave irresponsibly. Then, there was something else. Quinn, at first, obviously worshipped him, and implanted within him seeds of guilt. He attracted hero-worship – then punished it. For there was no core to him : other people were transplanted to become that core until he rejected them, merged with someone else. His friends and patrons he made temporarily a part of himself, but what seemed to them a most selfless generosity was his own need : the filling of emptiness.

So, from among the four of them – Augustus, Quinn, Symons and Miss Tobin – bound together by ties of reciprocal expediency, it was Symons, protected by an official certificate, who was least 'afflicted with intellectual vapours'.

9. ITALIAN STYLE, FRENCH FOUND

An epidemic of ambitious schemes infected the last three months of 1909. 'I am overwhelmed with work just now,' Augustus wrote to Alick Schepeler, 'and have to scorn delights (or pretend to) and live laborious days.' He had it in mind to prepare a catalogue of all his etchings, and to make a book about the gypsies of Europe; he would exhibit some paintings at the N.E.A.C. and drawings at Chenil; and then he would paint all his children, separately and together. He had already started a large new portrait of Dorelia – 'it ought to be one of the best portraits of a woman in the world', he told Quinn (4 January 1910), '– the woman at any rate is one of the best'. Newest and best of all were two other enterprises. 'There's a millionairess from Johannesburg [Mrs Lionel Phillips] who proposes sending me abroad to study and do some decorations for a gallery at Johannesburg which she is founding,' he wrote to Quinn (25 October 1909). 'If she is sufficiently impressed by what I will show her all will be well.' This opportunity had almost certainly come through Sir Hugh Lane, who was then forming the collection at the Johannesburg Municipal Gallery. Augustus had started work this autumn decorating Lindsay House, Lane's home in Cheyne Walk – 'exciting work', he told Ottoline Morrell (1 October 1909).

Suddenly, at the beginning of December, he was attacked by the most dreadful melancholia. 'I have been working at little Lane's walls,' he explained to Ottoline (4 December 1909). 'It is an absolutely futile thing to undertake that kind of work in a hurry. I should like to have years to do it in – and then it might *last* years. Lane himself is a silly creature and moreover an unmitigated snob. It seems my fate to be hasty but I have serious thoughts of quitting this island and going somewhere where life is more stable and beautiful and primitive and where one is not bound to be in a hurry. I want absolutely to grasp things plastically and not merely glance at their charms, and for that one needs time. – As for these commissions such as Lane's or Phillips', they are misleading entirely – one is not even asked to do one's best – merely one's quickest and convenientest.'

He continued to be misled for another fortnight of deepening gloom: then came the storm. 'I have made a drastic move as regards Lane's decorations,' he confided to Quinn (18 December 1909). 'I found doing them in his hall impossible, subjected to constant interruption and inconsequent criticism as I was. Lane himself proved too exasperating in his constant state of nervous agitation – he resembled more some hysterical old lady than a man. So I exploded one day and told him I'ld take the canvases away to finish – which I have done.'

` Lane's 'snobbishness', 'agitation' and 'inconsequent criticism' had not been provoked by anything Augustus had done on his canvases. In a letter Dorelia sent to Ursula Slade about this time, she reveals that Augustus had spotted 'a lovely gypsy girl and asked her to sit for him'. This sitting took place next day at Lane's house where the two of them were soon joined by 'a whole band of ruffians' who made merry in every room and 'nearly frightened Lane out of his wits'. When the danger had passed and they were gone, Lane 'was very angry and said it wasn't at all the thing to do'. It was after this protest that Augustus erupted with his reprimands against 'this island' and carried off his canvases; while Lane himself, in high dudgeon, descended into Monte Carlo.

Dissatisfaction spread everywhere. There was no light in England, and no space in Church Street. 'Il me faut de l'air, de l'air, de l'air,' he cried out to Wyndham Lewis. By Christmas, Robin had fallen ill with scarlet fever. He sat quarantined in one corner of the room with Dorelia's sister Edie, while the rest of them huddled in the opposite corner. When the Rothensteins, with implacable timing, called round bearing the compliments of the season they were shooed from the door. 'Our house', Augustus apologized (4 January 1910), 'was more hospital than hospitable, I fear.'

The crowded life began to tell on all their nerves. Even Dorelia's air of cheerful detachment faltered. She felt unwell and, to Augustus's fury, refused to see a doctor. It seemed almost as if she cherished her symptoms, like a list of unspoken complaints. In retaliation he developed catarrh : but as an argument it was hardly satisfactory. Dorelia's unnatural lethargy drained all energy from him, as if she were an electric current and he a mere bulb, growing dimmer. 'The days are leaden as a rule,' he confided to Quinn (18 December 1909). '... I don't seem to be cut out for family life. I can't help being convinced that the wear and tear on my nervous system is diminishing my activity by about half. The crisis which takes place at least weekly leaves me less and less hopeful as regards this ménage. It is a great pity as I am very fond of the missus and she of me.'

Despite all they had come through together, Augustus now felt that they must part. He would take a studio and live in it; she could remain at Church Street. They must see each other, but not live together. 'I think it would be fairer on us both to avoid the day to day test,' he wrote, 'and I should work with less preoccupation. You would scarcely believe the violence of the emotional storms I go through so often – and worst of all those gloomy periods that precede them.'[68]

Doubts redoubled, threatened to come between them, yet, with a curious adhesiveness, somehow kept them together. The discord was often loud but always it was resolved with tenderness, forgiveness to the point of forgetfulness. For it was not as though they were against each other : it was a common enemy they fought seeking to divide them.

'It was a horrible pity we got into that state,' he wrote to her after one row.

... I don't know what precisely brought it on. It was a kind of feeling you were tugging in the wrong direction or exhibiting a quite false aspect of your nature – not the real one which never fails to bowl me over, but like the moon suffers an occasional eclipse.

By living together too casually our manners deteriorate by degrees, 'inspiration' ceases to the natural accompaniment of irritation and dissatisfaction till at last the awful storms are necessary to restore us to dignity and harmony and equilibrium. You know very well that 'expression' in you or state of mind I shall always love as the most beautiful thing in the world and hate to see supplanted by something less divine and you know how mercurial I am, veering from Heaven to Hell and torn to pieces by emotion or nerves or thoughts – is it any wonder we can't always be happy? I acknowledge my grievous shortcomings as I acknowledge your superior vision to which I owe so much (that's what I meant by 'being useful'!). I never liked any 'tart' as a 'tart' but for some suggestion of beauty – and even some faint delusive charm is a concrete fact to a poor artist (!). I can't help thinking we *can* go on better than we have been by using our wits.

The explanation for Dorelia's 'false aspect' tugging 'in the wrong direction' was another pregnancy. Augustus needed all her devotion, faith, energy; he needed her as mother as well as mistress. But during pregnancy it was not biologically possible for her to provide all this. By the end of the year they had come, somewhat hesitantly, to the conclusion that during the second month of another pregnancy that December, she must have had a miscarriage.

'I have an ineradicable cold and am as discontented as a bear in a pit,' Augustus had complained to Ottoline (28 December 1909). But the New Year promised new hope. Quinn, who attributed their matrimonial difficulties to bad dentistry, had sent a Christmas cake to Dorelia and, to Augustus, his first cheque – a magic remedy. 'I feel by no means dreary now,' he replied (4 January 1910). '... Frank Harris has written me from near Naples[69] asking me to come out for a spell – I think I may manage a few weeks off profitably.'

By the second week of January they had drawn up a plan.

They would part – but only for a month or so. Augustus would
plunge south to escape the winter darkness and, putting Quinn's
money to good uses, explore the French and Italian galleries.
Edie, it was arranged, would mind the children, and Dorelia
would have an eye kept on her by her friend Helen Maitland.
Then, once she felt better, Dorelia would leave with Helen and
some children to join Augustus – while Edie, as a substitute for
her sister, went to stay with Lamb. Celebrating with a long
French holiday, they would all then enter a happier phase in
their lives.

The nine months Augustus spent abroad were to be of the
greatest significance. He set out by train in the middle of
January to discover the classic land of Provence of which he
had long dreamed. In bright sunlight he descended at Avignon
and 'as if in answer to the insistent call of far-off Roman
trumpets ... I found myself, still dreaming, under the ramparts
of the city by the swift flowing Rhône'.[70] To Dorelia he sent his
first vivid impressions of the place (10 January 1910): 'This is a
wonderful country and a wonderful town Avignon. I'm beginning to feel better ... The people are certainly a handsome lot
on the whole. I see beautiful ones now and then ... We could
camp under the city walls here.'
    Everything conspired to delight him. Across the Rhône the
white town of Villeneuve-les-Avignon shone like an illumination from some missal; and in the distance, as if snow-covered,
Le Ventoux unexpectedly raised its creamy head. Near by, like
a noble phalanstery rising straight and 'functional', stood the
Popes' Palace where Augustus would go to admire the fragmentary frescoes of Simone Martini. But it was not the works of
art that excited him most: it was the country and the people.
The sun would not be denied. 'I get tired of museums,' he wrote
to Dorelia (17 January 1910). 'The sun of Provence is curing me
of all my humours.' Of wonderful naïvety and charm were the
'gypsy children playing – Gitanos, I never saw such kids – one
of them especially broke my heart he was so incredibly charming, so ceaselessly active and boiling over with high spirits. He
was about Robin's age, but a consummate artist. I went down
first thing this morning to see them again but I fancy they have

disappeared in the night for one of their hooded carts had gone. It's so like them to vanish just as you think you've got at them.'

He did no work and his travels took in more encampments than art galleries. 'Nothing so fills me with the love of life as the medieval – *antique* – life of camps,' he had once (2 October 1909) told Scott Macfie, 'it seems to shame the specious permanence of cities, and tents will outlast pyramids.' Already he was feeling miraculously restored. 'I was in the last extremities of depression before getting here,' he wrote to Arthur Symons (January 1910), 'and now I begin to feel dangerously robust. The country is full of beautiful women.' From Avignon he advanced to Nîmes and then hurried on to Arles, once celebrated for the special beauty of its girls, where he was detained longer. 'The restaurant cafe where I am stopping here would not be a bad place for us to put up,' he told Dorelia. He was missing her. 'I can't sleep alone,' he complained, 'and when I do I dream of Irish tinkers and Lord Mayors.' Surely she would have to rescue him soon? 'What do you think about coming down here with P[yramus] and R[omilly]? I would love it. We would be quite warm in bed here.'

He made Arles his headquarters for the rest of this month. 'Arles is beautiful – Provence a lovely land,' he wrote to Ottoline Morrell (18 January 1910). '... What a foetid plague spot London seems from this point of vantage. It takes only this divine sunlight to disperse the clouds and humours that settle round in England. I never want to stop there again for all the winter.' But wherever he went in Provence he was tempted to stop – and would write to Dorelia telling her so. At Paradou he noticed 'an excellent bit of land to stop on, but we must have light wooded carts and tents – no heavy wagons please.' There were many such places in France. 'There's plenty of sand one could camp on all over the Camargue which is as flat as a pancake and mostly barren,' he reported to Dorelia (27 January 1910). 'I've been talking to a young man, a cocker, about getting a cart to move about in.' Meanwhile he walked huge distances – 'I have bought the largest pair of boots in the world' – and sometimes, in bourgeois fashion, travelled by train.

One village that enchanted him was Les Baux – 'an extraordinary place', he wrote, 'built among billows of rocks rather like Palestine as far as I remember. The people of Les Baux are pleasant simple folk – a little inclined to apologise for their ridiculous situation. We could have a fine apartment there cheap. There are plenty of precipices for the boys to fall over.' It was at Les Baux that he met Alphonse Broule, 'a superb fellow' who claimed to be a friend of the great Provençal poet Mistral whose statue, overcoat on arm, reared itself at Arles – 'a man singularly like Buffalo Bill'. This man – 'a poet', Augustus first hazarded: 'an absolute madman', he later concluded – offered to introduce him to the master, and a few days later they met near Maillane.

'The country I saw on the way made me wild,' he wrote to Dorelia,

– so beautiful – a chain of rocky hills quite barren except for olives here and there ... finally we came to Mistral's house; by this time my host was getting very nervous. But we found the master on the road, returning home with his wife ... and he was so feeble as to receive us into his house. Mrs Mistral was careful to see that we wiped our feet well first. My companion talked a lot and wept before the master, a large snot hanging from his nose. Mistral listened to him with some patience. On leaving I asked him if he would care to sit two seconds for me to draw him when I passed that way again. He refused absolutely and recommended me to go and view his portrait at Marseilles. I ... was enchanted with his answer which showed an intellect I was far from being prepared to meet.

Mistral later regretted having forbidden Augustus to do his portrait, he told Marie Mauron,[71] but their meeting had horrified him. First there was this man Broule with his voice-and-tears like some ceaseless breaking of waves in the depths of a hollow cavern; and then there was his companion, an extraordinarily flamboyant and forbidding fellow from whom Mistral shrank in alarm. Let a man like this begin to draw you, he had reflected, and you would find him living with you for the rest of your life.

'I don't see how Italy could be much better than this,' Augustus wrote from Arles. Nevertheless, with regret, he decided to 'go off to Marseilles to-day, and so to Italy and get through some of the galleries studiously'. The first stage of this journey was to yield a marvellous discovery. Leaving Arles for Marseilles, the railway skirts the northern shores of the vast blue Etang de Berre, bordered by far-off amethyst cliffs. As he travelled along this inland sea, through the pine and olive trees, the speckled aromatic hills, he saw from the window, in the distance, the spires of a town appear, built as it seemed upon the incredible waters. The sensation which this sight, now gliding slowly away, produced on him was like that of a vision. He made up his mind after Italy to return, and find out what this mysterious city might be.

At Marseilles another surprise: the town was teeming with gypsies. From the *terrasse* of the Bar Augas he watched groups of Almerian Gitanos lounging at the foot of the Porte d'Aix, staves in their hands, their jet-black hair brushed rigidly forward over the ears and there abruptly cut, like nuns from some unknown and brilliant order. His attention was particularly caught by one remarkable figure – a tall bulky man of middle age wearing voluminous high boots, baggy trousers decorated at the sides with insertions of green and red, a short braided coat garnished with huge silver pendants and chains, and a hat of less magnificence but of greater antiquity upon his shaggy head, puffing at a great German pipe. Recognizing him as a Russian gypsy, Augustus accosted him in Romany. He had just received from Quinn another fifty pounds and with some of this he proposed celebrating their meeting, in return for which he was invited back to their camp. They arrived, with a certain *éclat*, in a cab, ate supper round an enormous bonfire and ended the evening amid songs and dances in the Russian style. Augustus, who had come for dinner, stayed a week at this camp. 'I cannot tell you how they affect me,' he wrote to Ottoline Morrell (February 1910). '. . . I have an idea of dying myself chocolate pour mieux poser à Gitano.'

Last night Milosch and Terka, my hosts, showed me all their wealth – unnumbered gold coins each worth at least 100 francs, jewels, corals, pearls. This morning came 3 young men, while we were still lying a-bed on the floor, bearing news of the death of a Romany. Terka wept and lamented wildly, beating her face and knotting her diklo round her neck and calling upon God. At the station we found 20 or 30 Romanichels seated on the floor drinking

tea from samovars. Beautiful people – amongst them a fantastic
figure – the husband of the deceased – an old bearded man, refusing
to be comforted.[72]

Augustus did not draw much, feeling he gained more simply
from watching. 'I tried to draw some of them,' he told Dorelia,
'but they never look the same when they're posing. All the
same it's worthwhile trying.' What he hoped to do was to make
very rapid sketches from which to work later. 'When people
notice they are being drawn,' he explained to Ottoline, 'they
immediately change expression and look less intelligent.'

He was learning more Romany every hour, and sending
copious word-lists and notes on songs in the direction of Liverpool. What he jotted down in a few hours was enough to keep
the best gypsy brains there at work for months. Scott Macfie
was particularly gratified by the demoralizing effect of Augustus's researches. 'This new dialect seems pretty stiff stuff to
work out,' he wrote gleefully, 'and it is a pleasure to see signs
of exasperation in Winstedt's remarks. He complains that in
consequence of the strain his morals, his habits and his manners
have become disgusting.'

Augustus was happy – but Italy seemed as far off as ever.
'I'm not particularly impatient to do Italy,' he wrote to Dorelia.
'Already I've seen a good many sights, but no pictures it is true,
except the Avignon ones.' It is possible he would never have
crossed the border but for the fact that the gypsies had elected
to go there themselves.

'I may get off to-night to Genoa,' he eventually informed
Dorelia, 'as the Gypsies are going to Milan I shall see them again.
They also mean to come to London.* They could give a good
show in a theatre. Terka, the woman in whose room I am
staying, has a baby 10 months old who I think may die to-night.
We went to a doctor to-day who seemed anxious to get rid of
us. The little creature bucked up a bit to-night but was very
cold. I'm going back now with a little brandy, all I can think
of . . . I might take a room in Milan for a few weeks and try and
paint some of these folk.'

* They turned up in the summer of 1911 at Liverpool and were infiltrated by
several members of the Gypsy Lore Society in costume.

He travelled by night to Genoa, his head still full of gypsies, his bearded and bedraggled appearance itself very gypsylike. 'Why was I not warned against coming here,' he immediately complained to Dorelia. '... Wonderful things happened at Marseilles the last two days. I haven't had my clothes off for a week ... I'm sick of Italy.' But it was really Genoa he disliked. Though it had *sounded* warm, it was a cold place – 'a place to avoid'.[73] The streets crawled with people, like lice, and 'the pubs are horrid little places mostly art-nouveau'. Of course the country was better, and the Italian lower classes had wonderful faces – the faces of peasants, virile, martial, keen as birds. But the bourgeois, as elsewhere, were not fit to be mentioned: and they swarmed everywhere. 'I took a second class ticket – hoping to get along quicker,' he told Ottoline (11 February 1910), 'but I couldn't put up with the second-class people (not to speak of the first). I had to take refuge in the third class – and was happy then. The 3rd class carriages have a hard simplicity about them which was infinitely comfortable.' He aimed to 'get through' Italy as fast as he could – a week, he calculated, should do the job.

Since he intended rejoining the gypsies at Milan, he continued to cultivate a gypsy appearance – 'as to my handkerchiefs I have two with me, simply foul; socks I have given up; you could grow mushrooms in my vest'.[74] All this contributed to his Italian difficulties. His whirlwind flight, pursued everywhere by Quinn's venereal imprecations, lasted (owing to the slowness of Italian trains) a full fortnight, but had an effect out of all proportion to this time. Though he hated the big towns which, after the roughness of Marseilles, struck him as 'overcultivated', he loved the country. There were hillocks of brown earth on the way to Siena – 'things one might invent', he described them to Ottoline, 'without ever expecting to see'. The Tuscan landscape seemed not to have changed since the fourteenth century. 'You know those earthen mounds, gutted with the rains,' he wrote to Arthur Symons, '– and those mountains, like women in bed, under the quilts? What a lusty land it is!' From Siena, where he was greatly attracted by the work of Pietro Lorenzetti, he came to Orvieto – 'do you know it?' he asked Symons. 'Splendid! The frescoes there break your heart – so beautiful, so magnificent.' He sped on – to Perugia,* and then to Florence which, he told Ottoline (11 February 1910) was 'magnificent and uncomfortable for a vagrant like myself – and too much to see – too many masterpieces to digest at one meal'. All the same, simply because of the rush, he was seeing things with an extraordinary intensity that would keep these first impressions vividly before him.

He had decided to postpone Rome, turning north and travelling through thick gloomy mountains with half-melted snow on them, a grey mist hiding the sky, to Ravenna. 'The mosaics here are superb,' he wrote to Dorelia. 'Westminster Cathedral ought to be done in the same manner.' He had intended only to change trains at Ravenna, but it was difficult to relinquish the Court of Justinian and Theodora, and he stayed there several days. The Tomb of Theodoric evoked pre-natal memories of Gothic heroes – a semi-barbaric splendour compared with which the modern world seemed pale. Padua, his next halting place, and the paintings of Giotto also slowed down his progress. He had seen so much he was growing confused. 'Was it here I saw Piero della Francesca's majestic Christ rising from the tomb?' he wondered.[75] 'I think not.'

But what did it matter, the provenance? Italy, he was discovering, represented for him the great authentic tradition to which, undismayed by its splendour, he meant to dedicate himself. It was in Provence that he was to find another home – 'I love that patch of ground,' he told Symons – and it was to the Provençal landscape, and the landscape of North Wales that he would look for his finest pictures. In such an atmosphere, less charged with the accumulated glory of the past and where there were no masterpieces to overawe him, Augustus would set to work: but enriched by what he had seen during these two brilliant weeks in Italy. For to Giotto of Padua, to Duccio, Masaccio and Raphael, to Piero della Francesca wherever exactly his resurrected Christ might be, and to Botticelli whose *Primavera*, lovely beyond compare, was the brightest jewel of Florence, he would ultimately trace his own cultural beginnings.

* 'I went to Perugia this morning – no shape of a place. I did the whole shoot in an hour; nothing but some Perugino frescos, and Perugino as you know was rather a soft growth.' Augustus to Dorelia (February 1910).

And so to Milan. A vast assembly of gypsies – twenty tents of pleasure – occupied a field outside the city. Work was in progress when Augustus approached, and the air rang with the din of hammering and the cries of these wild tribes. To his astonishment he found not only his Marseilles friends but also the coppersmiths he had met two years previously in Cherbourg – and there was a grand reunion. That evening a party filled the principal tent. Black-bearded, wild-eyed, fierce and friendly, the men were dressed in the costumes of stage brigands. They carried long silver-bedecked staves, and their white-braided tunics were decorated with silver buttons as large as hens' eggs. The women were mostly in scarlet, and each had threaded twenty or more huge gold coins in her hair and on her blouse – a total, in sterling, of at least a hundred pounds. As the great celebration proceeded, these young girls were called upon to dance to music of accordions, while the men lifted up their voices in melancholy song. The dancers, without shifting their position on the carpet, agitated their limbs, hips and breasts in a kind of shivering ecstasy. Cross-legged at a low table, Todor, the elderly chief next to whom Augustus sat, beat time until the bottles leapt, sometimes in a sudden frenzy shattering his great German pipe – immediately to be handed another. Solid silver samovars littered the floor, and on the tables stood elaborately chased silver flagons a foot high and filled with wine and rum. A troop of old men were seated round them in a state of Bacchic inspiration, while outside the tent a crowd of *gâjos* looked on as if in some hypnotic trance. 'The absolute isolation of the Gypsies seemed to me the rarest and most unattainable thing in the world,' Augustus wrote to Scott Macfie (14 February 1910). 'The surge of music, which rose and fell as *naturally* as the wind makes music in the trees or the waves upon the shore affected one strangely. It was *religious* – orgiastic. I murmured to my neighbour "Kerela té kamav te rovav" ["It makes one want to cry"].'

Late that night, while the festivities were in full swing, he tore himself away and, returning the next morning to annotate some songs, found the party still going strong – together with the rattle of twenty hammers beating out copper vessels, and the yelling of youths with shining eyes swaying together in a multi-

embrace. 'If ever my own life becomes insupportable I know where to turn for another,' he wrote to Quinn (3 March 1910), 'and I shall be welcomed in the tents.'

Back to Marseilles. 'In some respect it beats Liverpool even,' he wrote to Chaloner Dowdall. The roughness of the place reflected the other side of his romanticism, and he began to relish it. 'You ought to let me take you round Marseilles one day,' he offered the Rani. 'There are things there to raise the hairs on Rothenstein's back.' Now he knew the night spots 'I feel ready to live here,' he told Dorelia. 'One sees *beautiful* Gitano girls about with orange, green and purple clothes ... Hundreds of people to paint ... One of the women, without being very dark, is as splendid as antiquity and her character is that of the Mother of God.'

But his letters to Dorelia were filled with anxiety. However urgently he wrote, she did not answer him. When, for example, he asked for a bundle of postal orders and blank cheques to be sent, a registered envelope arrived at the *poste restante* which, since he still travelled without a passport, could not be released to him. After summoning two stalwart gypsies to swear in strange tongues as to his identity, he was eventually allowed to open the envelope which was found to contain a dentist's bill. Soon he began to besiege her with telegrams. 'As you don't answer my three telegrams I conclude you have had enough of me.' What trickle of news had arrived worried him. 'You had better see a doctor about your poor tummy,' he had written near the start of his journey, '– and so leave nothing undone that might be good for you. Tell him you thought you had a fausse couche the other day. *Now do!*' The only information he had received since then was a note telling him she was suffering from mysterious pains in her side. 'Your belly is very enigmatic,' he replied. 'You'd better come this way at the next period and make sure. You'd don't want to have any more babies just yet. I don't suppose you'ld better Pyramus and Romilly. Don't forget to write ... Au revoir, my love, I wish you were here.'

Finally she wrote. 'I was overjoyed to hear from you,' he answered 'I was steeling myself for another disappointment.' The news itself was bad – and good. She *was* pregnant again : it had been a 'false miscarriage'. She would join him in Provence, together with Helen Maitland and a detachment of family. 'This is splendid news!' Augustus wrote back cheerfully. 'I hope it'll be another boy! Glad your belly has settled down to proper working order. I wonder what part of the babe will be missing. Its kâri perhaps, in which case it may turn out to be a girl after all.'

Dorelia herself seemed neither happy nor unhappy. Pregnancy was no mighty matter. 'The terrible thing is I am going to have another infant in August (I don't really mind),' she wrote to Ottoline (February 1910). '. . . It is sure to be another boy.'

In view of what was to happen, and of the criticism voiced by Henry Lamb and others to the effect that Augustus endangered Dorelia's life, as he had done Ida's, it is important to establish facts. An unusually intimate letter ('to no one else could I write so intimately') which Augustus sent Quinn (3 March 1910) gives a view of what happened that, because he seldom spoke of such things, was not appreciated by many who were close. It also reveals a concern over this new pregnancy that he was careful to keep veiled from Dorelia.

'The infernal fact is that she [Dorelia] is in for another baby sometime this summer. God knows I've got plenty of kids as it is, and worst of all Dorelia is not in robust health. Her inside bothers her. I tried my best to avoid this – but she hates interfering with nature. All I hope is that she will at least get strong here. She insisted on bringing 3 of the youngest kids here; 3 remain in London and go to school.'

But he was delighted she was coming. In his fashion he had been faithful to her. 'I went through Italy without sampling a single Italian female,' he gravely reassured Quinn. 'I saw, however, many with whom I slept (with my eyes open) in fancy.' He was to rejoin Dorelia at Arles. Travelling up there slowly from Marseilles, he wrote to Ottoline:

These really barren hills round here *enchant me* ... I visited this evening two bordels here ... the ladies were not very beautiful, strictly speaking – but I found them very aimable ... There was a mechanical piano which my acquaintance played with the utmost dexterity. I was thoroughly interested and lost more money than if I had been a 'client sérieux'.

At Avignon also I introduced myself into a bordel – 'une maison très sérieuse'. The ladies of those establishments are absolute slaves. The patron took all the money and the travailleuses are not allowed to quit the house without permission. However they don't complain – si le patron est gentil et pour une qu'il y aurait beaucoup de clients. They are excessively simple.

Two days later, 'looking incredible with some white veil over her head',[76] Dorelia arrived.

She came with Pyramus, Romilly and Edwin; and with Helen Maitland. Helen was now her closest friend and much influenced by her. She was a striking girl, with clear grey-blue eyes, a rosy complexion and finely formed features. Rather small, she held herself very upright and moved with a slow, trailing, purposeful stride that conveyed great dignity. The set of her face expressed a somewhat daunting determination; her tone of voice, flavoured with irony, was sometimes harsh : and she had a hard energy within. But it was her smile, radiant and welcoming, that was remarkable, softening her expression, sending out a challenge, a flattering air of complicity. And it was this smile, which she offered like a bouquet of flowers, that made people pour out their troubles to her. For herself, she hated sympathy and seldom spoke of her own difficulties. Like Dorelia, she was the most stimulating listener, the cause of good conversation in others.

Like Dorelia, too, she saw her life as a vocation to be fulfilled among painters. She was a woman who preferred, in a maternal fashion, to give love than to have the responsibility of receiving it. She was to marry, eight years later, the brilliant and burly Russian artist in mosaic, Boris Anrep – reputed to be the only man in London capable of standing up to Augustus in a fist fight; and in 1926 she was to leave him to live with Roger Fry,* many

---

* Like Augustus, Boris Anrep had landed himself with two wives in the same house – number two being useful for selecting books from the public library for Helen on the infallible principle of their not being the sort she would choose for herself. But he disappointed Helen 'by his literary philistinism and preference for legshows to those concerned more with the head', Romilly John remembers (29 July 1972). '. . . It was rumoured that she came from California which might account for her devotion to Culture and her eventual rejection of Boris and Hampstead in favour of Roger Fry and Bloomsbury.'

of whose ideas on modern art she 'invited' out of his head. But now, again following Dorelia, she was deeply in love with the satanic Henry Lamb.

Between her and Augustus, Lamb was the barrier.* It was galling to Augustus that, even though Helen's love might not primarily be a thing of the senses, she should prefer his understudy to himself. Besides, she was very loyal to Dorelia and, anxious that she should not be treated badly, over-ready to be critical of him. His sense of the ridiculous often reduced her to tears of laughter – but then she could not altogether take him seriously, being so serious herself. It was certainly galling for him. For though she laughed, she was not happy. Her love-affair was going badly and she blamed this on Lamb's philosophy which, she believed, he had picked up from Augustus. A strong feminist, she disapproved of an attitude that appeared to treat women simply as raw material for art. It was, she felt, merely another outpost of masculine self-assertion, and it provoked her own most aggressive streak. Men she treated as children, and children as nonentities. And she preferred men who were weak or in difficulties to those who seemed self-reliant. They sustained her belief that women, being the more practical sex, should run most things. It was a belief shortly to be tested.

They assembled, the six of them, at Arles and caught the same train south Augustus had taken the previous month along the Etang de Berre. Like a jewel in a chain changing colour and extending between the barren hills, the great lake seemed to mesmerize them all. 'I have seen this Etang de Berre looking wonderful,' Helen wrote to Lamb, 'it has these pale brown hills all around and it's small enough to get perfectly smooth the moment the wind is down and then the colours are lovely – very brilliant green one evening with a blue sky. All the way from Arles I was ecstatic with delight . . . simply speechless with astonishment at the curious light blue of one Etang we passed.

* In the first draft of his autobiography, Augustus referred to Helen as 'censorious', adding: 'I have always disappointed her, being somewhat earth-bound and unable to rise to the lofty stratosphere, where, without oxygen, she seems most at home . . . For, feeling myself accursed, her strictures left me subdued but with an inkling at least of higher things beyond my grasp.' Dorelia, however, considered these observations to be sarcastic and they were dropped from *Chiaroscuro*.

It was so bright that it made the sky look dull and dark. They had planted cypresses all along the line so we only saw it for a moment or two now and again through a break in them. But I doubt if any mortal could have stood such loveliness much prolonged. On the other side was a vast stony plain, quite limitless and bare except for sage bushes and sheep.'

They were en route for the town whose spires Augustus had briefly seen rising from the waters on his first journey into Marseilles. At Pas des Lanciers they descended, ate their food squatting in a circle on the platform, then changed to the little railway line that leads to Martigues. Their train skirted the Etang, passing close under hills of extraordinary shape, some very thin with jagged edges stacked one behind another and all bare except for aromatic grey herbs in patches – thyme, lavender and sage. At every orchard, at almost every cowshed, the train would stop. But at last they came to Martigues. There was no need to seek further.

'An enchanting spot this, situated in the water at the mouth of an island sea where it joins the Mediterranean,' Augustus wrote to Ottoline. '. . . The population are handsomer than the country folk. I have seen so many powerful women whose essential nudity no clothing can disguise. In the little port at hand are found sea-farers from all the shores of the Mediterranean.'

For several days they stayed at a hotel, then moved into 'an admirable logement unfurnished and unwallpapered, with a large room in which to paint'. This was the Villa St Anne, a house they were to keep, using it intermittently, for the next eighteen years. On the outskirts of Martigues, along the route to Marseilles, it stood upon a steep yellow bank overlooking the blue waters of the lagoon. From the terrace stretched a plantation of pine trees, and all around were trackless stones, and rocky grey hills interfused with heather and a million sweet-smelling herbs. To Dorelia's delight, they had a large wild garden with olives, vines, almonds, figs and 'weeds all over the ground which is covered in pale coloured stones'.[77]

For the time being they shared the villa with its proprietor, a hawk-faced Huguenot named Albert Bazin. He was a prime ex-

ample of that breed of eccentrics who clustered round Augustus
for most of his life, and he possessed one frustrated passion :
for flying. Over twenty years of ruthless experiments he had
constructed, to some secret ornithological recipe, a squadron of
aeroplanes, all of which *flapped their wings*. From time to time,
while Mme Bazin delivered a narrative of proceedings from the
shore, he would launch his latest model, like some enormous
gnat, across the waters where at a desperate rate it would rise
fractionally from the waves, sweep through a wide arc, then
plunge into the bosom of the lake. Although these machines
were reduced to salads, Bazin himself was always miraculously
unhurt. In such pursuits he had grown old, ill, bankrupt but
undismayed; for with the arrival of Augustus his aviation
fantasies soared to their highest altitude. He at once recognized
in him the perfect 'jockey' for his machines, and a vicarious
source of revenue with which to continue his inventive industry.
Augustus was delighted with this philosopher of the air and
promised to sound out various art patrons on his behalf. Bazin
needed, initially, a mere two hundred pounds to take off and 'it
must be found', Augustus told Ottoline (May 1910), since he was
the 'finest man and aviator in France'. But it was Quinn who,
through many months, bore the brunt of Augustus's enthusiasm.
In letter after letter he was buried under information about this
'real savant as regards flying matters', flooded with journals that
contained articles by Bazin proving that he 'has got ahead
theoretically at least of the other men', such as Blériot. Augustus's appeals took many forms. Would Quinn like 'to collaborate with him and his machine No. 8 which ought to be ready in
the autumn, if he finds the cash?' Could some 'American
energy' be harnessed for 'my bird-like neighbour'? Perhaps
someone from 'the Land of Enterprise' might investigate his
'case'. 'I wrote to you lately as longwindedly as I could about
Albert Bazin,' Augustus reminded him (23 May 1910). '... Do
not be bored with Bazin yourself but bore your friends as much
as you can.' Quinn alternated between physical alarm on Augustus's behalf – 'don't you attempt to go out on Bazin's machine'
– and financial alarm on his own : 'Personally I can't afford to
"take a flyer" now myself.' Although any appeal to bore his
friends was irresistible, he disliked such methods when applied

to himself. 'Say at once if you are not interested in the matter,' Augustus would beg him like someone stone deaf, and I will cease to bore you.' 'I am afraid it is hopeless!' cried Quinn. But Augustus, approaching the problem from a different angle, urged: 'He[Bazin]'s got a fine young daughter of 18 summers. The fact might as well be mentioned – in view of the collaboration.' 'I'd rather collaborate with his daughter than I would with the old man,' Quinn conceded – adding however that 'Marseilles seems to be far off'. But though the geography might be poor, the biology was strong enough, he insisted: 'I may tell you that not eating much meat and not drinking lessens the strain on the testicles ... I have doubled my efficiency since I quit eating so much and since I stopped drinking. If only I could cut out smoking entirely, I would treble my efficiency.'

The pattern of life at the Villa St Anne, though confused a little by good intentions, was straightforward. 'I am installed in this little house with a batch of family and hard at work,' Augustus promised Quinn (2 April 1910). 'The weather has been glorious and we have been out of doors all day for weeks.' They had bought a boat and spent many days dreamily rowing across the glasslike surface of the lake. 'From time to time, as with dread I looked down into the bottomless void beneath us,' Romilly John recalled, 'an enormous jellyfish of a yellowish grey colour sailed by, trailing in gentle curves long streamers decorated with overlapping purple fringe: it seemed to emphasize the spatial quality of the blue depths.'[78]

From a Catalonian gypsy Augustus also bought a donkey and cart, and while Dorelia took the children off to the sea, he would go on long sketching expeditions. 'One sees much more by these means,' he told Quinn (2 April 1910), 'and one doesn't go to sleep.' At night, while Dorelia cooked and the children eventually tumbled into bed, Augustus would read: gypsy literature from Liverpool, Provençal masters such as Daudet and Mistral, poems from Symons and Wyndham Lewis, the works of Léon Bloy, and old copies of the *New Age*.

Gypsies would often pass the door, be invited in for a drink and a talk, and stay several days. Somehow there was always enough food for them, and Dorelia enjoyed their company too. 'We had the house full of gypsies for about a week,' she wrote to

Ottoline (May 1910). '... It was great fun. They would dance and sing at any hour of the day.'

At intervals, when the supply of gypsies grew scarce, Augustus would take himself off to Marseilles and seek sanctuary with 'some Gitano pals' who were teaching him to play the guitar. From here he could keep watch on a waste piece of ground outside the town over which passed a strange procession: bear-leaders from the Balkans; wagon-loads of women; Russians 'fresh from Russia'; a pantalooned tribe of Turkish wanderers from Stamboul, 'in little brown tents of ragged sacking far from impervious to the rain', waiting for a boat to Tangier; a whole lot of Mumpers from Alsace – 'a low unprofitable company'; Irish tinkers, Dutch nomads, French Romanichels, gypsies from southern Spain, Bosnians, Belgians, Bohemians, Bessarabians – 'the travelling population of France is enormous'.[79] If only he could import some into Surrey, and let them breed!

His word-lists grew longer and his calligraphy more fevered. Of everyone he inquired about Sainte Sara and the gypsy pilgrimage to Saintes Maries de la Mer. 'This pilgrimage may be the last of the old pilgrim mysteries of the gypsies,' he assured Scott Macfie (14 May 1910). He ransacked the library at Aix; he reverently inspected the bones of the Egyptian saint at Saintes Maries. But beyond various stories of miraculous cures he could discover little. It did not matter. For though Sainte Sara was a problem to be solved by the Gypsy Lore Society, to Augustus she remained a symbol, and the annual fête at Saintes Maries a renewed act of faith. As such, it presented itself to him as a picture by Puvis de Chavannes, and was to dominate, tragically, the last years of his life.

Not all his pursuits were so scholarly. His letters to Scott Macfie intersperse gypsy investigations with exploits of another kind among the 'inveterate whores of Marseilles'[80] whom he now thought of introducing into his decorations for Hugh Lane. They were everywhere, like an army of occupation. To run the gauntlet of what he called 'this fine assortment of Mediterranean whores',[81] he resorted, Wyndham Lewis-style, to the protection of a voluminous cloak – 'a cloak albeit of stout fabric' – like a bandit. 'Why does the employment of a prostitute cause one's

last neglected but unbroken *religious* chord to vibrate with such
terrifying sonority?' he suddenly demanded (16 March 1910).
From Liverpool came little response to these Dostoievsky rumb-
lings, and Augustus was obliged to answer himself.

'As to whores and whoredom, considered from the purely
practical point of view (never really pure) as a utility it is an
abomination which stinks like anybody else's shit,' he volunteered (30 March 1910); 'considered morally it is a foul blasphemy which must make Christ continually sweat blood: but
without either point of view, there is an aspect of beauty to be
discovered – which indeed jumps at one's eye sometimes –
whores, especially at 20 sous la pusse, have often something
enigmatic, sacerdotal about them. It is as if one entered some
temple of some strange God, and the "intimacy" really doesn't
exist except to reveal the untraversable gulfs which can isolate
two souls.'

To 'know' someone in the Biblical sense, and to know them
otherwise not at all; to preserve the stranger-element in a
physical union; this symbolized, without speech, the loneliness
of human beings exiled on earth. Everyone *knew*, no one said
anything, and nothing was expected. The relationship was a
single act with no long descent into tedium, no race for disenchantment, no ugly clash of wills. It was the implications of
the act rather than the act itself that lived in the imagination.
A number of times this spring and summer Augustus took off
for Marseilles, drank whisky, 'misbehaved', and returned to
Martigues much the better for it all. But it was, he wrote to
Scott Macfie (3 April 1910), 'a dangerous subject'.

Two expeditions this summer were of particular interest. One
was to Aix-en-Provence where Augustus and Dorelia travelled in
their donkey cart from dawn to dusk to see Ottoline. She found
them sitting outside a café, Dorelia very beautiful in a striped
cotton skirt, a yellow scarf covering her head; Augustus, his
square-cut beard now pointed in the French manner, 'which
made him look like a dissipated Frenchman, as his eyes were
bloodshot and yellow from brandy and rum'.[82] Together they
went to Cézanne's house on the outskirts of Aix, which still
contained a number of his pictures including the murals of the

four seasons mysteriously inscribed 'Ingres'; and the next day
they explored the town, looking at churches and the tomb of
Joseph Sec. Augustus, Ottoline observed,

... was a bored and weary sightseer. In the afternoon when we
returned we found him sitting outside a café drinking happily with
the little untidy waiter from the hotel and a drunken box-maker
from the street nearby. In his companions he requires only a reflecting glass for himself, and thus he generally chooses them from
such inferiors. He seems curiously unaware of the world, too
heavily laden and oppressed with boredom to break through and
to realize life.[83]

Augustus's other expedition, to Nice – 'a paradise invaded by
bugs (human ones)'[84] – involved what he called 'some mighty
queer days' with Frank Harris. He had first met Harris in
Wellington Square, Chelsea, with Max Beerbohm, Conder, Will
Rothenstein and others. With his booming voice, baleful eye
and hardy wit, Harris imposed himself upon the distinguished
company by sheer force of bad character – or so it appeared to
Augustus, whose attention was much taken up with the stately
figure of Constance Collier, the flamboyant actress somewhat
improbably engaged to Max Beerbohm. While Harris was holding the floor, Augustus suggested to this 'large and handsome
lady' that she sit for him, adding, perhaps somewhat tactlessly,
that he would have to find a bigger studio. 'Why not take the
Crystal Palace then?' boomed Harris, suddenly exploding into
their conversation : and everyone laughed. He was, Augustus
rather sourly observed, very much the *pièce de résistance* of the
party, a position Augustus preferred to occupy himself. Like
Augustus, Harris presented a bold front to the world. 'Stocky in
build, his broad chest was protected by a formidable waistcoat
heavily studded with brass knobs,' Augustus wrote. 'With his
basilisk eyes and his rich booming voice he dominated the room.
Hair of a suspicious blackness rose steeply from his moderate
brow, and a luxuriant though well-trained moustache of the
same coloration added a suggestion of Mephistopheles to the
ensemble.'[85]

Harris took an apparently very flattering interest in Augustus,
claiming in return that 'he praised my stories beyond measure'
– the sort of high-flown approval he regretted being just unable

to accord Augustus's paintings. This was a preliminary exercise
in a most subtle piece of psychological outmanoeuvring. In fact
Augustus had not greatly admired Harris's fiction, but praised
The Man Shakespeare as 'a wonderful book'. To this literary
judgement Harris responded with a burst of artistic criticism:
'The quality of his [John's] painting is poor – gloomy and harsh
– reflecting, I think, a certain disdainful bitterness of character
which does not go with the highest genius.' Then, describing
Augustus as 'a draughtsman of the first rank, to be compared
with Ingres, Dürer and Degas, one of the great masters', he
bought a drawing, persuaded Augustus fulsomely to inscribe it
to him, then sold it for a nice profit to a dealer where, to his
irritation, Augustus later stumbled across it.

   In an unfair world, where it was always necessary to turn the
tables on those who were over-gifted, Harris saw Augustus as a
potentially superior version of himself – a superb Celtish actor, a
lover of women and a lusty drinker, a creature of fantasy and
of talent, and a rebel artist who disdained the social successes
that Harris had once coveted. Lunching at the Café Royal at the
time *The Man Shakespeare* was published (autumn 1909), Harris
was greatly struck by Augustus's height, beauty and 'great
manner' which, he wrote, 'swept aside argument and infected
all his hearers. Everyone felt in the imperious manner, flaming
eyes and eloquent cadenced voice the outward and visible signs
of that demonic spiritual endowment we call genius.'[86]

   Harris was then considering himself in the role of prosperous
gallery owner, and it must have been partly owing to this new
career that he acted quite so hospitably to Augustus. His
blandishments, mixed in with pious references to Jesus Christ,
continued to arrive by post that winter, first from Ravello, then
from Nice. And it was here that Augustus succumbed to an
invitation to stay with him. Their encounter was to strike sparks
that illumine odd corners in both their characters.

   Augustus arrived at Nice station dressed in corduroys and
with his painting materials in a small handbag. On the platform
he was met by Harris decked out in full evening dress, apparently disconcerted by his guest's lack of *chic*, yet determined to carry him off to the Opera House where he had a box
lent to him by the Princess de Monaco. Here his wife Nellie

awaited them 'attired for the occasion in somewhat faded and second-hand splendour'. The composer of 'the infernal din' to which they were subjected soon joined them and, taking a dislike to Augustus on sight, restricted his compliments to Harris. Augustus, who particularly resented exclusion from such exchanges, noticed that they 'vied with each other in mutual admiration', and 'I gathered that I was assisting at a meeting between "the modern Wagner" and "the greatest intellect in Europe".'[87]

What then happened later that night and on subsequent nights back at Harris's home was very peculiar. 'I was shown my room which, as Frank was careful to point out, adjoined Nelly's, his own being at a certain distance, round the corner ... Before many hours passed in the Villa, I decided I was either mad or living in a mad-house. What I found most sinister was the behaviour of Nelly and the female secretary. These two, possessed as it seemed by a mixture of fright and merriment, clung together at my approach, while giggling hysterically as if some desperate mischief was afoot.' Ten years later Nellie Harris hinted to Hesketh Pearson that she had repulsed Augustus's advances during this visit.[88] Whatever the actual facts, there is no doubt that Augustus came to interpret his unsatisfactory three days there as a fortunate escape from some deeply laid Harris plot.

'On the night of the third day our understanding came to an end, or rather I should say perhaps reached perfection. By this time I came to loathe the sight of this monster, and he knew it. I, it seems, had failed him, and his resounding eloquence was wasted on Nellie, who responded but with nervous giggles to the grandiose prospect her husband painted of a "European Courtesan's career".'

What is so strange in testing for the truth of this episode is that Harris was extremely possessive over Nellie; while Augustus, though he often gets details wrong (such as Harris's house at Nice) and embroiders facts with malice, had no gift for invention. It seems he had come to suspect that, by taking advantage of Nellie's night time propinquity, he would lay himself open to Harris's 'requests' for money. Thank God he – or perhaps Nellie – had failed! That Harris was keen on raising funds is undeniable, yet Augustus's interpretation of what was

in his mind must almost certainly have been wrong. A man of
liberal instincts, initially, Harris was, in the view of J. D.
Fergusson, a new Robin Hood robbing the rich in order (in due
course) to reimburse the poor. His vendetta was carried on
against the socially successful for the ostensible benefit of the
writer and artist. That he himself was poor and a writer enabled him to begin and end many of these charitable exercises
at home. But he would never have used an artist for blackmail.
So although Augustus, swelling himself up with optimism, could
congratulate himself on having 'failed' Harris, it seems more
likely that he played up perfectly.

From Carlyle onwards, Harris sought to humiliate, usually in
some sexual context, those he admired. Such men pointed the
way to all that Harris prized – power and the love of women –
but at their own risk, for Harris's route was paved with their
exposed lives. He resented that his own fame should depend
upon that of other men, that it should be a corollary to theirs.
Shakespeare was beyond his reach, if only in time; but his books
on Shaw and Wilde, and his series of contemporary portraits,
ring loud with this rival-complaint. His novels and short stories
demonstrate two other qualities: a lack of literary talent and
Harris's hopes of self-greatness. In *Undream'd of Shores*, for
example, there is an account of Akbar, the great Mogul ruler,
curiously similar to Harris. At one point he tells the girl he loves
that there are many men handsomer and stronger than he. But
she denies this hotly, asserting that he is the most splendid man
in the Court, for 'though he was only a little taller than the
average' there was, she reminds him, his 'black eyes and hair
and his loud deep voice'. Harris sought to lose the view of himself as he really appeared behind this vision of himself (here put
into the girl's mouth) as he wished to appear. The smoke
screen he used was puffed up with the fumes of competitive reassurance. In his writings and his life he set up situations which
allowed him to score off those who were publicly acknowledged
to be handsome, talented and romantic. Augustus unwittingly
presented himself as a sitting target. How conscious Harris was
of what he did it is impossible to say, but his Contemporary
Portrait of Augustus reveals his attitude of attraction-and-
resentment unashamedly.

'It was Montaigne who said that height was the only beauty of man, and indeed height is the only thing that gives presence to a man. A miniature of Venus may be more attractive than her taller sisters, but a man must have height to be imposing in appearance, or indeed impressive.'

Harris then goes on to portray Augustus as the perfect example of the male species.

'Over six feet in height,* spare and square shouldered, a good walker who always keeps himself fit and carries himself with an air, John would draw the eye in any ground. He is splendidly handsome with excellent features, great violet eyes and long lashes . . . he is physically, perhaps, the handsomest specimen of the genus homo that I have ever met.'

Yet this was the man who, three nights in succession, had been rejected by Nellie; who had failed precisely where Harris was successful. Throughout his pen portrait, he constantly returns to emphasize Augustus's fine looks together with 'his wonderful power of drawing and his weird and defiant looseness of living'. Such accomplishments apparently form a crescendo of praise, yet at the end we are suddenly turned against him – or rather what his physique represents – by an acrobatic moral twist. His pitfall, Harris insists, 'is not drink'. Jesus drank. No : if he fails 'it will be because he has been too heavily handicapped by his extraordinary physical advantages. His fine presence and handsome face brought him notoriety very speedily, and that's not good for a man. Women and girls have made up to him and he has spent himself in living instead of doing his work.'

Augustus brought up the full force of his boredom to meet Harris's challenge. But by the third night he had had enough and, shouldering his belongings, stole out at dawn and made his way down the hill to Nice harbour where he laid up in a sailors' café. 'Ah! the exquisite relief! To be alone again and out of that infected atmosphere, that madhouse! To be among common fellows and free to go as I pleased.'† It was an instance

---

* Augustus was just under six feet, but walked tall.

† 'I WENT TO NEECE TO STAY WITH SOME PEOPLE BUT I FOUND THEY WERE SO HORRIBLE I RAN AWAY ONE MORNING, EARLY, BEFORE THEY WERE UP NEECE IS A LOVELY PLACE FULL OF HORRIBLE PEOPLE.' Augustus to David John (March 1910).

of that 'certain abruptness of manner' without which, Harris gleefully noted, 'he would be almost too good-looking'.

In his amusing and urbane descriptions of Harris thirty years later, Augustus attempts to get something of his own back by taking it out of him *visually*. Harris, he observes, 'was looking his ugliest' by the third day; while Nellie (then in her thirties and not unattractive) is converted into a middle-aged matron. But when, in 1929, Augustus first read Harris's Contemporary Portrait of him, his tone was far from urbane: it was outraged. In a letter to Elmer Gertz (25 May 1929) he explains that he had left Harris's villa 'because I found the moral atmosphere of the place unbearable . . . I could not consent to stay as the guest of a cad and bully posing as a man of genius.' Besides, he went on, his host's habit of dragging the name of Jesus Christ into any conversation or piece of writing was obnoxious to him 'coming from a man of Harris's moral standards'.[89] Here, unmistakably, is the pompous tone of Edwin John, his father. He refused to let Gertz use these letters in his biography[90] to refute Harris's inaccuracies, partly because they revealed the extent to which he had been discomfited and partly because, Harris still being alive, he wished at all costs to avoid public controversy. His dealings with Harris, especially his sudden fear of blackmail, mark the first hereditary pull towards that caution and inflated air of authority with which, in later years, he sought to protect himself from a hostile world. 'It seems hopeless for me ever to attempt to conceal even the secrets of the water-closet from the outside world,' he complained to Wyndham Lewis (July 1910). 'There will still be an industrious person with a rake stationed at the other end of the sewer. It is true that I don't put myself out for secrecy . . .' – but the cuticle of secrecy, which would eventually cover and distort his life, had already begun to grow.

The effects of his visit to Nice lingered with Augustus like a bad hangover. 'I expect he would be less gloomy with just his Family,' Helen Maitland confided to Lamb. Soon afterwards she left Martigues to join him, having assured herself and Lamb that Dorelia 'seems better. She doesn't get a pain in her side anymore.'

A few weeks later, in the early morning of Monday, 1 May,

Augustus John. Self-portrait, about 1901 (chalk)

Victoria Place, Haverfordwest, 1870s

South Sands, Tenby

Thomas Smith

The four John children with
their nurse. Left to right:
Gwen, Winifred, Thornton
and Augustus

Augusta John

Edwin John

Thornton John

Winifred John

St Catharine's School, Tenby, 1893. Augustus John top left

Ida Nettleship and her parents

Left to right: Ida
Nettleship, Ursula
Tyrwhitt and Gwen
John. Drawing by
Augustus John about
1899

Augustus, Ida
(holding David) and
Gwen

John Knewstub

William Orpen

Augustus John

Ida John

Dorelia

Ida

A Slade School picnic, April 1899. Seated on the horse from
left to right are William Orpen, Augustus John and Gwen John.
Seated with foot on shaft, Albert Rutherston. Standing without
hat in centre, Edna Waugh. Seated to right, Alice Rothenstein
and, behind, William Rothenstein

Jury of the New English Art Club at the Dudley Gallery, 1904.
Left to right (standing) Walter Russell, David Muirhead, Alfred
Rich, Ambrose McEvoy, Henry Tonks, Augustus John,
D. S. MacColl, P. Wilson Steer, Muirhead Bone and Francis Bate;
(seated) Fred Winter, Fred Brown, Roger Fry and William
Rothenstein

Ida

Dorelia

Family
encampment.
Standing left
to right:
Caspar, Dorelia,
Augustus,
Robin, David;
sitting: Edwin,
Romilly and
friend

John

The Dowdalls

His Honour the Lord Mayor of Liverpool, and Smith (1909)

Alick Schepeler

Euphemia Lamb ('Lobelia')

Augustus John. Self-portrait, July 1955

Dorelia at Alderney Manor.
John's portrait is
reproduced by
permission of the
National Museum of Wales

Ambrose McEvoy

Trelawney Dayrell Reed

Dorelia, Vivien and
Poppet John

Mrs Cake and Old
Cake

John as a
Canadian major

Chiquita
photographed in
1924

Henry Lamb   Henry 'Elffin' John

Left to right: Poppet John, Vivien John, Lady Pansy Lamb (*née* Pakenham)

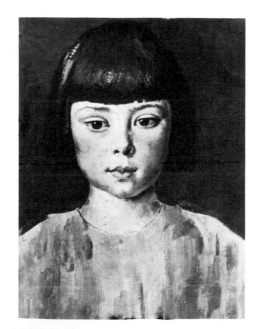

Two portraits of
Poppet by Augustus.
'The Girl in Red'
(below) is now
in the Art Gallery
of South Australia

Left to right, *sitting* : W. B. Yeats, Compton Mackenzie, Augustus John, Edwin Lutyens; *standing* : G. K. Chesterton, James Stephens, Lennox Robinson. This photograph was taken in summer 1924 at a garden party given by Oliver St John Gogarty at Ely Place, Dublin, on the occasion of a revival of the ancient Tailteann Games

Mortimer Wheeler and
Mavis de Vere Cole
(*née* Wright) on their
wedding day, with
Augustus as best man

With Sean O'Casey in
London

With James Joyce
in Paris

Movie queen in oils:
Tallulah Bankhead
and John (Keystone
Press photograph)

Cartoon by David Low (by
arrangement with the
London *Evening Standard*)

Augustus John

Max Beerbohm's rough
sketch for 'Annual
Meeting of Mr Stirling
Stuart-Crawford, Mr
Augustus John and
Lord Ribblesdale, to
protest against the
fashions for the
coming spring', 1909

Forty years on:
Augustus John in
1915 and
(photograph by
Cecil Beaton) in
1955

From left to right: Edwin and Romilly John, Mrs Beckles Willson,
Vivien John behind her, Augustus with Francis Macnamara
towering behind him, Trelawney Dayrell Reed, Constant Lambert,
Viva King, Robin and Poppet John; in front, Beckles Willson

With Matthew Smith

With Fiore
de Henriques
(photograph
by Felix
Fonteyn)

With Dorelia
in her garden
at Fryern
Court
(photograph
by Cecil
Beaton)

Augustus John (photographed shortly before his death by John
Hedgecoe)

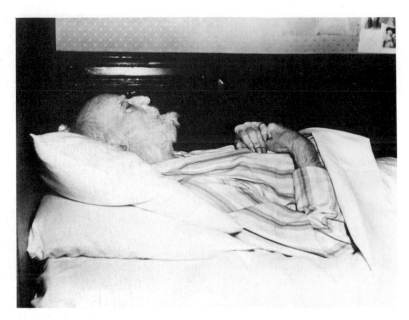

Augustus John: the last photograph

Dorelia gave birth prematurely to a dead child. Throughout
that day her life hung agonizingly in the balance. 'She *nearly*
died afterwards of loss of blood and was really saved by having
sea-water injected into her body,' Augustus wrote to Quinn (5
May 1910). '... The child, which was a girl, would have been
welcome 3 months hence. It had got displaced somehow.' Very
pale and weak, Dorelia kept to her bed for a month. 'Happily
she has more common sense than would be needed to fit out a
dozen normal people and doesn't worry herself at all, now that
she is comfortable.'

Augustus was less calm. The hideous threat of puerperal fever
terrified him – 'I know that demon already too well.' He was
seized with a panic of guilt and helplessness. Now that his
family was so scattered – three children in France, three in
London, and one, Henry, in Hampshire – he needed more than
ever a strong centre to his life. If Dorelia died, everything fell
apart. Being 'totally without help except for the neighbours', he
immediately wired Helen Maitland who, to his consternation,
returned bringing with her Henry Lamb. 'We made an amnesty
for these peculiar conditions,' Lamb explained to Ottoline. With
Dorelia and Helen in the house, Lamb assumed a very John-like
role, and it was difficult for Augustus to object, though he
feared, in Lamb's wake, a long line of gossip.* Only when it was
clear that Dorelia was 'on the high road to recovery' did Lamb
leave, after which Helen kept him informed by letter. 'Her lips
are dreadfully pale but I think she's getting better really' (19
May 1910). In another letter she observed: 'Dorelia, you know,
doesn't care for herself and if she thinks she does for other
people I am sure it's a mistake and it's something else that she
minds.'

Though she had brought a packet of tea with which to combat
the crisis, Helen was handicapped by being unused to children
and cooking.† Her meals may well have helped to subdue the

---

* 'I wired to a young woman to come and assist,' he gruffly explained to
Wyndham Lewis (July 1910), 'Lamb accompanied the young woman and spent
2 or 3 days in this town; possibly with the object of making himself useful or
perhaps with some purely sentimental motif or both.' In fact Lamb seems to
have spent about ten days there.

† 'One evening Helen experimentally served up an untried Greek vegetable
which I rashly pronounced delicious. A deathly silence ensued. It was as if I

boys, for they began to tell even on Augustus's redoubtable constitution. 'He is very saintly the way he eats the strange food
put before him and even finds ways of pretending to like it,' she
wrote to Lamb.

By 25 May, Augustus reported that Dorelia 'is getting strong.
She is gay to ravishing point.'[91] They had emerged at last from
their 'awful adventure' but, anxious to avoid any possibility of
a relapse, Augustus planned to import 'a sturdy wench' into the
house to do the work as soon as Helen left. 'We have an abominably pretty housemaid,' he was able to complain a little later
that summer.[92]

Dorelia's illness overshadowed the rest of that summer at
Martigues. For a time Augustus took a studio in Marseilles – 'an
astonishing town,' he assured Quinn (28 May 1910), 'probably
the dirtiest in Europe'; but he grew ill with a series of stomach
disorders cheerfully diagnosed by Dorelia as appendicitis,
cancer and ulcers – 'this is encouraging', he remarked to Quinn.
Personally he blamed the climate which was alternatively too
hot, too dry and too windy. By July the other four children
arrived – something Augustus strongly welcomed in theory –
and their complaints were added in chorus to his own. 'I have
my whole family over here now, and it's a good deal,' he conceded.[93] Regular cheques from Quinn and Hugh Lane arrived:
but he was more resistant to this medicine now. He was a
martyr, suddenly, to homesickness. 'There are no green fields
here,' he noticed (5 August 1910), 'scratch the ground and you
come to the rock ... a green meadow smells sweet to me ...
This place doesn't succeed in making me feel well – but I have
intervals of well being.'[94] A curious longing for the west of
Ireland swept over him, and for the people of Ireland with their
wry, ramshackle ways, so much more appealing than the com-
placent natives of Provence. 'These people are too bavard,' he

had praised Alma Tadema. Such are the pitfalls of associating with aesthetes!'
Romilly John wrote (29 July 1972). 'She was unable to leave children well
alone to get on with their insignificant lives, and one felt bound to come out
with some deep remark and continually to show promise . . . A tremendous
believer in talking things out, after a trying day with her little boy she would
go upstairs, wake him up, and reason with him about his conduct, finally leaving him in tears to reappear wreathed in smiles.'

told Ottoline (5 August 1910), 'too concrete – too academic even. They all look as if they've solved the riddle of the universe and lost their souls in the process.'

In this mood he decided to return to London before the end of September and, though he at once regretted this decision, it gave a zest to his last month there. He was working once more against time, and this suited him. Although little finished work had been possible – or so he believed – he had made a good many studies that would, he calculated, be useful for his Hugh Lane decorations. After a spell of defeat, he had begun something entirely new 'with all the lust and keenness of a convalescent'.[95]

'What I have been about here is rapid sketching in paint,' he told Quinn (25 August 1910), 'and I can say (with some excitement) that it's only during the last week or two that I have made an absolute technical step ... I want to live long!'

That November the fruits of Augustus's nine months abroad were shown at the Chenil Gallery in a one-man show entitled 'Provençal Studies and Other Works'. At the same time, a mile away, another exhibition had just opened: Roger Fry's 'Manet and the Post-Impressionists'.

6

Revolution 1910

I wish to God I was born with more method in my madness
– but it's coming.

AUGUSTUS JOHN TO ARTHUR SYMONS (MARCH 1910)

I. WHAT THEY SAY

There can have been few more unfortunate times for a British
painter to have been born than in the 1870s. At home, he would
have passed his youth in an atmosphere of genteel tranquillity
and then, at the onset of middle age, been overtaken by changes
unprecedented for their speed and significance. It was almost
impossible for such a painter not to be at some period out of
step with his age. For even in 1910 it was still easy to believe one
was living in the middle of the Victorian era. Nothing much
had changed – nothing that affected one. Victorianism had
hardened into a tiny Ice Age of its own, splendidly impervious
to the intellectual fires that were consuming the Continent.

Fear was the artificial stimulant that had kept Victorianism
alive so long beyond its natural life span: fear of national decline and the rise of the degenerate lower classes; fear of sex
and the spreading knowledge of birth control; fear that the very
implements of fear, poverty and religious superstition, were
losing their power; fear of foreigners.

Then, 'in or about December 1910 human character changed'.
The date was not arbitrary. Announcing[1] this change fourteen
years later, Virginia Woolf chose it so as to make 'Manet and
the Post-Impressionists' a symbol of the way in which European
ideas entered battle with English conservatism. Since then art-
and social-historians have sometimes tended to convert this
symbol into a reality. Time is a magnifying glass and through it,
as things recede, we seem to see them much more sharply. At
over sixty years' distance we have no difficulty in understanding
what happened. 'Manet and the Post-Impressionists' was a

watershed, and in or about December 1910 the character of British Art changed: indeed, it disappeared. The Second Post-Impressionist Exhibition which, two years later, admitted British artists, signalled the last opportunity for them to choose the path they would follow and the view posterity would take of them.

Like gossip for biographers, journalism is a rich but dangerous source material for historians. The 'awful excitement' which erupted after 'Manet and the Post-Impressionists' was a journalistic freak diagnosed by Roger Fry as another outbreak of British philistinism, more extreme than anything since Whistler's day. It was historic. The *Times* critic declared a state of anarchy;[2] Robert Ross warned readers of the *Morning Post*[3] that the exhibiting artists were lunatics, and Charles Ricketts wrote to congratulate him on his percipience. Doctors were called in publicly to pronounce on the pictures: Philip Burne-Jones saw in the show 'a huge practical joke organised in Paris at the expense of our countrymen', though Wilfrid Blunt could detect 'no trace of humour in it', only 'a handful of mud': and he summed up the exhibits as 'works of idleness and impotent stupidity, a pornographic show'. It was left to a Royal Academician, Sir William Richmond, to strike a note of pathos: 'I hope that in the last years of a long life', he wrote, 'it will be the last time I shall feel ashamed of being a painter.'[4]

It is when artists forget their own work and expend their energies on abusing other artists that art is most easily transformed into art-history. Historians pronouncing on this tempting subject, using it as a thread in their historical pattern, have an authority scarcely less extraordinary than that of doctors or psychiatrists. The special danger of the historical panorama is that it tends to widen the gap between appearance and reality. It is not necessarily the job of the artist to fix the destiny of kingdoms or to mirror social conditions, but to practise his art to the best of his ability wherever it may lead. The Post-Impressionist shows, which in their historical context have been used by some critics as a simplifying device, in fact greatly complicated the condition of art in Britain. That Sir William Richmond should find these exhibitions 'unmanly'; that Tonks would come to recognize in Fry the counterpart of Hitler and

Mussolini; and that Fry himself should emerge as the leader of a number of young and rebellious painters was all perhaps predictable. But the repercussions from these shows were felt most keenly by those artists who were embedded in their own times. Those whose work belongs to all time were generally less affected; while among others who, like Augustus, were half-in and half-out of their times, the reaction was highly unpredictable. 'The sheep and the goats are inextricably mixed up,' Eric Gill observed to Will Rothenstein.

Augustus is the prime example of an artist whose true position cannot clearly be defined in the perspective of an historical pattern. Within any general survey of the twentieth century it is impossible to place him neatly – unless he is depicted as a transitional figure in an age of transition, but moving diagonally. He was admired by Roger Fry and dismissed by Clive Bell, and he returned those feelings exactly; he was a pupil of Tonks, Fry's enemy, but provoked in the breast of Sir William Richmond, who called him 'loathesome', feelings of moral shame and outrage very similar to those stirred up by Fry himself. He admired Cézanne, was influenced by Gauguin, and disliked Matisse. Though he had seen and been impressed by Picasso's work and had travelled much in Europe, he could still in 1907 ask Henry Lamb who Van Gogh was. He exemplified nothing in British art that he could not just as well be made to contradict, and it is only when we examine him in relation to the particular, not the general, that a comprehensible likeness may be traced – that of a solitary figure occupying on the stage of British art a prominent position, yet to one side from the main events. It is an oblique view, and curiously revealing.

2. WHAT THEY SAID AT THE TIME

In the years before the First World War, Augustus's place in contemporary British art was unique. If Steer was the old king about to enter retirement, Sickert occupied the role of Regent: and Augustus was heir apparent. Whatever he did was news, and whatever he did added not so much to his achievement as to his promise. 'Promise' was the word that was invariably applied to his work; he was credited and debited with it; it hung round his neck like a label, and eventually like a stone. Ever since the Slade days, it was said, he had been dogged by an enviable and excessive facility. His admirers were encouraged to detect in his paintings signs of infinite potential. However good a particular painting might be – his 'William Nicholson', 'Yeats', 'The Smiling Woman', or his finest dream picture of Dorelia – it seemed only to add to the weight of his future. He was overburdened with promise.

For the last dozen years he had been constantly in the public mind, associated with something indefinably romantic, brilliant and slightly scandalous. The criticism and appreciation he attracted revolved round endless anecdotes that had little to do with his art. 'He is the wonder of Chelsea,' exclaimed George Moore in 1906, 'the lightning draughtsman, the only man living for whom drawing presents no difficulty whatever.' Two years later (10 June 1908) Neville Lytton was actually praising him for not allowing 'style to interfere with the spirit of life which is the one and only really essential thing for art'. Referring to him as 'an anarchistic artist', he told Will Rothenstein: 'I think John's daring and talent is an excellent example for us and shows us in which direction it is expedient for us to throw our bonnets over the windmills.' Some indication of the kind of fame he had achieved before 1910 is provided by an exhibition of Max Beerbohm's caricatures during May 1909 at the Leicester Galleries. One of these, as described by Max himself, shows Augustus 'standing in one of his own "primitive" landscapes, with an awfully dull looking art-critic beside him gazing (the art-critic gazing) at two or three very ugly "primitive" John women in angular attitudes. The drawing is called "Insecurity"; and the art-critic is saying to himself "How odd it seems that thirty years hence I may be desperately in love with these ladies!" '[5]*

* 'Max has done a very funny caricature of me – dozens of awful art students in the background,' Augustus wrote to Dorelia. Besides 'Insecurity' (now owned by the National Gallery of Victoria, Melbourne), Sir Rupert Hart-Davis has 'run to earth' another five Beerbohm caricatures of Augustus, including one (1909) protesting against the fashions for the coming spring; one as a war-artist in uniform coming across three barefoot gaily-clad women working on a farm; one leading a headless Lord Leverhulme by the arm; and one in the series 'The Old and the Young Self' (Ashmolean Museum, Oxford).

In 1942 Augustus became a member of the Maximilian Society, writing to

Max's ambiguous attitude to Augustus almost exactly reflects that of his contemporaries as a whole. At the Leicester Galleries his caricatures had been interspersed with pictures by Sickert and other artists – and 'John has a big (oils) portrait of Nicholson,' Max told Florence Beerbohm, '– a *very* fine portrait, and quite the *clou* of the exhibition.'[6] Four months previously Augustus and Max had dined with the Nicholsons and Max afterwards described Augustus as 'looking more than picturesque ... [he] sang an old French song, without accompaniment, very remarkable, and seemed like all the twelve disciples of Christ and especially like Judas!' Admiration for his personality, admiration for his painting: but both were shot through with suspicion. If his appearance suggested some betrayal, his painting often caused bewilderment. 'He [John] has a family group at the Grafton,' Max wrote to Florence (April 1909), '– a huge painting of a very weird family. I wish I could describe it, but I can't. I think there is no doubt of his genius.' Max considered 'The Smiling Woman' 'really great',* but many of Augustus's paintings, especially of women, struck him as crude and ugly. At the same time he believed, like his art-critic, that he would be 'converted' by them and that future generations would acknowledge them to be of lasting value. The 'promise' which he attributed to Augustus was therefore in a sense vicarious: it was the age that had not adjusted its focus yet to his particular vision.

To what extent this faith in Augustus's visionary power was buoyed up by an overflow from his personality to his painting is impossible to say. Paul Nash, who did not know him personally and had 'a deep respect for John's draughtsmanship especially when it was applied with a paint brush', observed that 'technical power rather than vision predominated'.[7] To swell the confusion, his work was extremely erratic, consistent only in its absence of dates: and he obeyed impulses that often

---

Alan Dent: 'I like best old and seasoned things. Max is old and seasoned. He was born so. Hence his endurance and indestructibility and the inviolable innocence of his genius.'

* 'In the Fair Women Show, by the way, John has a portrait in oils – a full length – of "A Smiling Woman" – which seems to me really great – quite apart from and above anything else there; and you behold in me a convert.' Max to Florence Beerbohm, March 1909.

provoked the public to fretful reactions – like that which had greeted his 'Lord Mayor of Liverpool'. By the young he was generally worshipped and, until the 1920s, remained a cult figure among art students. C. R. W. Nevinson, for instance, to whom Augustus was quite simply 'a genius', noted that 'though I am always called a Modern, I have always tried to base myself on John's example'.[8] To some other painters, and especially in retrospect, it appeared that he had achieved an instant and extraordinary success. Already, by 1900, at the age of twenty-two, he was comfortably sharing a long notice with Giorgione. And in 1907, in an article entitled 'Rubens, Delacroix and Mr John', Laurence Binyon wrote:

Mr John has shown such signal gifts, and has such magnetic power over his contemporaries, that he might to-day be the acclaimed leader of a strong new movement in English painting; only he seems to have little idea as to whither he is himself moving. Does he lack faith in himself? ... he will never know the fullness of his own capacities till he puts them to a greater test than he has done yet, till he concentrates with single purpose instead of dissipating his mind in easy response to casual inspirations of the moment ...[9]

The tone of this notice was very typical. No one questioned that here was a great draughtsman – but was he husbanding his talent as he should? – would he succumb to his own waywardness? – was he not more anxious to scatter than to build? By almost everyone his work was felt to be very 'unconventional'. It was not 'normal' to search for distortion as he persistently did. What was this 'affectation' that made him deliberately misplace 'the left eye in the "Girl's Head"?' asked the *Magazine of Fine Arts*; '... it is difficult to follow the aim of the artist'.[10] The critic of *The Times* (3 December 1907) expressed, in a genial way, what many established art critics thought about his work:

The artist, as is well known, is a favourite among the admirers of very advanced and modern methods; and, if he were a dramatist, his plays would be produced by the Stage Society. That is to say he is very strong, very capable, and very much interested in the realities of life, the ugly as well as the beautiful. Most of these drawings display the qualities mentioned, but it is only fair to add that in some of the pencil heads, especially the portraits, Mr John shows he can on occasion condescend to the taste of those old fashioned people who believe in beauty and charm.

Another critic of the same show, heralding what was to come, announced: 'One must go to Paris to see anything approaching the nightmares that Mr John is on occasion capable of.'[11]

By 1910 the Americans were discovering him.* When Quinn sent him a batch of notes from Philadelphia for Dorelia's 'scrapbook', Augustus replied (4 January 1910) that 'she don't keep one – when she *does* read my notices, it's with a smile'. She had begun, he added, to complain that they were no longer rude enough, and therefore not fun, and this coincided with his own feeling that during the previous year or two (1908) his work had started to tail off.

'I've never kept any of my press notices yet,' he wrote to Quinn (23 May 1910),

– doubt if I could find storing room for them, but I have a habit of sending some of them to my father, who likes it; reserving the scornful and abusive ones for my own delectation till I light my pipe or otherwise utilize them. I used to enjoy getting these latter kind but lately they are getting confoundedly dull and appreciative. It must be my fault of course; – Blague apart I am pleased as Punch when anybody admires my work *genuinely* and with *understanding* but the run of 'critics' are merely diplomatic journalists and even then 'admiration' would be unwelcome. The only ones who count are the inspired critic-clairvoyant and fearless – and the conscientious and equally fearless Philistine – and praise and blame from either are equally welcome and stimulating.

In another letter to Quinn that month (25 May 1910) Augustus admitted: 'I realise I have been fearfully constipated mentally for the last two years or so – in a thorough bad state and it has made my work dwindle and paralysed my activities.' It was during this period of constipation that his place in British art had apparently been sought and was to be defined. He now

---

* His portrait of William Nicholson was 'undoubtedly one of the strongest paintings' (John Beatty) at the International Exhibition held by the Carnegie Institute at Pittsburgh in 1910. Following this, a number of American critics became interested in his work and several American galleries offered to show it. At the famous Armory Show of 1913 he was strongly represented.

dominated the New English Art Club to an extent where even his failure to send in work to their exhibitions itself became headline news. Though still assailed by older critics for the wilful pursuit of ugliness – an opinion that seems incredible today – he was generally considered to be the most progressive artist in the country.

'There are two artistic camps in England just now,' W. B. Yeats advised Quinn in 1909, 'the Ricketts and Shannon camp which carries on the tradition of Watts and the romantic painters, and the camp of Augustus John which is always shouting its defiance at the other. I sometimes feel I am divided between them as Coleridge was between Christianity and the philosophers when he said "My intellect is with Spinoza but my whole heart with Paul and the Apostles".'

Quinn's intellect too, supported by his purse, was with Augustus, and as late as 1914 the wisdom of his investment was confirmed by the distinguished American critic James Huneker who declared that the three biggest talents among living artists were Matisse, Epstein and Augustus John.

If such estimates read strangely today it is partly because the reverberations that have echoed so loudly down the years from the two Post-Impressionist shows have deafened us to what was actually happening at the time. Many of the art critics who had written favourably of the impressionists and who, up to the autumn of 1910, had counted themselves among the progressives, now agreed with Wilfrid Blunt that the Post-Impressionist daubs were like 'indecencies scrawled upon the walls of a privy'. To us, therefore, it can easily appear that, in the last weeks of this year, the enlightened elite of Britain had been reduced to half-a-dozen Bloomsbury intellectuals drawn up about the frail but defiant figure of Roger Fry. It was not so. To many people Augustus's pictures at the Chenil Gallery in these weeks seemed more exaggerated than those of 'the Frenchmen at the Grafton'. Reviewing his show, which he summed up as being 'a mystery', The *Times* critic asked (5 December 1910): 'What does it all mean? Is there really a widespread demand for these queer, clever, forcible, but ugly and uncanny notes of form and dashes of colour? ... for our part we see neither nature nor art in many of these strangely-formed heads, these long and too rapidly tapering necks, and these blobs of heavy paint that sometimes do duty for eyes.' In notice after notice, critics linked him to the concurrent show of Post-Impressionists and, considering that the Chenil was situated far deeper within the territory of libel than the Grafton, the tone is often quite as hostile. 'At his worst he can outdo Gauguin,' wrote a critic in *The Queen* (10 December 1910), '... uncouth and grotesque ... It is unfortunate that Mr John should go on filling public exhibitions with these inchoate studies, instead of manfully bracing to produce some complete piece of work.' Two years later, when the Second Post-Impressionist Exhibition coincided with the showing of Augustus's 'Mumpers' at the N.E.A.C., it was the latter which was seen by many critics to be the turning-point in British painting. Public opinion in these two years had changed towards Post-Impressionism, but not in its placing of Augustus's work as more 'advanced' and, in some cases, more incomprehensible than the standard Post-Impressionists. For many he was the last word in modernity. 'After Picasso,' wrote one critic, 'Mr John.'[12]

In 1909 Augustus was *avant-garde*; by 1912 he had been relegated to the rearguard of British art: that, with the foreshortening of time, is how it can now appear. The younger artists had formed up behind him, but he had had nowhere to lead them and they turned instead to Fry. This is the judgement of history, and it has been influenced by the misinterpretation of two facts. The first of these was Augustus's description of 'Manet and the Post-Impressionists' as 'a bloody show'; the second was his refusal to send in any work to the Second Post-Impressionist Exhibition. Both are true. But they form only a portion of the truth.

The very year that he had begun to fulfil his much-trumpeted promise is the year that contemporary critics renewed their hostility to him and that, in retrospect, art-historians have removed him from the forefront of British art. For in 1910, working independently in France and taking his inspiration from Italy, he had launched a private revolution of his own.

3. WHAT HE SAID

The insularity that is blamed for the static nature of art in late-Victorian and Edwardian England could never, in strict geographical terms at least,* have applied to Augustus John. From an early age he had travelled widely in Europe; he had lived in France, met Picasso, seen the work of Cézanne in Provence and of Matisse in Paris. He had even read the novels of Dostoyevsky before they had been Garnetted. Yet in two respects insularity held him back. He had been trained in a climate so regulated that it admitted only two schools of rival art: the academic art taught by Tonks and Brown based on classical and Renaissance models; and the academizing process carried on by the Royal Academy 'by which', Harold Rosenberg has written, 'all styles are in time tamed and made to perform in the circus of public taste'.[13] Augustus had learnt his lessons well and it had taken him time to 'see' a non-academic form of art that matched his talent.

Despite all the time he had spent there, Augustus had remained something of a foreigner in Paris. But in Provence he had come home. There was something of Wales here, he felt, something to which he responded deeply and intuitively. The country was rooted in a past to which he himself belonged and with which he could connect the work of Puvis de Chavannes and the great Italian masters he had been studying. He saw himself, quite suddenly, as being part of a tradition in painting, of being able to add to that tradition; and this feeling of belonging gave him new stamina. Everything seemed to fall into place; what he had seen, where he was, who he was.

'I am certain I have profited greatly by my visit to Italy,' he told Quinn on reaching Martigues (3 March 1910).

My imagination and sense of reality seems to me just twice as strong as it was before – and no exaggeration ... I tell you frankly and sincerely, I feel *nobody* dead or alive is so near the guts of things as I am at present – and it's devilish hot. And, *what is sur-*

---

* 'Is it that the atmosphere of England is oppressive?' Augustus once asked Quinn (25 May 1910). 'Stendhal said a man lost 50% of his genius on setting foot on that island.' Almost fifty per cent of Augustus's post-Slade work had been done in France.

prising, together with this infallible *realism* my sense of beauty seems to: *has,* grown simultaneously. All this remains to be proved of course. I give myself till the end of the year to prove it up to the hilt. And this comes, it seems to me, from being suddenly *alone* for some months, and seeing – and rubbing against (without committing myself too far) new people and also seeing certain pictures which crystallize the overwhelming and triumphant energy of dead men – like Signorelli for instance.

At such moments of confidence the air was thick with resolutions. 'I have never really been captured by alcohol,' he admitted to Quinn on this occasion, 'and I'm not going to run after it. I think any sport can be overdone: and I'm taking a real pleasure in dispensing with that form of entertainment. In a short while I shall be able to get as drunk as I like on green tea. Besides I'm beginning to take a really miser's interest in my own value – and will grow less and less inclined to dissipate my savings.' It is easy to be too sceptical of such good intentions, often repeated, to his puritan, health-mad patron. There were, inevitably, events that confused this stern programme: drunken days with gypsies; the irrelevant sorties of his bird-like neighbour and the air-machines; the distressing ambush of hospitality prepared for him by Frank Harris; Dorelia's illness and interminable family troubles. Yet this season there was more optimism, more courage to say the word no. He admits to 'floundering' at times, but returns stubbornly to his proper work and makes genuine progress. One of his problems is that, in periods of mounting enthusiasm, he is inclined to turn away from his past to pursue anything new. 'I think little of my etchings so far,' he confided to Quinn (28 May 1910) who had bought almost all of them, '– but I'm keen to do a set of dry-points soon.' Temptation came to him in the form of an invitation to South Africa, where he was asked to found a school, decorate Parliament and paint ten portraits of South African celebrities – Joubert, Botha and others – for one thousand pounds. These offers he turned down.

He was helped in his resolution by a book that Quinn had sent him early in May: James Huneker's *Promenades of an Impressionist.* He had been prepared at first sight to dislike it. There were too many Parisian anecdotes, too many picturesque phrases, too many eulogies of bad artists such as Fortuny and

Sorolla. But it was characteristic of his new seriousness this year to get beyond first sight. He persevered and began to find it more and more stimulating. Huneker's large, genial, comprehensive outlook, his gargantuan appetite, might not be profound, but it was better than that: it was useful.

'He [Huneker] reminded me of many a thing I used to know but had, to my shame, forgotten,' he explained to Quinn (25 May 1910).

His fresh and unfailing enthusiasm for a crowd of merits lesser minds think mutually destructive, is splendid and unheard of ... it is the gesture of a generous and hearty man – who seems to overflow with intellectual energy and does not husband it like poorer men ... This book gives me the courage and humility of my boyhood. It is strong crude air after the finicking intellectuality of London which drives a sensitive spirit into subterranean caverns where thoughts grow pale like mushrooms. I have been assailed with manifold doubts and have taken refuge in dreams when I should have sharpened my pencil and returned to the charge. An artist has no business to think except brush in hand.

'I am keen on a good show in the autumn,' Augustus had told Quinn (19 May 1910). There were delays, but not serious ones. The show which opened in December contained thirty-five drawings and etchings in the upper rooms at Chenil's, and downstairs fifty small 'Provençal Studies' in oils. It was the drawings upstairs that tempered the hostility of critics with a tone of regretful wonder; but it was the oils that represented his new field of achievement. In certain moods he saw these panels as preliminary studies for a set of complete fresco works on a very large scale. In this he had been misled by the generous criticism of Roger Fry who, the previous year, had declared that 'it is quite evident that Mr John should have a great wall in some public building and a great theme to illustrate. In Watts we sacrificed to our incurable individualism, our national incapacity of co-operating for ideal ends, a great monumental designer. A generous fate has given us another chance in Mr John, and I suppose we shall waste him likewise. What would not the Germans do for a man of his genius if they ever had the chance to produce him?'[14] Such stirring words rang sweetly in Augustus's ears; but they were blind to his lack of consistency, the fact that he painted best when in the grip of some intense but fleeting mood – the intensity arising from its very transitoriness. Fry, in many ways the greatest and most influential critic of his age, had little idea of individual talent in relation to particular theories. Augustus was the last person to co-operate, publicly and for any length of time, for ideal civic ends. But Fry's appreciation had a heroic tone that echoed in Augustus's imagination for the rest of his life. In 1939, when opening an exhibition of photographs of contemporary British wall paintings at the Tate Gallery, Augustus said sadly: 'When one thinks of painting on great expanses of wall, painting of other kinds seems hardly worth doing.' And shortly afterwards, in a restaurant, he remarked to John Rothenstein: 'I suppose they'd charge a lot to let Matt Smith and me paint decorations on these walls.'[15] He was outraged when, in 1952, John Rothenstein referred to him as a great 'improviser' because this reflected adversely on his capacities as a painter on a monumental scale.

His oil sketches at the Chenil Gallery revealed, for the first time, a gift for colour. The pale hills of Provence with their olives and pines and their elusive skies, the summer light across the Etang mysteriously moving with sun and shade, seemed to have brought him into a more vivid contact with nature. These jewelled impressions tell no story: they are simply landscapes, or figures or groups of figures in a landscape setting who reflect life as in a ballet – the girl on the sea's edge poised like some dancer, her hand on the bar of the horizon. The colour is clear and untroubled, brushed on with hasty decision – there is no niggling detail: they are austere, these panels, in their simplicity – and often shamelessly unfinished. 'The technique appears to be, at its simplest, to make a pencil drawing on a small board covered with colourless transparent priming,' commented David Piper; 'then the outlines are washed in with a generous brush loaded with pure and brilliant oil colour – and there's a happy illogicality about it, for the lines of the drawing ... are those of any John drawing, subtly lapping and rounding the volume they conjure up, but they are obliterated by the oils, and the result for effect relies on the inscape of vivid colour, on contrasting colour, and the broad flattened simplified pattern.'[16]

Never in his work had the tension between dream and reality, the ideal and the actual, been presented so directly by means so simple; never had the content been raised so superior to mere imitation of nature. His method seemed far removed from the ordinary language of British art, and most critics argued that he was using a shorthand which was quite unintelligible. The most appreciative was Laurence Binyon, who wrote:

Somehow everything lives. Even the paint, rudely dashed on the canvas, seems to be rebelling into beauties of its own. Mr John tries to disguise his science and his skill, but it leaks out, it is there ... I do not know how it is, but these small studies, some of them at least, make an extraordinary impression and haunt one's memory. A tall woman leaning on a staff; a little boy in scarlet on a cliff-edge against blue sea; a woman carrying bundles of lavender: the description of these says nothing, but they themselves seem creatures of the infancy of the world, aboriginals of the earth, with an animal dignity and strangeness, swift of gesture, beautifully poised. That is the secret of Mr John's power. He is limited, obsessed by a few types ... his ideas are few ... But in it there is a jet of elemental energy, something powerful and unaccountable, like life itself.[17]

In the course of this review Binyon compared Augustus's instinct and the simplicity of his technique to that of Gauguin. Other critics compared this new work to that of Matisse,[18] Van Gogh[19] and Jules Flandrin,[20] all of whom were then exhibiting at the Grafton Gallery. This coincidence points to a parallel development that had been taking place in Augustus and Roger Fry. In the very month that Augustus had discovered the wall paintings of Luca Signorelli, Fry was writing of Signorelli as 'one of the family of the great audacious masters'.[21] The names of both Fry and Augustus had, in the past, been primarily associated with those of the Old Masters: they had been wary of the modern movement. But by the end of 1910 they were seen to be, quite separately, at the head of all that was most *avant-garde* in England. In neither case did this involve a rejection of what they had believed in before, for what they had discovered was the *modernity* of certain Old Masters, such as Masaccio and Signorelli, whose work was akin to the greatest of the Post-Impressionists. Their sudden flowering of enthusiasm for modern French painters sprang in each case from their new understanding of the Italian Primitives.

Augustus thought of Fry as a very skilful writer, a poor artist and a man of the most credulous disposition. He feared where this credulity might lead people in the future, but he saluted the 'wonderful things' Fry had seen which, by 1910, had brought him so close to his own conclusions.* Quentin Bell has written that it was 'remarkable' for a man of Fry's temperament and training to have realized that 'Cézanne and his followers were not simply innovators but represented also a return to the great tradition of the past, for such a conviction, which does not seem wonderful to-day, required an extraordinary effort of the mind in the year 1910'. Even more remarkable was for Augustus to have made an identical discovery at exactly the same time.

4. WHAT HE SAID ABOUT THEM

'A bloody show!' These shocking words have reverberated down the decades and, reaching the ears of art-historians, have been hailed as the first cry of the future Royal Academician.

He did say them – to Eric Gill who reported them by letter to Will Rothenstein, thus ensuring their immortality. They represented his first reaction, not so much to the pictures themselves but to the senseless chatter and vulgar journalistic outcry to which the show had given rise. From this time on he was to become increasingly touchy about publicity. It seems almost certain, from the date Gill must have written to Rothenstein, that Augustus had roundly denounced the exhibition before actually going to it. Certainly his first sight of it was distorted by all he had heard and read which, like a film, seemed to come between him and what he saw. He did not visit the Grafton until early December, after the show had been running a month. 'There is a show of "Post-Impressionists" now on here,' he noted

* It is this parallel course, as well as his own independence, that Augustus signified in a letter to Quinn (10 February 1911): 'I don't think we need Fry's lead: he's a gifted obscurantist and no doubt has his uses in the world. He is at any rate alive to unrecognised possibilities and guesses at all sorts of wonderful things.' Elsewhere in this letter he writes: 'If you sent him [Fry] a gilded turd in a glass case he would probably discover some strange poignant rhythm in it and hail you as a cataclysmic genius and persuade the Contemporary Art Society to buy the production for the Nation.'

in a letter to Quinn (December 1910), 'and my post-impression of it is by no means favourable.' That was all. But in the last week of the exhibition, when all the noise had died down, he went again. His true reaction to the pictures is set out in a long letter to Quinn (11 January 1911):

I went to the 'Post-Impressionists' again yesterday and was more powerfully impressed by them than I was at my first visit. There have been a good many additions made to the show in the meanwhile – and important ones. Several new paintings and drawings by Van Gogh served to convince me that this man was a great artist. My first view of his works disappointed and disagreed with me. I do not think however that one need expect to be at once charmed and captured by a personality so remarkable as his. Indeed 'charm' is the last thing to talk about in regard to Van Gogh. The drawings I saw of his were splendid and there is a stunning portrait of himself. Gauguin too has been reinforced and I admired enormously two Maori women in a landscape. As for Matisse, I regard him with the utmost suspicion. He is what the French call a fumiste – a charlatan, but an ingenious one. He has a portrait here of a 'woman with green eyes' which to me is devoid of every genuine quality – a vulgar and spurious work. While in Paris the other day I saw a show of paintings by Picasso which struck me as wonderfully fine – full of secret beauty of sentiment – I have admired his work for long ... I forgot to mention *Cézanne* – he was a splendid fellow, one of the greatest – he too has work at the Grafton.

As the example of Matisse shows, the work of some of these artists struck for him a dumb note. Later on (July 1913) he helped Quinn to buy a Gauguin ceiling he much admired, and he recommended (3 December 1912) work by Manet and Degas. But of Maurice Denis he wrote with discrimination to Quinn (17 May 1912:

I have known Mr Denis's work for long and have admired it from time to time ... I think Denis has a certain talent. I know he has, but I don't find it leads to much or is in the great sense, exciting. I think him an intelligent, ingenious, and sincere man who makes the most of his gifts within the contemporary field. He doesn't go beyond it. He is a well known and probably prosperous person and his recent works at Marchants have impressed me less than earlier ones. He is not, in my opinion, great by any means. Picasso now has genius, albeit perhaps of a morbid sort ...

Your feeling about Renoir is just. A wonderful man! That un-finished thing we saw at Durand-Ruels impressed me enormously. I may have said that 'Impressionism' was of the past – dead – but *impressionists* no!!! Renoir, Degas, Toulouse-Lautrec – etc. – will always be live artists. I wish we had gone to see Anquetin while in Paris. A man of immense gifts. Bye-the-bye if you come across a painting by Daumier, freeze on to it! One of the great Frenchmen. El Greco too is now coming into his own. A terrible, mysterious Spaniard – or rather Greek.

Certainly this is not the letter of an Englishman infected with the virus of insularity. Yet he was also extremely interested by his British contemporaries, writing copiously about their work to Quinn so that, in this way, he could help them without re-prisals of gratitude. Such methods appealed alike to his gener-osity and secretiveness, and accurately reflected his attitudes from 1910 until the 1920s. His taste was not at all what might be surmised. For himself he bought examples of work by, among others, Epstein, Wyndham Lewis, William Roberts and Christ-opher Wood. But about Ricketts and Shannon, artists who seem to have more in common with himself (such as a reverence for Puvis de Chavannes), he was lukewarm:

'I have never succeeded in feeling or showing any great interest in *his* [Shannon's] work tho' I have remarked that per-sonally he shows himself a man, one would say, of character,' he once (25 August 1910) wrote to Quinn. 'He has a reserve which contrasts with the funny effervescence of Ricketts – who is the cleverer chap; but as for him, he has lost his innocence, he is corrupt – and I doubt if even a good wash in Jordan would re-store his pristine purity. I mean that a man of his intellectual parts should keep himself straighter – at the risk of being stupid even.'*

* Another artist about whose pictures his feelings were mixed was Mark Gertler. He had recommended his early work – which hung alongside his own at the Chenil Gallery – but by 16 February 1916 he is telling Quinn that 'Mark Gertler's work has gone to buggery and I can't stand it. Not that he hasn't ability of a sort and all the cheek of a Yid, but the spirit of the work is false and affected.'

With Eric Gill it was the other way about. On 10 February 1911, he is advising Quinn against buying his work. 'Personally I don't admire the things and feel pretty certain that you wouldn't neither. I admit that Gill is an enter-

Since Quinn relied on Augustus for information about what was going on in the London galleries, their correspondence over the next half-dozen years gives much evidence of Augustus's opinions. The first artist whose work he recommended was naturally his sister Gwen. In her dealings with Quinn she is, in many respects, the very reverse of Augustus. From Quinn's point of view, it was like looking towards their pictures from across the Atlantic through opposite ends of a telescope: his seemed so near, hers so remote. And while Augustus is perpetually anxious for her to retain Quinn's goodwill, it was he in the end who forfeited it.

Among other artists he recommended were John Currie,* Epstein, Jacob Kramer, Harold Gilman, Charles Ginner, Spencer Gore,† Derwent Lees, C. R. W. Nevinson, Wilson Steer and

---

prising young man and not without ability. He has been a carver of inscriptions till quite recently when he started doing figures. His knowledge of human form is, you may be sure, of the slightest and I feel strongly that his experience of human beings is anything but profound. I know him personally. He carves well and succeeds in expressing one or two cut-and-dried philosophical ideas. He is much impressed by the importance of copulation possibly because he has had so little to do with that subject in practice, and apparently considers himself obliged to announce the gospel of the flesh, to a world that doesn't need it. Innes calls him "the naughty schoolmaster", Gore calls him the "precious cockney" and I call him the "artist of the Urinal" . . . I'll let you know when I see a thing of Gill's which I can really respect and desire. His present things are taking at first glance as they look so simple and unsophisticated — but, to me at least, only art at first glance.' Three years later his opinion of Gill's work has risen. 'I also ordered you one of Gill's things, a dancing figure in stone,' he wrote to Quinn (26 January 1914). '. . . Gill has made good progress and his things are admirable now, both in workmanship and idea.'

* John Currie, who appears as 'Logan' in Gilbert Cannan's novel *Mendel* (1916), shot himself and his mistress in a fit of jealousy. 'You remember Currie, some of whose works you bought?' Augustus asked Quinn (10 October 1914). 'He shot his mistress dead yesterday and then himself. He has since died of four bullet wounds in the chest. The girl was staying here [Alderney Manor] lately carrying on a futile love affair with another young man. We all got sick of her. She was an attractive girl or used to be when I knew her first, but seemed to have deteriorated into a deceitful little bitch.

'It is a terrible affair and it's a good thing I suppose that Currie died. He was an able fellow and would have had a successful career.'

† Spencer Gore, 'whose work I think good and promising', Augustus recommended to Quinn and continued to admire. In 1928 (*Vogue*, 25 July) he wrote: 'The work of Spencer F. Gore, although [attracting] the admiration of a small body of genuine picture-lovers, undoubtedly failed to reach its deserved

Walter Greaves.* Often he would write persuasively about painters working in styles very different from his own. Alvaro
('Chile') Guevara he described as 'the most gifted and promising
of them all' (16 February 1916), but he was also very impressed
by Gaudier-Brzeska, who, he wrote (3 April 1915), 'is a man of
talent. His things look as if they have been sat on before they
got quite hard. Some of them look like bits of stalactite roughly
resembling human forms. But they are wittily conceived.' Most
of all he wrote about David Bomberg. 'You ought to get more
Bombergs,' he advised Quinn† (26 January 1914), 'he is full of
talent.' Following the lead of Marinetti – 'a common type of the
meridional; naif, earnest, and ignorant. But we are very friendly'
– Bomberg's painting took a 'Futurist' course that was ultimately unsympathetic to Augustus. But, with reservations, he
continued to praise him (in company with 'another Futurist
called Balla who is good') – specifically his famous 'Mud-Bath'.[22]
'Would you like to invest in the unfathomable?' he invited
Quinn in a style suitably patronizing for a patron (24 June
1914). 'Bomberg has talent and ingenuity, but frankly his latest
things are too, too inhuman to provoke my whole-hearted enthusiasm. Still he is an amusing little type, and you might be
amused to have some of his inventions.'

There is no mention of Bomberg in *Chiaroscuro* or in *Finishing Touches*; and none, or almost none, of the other artists upon

---

favour with the general public on account of the war following so soon after his
death, which befell when he might be said to have arrived at the prime of his
accomplishment. But this unconscious injustice was repaired by the April
[1928] exhibition [at the Leicester Galleries], when it was realised that Gore
was one of the most notable landscape painters of his time.' And again in 1942
(*Horizon*, Vol. VI, No. 36, December 1942, p. 426) he wrote: 'The industrious
apprentice is a type to be admired rather than loved. In Spencer Gore's case,
however, immense industry was coupled not only with a rare and ever-
ripening talent: he possessed in addition an amiable, modest and upright nature
which elicited the deep affection and respect of all those who knew him.'

* 'He [Greaves] is a real artist-kid, with Chelsea in his brain. I shall never
cease to appreciate his work – *so* unlike Whistler's at bottom.' John to Quinn,
17 May 1912.

† On 29 December 1913, Augustus had written to Quinn urging him to buy
a Bomberg drawing 'extremely good and dramatic representing a man dead
with mourning family, very simplified and severe. I'ld like you to have it.'
Quinn bought it for fifteen pounds.

whose behalf he had secretly exercised himself. He had taken to writing only at the end of the 1930s, and by the time his fragments of autobiography were put together as books it was too late. He had become introverted, unwilling to study the unfamiliar, distrustful of his own good nature, a prey to disappointment and melancholia. His tone as well as the content of what he wrote is affected. Of Picasso, for example, he joked: 'Such ceaseless industry, leading to a torrent of *articles de nouveauté*, may seem to some, capricious and rootless, but it undoubtedly deserves its reward in the greatest snob-following of our time' – a sentence that was itself rewarded by Picasso's classification of Augustus as: 'The best bad painter in Britain.'

It can therefore be misleading to reconstruct the young man from what the older man wrote a long time in retrospect. Fortunately there exists in *Vogue* eight long articles[23] he wrote during 1928 on modern French and English painters – a series subsequently forgotten yet far more authentic as a guide to his artistic taste. These articles help to reconcile the old and the young man, and demonstrate how catholic and near-contemporary his taste still remained up to his early fifties – though he had grown resentful of the power of fashion in art, for which he blamed the dealers. The value of the French tradition was a thing beyond the ephemeral whim of fashion and depended upon 'the unceasing enthusiasm of French painters towards a personal expression'. The French painters he singled out as having created a climate that favoured modern innovations were Manet, Monet ('in the entrancing waterlilies of his later years'), Sisley and Camille Pissarro – 'these are the pioneers who led painting from the halting deliberation of David to the courageous or even risky contact with the open air. Monet, Renoir, Degas not tentatively, but with conscious authority, released that long-confined expression of instant response to the aspect of the visible world.' The battle of the Impressionists had long ago been fought and won, but he deplored the labelling of Post-Impressionism applied to the later romantics Van Gogh, Gauguin and Emile Bernard because 'their work and their own individuality was much more significant than, and much more distinct from, the work of the Impressionists themselves'. After the muscle-bound paganism of Gauguin, the reverent Christianity of Van Gogh, the next painters in the grand line of French art were rather less to his liking. The atmosphere had become too cultured. He praises, with reservations, the work of that lazy giant Derain, but deprecates his pedantry; while the developments since 1912 in the styles of Picasso and Matisse seem almost completely to have reversed his attitude to them. Picasso, whose Blue and Rose periods he had loved, appeared to be growing metaphorically false. 'Matisse remains the best, the most sensitive, of French painters, for Matisse having abandoned his early essays in imbecility, has by dint of assiduity and method achieved the foremost place in his generation as an exquisite paysagist and painter of *genre.*'

Among senior contemporary painters he singles out 'three old gentlemen', Bonnard, Forain and Rouault as being above competition – 'individual and isolated examples of the glory of French painting'. And among the younger ones he chooses Chagall for 'his admirable handling of paint', Antral, in whose best pictures 'one discovers a pure and architectural vision refreshingly distinct from the vinous romanticism of which Utrillo is the acknowledged master', Othon Friesz and, above all, Segonzac, who 'conceived the landscape in its fundamental unity and basic rhythm; escaping from a too direct naturalism, he rebuilds the essential structure, revealing the form in its organic fullness, and setting free its deep burden of emotion in low and thrilling cords of colour'.

These opinions give evidence of someone who could still look at new paintings and have reactions to them.* His criticism of British painters is more confused since it sews together paragraphs of friendship with passages of objective appreciation – the two sometimes embroidered with *double entendre*:

'With Mr Henry Lamb we have another type of mind, more self-conscious but less free [than Matthew Smith's]. He seeks, with an almost mathematical ingenuity, to invent new har-

---

* Over ten years earlier (10 February 1917) Roger Fry had written to Vanessa Bell: 'John turned up at the Omega t'other day and looked at our show. He seemed to me almost entirely stupid – to have no reaction whatever to pictures, but I don't know of course.' It is after this date that a note of disapproval enters Fry's criticism of Augustus's work. And it was after the war that Augustus began popularly to be represented as an embodiment of the past, without any active response to the present or curiosity over the future.

monies of colour in combination with a most searching analysis of character. This passionately serious painter, for whom any intellectual concession is an impossibility, remains still insufficiently recognised. For so many amateurs, an easy and comforting facility is more attractive than Mr Lamb's *intransigence* and the almost moral integrity of his art.'

The theme which emerges from the body of Augustus's art criticism is a belief in individual accomplishment entirely independent of art trends. It was, he reflected, a comforting thought that posterity amended the injustices of contemporary neglect, that no effort of real creative merit could fail to be recognized in the course of time: but he did not believe it. There was no sign, for instance, that the work of Paul Maitland or W. E. Osborn would ever be revived. Nor did Augustus expect his writing to dent this impervious system. Yet there was a certain luxury in protesting against the inevitable – a satisfaction of the soul.

His protest lay against Paris: not as a symbol and repository of the great French tradition of painting by which he himself had profited, but as a forcing house of the international picture-*bourse*. Paris had become the world's greatest stock-exchange for art, the Mecca of the amateur, the student, and above all the dealer. A great machinery for the encouragement of the young was centred there and people arrived from all over the world in search of revelation. That a great tradition had made Paris famous was taken to imply that it was Paris which had made the tradition. Yet many painters had had a bitter struggle to establish themselves in the city of which they were, after their deaths, the pride. Constantin Guys had been in Baudelaire's words 'le peintre inconnu'; Daumier a political suspect and journalist-illustrator to the end of his life. And so on. The Post-Impressionists found it no easier. Biographies of Cézanne, Gauguin and Van Gogh all told a similar story of derision, lack of understanding. Rousseau 'le Douanier' and Modigliani, whom in great poverty Augustus visited a few years before his death, were two recent victims of incomprehension on the part of 'the great art city of the world'. By the late 1920s their pictures all fetched enormous prices, and Paris, on their posthumous behalf, did herself great honour. Since there could be no guarantee that the centre of creative activity in painting still rested at Paris, the huge combination of studio and dealer's shop that had been constructed there, like some monument of piety or penance, was probably little better than an empty shell: the goddess of art had paused – and now moved on.

From this serious misreading of the past, Augustus suggested, there had arisen a dangerous contemporary mystique:

'It is possible seriously to question the wisdom of establishing a cosmopolitan usine d'art, however well equipped it be. For a French painter, to whom his own land is a natural source of inspiration, it doubtless affords considerable advantages, and, it is to be hoped, may save such lamentable examples of failures of appreciation ... But for painters of other countries, especially those who have a strongly defined native tradition, like England, there is a danger of the individual and national voice being lost in an international lingua franca.'

This became the basis of his complaint against Roger Fry, and it may be overheard in his criticism of the Bloomsbury Court painters Vanessa Bell and Duncan Grant, whose natural decorative gifts, he felt, had been misappropriated. Grant, for instance, had 'an innate sense of decoration [and] ... exhibits a natural lyricism in his work which appears to owe less to definite calculation than to irrepressible instinct for rhythmical self-expression'. But his instinct had been subjected to other people's calculation in such a way that his versatile temperament had absorbed 'with an ease nearly related to genius the most disconcerting manifestations of the modern spirit'. It was a case of a good artist being, so they said, rogered by Fry.

The right course, Augustus believed, was exemplified by another artist whose work had something in common with Duncan Grant's: Matthew Smith. He too had been influenced by the modern spirit, but had taken from it only what was germane to his special talent:

French influences are inevitably to be noted in his work, but the fulness of form which characterises so many of his figures has a distinct relationship with Indian and Persian drawings. With a cataract of emotional sensibility he casts upon the canvas a pageant of grandiose and voluptuous form and sumptuous colour, which are none the less controlled by an ordered design and a thoroughly learned command of technique. This makes him one of the most brilliant figures in modern English painting. Aloof and deliberately detached from the appeals of ordinary life, he sits apart and converts what to other men are the ever-partial triumphs of passion into permanent monuments of profound sensory emotion. In flowers, fruit and women he finds the necessary material for his self-expression, and from them he has evolved a kind of formula which represents his artist's inner-consciousness. And he has never risked the danger which threatens those who make bargains with society by attempting the almost impossible task of combining fine painting with satisfactory portraiture.

Of all Augustus's feelings for modern artists, this wonderful appreciation of Matthew Smith was by far the most consistent, lasting for over thirty years until his death. The nature of his admiration, suddenly revealed here, was partly a stick with which to beat himself. For he saw Matthew Smith's career as an example of the isolated and independent path the artist must climb in order, through long study, trial and many failures, to release the secret of his talent. The source of his own natural inspiration was South Wales, but he was temperamentally denied access there by the occupation of his father. Now he had found in Provence, and very soon would find in North Wales too, a landscape that absorbed his personality and, through a mysterious process of self-identification and self-abandonment, liberated his imagination. He had found also, in Primitive art, a means to escape from the boredom that overwhelms the half-civilized animal in the face of nature. Then, finally, he discovered an artist, another Welshman, whose imagination cross-fertilized with his own and with whom he now entered a brief period of mutual apprenticeship, radiant, and unique in his career.

5. WHAT HAPPENED

During 1910, that year of exceptional artistic ferment, the first of Augustus's Slade contemporaries, William Orpen, quietly joined the Royal Academy. This was the dull side of that brilliant Post-Impressionist symbol Virginia Woolf had coined. With extraordinary precision art-history was repeating itself and, to the rhythm of its thrilling monotony, the *enfants ter-ribles* of a decade ago were starting on their journey to become Grand Old Men. Their rebel headquarters, the New English Art Club, was now twenty-four years old. French-built to withstand the assaults of British Academicism, it now stood, a British fortress against the advance of French Post-Impressionism. What was needed, apparently, was a new, or still newer *Salon des Refusés* to oppose the old *Salon des Refusés* whose tyrannical rule was felt by the younger artists far more acutely than the remote indifference of Burlington House.

The first cumbersome expression of this need had been Frank Rutter's Allied Artists Association, a self-supporting concern modelled on the Parisian *Société des Artistes Indépendants*. All artists, by paying an annual subscription, could exhibit what works they pleased without submitting them to a censorious jury. Founded in 1908, in July of which year it held its first mammoth show at the Albert Hall, it soon gave birth to 'the Camden Town Group' and the 'London Group' which in 1914 was to swallow them both up. Augustus was a founder member of the Allied Artists Association, though he never exhibited with them. This paradox, which arose from the cross-currents of laziness and generosity, was explained by Rutter: 'John never does exhibit anywhere unless you go and fetch his pictures yourself ... He joined because, like the good fellow he is, he thoroughly approved of the principles of the A.A.A., and knew it would help others though he had no need of it himself.'[24]

The idealism of the Allied Artists Association soon descended into combative art-politics. On Saturday nights they would meet at a little hotel in Golden Square – usually Augustus, Bevan, Gilman, Ginner, Gore, Lucien Pissarro, Rutter and Sickert – and go on afterwards to the Café Royal. And almost always, at some hour of the evening, the talk would turn, and return, to the question of whether they should capture the New English Art Club or secede and set up a rival society. Augustus was what Rutter called 'consistently loyal' to the N.E.A.C. In several respects his position was closest perhaps to the Protean figure of Sickert. Both were opposed to 'capturing' the New English, and Augustus believed furthermore that any other group they might found must be truly independent rather than a rival. Only in that way could it faithfully represent their ideal of exhibiting freely, and steer a course of tolerance and diversity between the various rocks of art-fashion. The result of these talks was the formation in 1911 of the Camden Town Group, dominated by Gilman, Ginner, Bevan and Gore, and watched over by the benevolent eye of Sickert. Though unconnected with Camden Town, Augustus was admitted to this group which marked an important defection from the New English whose original aims it nevertheless almost exactly reproduced. He exhibited only once with them, though he liked to look in on their weekly meetings at 21 Fitzroy Street, and surreptitiously buy pictures both for himself and for Quinn.

Then, in 1912, two things happened: he turned down Clive Bell's invitation to show work at 'The Second Post-Impressionist Exhibition'; and, in the words of Quentin Bell, he left the Camden Town Group and 'flew back to the New English'. Both actions have been interpreted as retrogressive steps marking his end as an imaginative artist. When, in 1914, the London Group emerged as the spearhead of modernity, Augustus's name was, for the first time, not among Britain's *avant-garde*.*

Because of Augustus's circumstances, which at this period were unique, it is easy to draw from these two acts a wrong conclusion. He was prolific; he had a wealthy American patron; he had the use of a London gallery where he could show his pictures at any time. Although, with his large family, he needed more money than most other artists, his work was now fetching good prices – the small oil panels at Chenil's had sold for forty pounds each and some of them were soon changing hands for seventy and eighty. The considerable trade union spirit he felt for his fellow artists was uncorrupted by art-politics – he saw no reason why the Vorticist should not lie down with the Omega. He would have liked as many alternatives as were practicable to be available for all of them, involving numerous exhibitions where, irrespective of style, they could display and sell their paintings. But the Camden Town Group – named, in deference to Sickert, after the drab working-class area which provided subject matter for many of

* He was, however, elected with Oscar Kokoschka and Jack Yeats as an honorary member of the London Group in the Second World War.

the members' pictures – though it might contain better painters, was narrower than the untidy pell-mell of the New English. Besides, the theme of his landscapes represented everything that was remote from suburbia and was quite out of place in a Camden show. In fact he had never broken with the New English – his tepid relations with them were still intact. The decision to show nothing at their two exhibitions in 1910 had not been one of deep art-policy but simple geography : no one could 'go and fetch his pictures' while he was abroad almost all that year. The year had ended with his one-man show at Chenil's for which he reserved all his recent work; but in 1911 he was again exhibiting with them. Nor had he broken with the Camden Town painters, whose work, as we have seen, he continued to recommend to Quinn. For him these various clubs and societies were not exclusive alternatives but additional platforms from which all artists might perform.

Yet behind his decision to withhold work from the 'Second Post-Impressionist Exhibition' there lay Augustus's involuntary involvement in a sudden clash between Roger Fry and Will Rothenstein. The enmity which flared up between these two didactic painter-politicians seems partly to have arisen from Rothenstein's attitude to the new power Fry was exercising on behalf of contemporary artists, especially the younger ones. Fry had been given temporary control of the Grafton Gallery which, he innocently told Rothenstein, 'seemed to me a real acquisition of power'. He planned to stage there a large exhibition by living British artists and, very late in the day, invited Rothenstein to submit – adding by way of inducement: 'John has promised to send.'[25] This invitation, however, was not only delayed but also restricted to Rothenstein's recent Indian work which Will knew in his heart was far from being his best. Worse still, he himself had been pondering upon a similar plan; but while he pondered Fry had gone ahead with his own arrangements without benefit of Rothenstein's collaboration. Many years later (27 July 1920) he admitted to Virginia Woolf that 'I used to be jealous of Prof. Rothenstein, who came along about four years after me and at once got a great reputation, but,' he added triumphantly, 'I wouldn't change places with him now.'[26] From all sorts of people – Desmond MacCarthy, Eric Gill and others – Rothenstein was hearing rumours of Fry's schemes, and he was deeply offended by this neglect. 'I have heard no details of your Grafton schemes at all and was waiting to hear what it is you propose,' he pointed out to Fry (30 March 1911) '... You have been too busy to tell me of a thing which is of some importance.' Fry, however, seems to have been anxious to establish his Grafton Group to a point where Rothenstein, once admitted, could not alter it. 'Do let us, however, get rid of misunderstandings,' Rothenstein pleaded under the threat of being left out altogether (4 April 1911); 'we are both of us working for the same thing and it seems absurd that there should be anything of the kind ... But I don't think you realise how ignorant I am of your intentions and of your powers.'

It was the fact of their 'working for the same thing' that drove them apart. Rothenstein felt that if Bloomsbury was sponsoring the Grafton group, he would be at a disadvantage. He therefore sought, with some success, to discover a point of principle with which to misunderstand Fry's intentions. Since Steer and Tonks had already refused to let their pictures be shown in company with those of younger artists, there seemed a good chance that, by laying down enough barbed wire of high principles, Fry's rival scheme could be halted altogether. The particular point of principle that Rothenstein turned up concerned the selection of the show, which apparently was to be made by Fry alone. In place of such dictatorship, Rothenstein suggested an 'advisory committee of artists', and recommended the sort of people – Augustus, Epstein, Eric Gill, Ambrose McEvoy – who might sit on it. These were all artists friendly to Rothenstein whose work Fry wanted to include. By refusing this suggestion Fry ran the risk of alienating them altogether. In his reply to Rothenstein (13 April 1911) he insisted that it was

inevitable that I should appeal to various artists to trust me with large powers since I have the actual control and responsibility on behalf of the Grafton Galleries. Now you know me well enough to know that I am not unlikely to listen to advice from you and that I should give every consideration to any suggestions which you or John or McEvoy might make and I should be delighted if you would co-operate; at the same time I could hardly go to the other groups of younger artists, who are quite willing to trust me personally, and

say to them that their work must come before such a committee as
you suggest for judgement; nor can I possibly get rid of my responsibilities to the Grafton Galleries.

The tone and language of this letter declare it to be a political
document; but it was not a document of diplomacy. Rothenstein
resented being made, as it were, a mere minister without port-
folio in Fry's new government: he wanted at least a cabinet
post – preferably that one occupied by Clive Bell. Was it not he,
Will Rothenstein, who had first established lines of communication between France and England while Fry was merely potter-
ing through the galleries? And was he now, summarily, to be
ousted? Although, in the past, Fry had written generously in
praise of his work, Rothenstein refused to trust his judgement.[27]
Didn't everyone know how naïve he was, how credulous? It
was impossible to serve under him in only a minor advisory
capacity. Fry, with some intransigence, maintained he was at a
loss to account for Rothenstein's non-co-operation. 'I gather you
are very much annoyed with me,' he wrote to him (13 September 1911), 'but I simply can't disentangle the reason. No
doubt it is all quite clear in your mind, but I haven't a clue.'

Although Rothenstein was out of things after he left for
America in October 1911, his tactics had helped to alter the
nature of Fry's 'Second Post-Impressionist Exhibition' which
eventually included only a small British group among French
and Russian sections. If McEvoy seems to have been a pawn in
the complicated chess game that had developed between these
two painter-impresarios, Augustus had been a knight who found
himself being moved strongly about the board forwards and
sideways on behalf of Rothenstein's team. Great efforts were
made to capture him. As late as the summer of 1912, Fry was
writing to Clive Bell: 'I'm delighted that John wants to show';
but in the event he did not do so, and his absence from the
exhibition was remarked upon by some as being a sign of its
absurdity. His letter of refusal had been sent not to Fry but to
Clive Bell:

Dear Bell,
I received your very enigmatic letter. I am sorry I cannot promise
anything for the 'Second Post-Impressionists'. For one reason I am
away from town, and for another I should hesitate to submit any

work to so ambiguous a tribunal. No doubt my decision will be a relief – to everybody.

Yrs truly, Augustus John.[28]

It was a relief, primarily, to Augustus himself. 'I am conscious that the various confabulators find the question of my inclusion embarrassing,' he had confided to Wyndham Lewis, 'and I would wish to liberate their consciences in the matter if I could find adequately delicate means of doing so.' Once he was clear of the whole bloody show he felt marvellously disencumbered. He had owed some loyalty to Will Rothenstein in the same sense that he was 'consistently loyal' to the New English Art Club – though in spirit he might feel closer to Fry and some of the Camden painters. He was not, however, close to the 'highbrow' critic Clive Bell, who after a long interval of silence was to launch upon his pictures a most bitter and brilliant attack,* evaluating them, with care, as 'almost worthless'. Perhaps this was one of those examples of Clive Bell's journalism that, Fry complained,† 'have done me more harm than all the others'. In any event, Augustus reflected, with Bell as his lieutenant Fry might be

* 'Seriousness' by Clive Bell, *The New Statesman and Nation*, 4 June 1938, pp. 952–3. 'If only Augustus John had been serious what a fine painter he might have been . . . in my opinion "the latest paintings of Augustus John" at Tooth's gallery in Bond Street are almost worthless.

'They are not serious: in the strict sense of the word they are superficial. The painter accepts a commonplace view and renders it with a thoughtless gesture. And even that gesture is not sustained . . . the picture crumbles into nothingness. Nothingness: at least I can find nothing beneath the general effect . . . there is less talent than trick; and there is no thought at all . . . the master has preferred carelessly to dash on the canvas a brushful of colour which at most indicates a fact of no aesthetic importance . . .'

Elsewhere in the article, which refers to John's talent, charm, personal beauty, detestation of humbug and, perhaps optimistically, his sense of decency and magnanimity, and calls him 'a national monument', his work is unfavourably compared to that of Paul Nash, Xavier Roussel and Claire Bertrand.

† Roger Fry to Jean Marchand, 19 December 1921. *The Letters of Roger Fry*, Vol. II, p. 519. 'I do not exactly find him [Clive Bell] spiteful. He hasn't much personal judgement and he's a terrible snob . . . it is not by personal antipathy that he castigates a painter but rather by his over-preoccupation to show himself in the forefront of the trend. And since he is an admirable journalist and expresses himself forcefully he inflicts much distress without exactly meaning to.' Later in this letter, Fry suggests that Bell was not fundamentally a 'serious' art critic – 'he does not make a serious effort to understand it but collects hearsay and remarks from other artists etc.'

pushed anywhere. It seemed to him ironical to insist, as an Allied Artist, that no censor should come between the painter and his public and then, as a 'Post-Impressionist', to sanction Fry's censorship. In fact he admired a number of painters exhibiting among the English group which included Spencer Gore, Henry Lamb, Wyndham Lewis and Stanley Spencer. But the best way he could help such painters was via Quinn; otherwise he could only join them at the expense of Will Rothenstein, the New English and his own independence – and with the uncomfortable feeling of having betrayed a part of his past.

He needed, too, the right background. Fry's habit of herding artists together into groups, societies and clubs, always with the finest motives, did not fit Augustus. Since he could not work within such closely knit units, he began to feel that probably he should not be identified with them. It was as much a matter of instinct as of reason: he was simply out of place. His right place was far away from the metropolitan art world, in North Wales or southern France, not alone, but with his new friend, the painter J. D. Innes.

James Dickson Innes was nine years younger than Augustus.* His parents were 'old-fashioned folk' addressing each other, when they spoke at all, as Mr and Mrs Innes. But from the earliest days 'Dick' Innes was a romantic. 'Born and bred in Wales,' Augustus wrote, 'to which country he felt himself bound by every tie of sentiment and predilection',[29] he had nevertheless practised eating black ants at school in order to establish his French ancestry.[30] In 1905, from the art school at Carmarthen, he won a scholarship to the Slade and by the autumn of 1907, when he first met Augustus, was living in Fitzroy Street.† He presented at this time a remarkable looking spectacle: 'a Quaker hat, coloured silk scarf and long black overcoat set off features of a slightly cadaverous cast with glittering black eyes, wide sardonic mouth, prominent nose, and a large bony forehead invaded by streaks of thin black hair. He carried a Malacca cane with a gold top and spoke with a heavy

* He was born on 27 February 1887, one of three sons.

† At either 8 or 9 Fitzroy Street, to which he had moved from 125 Cheyne Walk in order to be near the Slade.

English accent which now and then betrayed an agreeable Welsh sub-stratum.'[31]

His early paintings reflect his admiration for Wilson Steer. Working *en plein air*, in the suppressed light of evening or dawn, and using luminous colours, he would explore the blurring of detail caused by a wide variety of atmospheric effects. But it was during his first visit to France with John Fothergill* that his short painting life really began. The impact of southern light upon him increased his awareness of colour and intensified his romantic involvement with Nature in a manner very close to Augustus's experiences two years later in Provence. Having fallen ill, apparently with spots encouraged by his failure, over a long period, to wash, he returned alone via Dieppe and was found to be suffering from tuberculosis. It is not easy now to understand the significance of such a diagnosis: probably it meant death. The 'White Scourge', as it was called, was one of the great killers; there were no antibiotics and almost the only recommended treatment was unending rest. Innes was not the person to accept such passive medical advice and he grew increasingly restless. The T.B. had attacked his teeth so that he could not masticate properly: but he could drink, and in the intervals between intense activity, he did so heavily. One other pleasure at least the disease did not quench (as a romantic adventure with a young Algerian carpet weaver was to demonstrate): tuberculosis is said to fortify potency.

Early in 1909 Innes had visited Paris with Matthew Smith, but does not seem to have been particularly interested in the French painters who (some of them posthumously) were about to invade England. Once again illness cut short his visit and he was sent to convalesce at St Ives. But in the spring of the next year he was back in Paris and it was here, in a café,† that he met and fell passionately in love with Euphemia Lamb. Together they made their way, largely on foot, to Collioure, revisiting the places Innes had first seen with Fothergill – Euphemia dancing in the cafés to help pay for them.

* Innes was in South Wales early in 1908. Then, during April and May, he travelled with Fothergill to Caudebec, Boxouls and Collioure where Matisse and Derain had worked in 1905–6.

† At 25 Boulevard du Montparnasse in May 1910.

As with so many British artists, this year, 1910, was crucial for Innes. He had returned to the Slade as a teacher, but finding himself in disagreement with Tonks and Brown, had looked for guidance to John Fothergill. Now, early in 1910, he broke with Fothergill. The reasons for this break, which had serious consequences on Fothergill's short book[32] about Innes, have never been explained. It seems clear that Fothergill's relationship with Innes was to some degree possessively homosexual. A misfit in modern civilization, Fothergill prided himself on his elaborately civilized manners, but seems to have derived most satisfaction from ticking off, and being abused by, the uncivilized. There was almost a self-destructive aspect to this artist, gallery proprietor and classical archaeologist's decision to take up, of all occupations, innkeeping. Such a masochistic vein Innes, with his violent Swiftian imagery, was the perfect man to exploit; and there was soon much for Fothergill to lament:

'[Derwent] Lees tells me strange things about Innes,' he complained to Albert Rutherston, '– in short – [Euphemia] Lamb off – (sounds like 11 o'clock P.M. at a nasty eating house) and also his allowance from mother – gone to Paris, his savings gone also. Knocked a bobby on the head and arrested. He was also wounded in the head in a back street in Chelsea along with John in a fight. What stupidities some people allow themselves to indulge in because they call themselves artists.'

And the company he kept! Bohemians, drunkards, practical jokers, known eccentrics. No wonder his mother had cancelled his allowance – Fothergill knew just how she must be feeling. Even worse goings-on were to follow. One day, for example, when Innes, Horace Cole and Augustus were in a taxi they

bethought themselves of the rite of 'blood brotherhood', and at once put it into practice. They mingled their blood freely enough. Innes drove a knife right through his left hand. One of the others [Augustus] stabbed himself in the leg and was laid up for some time afterwards. Cole made a prudent incision, sufficient to satisfy the needs of the case. The driver was indignant when he saw the state of his cab and its occupants, but the rite had been performed and no lasting damage was done.[33]

Fothergill's place in Innes's life was 'for a season' taken by Albert Rutherston who, in 1909, had suffered some sort of

nervous breakdown. Something, perhaps, of Rutherston's delicate tracery may be detected in his later work, but already the
most important living influence on him was that of Augustus.
According to Charles Hampton, Innes particularly admired the
lyricism of his nude figures. As early as 1909 some John-like
figures – nudes disporting themselves in a sandy pool – have
made their appearance in Innes's imaginative pictures, though
they tend to be much more primitive and awkward.

It is often assumed that Innes influenced Augustus by his
example of flattening landscape in his use of colour so as to
escape the strait-jacket of Nature; while Augustus taught Innes
how to work in figures so that they appeared to grow out of
the landscape. There may be some truth in this, but Augustus
was certainly employing the flat-colour technique and non-
figurative design in 1910 before there is any biographical
evidence to suggest that Innes's work was well known to him;
while, on the whole, the least successful parts of Inne's pictures
are his figures, since in his passionate involvement with Nature,
the landscape itself became, as it were, a woman, and the
human form a tautology.

What is perhaps more interesting is the extraordinarily
similar position each had achieved. As John Rothenstein has
noted,[34] both were obsessed 'by a highly personal conception of
the ideal landscape which also haunted the imaginings of Puvis
de Chavannes'; both, in the Mediterranean light, had rediscovered what they had first known as children in Wales; both
observed and sought, using more primary colours, to reproduce
the poetry of Nature. Yet there were differences. Augustus
searched for a lyrical simplicity that would convey in essence
and by the most direct means, his feelings for the wild and
barren country into which he sowed his fertile mothers-and-
children. Innes was more formal in his methods. His structural
principles of composition were strongly influenced by Japanese
prints, and the foregrounds of his landscapes (often designed
against a naturalistic distance) are, in their bold rhythmical
manner of foreshortening, abstract patterns.

It was in the autumn of 1910 that Innes and Augustus began
to see a lot of each other. Augustus's exhibition at Chenil's in
December 1910 was followed by a one-man show of Innes's

work, and Augustus immediately wrote to Quinn advising him to buy some of them.

'He's a really gifted chap and shows a rare imagination in his landscapes. It is true he has not done much yet, being quite young, but if he can keep it up there can be no doubt about his future. London doesn't do for him and he's off to Wales and later to the south.'[35]

Innes preferred the country but visited London for exhibitions and would sometimes stay on, obeying what he called the 'stern call of dissipation'. He was by now a bearded, unkempt figure, still with his wide black hat, but permanently covered with paint, permanently ill and permanently out-of-doors – he preferred even to sleep in the open. Wandering one night upon the moors of North Wales between Bala and Blaenau Ffestiniog, he had come upon the lonely inn of Rhyd-y-fen and, though destitute and forlorn, had been cared for by its landlord, Washington Davies – a playboy of Northern Wales – who fed him on Welsh mutton and, in the evenings, danced Welsh jigs. It was then that Innes had seen the mountain of Arennig, and made it his own. On and around this rock of porphyry he did his most inspired pictures. 'His passionate love of Wales and the mountains of Wales was the supreme mainspring of his art,' Augustus wrote, 'and though he worked much in the south of France, mostly in the neighbourhood of Mount Cagnion, Mynedd Arennig remained ever his sacred mountain and the slopes of the Migneint his spiritual home.'[36] Upon the summit of this mountain, under the cairn, he was to bury a silver casket containing his letters from Euphemia, whom he always associated with Arennig. He did not paint her poised against its precipitous contours as Augustus might have done; she *was* Arennig and Arennig her. Though emotional storms might sometimes shake and agitate him, here was the magnetic point to which, like the needle of a compass, his heart would always turn.

Compelled, like a lover, to broadcast his feelings, Innes confided to Augustus about Arennig, and the two of them made a plan to meet at Rhyd-y-fen that March. 'Our meeting was cordial,' Augustus remembered, 'but yet I felt on his part a little reserve, as if he felt the scruples of a lover on introducing a friend to the object of his passion.'[37] Behind the inn rose the slopes of Arennig Fach, and beyond the little lake of Tryweryn they could see in the distance the peaks of Moelwyn. It was an ideal place,* and they decided to look for a cottage near by. At last Innes came across one, about three miles from Rhyd-y-fen on the slopes of the Migneint by a brook called Nant Ddu. They furnished it sparsely and moved in when Augustus returned during May. 'I think Innes was never happier than when painting in this district,' Augustus recalled.[38]

But this happiness was not without a morbid side for his passionate devotion to the landscape was also a way of escape from his consciousness of the malady which then was casting its shadow across his days, ignore it as he might appear to do in an effort of sublime but foolish self-deception. This it was that hastened his steps across the moor and lent his brush a greater swiftness and decision as he set down in a single sitting view after jewelled view of the delectable mountains he loved before darkness came to hide everything except a dim but inextinguishable glow, perceived by him as a reflection of some miraculous and eternal City of the West.

Innes's activity was prodigious. Rarely did he return at dusk without at least two panels completed. Though rapidly done, they had often entailed long expeditions over the moors in search of that magical moment of illumination which would suddenly burst upon him through the ever-changing procession of clouds. Like a man condemned, he worked with feverish speed: he simply did not have the time for mistakes. The effect of this upon Augustus was extraordinary. Never before had he met someone whose swiftness and decision exceeded his own. What he had once done at the Slade for others, Innes, acting as a pacemaker, could now do for him.

But there was another way in which Innes helped. 'He was an original, a "naif",' Augustus wrote[39] – and in a letter to Quinn (15 June 1911) he describes him as an 'entirely original chap and that's saying a lot. He is not the sort who learns anything.

* 'This is the most wonderful place I've seen,' Augustus wrote to Dorelia (March 1911). '. . . The air is superb and the mountains wonderful . . . We are now off for a week to see a waterfall that falls 400 feet without a break.' This was possibly the subject of Innes's waterfall picture done the previous autumn and now in the Tate Gallery (3804).

He will die innocent and a virgin intellectually which I think a very charming and rare thing.' Augustus did not copy Innes or seek to learn from him any very painterly secrets. It was Innes's example that inspired him. He had felt recently that his own innocence, the quality which W. B. Yeats had found so remarkable in him, was in jeopardy. Innes encouraged him to reestablish it – so much is evident from his letter to Quinn in which, passing from Innes to himself, he adds: 'I am on my way I think to get back (or forward) to a purely delightful way of decorating which shall in no way compete with the camera or the coal-hole. But one has a lot to unlearn before the instinct or the soul or what you call it can shine out uninstructed.'

It was ironic that their sole disciple should be a copycat of genius, Derwent Lees. He could paint McEvoys, Inneses* or Johns[40] at will and with a fluency that sometimes makes them almost indistinguishable from their originals – though his figures with their great dense areas of cheek and chin do have originality. An Australian, he had come from Melbourne, after a duty stop in Paris, to London, and now taught drawing at the Slade. A strange, fair-complexioned man, rather thin, he somehow – possibly it was the way he dressed – gave the impression of plumpness. But he was chiefly remarkable, in the days when artificial limbs were still unusual, for a fine and exciting false right foot, complete with wooden toes in which, amid much giggling, a Slade girl once got her finger caught.

The paintings which these three did in the four or five years before the war mark a unique phase in British painting which, though it has been generally labelled 'post-impressionist' belongs more properly to the alternative tradition of the symbolist painters.

The war signalled the end of this visionary period of landscape painting. It was during the war that Lees succumbed to an incurable mental disease which terminated his painting career. And it was on 22 August 1914 that Innes died of his tuberculosis. In his first draft of the introduction to an Innes Memorial Exhibition at the Chenil Gallery in 1923 Augustus laments not just the death of so promising a talent but, by

* 'I tire of seeing my own subjects so many times,' Innes once wrote of Lees's pictures.

implication, the fading of his own which, he sometimes suspected, would have been better served by a fate like Innes's.

'In his short lifetime, though handicapped and tortured by the remorseless disease which finally put an end to him, he managed by heroic effort to make a name for himself as one of the foremost figures of his time in the art of landscape painting. He cannot be said to have fulfilled himself completely; he died too young for his powers to have reached their full maturity – and for that matter does not everyone? But by the intensity of his vision and his passionately romantic outlook, his work will live when that of many happier and healthier men will have grown, with the passing years, cold and chill and lifeless.'

6. WHAT NEXT?

'It was cruel to leave Provence,' Augustus had complained to Ottoline on his arrival back in England in September 1910. Only a month before, in France, he had started to feel homesick – but for what home? London suited neither Dorelia, nor himself, nor the children who (especially David) fell far too readily under the sway of Mrs Nettleship. 'Dorelia (my missus) is very keen on a house in the country,' Augustus reminded Quinn (December 1910), 'and we shall have to look out for one soon. She tends to get poor in London.'

He had recommended work on Hugh Lane's decorations – but no longer in Lane's house. Instead he had taken a studio at the Chenil Gallery. 'I think you will find Chenil's quite a good place now,' he reported with some optimism to Will Rothenstein, 'and Knewstub is improving.' Determined to get Lane's pictures done by the spring 'or perish', he several times gave up 'touching a drop of liquor' and admitted feeling 'exceedingly good'.

Having Chenil's as his office brought some alleviation to their Church Street problems, but it fell far short of solving them. All the old difficulties crowded in and it seemed possible once more that they could not continue living together very long. 'Do you want a ring,' Augustus suddenly asked Dorelia: but answer came there none. Like some General, he had moved up his squadron of caravans to Battersea 'so that we may turn into the van any hour'. As soon as the winter was done with they could trek all over England: the possibilities were endless.

These next twelve months were feverish. Augustus spent more and more time at his office and it was there, rather than at home in Church Street, he would entertain his friends. Some days he would leave for Chenil's in the morning – a distance of at least five hundred yards – and not return that night at all. Next day Dorelia would receive a note from Essex, Berkshire or Brittany: 'The country is so beautiful – you wouldn't believe – I suddenly quitted London.' In October he had gone to France; in November he took off to see Eric Gill at Ditchling, discussing there the question of a New Religion and a co-operative scheme (which came to nothing) for taking a house from which their work could be sold independently of the dealers. In December he hurried off twice to Charlie McEvoy's 'pig-stye' at Wantage: 'Mrs McEvoy frequently wishes you were here,' he wrote to Dorelia – adding hastily: 'So do I.'

A family Christmas at Church Street being obviously unsupportable, he once more set off for the Chenil and arrived this time in Paris. 'I have been so embêté lately and have taken refuge in Paris and have neglected all my pleasures,' he explained to Ottoline (27 December 1910). '... I found London quite deadly and think of going south again till England becomes more habitable. I hear Lamb has been doing your portrait* – le salaud!' He dined with Royall Tyler off stuffed pigs' trotters and met his new wife – 'a horror'; saw Epstein and Nevinson, and squared up to Boris Anrep;† searched in vain for

* 'My immense picture of Ottoline is to begin: so my respiration may be audible in Dorset,' Henry Lamb to Lytton Strachey, 10 April 1910.

† Boris Anrep recorded this first encounter with Augustus (in a letter to Henry Lamb) thus: 'If you could creep in my heart and memory which you honoured by some particulars of your relation to John's – you would feel sike and poisoned by the byle which turns round in me when I first saw John. That was a night-mare, with all appreciation of his powerful and mighty dreadedness, and some ghotic beaty, I could not keep down my heat to some beastly and cruel and vulgar look of brightness which I perceived in his face and demeanour . . .' Augustus relished Anrep's personality and admired his work. In 1913 he persuaded Knewstub to arrange an exhibition of Anrep's drawings at the Chenil Gallery, and in later years put him in the way of several commissions, from Lady Tredegar and others, for his mosaics. Once, in 1928, he suddenly telephoned Anrep in a highly emotional state to say: 'Boris, you are a great artist.

Gwen; attempted to teach Lobelia to ride a bicycle; was chased
by an Austrian tiger woman from whom he eventually escaped
through a smoke-screen of Horace Cole's practical jokes (including, apparently, a mock-operation for appendicitis), and in
all devastating innocence concluded: 'Paris is certainly preferable to Chelsea. I think I'd like to live here.'[41] It was as if the
past had never been.

For most of this time he stayed at 40 Rue Pascal with Fabian
de Castro, the Spanish guitarist who, with the cunning of the
devil, had outwitted his gaolers in Madrid and was now writing
his autobiography. 'He has wandered all over Europe,' Augustus
warned Quinn, 'and even across the Caucasus *on foot* and
speaking only Spanish – and has done everything except kill a
man.'

It was almost in parody of himself that, having determined
to go south to Marseilles with a Miss George* who, he consoled
Dorelia, 'might be useful, posing', Augustus straightaway returned to London leading, like small deer behind him, a troupe
of his cronies right up to the front door of Church Street. What
with the cook's two children to reinforce Augustus's six, and
the intermittent appearances of Helen Maitland and Edie
McNeill to reinforce that of Fabian de Castro and other friends,
the place was crowded as for war. One packed night during the
first week of January 1911, fire broke out in the house, and
Augustus, wakened by screams, 'leapt out of the room half-
crazy and found our servant on top of the stairs burning like a

---

want you to know that I think so' – and then rang off. This must have been at
the time he was writing 'Five Modern Artists' for *Vogue* (3 October 1928), in
which he said of Anrep: 'In those works with which he has adorned our public
buildings he has performed a permanent and most signal service to the life of
our time. Alone among living artists he has practically restored a lost art, and
revived the traditions of the golden age of Christian art in this particular
medium. Affected both by the early Byzantine traditions still surviving in
Russia, together with the magnificent examples to be seen in Sta. Maria
Maggiore in Rome, and those of Ravenna and Palermo, he has succeeded in
expressing modern conditions in terms which have too long been considered
obsolete.'

* Possibly Teresa George who, he tells us in *Chiaroscuro* (p. 17), called on
him in London and told him that his father was seeking her hand in marriage.
'He and I had something in common after all, then!' Augustus concluded.

torch. I happened to have been sleeping in a dressing-gown by
some happy chance and managed to extinguish the poor girl
with this. But it was a terrible moment . . . fortunately her face,
which is a good face, was untouched. She was burnt about the
arms, legs and stomach . . . She had come up the stairs from
the dining-room, blazing – the smell nearly made me faint afterwards. It was the hottest embrace I've ever had of a woman.'[42]
They summoned a 'smart little doctor' to do the repairs both
to the girl and to Augustus himself, whose left hand and leg
and more pertinent areas had got severely toasted without, he
was anxious to demonstrate, putting him 'out of action in the
slightest degree'.[43] He was, however, ordered to stay in bed. 'This
will mean keeping quiet for a few days,' he told Quinn (5
January 1911), 'after which I want to take one of my vans on
the road for a week or so and then get back to work with full
steam up.'

It was less these conflagrations than the convalescences that
were, for Dorelia, most arduous; not the rows but the periods
of 'keeping quiet'. She, who could enjoy-and-endure so much of
the heroic found herself strangely vulnerable to the trivial. A
small thing it was that finally cracked her cheerful detachment:
spitting. By all accounts Fabian de Castro was a splendid
guitarist, but he *would spit in the bath*. This accomplishment
infuriated Dorelia beyond reason. She lay awake thinking about
it, and finally she put up a notice: PLEASE DO NOT SPIT IN
THE BATHROOM. And when he took no notice of it, she left.

She left for Paris, and she left with Lamb. It was a casual
business. 'Dorelia is in Paris for a few days and I in London,'
Augustus remarked in the course of a letter to Michel Salaman
about the more pressing matter of ponies. But it was not casual
for Lamb. 'I stayed more than a week,' he wrote to Lytton
Strachey (1 February 1911): 'seeing for the first time the city in
all its glamour of history, art and romance. But I should explain
Dorelia was there and that I came back with her in a motor car
belonging to an American millionairess [Mrs Chadbourne]. Now
I am completely rejuvenated and working with tenfold industry.' Invariably Dorelia would have this inspiriting effect on
him, but she caused him much pain that, though he bore it
uncomplainingly, may itself have contributed to the pain he

inflicted on those who fell in love with him, and eventually on Dorelia herself. On the evening of their return, after they had parted, Lamb wrote to Ottoline:

I arrived about 6 this evening having travelled since very early on Sunday with Dorelia, Pyramus and Mrs Chad, in her motor. The excitements of Paris came in an unusually trebled dose, and the final shaking of the journey have reduced me too low ... I have lived too giddily these last days to give them the thought they must have. It is an odd and desolate sensation to spend the evening alone. I must turn into bed immediately in the hope of a braver morning moral.

By the time Dorelia arrived back in Church Street, 'full steam' was up. Augustus and his friends had journeyed into Essex for a gypsy evening during which Lobelia executed a fantastic belly dance, writing her name and address on the shirt fronts of those she took to as she whirled past them; and Augustus got 'mad drunk' after another spell of total abstinence; and Fabian de Castro lost himself. Then, on their return, Horace Cole charged his motor car into a cart-load of people injuring many, one severely. Innes, too, had 'been doing la Bombe lately by all appearances', Augustus advised Dorelia; and McEvoy, in her absence, had sprouted 'a moustache like an old blacking brush'. And now there was the Gauguin Ball in London; and after that Lady Gregory had invited him back to Coole. But first, he decided (10 February 1911), 'I want to go south again and work in the open'. This was his way of announcing the expedition to meet Innes in North Wales. After he returned, Dorelia again left, joining Lamb at the Dog Inn at Peppard and then in London. 'Dorelia did come the last day at Peppard,' Lamb wrote to Strachey (11 May 1911); 'we walked through divine woods and lunched in an exquisite pub with the politest of yokels and I ... got of course quite drunk. Then I had another evening with her all alone at Bedford Square. It was more than the expected comble.'

In a letter to Ottoline, Lamb had once suggested (10 May 1910) establishing 'a discreet form of colony'. With an amoeba-like drawing he outlined a community of Johns, Maitlands, Morrells and himself, adding: 'I could double myself no doubt

and general reunions could be arranged at suitable intervals.' It
was a fantasy that had nearly been translated into fact. Like a
rock-pool by the sea, the colony was sometimes teeming, sometimes almost empty. Innes and Lobelia and Epstein; Alick
Schepeler and Wyndham Lewis and Mrs Strindberg – all these,
and others – countless others – would float in and be carried out
from time to time, causing a little ripple. But for Lamb there
was no one so important as Dorelia. In his letters he does not
gossip about her, but writes in a tone – rueful, tender, oblique –
he reserves for no one else. He saw and heard too little of her;
but he felt hopelessly in her debt.

When Augustus returned to North Wales in May he took
Dorelia with him. But the journey was not a success and she
came back alone. 'We are getting restless about moving,' Augustus had confided to Quinn (10 February 1911). For Dorelia this
had by now become a matter of urgency. Cut off from the
country she seemed to lose strength. Their sardine-life together
held no nourishment for her. There was no sun in London, no
air, no time, no involvement with real things that made sense
by multiplying and returning the energy you put into them.
The very atmosphere was clogged with 'important' matters that
people confused with reality. She had to get away.

They had written to a number of friends asking them to look
out for a house in the country, but so far their investigations
had been worse than unsuccessful. Pursuing a house in the west
with Charlie Slade, Augustus tripped, fell, damaged his leg and
returned home a convalescent again. 'Please get me a house,
John,' he had desperately cried from bed to his friends the
Everetts. In reply he received a list of questions with intervening
spaces, which he loyally filled in and sent back. Shortly afterwards, Katherine Everett came upon Alderney Manor, a
strangely fortified bungalow larger than most houses, that had
been built by an eccentric Frenchman. It was set in sixty acres
of woodland near the Ringwood Road outside Parkstone in
Dorset, included a walled garden, cottage and stables – all for an
incredible rent of fifty pounds a year. Lady Wimborne, the
landlord, a keen Liberal and Evangelical leader, insisted in conversation with Katherine Everett that 'we should be pleased to
have a clever artist for a tenant'.[44] Dorelia was so desperate to

leave London she was ready, it seemed, to take the house sight
unseen, but Augustus, in the guise of a practical man, advised:
'The house is no doubt lovely in itself, but it must be seen – so
much depends on the placing of it.' They therefore went down
to spend a few days with the Everetts, who lived some three
miles from Alderney.

'I can still visualize the group coming up our pine-shaded,
sun-dappled drive,' Katherine Everett wrote. 'Mrs John, who was
leading a grey donkey with a small boy astride it dressed in
brilliant blue and another equally vivid small boy at her side,
wore a tight-fitting, hand-sewn, canary-coloured bodice above
a dark, gathered, flowing skirt, and her hair very black and
gleaming, emphasized the long silver earrings which were her
only adornment.'[45]

Augustus and Dorelia took to Alderney Manor at once. 'It's a
good find,' Augustus informed Quinn, 'any amount of land with
pine woods goes to it, and inexpensive.'[46] Some repairs and
alterations were needed and, while these were being arranged,
the Johns camped in the Everetts' grounds, amusing themselves
by decorating the small empty gardener's cottage where they
ate, painting the walls black and the furniture scarlet.

'One afternoon,' Katherine Everett remembered, 'the children
decided to get the red and black paint off their persons, so they
all undressed and, with turpentine soap and scrubbing brushes,
set to work to clean themselves up. It was while they were so
occupied that Lady Wimborne paid her first call.'[47]

For a moment Alderney seemed to tremble in the balance, but
Lady Wimborne, her liberal principles fully extended, sailed
past this test and everything was quickly settled. Over these
summer months, Dorelia spent much of her time preparing for
their move to the house. 'D. has gone to live for ever near
Poole,' Lamb wrote in despair to Lytton Strachey. But already,
in the second week of July, he had joined her there for what
he called 'a supreme time'. In a letter to Strachey (24 July
1911) he described what was to become for him a second
home.

'She [Dorelia] lives in an amazing place – a vast secluded park
of prairies, pine woods, birch woods, dells and moors with a
house, cottages and a circular walled-garden. And, pensez, all

these you could have possessed for £50 a year – *we* could have possessed them!! It was very hot when I was there and lovely naked boys running about the woods. John was away. In the course of some almost endless conversations with D. I thought her as superior as ever, but in danger of becoming overgrown in such isolation.'

On leaving Alderney, Lamb crossed over to France, a sudden enterprise inciting him to carry off with him Dorelia's sister 'poor picturesque Ede' – a scheme he almost instantly regretted.

While Lamb lingered at Alderney, Augustus had been in Liverpool finishing his portrait of Kuno Meyer. 'Funny things continue to happen,' he told Ottoline (14 July 1911). Charles Reilly, the architect, was roused from sleep by the figure of Augustus, in flight once more from the 'Walking hell-bitch of the Western World',[48] climbing through his bedroom window; Granville-Barker was surprised at finding himself cross-examined over dinner on the subject of 'a horse and trap'; Innes was infuriated on being joined at Nant Ddu by Albert Lipczinski and his beautiful Doonie, sent expressly from Liverpool – 'they are incredibly poor', Augustus explained; the Sampsons and Dowdalls were visited, and Susan their maid. And all Liverpool was praised and blamed: 'The Mersey is a grand thing. The ordinary Li-pool population is awful – hopeless barbarism.'[49]

Though nothing appeared to have altered, Alderney marked the positive beginning of a very different pattern in Augustus and Dorelia's lives. They moved in during August, though Augustus still kept on his studio at the Chenil Gallery. 'We have left Church Street for this place which does well for the kids,' he announced to Quinn (16 August 1911). '. . . My studio here is still unfinished and this has lost me a lot of work. My missus is well and gay but I very much fear she is in for something rather unnecessary.'

They had, it seemed, solved their problems by altering the geography of their lives together. A new phase in Augustus's career was about to start. Though composed of the same parts as before, it would increasingly re-arrange the kaleidoscope of his life; and, as with all change, he responded optimistically to the prospect.

But to Henry Lamb the future seemed black: 'One of the chief temptations,' he confessed, '[is] to succumb to the general pressure of the news that Dorelia is enceinte again, which means she may die at any minute.'[50]

PART TWO

The Years of Experience

7

Before the Deluge

I saw in Augustus and Dorelia two of that rare sort of
people, suggestive of ancient or primitive times, whose
point lay rather in what they were than in what they said
or did. I felt that they would have been more at home
drinking wine under an olive tree or sitting in a smoky
mountain cave than planted in this tepid English scene.
But at least they were bohemians and kept up with style
and lavish hospitality the old tradition of artistic life that
had come down from William Morris and Rossetti. This I
thought was important...'

GERALD BRENAN. *A Life of One's Own*

I. A SUMMER OF POETRY

That summer of 1911 was oppressively hot. The heathlands of
the Wimborne Estate were turning brown, and from time to
time fires would break out sending columns of smoke far up
into the blue skies.

The carts and wagons, with their wildly singing children,
rattled past in the sun. Then, swerving off the narrow road, they
entered a drive lined, like a green tunnel, with rhododendrons
tall as trees. They turned left; and there, before them, lay a
curious low pink building, an elongated bungalow with Gothick
windows and a fantastic castellated parapet: Alderney Manor.

It looked, at first sight, like a cardboard castle from some
Hans Andersen story – a fragile fortress, strangely misplaced,
which an army of toy soldiers might suddenly emerge from, a
puff of wind knock flat. The smooth stucco surface, once a
proud red, had faded leaving patches here and there of the
cardboard colour. With its single row of windows pointing
loftily nowhere, the house seemed to be smiling, full of teeth, as
if embarrassed by its own absurdity. 'But its poetry even outdid
its absurdity ... There was something fantastic and stunning
about it.'[1]

Alderney was to be the Johns' home for sixteen years. Like Fryern Court, into which they moved afterwards, it became Dorelia's creation and the most eloquent expression of her personality. The rich colours – yellows,, browns and mauves – the arrangements of flowers everywhere lighting up the rooms, the delicious meals – huge soups, stews and casseroles with rough red wine, and Provençal salads with plenty of garlic, tomatoes and olive oil – the wood fires filling the air with their fragrance, contributed to a pagan love of the beautiful. They were not tidy places, these houses. A happy disorder embellished the scene – Lord David Cecil remembers leaving his hat on the floor one evening, and returning six weeks later to find it undisturbed. Nor was the régime formal : guests were seldom introduced to one another and might be confronted on arrival by an animal silence from the whole John pack. Sometimes, having accepted a pressing invitation, visitors would turn up to find no one in the house at all, though all doors and windows lay open as if everyone had just vanished through them. When the Spencer brothers, Gilbert and Stanley, came to stay

we found the children frightening. At bed time everyone seemed to fade away but no one attempted to 'show us to our bedrooms' until we decided that you slept as you fell but took the precaution of falling on odd pieces of furniture which made things easier ... Requiring a lavatory I decided to seek one unaided. Having no luck I opened the front door very quietly and crept out into the darkness. Dorelia went into another room and noticing a bowl of dead flowers, opened a window and flung them out smack into my lap.[2]

Yet the atmosphere had a magic quality that cast its spell on almost everybody. 'The life, the atmosphere, the freedom, the presiding figures were all unique and irresistible,' wrote Romilly John : 'it was like a royal household in the heroic age, at once grand and simple'.[3] For many it became a place to run away to, a place where someone, calling for tea, might stay a week, a month, even a year. These guests perpetually filled Alderney, overflowing into the blue and yellow caravans and the 'cottage' – a mellow red-brick building, actually larger than the 'Manor', standing invisible a hundred yards off behind a range of rhododendrons. 'This intervening vegetation made comings and

goings difficult on wintry nights,' Romilly recalled: 'those unfamiliar with the route would bid a cheerful good night to the
house-dwellers, launch out into the dark, and presently find
themselves struggling amid a wilderness of snaky boughs.'

At one end of Alderney was the dining-room with its long
oak table and, on one side behind the benches, a row of
windows through which, at mealtimes, the horses would poke
their heads, and doze. At the other end, looking on to beech
trees, towards the orchard and the walk to the sand-pit, was
the kitchen. In between lay the bedrooms, and below the
capacious cellars.

The kitchen, noisy with helpers, full of the savour of bubbling stock, crusty bread baking in the oven, was ruled over by
Dorelia's sister Edie. Small, with very dark hair, a mixture of
black and brown; large brooding eyes, their upper lids curiously
straight giving them a strange rectangular shape; a mouth rather
prominent, curving downwards: Edie's expression was sardonic
yet vulnerable – an index of her life to come. Into her care were
given the youngest children and much of the cooking.

By helping to run things inside the house, Edie enabled
Dorelia to devote herself more to the gardens. Under her
management, Alderney became an almost self-supporting community, flowing with milk and honey. Her first venture was,
appropriately, an Alderney cow which gave them colossal
quantities of cream so rich it had the taste of caramel. This cow
was soon followed by 'a large black beast called Gipsy, an
adept in the art of opening gates and leading off the increasing
herd to unimagined spots in the remote distance,'⁴ to which a
team of children would be sent off to shepherd them home. The
children were also trained to help Dorelia milk the herd, to
skim the milk, and – an eternal task – make the butter with a
hand-operated churn.

To the cows, at one time or another, were added, less successfully, a dovecote of pigeons (which all flew away); and, briefly,
a 'biteful' monkey; then an entire breeding herd of pedigree
saddle-back pigs; various donkeys, New Forest ponies and cart-
horses, all with names; miscellaneous groups of dogs and,
among the teacups, endless cats – Siamese, white, tabby and
black – which bore unheard-of relationships to one another.

Finally came twelve hives of dangerous bees that stung every-one abominably.

People who were staying at Alderney would come and watch the operations from a distance, whereupon a detachment of bees made a bee-line for them, alighting on their noses and cheeks and in their hair, which would cause them to rush round and round the field beating their heads like madmen. The next day everybody would present an extraordinary and uncharacteristic appearance. People who had usually long solemn faces would appear with perfectly round ones, and a perpetual clownish smile. Eyes would vanish altogether, and once or twice the victims retired to bed with swollen tongues, convinced ... they would be choked to death ... At last we resorted to a couple of old tennis racquets ... Anybody at a little distance might have imagined that we were playing some very intricate kind of tennis, with special rules and invisible balls.[5]

In all things Dorelia seemed to rely on instinct rather than planning. She invented as she went along, and although there were occasional disasters, she seemed to have an innate gift for knowing what was right. 'With an air of complete ease and leisure, without hurrying or raising her voice, her long Pre-Raphaelite robes trailing behind her as she moved, she ran this lively house, cooked for this large family and their visitors, yet always appeared to have time on her hands,' wrote Gerald Brenan. '... I remember her best as she sat at the head of the long dining-table, resting her large, expressive eyes with their clear whites on the children and visitors and bringing an order and beauty into the scene.'[6] She seemed perfectly at one with her surroundings, and from them to derive a natural co-ordination, the faculty for effortless action compared with which others appeared bustling and vociferous. Nature and human nature, garden and house were perfectly combined. The windows at Alderney stood open, and into the house flowed the produce of Dorelia's 'home farm' – piles of fresh vegetables from the kitchen gardens; blue and brown jugs of milk and cream; jars of home-made mead tasting like a light white wine; the honey and the butter; lavender in the coarse linen – and everywhere a profusion of flowers.

Flowers she loved. Almost every kind of tree and shrub flourished at Alderney with an abnormal vigour: ilex and pine, apple and cherry and chestnut, pink and white clematis, old-fashioned roses. The circular walled-in garden with its crescent-shaped flower-beds over which simmered the bees and butter-flies became an enchanted place. 'The peculiar charm of that garden was its half-wild appearance,' wrote Romilly John :

> The grass was seldom as closely shaven as orthodoxy demands, and great masses of lavender and other smelling plants sprawled outwards from the concentric beds, until in some places the pathways were almost concealed. Tangled masses of roses and clematis heaved up into the air, or hung droopingly from the wall. The pond in the middle became hidden by the high screen of flowering vegetation ... In summer the composite smell of innumerable flowers hung upon the still air. The wall was overtopped most of the way by a thick hedge formed by the laurels that grew outside, and a eucalyptus, which had escaped the frosts of several winters, lifted high into the air its graceful and silvery spire.[7]

Dorelia's influence extended far beyond the walls of this garden, affecting many she never met. For three decades her taste in clothes became the fashion among art-students. She ignored the genteel manners and sophisticated fashions of London and Paris, and the brash styles that succeeded them. Her style was peculiar to herself and no one could carry it off with such hypnotic dignity.* She was a skilled dressmaker. From cotton velveteen or shantung in bright dyes and shimmering surfaces; from unusual prints, often Indian or Mediterranean in origin, she evolved clothes that followed the movement of the body, timelessly, like classic draperies. Her long flowing dresses that reached the ground, with their high waistline and long sleeves topped by a broad-brimmed straw hat, its sweeping line

---

* 'To have known Dorelia was the most important experience of my whole life,' Kathleen Hale wrote to the author. 'She was the most beautiful woman I have ever seen . . . I remember one Christmas at Alderney, when all the decorations were fixed and everything set for the fun and sing-song, the last to arrive was Dorelia. She appeared on the top step of the room in a white woollen gown, her dark hair looped and braided as always, but so different to the arty hair-do's of the artistic set. Her warm brown skin glowed in the whiteness of her softly gathered white bodice. Translucent green earrings dangled from her ears – they may have been only of glass but no emerald could have been more beautiful. They were the only colour she wore. She stood quietly surveying us, unaware of the impact she made.'

like those of the French peasants, became a uniform adopted by nearly all the girls at art colleges, and a symbol, in their metropolitan surroundings, of an unsevered connection with country things.

For the boys she also invented a costume which, with its long-belted smock over corduroy trousers, together with their bobbed hair, gave them the appearance of fierce dolls. 'Our hair was long and golden,' Romilly remembered, 'with a fringe in front that came down to our eyebrows; we had little pink pinafores reaching to just below the waist, and leaving our necks bare; brown corduroy knickers, red socks and black boots completed the effect.'[8] Later on, Dorelia dressed her daughters in buff-coloured woollen dresses, rather draughty, with thin criss-cross lines, saffron-yellow ankle socks and square-toed black slippers. Their hair, also bobbed, was shoulder-length, and their frocks, which they learnt to manipulate with dexterity when climbing off floors or clambering into chairs, reached almost down to their feet. It was as if Augustus's pictures had come alive and were walking about. Here, in a coach-house converted to a studio, he painted 'Washing Day',[9] 'The Blue Pool',[10] numerous drawings and panels of the children alone or in groups, portraits of the many visitors from Francis Macnamara[11] to Roy Campbell,[12] and studies for the figures in his large decorative groups 'Forza e Amore',[13] 'The Mumpers'[14] and 'Lyric Fantasy'.[15]

At Alderney, Augustus kept himself in the background. His presence, like that of a volcano, was often silent, sometimes threatening, always impressive. A quiet, swiftly-moving, dark-bearded figure, with a wide-brimmed hat, tweeds and a pipe, he patrolled Alderney, watching everyone with intentness, disconcerting them with his stare, his sudden eruptions. No longer was he the wild youth 'Gus John'; he had flowered into the full magnificence of 'Augustus John', soon to be truncated to the moody, monosyllabic 'John'. On many mornings he was morose, merely issuing a rumbling summons 'Come and sit!' He would collect some guest, or two or three children, take them off and by lunch produce a panel of one of the boys with a bow-and-arrow, or Dorelia leaning against a fir tree, or a series of drawings.

As the day wore on his mood lightened. Often he would suggest taking out the pony trap and driving through the country lanes to the White Hart or King's Arms, small favourite pubs with sawdust on the floors and the reek of shag and cool ale, where he would play shove-ha'penny and drink beer. But it was in the evening, seated at the head of the refectory table, that he came into his own. Within the arena of this hospitality, his melancholy would thaw, allowing his natural good humour to come out. Sometimes he would permit the children to stay up on these gorgeous occasions so as to wait at table. 'The table seemed to groan under the weight of innumerable dishes,' Romilly remembered, 'and to be lighted by a hundred glittering candles in their shining candlesticks of brass. Dorelia and John appeared, for the first time in the day, in their true characters and proportions; they were like Jove and Juno presiding over the Olympian feast.'[16] Sometimes, too, there were terrific parties with bonfires and dancing, and John, rolling his lustrous eyes like marbles, a wild enigmatic smile on his face, would sing songs between long puffs of pipe-smoke.

> In Jurytown I was bred and bornn
> In Newgate gaol I'll die in scornn

He threw himself into these highwayman's songs with intense concentration; but it was a strange thing, one of his listeners noticed: 'as he sang his body seemed to grow small. It was as if it all went into his voice. He dwindled.'[17]

> At seventeen I took a wife
> I loved her as I loved my life.

It was often a point of honour that these parties continue till early morning, and so many people came that huge wigwams had to be constructed from branches and brown blankets, like the tents in *Prince Igor*, to accommodate everyone in the garden. On hot nights they would make up a communal bed in the orchard, nine-wide and full of bracken that crackled when anyone moved. Then, first thing in the morning, John would arrive and, while the others were still lying where they had fallen, lead off some girl or child.

The children played a natural part in this community. They

were always out-of-doors, immersed in their secret games in the dark undergrowth. They would shin up the trees in bare feet, run with a pack of red setters, wander into Dorelia's enchanted garden, plunge into the frog-laden pond and, to the distress of the parson, dash naked about the place getting dry. Sometimes they played hide-and-seek on the horses, or harnessed a tin bath to one of the pigs which towed them across the grass. One favourite place was the brick-yard over the road with its great clay-pit and little trolleys pulled along miniature railway lines; and another, a large sand-pit enclosed by pine trees. The many-shaded sand-cliffs could be tunnelled into and carved out in paths and bear-holes. At the top where the sand joined silver-grey and black earth, the smell of heath and dank sand seemed to give the aroma of heaven. They would set up shop here with different coloured sands, an absorbing game: then the lunch bell, erected at the top of a high post at the back of the house, echoed across the fields, and they would pelt back through the orchard, naked or otherwise, and greedily line themselves along the refectory table. On windless days this bell could be heard all over the estate, alerting whole troops of poachers and stealers of wood, who had to be chased off between courses.

After lunch, they were off again, fighting a fire on the heath or, more mysteriously, entering their private world of rites and humours, games of their own invention such as 'Bottom First' inaccessible to the untrained mind, and cults that embraced strange moaning choruses, 'Give us our seaweed!', accompanied by side-splitting yells of laughter.

They were not pampered, these children, but increasingly as time went on put to work sawing logs, digging, grooming the horses, collecting hens' eggs, tarring fences, minding the farm, doing all the chores of the house and, from time to time, answering the patriarchal summons to sit. It was a hard, unorthodox upbringing, permissive yet oppressive. But this first summer, while the house was still empty and they slept in tents and every day the sun shone, Alderney seemed idyllic.

2. THE SECOND MRS STRINDBERG

Dorelia made Alderney a harbour. John kept on his studio at the Chenil Gallery and would stay there for much of the week; then, at week-ends, or in moments of sudden revulsion from town life, he appeared at Alderney to continue his work inside the converted coach-house. It suited him in many ways, this dual existence, giving a constructive pattern to his restlessness, a momentum supporting his work : and it enabled Dorelia to look after him without obviously appearing to do so. She was an anchor, discreetly out of sight.

'He behaves very well,' she admitted to Charles Tennyson, ' – *if I keep my eye on him.*' The eye she kept on him was at first pretty fierce. Over the early years at Alderney a pattern of existence developed between them that became roughly acceptable to both. He carried on two lives; and so, eventually, did she. In London he enjoyed affairs with models, art-students, actresses, dancers – anyone new. These amatory exercises seemed almost obligatory. 'The dirty little girl I meet in the lane,' he declared, 'has a secret for me – communicable in no language, estimable at no price, momentous beyond knowledge, though it concern but her and me.'[18] It was of some concern to Dorelia, nevertheless, when these girls appeared down at Alderney. For she would surrender to nothing easily, knowing that were she to do so John, like a child, would seek to push things further. It was a struggle to test who, finally, controlled whom. 'I want to live with you when I come down,' John wrote from London, 'but I don't like imposing myself on you.' From Dorelia's point of view this seemed a promising start. Her most useful card was Henry Lamb. Whenever Lamb wanted to see her, she would ask John, almost formally, whether he minded. Surprised, he would disclaim any objection to 'the poor agneau' coming to Alderney – provided, of course, Dorelia didn't mind. But when he inflicted his girls on her, or inconsiderately hared off in pursuit of them, he would find at moments particularly inconvenient to himself Lamb happily installed there again. He hadn't imagined Lamb's company was so 'indispensable', he sarcastically remarked.

The guidelines Dorelia laid down were swept aside whenever

John was suddenly taken over by some infatuation. Many of these romances were short;* others, drifting into the shallower waters of affection, lasted years. 'You may be sure I want you a great deal more than any other damsels,' he once wrote to Dorelia: but he wanted them as well. In all his painting, whether landscapes or portraits, he depended upon some instinctive relationship to develop that would take hold of him and guide his brush. In the case of women, this miracle was almost impossible to achieve if his concentration was constantly fretted by unsatisfied physical desire. Under such unnatural conditions, his shyness stood like an intolerable barrier between him and his sitter. It was to this argument, which it is perhaps over-easy to caricature, that Dorelia listened with most attention. No worthwhile man, she once told Amaryllis Fleming, was easy. By such a definition John was extremely worthwhile. There were those who wondered how, stoical and acceptant of life as she was, Dorelia could put up with as much as she did. She did not do so without a struggle. In their long tug-of-war, the rope between them almost snapped. Although John felt more for Dorelia than for anyone, this did not stop him, when the evil was upon him, from purging his guilt by wounding her. She endured this not for love but from belief. She believed he was a great artist whose vocation demanded that he throw himself into every form of life. She scorned people's conventional indignation, often expressed on her behalf, about his 'goings-on'. But if he were not to prove a great artist, she once told Helen Anrep, then her life had been wasted. Her strength –

---

* The painter Jean Varda remembers a characteristic affair with the extravagant dancer Lady Constance Stewart-Richardson – reputedly 'the worst dancer in the world but one of the most remarkable athletes', as described by Aldous Huxley, 'whose strength is as the strength of ten'. Their liaison began in 1914 and 'for being unrequited lasted longer than his [John's] periodic infatuations. At Lady Constance's studio (in her performance of the sword dance) he took a violent dislike to me and in fits of prodigious eloquence cursed me with a wealth of abuse and vituperation, the like of which I never encountered in my life . . . It was a great treat to hear these gorgeous syllables delivered with the grandiose emphasis of a Mounet Sully of the Comédie Française.' Varda at that time was Lady Constance's perspiring partner in the dance. A few years later a calm seems to have descended and at Evan Morgan's birthday party in July 1917 Aldous Huxley records: 'in one corner of the room Lady Constance supported John on her bosom'. She was, he adds, 'profoundly exhausting company'.

or at least her calm – was fed by another world into which she would often disappear. For like him she led a second life – not among people or in London, but lost in her garden with her flowers and growing things.

She saw her job as lifting some of the responsibilities, irrelevant to painting, from his shoulders. She would untie the cords and give him back his freedom. When he had illegitimate children she did not leave him, but sometimes helped to look after them. He could go where he wanted, do what he wanted, return when he wanted. If he needed clothes or tobacco, she got them. But everything ultimately depended upon him.

It seemed, at times, as if Dorelia had entered the plant world more completely than the world of human beings, as if flowers meant more to her than people: perhaps, eventually, they did. There were interruptions in her calm – violent, terrifying fights with John: but over such issues as (to take an actual example) whether or not, on some half-forgotten occasion, Caspar had had toothache. She examined small things under a microscope; but the large events of life she appeared to look at, as it were, through the wrong end of a pair of binoculars so that they never overwhelmed her, never came too close. This protective philosophy is well caught by a conversation she had in about 1939 with Richard Hughes. One afternoon, when the two of them were walking in the garden with a boy of about four believed to be John's youngest illegitimate son, Dorelia suddenly came out with: 'There's one thing about John I've never got used to, not after all these years.' Richard Hughes glanced apprehensively at the child, but she continued: 'I don't know what to do about it. Time after time, *he's late for lunch.*'

The girls John brought down to Alderney were accepted with suspicion by Dorelia and were not helped much by John himself. She tolerated them, half-ignored them, almost as if they knew a different John, while, in the words of Iris Tree, 'she guarded his higher ghost'. Some she positively frightened, being known by them as 'the yellow peril'; others, through exceptional qualities, she came to accept as allies.

But there were limits. Her censure usually fell hardest on the girls themselves rather than on John, for it was not justice that interested her but practicality. A friend who lived near by remembers one incident that shows her shorthand methods of dealing with anything unacceptable:

One afternoon I had gone up to Alderney Manor to learn from Dorelia how to 'turn a heel', so I would be able to knit socks for my two boys. We were having tea when a vehicle came to the front door. Dorelia went to see who it was, some luggage was dumped in the passage, a girl was brought in, introduced, and politely asked to have some tea. The conversation dragged, neither Dorelia nor I were any good at 'chatting'. Soon I got up to go, but Dorelia asked me to stay on ... Dorelia then turned to the girl. 'What train are you catching?' she said. The girl looked surprised. 'There is a good train to Waterloo you can get if you go now, the next one is much later. I will see that you are driven to the station.' Before Dorelia had reached the door, the girl blurted out in an offended voice: 'Augustus asked me to stay.' 'But Augustus is not here,' answered Dorelia calmly, and went out ... She politely and firmly got the girl and luggage out of the house without raising her voice, without losing her temper, without even looking upset, so it all seemed a most ordinary affair. 'I am not going to have Augustus's girls here when he is not present' – that was all she ever said about that interlude.[19]

It was this version of a welcome (emphasized by an adhesive. dart shot at her by one of the children) which was extended to that 'Walking hell-bitch of the Western World', the second Mrs Strindberg, who, rising vigorously from her death-bed in the Savoy (upon which, she boasted, John had deposited her), called on Dorelia one Christmas Eve. Her visit, wearing a nightdress, was brief and represented the latest in 'a long series of grotesque and unedifying adventures'[20] to which this tiger-woman from Vienna was, John claimed, subjecting him. For two years, in Paris, Liverpool and London, she had dogged his heels, buying up pictures that were not for sale and presenting in various directions large cheques that baffled Knewstub, infuriated Quinn, and eventually found their way, via her maid, back into her own pocket.*

By all accounts Frida Strindberg was a remarkable woman. After ten years in a convent 'among the brides of Christ', she had been let out to serve, for a further two years, as 'the beauti-

---

* Once, when she was bartering with notes, John put them in an envelope and forwarded them to Bazin, the bird-man of Martigues.

ful jail keeper' of Sweden's chief dramatist. Their marriage had
been an exhausting comedy of love, the tone of which was set
at the wedding when the parson, addressing his question to
Strindberg rather than to Frida, demanded: 'Will you swear
that you do not carry another man's child under your heart?'
While Strindberg nervously denied being pregnant, Frida interrupted with volleys of hysterical laughter.

In the tilts of untarnished romance Frida was anybody's
superior. A determined admirer of the hero in man, she had
sharpened up a ravenous appetite, given somewhat to indigestion, for men of genius. On catching sight of such a specimen
she would burrow ruthlessly under his spell, and there was little
he might do to extricate himself from the rigours of such devotion. For the quality of her worship was not meek. Melodramatic even at the age of nineteen, she had as she grew older
gathered force until she arrived in London an Amazon. The in-
heritance of a large sum of money had done nothing to reduce
this velocity. Never a woman for compromise, she had become
aware within herself of brilliant gifts as a journalist – a breed
allergic to John – and now conducted her life as if it were the
daily material for front-page headlines. In 1910, while on the
track of the fleeing Wyndham Lewis, she had called at Church
Street and, expecting to quarry him there, found herself briefly
in bed with John. 'I then dismissed the incident from my mind,'
John recorded,[21] 'but it turned out to be the prelude to a long
and by no means idyllic tale of misdirected energy, mad incomprehension, absurdity and even squalor.'[22]

What happened over the next two years has been brilliantly
summarized by Strindberg's biographer John Stewart Collis:

John frequently made elaborate efforts to evade her. In vain, it appears. He came to the conclusion that she possessed second sight and
the gift of obliquity. If, without telling a soul where he was going,
he sought refuge in some obscure café in Paris or London, Frida
would know and appear on the scene. If he boarded a train for the
country, there she would be on the platform to bid him good-bye or
to follow him. And it was advisable for him to watch his step in his
treatment of her even when dining with her in company, for if he
were discovered paying too much attention to another female member of the party she would pay a man to take up a concealed posi-

tion and aim a champagne bottle at his head; and on one occasion, in Paris, when he imagined that he had been successful in eluding her by a series of swift changes of scene, he was informed through an anonymous and illiterate note that he would *again* be beaten up if his behaviour towards a certain lady did not improve – for evidently someone had been mistaken for John and had innocently suffered the attack.[23]

There is no record of John having drawn or painted Mrs Strindberg – for she saw herself not as another model but as his benefactress and saviour. In her late thirties, she was still a very cordial woman, her good figure ill-concealed, her face wreathed in dangerous smiles and, we are told, 'eyes of that shade of dark and lively brown which so often prove irresistible to men'.[24] Perfect beauty intimidates – but seldom to the extent to which John felt intimidated. 'I admit', he conceded, 'that the sight of Mme Strindberg bearing down on me in an open taxi-cab, a glad smile of greeting on her face, shaded with a hat turned up behind and bearing a luxuriant outcrop of sweetpeas – this sight, I confess, unnerved me.'[25] He held his ground – then ran; but whichever way he went, there she was with arms outstretched to welcome him. Sometimes he ran directly towards this apparition, and still failed to avoid her. He was never safe, and nor was she. Their reproaches were often antiphonal: 'I am worn out!' she cries. 'I am suffering more than I have strength to bear!!' But he too is suffering: 'Can you seriously think I *enjoy* this business,' he asks, 'that I glory in it???' Their complaints and punctuation marks multiply. She speaks eternally of love and death, and swears that he does not understand her. He hears only the voice of power, and objects: 'It is this *constant* misunderstanding of my character which is the fatal element in the whole affair. When you are not annoying me with hyperbolic eulogies you are outraging me with the vilest suspicions and accusations.' Their accusations turned simultaneously into the avenues of law. 'They are serving you a subpoena or will try to do so to-day,' she promises him. 'I want to attack you by the Law!!!' he bursts out.

What has survived of their correspondence reveals the secret of Frida's ubiquity. When unable to accompany John on his wild flittings to and fro, she would arrange for him to be shadowed by a private detective. He was never lonely. Frida's letters to him were often prompted by this detective's reports rather than anything John had written, and it is round the competence of this man's work that many of their arguments revolve.

Each claimed that the other was making a public exhibition of them both. 'If all Chelsea is aware of your existence it is simply because you have a genius for advertising it,' John blandly concluded. Frida's chief complaints centred on the company he kept other than her own. 'You write love letters to all the girls in London, which they all read aloud,' she objected. One girl, in a leopard skin, had recited nine pages to music the other night; and another, unaccompanied, had danced a dance of jealousy. Was it any wonder, then, that Frida 'felt like murder yesterday – I was mad, mad, mad'. In the intoxication of this madness, she persistently denied the most extravagant charges, assailing John (sometimes as late as 1.30 in the morning 'when I was in bed and disposed to sleep') with her eloquent defences. It was untrue, she suddenly protested, that his girl friend Edith Ashley ('a silly Kensington girl from a penny novel') had 'been bribed by me not to see you, that I had twice tried to murder her, once by poison, once by pushing her from a cliff'. All this, she repeated, was positively untrue.

John refused to disbelieve her. These inventions 'have rekindled your imagination to fresh horrors,' he told her, '. . . as a means of revenge for quite hypothetical injuries, you are determined to be melodramatic to the last!' Nevertheless he felt imperilled by these non-confessions and threats of love, recognizing in her gratuitous pleas of not guilty 'an audacious attempt at intimidation'. For she had sensed his fear of publicity and was constantly playing on it. 'I was born as the only woman of one man,' she was to write in her autobiography.[26] For all time (for the time being) that man was John. She therefore refused to be supplanted by other women who, unlike herself, did not share John's Creative Urge.

John, dear, dear John – *What* have they made of you – what have you made of *me*? You say my dignity is gone. Yes, John – far, far away. You tore it down over a long year to the ground, in the mud – and I let you, as I let you do everything . . . You have gone so far

with them all that it is scarcely possible for you to come back -
unless I publicly unmask them all. I have shunned it until now for
your sake.

Accompanying such threats were erratic demands to 'help
me, befriend me . . . for heavens' sake, for your wife and children's sake'.

John read her message plain. Either he had to live with her in
London or else she would, by means of the courts and press,
disrupt his life, so lately established, at Alderney. To forestall
this he had already made Frida into a figure of fun for Dorelia
– a process he exploited still further in *Chiaroscuro*. It was not
so much what Frida might reveal about herself as about others
that he feared. She had one very potent weapon: death. It
happened that she was very strong on suicide. She thrived on
regular doses of veronal, swallowing them down with Bovril,
then dispatching her abominably pretty maid to John with the
news that she had tossed down this fatal cocktail and was about
to die. Indeed, she was dying – but only to see John.* For
when, in terror of some farewell message for the coroner and
press, he hurried to her bedside, there would always ensue an
intolerable interview; and on one occasion, having seized his
hat and bolted down the hotel corridor, he was overtaken by
the dying woman in the lift.

In *Chiaroscuro* John makes well-rehearsed comedy out of such
episodes, though it appears from contemporary documents that
he was sometimes seriously disturbed by them. To John Quinn,
revisiting London at the beginning of September 1911, he un-
burdened himself. Quinn's diary entry for 3 September records
that John, at the Café Royal, 'sober but normal looking', told
him that, in response to four or five pleading letters from
Frida, he had just gone to see her at the Capitol Hotel. He was
resolved that, however tempted, he must not lie. Nor did he. He
advised her that she had made 'a damnable nuisance of herself',
and that their relationship must end. She 'clutched and raved',

---

* 'When I was ill in December, on the day on which I regained consciousness,
I thought I should not outlive it . . . I was dying – to see you, my dear man . . .
there was nothing to which I should not have forced myself only to see you
once again ! ! !' Frida Strindberg to Augustus John (undated).

but though he felt sorry for her, he steeled himself not to surrender. Later that night, in his studio at Chenil's, he learnt that she had again killed herself and was not feeling well. Next morning Quinn called round : 'Awful tale about Madame Strindberg all right,' he confirmed in his diary. '... Mme S. had taken poison and the doctor said she would not last the night. John shaken but game & determined not to give in. I felt sorry for him and did my best to brace him up. I don't think he had slept very much. This damned Austrian woman has wasted John's time – upset his nerves – played hell with his work ...' At two o'clock that afternoon Innes arrived, his black hair flat over his forehead, like Beardsley, his face very pale, his teeth missing, wearing a dark green tie and a big black felt hat. 'A lot of talk about the Austrian woman,' Quinn wrote, '– John very quiet & Innes a little scared. Both felt very sorry for her as a human being. John sent wire and we all walked to the Queen's restaurant near Sloane Square ... I advised John if Mme S. *did* die to "beat it" – clear out of the country. I amused Innes and John by a description of John in the witness box ... Both laughed like kids. John is really a combination of boy and man – but a man of the highest principle.'

As a result of their discussion, John made up his mind, whatever happened, to accompany Quinn to France. 'I find it difficult to decide to go,' he wrote to Dorelia. '... Would you come over too? ... we could persuade Quinn to eat in modest restaurants.' But Dorelia was involved in her garden and could not join them. Disappointed, John met Quinn at the Café Royal next evening determined to call the journey off, but reports of Frida Strindberg's worsening condition altered his mind very wonderfully. Instead of Dorelia, he arranged for the two of them to be accompanied by Euphemia Lamb and another model, Lillian Shelley, 'a beautiful thing ... red lips and hair as black as a Turk's, stunning figure, great sense of humour'.[27] Exhilaration and exhaustion struggled for possession of Quinn, but he was increasingly under John's spell. At midnight, he allowed himself together with Innes, Shelley and Euphemia Lamb, to carry on their celebrations in John's studio. 'All drunk,' he rejoiced, 'and John sang and acted wonderfully. Two divans full – L[illian] the

best natured'. After breakfast Quinn ordered four tickets, and
John (whom he had just paid two hundred pounds for some
pictures) bought 'a swell automobile coat & cap'.[28]

John was looking forward to 'a few days' peace'; Quinn, more
nervously, hoped that 'the trip will be pleasant'. The two of
them arrived punctually at Charing Cross station, but the girls
did not. Instead, upon the platform stood Frida Strindberg, her
only luggage a revolver. Quinn's notes at this stage become
shaky, though the word 'carnage' is deceptively clear. From
John's account it appears that she urgently pressed upon them
the favour of her companionship. 'Only by appealing to the
guard and the use of a little physical force were we able to preserve our privacy.'[29]* Undeterred she followed them on to the
boat at Dover. John hurriedly locked himself into his cabin,
but Quinn, relishing this contact with Bohemian life, bravely
offered the huntress a cup of tea. John was appalled when he
heard of this errand: 'She spoke to Quinn on the boat and
tried to get him into partnership with her to run me! !' he protested in a letter to Dorelia. To this purpose she had made an
appointment to see Quinn the following day in Paris. But in
the interval, possibly with John's aid, Quinn's ardour cooled and
instead of keeping his appointment he took John to the Hotel
Bristol to meet an American copper king, Thomas Fortune Ryan;
a tall elderly southerner who talked wearily in immense sums of
money and pessimistically chewed upon an unlit cigar. That
evening they went to the Bal Tabarin and were joined by a
young Kabyle woman. 'This dusky girl's whole person exhaled a
delicious odour of musk or sandalwood. A childlike candour
illuminated her smouldering eyes.'[30] At two o'clock that morning they returned to their hotel: 'finally to Pl. Panthéon,' Quinn
noted wearily, '& John went with the girl'.

By now Madame Strindberg was also at their hotel and,
mortified by these events, committed suicide. Since she was
never more active than when laid out on her death-bed, they
hurriedly borrowed Ryan's seventy-five-horsepower Mercedes
touring car, manned by 'the best chauffeur in Europe',[31] a

* In *Chiaroscuro*, John was careful to write of 'passive yet firm resistance' at
the railway station. But in a letter to Dorelia he is more direct: 'I shoved her
out.'

German. There was not a moment to lose. Setting off at once they 'careered over France ruthlessly'.[32]

The prospect of a week with Quinn in such delightful country depressed John unutterably, and he proposed reviving their earlier scheme by fetching over Shelley and Euphemia. Quinn was game, but Dorelia, to whom John suggested this by letter, was not: and the scheme was reluctantly abandoned. For much of the ensuing time John was sullen; silent sometimes and at other times attempting, it seemed, to provoke a quarrel. 'O these Americans ! ! !' he burst out. 'I don't think I can stand that accent much longer ... their naiveté, their innocence, their banality, their crass stupidity is unimaginable.'[33] Yet Quinn stayed doggedly optimistic. 'John and I had a great time in France,' he loyally declared.[34]

What they achieved in this breathless ellipse to and back from the Mediterranean was a forerunner of the modern package tour.* 'It was like a nightmare.' From the start they fuelled themselves against the ordeal with prodigious quantities of champagne. 'The first day out we started on champagne at lunch,' Quinn told James G. Huneker (15 November 1911):

> That night at dinner, feeling sure that I would be knocked out the next day, I might as well go the limit and so we had champagne at dinner. I slept like a top, woke up feeling like a prince, and did a hundred and fifty miles next day, and from then on and every day till we returned to Paris we had two and sometimes three quarts of champagne a day – champagne for lunch, champagne for dinner, liqueurs of all kinds, cassis and marc, vermouth, absinthe and the devil knows what else.

For John, who had counted on Quinn retiring to bed most days with a hangover, such resilience was disappointing. But there were many hair-raising misadventures to enliven this ex-

---

* In a letter to Huneker (15 November 1911) Quinn gave the inventory of this tour. 'We did Chartres, Tours, Amboise, Blois, Montélimar, Le Puy (a wonderful old place), Orange, Avignon, Aix en Provence (where we saw some of the most wonderful tapestries in the world), Marseilles, Martigues (where John spent over a year), Aiguemortes, Arles and Nîmes; back by way of Le Puy, St Étienne, Moulins, Bourges and into Paris by way of Fontainebleau. John knew interesting people at Avignon, Aix, Marseilles, Martigues, Arles and Nîmes ... We careered through the heart of the Cévennes twice ...'

cursion 'into that labyrinth of platitude and bluff, the American
mind'.[35] Their progress was punctuated by several burst tyres
and encounters with chickens and dogs. At one place they
knocked down a young boy on a bicycle and themselves leapt
wildly down a steep place into a ploughed field. 'We landed
after about three terrific jumps,' Quinn reported, '... just missed
bumping into a tree which would have smashed the machine
... the kid's thick skull that got him into trouble saved him
when he fell'.[36] Having taken the child to a doctor, they raced
on expecting at every town to be arrested. 'Quinn's French
efforts are amazing,' John wrote in a letter to Dorelia. 'Imagine
the language we have to talk to the chauffeur. Desperando!'
Descending a tortuous mountain road, Quinn had inquired the
German for 'slow'. 'Schnell', John replied. 'Schnell!' Quinn
shouted at their burly driver who obediently accelerated.
'Schnell! Schnell!' Quinn repeatedly cried. They hurtled down
the mountain at breakneck speed and arrived at their hotel 'in
good time for dinner' – though on this occasion Quinn retired to
bed at once.

In a letter to Conrad[37] Quinn recalled 'feeling like a fighting
man' during this journey. But the points were building up in
John's favour, and Quinn's nerves grew badly frayed. At night
he was haunted by 'horrible shapes – stone houses, fences, trees,
hay stacks, stone walls, stone piles, dirt walls, chasms and precipices advancing towards us out of the fog all to fade away into
grey mist again'. On one occasion, John recounts in *Chiaroscuro*,
'when the car was creeping at a snail's pace on an unknown
road through a dense fog in the Cevennes, the attorney suddenly
gave vent to a despairing cry, and in one masterly leap precipitated himself clean through the open window, to land harm-
lessly on the grass by the road-side! He felt sure we were going
over a precipice.'[38]*

Quinn secretly, and John openly, were much relieved when
their tour came to an end. 'We were not quite a success as

---

* Quinn's biographer, B. L. Reid, seems sceptical of this incident. 'Quinn's
journal says nothing of this,' he points out (p. 106). But in a letter to James
Huneker (15 November 1911) Quinn describes it in full: 'I threw myself out
of the machine and somehow landed on my feet, but I turned a complete
somersault. How I did it without breaking my neck or leg or arm is a mystery.'

of education from which he himself had benefited. On 16 August 1911 he reported to Quinn that 'I have just secured a young tutor who really seems a jewel'; and a month later[41] he was telling Ottoline Morrell that 'our tutor is an excellent and charming youth'.

His name was John Hope-Johnstone, and he was then in his late twenties, a man of many attainments and no profession. He had been educated between Bradfield, Hanover and Trinity College, Cambridge, which he had been obliged to leave prematurely when his mother abandoned her second fortune to the roulette wheel. From this time onwards he lived, pennilessly, by his wits. But, as Romilly John observed, 'he was very unfortunate in combining, at that time, extreme poverty with the most epicurean tastes I have ever known'.[42] He had a hunger for the possession of knowledge that ranged from the intricacies of pronouncing Arabic to the address of the only place in Britain where a certain toothpaste might be bought. There was nothing haphazard about all this: it was part of a relentless programme of theoretical self-perfection to which he had dedicated himself pending the death of eleven persons which, he had mathematically calculated, would bring him into a fortune and, more dubiously, a title. As a believer in the beauty of uselessness, he strove to make himself its chief embodiment. Undeterred by a complete lack of 'ear', he mastered the penny whistle and then, by sheer perseverance, the flute.* His abstract enthusiasms and remoteness from ordinary human desires gave him an aura of romance. He was a confirmed wanderer. Before taking up his post as a

* He even became, with Compton Mackenzie, joint-editor of *Gramophone*, in which he reviewed the latest records under the pseudonym 'James Caskett'. In Octave 5 of *My Life and Times*, Compton Mackenzie recounts that he first met Hope-Johnstone in Greece in 1916. 'John Hope-Johnstone had arrived by now from Corfu with a kitbag containing a few clothes, one top-boot, several works on higher mathematics and two volumes of Doughty's *Arabia Deserta*, a pair of bright yellow Moorish slippers, a camera and a flute. He was ten days older than myself and among the friends with whom I've enjoyed good conversation I bracket Hope-Johnstone with Norman Douglas at the top . . . When war broke out he was more than halfway on a journey to Baghdad and in spite of having to wear very strong glasses nothing escaped him. He enlisted at the beginning of the war, somehow cheating the military authorities over his eyesight; then his myopia was discovered by his having saluted a drum he had mistaken for the regimental sergeant-major.'

travelling companions,' John conceded.[39] The motor car, he thought 'is a damnable invention'. Travelling on foot or by diligence was the only proper progress for a painter. 'Motoring is a fearfully wrong way of seeing the country but an awfully nice way of doing without railway trains,' he instructed Dorelia. 'It makes one very sleepy.' Nevertheless, it had been impossible to overlook everything, the countryside, the cathedrals at Bourges and Chartres 'veritably miraculous and power-communicating. The Ancients,' he told Will Rothenstein, 'did nothing like this.'

Another success had been their final shaking-off of Mrs Strindberg. Two days after their return, Quinn embarked for New York; and John, having heard that Frida was again becoming 'very active in London', slipped quietly down to join Innes at Nant Ddu. 'It has been impossible to do any work travelling this way,' he had written to Dorelia from a brothel in Marseilles, 'but one can think all the same'. Now, in the peace of Wales, he could transfer these thoughts to paint.

3. CAVALIERS AND EGGHEADS

One of the earliest visitors to Alderney was John's father. He was a model of patience. For hours he would sit strictly motionless and then move quietly about the garden, hoping to be photographed. Every day he put on the same costume he wore for promenading the beach at Tenby: a sober suit, leather gloves, dark hat, wing collar and spats. He too had recently moved, a distance of several hundred yards, to 5 Lexden Terrace overlooking the sea. In this desirable residence he was to linger a little uncertainly some thirty years, with the weather, a few illnesses and his 'specimens of self-photography' as constant companions. Occasionally he was visited by grandchildren, and more occasionally by John himself. It was a life spent waiting.

From Dorelia's family there came, among others, her mother – a very straight-backed old woman with shiny white hair and a comforting round farm face. She spent her days quilt-making, and in the evenings would take a hot brick from the fireplace, wrapping it in cloth to warm her bed.

From 1912 onwards the guests, permanent and recurring,

began to assemble at Alderney. There was Iris Tree, with her freckles and blue shadows, gliding between the trees in a poetic trance; Lytton Strachey who came chiefly to see Dorelia and who amazed the children by claiming he felt so weak before breakfast that he found it impossible to lift a match; Fanny Fletcher, a poor art-student later revered for her potato wall-papers, who arrived for a few weeks, knitted herself into the household with her cardigans and gained the reputation for being a rather inefficient witch whose salad dressings were said to contain spells; there was also a Polish doctor of music, Jan Sliwinski, who became expert at tarring fences, mending walls and cataloguing books; the Chilean painter Alvaro Guevara with tales of terrific boxing-matches in Valparaiso where he had been a champion; and an Icelandic poet who had written a play in which angels somehow figured and who was now heavily in-volved in defeating the law of gravity. Very often Henry Lamb would ride over on a pony-cart to play duets with Dorelia at the upright piano. Sounds of Mozart and of Bach fugues would float out of the open windows into the garden, sometimes fol-lowed by heated words as to who had played the wrong note and, more implausibly, whether or not there was a deity – for Dorelia was an agnostic, staunchly vague, and Lamb an atheistic God-botherer, and the two of them would often argue over what neither of them believed. Horace de Vere Cole, the country's most eminent practical joker, who claimed descent from Old King Cole, was another visitor. More cavalier still was the farmer, archaeologist* and anti-aircraft pioneer, Trelawney Dayrell Reed, who dropped in for a cup of tea one afternoon, hung on a few years, then bought a farm near by into which he settled with his grim mother, unmarried sister and some eighteenth-century furniture. Black-bearded and fanatic, he looked like a prince in the manner of El Greco, and was much admired for the violence of his Oxford stammer, his endless

* He was the author of *The First Battle of Britain* and *The Rise of Wessex*, two extraordinary archaeological works interspersed with pages of his own poetry. Later he became curator of the Farnham Museum, from where he waged war against the archaeological establishment. In the opinion of Stuart Piggott (to whom he introduced John) his archaeological work was 'crazy, but occasion-ally contained passages of inspired instinct'. He also published a useful manual on shove-ha'penny.

loud check tweeds, and socks of revolutionary red. casional poet, he also took to painting, executing in hi house a series of vigorous and explicit frescoes. He wa ded by two spaniels and his 'man', a wide-eyed factotum Ernest, and would assume in this company an air of utm finement which regularly infuriated John. 'Huntin' does gi the opportunity of dressin' like a gentleman,' he would d adding 'But I've always thought the real test was how to un like a gentleman.'* In song his voice was powerful and tune assisted by free-flowing exotic gestures with which he w conduct ballads of extreme bawdiness. A great hero to children, he was master of many accomplishments from da to the deepest dialect of Dorset. He was also a professional lar scape-and-market gardener and a scholar, in Latin, of hollyhoc and roses – his chief love. It was in defence of these blooms, h dogs, pigs and an apple-tree that he served his finest hour. Ever afternoon he would go to bed to nurse his ill-health; and every afternoon he was woken by aeroplanes which had selected his cottage as a turning-point in their local races. He wrote letters, he remonstrated, he complained by every lawful means : but the flying monsters still howled about his chimney pots, creating havoc among his household of cattle and female relatives. Then, one afternoon, awakened by a deafening racket, he sprang from his bed and, rushing into the garden, let fly with a double-barrelled shotgun, winging one of the brutes. Although no vital damage was done, Trelawney was arrested and tried at Dorches-ter Assizes on a charge of attempted murder. In opposition to the judge, a man much loved for his severity, the jury (being composed mostly of farmers like himself) acquitted Trelawney : and there was a grand celebration.

To be brought up amid such people, it might be thought, con-stituted an education in itself. John, however, pressed matters to extremes : he hired a tutor. As long ago as May 1910 he had been persuaded that 'the immediate *necessity* seems to be an able tutor and major-domo for my family'.[40] If the search had been long and hesitant, this was because he needed someone re-markable whom he could trust not to give his children the sort

* Trelawney was a country homosexual. When asked once whether he had pigs on his farm, he replied: 'No. The boys have the pigs. I have the boys.'

tutor, he had spent some years pushing a pram charged with grammars and metaphysical works through Asia reputedly in pursuit of a village where chickens were said to cost a penny each.

He never found it, but arrived instead at Alderney into which, for a time, he fitted very well. Slim and well built, with finely cut features, dark hair and ivory pale skin, he wore heavy horn-rimmed spectacles, an innovation at the time. It was not long before he conceived an immense admiration for John and Dorelia and the romantic life they led in and around their absurdly battlemented bungalow. With their *entourage* of gypsy caravans and ponies and naked children they belonged in his imagination to the race of Homeric gods. As a mark of admiration he took to wearing a medley of Bohemian clothes – buff corduroy suits cut by a grand tailor in Savile Row after the style of a dress suit, with swallow tails behind, a coloured handkerchief or 'diklo' round his neck and, to complete the bizarre effect, a black felt hat of the kind later made fashionable by Anthony Eden, though with a broad rim. To John's eyes he was every inch a tutor.

It is doubtful if his pupils benefited as much as John and Dorelia did from the tutelage of this walking encyclopedia. 'For Hope the argument – long, persistent, remorseless, carried back to first logical principles – was an almost indispensable element in the day's hygiene,' his friend Gerald Brenan recorded.[43] It began at first light. He would sit over the breakfast table dilating upon Symbolic Logic or Four Dimensional Geometry while the children fled on to the heath. Then Dorelia, who in any case did not believe in education, would murmur: 'Never mind. Leave them for to-day,' and the tutor would be free to retreat into the cottage kitchen, which he had converted, with retorts and bottles of coloured fluid, into a laboratory for his malodorous chemical experiments. At other moments, possibly when it was raining, he would lead the older boys off into their sanctum of learning and propound to them the Latin gender rhymes and the names of the Hebrew kings. He also made a speciality of the Book of Job, parts of which he made them learn by heart in order to train their ears for sonorous language, provide them with a sense of the remote past, and instil patience.* He was not entirely popular however with the children, chiefly because of his greed. At table, when the cream jug was passed round, he would 'accidentally' spill most of it over his own plate, leaving nothing for them.

To Dorelia, with whom he was a little in love, he made himself more helpful. He was a scholar of ancient herbs and jellies, and she made use of his extensive book-knowledge in the kitchen and when laying out her garden. To John also he tried to make himself of value by persuading him to buy an expensive camera with which to photograph his paintings. But Hope's technique perfected a gradual fading away of all the prints into invisibility. It was an accurate record at Alderney of his waning popularity. John had warmed to him at first as someone magnificently irrelevant to modern life – an authentic eighteenth-century dilettante. He had been impressed by his reputation as a mathematical genius and amused by his amazingly well-informed conversation – there must have been few people who could speak with such perceptible pleasure on Phonetics, for instance, exploring all the entertainment the subject provided. He had liked, too, the way the tutor dived into their rigorously easygoing way of life, accompanying, unshaven, the barefoot boys through the Cotswolds to North Wales with a pony and cart. Then John began to tire of him, as he did of everyone whom he saw regularly. He had encouraged Hope as an entertainer, and within a year his repertoire of tricks and stories had run out. John was never one for *encores*: they bored him, not just negatively but with a burning antagonism; the tutor did not find it difficult to fan this. His capacity for absorbing knowledge, which appeared limitless, was replenished by his growing library and by John's depleted one. As a future editor of the *Burlington Magazine*, it was necessary that he should study art closely, but not perhaps by the method of absconding with John's own pictures, of which he amassed a fine private collection. His passion for argument pierced through the barrier of John's deafness and especially when it developed into vast literary quarrels with Trelawney or with Edie, whose reading

* 'Hope-Johnstone used to try and explain relativity to me when I was about 10,' Romilly John admitted. 'I still remember the horror of his subsequent discovery that I had not yet wholly mastered vulgar fractions.'

was confined to the *Daily Mirror* and romantic novels from
Parkstone Station lending library. So it was with some relief on
all sides that in the last week of August 1912, with his entire
capital of £16, a camel-hair sleeping bag and a good many
grammars, he wheeled his perambulator off once more in the
direction of China. Although he had been tutor for little more
than a year, he was regularly to re-enter the lives of the Johns,
in Spain, in Italy, at the corner of Oxford Street. Gerald Brenan,
with whom he set out for the borders of Outer Mongolia, gives
as Hope's reason for this sudden journey the rainy weather in
North Wales, where he had passed a few weeks with the
Johns. Another more pressing reason, it was inaccurately suggested, was a plan John had hit on to marry him off to one of
his models who, about this time, gave birth to a child.

After Hope's disappearance the children's education stumbled
on along slightly more conventional lines. 'The boys go to a
beastly school now and seem to like it,' John complained to
their ex-tutor (20 November 1912). Dane Court was a new
school, not outstandingly orthodox, that had been started by a
newly married comic couple, Hugh and Michaela Pooley. Hugh
Pooley, a hearty player of the piccolo and owner of a rich baritone voice, took music classes. When not playing or singing, he
was usually laughing; and when doing none of these things he
was incomprehensible. 'He lectured us in the dormitory on the
dangers of masturbation I now realize,' recalled Romilly,
'though I was puzzled at the time.'[44] If Hugh was the symbol of
a headmaster, his wife, a tremendous devotee of bicycling and
an emotional speech-maker, was the 'progressive' force in the
school. She had the enviable ability to miss church on Sunday,
and busied herself on weekdays in French. She was a Dane*

---

* 'We considered her rather a witch-like figure, though I daresay she was
quite handsome in a Danish way,' Romilly John recalled. '. . . On parents' day
Mrs P. invariably gave the same speech, in which she told, with considerable
emotion, how she was enlightened as to the meaning of the word "gentleman",
presumably there being no equivalent in Denmark either of the word or the
thing. One day she had seen from an upstairs window one of the 12 older boys
(*not* a John) stealing gooseberries. This boy had subsequently owned up to the
theft, an instance of gentlemanliness the like of which Denmark could afford no
equal. It was this boy who at a later date was employed as a tutor to Edwin and
me.' Romilly John to the author, 15 November 1972.

and the daughter of an artist and museum director 'so,' she concluded, 'the Johns' home came as a refuge to me'. On the
strength of her parentage she would bicycle up uninvited to
Alderney with her husband and a tin of sardines to supplement
the rations, and seemed deaf to the loud groans which greeted
her arrival. While Hugh sang in his baritone for supper,
Michaela would swivel her attentions upon John himself, whom
she treated as one of the more backward boys in her class. The
retired colonels and civil servants with which Hampshire and
Dorset seemed brimming over were, she conveyed, very little to
her *smörgasbord* tastes, whereas John was an 'attractive man,
who made one feel 100% woman – a quality I missed in most
Englishmen at that period'.

Dane Court had eleven pupils and, since its future depended
upon swelling this number, the Pooleys had been delighted to
receive one morning a letter of inquiry from Alderney Manor –
a large place, they saw from the map, on Lord Wimborne's
estate. An interview had been punctually arranged, and the
Pooleys had prepared themselves to meet some grand people.

'From our stand by the window we saw a green Governess
cart drawn by a pony approaching up the drive,' Michaela
Pooley remembered.

A queer square cart – later named 'The Marmalade Box' by the
boys in the school – and out stepped a lady in a cloak with a large
hat and hair cut short ... After her a couple of boys tumbled out,
their hair cut likewise and they wore coloured tunics. For a moment
we thought they were girls ... It was soon fixed that the three boys
aged 8, 9, 10 should come as day boys. When Mrs John was going,
she turned at the door and said: 'I think there are two more at
home, who might as well come.'[45]

That was the beginning and it was not easy for them, knowing only the Latin gender rules and part of the Book of Job. But
they were quick to learn, being, the Pooleys judged, 'a fine lot
... intelligent and sturdy, good at work and good at games'.
With their long page-style hair and belted pinafores (brightly
coloured at first, then khaki to match the brown Norfolk suits
the other boys wore) they felt shamefully conspicuous. Yet
since they numbered almost half Dane Court and stood
shoulder to shoulder against any attack, their entrance into

school life was not so painful as it might have been. They formed a community of their own, a family circle with doors that could be opened only from inside. But gradually they edged these doors ajar and exerted a considerable influence on the school, Eton collars giving way, under Michaela's reforming spirit, to allow corduroy suits and earthenware bowls to become the order of the day.

'David and Caspar now are expert cyclists,' John reported to Mrs Nettleship after their first term (8 January 1913). '... Mr Pooley wants them to be weekly boarders, he thinks they'd get on much faster – and I think it's no bad idea.' First the three eldest, then the others boarded and immersed themselves more deeply in an atmosphere altogether different from that of Alderney. They grew more self-conscious, more vulnerable to parent-embarrassment at sports days. So far as was possible they tried to keep the two parts of their lives – and the Nettleship part too – within separate compartments. Details of their home life were guarded from their friends, while about Dane Court they were seldom pestered for information by John and Dorelia.

'I was especially afraid that one of my brothers would let out some frightful detail of our life at Alderney, and thus ruin us for ever,' wrote Romilly; 'a needless alarm, as they were all older and warier than I. I contracted a habit of inserting secretly after the Lord's Prayer a little clause to the effect that Dorelia might be brought by divine intervention to wear proper clothes; I used also to pray that she and John might not be tempted, by the invitation sent to all parents, to appear at the school sports.'[46]

The boys did well at school; especially David, who was head boy for two years. As the eldest he felt himself to be at least as much a Nettleship as a John and was more successful when away from Alderney : but it was Caspar, the second son, who cut loose. He had been given a copy of *Jane's Fighting Ships* and, looking through the lists of warships, two-thirds of them British, came to the conclusion that 'here was a new and orderly society ... This was the world for me'.[47] With Hugh Pooley's encouragement, he eventually approached his father with the notion of making the navy his career. It was a difficult interview. Since John plainly thought it stupid voluntarily to subject oneself to such harsh exterior discipline, he did not scruple to say so. 'Think again,' he advised, and brushed the idea aside. When Caspar persisted he came up against other obstacles – the naval cadet uniform alone cost a hundred and fifty pounds. But once John appreciated that his son was set on the navy, he paid all bills without objection. Almost certainly it was Dorelia who engineered this change of mind. She had no more interest in the sea than in schooling, but she wanted to get at least one boy off her hands and see him settled. So she organized everything, eventually driving him to Portsmouth – to make sure.

Caspar was the only one of John's children brought up at Alderney who, like Thornton, Gwen and Winifred from Wales, left home and made for himself a life that became rooted elsewhere. The others left too late or too incompletely, as John himself had done. Although one or two of his later illegitimate children, raised with their mothers, felt themselves deprived by not living at Alderney or Fryern, Ida's and Dorelia's children needed to escape these places – and for many of the same reasons that old Edwin John's family had fled Tenby. The atmosphere was very powerful and, as the boys grew older, it seemed to become less sympathetic. John loved babies. When they were very small he used sometimes to bath them, and in such a role they preferred him to anyone else. But, as a man of strong vitality, he found it hard to bear the physical presence of his maturing sons. Overawed by his great presence they fell, one by one, into privacy and other lines of self-preservation. It was the beginning of a long defensive war no one could win. Even now, he ruled them, so Caspar recalled, 'with a rod of iron',[48] so that there was not 'a great deal of sympathy' in the climate at Alderney. Partly this was due to Dorelia who, at least under John's influence, was not overtly a loving person. Ida had been warmer, and with her death her children were deprived of this physical warmth. It was not that Dorelia was unfair, but that only her own children seemed able to sense her fondness for them. John was inhibited from expressions of tenderness. 'He intensely disliked seeing parents *fondling* their children and this may partly have accounted for my mother's inhibitions in respect of us children,' remembered his daughter Vivien. 'In fact we never embraced our mother until the ages of 12 and 15, when Poppet and I made a pact to break this "spell" in order to be like other families'.[49] But this was later, and for the most part Dorelia acquiesced in this bleak régime. So the atmosphere, for all its perfume of Bohemianism, was almost Victorian in its rules of reticence.

The current of children to and from Alderney over the next years was continuous. Dorelia's pregnancy, in the autumn of 1911, was against her doctor's advice and the cause of some anxiety. In the event everyone except Dorelia fell ill.[50] By the end of February 1912, John was already confessing to 'feeling so sick ... Dorelia is expecting a baby momentarily ... Pyramus mysteriously ill'. In the following week this illness was diagnosed. 'Little Pyramus is fearfully ill – meningitis, and I can't believe he can recover, though I do hope still,' John wrote to Ottoline Morrell (5 March 1912). 'Last night I thought he was about to die but he kept on. Dorelia behaves most wonderfully – though she is expecting her baby at any moment. It will be terrible to lose Pyra ...' In desperation John had tried to get 'the best specialist in London, perhaps in Europe,' but the man was in Europe, not London – and besides what was there he could do? 'There is no treatment for the disease.'[51]

On 8 March Dorelia's labour pains began and she 'had to take leave of Pyramus and go and have her baby' which 'turned out a big nice girl'. They told Dorelia that Pyramus was already dead, but for four more days the child lay on his bed quite close to her, still just alive. 'Pyra is still breathing feebly but happily has been unconscious for the last 2 or 3 days,' John told Ottoline on 10 March. 'I do not think he will outlive to-day. He was indeed a celestial child and that is why the Gods take him ... The mind refuses to contemplate ... such an awful fact.' While Dorelia grew stronger, John continued to sit by their son, without hope, waiting for the end. 'It was a terrible event,' he wrote afterwards (9 May 1912) to Quinn. '... I must say the Missus behaved throughout as I think few women would – with amazing good sense and a splendid determination not to give way to the *luxury* of the expression of grief.' It was this silence, outwardly, they shared. 'I can't talk about Pyra,' Dorelia told Ottoline a year later (10 March 1913); and John wrote to Albert Rutherston: 'It is indeed a terrible thing to have lost darling little Pyramus – the most adorable of children. Of course I can't find words to say what I feel.' But their silence was not the same. Dorelia's was natural, and her grief private. John admired this: there was no falsity to it. When he spoke of feeling, as from time to time he was tempted to do, he always regretted it for the words seemed to let him down, making the reality something acted. When unhappiness threatened, he feared giving way to it because he knew the depths of depression of which his nature was capable. He concentrated therefore on the birth of his daughter: 'Le roi est mort, vive la reine'.[52] They called her Elizabeth Ann – at least that was their intention. But somehow these names never stuck. Then, one day, after contemplating her some time, Caspar chanced to remark: 'What a little poppet it is!': after which she was always known as Poppet.

Pyramus was cremated at Woking. Returning by train with the ashes – 'one more urn for my collection'[53] – John placed the receptacle carefully on the rack above his seat, and then forgot it. It was later found, and sent to Alderney.

4. CHRONIC POTENTIAL

'All are well at home,' John reported philosophically, ' – the baby-girl a god-send. My missus keeps fit. We have disturbances of the atmosphere occasionally but have so far managed to recover every time.'[54] He seldom stayed at Alderney long. For one of his temperament it was insufferable to be tied to a large family, however elastic the bonds. He preferred to visit rather than to live with them. 'It is pleasant enough down here,' he remarked to Ottoline Morrell (25 July 1913), 'but a little uninspiring.'

Inspiration lay further off, waiting to be taken by surprise. In the summer of 1912 he had set off with his family to Wales – then, abandoning them at Nant Ddu, hurried on by himself to Ireland. 'Like a lion' he entered Dublin, remembered St John Gogarty;[55] 'or some sea king' ...

> 'Or a Viking who has steered,
> All blue eyes and yellow beard.'[56]

This was John's first meeting with stately, plump, buck Gogarty, professional Irishman of many parts – quick-witted and long-talking, a poet and busybody, surgeon, litigant and aviator, wearer of a primrose waistcoat and owner of the first butter-coloured Rolls-Royce. John had sought him out in the Bailey Restaurant, Dublin's equivalent of the Café Royal, on the advice of Orpen and, despite Gogarty's 'ceaseless outpour of wit and wisdom', confessed to being 'immensely entertained'[57] by him. Gogarty, 'all agog with good humour', fell headlong under John's spell, describing him as 'a man of deep shadows and dazzling light ... When I saw him for the first time I noticed that he had a magnificent body ... He was tall, broad-shouldered and narrow-hipped. His limbs were not heavy, his hands and feet were long.'[58] 'The aura of the man! The mental amplitude!' It was extraordinary. Overwhelmed by these sensations, Gogarty suspected he had trespassed into 'the majesty of genius'.[59] Even so, he could not fail to notice that John was 'a moody man'. There was always the problem of what to do with him. In his Ode 'To Augustus John', he explains the open-mouthed effect it had on him:

> You who revel in the quick
> And are Beauty's Bolshevik;
> For you know how to undress
> And expose her loveliness ...
> Suddenly profoundest gloom
> Wrapped you as you gazed apart,
> And not one of us had heart
> To inquire what was the matter.
> So we kept our frantic chatter
> up to save an awful pause
> Guessing what could be the cause
> Of your sudden, silent mood,
> What in daylight made you brood ...
> Enough!. There is no need to tell
> How I broke the gloomy spell,
> What I was inspired to give –
> By bread alone does no man live,
> And water makes a man depressed:
> Maybe silence had been best.

But Gogarty was incapable of silence: his tongue could not master it. Being in his company was like crossing a Sahara of words – hectic, brilliant, utterly exhausting. His friendship with John was largely an ear-and-mouth affair. As an ear-nose-and-throat specialist, he once examined John's ears and pronounced them to be the very Seat of his Melancholy : in which case, John felt, he had much to answer for. Gogarty was not simply a raconteur but a verbal exhibitionist and monopolizer of all conversation. If he did not have enough words of his own, he borrowed other people's, so he was never at a loss. Only once did John arrest him – and then drastically by flinging in his face a bowl of nuts.[60] Usually he would accept Gogarty's injunction to 'float his intellect' while in Dublin, and drink huge tumblers of whisky until the chatter retreated to a distant murmur. John Jameson was what Gogarty was 'inspired to give' with almost sinister generosity. 'It was very pleasant, this bathing in the glory of Augustus,' Gogarty remembered[61] – adding, to John's chagrin : 'I felt myself growing so witty that I was able to laugh at my own jokes'.

But still there was the problem of what to do with John. Gogarty put him up in lodgings next to the Royal Hotel, Dalkey, overlooking Shanagolden Bay. His presence there, at the window, was a constant invitation to take the day off. 'We would pick up Joe Hone, who lived at Killiney, and go to Glendalough, the Glen of the Lakes, in Wicklow,' Gogarty wrote. '... On through the lovely country we went. Augustus, who was sitting in the back, could not be distracted by scenery, for beside him sat Vera Hone.

'... We bowled along the Rocky Valley. Suddenly I heard the word "Stop". As it evidently was not meant for me, I didn't stop. Joe Hone did not turn his head, so why should I?'[62]

This was the propitious beginning to a lifelong, infuriating friendship commemorated by John with two fine portraits* of

---

* Painted in August 1917, the best-known portrait depicts Gogarty as a rather flagging dandy lit up with what Ulick O'Connor called 'elfin vitality' – though to Gogarty himself this image looked

> like Caesar late returned
> Exhausted from a long campaign.

In his poem 'To My Portrait, By Augustus John', he reveals that the painting provoked some deep questions.

> Is it a warning? And, to me,
> Your criticism upon Life?
> If this be caused by Poetry
> What should a Poet tell his wife?

Gogarty, and by Gogarty with two fine 'Odes and Addresses'.
The fascination Gogarty felt for John did not diminish with the
years, and in a tiny fragile verse at the end of his poem 'To
Augustus John', he set down how much, despite all its difficulties, this friendship meant to him:

> When my hawk's soul shall be
> With little talk in her,
> Trembling, about to flee,
> And Father Falconer
> Touches her off for me,
> And I am gone –
> All shall forgotten be
> Save for you, John!

But still there was the problem of what to do. He had been
offered the freedom of the island by another new friend, Francis
Macnamara, 'poet, philosopher and financial expert',[63] and
though payment for such freedom could be heavy, he willingly
accepted it. Macnamara was another 'bright gem' John now
added to his adornment of friends. From a career in the law,
from Magdalen College, Oxford, from his father the High
Sheriff of County Clare, Francis Macnamara had violently rebelled in order to devote himself to speculations of a literary
and philosophical complexion. He had married a girl very pretty
and small, Quaker and quite French, and lived with her, an even
prettier sister-in-law, and a multiplying family of blond and
beautiful children. Over six feet tall, golden-haired and with
bright blue eyes, he carried himself (as John's portrait of him
clearly reveals) 'like a conqueror'.[64] Famous for his courage and
wild deeds, he subsisted on theories which embraced every
subject from Bishop Butler to tar water, admitted to being (by
vocation) a poet, and claimed, by way of trade, to teach poetry.
'He has shown me a manuscript which seems to me most remarkable,' John confided to Quinn (6 August 1912). 'He has put
soliloquies into the mouths of personages from the Irish legends
and he has made them talk quite modern language albeit in free
verse – the result is amazingly vivid and vital. The people live
again!'

Macnamara had a talent for procrastination. 'There were
schools of poetry in Ireland where the pupil had to study for

fourteen years before he was considered proficient,' Gogarty records. 'Francis studied all his days,' he had assumed, perhaps too precociously, the cumbersome mantle of the sage, but 'would sometimes divest himself of this,' John noted, 'together with his messianic responsibilities, and warmed by what he called "the hard stuff" became popular, genial, and even, as the police were apt to think, dangerous'.[65]

It was Francis's pride, his daughter Nicolette later wrote with a little exaggeration, 'to introduce Augustus to Ireland, to County Clare, Galway and Connemara; the land the Macnamaras had roamed since history began.'[66] Though living in London, he owned a house in Doolin, a small fishing village 'seven Irish miles away from Ennistymon', and it was here that John arrived at the end of July.

It was a lonely place, and wild. The troughs and furrows of the land, 'like an immobilized rough sea',[67] were crested with outcrops of grey rock and ridden by a net of stone walls. Except for a few obstinate trees, stunted and windswept like masted wrecks, and sudden calm surges of lush green grass, it was a barren landscape, frozen from times of primitive survival: the very place for painting. When the mood was on him, Macnamara would harness his horse and cart and ride off with John for days on end, explaining the countryside. Several times, either by steamship or, more recklessly, by native currach, they crossed over to the Aran Islands. The great Atlantic waves that thundered in from Newfoundland and Greenland and charged into the granite boulders of the Doolin coast had protected the islanders from invasion by the monsters of modern civilization. They remained part of their Island, living naturally among the same rocks and wind and weather that had always enveloped them. They were, as John felt himself to be, throwbacks to an earlier century. Grave, dignified people, speaking English when unavoidable with a rich Elizabethan vocabulary, these heirs of an ancient people wove their own garments and supported themselves without interference from the mainland. 'The smoke of burning kelp rose from the shores,' John recorded. 'Women and girls in black shawls and red or saffron skirts stood or moved in groups with a kind of nun-like uniformity and decorum. Upon the precipitous Atlantic verge some forgotten people had disputed a last foothold upon the ramparts of more than one astounding fortress ... who on earth were they?'[68]

It was a mystery he shared with them and which, with the bleakness of their lives, made them beautiful to him. Yet because there were so many unco-ordinated sides to his personality, John could not live in such a place: he could only remember and revisit. Their simplicity represented an ideal, a dream without a dream's exactness, visionary and insubstantial. His own life was about to grow more complex, episodic. But like a religion that rises above human performance, the Aran Islands would remain inviolate, floating in his imagination where, gradually deprived of nourishment, they grew vaguer, though never disappearing.

To these islands, to Doolin as the guest of Macnamara, to Galway and the speckled hills of Connemara where Gogarty owned a house John already felt impatient to return, he told Quinn, to paint the landscape and 'some of the women'.[69]

But in order to return he had first to leave. Innes, who was staying with Lady Gregory, had suddenly appeared – 'God knows how'[70] – and together the two painters crossed back into Wales. John had been invited by Lord Howard de Walden, the amateur of all trades and descriptions, to go to Chirk Castle and paint his wife. Having separated from Innes and returned his family, safe and disgruntled, to Alderney, he rushed back to Wales again from the other direction to find Lady Howard de Walden, powerfully pregnant, ready and waiting for him. No foreigner to this condition, he did not hesitate, but took up his brushes and started to paint her, full length. But on seeing what he was up to she was horrified, protesting that the picture was cruel, while he endeavoured to explain that 'lots of husbands want it like that, you know'.* In the saga of this picture, and John's many visits to Chirk in order to complete it, lies much of

* John had painted a full-length portrait of Ida when she was pregnant. It is now in the National Gallery of Wales, Cardiff. 'It is a picture of a pregnant woman, painted with the assured brushwork of Hals or Manet, and a tenderness reminiscent of Rembrandt's,' wrote R. L. Charles, the Keeper of Art: 'mastery, depth and intimacy combined in a way hardly paralleled in British painting of its time.' *Amgueddfa*. Bulletin of the National Museum of Wales. 12. Winter 1972, p. 29.

the pattern his life would follow. After this first visit he wrote to Quinn (11 October 1912): 'I enjoyed my stay at the medieval Castle of Chirk. I found deer stalking with bows and arrows exciting. Lord Howard goes in for falconry also and now and then dons a suit of steel armour . . .' In such an atmosphere there was room for his ideas to expand. 'Howard de W ought to be taken in hand,' he was soon telling Dorelia. His host had allowed second-rate people to 'impose themselves on him'. By way of a new regime he suggested substituting himself in their place as artist-in-residence. He would decorate, on a vast scale, the Music Room at Chirk : it was a grand scheme. But first there was the problem of her ladyship's portrait. It was, he told Quinn, extremely promising. He waited patiently till after the birth of her twins, started again, exhibited it half-finished, re-commenced, changed her black hair to pink and threatened to 'alter everything'. Years went by: wars came. Her ladyship's nose, John complained, was an enigma. Finally he spoilt the painting beyond redemption, offering her in its place another picture. The Music Room was never begun. But he was not idle at Chirk; he painted all the time – small brilliant panels of the Welsh landscape which he conceived to be preliminary studies for his big non-existent Music Room decorations.

Chirk was a precursor of his later career. It saw a preliminary miscarriage before his birth as erratic portrait painter of fashionable and aristocratic sitters;* and, more indirectly, it saw too his death as a brilliant symbolist painter. 'Do you mind if I bring a friend?' he once asked Lady Howard de Walden. This was Derwent Lees. Recently John's opinion of Lees's work had risen. Despite his wooden leg, Lees had climbed up the outside of the Chenil Gallery and entered upon a seven-round combat with Knewstub :† it was impossible to think badly of such a man even when, to everyone's surprise, he suddenly got himself married to a model. 'I too was astonished by the Lees marriage,' Innes admitted to John (4 August 1913). '. . . I think

---

* 'I would much rather just do the things I want to do and leave people to buy if they want . . . I am not likely to make a success of fashionable people even if I tried to.' John to Quinn (29 September 1913).

† On another occasion Orpen aimed a gun at Knewstub, fired it, but missed him and shot a hole through one of his own pictures.

I felt rather jealous of him. Well they looked very happy and so good luck to them.' A year later Innes was dead, but Lees could not take his place. He looked lost and white when John brought him to Chirk during a very smart week-end party and, it later transpired, was under the impression he had arrived at an expensive lunatic asylum. At night he would stand rigid in the corridors, a helpless pyjama'd figure, and when called upon for some explanation, whisper: 'Frightened. Can't sleep.' He had developed a shorthand method of speaking, like a child. 'Want to go for walk,' he would say. But when Lady Howard de Walden soothingly offered to accompany him, Lees objected: 'Can't. No gloves.' He did not feel safe without gloves. It was a symptom of the mental illness that by the end of the war put an end to his career as a painter and eventually killed him.

Although John obstinately admired the simple life, everything conspired to complicate his own. Chirk Castle was a fine example of this process. For his security John needed plans; but he also needed to avoid the implications of these plans unless they were to become prisons for the future. He could not edit life, had not grasped the trick of saying no. He was impelled to say yes even when no one had asked him anything. He said yes now to the prospect of Lord Howard de Walden becoming a new patron. The difficulties that might follow with Quinn or even with Hugh Lane, whom he had similarly elected, were of no account. He looked only at the attractive side. He would need, for example, a new house – somewhere close to Chirk. On his first visit he had been introduced to the composer Joseph Holbrooke, 'an extraordinary chap ... funniest creature I've ever met'.[71] With Holbrooke's friend, the artist Sidney Sime, they had set off on a number of wild motor rides around Wales, knocking up Sampson at Bala, descending on Lees at Ffestiniog, resting a little with Innes at Nant Ddu 'where I always keep a few bottles of chianti'; then scaling the Park gates at Chirk at three o'clock in the morning. 'The country round Ffestiniog was staggering,' he reported to Dorelia (September 1912), '... I have my eye on a cottage or two ... I feel full of work.'

Having exhausted the possibilities at Nant Ddu, John decided to throw in his lot with Holbrooke and Sime, and the three of them took Llwynythyl, a corrugated-iron shanty consisting of a large kitchen, a living-room and four small cabins containing bunks, the upper ones reached by wooden ladders. On the inside it was lined with tongued and grooved pinewood plank-ing, lightly varnished but otherwise left its natural colour. Into this remote bungalow in the mountains above the Vale of Ffestiniog, Holbrooke (who collaborated with Lord Howard de Walden on an operatic trilogy) imported a piano, and John imported Lily Ireland, a model of classic proportions who had never before strayed beyond the slum pastures of London. It was a desolate place, reached by a steep climb from Tan-y-grisiau, the nearest station, up an old trolley-shaft with a broken cable-winch at the top. The bungalow stood on a small plateau and commanded an extraordinary view across the valley to the range of mountains on the other side, above which the endless drama of the sky unfolded itself, and below the breathing land was draped in purple or shone suddenly in a dazzling corusca-tion of blue and gold.

The place was almost ready, and John prepared himself for a long painting expedition. In December he set off: for France. The weather was so gloomy he had decided to go south 'with the intention of working out of doors'.[72] At the New Year, Epstein reported him passing through Paris 'in good spirits'.[73] He planned to link up with Innes and Lees in Marseilles. From the Hôtel du Nord he wrote to Dorelia:

Innes came yesterday morning. He looks rather dejected. Lees doesn't appear to be well yet. He is going back to London. We have been wandering about Marseilles all day. When you come we might get another cart and donkey. I have advised Innes to go to Paris and get a girl as he is pretty well lost alone and must have a model ... I don't know who you might bring over. Nellie Furr, that girl you said one day might be a bore although she has a good figure and seems amiable enough. It could of course make a lot of difference to have several people to pose.[74]

Marching off each day into the country to 'look about', John would return late at night to Marseilles – and to Innes who, though invariably talking of his departure, would not leave. 'He is insupportable – appears to be going off his head and stutters dreadfully,' John complained. 'He wanted to come and work with me but I can't stand him for long.'

It was now Dorelia's turn to come south, bringing with her money, underclothing, a paintbox, some hairwash – but no model: and the three of them moved, in some dejection, to the Hotel Basio at St Chamas. 'It is a beautiful place,' John told Mrs Nettleship, 'on the same lake as Martigues but on the north side.' No sooner had they settled in than Innes fell seriously ill. 'He had had a very dissipated time at Perpignan and was quite run down,' John explained to Quinn (2 February 1913). 'Finally at St Chamas ... he was laid up for about a week after which we took him back to Paris and sent him off to London to see a doctor ... The company of a sick man gets on one's nerves in the end.'

Though he spent part of August in Paris in the strange company of Epstein, J. C. Squire and Modigliani (from whom he bought 'a couple of stone heads'), John did use his new Welsh cottage during 1913, passing all July there and all September. The paintings he did in these two months were exhibited during November in a highly successful show at the Goupil Gallery. His letters show that he was working in tempera, a technique of painting that had the advantage of putting him physically in closer touch with the fifteenth-century Italians from whom he sought inspiration, and his own recipe for which he passed on to younger British artists such as Mark Gertler.* He was also attempting to work on a larger scale than before. At the end of 1911 his large 'Forza e Amore' had been hung at the New English Art Club to the bewilderment of almost everyone. At the end of 1912 he showed 'The Mumpers'. 'The N.E.A.C. has just been hung,' he wrote to John Hope-Johnstone (20 November 1912). 'I suddenly took and painted my cartoon of Mumpers – in Tempera, finished it in 4½ days, and sent it in. In spite of the hasty workmanship, it doesn't look so bad on the whole. I have

---

* In the summer of 1912, Gertler wrote that John 'proceeded to give me some very useful "tips" on tempera,' and by September he was writing: 'Just think, I have actually done a painting in that wonderful medium tempera, the medium of our old Great friends! . . . I love tempera.' See *Mark Gertler* by John Woodeson, pp. 81, 100.

also an immense drawing of the Caucasian Gypsies [Calderari].'
Again, at the late New English show of 1913, he exhibited another huge cartoon, 'The Flute of Pan', which was the 'chief
attraction'.* All these years, too, he had been struggling with
Hugh Lane's big picture, subsequently called 'Lyric Fantasy'. On
28 October 1913 he was writing to Ottoline Morrell: 'I am
overwhelmed with the problem of finishing Lane's picture.' He
had hoped to show it at the next New English. On 29 December he confided to Quinn that it 'will soon be done'; and
again on 16 March 1914 he is 'actually getting Lane's big picture
done at last'. So it went on until, in 1915, Lane was drowned on
board the *Lusitania*, at which opportunity John abruptly ceased
work on it altogether. Had Quinn himself had the tact to die
prematurely, there seems every likelihood that his big picture
'Forza e Amore' would have survived.† Despite this epidemic
of long unfinished pictures, John was working harder than ever
before and producing much of his best work. This was often
achieved as an offshoot to what he considered really important
– as preliminary studies for larger decorations, panels knocked

* John Currie to Mark Gertler. It comprised three female, four male figures,
and a boy, all life size. 'Some say it is the best thing I've done and some the
worst,' John told Quinn (26 January 1914).

† This picture had originally been promised to Quinn in 1910. Quinn's
inquiries about it met with little response until 19 February 1914 when John
announced that he was now able to 'simplify the problem by confessing that I
have *painted it out* some time back. I had it down here [Alderney] to work on,
and after reflection decided I could not finish it to my satisfaction (without the
original models) and thought I would paint you another picture which would
be a great deal better. The cartoon lately at the N. English (The Flute of Pan)
was started with that object. In course of doing it I added the right portion of
the design, consisting of landscape which makes it about a third larger than
"Forza e Amore". As to Lane's claim to this last – it originally formed part of a
much larger scheme which on my break with him I did not carry out . . . I am
damn sorry you were so set on the "F. e A." I was merely conscientious in
painting it out as I did. But you will like The Flute of Pan better and the price
of course will be the same.'

Quinn was horrified at this news, and John assured him (16 March 1914) he
was not alone. 'I was at Lane's lately and told him I had painted out "Forza e
Amore". Words failed him to express his horror . . . He implored me to send
it up to him and let him have the coat of white I gave it taken off. Shall I? I
suppose I was a bloody fool to do it.' Three months later (24 June 1914) he
confirmed that Quinn had 'the only real claim to the picture' – adding that he
was now certain the white coat could not be removed successfully.

off while on holiday, or pictures done as designs for Dorelia's embroidery. His output was prodigious. He held shows almost every year at Chenil's, sometimes covered whole walls at the New English, struggled on with his private commissions, and regularly sent work in to the Society of Twelve and the National Portrait Society of which, in February 1914, he was elected President. What caused the muddle in his life was also midwife to his best work – a sense of urgency, assisted very often by financial pressure. So as to grapple with his problems John made a habit of externalizing them. But what he grappled with was some phantom rather than the problem itself, at best a symptom. Whenever he felt dull or ill he fixed the blame on people and places, and would demand a change. These changes often brought with them an immediate lifting of his spirits, but would quickly lead to complications even worse than those he had fled from.

For a short time early in 1913 he populated a bewildering number of houses acquired through this process of change. There was Alderney which he shared with Dorelia and his family; Nant Ddu which he shared with Innes; Llwynythyl which he shared with Holbrooke and Sime; the Villa St Anne at Martigues which he shared with the mad bird-man Bazin; and 181A King's Road, Chelsea, which he shared with Knewstub. He felt restless. The cure he settled on was a new London house and studio. Entering a public house in Chelsea, he demanded to know whether there was an architect present and then commissioned a Dutchman he had never met before who happened to be drinking at the bar. The simple part of the business was now over.

Van-t-Hoff, as this architect was called, 'takes the studio very seriously', John promised Dorelia. '... He is going back to' Holland to *think hard.*' After a long interval of slumbering thought, John was obliged to summon him back by cable. By 13 May 1913 he confidently reported to Quinn : 'My Dutch architect has done his designs for my new studio with living rooms – and it will be a charming place. They will start building at once and it'll be done in 6 months. How glad I shall be to be able to live more quietly – a thing almost impossible in this studio. My lawyer strongly urges me to try and find the money for the building straight away instead of saddling myself with a mortgage. The building will cost £2,200.' John would have liked to offer all the responsibilities for this property to others – looking in from time to time to pass, over the rising pile, his critical eye. But lawyers, estate agents, builders and decorators were constantly importuning him. 'I can't be rushing all over London and paint too, not having the brain of a Pierpont Morgan,' he complained to Dorelia. Nor was it just his time for which these people were so greedy. 'I shall want all my money and a good deal of other people's,' he explained to John Hope-Johnstone (8 September 1913). His letters to Quinn are congested with money proposals, the nicest of which is a scheme to save costs by building two houses, the second (at some considerable distance from the first) for his patron. 'The materials will be of the best,' he assures him, 'and I think it will be a great success.' His own house continued to rise, his funds to sink and his spirits to oscillate between optimism and despair. He had decided to move in during the autumn, but when autumn came the house still had no roof. 'It'll be ready in January,' he declared: adding with some desperation, 'I feel rather inclined to try another planet.'[75] By February 1914 he had not retreated an inch. 'The house is getting on well and will be done in three weeks Van-t-Hoff thinks,' he informed the silent Dorelia (26 February 1914). Three weeks later it was 'nearly done' and being 'much admired'. By April John is again ready to move – but to Dieppe where he aims to hold out until the house is equipped to receive him. After what turns out to be a fortnight round Cardiganshire and, in June, one week at Boulogne he returns to Chelsea and, though the house is still incomplete, decides to occupy it and hold a party 'to baptize my new studio'.[76] This party, a magnificent affair in fancy dress, lasts from the first into the second week of July.

'The company was very charming and sympathetic, I thought,' wrote an early guest, Lytton Strachey,

– so easy-going and taking everything for granted; and really I think it's the proper milieu for me – if only the wretches had a trifle more brain ... John was a superb figure. There was dancing – two-steps and such things – so much nicer than waltzes – and at last I danced with him [John] – it seemed an opportunity not to be missed. (I forget to say I was dressed as a pirate). Nini Lamb was there, and made effréné love to me. We came out in broad daylight.[77]

The site on which John had raised this house was in Mallord Street,* parallel to the King's Road and just off Church Street, where he had lived six years before. It was like a dolls' house, a charming, impractical square place, beautiful but unfitted to contain John and his family. Steep steps led up to the front door, behind which the rooms were poky and, in spite of the sun streaming in from the south over the market gardens, dark. The windows were long and thin and well-proportioned; yet they appeared almost unopenable and, when children appeared behind them, looked like iron-barred cages. With its mid-tone panelling it was a gloomy, if not unfriendly, interior. The best feature was the staircase which, copied from Rembrandt's house, floated gracefully upwards. In the drawing-room Boris Anrep designed a superb mosaic, a pyramid of the wives and children with John at its apex, that glowed a dull green as if from the depths of the sea. At the back lay the great studio. With its sloping ceiling, deep alcove, two fires burning at opposite corners, it conveyed a sense of hemmed-in space, like the exercise yard of a prison. 'The studio looks fine,' John told Quinn (24 June 1914). But even in these early days he recognized the prison-like atmosphere of the place. 'It is quite a success I think. It has nearly ruined me,' he wrote to John Hope-Johnstone. '. . . It certainly is rather Dutch but has a solidity and tautness unmatched in London – a little stronghold. I hope I shall find the studio practical.' The studio was perhaps the most practical area – a good place to paint and an excellent arena for parties. But within two years the 'little stronghold' had crumbled into 'this damned Dutch shanty'.[78] John felt incarcerated there and his dissatisfaction, which he attributed to the Dutchman's 'passion for rectangles',[79] was added to by Dorelia's dislike of the place – even the roof garden faced north.

By this time he had shed his two Welsh cottages. Nant Ddu went first. Between February 1913 and August 1914 he did not see Innes who, in an attempt to regain his health, had gone to

* It was originally No. 5, but the numbering was changed later that year and it became No. 28.

Tenerife with Trelawney Dayrell Reed. Llwynythyl was given
up in 1914.* The place had gone sour on him. He tracked down
the source of this feeling to the presence of Joseph Holbrooke
and the noise he made at meals. 'I don't think I can stand him
and will probably leave at the end of the week . . . I could get on
with Sime but Holbrooke is too horrible.' While Holbrooke, it
appeared, had 'a tune constantly playing in his left ear', the
'man Sime' seemed one of Nature's gentlemen – strongly built,
with a cliff-like, overhanging, tyrannous forehead, eyes of super-
lative greyish-blue and a look (which grew fixed at Llwynythyl)
of pathetic patience.[80]

In place of Wales, John had hit upon 'the only warm place
north of the Pyramids'[81] during winter: Lamorna Cove, near
Penzance in Cornwall where he met 'a number of excellent
people down in the little village . . . all painters of sorts'[82] – John
Birch, Harold and Laura Knight, and Alfred Munnings† – 'and
we had numerous beanos'. These 'beanos', which led to invitations to continue them in London, were terrifying affairs. 'We
feared,' Dame Laura Knight recalled, 'to shorten our lives.'[83]
John would perform all manner of amazing tricks – opening
bottles of wine, tenderly, without a corkscrew; flicking, from a
great distance, pats of butter into people's mouths; dancing, on
point in his hand-made shoes, upon the rickety table, and other
astonishing feats until dawn. Then, while the others collapsed
into exhausted sleep, out he would go in search of Dorelia, and
do little studies of her in various poses on the rocks: 'He never
did anything better'.[84] The local community was much agitated

---

* Llwynythyl was later taken by the composer Granville Bantock. His
daughter remembers that John 'had drawn an enormous mural in white chalk of
angel figures covering the entire end wall of the sitting-room . . . We discovered a whole pile of discarded oil paints and brushes, together with many
crumpled sketches. We salvaged and smoothed out two of these sketches and I
still have one of them . . . an amusing cartoon of a woman sitting at a table and
trying to work; around her pots and pans are flying through the air, a tradesman
presents bills and a half-naked baby screams on the floor.'

† John went out sketching with Munnings, listening carefully to Munnings's
theory that a horse's coat reflects the light of day, and then, after silent reflection, gruffly demanding: 'If you see a brown horse, why not paint it brown?'
Many years later John told E. J. Rousuck that Munnings's horses had 'better
picture quality, better groupings' than Stubbs's. See *The Englishman* by
Reginald Pound, pp. 50, 51, 201.

by these parties, by the mortal sin of Sunday painting and Dorelia's brazen habit of walking abroad on that day without a hat. But John was delighted with the place. 'I found Cornwall a most sympathetic country,' he wrote to Quinn on his arrival back at Alderney (19 February 1914). '... There are some extraordinarily nice people there among the artists and some very attractive young girls among the people.'

John was in the Café Royal the night war was declared. 'I remember our excitement over it,'[85] he wrote. One of their friends carried the news among the waiters, and John, very perturbed, turned to Bomberg: 'This is going to be bad for art.' Much of that August he spent with Innes, who, indifferent to the tremors of war, was dying. To John himself the war threatened to make little personal difference: a disappointing prospect. With Dorelia pregnant once more and, also by John, one of his models, the future seemed to promise simply more of the same. But though he took no exaggerated part in this war, it was to affect him permanently.

8

How He Got On

'Kennington and John: both hag-ridden by a sense that
perhaps their strength was greater than they knew. What
an uncertain, disappointed, barbarous generation we war-
timers have been. They said the best ones were killed.
There's far too much talent still alive.'

T. E. LAWRENCE TO WILLIAM ROTHENSTEIN
(14 APRIL 1928)

I. MARKING TIME

'Wadsworth, along with Augustus John and nearly everybody,
is drilling in the courtyard of the Royal Academy, in a regiment for home defence,' wrote Ezra Pound that autumn to
Harriet Monroe. It was the last occasion John would find himself
so precisely in step with other artists. The war's immediate
effect on him had been to clarify life. His letters grew more
portentous, nearer in tone to those of his father: full of the
stuff to give the troops. Already in the first month, the sight of
fifteen hundred territorials plodding up Regent Street swells
him with pride: 'they looked damn fine'.[1] And by the end of the
war he was to feel anxiety lest the Germans be let off too
lightly. 'The German hatred for England is the finest compliment
we have been paid for ages,' he assures Quinn on 12 October
1914. To some extent he seems to have fallen victim to war
propaganda, though never to war literature. 'The atrocities of
the Germans are only equalled in horror by the war poems of
the English papers,' he writes to Ottoline Morrell in 1916. 'What
tales of blood and mud!' In addition to what he reads in the
papers, he absorbs confidential matter from his various khaki
sitters, repeating strange stories of lunatic generals on whom he
fixes the blame for all defeats. 'As for the men, they are beyond
praise.'[2] By the spring of 1916 he is looking forward to being
able to 'swamp the German lines with metal'.

John's attitude to the war remained consistent: but his emotions, as he lived through it, veered hectically. At first he is excited; by the end it has aged him, and he is no longer the same person. He started out smartly in step, but it left him far behind, marching on to build a world where he could never feel at home. From the beginning he wanted to 'join in' – 'it's rather sickening to be out of it all'.[3] His predicament is set out in a letter (10 October 1914) to Quinn:

I have had more than one impulse to enlist but have each time been dissuaded by various arguments. In the first place I can't decide to leave my painting at this stage nor can I leave my family without resources to go on with. I feel sure I shall be doing better to keep working at my own job. Still all depends on how the War goes on. I long to see something of the fighting and possibly may manage to get in [in] some capacity. I feel a view of the havoc in Belgium with the fleeing refugees would be inspiring and memorable. Lots of my friends have joined the army. The general feeling of the country is I believe quite decent and cheerfully serious – not at all reflected by the nauseating cant and hypocrisy and vulgarity of the average Press. There is no lack of volunteers. The difficulty is to cope with the immense number of recruits, feed and clothe and drill them. There are 20,000 near here, still mostly without their uniforms but they have sing-songs every night in the pubs till they are turned out at 9 o'clock.

The war intensified John's sense of exclusion; and by curtailing freedom of movement it aggravated his tendency to claustrophobia. Apart from a vain trip to Paris in December 1914 to persuade Gwen to come back to England for the duration of the war,* he did not return to France for three-and-a-half years. 'I feel the nostalgie du Midi now that there's no chance of going there,' he told Ottoline. '... I commence the New Year rather ill-temperedly.'[4] The dark days, from which there was now no escape, made work uncertain. He began to develop numerous symptoms about the head and legs that 'put me quite out of action'[5] and accounted, as it were, for his long civilian incarceration.

---

* 'I offered to fetch her [Gwen John] over to England but she refused to leave Paris,' John wrote to Quinn on 10 October 1914. Two months later he went over and repeated his offer – 'otherwise she is likely to suffer great hardship' – but Gwen, as he had predicted, stayed on.

Ireland now took the place of France. He made several visits
to Dublin, to Galway and Connemara – but even here there was
not the same independence as before. The men were going off
'to fight England's battles', and there was a great wailing on the
platforms as their women saw them off. 'I have found a house
here,' he wrote to Dorelia from Galway City,[6] 'with fine big
rooms and windows which I'm taking – only £30 a year ... I
had a bad attack of blues here, doing nothing, but the prospect
of soon getting to work bucks me up.' This house was in Tuam
Street and owned by Bishop O'Dea who leased it to John for
three years on the understanding that no painting from the nude
was to be enjoyed on the premises. John's plan was to execute a
big dramatization of Galway bringing in everything characteristic of the place. He explained this scheme to Dorelia (5 October
1915):

I'm thinking out a vast picture synthesizing all that's fine and
characteristic in Galway City – a grand marshalling of the elements.
It will have to be enormous to contain troops of women and children, groups of fishermen, docks, wharves, the church, mills, constables, donkeys, widows, men from Aran, hookers* etc., perhaps
with a night sky and all illuminated in the light of a dream. This will
be worth while – worth the delay and the misery that went before.

He went out into the streets, staring, sketching: and was at
once identified as a bearded spy. Bathing – 'the best tonic in
the world' – was reckoned to be a misdemeanour in wartime;
and sketching in the harbour a treason – 'so that is a drawback
and a big one'. In a letter to Ottoline Morrell, with whose
portrait he was attempting to wrestle from memory, he complained: 'There are wonderful people and it is beautiful about
the harbour but if one starts sketching one is at once shot by
a policeman ... It would be worth while passing 6 months here
given the right conditions.'

But the right conditions for John's type of work were elusive.
The spirit of the place seemed to be evaporating. Without disobeying the letter of Bishop O'Dea's injunction, 'I had two girls
in here yesterday,' he admitted to Dorelia, 'but they didn't give

* A two-masted fishing-boat of Dutch origin used off the west coast of
Ireland. John had a scheme for buying one for fifty pounds.

the same impression as when seen in the street. I could do with some underclothing.' He was desperately anxious not to return to Alderney 'till I've got something good to take away'. Every day he would go out and look, then hurry back to Tuam Street and do some drawings or pen-and-wash sketches. 'I've observed the people here enough,' he eventually wrote to Dorelia. 'Their drapery is often very pleasing – one generally sees one good thing a day at least – but the population is greatly spoilt now – 20 years ago it must have been astonishing ... Painting from nature *and* from imagination spells defeat I see clearly.'

Imagination meant in practice memory. His imagination was kindled, by some perception of beauty, instantly: then the good minute went. He had to catch it before it began to fade, rather than try to recollect it in tranquillity. Yet now there seemed no alternative to a retrospective technique – what he called 'mental observation'.[7] After vacillating for weeks between the railway station and the telegraph office, he left. 'It was in the end,' he explained to Bernard Shaw, 'less will-power than panic that got me away.'[8]

He had been at Galway two months. After his return to Alderney he began to work feverishly at a large cartoon, covering four hundred square feet in a single week. Once again he was racing against time. He wanted, before they had clouded over, to use his actual observations – all those one good things a day – to build up a composite picture of an ideal Galway: a visionary city locked deep in his imagination to which, all his life, he was searching to find the key.

War offers some painters a unique opportunity to record and interpret unusual sights. Lamb, Lewis, Paul Nash, C. R. W. Nevinson, William Roberts and Stanley Spencer were among the artists who seized this opportunity and contributed to a group of pictures unexampled in modern British painting. Many of John's friends, such as McEvoy and Orpen,* had long ago

---

* 'McEvoy is in a state of exultation bordering on hysteria – the result of painting duchesses and other nobilities.' John to Dorelia (1915). Many years later, on 5 January 1944, John wrote to D. S. MacColl: 'I have always thought the absurd superstition that Orpen was in any sense an artist should be scotched. Personally he had nice qualities though he had all the disadvantages of arrested growth.'

succumbed to an unnourishing diet of fashionable portraiture. John, like William Nicholson, also painted commissioned portraits to earn money; but they were not especially fashionable and he had never been corrupted by them. By 1914, in a hit-or-miss fashion, he was still painting in his best vein. 'Of course painters as good as John will always sell,' Sickert assured Nan Hudson, 'war or no war.' But the war put pressures on him. 'I am afraid we are in for thin times over here,' he explained to Quinn. 'No one will want luxuries like pictures for awhile.'[9] Nevertheless he continued to paint those pictures, such as 'Galway', for which, he felt, his talent was best suited: landscapes, decorative groups, paintings of his family. In the past he had sold such work better than any of his contemporaries, but after 1914 this was no longer possible. Partly for financial reasons, but partly also because he did not want his work to be wholly irrelevant to the business of the war, he began to paint a different sort of picture. 'I am called upon to provide various things in aid of war funds or charities connected with the war,' he told Quinn.[10] Among his sitters were several staff officers and in 1916 the bellicose Admiral Lord Fisher who brought in tow the Duchess of Hamilton,* to whom John transferred part of his attentions, while Fisher, with measured quarter-deck stride, explained how to 'end the war in a week'.[11] When this portrait was shown at the N.E.A.C., Albert Rutherston noted that it was 'careless and sketchy',[12] and the *Times* critic observed that John had really painted a zoo picture of Fisher as a 'Sea-Lion ... hungering for his prey'.[13] On the whole these public portraits of war celebrities are not good, perhaps because John could not

---

* This commission to paint Lord Fisher had come through Epstein, who had recently done a bust of Fisher for the Duchess of Hamilton. 'Fisher, while I was doing the bust, asked me if I knew of a painter who I thought would do a portrait of the Duchess for him; and said he thought of getting Laszlo the Austrian to do it,' Epstein wrote to Quinn (14 June 1916); 'but I told him he *must get John*, so I've been arranging to have John paint the Duchess's portrait ... I couldn't see Laszlo preferred to him.' When the proposal reached John, it was to do a portrait of Fisher — with a chance of painting the Duchess of Hamilton afterwards if there was time: an arrangement that may have accounted for his rather hurried treatment of the Admiral. John began a portrait of the Duchess and visited her on several occasions.

match his public sentiments with private feelings. In his correspondence he is often generously approving of these bold statesmen and soldiers; but when he actually came face to face with
them he felt unaccountably bored. In the circumstances he did
not think it proper to caricature them as he had done the Lord
Mayor of Liverpool. Some satire, in a muted form, does come
through: but seldom convincingly.

Perhaps the most interesting of these war pictures was that of
Lloyd George. It was towards the end of 1915 that Lloyd George
surrendered to the proposal that John should paint him. A suitable canvas had been bought by Sir James Murray in aid of Red
Cross Funds, the arrangement being that John would paint
whomever Murray, a friend of Lloyd George, designated. Like
some marriage broker, Murray settled up the agreement between them, then discreetly retired, confident that the two
Welshmen would get on like fireworks. In fact, since they had
just the wrong things in common, they did not take to each
other. The poetry of their natures was rooted in Wales: England had magnetized their ambitions. But their ambitions were
different. Happy as a child, pampered by his family, Lloyd
George was greedy for the world's attentions. John in his childhood had felt deprived of love, and sought to evoke an ideal
world set in those places of natural beauty politicians call the
wilderness. 'I feel I have no contact,' Lloyd George once told
Frances Stevenson. John too had no contact by the end: but he
had been reaching for other things.

In public, at least, John admired Lloyd George. He was 'doing
good work over Munitions' and would surely have made a better
business than Asquith of leading the country to victory. 'One
feels that what really is wanted is a sort of Cromwell to take
charge,' he told Quinn, 'having turned out our Parliamentarians
into the street first.'[14] The Welsh wizard who was to play the
part of Cromwell does not seem to have dazzled John when
they first met a year before in Wales; and as a sitter he was
highly unsatisfactory. He had agreed 'to sit for half an hour in
the mornings' but, John complained, was 'difficult to get hold
of'.[15] The portrait lurched forward in short bursts during
December, January and February. On 16 February 1916 John

wrote to Quinn : 'I have finished my portrait of Lloyd George. He was a rotten sitter – as you say a "hot-arse who can't sit still and be patient".' It was a restlessness, eventually dissolving into incoherence, that consumed them both. Lloyd George may not have appreciated being placed, in order of priority, behind the actress Réjane whom John was then also painting, and indiscriminately shoulder to shoulder with 'some soldiers'. According to Lloyd George's mistress, Frances Stevenson, 'the sittings were not very gay ones'.[16] Lloyd George was 'in a grim mood', suffering, in addition to toothache, from the latest Serbian crisis. Nevertheless, this cannot wholly account for his testy expression – 'a hard, determined, almost cruel face,' Frances Stevenson noted angrily in her diary, 'with nothing of the tenderness & charm of the D[avid] of everyday life'.[17] 'Do you notice what John says about pictures which he does not like?' he had asked her. 'Very pleasant!' He was 'upset', she realized, 'for he likes to look nice in his portraits!' Another worry was Frances herself. Though professing to find John 'terrifying', she acknowledged him to be 'an uncommon person ... extraordinarily conceited ... nevertheless ... very fascinating'. Lloyd George responded to this threat with a most practised performance. He discouraged her from having her own portrait painted by John (though she generally admired his work) and, to her disappointment, expressly prohibited her from accepting invitations to his parties. Confronted by John's 'unpleasant' portrait he reverted to nursery tactics, gathering his family round him (much to John's irritation) in a chorus of abuse over the object, and provoking in 'Pussy' Stevenson her most protective vein. To account for the cunning, querulous expression, he suggested in public entitling the picture 'Salonika'. Then, having wrapped up this awkward incident, he affected to forget about it.[18] But John remembered. Announcing his first portrait to have been 'unfinished', he caught up with Lloyd George nearly four years later in Deauville,* rapidly drew his brushes and began a second canvas. Under his fierce gaze Lloyd George grew restless again, hurried back to London and, wisely, did not honour his promise to continue the sittings at Downing Street. For John this was a foretaste of how his career as a professional portrait painter,

* At the Villa la Chaumière in September 1919.

particularly of men in public life, would proceed.* As his powers waned, so increasingly he relished the prospect of meeting the famous. But invariably the prospect was better than the experience – except, sometimes, in the case of other artists and writers.

These portraits, especially of writers, comprise a separate section of his work – not private in the same way that 'Washing Day' or 'The Red Feather' are private, but not to be classed among what Quinn fretfully described as his 'colonels and fat women, and ... other disagreeable pot-boilers'.[19] Among the writers who sat to him in the war years were W. H. Davies,[20] Ronald Firbank, Gogarty and Arthur Symons. The most celebrated was Bernard Shaw, of whom, during May 1915, he did three portraits in oil.

Shaw was staying at Coole over Easter with Lady Gregory when his unresting industry was suddenly halted by an atrocious headache. 'Mrs Shaw was lamenting about not having him painted by a good artist,' Lady Gregory wrote to W. B. Yeats, 'and I suggested having John over, and she jumped at it, and

* In Winston Churchill, whom he drew after the Second World War, John observed the same strange inability to keep still. Under John's scrutiny, Churchill seemed reduced to the condition of a restless child. His concern, like that of Lloyd George, was for his 'image'. How else to explain, John wondered, 'these fits and starts, these visits to the mirror, this preoccupation with the window curtains, and the nervous fidgeting with his jowl?'

A less quick-footed target was Ramsay MacDonald whom John vainly attempted to paint on a number of occasions. The difficulty here seems to have been that the sitter proved too dim a subject to illuminate the romantic interpretation of a 'dreamy knight-errant, dedicated to the overthrow of dragons and the rescue of distressed damsels' which John, perverse to the point of irony, insisted upon trying to fix on him. 'John's portrait was a melancholy failure,' Ramsay MacDonald admitted to Will Rothenstein (23 August 1933). 'It really was a terrible production, and everybody who saw it turned it down instantly. He wants to begin again, but I am really tired. The waste of my time has been rather bad. He made two attempts and an earlier one some time ago. In all I must have given between 20 and 30 sittings of 1½ hours' average, and I cannot afford going on unless there is some certainty of a satisfactory result . . .'

The most satisfactory result among John's flock of prime ministers was achieved at the expense of A. J. Balfour who, under the acid test of his pencil, fell asleep. His philosophy of doubt, which always appealed to John, seemed to coincide with his appearance and reached a culmination in his slumbering posture. 'I set to,' John records, 'and completed the drawing within an hour.'

Robert [Gregory] is to bring him over on Monday.'[21] In the event
John seems to have travelled more erratically, catching 'a kind
of cold'[22] in Dublin on his way and arriving very morose. His
symptoms deepened on discovering that Lady Gregory had
used Shaw as bait for a portrait of her grandson 'little Richard'*
whom, until now, he had successfully avoided. Although John
made no secret of his preference for little Richard's sister, Anne
Gregory, 'a very pretty little child with pale gold hair,' Lady
Gregory insisted that it must be the son of the house who was
honoured. So he began this 'awful job', producing what both
children found 'a very odd picture . . . [with] enormous sticky-
out ears and eyes that sloped up at the corners, rather like a
picture of a chinaman . . .'[23]†

Meanwhile, in his bedroom, Shaw was preparing himself. He
had recovered from his headache to the extent of having his
hair cut, but in the excitement, Lady Gregory lamented, 'too
much was taken off'.[24] Despite Shaw's head and John's cold,
both were at their most winning by the time the sittings
began.

Each morning John would strip off his coat, prop his canvases on the best chairs and paint several versions at one sitting.
Whenever he was dissatisfied he washed the whole canvas clean
and started another in its place. 'He painted with large brushes
and used large quantities of paint,' Shaw remembered.[25] Over the
course of eight days he painted 'six magnificent portraits of me,'
Shaw wrote to Mrs Patrick Campbell.[26] '. . . Unfortunately as he

---

* Lady Gregory remembered this rather differently. In *Coole*, she wrote:
'John asked while he was here if he might paint Richard, and I, delighted,
reading a story to the child, kept him still for the sitting. I longed to possess the
picture but did not know how I could do so without stinting the comforts of
the household, and said no word. But I think he must have seen my astonished
delight when he gave it to me, said it was for me he had painted it. That was
one of the happy moments of my life.' She also added: 'I had from the time of
his birth dreamed he might one day be painted by that great Master, Augustus
John, yet it had seemed but a dream.'

† 'Augustus John had been very annoyed at being thwarted, and had given
Richard that funny look to pay Grandma out! The picture of Richard was hung
in the drawing-room, on the left of the big fireplace.' Anne Gregory also
remembered that John 'was large and rather frightening to look at, and we felt
he might step on us, as he seemed to stride about not ever looking where he was
going'. *Me and Nu*, Chapter VIII.

kept painting them on top of one another until our protests became overwhelming, only three portraits have survived.'

Between sittings John went off for 'some grand galloping'[27] with Robert Gregory, or, more sedately, would row Mrs Shaw across the lake. 'Mrs Shaw is [a] fat party with green eyes who says "Ye-hes" in an intellectual way ending with a hiss,' he divulged to Dorelia. Over thirty years later, in *Chiaroscuro*, John described Shaw as 'a true Prince of the Spirit, a fearless enemy of cant and humbug, and in his queer way, a highly respectable though strictly uncanonical saint'.[28] In his letters to Dorelia at the time he refers to him as 'a ridiculous vain object in knickerbockers' and describes the three of them – Lady Gregory and the Shaws – as 'dreadful people'. Such discrepancies were odd notes played by John's violently fluctuating moods which, from about this time onwards, were to grow more exaggerated. Together they orchestrate his personality on an increasingly discordant pattern : but in isolation they are almost meaningless – unconnected points in a contour-map that, to the untrained eye, can be misleading. It is the published, retrospective account that, strangely, gives more of the truth than the correspondence. What lies concealed under a patina of public deference is the extraordinary inconsistency that was becoming so characteristic of him. His admiration of Shaw was qualified by the extreme awe radiated towards him from the women in the house. This veneration combined with John's hearty silence to stimulate in Shaw the kind of brilliant intellectual monologues to which John (only partly for reasons of vanity) was allergic. What, after all, is more boring than 'brilliance'?

'I find him [Shaw] a decent man to deal with,' John notified Quinn,[29] after Shaw had decided to buy one of the portraits for three hundred pounds – the one with the blue background.* His head, as Shaw had pointed out, had two aspects, the concave and the convex. John produced two studies from the con-

---

* Of the three portraits Shaw temporarily owned two. In 1922 he presented one of these to the Fitzwilliam Museum, Cambridge. 'I note that you are keeping the best – with the blue background – which I suppose still adorns one of the top corners of your room at Adelphi Terrace,' John wrote to him (24 March 1922). This portrait is now at Ayot St Lawrence and belongs to the National Trust.

cave angle, and a third (with eyes shut as if in deep thought) from the convex – 'the blind portrait' Shaw called it: adding in a letter to Mrs Patrick Campbell that it had 'got turned into a subject entitled Shaw Listening to Someone Else Talking, because I went to sleep ...'[30] With this sleeping version John was never wholly satisfied. 'It could only have happened of course in the dreamy atmosphere of Coole,' he suggested to Shaw.[31]*

On the whole Shaw was delighted with these portraits, especially the one he held on to all his life – 'though to keep it in a private house seems to me rather like keeping an oak tree in an umbrella stand'.[32] In the regular Irish manner, like Yeats, he boasted that 'John makes me out the inebriated gamekeeper'; but in later life he would tell other artists wishing to paint him that since he had been 'done' by the two greatest artists in the last forty years, Rodin and John, there was no room for more portraits.†

John exhibited the portrait with the blue background at the summer show of the N.E.A.C. in 1915; and in February 1916 he held an exhibition of twenty-one paintings and forty-one drawings at the Chenil Gallery. It was, perhaps, his last effort to pursue something of what he had been doing before the war. The tone of many reviews was caught by the *Times* critic who, under the heading 'Empty Accomplishment', concluded that 'Mr Augustus John continues to mark time with great professional

* He attributed the expression to Shaw's intake of midday vegetables, though admitting (16 May 1915) that 'the one in which you have apparently reached a state of philosophic oblivion is perhaps liable to misinterpretation'. It was originally credited with the title 'The Philosopher in Contemplation' or 'When Homer Nods'. It was bought by an Australian who later sold it in London where it was purchased by the Queen. It now hangs in Clarence House.

† Between John's portrait and Rodin's bust, which had been done a few years earlier, Shaw differentiated. 'With an affectation of colossal vanity, Shaw gestured and genuflected before the Rodin bust of himself when I once visited him,' Archibald Henderson wrote (*George Bernard Shaw: Man of the Century*, 1956 edn., p. 789); 'but during a later visit delightedly rushed me into the dining-room to see the Augustus John poster-portrait, in primary colours – flying locks and breezy moustaches, rectangular head, and caricaturishly flouting underlip. To the John portrait he pointed with a delicious chuckle: "There's the portrait of my great reputation"; then pointing to the Rodin bust, he breathed: "Just as I am, without one plea".' But it is arguable that, by 1915, Shaw's protective covering was complete, and G.B.S., the public personality, had eclipsed the man as he was.

skill'. The eyes of critics and painters were now fixed on him to
see in what new direction he would set off.

2. THE VIRGIN'S PRAYER

'A house without children isn't worth living in!' John had once
pronounced. His sons, no longer to be classed simply as children,
now passed much of their time at schools and colleges: but the
supply of fresh children to Alderney went on unchecked. In
March 1915, in a room next to the kitchen, John presiding,
Dorelia gave birth to a second daughter, described as 'small and
nice',[33] whom they named Vivien. By the age of two she had
grown into 'a most imposing personage – half the size of Poppet,
and twice as dangerous'.[34] Through the woods she liked to
wander with her nanny, 'a beautiful Irish setter called Cuchulain
... he patiently bringing me home for meals at the toll of the
great bell'.[35] Unlike the boys, neither Poppet nor Vivien was sent
to school. 'We roamed the countryside,' Vivien recalled, 'and a
tutor cycled over from Bournemouth to teach us. Finally we
punctured his bicycle ...'

In 1917 four more children had joined the Alderney gang –
John, Nicolette, Brigit and Caitlin. These were the son and
daughters, 'robust specimens' aged between seven and three, of
Francis Macnamara, who, after seven years of happy and un-
faithful marriage, had left home permanently to live with
Euphemia Lamb (who had briefly left someone else's home to
live with him). Cut adrift, his children had circled slowly in
the wake of their mother who, helpless and half-French, was
eventually towed down to Alderney out of reach of the zep-
pelins. Because of this splintered upbringing one of the children,
Nicolette, elected John as her second father. On the strength of
her stay at Alderney over one summer she invented Alderney as
her new home and conceived for the John ménage an exaggerated loyalty not always wholeheartedly appreciated by them.
Yet her feelings give an intensity to her memories of Alderney,
despite some lapses from fact:

In my memory the bedrooms were small boxes with large double
beds. Poppet and Vivien shared one of these. On occasions we three

Macnamara girls squashed in beside them for the night. In the morning we always woke up with hangovers from an excess of giggling...

... Poppet and Vivien, the younger boys, my sisters, splashed naked in the pond, while my mother and Dodo stood by with their arms full of flowers. Edie held out a towel for a wet child. And like some mythical god observing the mortals, Augustus the Watcher sat on a bench leaning forward, his long hair covered by a felt hat, his beard a sign of authority.

It was in this garden that I first experienced ecstasy. And to-day the memory of this impact of ecstasy is as fresh as it was at the time. There has never been another garden like it; it excited me in such a way that it became the symbol of heaven.[36]

For those who, like the Macnamara or Anrep children, continually came and went, Alderney might seem an Eden; but for the John children themselves it was an Eden from which they needed to be expelled in order to be fully born into the world outside. While for a third group, a race of demi-Johns, it was also an Eden, but, seen from a place of exile, a purgatory.

The first of this race 'not of the whole blood' was the daughter of a music student of generous figure and complexion called Nora Brownsword, twenty years younger than John and known, bluntly, by her surname. On a number of occasions she had posed for him mostly for wood panels, and on 12 October 1914 he wrote in a state of some financial panic to Quinn: 'By-the-bye I've been and got a young lady in the family way! What in blazes is to be done?' Quinn suggested exporting the lady to France. This advice, which arrived safely at Alderney almost five months later, was invalid by the time John read it. Yet the problem remained. What in blazes *was* to be done?

John explained the position as clearly as he could in another letter to Quinn: 'Some while back, I conceived a wild passion for a girl and put her in the family way. She has now a daughter and I've promised her what she asks: £2 a week and £50 to set up in a cottage. I never see her now and don't want to, but I'm damned if I see where that £50 is to be found at the moment. Her father is a wealthy man. He has just tumbled to the situation and I suppose he'll be howling for my blood.'[37] Dorelia's attitude was one of sternness and calm. If matters were made too easy, then the same thing might happen over and over again. So she hardened herself. In John's letters to her at this time there is a new note of diffidence mingling with reminders that 'I cannot exist without you for long, as you know'. He is apologetic too for not meanwhile having painted better. 'Sorry to be so damn disappointing in my work. It must make you pretty hopeless at times, but don't give me up yet. I'm going to improve.'

In Dorelia's eyes he could only exculpate himself through his work: and that was fair. But if the work did not improve, then his guilt would rise up and stifle him. As a civilian in wartime he felt as if at the dead centre of a hurricane. It was this awful sense of deadness that tempted him to rush into new love-making, as the only excitement, the only means of self-renewal available. Extricating himself from the consequences of his affair with Brownsword seems to have taken considerably longer than the affair itself, and was the antithesis of excitement. Brownsword had often visited Alderney during her holidays from music college; after the birth of her daughter she never went back there. The romance was over. 'She must on no account come to Alderney,' John instructed Dorelia. '... For God's sake don't worry about it – don't think about it.'

This advice, for Dorelia somewhat tautological, John made many lusty attempts to pursue himself. It was not easy. Brownsword had been anxious to shield the news from her parents – which, since they could far better afford to look after the child than he, irritated John. In due course she went to live in Highgate, where John sometimes turned up – Brownsword hiding herself away at his approach. She had become extraordinarily elusive and when John did catch up with her he felt doubly impatient. 'I dined with her and wasn't too nice,' he admitted to Dorelia, 'but tried to keep my temper and it's no use allowing oneself to be too severe ... She showed every sign of innocent surprise when I asked her why she had bunked away without warning.' In a less severe mood still, he confided on one occasion to Theodosia Townshend: 'I'd marry her if necessary – Dodo

wouldn't mind.' To what extent he believed this it is impossible
to be sure: probably a little, once it was out of the question.
Certainly it was not more fantastic than some of the other plans
which, unknown to Brownsword herself, were manufactured to
meet the crisis. 'The Tutor's plan I think the best,' John had
affirmed in another letter to Dorelia. The boys' ex-tutor, John
Hope-Johnstone, stopped in his tracks somewhere in Europe by
the world war, had re-appeared in London and secretly offered
himself in the rôle of the baby's legal father. 'I must say,' John
acknowledged, 'the tutor is behaving with uncommon decency.'
From Brownsword's point of view this 'best plan' contained disadvantages. Although Hope-Johnstone entertained some romantic attachments for young men of under twenty, he was physically attracted to girls – but of ten or twelve, towards whom he
would proffer timid advances, placing his hand on their thighs
until, their mothers getting to hear of it, he was expelled from
the house. The prospect of having a young daughter in his own
house was certainly inviting; and it seems probable that he
sniffed money in this *mariage blanc* – to the extent at least of
buying a household investment, 'a most expensive frying pan'.
But Brownsword was not a party to this. The punning surname
she gave her daughter Gwyneth reflects the fact that hope never
entered this relationship.

In his letters to Dorelia, John makes no single reference to
Nora Brownsword that can be construed as sympathetic. He
appears to have believed that he offered her money, but that she
accepted nothing. She remembers asking for £4 a week for the
baby, not herself: and receiving nothing. That nothing positively
changed hands on a number of occasions appears indisputable.
Having a musical degree she was just able to support herself
and her daughter, and their independence was complete. It was
only casually, years later, that John learnt she had married. As
for Dorelia, she provided Brownsword with a ring; and within
limits she was kind. But her aloofness was not welcoming:
deliberately so. Everyone must sink or swim – that was her
philosophy. Against her dislike there was no appeal on whatever
grounds. Like God, she allowed help only to those capable of
helping themselves. She offered to take the baby and bring it up
as one of the family, provided Brownsword never saw it again.

But since this was unacceptable to Brownsword, she took no further interest in the matter.*

The Brownsword affair shot a warning across John's bows, but though his progress became more rocky it did not slacken. Through the deep gloom of war he needed, like pilot lights, a girl to ring and a girl to play. But soon the process had cemented itself into a formula. After one party at Mallord Street, Dorelia and Helen Anrep could hear him shuffling about in the entrance hall and, with hushed intensity, confiding to a procession of female guests: 'When shall I see you again? You know how much it means to me.' Each time, for a moment, the tone carried conviction. His need seemed, if almost indiscriminate, almost real. Without these girls he was in the dark. He was not hypocritical, but being self-deceived, constantly deceived others, and could not stop himself. At the beginning and in the end, he drank: first to make contact, then to forget; finally to destroy himself.

The roll-call reverberated on. Lady Tredegar with her strange gift for climbing into trees and arranging nests in which polite birds would later settle; Iris Tree, with her pink hair and poetry, 'someone quite marvellous'; Sylvia Gough, with her thin loose legs, who later paid him the compliment of including his name among the list of co-respondents at her divorce case; Sybil Hart-Davis, nice and apologetic and 'determined to give up the drink';[38] a famous Russian ballerina, from whose Italianate husband John was said to have 'taken a loan of her': these and others, many others, were among his girl-friends or mistresses over these few years. Not all the voluminous gossip that rose up round him was true, not all: but the smoke did not wholly obscure the flames. Even before the war his reputation, along with that of the solo-dancing, velvet-jacketed American poet Ezra Pound, had been popularly celebrated in the 'Virgin's Prayer':

* Some years later, when John was visiting the composer' Jack Moeran in Norfolk, he called on Brownsword; and continued to see her later still after she was widowed, 'always on friendly terms'.
   'Gwyneth became a talented painter, and mixed with the Johns after she had grown up, but remained outside the family circle, although she was always very fond of Augustus, and would frequently see him in London, and lent him her studio to work in occasionally.'

Ezra Pound
And Augustus John
Bless the bed
That I lie on.[39]

Of such notoriety John was growing increasingly shy. 'The only difference between the World's treatment of me and other of her illustrious sons is that it doesn't wait till I am dead before weaving its legends about my name,' he complained (February 1918) to Alick Schepeler. By becoming more stealthy he did not diminish this legend, but gave it more zest. The addict's spell is written in the many moods of revulsion and counter-resolution, the promises, promises, that chart his downhill fight. Sometimes it seemed as if Dorelia alone could arrest this gradual descent. 'If you come here I'll promise to be good,' he wrote to her from Mallord Street at the end of the war, '. . . I am discharging all my mistresses at the rate of about 3 a week – Goodbye Girls, I'm through.'

3. CORRUPT COTERIES

Alderney had changed since the beginning of the war. Vague visitors no longer floated in and out in such abundant numbers. Henry Lamb had left, and the piano duets were stilled. After drawing up his first Will and Testament, and solemnly handing it to Dorelia during a miserable farewell party at Alderney,* he had gone, looking 'very sweet in his uniform', to serve as an army doctor in France. Deprived of 'poor darling Lamb',[40] Dorelia dug herself more deeply still into the plant world. She had been assured by John that 'in a week or two there'll be no money about and no food,' so now she surrounded herself with useful vegetables. They clustered thick about her, giving com-

---

* In the last week of January 1915. Lamb had been in Guy's Hospital for an operation. 'I have written to Dodo to know if she can pick me up . . . It all depends on whether J[ohn] will be gone: his temper not being considered good enough to stand the strain of a visit from me,' Lamb had explained to Lytton Strachey (15 January 1915). After his visit, he wrote (31 January 1915): 'They have been discussing the moral effects of being in hospital, saying that one's sensitiveness is apt to become magnified. I wonder if that is the reason why I was miserable at Parkstone.'

fort. 'It's rather a sickening life,' she confessed to Lytton Strachey, 'but the garden looks nice.'[41]

God came to Alderney less often these days: God was Dorelia's new name for John. The war had thrown shadows over both their lives, and between them. 'Do you feel 200?' he asked her once, '– I feel 300'. But superannuation affected them differently. While Dorelia immersed herself in the non-human life of the soil, John sought distraction at the clubs and parties in London. Though he still drank elbow-to-elbow with poets and prostitutes under the fly-blown rococo of the Café Royal, the place was beginning to revolve almost too crazily. There were the raucous-voiced sportsmen; the grave contingent from the British Museum with their academic squeaks, like bats; the well-dressed gangs of blackmailers, bullies, pimps and *agents-pro-vocateurs* muttering over plans; the intoxicated social reformers and Anglo-Irish jokers with their whoops and slogans; the exquisite herd of Old Boys from the Nineties 'recognizable by their bright chestnut wigs and raddled faces' whispering in the sub-dialect of the period; a *schlemozzle* of Cubists sitting algebraically at the domino tables; and, not far off, under the glittering façade of the bar, his eye fixed on the fluctuating crisis of power, the leader of the Vorticists keeping company with his lieutenants. Decidedly the place was getting a bit 'thick'.[42]

Throughout London a bewildering variety of clubs and pubs had sprung up offering doubtful consolations. First among these was the astonishing 'Cave of the Golden Calf', a cabaret club lodged deep in a Soho basement where the miraculous Madame Strindberg was resurrected. As Queen of this vapid cellardom, wrapped in a fur coat, her face chalk white, her hair wonderfully dark, her eyes blazing with fatigue and laughter, she drifted among her guests diverting their attention from entertainments that featured everything most up to date. Under walls 'relevantly frescoed' by Spencer Gore and Charles Ginner, beside a huge and hideous raw meat drop curtain designed by Wyndham Lewis, and watched over by the heads of hawks, cats and camels that, executed by Epstein in scarlet and shocking white, served as decorative reliefs for the columns supporting the ceiling, couples sagged through the latest obsolete dances, the Bunny Hug and Turkey Trot. Between dances there were

violent experiments in amateur theatre, assaults upon foreign
folk songs led by an Hungarian fiddler and the spectacle of performing Coppersmiths. Everything was expensive, but democratic. Girls, young and poor, were introduced to rich men on
the periphery of the art world; various writers and artists, including John, found themselves elected honorary members 'out
of deference to their personalities' and given the privilege of
charging drinks to non-artistic patrons in their absence. Into
this vicious, pleasant establishment slunk the Vorticists,
'Cubists, Voo-dooists, Futurists and other Boomists'[43] for whom
it was transfigured into a hole-and-corner headquarters. But not
for long. As war advanced from the East, so Madame Strindberg
went west. 'I'm leaving the Cabaret,' she wrote to John.
'Dreams are sweeter than reality.' Stripping the cellar of everything she could carry, she sailed for New York. 'We shall never
meet again now,' she wrote from the ship.* '. . . I could neither
help loving you, nor hating you – and . . . friendship and esteem
and everything got drowned between those two feelings.'

Long before Madame Strindberg left, John had absconded to
help set up a rival haunt in Greek Street. 'We are starting a new
club in town called the "Crab-tree" for artists, poets and musicians,' he wrote to Quinn. 'It ought to be amusing and useful
at times.' The Crabtree was opened, at John's instigation, in
April 1914, and for a time it tasted sweet to him : the only
thing wrong with it, he hinted darkly, were the crabs. Like the
'Cave of the Golden Calf' it was a very democratic affair, and

---

* In *Chiaroscuro* John records: 'I received a letter from her, written on the
ship. It was a noble epistle. In it I was absolved from all blame: all charges, all
imputations were withdrawn: she alone had been at fault from the beginning:
though this wasn't true, I was invested with a kind of halo, quite unncessarily. I
wish I had kept this letter; it might serve me in an emergency.' This letter,
written from the R.M.S. *Campania*, has since come to light. In it she writes:
'The chief fault others had, who interfered with lies and mischief. The rest, I
take it, was my fault – and therefore I stretch out my heart in farewell . . . You
are the finest man I met in this world, dear John – and you'll ever be to me
what the Sun is, and the Sea around me, and the immortal beauty of nature.
Therefore if ever you think of me, do it without bitterness and stripe [*sic*] me of
all the ugliness that events have put on me and which is not in my heart . . .
Goodbye John. I don't know whether you know how awfully good at the
bottom of your heart you are – *I* know. And that is why I write this to you –
Frida Strindberg'.

provided customers with what John called 'the real thing'. Euphemia Lamb, Betty May, Lillian Shelley and other famous models were there night after night wearing black hats and throwing bottles : and for the men there were boxing matches. Actresses flocked in from the West End theatres to meet these swaggering painter-pugilists and the atmosphere grew wildly extravagant. 'A most disgusting place!' was Paul Nash's recommendation in a letter to Albert Rutherston, 'where only the very lowest city jews and the most pinched harlots attend. A place of utter coarseness and dull unrelieved monotony. John alone, a great pathetic muzzy god, a sort of Silenus – but alas no nymphs, satyrs and leopards to complete the picture.'

Much the same spirit of tense tedium and relaxed excitement saturated the atmosphere of the Cavendish Hotel in Jermyn Street which outlasted all these clubs. This was owned by Rosa Lewis, a kind and sinister nanny, who ran it along the lines of a plush lunatic asylum in her own Welfare State. For those who went to bed early and locked their doors, it was possible to detect little that was different from the expensive mediocrity of the usual hotel. But for connoisseurs there was nothing like the Cavendish, its multitudinous pictures; its acres of faded red morocco, and hideous landscape of battered furniture, massive and monogrammed; its perpetual parties. Beneath every cushion lay a bottle, and beside it a girl. The place flowed with brandy and champagne, paid for by innocent millionaires who had been equipped with mistresses. Much of this money came from America, among whose well-brought-up young men, bitten with the notion of being Bohemians Abroad, Rosa Lewis became a legend. Financially it was once again the artists, models and other poorer people who benefited : but for those who did not own John's constitution it was a risky lair. John himself scented no danger, and continued intermittently to use it over many years.[44]

In quieter vein, he would appear at the Café Verrey, a public house in the Continental style in Soho; then, for the sake of the Chianti – though he always 'walked out nice and lovely' – at Bertorelli's; and, a little later, also in Charlotte Street near the Scala Theatre, at the Saint-Bernard Restaurant, a small friendly place with an enormous dog, the mascot and name-giver, that filled the alley between the tables to the exclusion of the single waiter and Signor del Fiume, the gesticulating owner. But of all these restaurants the most celebrated was the Eiffel Tower in Percy Street, 'our carnal-spiritual home' as Nancy Cunard called it.[45] The story is that one stormy night, John and Nancy Cunard found refuge there, and taking a liking to its genial Austrian proprietor Rudolph Stulik, transformed the place during these war years into a club patronized chiefly by those who were connected with the arts. Something of the Café Royal atmosphere was transported, but on a scale much simplified. Its series of windows, each with a daffodil-yellow half-blind looking wearily up Charlotte Street, became a landmark of the metropolitan art-and-vulture world until the Second World War. The décor was simple, with white table-cloths, narrow crusty rolls wrapped up in napkins beside the plates and long slender wine glasses. The food was elaborate ('Canard Pressé', 'Sole Dieppeoise', 'Chicken à la King' and 'Gâteau St Honoré', a large circular custard tart ornamented round its edges with big balls of pastry, were among its specialities); and it was costly. For the art-students and impoverished writers drinking opposite in 'The Marquis' it represented luxury. To be invited there, to catch sight of the elegant figure of Sickert amid his entourage; of the Sybil of Soho, Nina Hamnett, being helped home, a waiter at each elbow; of Herbert Asquith in poetic travail; of minor royalty slumming for the evening; of actresses and Irishmen, musicians, magicians, cosmeticians; of a pageant of Sitwells, some outriders from Bloomsbury, a yapping kennel of politicians: to be part of this glorious constellation even for a single evening was to become a man or woman of the world.

Those who were well looked upon by Stulik could stay on long after the front door had been closed, drinking into the early hours of the morning mostly German wines known collectively as 'Stulik's Wee'. Stulik himself spoke indecipherably in galloping, broken-back English, hinting that he was the result of an irregular attachment 'in which the charms of a famous ballerina had overcome the scruples of an exalted but anonymous personage' – a story that, reduced to the commonplace, became that he had once been chef to the Emperor Franz Josef to whom he bore an uncertain resemblance. He was assisted in the running of the place by a team of tactful waiters, a parrot and a dog. Upstairs, touched by the paintbrush of Wyndham Lewis, lay the private dining-room, small, stuffy with aspidistras, glowing dully under a good deal of dark crimson. Here secret liaisons were intended to take place, grand ladies entering by the side-door and ascending the hen-roost stairs for private debauches with raffish character-actors. Those modestly sitting below could feel tremors of equivocal excitement and, late at night, hear mouse-scufflings up and down the narrow staircase.

Then, on the topmost floors, 'dark and cluttered with huge articles of central European furniture',[46] were the bedrooms, between which a vigorous scampering to and fro was carried on – and no questions asked.

The high prices were partly subsidized by young diplomats on leave, and the tariff was tempered to the visitor's purse. John was a popular host, sometimes even in his absence. 'Stulik's friends could run up enormous bills,' Constantine FitzGibbon recalls.

Augustus once asked for his bill after a dinner party, Stulik produced his accumulated account, and Augustus took out £300 from his pocket with which to pay it. One result of this was that Stulik himself was sometimes penniless. On one occasion when John Davenport ordered an omelette there, Stulik asked if he might have the money to buy the eggs with which to make it. On another occasion, when Augustus grumbled at the size of his dinner bill, Stulik explained calmly in his guttural and almost incomprehensible English that it included the cost of Dylan [Thomas]'s dinner, bed and breakfast the night before.[47]

Such bursts of generosity were followed by periods of financial remorse deepened by the weight of Dorelia's disapproval. But for John money was an exit, and he could not tolerate being imprisoned by the lack of it. As his correspondence shows, money worries buzzed about him like flies, persistent though unstinging. A request by post from a deserving relative, if it arrived in the wrong hour, would detonate a terrifying explosion of anger. But he did not covet money. It was not beyond him to bargain over a price for a picture, obtain it, then absent-mindedly light his pipe with the cheque. And once, at Mallord Street, when he was grumbling about having so little money available, his friend Hugo Pitman offered to search through the house and came up with, in notes and uncashed cheques, several thousand pounds.

His generosity was unpremeditated. He preferred to give in kind rather than in cash. Money was important to him for his morale not his bank account. He needed it about his person. All manner of creditors, from builders to schoolmasters, would queue many months for their bills to be paid, while he graciously entertained his debtors at the Eiffel Tower. In times of war, he would explain with some severity, it was necessary for everyone to make sacrifices. But he himself could not sacrifice popularity. Among the art-students he was a fabled figure, a king of Chelsea, Soho and Fitzrovia. 'I can see him now walking ... beneath the plane trees,' recalled Sir Charles Wheeler.

... He is tall, erect and broad-shouldered, wearing a loose tweed suit with a brightly coloured bandana round a neck which holds erect, compelling features ... He is red-bearded and has eyes like those of a bull, doubtless is conscious of being the cynosure of the gaze of all Chelsea and looking neither to the left nor the right strides on with big steps and at a great pace towards Sloane Square, focussing on the distance and following, one imagines, some beautiful creature he is intent on catching ...[48]

Dorothy Brett remembers her first sight of him from a bus in the King's Road – 'Tall, bearded, handsome, shaggy hair with a large black homburg hat at a slight angle on his head, some kind of black frock coat. I think I must have been staring with my mouth open at him, he shot me a piercing look, and the bus rolled away.'[49] Later on, he would call at the Slade for Brett and two other students, Ruth Humphries and Dora Carrington, and take them to the Belgian cafés along Fitzroy Street, and once to call on a group of gypsies 'beautiful, dark-haired men and women and children, in brilliant-coloured clothes,' Brett recalled, in a room full of bright eiderdowns.

Best of all were the parties in Mallord Street. Invitations would arrive on the day itself – a telephone call or a note pushed under the door or a shout across the street urging one to 'join in' that evening. Carrington, in a letter to Lytton Strachey (23 July 1917), gives a voluptuous description of one of these events:

It had been given in honour of a favourite barmaid of the Pub in Chelsea, near Mallord St, as she was leaving. She looked a charming character, very solid, with bosoms, and a fat pouting face. It was great fun.

Joseph, a splendid man from one of those cafés in Fitzroy St, played a concertina, and another man a mandoline. John drunk as a King Fisher. Many dreadfully worn characters, moth eaten and decrepit who I gathered were artists of Chelsea ...

John made many serious attempts to wrest my virginity from me. But he was too mangy to tempt Me even for a second. 'Twenty years ago would have been a very different matter my dear sir' ... There was one magnificent scene when a presentation watch was given the barmaid, John drest in a top hat, walking the whole length of that polished floor to the Barmaid sitting on the sofa by the fireplace, incredibly shy and embarrassed over the whole business, and giggling with delight. John swaggering with his bum lurching behind from side to side. Then kneeling down in the most gallant attitude with the watch on a cushion. Then they danced in the middle of the room, and every one rushed round in a circle shouting. Afterwards, it was wonderful to see John kissing this fat Pussycat, and diving his hand down her bodice. Lying with his legs apart on a divan in the most affected melodramatic attitudes!! [50]*

The spirit of London during the war, its spiral of gaiety and recrimination, is wonderfully caught by the affair of the Monster Matinée performed on 20 March 1917 at the Chelsea

* Of another party, Carrington wrote (2 November 1920): 'How it brought back another world! ... Dorelia like some Sibyl sitting in a corner with a Basque cap on her head and her cloak swept round her in great folds, smiling mysteriously, talking to everyone, unperturbed watching the dancers. I wondered what went on in her head. I fell very much in love with her. She was so amazingly beautiful. It's something to have seen such a vision as she looked last night ... I had some very entertaining dialogues with John, who was like some old salt in his transparent drunkenness.

' "I say old chap will you come away with me?"
D.C. "But you know what they call that."
"Oh I forgot you were a boy."
D.C. "Well don't forget it or you'll get 2 years hard."
"I say you are insinuating," drawing himself up and flashing his eyes in mock indignation, "that I am a Bugger."
D.C. "My brother is the chief inspector of Scotland Yard."
"Oh I'm not afraid of him." But in a whisper. "Will you come to Spain with me? I'd love to go to Spain with *you*."
D.C. "This year, next year, sometime."
John. "Never." Then we both laughed in a roar together.'

Palace Theatre.[51] This jumbo pantomime had been organized in aid of Lena Ashwell's Concerts at the Front. 'It was to be a sort of history of Chelsea,' Lady Glenavy wrote, 'with little plays about Rossetti, Whistler and others, with songs and dances ending up with a grand finale in praise of Augustus John.' Everyone in the polite world was soon elbowing his way into this charity-rag; a Committee of Duchesses gave birth to itself; and the arrangements spread up a crescendo of smart houses – John himself being given the scent to hunt out a musician. During rehearsals fashionable ladies gathered together for gossip about him, vying with one another to tell the most succulent story of his dreadful deeds. But when he appeared, 'Birdie' Schwabe noticed, such was his presence that they would all stand up to greet him with their best smiles. The last scene of the show featured 'Mrs Grundy and the John Beauty Chorus',* in which a band of Slade girls – Brett, Carrington, Barbara Hiles and others – shouted out:

John! John!
How he's got on!
   He owes it, he knows it, to me!
Brass earrings I wear,
And I don't do my hair,
   And my feet are as bare as can be;
When I walk down the street,
All the people I meet
   They stare at the things I have on!
When Battersea-Parking
You'll hear folks remarking:
   'There goes an Augustus John!'[52]

But not everyone was approving. Peering out from the jungle of the art world, Epstein sniffed a plot within the matinée, with John its Machiavelli. At the start of the war Epstein had written to Quinn: 'My business as I see it is to get on with my work and to get things in hand finished ... Everybody here is war-mad. But my life has always been war, and it is more difficult I believe for me here to stick to the job, than go out and fight or at least get blind, patriotically drunk'.[53] He seemed determined to be disliked: 'As an artist I am among the best-hated ones

* See Appendix Four.

here,' he boasted, 'and the most ignored.'⁵⁴ Perhaps through negligence, John and he seem to have remained on good terms. In January 1917 Epstein did a portrait of John which, seen from a certain angle, gives him the aspect of a devil;* and this, a little later that year, was what he became. Compulsory conscription had now been introduced and Epstein found himself called up. It was obviously the result of this monster pantomine – he saw that clearly:

My enemies have at last succeeded in forcing me into the army. I have not been averse to joining, but [I] really am too important to waste my days in thinking of matters military. When the last tribunal gave me three months' exemption there was organized a deliberate conspiracy in the press against my exemption; bad painters and bad sculptors wrote and howled, men like Brangwyn. One Sir Philip Burne Jones, a son of old B.J., a social nincompoop, and sculptors whose names you've never even heard of; but the actual organizing of this conspiracy to commit me to the army was mainly engineered by a sycophant of John, and it is him I blame chiefly for the whole affair. John has been behind the whole nasty business ever since the war started, but I first found it out when in a theatrical show got up for charity, he had me caricatured on the stage; he was one of the chief organizers of this dastardly business and ever since then I understand the low, base character of the man. This so-called charity performance was the work of our 'artists' mostly hailing from Chelsea, and I was chief butt, partly on account as I take it, of the great public success of my exhibitions of sculpture at the Leicester Gallery ... To be attacked in the press is now my almost daily portion. I loom too large for our feeble small folk of the brush and chisel. Even my existence is a nuisance to them. They shall have their reward.⁵⁵

This outpouring was the result of a collision between two gifted paranoiacs. The conspiracy, to the extent that it existed, was a conspiracy of one – the professional joker Horace de Vere Cole. Making a tour of rival sculptors, he had guided their hands in the writing of some extraordinary letters to the *Sunday Herald*⁵⁶ opposing Epstein's military exemption. Walter Winars, a sculptor of horses, wrote from Claridges; Derwent Wood

* 'I wanted to capture a certain wildness, an untamed quality that is the essence of the man,' Epstein wrote. *Epstein. An Autobiography* (Hulton Press 1955), p. 89.

went on record as disliking Epstein personally, and John Bach came up with the notion that there were too many artists in the country anyway. In a sane world, such a correspondence could have done no harm to Epstein. But the world was not sane, it was at war; and Epstein came to believe that, back in 1914, it must have been Cole who, travelling widely, had actually initiated that war. In any event, the anti-Epstein conspiracy was now rampant, and this deeply laid pantomime revealed its leader to be the most popular artist of the day, Augustus John. Nothing less would satisfy Epstein.

John was certainly capable, when the mood was on him, of doing ugly things. But he was allergic to conspiracies and could never have sustained over years a campaign of hate. In fact he had no part in Cole's joke, and his letters show that he actually wanted Epstein to escape conscription. Quinn, who gave generous support to Epstein's fantasy, calling John 'malicious, for what you describe is pure malice and meanness and dirt', failed to tell Epstein that John had written to him on 18 August 1916: 'I saw Epstein lately: he is in suspense about being taken for the army. I sincerely hope they'll let him off.'

Friends did bring the two artists together again following this pantomanic break and a reconciliation was arranged at a hotel in Brighton. Unfortunately a parrot belonging to the hotel exploded with some abusive remarks just as Epstein entered the restaurant, and he rushed out swearing that John was up to his tricks again.*

Epstein had objected both to John's singular place among British artists at this time, and to his untroubled exemption from conscription. While in Ireland with Gogarty, John had injured his knee jumping a fence. Despite months encased in plaster of paris, the knee had not mended and he consulted Herbert Barker the specialist in manipulative surgery. 'The celebrated "bone-setter" having put me under gas ... carrying

---

* Information from Sir Sacheverell Sitwell. Later in life, while not seeing much of each other, Epstein and John remained friendly. Lady Kathleen Epstein remembers that they met once in a street and, in answer to a question, Epstein said he was doing good work but could not sell it and was very poor. John at once took out a cheque book and wrote him a cheque 'which we will never refer to again'. This was in the 1930s.

my crutches, I walked away like the man in the Bible.'⁵⁷ Not
long afterwards, with another insufficient leap, he successfully
damaged the other knee – 'bang went the semi-lunar and I
nearly fainted'. Again he sought out Barker, this time at a
remote village in North Devon.

'I invited him to my private sitting-room and examined his
knee,' Barker records. 'It was swollen, bent to a considerable
angle and both flexión and extension were painful even to attempt. It was a typical case of derangement of the internal semi-
lunar cartilage.'⁵⁸ This time there was no anaesthetic and the
knee snapped back into place while John smoked a cigarette. 'I
feel rather like a racehorse come down in the world and pulling
a fourwheeler must feel,' he wrote afterwards (18 August 1916)
to Quinn. 'But both knees will get strong again in time.'*

They were not strong enough for the medical authorities who
examined him later that year at Dorchester barracks and who,
while insisting that he be re-examined periodically, rejected him
for military service. There followed a year in limbo, with the
constant threat of being compelled to do office work – a prospect more alarming than trench warfare. On the bright surface
of things he was enjoying a brilliant career in London, admired
by the young and lustfully pursued by the smart. But below this

* By way of payment John offered to 'do a head' of Barker. 'If you will rattle
my bones, I should be more than repaid!' This portrait, the first of two painted
during the war, is now in the National Portrait Gallery, London. Barker, who
often slept during the sittings, nevertheless observed: 'It was a wonderful thing
to watch John at work – to note his interest and utter absorption in what he
was doing . . . The genius of the born craftsman was apparent in every look and
movement. He had a habit when most wrapped up in some master-stroke or
final touch of running backwards some feet from the canvas with his critical
eyes bent upon the painting. Once when doing this he tripped and almost fell
heavily over the stove near by.' The portrait used to hang in Barker's waiting-
room to encourage the patients. Variously described as 'Satanic' or like 'a
Venetian Doge', it was, Barker bravely maintained, one of John's 'best male
portraits': adding 'I look upon John as one of the greatest portrait painters who
has ever lived'. John himself described the painting, in a letter to Hope-Johnstone, as 'just like him, stuffy and good'. Early in March 1932 John saw Barker
again, this time in Jersey. 'You have always done me good, and I feel it is high
time I put myself in your hands again,' he had written (17 September 1931).
During this visit he began a third portrait. See *Harley Street* by Reginald Pound
(Michael Joseph, 1967, pp. 80, 123–4). Also unpublished correspondence at
the Royal College of Surgeons.

surface, a lake of despair was forming. He was petted and flattered; he still roared, but he had been coaxed, it seemed to some, into a cage and the door was closing behind him. All the sweetmeats poked through the bars he gobbled up at once: he liked them, but they did not satisfy him, so he ate more until they began to sicken him. He was painting less well, and though he could blink this fact he could not blind himself to it. 'I wish it were not necessary to depend so much on rich people,' he confessed to Handrafs O'Grady. 'They don't really buy things for love – or rarely'. He had developed a technique of 'boldly accelerated "drawing with the brush".'[59] Once he had mastered this, he could almost never unlearn it because anything else was slower.

In November 1917, at the Alpine Club, he held the largest exhibition of his pictures ever assembled. He was now, in the words of *The Times*, 'the most famous of living English painters'.[60] But he had reached a watershed in his career. He did not paint to please the public nor, wholeheartedly, to please himself: but as if he were simply passing the time. He seemed poised between two worlds, uncertain of which to enter and unable, eventually, to enter either.

'He seems to have, with the artistic gifts of a man, the mind of a child,' wrote one critic of this show.

... Life to him is very simple; it consists of objects that arouse in him a *naïve* childish curiosity and delight; but he has been artistically educated in a modern, very unchildish, world, and has learnt very easily all the technical lessons that the world has to teach. The consequence is that he is too skilful for his own vision, like those later Flemish Primitives who were spoilt by acquiring the too intellectual technique of Italy. Constantly one feels the virtuoso obtruding himself into a picture that ought to be as *naïve* in execution as it is on conception; and often, where there is no conception at all, one sees the virtuoso trying to force one.

The change that was spreading over his pictures may be measured by the kind of enthusiasm they provoked. Shortly before the war Osbert Sitwell had visited the Chenil Gallery.

and saw a collection of small paintings by Augustus John: young women in wide orange or green skirts, without hats or crowned with large straw hats, lounging wistfully on small hills in undulating and monumental landscapes, with the feel of sea and mountain in the air round them ... By these I was so greatly impressed that I tried to persuade my father to purchase the whole contents of the room ... Alas, I did not possess the authority necessary to convince him ...[61]

The new exhibition this autumn was also impressive, but in a manner less painterly and to a different public. 'If you will go to the Alpine Club on Mill Street off Conduit Street you will see an unprecedented exhibition of paintings of Augustus John,' wrote Lord Beaverbrook to F. E. Smith (28 November 1917). 'Every picture in the room is painted by John. If you judge for yourself you will conclude that John is the greatest artist of our time and possibly of any time. If you refuse to follow your own judgement you must listen to the comments of your fashionable friends who are flocking to John's Exhibition. I saw some of the female persuasion there to-day gazing on John rather than on his pictures.'

It was Sickert, the previous year, who had warned his fellow painters against the mistake of inverted snobbery: 'you are reflecting whether it is not high time to throw Augustus John, who has clearly become compromising, overboard. Take my tip. Don't!'[62] But the war had dimmed his imaginative world: suddenly he was an artist with a past and little future. The future lay with those who were abandoning Naturalism and tradition and who demanded a new art modelled on the functions of the machine in place of the organic forms of nature. The war, even the threat of war, had been recognized as an enemy common to all artists, and they had come together in a profusion of groups and movements.

They had come together: collided: flown apart. Marinetti's Futurists, Wyndham Lewis's Vorticists, Roger Fry's Omega Workshops: all were adjusting to an industrial age, to discord, to the conditions of war – and all were to be extinguished by the forces that had brought them into being. In the histories of modern art, John has no place with these movements, and it is true that he saw them as revolutions in journalism as much as in art. But he did maintain an important contact on the periphery. When in the autumn of 1914 Wyndham Lewis's Rebel Art Centre in 38 Great Ormond Street destroyed itself, another less

well-publicized centre at 8 Ormonde Terrace sprang limping up.
It was led by Bomberg, Epstein and William Roberts: and John
was asked to be its first president. In their derelict house, leased
by 'a dear old humourist with a passion for vegetables',[63]* these
artists took aggressive refuge from the war, teaching and employing the rooms as studios. In a letter to Evan Morgan, John
(who refused the Presidency) explained his views in a manner
that defines his relation to almost all the new movements:

I confess I was always shy of the Ormonde Terrace schemes when
approached before ... *I do still think the idea is a very good one.* I
only have my doubts of our carrying it to success when hindered by
certain personalities – given a nucleus of serious and sensible persons or enough of such to *predominate* I would not refuse my name
for any useful purpose. It was for this reason I was so keen to get
Ginner and Gilman on the Committee. They are both able men
especially the former and would not be likely to wreck or jeopar-
dize our plans by childish frivolity or lack of savoir-faire. Given such
conditions, I say, B[omberg] and the rest could take their chance ...
I am quite game to go on with the affair and do all I can. But I
can't go and identify myself publicly with a narrow group with
which I have no natural connexion. You must see that I have arrived
at greater responsibilities than the people we are dealing with. My
own 'interests' lie in *isolation* as complete as possible. I have never
studied my interests but experience teaches me at least to avoid
misunderstandings. I would be quite ready to waive my 'interests'
damn them! pour le bon motif, but I don't want a fiasco ... It's impossible for a painter to be also a politician and an administrator.
We ought to have [A. R.] Orage as dictator ... I was loath to act as
captain to a scratch crew and seeing nothing but rocks ahead.[64]

This letter points to several developing strains in John: the
almost medieval fear of failure, of contagious 'bad luck', and
an impatience with himself for succumbing to this; an apprehension of press and publicity; the film of 'greater responsibilities' that was clouding his natural vision; common sense and
a sure instinct as to where his talent lay. Only isolation could
uphold this talent, but to isolation he was by temperament
unsuited. The groups and movements he so sensibly shunned
had, as they exploded, flung their adherents into the forefront

* Stuart Gray, an ex-lawyer, hunger-marcher and future 'King of Utopia'.

of the war where, instead of the despondency they expected, they found inspiration, John too had long wanted to hurry to the front.

'I have had the idea of going to France to sketch for a long while and I have hopes now of being able to do so,' he had written on 26 April 1916 to Will Rothenstein.

> But I am still in suspense. I have applied for a temporary commission which I think indispensable to move with any freedom in the British lines where the discipline is exceedingly severe ... there's enough material to occupy a dozen artists. Of course the proper time for war is the winter and I very much regret not having managed to go out last winter. I cannot say I have any personal influence with the powers that be ... I have been advised at the same time to keep my business quite dark. You might suppose I could do something with Lloyd George but I fear that gentleman will never forgive me for painting a somewhat unconventional portrait of him ...

Another winter came and went, and John continued to keep his business dark, remaining sombrely at home. During 1917 he began to drift, not altogether gracefully, into the McEvoy world of 'Duchesses'. One sitter who occupied him that year was Lady Cynthia Asquith,* some of whose diary entries give revealing glimpses of him in this new milieu.

Friday 27 April 1917.
... I had never met John before. He is very magnificent-looking, huge and bearded. His appearance reduced Margot [Asquith]'s two-year-old girl to terrified tears. I like him but felt very shy with him ... Mary [Herbert] and I both exhibited our faces, hoping he might want to paint us. He is doing a portrait of Margot and at one time asked her to sit for the 'altogether', saying she had such a perfect artist's figure ...
... Margot once asked John how many wives he really had (he is rather a mythical figure), saying she heard he was a most immoral man. He indignantly replied, 'It's monstrous – I'm a very moderate man. I've only got *one* wife!'

Tuesday 9 October 1917.
... He has a most delightful studio – huge, with an immense window, and full of interesting works. The cold was something excruciating ... I felt myself becoming more and more discoloured.

* She also sat persistently to McEvoy, and to Sargent and Tonks.

His appearance is magnificent, straight out of the Old Testament – flowing, well-kept beard, hair cut *en bloc* at about the top of the ear, fine, majestic features. He had on a sort of overall daubed with paint, buttoning up round his throat, which completed a brilliant picturesque appearance. He was 'blind sober' and quite civil. I believe sometimes he is alarmingly surly. Unlike McEvoy, he didn't seem to want to converse at all while painting and I gratefully accepted the silence. He talked quite agreeably during the intervals he allowed me. He made – I think – a very promising beginning of me sitting in a chair in a severe pose : full face, but with eyes averted – a very sidelong glance. He said my expression 'intrigued' him, and certainly I think he has given me a very evil one* – a sort of *listening* look as though I was hearkening to bad advice.

Thursday 1 November 1917.
Bicycled to John's studio. John began a new version of me, in which I could see no sort of resemblance to myself. The [D. H.] Lawrences turned up. I thought it just possible John *might* add another to the half dozen or so people whose company Lawrence can tolerate for two hours. It was quite a success. John asked Lawrence to sit for him,† and Lawrence admired the large designs in the studios, but maintained an ominous silence as regards my pictures. He charged John to depict 'generations of Wemyss disagreeableness in my face, especially the mouth', said disappointment was the keynote of my expression, and that what made him 'wild' was that I

* 'You are too much like the popular idea of an angel!' John wrote to her (5 October 1917), '(not *my* idea – which is of course the traditional one).' This portrait (oil 34 by 25 inches) was bought in 1933 from Arthur Tooth and Sons for £1,400 by the Art Gallery of Ontario. 'At the time of the purchase we were requested to hang it as *Portrait of a Lady in Black*,' the Curator wrote, 'and not refer to the fact that it was a portrait of Lady Cynthia.' In 1968 it was reproduced as the frontispiece to Cynthia Asquith's *Diaries*.

† In *Chiaroscuro* John reveals that Lawrence, despite his eagerness to have Cynthia Asquith portrayed disagreeably, protested that he himself was 'too ugly' to be painted. 'I met D. H. Lawrence in the flesh only once,' John wrote, and adds that Cynthia Asquith 'treated us to a box at the Opera that evening'. In fact they met twice, the visit to *Aida* taking place twelve days later, on 13 November – a meeting Cynthia Asquith describes in *Haply I May Remember* and Lawrence in *Aaron's Rod*.
Of John's portrait Lawrence remarked that it had achieved a certain beauty and had 'courage'. In 1929, when Lawrence's pictures were seized from the Warren Gallery and a summons issued against him, John added his name to the petition in Lawrence's support and stated that he was prepared, if it came to trial, to go into the witness box.

was 'a woman with a weapon she would never use' ... He thought the painting of Bernard Shaw with closed eyes very true symbolism.

'*Come quickly*, like Lord Jesus,' John had urged her, 'because I've got to go away before long.' After eighteen months at the starting line he was still hourly expecting his call to the Front – or if possible to several Fronts in succession, with intervals at home during which he would work up the results of his sketching into pictures. 'I very much want to do a great deal in the way of military drawings and paintings,' he told Grant Richards,[65] who had written to him proposing a book of such drawings. The authorities, however, held out against permanent exemption being granted to him. Its rule was that all artists must be called up, after which the War Office could then apply to the army for their artistic services. Because of his recurring exemption, John was unable to force his way into the army in order to get seconded out of it. He had become the centre of a bureaucratic stalemate.

On 7 September 1917 he underwent another medical examination. 'I was not taken on the 7th,' he wrote to Campbell Dodgson. 'On leaving, my leg (the worst one) "went out" so I had physical support for spiritual satisfaction.'[66] He had already informed the War Office that he had no objection to his work being used for Government publications, and had produced for a Ministry of Information book, *British Aims and Ideals*, a hideously symbolical lithograph, 'The Dawn'. In a letter to C. F. G. Masterman, Campbell Dodgson wrote: 'I am of opinion that it might be the making of John to be brought into contact with reality and the hard facts of warfare, instead of doing things out of his own head as he does at present, except when he has a portrait to paint.' Impressed by these arguments, and by John's obvious eagerness, the War Office capitulated, inviting him to act as one of its official artists: and John refused.

The invitation had come just too late. Through the good offices of P. G. Konody, John had volunteered to work for the Canadian War Memorials Fund, a scheme started by Lord Beaverbrook (then Sir Max Aitken) to assemble a picture collection that would give a record of Canada's part in the war. The Canadian War Records Office now granted him, with full pay, allowances and an extra £300 expenses, an honorary commission in the Overseas Military Forces of Canada, in return for which John agreed to paint a decorative picture of between thirty and forty feet in length. 'I had almost forgotten about this project which Konody talked to me about some months ago. I had given up hope of it,' John explained to Campbell Dodgson. '... The Canadians would be, I imagine, far more generous than the British Government.'

London that autumn saw the sight of John attired as a Canadian major. 'I have lunched in the Café Royal with Major John in Khaki!' exclaimed Arthur Symons in a letter to Quinn. 'The uniform does not suit him ... I never saw John more sombre and grave than to-day. He is brooding on I know not what.'[67] Lytton Strachey, who had observed him looking 'decidedly colonial' at the Alpine Club, took a more hostile view of this development. 'Poor John,' he lamented. '... Naturally he has become the darling of the upper classes, and made £5,000 out of his show. His appearance in Khaki is unfortunate – a dwindled creature, with clipped beard, pseudo-smart, and in fact altogether deplorable.'[68]

Strachey was one of those who 'joined in' a farewell party at Mallord Street – a fantastic all-night affair, very much en bohème. Early next morning, John's military figure, immaculately great-coated and spurred, with leather gloves, a cane, and riding boots laced up to the knee, picked his way nimbly between the prostrate bodies, and strode off to the war.

4. AUGUSTUS DOES HIS BIT

'John is having a great time!' William Orpen wrote excitedly from northern France. '... in the army [he] is a fearful and wonderful person. I believe his return to "Corps" the other evening will never be forgotten – followed by a band of photographers. He's going to stop for the duration.'[69]

He was billeted at Aubigny, a small village that had been designated a 'bridgehead'. Though there were intermittent shelling and occasional raids, one of which removed the roof of the château where he lived, John discovered Aubigny to be a dull place. Nevertheless he was 'overjoyed to be out here'.[70] The old

London life that had clung to him so damply seemed to be dissolving, and he felt renewed. Over the last two years his letters had been weighed down with confessions of a despair that leaves 'me speechless, doubting the reality of my own existence'.[71] He complained of a 'sort of paranoia or mental hail-storm from which I suffer continually',[72] and of curious states of mind when he was 'not myself'. Often he felt 'horribly alone',[73] knowing that 'there is no one I can be with for long'.[74] In a letter to Cynthia Asquith he accused himself of owning 'a truly mean and miserable nature. Obviously I am ill since I cannot stand *anybody*.' This meanness infected everything with which he came in contact and he could see 'no good in anything.'[75] While submerged in such moods he had a way of hopelessly shaking his head. There were other signs, too, of this devouring melancholia. In August 1917, after observing him closely one evening at the Margaret Morris Theatre 'with two very worn and *chipped* ladies', Katherine Mansfield wrote to Ottoline Morrell:

I seemed to see his [John's] mind, his haggard mind, like a strange forbidding country, full of lean sharp peaks and pools lit with a gloomy glow, and trees bent with the wind and vagrant muffled creatures tramping their vagrant way. Everything exhausted and finished – great black rings where the fires had been, and not a single fire even left to smoulder. And then he reminded me of that man in *Crime and Punishment* who finds a little girl in his bed in that awful hotel the night before he shoots himself, in that appalling hotel. But I expect this is all rubbish, and he's really a happy man and fond of his bottle and a goo-goo eye. But I don't think so.[76]

It was the business of the artist, John believed, to be young. But he was now in his fortieth year, and age had begun to inflict upon him its humiliations. 'I am waiting for a magic elastic belt to prevent me from becoming an *absolute wreck* at 35!' he had written to Ottoline. 'It doesn't sound very romantic does it?' His deafness too had worsened and partly accounted for his great bravery during air-raids. 'I'm stone deaf myself,' he shouted at Dorothy Brett, 'besides having a weak knee and defective teeth and moral paralysis.'[77] This last condition was a wartime virus. 'As for me I can only see imminent ruin ahead – personal I mean, perhaps even general,' he had confided to

Evan Morgan. Inevitably the war had subordinated the individual to the State, and in such an atmosphere John could hardly breathe – he was 'neither fish, flesh, fowl nor good red herring'.[78] His work too afforded him little certainty – painting for money, against time: an abuse of his skill. Some break had to come. His translation into a Canadian major appeared to offer him a new life, a fresh stimulus for his painting. It had arrived just in time.

The relief was enormous – to be caught up by events, to be on the move again. The blood began to surge more rapidly through his body; cheerfulness broke through. With his elevated rank came a car and a batman, and before long he was energetically patrolling the Vimy Front. 'I go about a good deal and find much to admire,' he wrote to Evan Morgan.[79] In particular he had discovered 'quite a remarkable place which might make a good picture'. This was a medieval château, converted into a battery position, with towers and a river running through it, at Lieven, a devastated town opposite Lens. Near by were several battered churches standing up amid the general ruin and, further off, a few shattered trees and slag-heaps, like pyramids against the sky. It was here, among this strange confusion of ancient and modern, that he planned his big 'synthetic' picture, bringing in tanks, a balloon, 'some of the right sort of civilians', and a crucifix. 'There is so much to do out here,' he wrote to Arthur Symons. 'All is glittering in the front; amidst great silence the guns reverberate. I shall take ages to get all I want done in preparation for a huge canvas. France is divine – and the French people.'[80] The desolation seemed to exhilarate him. It was 'too beautiful', he told Dorelia, adding: 'I suppose France and the whole of Europe is doomed.'

Also stationed at the Château, in the transparent disguise of an ex-battery officer, was Wyndham Lewis. For both these war-artists it was an untypically peaceful time: guns were everywhere, but for painting not firing. John, Lewis noted with approval, did not neglect the social side of military life and was everywhere accorded the highest signs of respect, largely on account of his beard. 'He was the only officer in the British Army, except the King, who wore a beard,' Lewis explained. 'In consequence he was a constant source of anxiety and terror wherever he went. Catching sight of him coming down a road any ordinary private would display every sign of the liveliest consternation. He would start saluting a mile off. Augustus John – every inch a King George – would solemnly touch his hat and pass on.'⁸¹

On one occasion, after a specially successful party, the two war-artists commandeered a car and careered off together almost into enemy lines. It was the closest John ever got to the fighting, and Lewis, the ex-bombardier, was soon poking fun at his friend's mock-war experiences. But John, noticing that Lewis had retreated home following their exploit, pursued him vicariously. 'Have you seen anything of that tragic hero and consumer of tarts and mutton-chops, Wyndham Lewis?' he asked Alick Schepeler. 'He is I think in London, painting his gun pit and striving to reduce his "Vorticism" to the level of Canadian intelligibility – a hopeless task I fear.'

Occasionally John would 'run over' to Amiens, Paris or, more surreptitiously, back to London. At Amiens he had 'found Orpen',⁸² whose welcome seemed a little agitated. 'They are trying to saddle me with him [John],' Orpen protested to Will Rothenstein, '– but I'm not having any! Too much responsibility.'

In Paris he called persistently on Gwen, catching her at the fourth call 'and borrowed a fiver off her ... She says my visit did her a lot of good', he told Dorelia. '... One might send her some photographs, and perhaps a Jaeger blanket as she admits the cold keeps her awake at night. The Lord only knows how she passes her days.'

He was staying at the Palais d'Orsay and being escorted everywhere by Lord Beaverbrook, who had arranged some extra special entertainment for his 'Canadians' in a suite at the Hotel Bristol.⁸³ At supper, John recalled, 'the guests were so spaced as to allow further seating accommodation between them. The reason for this arrangement was soon seen on the arrival of a bevy of young women in evening clothes, who without introduction established themselves in the empty chairs.' These girls, the pick of the local emporium, came strongly recommended for their efficiency: 'one or two of them were even said to be able to bring the dead to life'. Beaverbrook, at this critical moment, tactfully withdrew, and was hurriedly followed by the impetuously cautious Orpen. Bottles of champagne were then handed round and the atmosphere became charged with compulsory conviviality. 'Yet as I looked round the table, a curious melancholy took possession of me,' John recorded. '... I had no parlour tricks, nor did my companions-in-arms seem much better equipped than I was in this line; except for one gallant major, who, somehow recapturing his youthful high spirits, proceeded to emit a series of comical Canadian noises, which instantly provoked loud shrieks of appreciative laughter.' To keep his melancholy at bay, John also attempted an outburst of gaiety, raising 'in desperation' one of the girls to the level of the table and there effecting 'a successful *retroussage*, in spite of her struggles'.

Despite all this 'rich fun', he felt curiously islanded. The conditions of war were forcing a crisis within him. Before starting out, he had promised Cynthia Asquith to keep a diary while at the Front, but 'the truth is I funk it!'

'I am in a curious state,' he explained,

– wondering who I am. I watch myself closely without yet being able to classify myself. I evade definition – and that must mean I have no *character* ... To be a Major is not enough – clearly – now if one were a Brigadier-General say – would *that* help to self-knowledge if not self-respect ...? I am alone in what they call the 'Château' in this dismal little town. I am very lucky, not having to face a *Mess* twice a day with a cheerful optimistic air. When out at the front I admire things unreasonably – and conduct myself with that instinctive tact which is the mark of the moral traitor. A good sun makes beauty out of wreckage. I wander among bricks and wonder if those shells will come a little bit nearer ...

The wearing of a uniform seemed to have imposed another self on him, and he had no centre from which to combat this. He reflected the devastation of the fields and trees. The military rhythm of his life was destroying even the reassurance of habit. In company, at Beaverbrook's party or in the mess, he could not lose himself; alone, in the château where there was 'no romance', he felt characterless. Yet he knew that to paint well he had to establish a strong sense of character, and if he could not do this then it might be better to be killed, suddenly, pointlessly, by some shell. He watched himself. The crisis mounted until culminating in a sudden act of self-assertion when he knocked out one of his fellow officers, Captain Wright. 'The gesture had only an indirect relation to my codpiece,' he assured Gogarty.[84] Unwittingly Captain Wright had said something that, interpreted by John as an insult, acted as the trigger movement for this explosion. The situation was serious and John was rushed out of France by Lord Beaverbrook. 'Do you know I saved him [John] at a Court-martial for hitting a man named Peter Wright?' Beaverbrook complained in a private letter to Sir Walter Monckton (30 April 1941). 'I cannot tell you what benefits I did not bestow on him. And do you know what work I got out of John? – Not a damned thing.'

John arrived back in London at the end of March 'in a state of utter mental confusion'.[85] There was no chance of returning to France, and for four months the threat of some military humiliation hung over him. 'I think this trouble must be over,' he eventually wrote to Gogarty on 24 July 1918. 'The Canadian people seem to think so, and it's now so long since.'

It remained to be seen whether he could salvage something from his few months at the Front. 'I am tackling a vast canvas,' he had told Innes Meo (22 February 1918), '– that is, I shall do'. Cynthia Asquith, who saw this canvas on 29 July, recorded her impressions in a diary: 'It is all sketched in, but without any painting yet. I was tremendously impressed. I think it magnificent and it rather took my breath away – splendid composition, and what an undertaking to fill a forty-foot canvas!' This canvas went on view in January 1919 when the *Observer* art critic P. G. Konody organized a Canadian War Memorials exhibition at Burlington House. 'Even Mr Paul Nash may grow old-fashioned with the years,' commented *The Times*, 'but it is hard to imagine a time when Major John's cartoon (not yet finished) "The Pageant of War" will not interest by its masterly suggestion of what war means.'[86]* Intermittently during that year John

---

* John Singer Sargent was less impressed. 'I have just come from the Canadian Exhibition, where there is a hideous post-impressionist picture, of which mine ['Gassed'] cannot be accused of being a crib,' he wrote to Evan Charteris. 'Augustus John has a canvas forty feet long done in his free and script style, but without beauty of composition. I was afraid I should be depressed by seeing

grappled 'with my Canadian incubus ... I must try to get quit of the whole business. No more official jobs for me.'[87] By January 1920, while altering its name from time to time, the picture was no further off from completion. The erection of the art gallery in Ottawa, planned to house the entire Canadian War Memorials collection, had been postponed. Forty years on Beaverbrook and John were still in close correspondence about this, Beaverbrook asking after the picture, John parrying with inquiries about the gallery.* When John died the painting was still obstinately unfinished; and by the time Beaverbrook died his gallery remained stolidly unbuilt. But he had erected a gallery at Fredericton, and John had completed several smaller war pictures, some of which went to the Canadian National Gallery at Ottawa. Among these were numerous solid and precise drawings of soldiers, and some oil portraits done in thick juicy textures – studies in military boredom.

But there is one large oil painting, 'Fraternity',[88] that justifies the time he spent in France. Executed in muted greens and browns, it depicts three soldiers against a background of ruined brickwork and shattered trees, one giving another a light for his cigarette. It is a touching picture, emotionally and literally in the swirl of arms and the two cigarettes held tip to tip: a gesture, unexpectedly moving.

The war was over. On Armistice Day, John made his appearance at an endless party at Montague Shearman's flat in the

---

something in it that would make me feel that my picture is conventional, academic and boring – whereas.' For a different point of view by another artist on this exhibition see William Rothenstein's *Men and Memories*, Vol. II, p. 350.

* 'My dear Comrade,' Beaverbrook wrote to John on 26 August 1959, ... I was quite willing to build a Gallery in Ottawa but the Canadians did not have a suitable site and also there seemed little enthusiasm for the project.

'Now there is a beautiful Art Gallery by the River in Fredericton built by me and in it you will find two John drawings and two John paintings with a third on the way.

'How I wish that big picture might be handed over to us for exhibition there.'

Among those pictures owned by Beaverbrook Foundations is a small version oil on canvas $14\frac{1}{2} \times 48$ inches) of his large war picture, entitled 'Canadians at Lieven Castle'. The cartoon was rescued by Vincent Massey who took it to Canada.

he gave it an appropriate epitaph: 'I hope to get ahead with it as soon as the Canadian picture on which I am now engaged is finished.'

In April he had moved from Gandarillas's apartment to a private house belonging to the Duchess of Gramont whose portrait he was painting. By May he resolved to quit Paris. He had been spoilt, pampered, dazzled. But now he had had enough: strangers would make better company, or perhaps solitude itself might be best. 'Life in Paris was too surprising,' he afterwards confided to Cynthia Asquith. 'I long for some far island, sun and salt water.' Financial cares anchored him to these northern lands. He had too much work of the wrong sort dotted through France and England, and felt unequal to organizing it all. 'I am very helpless and desolate,' he confessed.[96]

He was still in khaki. Until the autumn of 1919, and increasingly to everyone's consternation, he continued to receive pay and allowances from the Canadians, and for almost seven months from the British War Office also. 'I must drop this commission and get into walking clothes again,' he told Dorelia. 'Would it not be more satisfactory for you to be demobilized?' the authorities tactfully persisted. But every time he prepared to return to civilian life a curious reluctance, not wholly financial, overcame him.* Had he not been 'going for a soldier' even before deciding on the Slade? The uniform, which had caused such embarrassment in Montparnasse, had given him confidence in the Champs-Élysées, and he enjoyed the pantomime.

The inability he experienced to finish either the Canadian War or Paris Peace pictures† made him feel 'very unstable'. He tried several methods of restoring this stability. He began to travel again – to Rouen‡ ('nearly died of depression') and, in

* His secondment for duty with the War Office was terminated on 22 September 1919; and then, without delay (on 23 September) he was struck off the strength of the Canadian War Records – though with two medals: the British War Medal and the Victory Medal.

† To reimburse the British Government for the expenses it had paid him on his never-to-be-painted Conference picture, he gave the Imperial War Museum eight drawings relating to the war, and allowed the museum to buy at an almost nominal price (£140) his painting 'Fraternity'.

‡ In May 1920, with two of his sons, Edwin and Romilly, whom he was sending to a French school.

Adelphi 'amid cheers, in his British [*sic*] officer's uniform, accompanied by some land-girls in leggings and breeches who brought a fresh feeling of the country into the overheated room'.[89] He seemed to be enjoying himself, and communicating enjoyment, more than anyone. The following month he wrote to Quinn: 'London went fairly mad for a week but thank the Lord that's over and we have to face the perils of Peace now.'

His 'bad period', that had begun in France, was still with him. 'Rather dreadful that feeling of wanting to go somewhere and not knowing where,' he noted. 'I spend hours of anguish trying to make a move – in some direction.'[90] In this whirlpool of inactivity he grew more dependent on other people. One was Lady Cynthia Asquith. 'Of you alone I can think with longing and admiration,' he declared. 'You have all the effect of a Divine Being whose smile and touch can heal, redeem and renew.' For Cynthia Asquith, herself close to a nervous breakdown, admiration was a medicine to be swallowed as 'dewdrops' – though when it took the form of 'an advance – clutching me very roughly and disagreeably by the shoulders – I shook myself free and there was no recurrence'.[91] What John responded to, felt companionship with, was the unhappiness far below her giddy exterior. He understood her need for such an exterior, could relax with her, talk. 'I bucked up somewhat,' he told her. 'Such is the benefit we get from confessing to one another.'

The war was over, but the trappings of war remained. In the spring of 1919 he was invited to attend the Peace Conference in Paris. Lloyd George had proclaimed that the conference should not be allowed to pass 'without some suitable and permanent memento being made of these gatherings'. The British Government had therefore decided to 'approach two of the most famous British artists and ask them to undertake the representation of the Conference'. The two selected were John and Orpen, and both accepted. Terms were generous. They were to get a subsistence allowance of £3 a day, expenses, a Government option to purchase each of their pictures for £3,000, and a £500 option price for the portraits of visiting celebrities, many of whom, Sir George Riddell assured the Government, 'are most anxious to be painted'. In John's case there was an immediate obstacle. Unaccountably he was still in the Canadian Army, and special arrangements were rushed through enabling him officially to be 'loaned to the War Office'.

He dreamed of being flown to France but, after three days of waiting in foggy weather, went like everyone else by train, finding himself in 'a charming flat ... almost too dream-like' on the third floor of 60 Avenue Montaigne. Here as the guest of Don José-Antonio de Gandarillas, a charming opium-eater with dyed hair, attached to the Chilean Legation, he stayed during February and March. The conference hall was just across the river and he at once rushed over in search of profitable celebrities. 'A certain delay at the start is to be expected no doubt,' he hazarded in a letter to Frances Stevenson.[92] It was Gandarillas who put delay to flight. He knew everyone, and invited everyone to his flat. The parties they gave in the Avenue Montaigne became the talk of Paris. 'My host Gandarillas leads a lurid and fashionable life,' John admitted.[93] An orchestra played ceaselessly all night and the spacious apartment was thronged with the *beau monde*. Rather nervously John began to infiltrate these parties, entering for the first time 'as dream-like a world as any I had been deprived of'.[94]

He had not thought of obtruding himself – certainly he had no wish to dance: he had come prepared to 'stand apart in a corner and watch the scene'. What happened astonished him. He talked, he laughed, he danced: he was an extraordinary success. Paris this spring was the hub of the social and political world; and amid the galaxy gathered there this son of a Pembrokeshire solicitor was acknowledged to stand out as 'easily the most picturesque personality', Frances Stevenson recorded. 'He held court in Paris.'

All red carpets led to him. The prime ministers of Australia, Canada and New Zealand submitted to his brush; kings and maharajahs, dukes and generals, lords of finance and of law froze before him; Lawrence of Arabia took his place humbly in the queue – and Dorelia wrote to inquire whether he had yet been knighted. More wonderful still were the princesses, duchesses, marchesas who lionized him. His awkwardness departed, confidence surged through his veins. They were, he discovered, these grandiloquent ladies, all too human: they 'loved

a bit of fun'. Under a smart corsage beat, as like as not, 'a warm, tender even fragile heart'. It was a revelation.

He had been born quite suddenly into a new world, but it did not take full possession of him. Even now, at the height of his triumph, his 'criminal instincts' reasserted themselves; he hurried away to 'my old and squalid but ever glorious quarter ... and sat for a while in the company of young and sinister looking men with obvious cubistic tendencies.'[95] A few old friends still roamed Montparnasse, but it was not the same. Something was being extinguished, something was vanishing for ever. Jean Moréas was dead; Modigliani too; Paul Fort had become respectable and the *cercle* of the Closerie de Lilas was disbanded. Maurice Cremnitz was there, only slightly damaged by the war; but he, who had once likened Augustus to Robinson Crusoe, now gazed at Major John with suspicion. 'I was conscious of causing my friends embarrassment,' John admitted. A doubt sailed across his mind, and vanished. Was he too becoming respectable?

He was doubtful also about his painting. He had begun the peace portraits grudgingly, but his accelerated technique worked well. 'I think I have acquired more common skill,' he wrote to Cynthia Asquith on 24 July 1919, '– or is it that I have learnt to limit my horizons merely?' In the immense conference hall he had found a room with a high window-niche, and from here he made sketches of the delegates. It was uninspiring labour. Smuts appeared overcome with misgivings; Massey described the proceedings as farcical; Balfour slumbered; the prime minister of Australia, looking like a jugged hare, was learning French. Speech followed speech in a multiplicity of languages: the assembly wilted in boredom. For John these interminable rows of seated figures offered no pictorial possibilities. But he badly needed the three thousand pounds and decided to attempt a more fanciful interpretation of what he saw. 'I do not propose to paint a literal representation of the Conference Chamber,' he promised the Ministry of Information, 'but a group which will have a more symbolic character, bring in motifs which will suggest the conditions which gave rise to the Conference and various interests involved in it.' So far as he could see, it was Conference in Spain, and from the point of view of his pic

September 1919, to Deauville as the guest of Lloyd George.

'What a monde he lives in!' he wrote to Cynthia Asquith. '... My fortnight here has been fantastic ... It's a place I should normally avoid. I have been horribly parasitical. I began a portrait of a lady here which promised well – till I gathered from her that if I made her *beautiful*, it might turn out to be the first step in a really brilliant career.'[97]

In March 1920, once more at the Alpine Club Gallery, John exhibited his war and peace portraits – statesmen, generals and fine ladies. They were not flattering likenesses, nor were they malicious: with few exceptions (mostly the ladies) they were neutral. The tedium released by the company of such public persons is very adequately recorded, and to that extent he remained uncorrupted by this 'exalted company'.[98] But, mainly for financial reasons, he had succumbed to the temptation to waste time. His two exhibitions at the Alpine Club were exercises in the higher journalism of art – pot-boiling commissions that gave little evidence of his genius. John knew this himself. No amount of social success could conceal the truth for long. His fits of melancholia persisted, sometimes smothering him with a blanket of depression. In April 1920 he entered the Sister Carlin Hospital for an operation on his nose which he counted on to make breathing easier. He had been 'in a state of profound depression', he told Ottoline Morrell. '... I feel always as though practically poisoned and must not shirk the operation. I look forward to it indeed as a means of recovering my normal self.'[99] It was essential to keep morale high. 'It took an uncommon amount of ether to get me under,' he bragged to Eric Sutton.[100] Under the ether, with a deep sigh, he uttered one remark: 'Well, I suppose I must be polite to these people.' He recovered with his usual facility. 'I am doing rather brilliantly,' he trumpeted.[101]

Later that year, following a convalescence, he went with Dorelia and some of the family to stay with his father back in Tenby. A new age was dawning in Britain, and many were curious to know what part John would occupy in it. He was no longer the leader, as the *Observer* art critic had reported in 1912, of 'all that is most modern and advanced in present day British

Art'. Nor, in his forty-third year, was he yet a Grand Old Man. To the younger artists he had been the apostle of a new way of seeing; now he was the fugleman for a way of living. If commissioned work had helped to cloud his vision, it did not seem likely he would be content merely to repeat himself. It was time to start again. 'I want to dig myself up and replant myself in some corner where no one will look for me,' he stated to Cynthia Asquith. 'There perhaps – there in fact I know I shall be able to paint better.'

9

Artist of the Portraits

'Having been regarded as a kind of "old master" for a long time I am now hailed as a "modern" which you must admit is very satisfactory.'

AUGUSTUS JOHN TO CONGER GOODYEAR
(4 JANUARY 1928)

'I don't find it at all amusing to paint stupid millionaires when I might be painting entirely for my own satisfaction.'

AUGUSTUS JOHN TO ADA NETTLESHIP (1928)

I. EVERYBODY'S DOING IT

> Après la guerre
> There'll be a good time everywhere.

And there was. Everyone wanted to be young. People had grown weary of big guns, big phrases: they needed to forget — not just the war but those feigned ideals that had gone down in it. Enjoyment was to be the new currency — enjoyment spent as an unprecedented freedom to act, to feel, to travel. The Continent became transformed from a battlefield into a playground. It was as if youth had suddenly been invented and pleasure become compulsory. There was no one unaffected by those four years of terrible fighting: the whole country had been scorched. Now it set about applying a miraculous balm.

To no category of people did this fashionable freedom apply more directly than the New Woman. During the war her masculine capabilities had been astonishingly displayed as policemen, postmen, commissionaires, as workmen in munition factories, gasworks and on the land. In the twenties she grew into a little boy. No longer did she take up her hair and let down her hems to signify at sixteen that she was an adult: her hems went farther up and her hair was cut, insisting on a refusal to grow up.

To revive jaded palates new entertainments were explored – night clubs, cocktails, cinemas, open-air breakfast parties and the *thé dansant*. 'I have a thé dansant to-morrow,' John announced from Mallord Street, '– about 3,000 people are coming.' Parties were more informal and gyrated to more syncopated rhythms, jazz on the gramophone, and exotic dances – the shimmy, the charleston, the black bottom, the fox trot. The handsome woman in the hansom cab had been overtaken by a fast woman in a fast car. She stepped out of the shadows, glittering with painted face and nails, a vibrant brunette or red-head. Glamour had come to London. There was a whirl of glass beads and pearls, sparkling paste, plucked eyebrows, rouge, brilliantined hair, sticky scarlet lips, surprised faces. Coloured underclothes broke out in shades of ice-cream: peach, pistachio, coffee. Young men sported plus-fours, big bow ties, motoring caps, gauntlets, co-respondent's shoes. John himself sprouted a waistcoat and suits of decisive check tweed.

There was an epidemic of health. 'Vapours' were no longer admired, neurasthenia went out of date. Young wives drilled themselves in natural childbirth exercises, practised art and craftwork for charity. At week-ends everyone stayed with everyone else in draughty country houses, playing bridge and tennis. Nature was again important: a million women cycled out beyond the suburbs.

The twenties was not a cynical but a sentimental decade. Under the high kicks lay a deep disillusionment, beneath the quick-step slow disintegration. Social divisions were being, creakingly, re-adjusted. The social centre of gravity in Britain was on the move and for this brief artificial period it lodged with the upper-middle class.

To the Old Guard, those dinosaurs from Victorian and Edwardian England, Augustus John was still 'disgusting John', a rascal in sinister hirsute league with those other dangerous spirits – D. H. Lawrence, Bernard Shaw, Lytton Strachey – all of them plotting to do away with what was decent in the country. But to the Bright Young Things, John was a ready-made hero, one of the pioneers of the new freedom.

Although by no means an ideal age for him, the twenties seemed more sympathetic to John than any decade that was to follow. He appeared to recover himself and gain a second wind. He travelled further, drank more, made more money, did more portraits. He painted popular people: film actors, airmen, matinée idols, beauties and beauticians, Greek bankers, Infantas, Wimbledon champions, novelists, musicians. The Emperor of Japan called one morning and was polished off in an hour. One problem was that the new cosmetics made a false barrier between the painter and his subject, but he knew about barriers, responded to their painted happiness. His most glittering portraits – of the Marchesa Casati, of Kit Dunn as the arch-flapper, and of Poppet as a provocative sex-kitten – are extraordinarily vivid.

The spirit of the age was a fairweather friend to John. The sun shone, the breeze blew, he sped along: it did not matter where. He was invited everywhere, though his own incompetence and the dark weather of his moods forestalled a measure of temptation. Wherever he went, his gift for boredom dramatically asserted itself. 'What a damnable mistake it is to go and stay with anybody,' he cried out in one letter to Dorelia. Many of the smart London hostesses were too sophisticated for his appetite. He was sometimes abominably rude to them, but his apologies were full of charm, and all was forgiven this half-tamed society artist.

He had become one of the most popular men in the country. In Soho restaurants 'Entrecôte à la John' was eaten; in theatres any actor impersonating an artist was indistinguishable from him; in several novels he was instantly recognizable as 'the painter'.[1] He began to use a secretary. 'Is there room for Kathleen Hale?'[2] he asked Dorelia somewhat desperately. There was, and he started to employ this young girl (later to become celebrated as the creator of a marmalade cat, 'Orlando') primarily, he explained, gesturing with his hand across his stomach as though guarding against onslaught, to provide a barrier between him and the hostesses, journalists and probationary models who ceaselessly solicited him.

Nowhere was the popular legend of John seen more clearly than at his Petronian parties in Mallord Street. They would begin at five and last till five, and they had what Christopher Wood called 'a remarkable feature ... there was not one ugly

girl, all wonderfully beautiful and young'. Though they regularly ended 'in the most dreadful orgy I have ever seen',
Christopher Wood concluded: 'One always enjoys oneself so
much at his house, he is such a thorough gentleman.'[3] More
coveted still was an invitation to Alderney.

'He has lots of ponies, dogs and all kinds of animals which
roam quite wild all round the house,' Christopher Wood told
his mother (11 October 1926).

... we arrived to find old John sitting at his long dining table
with all his children and family followers. We took our places quite
naturally at the table where there was a perfect banquet with all
kinds of different drinks, which everyone – even the children going
down to ten years of age and even seven, and all the cats and dogs
partook of. Afterwards we took off our coats and waistcoats and
had a proper country dance. John has a little daughter of fifteen,
like a Venus, whom he thinks a lot of ... [He] is the most delightful
person, the perfect gentleman, most charming in every possible
way.

Dancing and motoring were the obsessional hazards of the
twenties, and together they match the rhythm of the age.
Dorelia never danced, though she was often near by, watching
and smiling. John could not be prevented from taking the floor.
'The tango can't be resisted,' he admitted. More irresistible still
were motor cars. He had first been infected with this virus in
1911 when chauffeured through France in Ryan's Mercedes. 'It
can't be denied there's something gorgeous in motoring by night
100 kilometres an hour,' he had told Ottoline Morrell.[4] He had
never driven himself until, one day in the year 1920, he
acquired, in exchange for a picture, a powerful blue two-seater
Buick with yellow wheels and a dicky. After enduring half an
hour's lesson in London, he filled it with friends and set off for
Alderney. Apart from barging into a barrel-organ and, so far as
the passengers could judge, de-railing a train, the car enjoyed an
immaculate journey down – and this despite the fact that John's
lesson had not touched upon the philosophy of gear-changing,
so that it had been in first gear from start to finish. 'The arrival
at Alderney was rightly considered a great triumph,' Romilly
John recalled.

I insisted on being taught to drive immediately, and David, who had never driven a car in his life, but who had had much experience with a motor bicycle, undertook the task. I had often observed other drivers, and was therefore a qualified chauffeur in theory, so that after about half an hour I was considered competent to drive out by myself. It was then Dorelia's turn. By the evening the house was full of newly-fledged drivers, and in a few days it was considered a mere nothing to go spinning along at sixty miles an hour ... After that we always seemed to be whizzing – the right word for our mode of transit – up to London. In those days the roads were still fairly empty, and motoring was still a sport. We nearly always came up with another fast car, also on its way to town, and then we would race it for a hundred miles. No matter who was driving, we made it a point of honour never to be outdone, and we very seldom were. When our car and its rival had passed and repassed each other several times, emotion would work up to a white-heat, and every minor victory was the signal of a wild hilariousness.[5]

Though the family inherited his talent, the John style of motoring was seen in its purest form whenever Augustus took the wheel. In fine country, on a good day, he was apt to forget he was driving at all, allowing the car to pelt on ahead while he stared back over his shoulder to admire some receding view. Under this *laisser-aller* the car often performed better than when he bent upon it his fullest attention. Then, roaring like a wounded elephant, it would mount hedges, charge with intrepid bursts of speed towards corners, or simply explode with punctured tyres. Passengers were called upon to assist only during emergencies. Once, when hurtling towards a fork in the road, John demanded which direction to take, and, his passenger hesitating a moment, bisected the angle, accelerating straight into a ploughed field until brought to a halt by the waves of earth. Another time, he 'awoke to find himself driving through the iron gate of a churchyard'.[6] Because of feats like these, the car soon began to present a dilapidated appearance, like an old animal in a circus : the brakes almost ceased to operate, and the mechanism could only be worked by two people simultaneously, the second taking off the hand-brake at the precise moment when the first, manipulating the knobs, buttons and handles as if performing on an organ, caused the engine to engage with the wheels. Sometimes, 'like a woman', the car refused to respond at all and had to be warmed up, cajoled, petted, pushed. At last, yielding to these blandishments (again like a woman), she would jerk into life and, with her flushed occupants, drag herself away from the scene of her humiliation to the dispiriting cheers of the assembled *voyeurs*. In her most petulant moods she would react only to the full frontal approach. But once, when John was winding up the crank (the car having been left in gear on the downward slope of a hill), she ran him down. His companion, a music critic, 'frantically pushing and pulling every lever I could lay my hands and feet on,'⁷ was carried off out of sight, their elopement being eventually arrested by a brick wall.

Though accidents were plentiful there were almost no deaths and the Johns themselves seemed marvellously indestructible. They were, however, extremely critical, even contemptuous, of one another's skill. Dorelia, for example, failed to applaud John's inspired cornering; while he irritably censored her triumphant use of the horn. None of them 'felt safe' while being driven by any of the others, and did not scruple to hide this. 'I will not attempt to conceal,' wrote Romilly John, 'that some of us were secretly glad when some others incurred some minor accident.'⁸

Towards people outside the family, though dismissive of their ability, they were nervously polite. An episode from Lucy Norton's motoring career shows John's kindness on wheels at its most characteristic:

The incident happened in 1926 or 1927 when I was 23 or 24. I had recently purchased a motor-car, and John thought a long country drive would be the thing to give me experience. Night-driving experience, he said, was very important. I picked him up at Mallord Street early on a May morning. He appeared in a beautiful Harris-tweed coat, his usual large gypsy hat, several scarves with fringed ends, a bottle of whisky in case of need, and a bottle of gin for a friend.

All seems to have gone well until we reached Winchester, when I was turning to the right as John was saying 'turn left', and we mounted, very slowly, a lamp-post. John said nothing but I could see he was shaken. We proceeded to Ringwood, had a superlative lunch and about six o'clock started for home.

I suppose we must have gone about ten miles or so, when I was overcome with the strong suspicion that the back door of the four-doored Morris Cowley (I had bought the cheapest car, so that it would not matter if I hit things) was not shut. I turned to shut it – not realising that, as I pivoted with one hand back, the other on the steering wheel would follow me round. The next thing was a mildly terrific crash, as the car hit the soft bank at right angles on the other side of the road. John rose upright in his seat, lifted me also to a standing position behind the wheel, and clasping me to his shoulder said in tones of sympathetic disgust: 'You simply cannot trust the steering of these modern cars! It's too bad!'[9]

Such imaginative courtesy was often useful in Court. Montgomery Hyde, who happened to be passing one day, observed how John, coming out of his drive 'fairly rapidly',[10] cannoned into a steamroller which was doing innocent repairs to the road outside his gate. Very correctly John reported this incident but the police, having their own ideas, replied with a summons. In due course he appeared before the local Bench but was acquitted because, the magistrate explained, he 'behaved in such a gentlemanlike manner'.

As it whizzed through the twenties this car took on many of John's characteristics. It became, in effect, a magnified version of himself, and its exploits drew attention to a developing feature of his life. He seemed to have no nerves or sensitivity to danger. 'How we never got killed in this car was a miracle,' Poppet recalled.[11] The detached feeling that had first invaded John at the Front – the calm knowledge that he might be struck dead at any second – grew more established. 'He might easily have been killed,' wrote Cecil Gray of one motoring adventure, '... but Augustus has always lived a charmed life where cars are concerned ... I recommend anyone suffering from suicidal depression or a distaste for life to induce my illustrious friend to take him for a spin in the country and I guarantee that when he returns – if he ever does return, which is problematical – it will be as a yea-saying Nietzschean lover of life.'[12]

To more than one person in his later years John spoke of
suicide: how he must resist the temptation to give into it. He
would not kill himself, but need he

> strive
> Officiously to keep alive?

His carelessness seemed deliberate, an invitation for Fate to
intercede. The irony was that his negligence was exactly
cancelled out by Dorelia's diligence. As the 'femme inspiratrice',
attaching herself to Augustus so as to nurture his genius, she
helped to keep him alive over the thirty years in which he
painted his worst pictures. Sometimes he longed – or so it
appeared – to make what haste he could and be gone: but she
would never let him.

So he drove on, recklessly, not knowing where to go. And
nothing happened. In spite of all vicissitudes, the Buick continued noisily to function 'and was only abandoned at last,'
Romilly remembered, 'somewhere near London, upsidedown
and in a state bordering on the chaotic'.[13]

2. WOMEN AND CHILDREN: AN A TO Z

He had said good-bye to his mistresses and also, by the end of
the war, to many friends who had been killed. 'What casualty
lists!' he exclaimed in a letter to Quinn.[14] 'How can it go on
much longer? Among my own friends, and I never had many
– [Dummer] Howard, [Ivor] Campbell, Heald, Baines, Jay,
[Tudor] Castle, Rourke, Warren, Tennant ... We must be
bleeding white – and it seems the best go down always.' The
eccentrics survived: Trelawney Dayrell Reed, aloof and stam-
mering, to be the perfect subject for John's El Greco phase;
Horace de Vere Cole, to become a victim of his own practical
jokes; Francis Macnamara, John's replica-rival, surrounded by
logbooks, bottled ships, thundering treatises, and supported by
monkey-glands, to emerge first as Romilly's theological tutor,
then (by scooping up Edie McNeill and marrying her) as
Dorelia's brother-in-law and after that as the father-in-law of
Dylan Thomas. The boys' old tutor, John Hope-Johnstone, also

danced back 'like an abandoned camel'[15] and promptly re-engaged himself as Robin's philosopher and guide.

In the eyes of many, John appeared superior to the needs of ordinary friendship. 'Is it because I seem an indifferent friend myself?' he asked Will Rothenstein. 'I know I have moods which afford my friends reason for resentment; but I love my friends I think as much as anybody – when they let me.'[16] What he needed in the way of friends was variety, from which, like notes on a piano, he could select any tune of his choice. Though many had gone down, more were stepping forward, like the fresh row of a chorus, to fill their places. There was Joe Hone, rare phenomenon, an Irishman of impressive silence; Roy Campbell, the big action maverick poet from South Africa, with his black cowboy hat, white face and flashing blue eyes, dressed in clothes that 'appeared to have been rescued from the dustbin';[17] T. W. Earp, ex-President of the Oxford Union, a soft-spoken, gently humorous man, his hair close-cropped, his head shaped like a vegetable, who had taken his lack of ambition to the extreme of becoming an art-critic; Ronald Firbank,[18] wrestling with a shoot of asparagus, his nervous laugh like the sound of a clock suddenly running down, his hands fluttering with embarrassment, trying to live down 'the dreadful fact that his father had been an M.P.'; and A. R. Orage, John's 'man of sense',[19] the brilliant wayward editor of the *New Age*, who, like a Mohammed always changing his Allah, had first elected Nietzsche as god, then ousted him with the Douglas Credit Scheme which gave way before the deity of psychoanalysis, and was finally replaced, in New York and Fontainebleau, by Gourdjief's box of tricks – at which point John lost him. Like John, he had the mind of a disciple and the temperament of a leader, which led even this last association with Gourdjief to break up. Between the extremes of rhetoric and literature, honesty and sophistry, he passed his life, stimulating where he could not nourish and testifying by his persistent search to the existence of what he could not find.

Such friends provided new worlds for John. Being rootless himself, he was easily transplanted. Having been a Welshman, gypsy, sartorial soldier and leader of the British School of Promise, he was soon to turn academician, stage designer for

Sean O'Casey and for J. M. Barrie, illustrator for Ronald Firbank. He had been on friendly terms with Bloomsbury, still maintained good relations with the Sitwells and, intermittently, with Wyndham Lewis. But in the 1920s he moved for the first time into the land of the rich and aristocratic – of Napier Alington, Evan Morgan, Gerald Berners. It would not be true that he never looked back – such was not in his nature. But the distance over which he had to look to connect other parts of his life lengthened.

He had crossed the border into this elevated world at the Paris Peace Conference. It was here that his friendship began with T. E. Lawrence who, singling him out as the perfect image-maker, returned again and again (concealing his hideous motor-bike behind the bushes) for 'fancy-dress'[20] portraits of himself as Café Royal Arab or pale plaintive aircraftsman. But it was the Marchesa Casati, of the archaic smile and macabre beauty, who beckoned him into international society. As Luisa Ammon, daughter of a Milanese industrialist, she had been, it was said, a mousy little girl. As the young wife of Camillo Casati, noblest of Roman huntsmen, she pounced like a panther on to life: and overshot it. The mousy hair burst into henna'd flames; the grey-green eyes, now ringed with black kohl, expanded enormously, amazing false eyelashes spreading and waving before them like peacock's feathers. Her lips were steeped in vermilion, her feet empurpled, her face, transformed by some black-and-white alchemy, became a painted mask, a sphinx. By taking thought she added a cubit to her stature, raising her legs on altitudinous platform heels, and crowning her head with top hats of tiger skin and black satin, huge gold waste-paper baskets turned upside down, or the odd inverted flowerpot from which gesticulated a salmon-pink feather. It was for her that Léon Bakst, soaring on his most extravagant flights of fantasy, designed *incroyable* Persian trousers of the most savage cut; for her Mariano Fortuny invented his finest fabrics – long scarves of oriental gauze, soaked in the mysterious pigments of his vats and 'tinted with strange dreams'.[21]

She lived, this decadent queen of Venice, in the roofless 'Palazzo Non Finito',* there conducting entertainments of sur-

* Subsequently converted into the Guggenheim Institute.

realist splendour. Disguised as an animal-tamer in leopard skins from neck to ankle, she would appear with a macaw on her shoulder, an ape on one arm, or a few cobras. As background for these appearances she redesigned her ballroom with caged monkeys which gibbered among branches of lilac as she floated past pursued by a shoal of Afghan hounds and a restive ocelot held on its leash by the Negro keeper, his hand dripping with paint. Whenever the guests overflowed she would take over the Piazza San Marco, illuminating it with torches brandished by near-naked slaves. But there were failures. The slaves, painted with gold, expired; her costume – an affair of armour pierced with a hundred electric arrows – short-circuited. By the spring of 1919 she had left Venice and her husband, achieved poetic status as the mistress of d'Annunzio and, having exhausted one huge fortune, was preparing to demolish a second.

Casati's witchlike aspect often provoked terror in her admirers: but John, unlike most of these cavaliers (whom she treated with glorious contempt) was a romantic only by instalments. Visually she stimulated him, but in other ways caused him (between yawns) to 'laugh immoderately'.[22] Where T. E. Lawrence had beheld a 'vampire', John saw only 'a spoilt child of a woman' ringed about with the credulity and suspiciousness of a savage. Taken in small draughts, her presence, with all its malice and extravagance, intoxicated him.

She had been painted by innumerable artists. To Marinetti and the Futurists, she was their Gioconda; to Boldini, who portrayed her smothered in peacock feathers and arched over cushions like a pretend-panther, she was Scheherazade. To John, who painted her twice in April 1919, she was something else again: a truncated, pyjama'd figure,* fantastically mascara'd, and poised, vamp-like, before a view of Vesuvius where, as the unbidden guest of Axel Munthe, she overstayed her welcome by some fifteen years. For once romanticism and irony were perfectly blended to produce what Lord Duveen was to call 'an outstanding masterpiece of our time'.[23]

'He painted like a lion,' sighed Casati. 'Le taxi vous attend,' he writes to her from Paris. 'Venez!' They flung themselves to-

---

* It was, Sir Evan Charteris wrote, 'originally full-length in pyjamas and was cut in half by John himself'.

wards each other, but the romance, a brilliantly casual performance, seemed sadly under-rehearsed. Sex was not the real attraction between them. Casati took other people's admiration for granted, using it as an orchestration to her life, a perpetual chorus singing invisibly while she stood on stage alone. Otherwise love-affairs threatened to interfere with her passionate self-love. For she was intensely narcissistic, rather under-sexed and without actual intelligence. As an exhibitionist she needed partners only for her audience. Yet somehow John felt a kinship with her. Like him, she was outrageously shy, concocting, in place of real life, a pantomime.

She wanted for nothing until the 1930s when the last penny of the last fortune had been squandered and the curtain came down on her performance. As Cagliostro at a Magicians' Ball she tempted the Devil once too often. A dreadful storm scattered her guests and she fled from her Palais Rose at Neuilly, penniless, to England. From those who had shared her costume ball career throughout the Continent she knew with a peasant's sharp instinct there would be no compassion, no cash. In England there was charity, a pale but persistent kindness, first from Lord Alington, then, for the last dozen years of her life from a Wodehousean platoon of old fellows – the Duke of Westminster, Lord Tredegar (Evan Morgan) and John himself. 'Je serai ravi de vous revoir, carissima,' he gallantly welcomed her, enclosing 'un petit cadeau'. He warned her that 'Londres n'est pas gai en ce moment', but she knew there was nowhere else she could shelter. She lived in a small dirty flat within, however, a house that had once been Byron's. The layers of powder grew thicker; the stories of Italy longer; her clothes more faded and frayed; her leopard-skin gloves spotted with holes; her thin figure, like a scarecrow, into a bag of bones. But she had never valued mere comfort and did not miss it now. Despite the squalor, she played, to the last notes, this ghostly echo of the d'Annunzian heroine. 'Bring in the drinks!' she would call, and a bent Italian servant would shuffle forward with a half-empty bottle of beer. What money came in she tended to spend at once, shopping by taxi in Knightsbridge and Mayfair for Spider, her Pekinese. Her one asset was absolute helplessness, which threw responsibility for her survival on to everyone else. To ensure that their help was practical, her friends paid an allowance each week into her bank from where, by taxi, she would grudgingly collect it. Her bank accounts show that, for over a decade, John was her most persistent source of income. She did not need very often to beg from him: he gave spontaneously, regularly, small sums with a there-but-for-the-grace-of-God generosity. 'Ayez courage, carissima, et croyez à mon amitié sincère.' It did not occur to her to do otherwise. 'Je suis bien triste que vous êtes toujours dans les difficultés,' he wrote again, with more apprehension. But when, during the early 1940s, she asked for more money to remove these difficulties, he fell back into explanations: 'Le gouvernement prend tout mon argent pour ce guerre et j'ai des grandes dépenses comme vous savez.' The aphrodisiac notes now gave way before a crisp commercial correspondence – 'Voici le chèque.' But she did not embarrass him with gratitude and they remained friends until her death. Meanwhile she had been overtaken by a desperate faith in occult power, no longer wasting her time writing letters to her friends but receiving them from the other world; documents in disguised handwriting that prophesied all manner of miracles – the foul death of her enemies; presents of brandy and jewels.

The mercurial Casati occupied a unique place within the latter part of John's life. She should, he once suggested to Cecil Beaton, have been shot and, like Spider, stuffed – she would have looked so well in a glass case. The other women in his life were for more active employment and, from the 1920s onwards, began to arrange themselves into a pattern. There were the occasional models; there was the chief mistress who looked after him in town and abroad when Dorelia was absent; and there was the Grand Lady, to be defined neither as model nor mistress, who conducted his life in society.

John's principal mistress during these years was Eileen Hawthorne, 'an uncommon and interesting type', he suggested to Maurice Elvey, ' – at any rate she would like to do some work in films'. Young and very beautiful, she did most of her work for artists, with whom she was extremely popular. Pictures of her constantly appeared in the press – a new portrait by Lewis Baumer or Russell Flint; an eager advertisement for bathcubes, lingerie, eau-de-cologne; or simply as 'Miss 1933'. The most extraordinary feature of these pictures was that none of them looked in the least alike. She had developed a most versatile appearance, and as queen of the magic world of cosmetics she could change her looks from day to day. This was her 'mystery'. She was known by the newspapers as the girl of a thousand faces. Each morning she re-created herself, and again each evening. Superficially, it was impossible to tire of her.

She was not a good model for John. Hardly had he begun to apply his brushes than her features would wobble, start to dissolve and, so it seemed, re-form themselves into a different shape. She tried to appear consistent but, having no enthusiasm for it, always painted herself more fluently, it was said, than he did.

There were other problems too. He suspected that she did not possess a flair for discretion. The man who, twenty years before, advised Sampson to 'sin openly and scandalize the world' had grown timid of scandal himself. Experience, like a great wall, shut off his return to innocence. His letters to Eileen Hawthorne exhibit more anxiety than enjoyment. He asks her, because of Dorelia, not to telephone him in the country; he begs her to avoid journalists – especially on those occasions when she happens to be missing a tooth or unable to conceal a black eye, marks which, he warns her, will inevitably be credited to his infernal 'legend'. He wishes he could trust more wholeheartedly her ability to hide things: for example, pregnancies. Though he shared her favours with the musician E. J. Moeran, it was John who, after some grumbling, paid for the abortions. He had no choice. Otherwise her mother would get to hear of them, and then the world would know.

This climate of secrecy did not suit John, but it was necessary. He divided his life into compartments. It is unlikely, for instance, that Eileen Hawthorne ever met the redoubtable Mrs Fleming who, during the 1920s and 1930s, made herself responsible for much of John's social life. She was the widow of Valentine Fleming, a Yeomanry officer and Member of Parliament for Henley, who had been killed after winning the D.S.O. in the First World War. She was rich; she was handsome – dark, with a small head, large eyes and an affluent complexion. John and she overwhelmed each other. The three portraits he painted of her in her forties show 'a Goyaesque beauty, hard, strong-featured, the self-absorbed face of an acknowledged prima donna used to getting her own way'.[24] Upon her four sons – Peter the author and explorer, Ian the creator of James Bond, Richard a prosperous banker and Michael who died of wounds as a prisoner-of-war after Dunkirk – she laid an obligation to succeed. She believed in success, and herself led an extremely successful life in society. In 1923 she moved to Turner's House at 118 Cheyne Walk, Chelsea. It was a beautiful place, superb for entertaining, with a large studio at the back, all drastically improved since the days when Turner had lodged there. Sitting at the bar of the public house next door 'fortifying the inner man' against his entry into Mrs Fleming's luncheon parties, John sometimes thought of Turner – how he would have preferred the grosser amenities of Wapping. John's own sympathies lay in a similar direction. Often he needed more drink to confront these social occasions, but the money, the aura of success, the opportunities – these could not be denied. Mrs Fleming admired him, he admired her and many people came to Cheyne Walk and admired them both. In such company it was possible temporarily to forget a bad day's work.

In his biography of Ian Fleming, John Pearson describes Mrs Fleming as 'a bird of paradise', extravagant, passionate, demanding, a law to herself. She was, he wrote, 'a rich, beautiful widow – and, thanks to the provision of her husband's Will, likely to remain one'. Nevertheless, at one critical point in the 1920s, she seems to have entertained the possibility of marriage to John. This notion, which offended Dorelia, had as its object the solution to a very real problem that was then advancing upon them.

John Hope-Johnstone had turned up on the doorstep of Mallord Street one afternoon in the late spring of 1921 with a girl. She was just sixteen, he explained. He had caught sight of her at the Armenian café in Archer Street, introduced himself, then taken her in a cab to meet Compton Mackenzie. They'd had a grand time. Now, since she was an avid admirer of John, they'd come to see him too. Her name was Chiquita. John grunted and let them in.

She was an engaging creature, *mignonne*, very tiny, with a dark fringe and low rippling laugh. Her passport was charm, and

she specialized in 'cheekiness'. While the men growled in conversation, she flitted round the enormous studio, aware of
John's eyes, like searchlights, travelling all over her as she
moved. Soon she began to chatter, telling stories about herself
– how her mother had run away to New Orleans with a Cuban
leaving her to be brought up by a funny old man with whiskers;
how she had been a tom boy, climbing trees, stealing apples,
getting spanked and, at the age of fifteen, ran away from school
to join a travelling theatre company . . .

'When can I paint you?' John interrupted. 'Come to-morrow
at four.'

'I'll come at five,' Chiquita retorted.

It was agreed that she should wear the same clothes – a blue
blouse, black stockings, red skirt – and that he would pay her a
pound for each sitting: handsome wages. She came at five,
carrying as a weapon and badge of her sophistication a long
cigarette holder.

John's oil portrait of Chiquita proclaims her to have been a
stimulating model. But as a sitter she was frightful. She talked
all the time, while John's expression darkened dreadfully. She
could not understand why he seemed so 'terribly ratty'. One
afternoon he said he would like to draw her, and demanded to
know whether she would take off her clothes. She agreed, provided there was somewhere private to undress. She re-entered
the studio wearing a dressing-gown. He began to work – then
after a few minutes, while she lay there nakedly chattering, he
pounced. She remembered him being so old, the coarse beard,
smell of whisky and tobacco, no words, just grunting and
snorting . . .

Later, on discovering she was pregnant, Chiquita approached
Dorelia. It was arranged that she should have an abortion, but
Chiquita did not take to the specialist and eventually refused to
go through with the operation. 'It was a very drastic time in my
life but I was too young to be unhappy,' she remembered.[25] The
atmosphere at Alderney was wonderfully comforting. She felt
free, yet cared for. 'It was a lovely summer,' she recalled, 'and
we slept outside in the orchard in the communal bed there . . .
We used to light a little bonfire down our end . . . it was fun –
there weren't any strict rules, one could get in through the

window without being nagged at.' Pigs and red setters stalked
the garden; there were picnics, rides in the pony cart and, under
a sign that read 'Bathing Prohibited', there was bathing. Dorelia
was always near 'and she always looked pretty super especially
when she wore her sun bonnet and picked currants'.[26] Dorelia
never referred to her pregnancy, suggesting, after a few months,
that Chiquita wear a cloak 'because she would look so fine in
one, and they were becoming very fashionable'.

At the beginning of March they took her to an expensive
nursing home where, on 6 March, she gave birth to a daughter
whom she called Zoë. John arrived bringing masses of flowers,
but when Chiquita came out he had tactfully withdrawn to
Spain.

She had a little money, and quickly got some jobs as a photographer's model. Zoë meanwhile was billeted in Islington with
a policeman and his wife whose daughter, 'Simon', was later to
marry Augustus's eldest son David. One day Chiquita received
an invitation to call on Mrs Fleming. The meeting was not easy.
Mrs Fleming's imperious personality brought out everything
that was rebellious in Chiquita, and when she offered to adopt
the baby, provide it with a good home and education, Chiquita
refused – though accepting some clothes and the assistance of a
nanny. There seems little doubt that Mrs Fleming hoped to build
up this pressure of persuasion, but before she had any real
opportunity a row broke out over the clothes, all of which
were marked 'Fleming'. From this time on the two women
stood revealed as enemies. 'If she [Chiquita] had a million
pounds a year, I still should not alter my opinion that she ought
not to have the bringing up of that baby or of any other,' wrote
Mrs Fleming.[27]

Each weekend Chiquita would call at Islington and pick up
Zoë. One Saturday the baby was collected early – by Mrs Fleming, who rushed her off to North Wales in the hope that
Chiquita would not trouble to pursue them. Over the crisis
lawyers now began to circle and the dry corpses of legal correspondence rapidly accumulated. John, on his return from Spain,
was horrified. He had supported, in his absence, Mrs Fleming's
plan and arranged anonymously through her and a solicitor to
pay Chiquita £20 down and £1 a week thereafter in exchange

for the baby. But instead of this sensible 'baby agreement' he was faced with a *cause célèbre*. It was possibly his influence that helped to persuade Mrs Fleming to return the baby.

But Chiquita had other allies, in particular Seymour Leslie to whom she blurted out her story one evening at the Eiffel Tower. She was determined to 'fight like a tiger' to keep Zoë, she insisted. 'I trust no one with Zoë's happiness as I do myself. I am waiting for Mrs Fleming to return. I would like to kill her ...' Vowing indignantly to help, Seymour Leslie called for pen and ink and drew up a contract, signed by Stulick and the head waiter Otto, undertaking to pay for Zoë provided Chiquita agreed to live with him as his mistress. This settled, they hurried off to Paris for four days of celebration.

The arrangement lasted some six months. 'I used to lead him a pretty good dance,' she recalled, '. . . tho' he made me happy in a strange sort of way.' He let her have fun, but what she really wanted was marriage. When Seymour Leslie returned from a visit to Russia in the autumn of 1923, he found her married to Michael Birkbeck, a friend of John's and living with him and Zoë in the country.*

Mrs Fleming was not used to being worsted: it unnerved her. 'My dreams of a happy home,' she wrote, '. . . have fallen to the ground.' In their place she was surrounded by clouds of 'reprehensible gossip'. 'It seems to be a mistake to be the good Samaritan or to feel things,' she complained bitterly to Seymour Leslie. 'People don't seem to understand either, and only to imagine the worst motives for one's actions.' The deplorable affair had made her ill. 'I have done my best,' she declared, 'and have had to retire to bed, really exhausted with this worry.' At night she would dream 'of drowned babies with dead faces and alive eyes looking at me'. She had four sons, but she wanted a daughter: John's. It should have all been so easy, so private. John himself felt exasperated by these women. 'I'm so horribly complicated and there's no peace for a *man* at all,' he complained to the Rani. Had Ida lived, he sometimes thought, it might have all been different. 'Failing her, one simply tries all the others in rotation – I've nearly reached the limit.'

Once begun, the ridiculous game had to be played out 'to the

* John gave the Birkbecks £1,000 to be invested for Zoë.

last spasm'. Mrs Fleming wanted a child – she should have one. One day she announced that she was going on a long cruise. When she returned, some months later, sure enough it was with a baby – a girl: Amaryllis. Amaryllis's childhood was very different from Zoë's. This 'rare bird'[28] was discreetly hidden away in Turner's House and, in a vague way, it was understood that she had been adopted.*

Zoë and Amaryllis both adored Augustus. In the 1930s and later each of them often stayed with him and Dorelia at Fryern. Once they turned up there on the same day, and John, his eyes glinting, introduced them: 'I believe you two are related.' Amaryllis's success as a 'cellist gave him much pleasure. He listened to her on the radio, wrote her letters of congratulation, attended her first concert where he judged her triumph in terms of the number of people in tears during the slow movement. He felt proud that she with her red hair and the black-haired Zoë were such fine-looking wenches. Each of them sat for him. 'I could paint you on your back . . .' he offered Amaryllis. Zoë, too, who had gone on the stage and was everybody's understudy, was 'a first-rate sitter, and useful', he judged, 'in other ways too'.[29]

3. FACES AND TALES

'Augustus John, whose brain was once teeming with ideas for great compositions, had ceased to do imaginative work and was painting portraits,' wrote Will Rothenstein of these years between the wars.[30] Though he was to return in the next two decades to 'invented' landscapes on a large scale, and though he continued to paint at all times from Nature, adding, on Dorelia's instructions, flower pictures to his repertoire in the 1920s, portraits dominated John's work until the Second World War. He was always 'dying to get through with them and tackle other things', but in vain. 'Alas! that seems to be my perpetual state!'[31]

By popular consent, the finest portrait of this period was of Guilhermina Suggia, the famous Portuguese 'cellist. John began

* John Pearson refers to her as adopted in his *Life of Ian Fleming*, and so does Cecil Roberts in the fourth volume of his autobiography *Sunshine and Shadow*.

this work early in 1920 and, after almost eighty sittings, finished it early in 1923.[32] It took so long and involved her calling at Mallord Street so incessantly that a rumour spread that they were living there together.

'To be painted by Augustus John is no ordinary experience,' Suggia allowed. '. . . The man is unique and so are his methods.'[33] Throughout the sittings she played unintermittent Bach, and this, in the most agreeable manner, forestalled conversation – John continuing to hum the music during lunch. 'Sometimes,' Suggia noticed, 'he would begin to walk up and down in time to the music . . . When specially pleased with his work, when some finesse of painting eyelash or tint had gone well, he would always walk on tiptoe.'* As a rule she posed for two hours a day, but by the third year, when John was growing desperate to complete the picture, she would sit for another two in the afternoon.

Those who visited the studio during these years were aware that a terrific struggle was taking place. John was attempting to paint again: that is, not simply draw with the brush. From week to week the picture would change: sometimes it looked good, sometimes it had deteriorated, and at other times, in spite of much repainting, it appeared almost unchanged. As with a tug-of-war, tense, motionless, no one could tell which way it would go.†

'Suggia' challenges comparison with 'The Smiling Woman' of fifteen years earlier. There is something of the same monumental quality in both paintings, though the mood of 'Suggia' is more dignified than the provocative study of Dorelia. The colour schemes too are similar – dull reds and greens – even if, as Mary Chamot has observed, the 'colours [of 'Suggia'] are no longer as clear cut – there is more fugue in the design'.[34] Suggia herself was 'more delighted with the result than I should have thought possible'. The painting had a strength of composition

* Suggia continued: 'Directly I heard his footsteps hush and his tread lighten I strained all my powers to keep at just the correct attitude. In a picture painted like this, a portrait not only of a musician but of her instrument – more of the very spirit of music itself – the sitter must to a great extent share in its creation. John himself is kind enough to call it "our" picture.'

† The picture was first shown at the Alpine Gallery in March 1923, and the following year won first prize at the Pittsburgh International Exhibition.

(the long elaboration of the dress acting as a perfect balance to the awkward shape of the 'cello) that was undeniable.

Something seemed to have snapped in John as a result of the extended effort he put into this picture. Never again did he seriously attempt anything so 'painterly'. The portrait of Thomas Hardy, for example, done some six months after the completion of 'Suggia', is a dry impasto laid straight on to the canvas, which is barely covered in parts (the hairs of the moustache are attached not to the face but to a piece of un-primed canvas). In treatment and colour-scheme it is reminiscent of his three studies of Bernard Shaw.

John had met Hardy at Kingston Maurward on 21 September 1923 and, after several visits to Max Gate, polished off the portrait by the middle of the following month. Hardy was then eighty-three. 'An atmosphere of great sympathy and almost complete understanding at once established itself between us,' John recorded.[35] They did not talk much, but John felt they were of a kind : * 'I wonder which of the two of us was the more naïve!' He painted Hardy seated in his study, a room piled to the ceiling with books 'of a philosophical character'. Hardy wears a serious, querying expression; he looks stiff, but bearing up. It is the portrait of a shy man, full of disciplined emotion. On seeing it, he sighed: 'I don't know whether that is how I look or not, but that is how I *feel*' – a fine tribute for any painter.[36]

In a letter to Hardy, John suggested that this portrait was 'merely preparatory to another & more satisfactory picture which I hope to do with your help, later on'.[37] It was only by labelling his paintings as preliminary studies for more elaborate compositions that he could agree with himself to stop working on them. Where there was infinite time there was infinite delay, infinite painting out and indecision. Critics have interpreted this dissatisfaction as a quest for perfection, but his search was joined to a temperament that frustrated this quest. He could not adjust to difficulties. He painted on without premeditation, sometimes asking his sitters what background colour they would

---

* In a letter to John, Florence Hardy wrote (8 February 1929): 'He [Hardy] had the greatest respect and *liking* for you not only as an artist but as a man. I can think of few people he liked so much.'

like, whether they thought he should introduce a flower or a bowl of fruit, or posing some ironic demand such as: 'Tell me what's wrong with this arm'. Such appeals, it was alleged, spoke of an amazing modesty. But they told too of the failure of artistic purpose. When Lord David Cecil inquired what aesthetic motive there had been for making the colour of his tie darker that it actually was, John replied that some black paint had accidentally got into the red, and he thought it looked rather good. He had little conscious idea of how a portrait would turn out, though he liked, starting perhaps with an eye, to exaggerate the figure as he worked downwards, as El Greco or Velasquez might, for grand manner. His unfinished work is often better because it manages to convey powers, latent in him, on which he could no longer call. It must be 'hard', T. E. Lawrence sympathized (9 April 1930), 'to paint against time'. But time was a false friend to John – a substitute for deep concentration. It remained to Dorelia and close brave friends to rescue, by one subterfuge or another, what pictures they could before they were painted into oblivion.

The longer he worked the more difficult it became to persuade him to stop. With commissioned portraits there was usually some limitation that imposed a discipline, though it afforded little pleasure. Of all these 'board-room' portraits, his favourite was of Montagu Norman, Governor of the Bank of England. Begun on 1 April 1930, it was completed a year later, Norman's hair subsiding in the interval from grey to white. To John's mind he was 'an almost ideal sitter', taking apparently no interest whatever in the artist or his picture. 'It was in a spirit of severe reserve that we used to part on the doorstep of my house,' John recorded, 'whence, after looking this way and that, and finding the coast clear, Mr Norman would venture forth to regain his car, parked as usual discreetly round the corner.'[38] What John did not know was that, on arriving back at his office, Norman was transformed, regaling everyone with envious and excited descriptions of the Great Artist at work. 'It's marvellous to watch him scrutinizing me,' he would rhapsodize, '... then using a few swift strokes like this on the outline and dabbing on paint like lightning. What a heavenly gift!'[39]

John represents the two of them as sharing one quality: a

sense of isolation. Norman's air of preoccupation conveyed that
he was 'troubled with graver problems than beset other men',
and it was not difficult, John recalled, 'to offset Mr Montagu
Norman's indifference to my activities by a corresponding disregard of his'.[40] At rare moments 'our acquaintance seemed to
show signs of ripening,' and then, so he told Michael Ayrton, an
immense attraction would sweep over him for this dry, semi-
detached figure. 'Could there,' he hazarded, 'have been something *Greek* about it?' To John Freeman he later remarked: 'It
seemed to give him pleasure.' But he was referring to the sittings,
not the portrait itself which, with its hard eyes, nervously taut
mouth and haunted expression shocked Norman so much that
he refused to let it hang either in his home or at the Bank of
England.*

'Sometimes,' John recalled, 'Lord D'Abernon would come to
chat with my sitter. The subject appeared to be High Finance. I
was not tempted to join in these discussions.'[41] D'Abernon was
another of John's subjects, whose portrait, completed after
Montagu Norman's, had been started early in 1927. As only the
second ceremonial portrait of John's career, it invites comparison with the 'Lord Mayor of Liverpool' but falls incomparably short. It is neither caricature nor straight portrait study: it
is a false creation. John himself affected to believe it a finer
painting than 'Suggia', but this judgement rested on the greater
time it had taken him, and on his wish to obtain for it the same
price – three thousand pounds. Sometimes, during this five years
marathon, he was tempted to give up: then another cheque, for
£500 or £1,000, would arrive and he was obliged to paint on. To
gain wind it was necessary for him to fabricate vast enthusiasm
for the ordeal. On 18 December 1927 he writes to D'Abernon
that the portrait was 'too fine a scheme' to take any 'risks' with.
Since Lady D'Abernon had a villa in Rome, might it not be 'a
practical plan', John wondered, 'for me to come to Rome in
February where I could use a studio at the British School'.[42] Two
years later, on 8 December 1929, Lord D'Abernon notes in a
letter to his wife: 'The Augustus John portrait at last improving
– the face less bibulous. Seen from five yards off – it is a fine
costume picture.'[43] John had brought in a stalwart Guardsman

* Where, nevertheless, it now hangs.

to stand wearing the British Ambassador's elaborate uniform, but eventually this soldier collapsed and John fell back on a wooden dressmaker's model, the character of which is well conveyed in the completed work. Like Macbeth, he had reached a point from which it was as tedious to retreat as to go on. He put the best face he could on it: 'Things bad begun make strong themselves by ill.'

The portrait, now in the Tate Gallery, is dated 1932, in which year it was finally handed over to Lord D'Abernon. 'There are only two styles of portrait painting,' says Miss La Creevy in *Nicholas Nickleby*; 'the serious and the smirk.' 'Lord D'Abernon' is neither. It is a masterpiece of elongated confusion, pleasing no one. In making a solemn attempt to be obsequious John had painted a uniform.

On other occasions, when his soul revolted against such work, he could be less accommodating. After finishing the portrait of the Earl of Athlone, he agreed to show it the following day to the sitter's wife. She arrived with her husband and went into his studio. Two minutes later they burst out, looking furious. John stood in the doorway quietly lighting his pipe as they drove heatedly off. Egerton Cooper, who had watched the incident from his studio near by, hurried over to ask what was wrong. 'I tore the painting to pieces,' explained John. 'I suddenly couldn't bear it.'

Another time it was the sitter who dismantled a portrait. During part of the summer of 1920, John had been at work on 'His Margarine Majesty', the fish and soap millionaire, Lord Leverhulme. Although 'strongly inclined' to have his portrait done by John, Leverhulme had begun the first sitting by warning him he could spare little time and that he was an almost impossible subject, no artist (excepting to some degree Sir Luke Fildes) having done him justice. When the time was up, great pleasure was lavished over the picture: by John. It seemed, he proclaimed, to breathe with life and self-satisfaction and only lacked speech. Leverhulme himself did not lack speech, and finding the portrait very 'humbling to pride' and a 'chastening'[44] reflection, argued that neither the eyes, nor the mouth, nor yet the nose were his – at which, proffering his palette, John invited his Lordship to make the corrections himself. This offer was declined and the picture, with all its alleged faults, paid for and dispatched.

John had then gone down to Tenby. Returning to Mallord Street late in September he discovered the portrait had been returned to him – at least that part representing Lord Leverhulme's trunk, shoulders, arms, hands and thighs, though not his head which had been scissored out. That evening (31 September 1920) John sat down and wrote: 'I am intensely anxious to have your Lordship's explanation of this, the grossest insult I have ever received in the course of my career.'

Leverhulme's reply four days later shone with friendliness. He felt 'extremely distressed at the blunder that has occurred', but added: 'I assure you it is entirely a blunder on the part of my housekeeper.' He had intended hanging the painting in his safe at Rivington Bungalow, he explained, but had overlooked 'the fact that there were internal partitionings and other obstacles that prevented me doing this'. After a bold prognosis, he settled on a surgical operation, removing the head 'which is the important part of the portrait', and storing it safely away. This letter, culminating with an urgent request to keep the matter dark, was succeeded by an invitation to 'dine with my sister'. To his surprise, John appeared dissatisfied with this answer, and the correspondence between them persisted in lively fashion over the next ten days until suddenly appearing in full on the front page of the *Daily Express*.[45] It was a case of the Baronet and the Butterfly in reverse. Leverhulme insisted that he had a right to deal with his own property – a little trimming here or there – as he chose. Even the copyright, he hazarded, belonged to him. As for this publicity, it served no purpose and was not of his choosing: 'all that I am impressed by is that Mr John can get his advertising perfectly free ... whereas the poor Soap Maker has to pay a very high rate for a very bad position in the paper'.

For John it had begun as a matter of principle. He took the Whistlerian view that money purchased merely the custodianship of a picture. After Leverhulme, a self-appointed art patron, had dismembered his portrait he had felt genuinely shocked. Whatever the legal rights, he was convinced of his moral right.

The excitement provoked by this beheading was tremendous. Newspapers throughout Britain, America, on the Continent and as far off as Japan trumpeted their reports of the affair. Public demonstrations sprang into being. Students of the London art schools marched on Hyde Park 'bearing aloft a gigantic replica of the celebrated soap-boiler's torso, the head being absent'.[46] In Paris there was furore; in Italy a twenty-four hour strike was called involving everyone connected with painting – even models, colourmen and frame-makers. 'A colossal effigy entitled "IL-LE-VER-HUL-ME" was constructed of soap and tallow, paraded through the streets of Florence, and ceremoniously burnt in the Piazza dei Signori, after which, the demonstrators proceeded to the Battisteria where a wreath was solemnly laid on the altar of St John.'[47]

Appalled by the rumpus he had invoked, John backed away to Lady Tredegar's home, near Broadstairs; but the reporters discovered his hiding place and besieged him there. 'I did not want this publicity,' he prevaricated. 'I get too much as it is.' Nevertheless some papers were announcing that he intended to press the matter to the courts so as to establish a precedent for the protection of artists. 'The bottom fact of the case is that there is something in a work of art which, in the higher equity as distinct from the law, you can not buy,' declared the *Manchester Guardian*. '. . . whatever the law may allow, or courts award, the common fairness of mankind cannot assent to the doctrine that one man may rightfully use his own rights of property in such a way as to silence or interrupt another in making so critical appeal to posterity for recognition of his genius. The right to put up this appeal comes too near those other fundamental personal rights the infringement of which is the essence of slavery.'

The country waited for this Wilberforce of the art world to act. There had been a great roll of drums: then nothing. For John, unlike Whistler, had no relish for court work. He did not even have the stamina of his own indignation, and his sense of humour outran his sense of honour. At last the affair subsided into a joke, signalled by John's exhibiting his portion of the portrait above the title 'Lord Leverhulme's Watch-chain'. For many years he patiently preserved this decapitated torso while the missing head continued to blush unseen in its depository. Then, in 1954, by what Sir Gerald Kelly described as 'hellish ingenuity',* the two segments were sewn together and the picture elevated to a place of honour in the Leverhulme Art Gallery.

John's portraiture attracted controversy. 'I painted what I saw', he remarked of Lord Spencer's portrait. 'But many people have told me I ought to have been hung instead of the picture.' Men he was tempted to caricature, women to sentimentalize. For this reason, as the examples of Gerald du Maurier and Tallulah Bankhead suggest, his good portraits of men were often less acceptable to their sitters than his weaker pictures of women.

John had painted du Maurier in four sittings during 1928, but the picture had lain in his studio in Mallord Street until Tallulah Bankhead rediscovered it there early in 1930. At her insistence it was shown, with her own portrait, at the Royal Academy Summer Show that year when together they caused a sensation. Tallulah reserved her portrait for the special price of one thousand pounds, but the du Maurier was for sale. Since his knighthood in 1922, du Maurier had become the acknowledged sovereign of the British theatre. He was a figure of much personal charm and decorum. But in John's portrait, one of his most sombre and remorseless studies, there was an expression that seemed almost criminal. Du Maurier had prayed never to see the picture again, and after it was exhibited at Burlington House he issued a vividly distressed statement proclaiming that it 'showed all the misery of my wretched soul ... It would drive me either to suicide or strong drink.'[48] John, apparently at a loss to account for this response from so fashionable an actor, suggested that perhaps it was insufficiently permeated with sex allure: 'In my innocence I had omitted to repair his broken nose.'[49]

John had imagined the picture hanging at the Garrick Club, but Tallulah herself bought it ('even though I had to go in hock'[50]) and carried it off to America. It was, however, her own portrait that, as her legend grew, became the more celebrated. 'My most valuable possession is my Augustus John portrait,' she wrote in her autobiography:[51] and since Lord Duveen had offered her one hundred thousand dollars for it, this may have

* The operation was performed by a Dr J. Hell.

been literally true. Opinion since then has moderated. The judgement of one critic in 1930 – that it was 'the greatest portraiture since Gainsborough's "Perdita" ' – now looks excessive.[52] According to some who saw it, John's first image of Tallulah – a thin face blown lightly on to the canvas – had been exquisite. But, as he himself acknowledged, the finished work was something of a disappointment. 'Perhaps she has just that initial quality and no follow through,' T. E. Lawrence tactfully suggested.[53] Tallulah's friends objected that the baleful fragility of the painting had little connection with her ravishing beauty – the blue eyes, voluptuous mouth and honey-coloured hair falling in waves on to her shoulders. Yet over the years she suffered a curious change into the very replica of this picture – either an act of will on her part or, on his, of foresight.

Public portraits often paid John well, but they gave him endless trouble. 'I'm not a fashionable portrait painter,' he told John Freeman.[54] The climax of this unfashionable career, and perhaps the most endearingly deficient picture of his life, was the painting of the Queen he failed to finish between the years 1939 and 1961.

John's name had been tentatively advanced as a royal portrait painter by Lord D'Abernon as early as 1925. In his shocked rejection, the King's private secretary Lord Stamfordham replied (11 December 1925): 'No! H.M. wouldn't look at A.J.!! and so A.J. wouldn't be able to look at H.M.!!' The notion merited only a joke. Then, in about 1937, shortly after George VI had come to the throne, Hugo Pitman nervously invited John to meet the new Queen – provided he arrived dead sober. The implications of this proviso angered John. For a moment he looked murderous, then, his face clearing, he inquired: 'Must I be dead sober when I leave?' One way or another the meeting had gone well. The possibility of a portrait had been mooted, though nothing immediate ensued. 'It is very nice to know that the Queen still wants me to paint her,' John wrote to Maud Cazalet two years later. 'Needless to say I am at her service and would love to do her portrait whenever it is possible.' In September the outbreak of war seemed to put an end to this plan, which in any case had perhaps been a day dream. 'No chance of doing Her Majesty now ...'[55]

But to John's surprise, the Queen did not see the war as any obstacle. In fact it was the catalyst their lethargic negotiations had called for. At this time of crisis, an inspiring new picture of the Queen in Garter robes was what the Nation needed. John, who had overlooked the national significance such a portrait might have, was thinking more informally. His imagination raced away along tracks of private fantasy. The Queen could sit, he thought, during week-ends at Windsor Castle – it would be 'a well-earned rest' for her. 'I would stay in some pub,' he explained to Mrs Cazalet, 'and no doubt there's a suitable room at the castle for painting.'[56] If not, doubtless there'd be something at the pub – 'one could keep it very dark'. The Queen, he hoped, would wear 'a pretty costume with a hat' : something 'decolletée'. She would be a tremendous success in Hollywood – the destination he vaguely had in mind for the portrait.

Arrangements were completed in October. The portrait was to be painted in Buckingham Palace where a room with a north-east aspect had been set aside. All painting equipment should be dispatched in advance. John himself must seek admittance by the Privy Purse entrance. It was possible that Her Majesty might be graciously pleased to accept the picture as a token of the artist's 'deep admiration and respect'. The first sitting was scheduled for Tuesday 31 October at eleven o'clock, but the Queen would consent to receive him at 2.45 p.m. on the Monday for a preliminary interview.

John was horrified. By the time Monday came he felt 'very odd' and, finding that he had forced up his temperature, wired to call the meeting off. It had been, he diagnosed, an attack of the influenza, though with a slip of the pen he described himself as suffering from 'the influence'.

The Palace, meanwhile, awaited news from him 'to say when you will feel yourself available again'.[57] Sittings began next month. 'I'm dreading it,' John told Egerton Cooper as he set off in a taxi. What should the Queen wear? At last an evening gown was agreed on, but an extraordinary eagerness to discover fresh difficulties possessed John. 'Is there a platform available at the Palace?' he suddenly demanded. 'It should be a foot from the ground or slightly more.' Could they, he wanted to know, import an easel with a *forward lean*? By the beginning of 1940,

the sittings were transferred to another room, where John had
installed a new electric day-light system. 'I feel sure it will prove
a success and will illuminate Your Majesty in a far more satisfactory way besides rendering one independent of the weather.'
It was the weather,[58] nevertheless, that offered the next interruption. 'The temperature in the Yellow Room is indistinguishable to that reported in Finland,' the Queen's private secretary
advised, 'and Her Majesty would like therefore to wait until
some temperature more agreeable . . . makes resumption of the
portrait possible.' There was no difficulty here: John knew how
to wait. But when sittings started again in March fresh difficulties had bloomed. 'There is a great lack of back-ground,' John
ejaculated. '. . . what is wanted is a tapestry of the right sort –
with a bit of sky and landscape. Perhaps I shall have to invent
one.' The Palace, anxious for John to avoid invention, hurried
in tapestries and decorations from Lenygon and Morant. These,
at John's request, were subsequenty removed, then more subsequently at John's insistence returned. With and without them,
the painting struggled on from one crisis to another. John felt
persecuted by kindness. In a panic of claustrophobia he began
to perceive spies. 'I wouldn't be surprised if people have been
peeping at the beginning of it and seeing it merely sketched out
in *green*', he suspected. '. . . I loathe people peeping . . .' Green,
he had decided, was a mistake. But when he arrived at the
Palace to change it to blue, Her Majesty was not there. 'As the
Queen understood from you that you were going to have your
tonsils out, Her Majesty made other arrangements,' her secretary explained.

The source of all these difficulties was John's paralysing shyness. He could not overcome it. 'She has been absolutely angelic
in posing so often and with such cheerfulness,' he told Mrs
Cazalet on 13 June 1940. But he could make no contact with her
– she was not real. He wanted to make her real . . . Good God!
It was an impossible situation!

Something of these inhibitions was sensed at Buckingham
Palace. In next to no time sherry was introduced into the
sittings; and then, in a cupboard reserved for John's painting
equipment, a private bottle of brandy. As a further aid to relaxation, the Griller Quartet (unnervingly misheard by John as the

'Gorilla Quartet') was wheeled into an anteroom to play works by old English composers. Eventually it was Hitler who came to the rescue, his blitz on London providing the ostensible motive everyone had been seeking to end the ordeal. 'At this moment, what is described as "the last sitting" is proceeding,' the Queen's private secretary wrote on 26 June 1940. John puts his bravest face on the matter: 'it looks very near done to a turn,' he told Mrs Cazalet.

That autumn the portrait was moved to his studio in the country where he continued to brood over it. 'I can see a good Johnish picture there – *not* a Cecil Beaton creation or anything of that sort,' he had claimed. Later, on 10 February 1941, he evolved a new plan 'to bring Mr Cecil Beaton to the Palace to take some photographs of Her Majesty, which should help me to complete her picture'. The Queen agreed to this: she did more. The following year she wrote to remind John of her portrait. 'If you are in London, I could come to your studio if you have any windows, for we have none in Buckingham Palace, and it is too dark and dusty to paint in anyway.'

John felt acutely his sense of failure. He had shut away the portrait and no one was allowed to see it. In December 1948, the Queen wrote again suggesting a drawing of her daughter Margaret: 'I could easily bring her to your studio, and I promise that I won't bring an orchestra with me!' Nothing came of this, and it was not until 1961 that the Queen Mother, as she had become, finally took possession of the portrait. Under thick dust and massed cobwebs, in a world of rats and spiders, it had lain with canvases from all periods, in one of the cellars below John's studio. Here a foraging West End dealer stumbled across it and, at a show of John's 'Paintings and Drawings not previously exhibited' in March 1961, revealed it to the public. Shortly afterwards a shipping company, to commemorate the launching of a large tanker, presented it to the Queen Mother. 'I want to tell you what a tremendous pleasure it gives me to see it once again,' she wrote to John on 19 July 1961. 'It looks so lovely in my drawing-room, and has cheered it up no end! The sequins glitter, and the roses and the red chair give a fine glow, and I am so happy to have it ...'

After almost twenty-two years the portrait had come home

where, greatly loved, it has remained. It is not the picture of a queen, nor of a woman : but of a fairy princess. It is disarmingly unfinished; it is no masterpiece. Stern critics have condemned it. Yet, as Tallulah Bankhead did in her portrait, the sitter has seen something to which others are perhaps blind. And who is to say that she is wrong?

4. METHODS AND PLACES

It has been claimed that John prostituted his talent to catch the likenesses of dukes, actresses and millionaires; that, in pursuing such people, he went over to 'the other side'. More ambiguously it has been urged on his behalf tht he did not prefer the company of titled people : he simply wished everyone owned a title.

Although contemptuous of conformity, John responded to the more spectacular side of the establishment. The obverse of this romanticism was a cynical view that saw in a smart clientele his most promising source of money. Yet the exercise of amassing money never excited him, and when an agent once brought him a list of twenty rich prospective sitters, he crossed off all but one name, that of an exceptionally pretty girl.

His greatest portraits are not generally of the great – unless in the field of the arts. From commissioned portraits, with all their rules of vanity and forced politeness, he turned with relief back to the ranks of his family. For them there was little relief. The ordeal of sitting began at the age of two-and-a-half. To the girls, Poppet and Vivien, he was a fearful figure. Each morning they would wait to discover which of them was doomed for the day. Tears were stemmed with lumps of sugar : and the painting went remorselessly on. At all times John insisted upon absolute immobility, the slightest movement of the head or body being corrected with the point of the brush used like a conductor's baton.

The studio was John's battlefield, and his preparatory drill was always the same. Though he might debate with a woman about the wearing, or not, of a particular dress, he seldom posed his subjects. 'Sit down!' was his usual instruction to men on leading them up to the platform. After that a curious impersonality tempered the proceedings, as if the sitter was merely an 'object', a basket of apples. John would come up very close, too close, and stare. It was difficult not to start back at the ferocity of that stare, the eyes, an inch away, seeming like X-rays to pierce through the skull. Then with a grunt he retreated, and battle began.

He painted with intense physical concentration. He worked without words, breathing heavily, occasionally stamping his foot, drawing on his pipe which gave out a small bubbling sound. Sometimes it appeared as if he had stopped breathing altogether, and then everything seemed to stop – the bees, the birds on the trees. Perspiration broke out on his temples, the pipe trembled between his lips, and the only sound for miles was the brush jabbing on the canvas. Suddenly he would explode, jump backwards knocking over a chair; there was a crash and a curse, and, letting go of his pipe, he would begin pacing back and forwards. The sitter, his body aching as if on the rack, seemed wholly forgotten. Finally a rest was called, like half-time at a football match, and John would sit down for a long look at the canvas. Then, after two or three minutes, he was up and at it again.

There were variations in this drill. Occasionally he played music on the radio, or if things were going well the silence might be splintered with a Welsh poem or a snatch of song. Sometimes he smoked cigarettes instead of a pipe, and as he advanced and retreated before the canvas, he would throw the stubs into a corner, unerringly missing the ashtray and waste-paper basket, and once or twice starting a small fire. For those who were practised sitters it was possible to tell which part of them he was working on, and to keep that part alive: and always when he came to the mouth he would summon his own lips into a rosebud.

Whatever the variations, it was the bursting effort to concentrate that impressed his subjects. The studio seemed to throb with energy as he worked. But somehow the moment of finishing never quite arrived and then, at the bell for tea, he would stop instantly, like a cricketer drawing stumps.

These were unorthodox methods for a painter who was presumed to be growing more conventional: the methods almost of an action painter rather than the Royal Academician he had recently become. Over a number of years his election as an Associate had been painfully imminent – so much so that it had became his habit to leave the country at the time elections took place. 'Noticed with the greatest relief that I was not elected,' he wrote from Dieppe to Cynthia Asquith in May 1920. Yet by this time his persistent non-election had in itself become considerable news, pulling the headlines from under the feet of those who had been chosen. 'We learn', announced *The Times* in 1920, 'that Mr Augustus John has received no direct intimation of any decision of the Royal Academy to open its doors to him.'[59] People looked to his election as a symbol of Burlington House being prepared to accept what was called 'broader views and wider sympathies'. When the offer did come in April 1921 he decided to accept: then grew defensive. 'To many', he wrote, 'it seemed to be not a triumph but a surrender. Had I not been a Slade student? Was I not a member of the New English Art Club? Did I not march in the front ranks of the insurgents? The answer to these questions is "Yes". But had I cultivated the Royal Academy in any way? Had I ever submitted a single work to the Selection Committee? . . . History answers "No". Without even blowing my own trumpet the walls of Jericho had fallen! . . . I acknowledged and returned the compliment.'[60]

Then, in December 1928, he was elected to full membership and the process of 'self-sacrifice' as he called it was complete. But his passage with the R.A. was far rougher than his autobiographical writings allow. To start with – and that was terrible – his father congratulated him on achieving the crown of his career. Then Sean O'Casey wrote to commiserate, suggesting he was now 'soiled' by contact with the World, the Flesh and the Devil – 'three excellent things,' John retorted. '. . . I assure you that it won't make the slightest difference to me,* unless by stimulating me to greater freedom of expression . . . Perhaps, at any rate, it will be a useful disguise. Cézanne longed

---

* In a letter to his mother, Christopher Wood wrote (22 May 1922): 'Augustus John has been admitted to the Academy this year. They wouldn't have him before. I don't think he takes this as an honour in the least, as it doesn't matter much to him whether he is an A.R.A. or not. He is unquestionably the greatest painter in England to-day and if he hadn't drunk so much would have been greater than Leonardo da Vinci or Michelangelo.'

for official recognition and the Legion of Honour – and didn't get either. Van Gogh dreamt of electric light, hot and cold water, w.c's and general confort anglais. I have them all and remain unsatisfied.'[61]

The chief use of Burlington House lay in providing a new market for his wares at a time when the New English Art Club had faded. John's attitude to it depended very largely upon the personality of its President. In 1928 he was reasonably happy and exhibiting pictures there; in 1938 he rebelled. It was this year that Wyndham Lewis painted his portrait of T. S. Eliot. In the spring it was submitted to the hanging committee of the Royal Academy which, much to Eliot's relief and Lewis's indignation, rejected it. On learning this, John at once issued a statement full of powerful negatives for the press :

I very much regret to make a sensation, but it cannot be helped. Nothing that Mr Wyndham Lewis paints is negligible or to be condemned lightly. I strongly disagree with this rejection. I think it is an inept act on the part of the Academy. The rejection of Mr Wyndham Lewis's portrait by the Academy has determined my decision to resign from that body ... I shall henceforth experience no longer the uncomfortable feeling of being in a false position as a member of an institution with whose general policy I am constantly in disagreement. I shall be happier and more honest in rejoining the ranks of those outside, where I naturally belong.

This statement provoked an extraordinary response in the press in Britain, America and, breaking through the walls of art insularity, France. 'Premier May be Questioned,' ran a headline in the *Morning Post*. Elsewhere, with more bewilderment, it was reported that the Academy itself had received no notification of John's resignation. In fact he had written a formal letter to the President Sir William Llewellyn three days beforehand, but neglected to post it. 'After the crowning ineptitude of the rejection of Wyndham Lewis's picture I feel it is impossible for me to remain longer a member of the R.A.,' he told Llewellyn. Although in all the press anouncements John confessed to great 'reluctance' in coming to his decision, he had in fact been searching round for an avenue of escape from the Academy, partly because he disliked Llewellyn. The Eliot portrait provided him with a perfect motive, and he wrote to Lewis to thank him :

'I resign with gratitude to you for affording me so good a reason.'

Lewis was delighted, suggesting that all sorts of politico-artistic activities should issue out of this rumpus, including the formation by the two of them of a new *Salon des Refusés*. But John demurred, delivering instead a neatly placed blow, just below the belt, when he let it be known that he had not seen the portrait of Eliot at the time of its rejection but on doing so later felt inclined to agree with the Academy. 'I wasn't thinking of doing anybody a kindness and I don't give a damn for that picture,' he assured Laura Knight, 'but I acted as a better R.A. than you and others who let the show go to pot from year to year. I know I haven't done anything directly to affect the policy of the Institution. It seemed pretty hopeless to oppose the predominant junta of deadly conservatism which rules. If by my beastly action I shall have brought some fresh air into Burlington House I shall feel justified.'[62]

Though anxious not to offend his new friends within the Academy, he kept up these attacks from outside. 'The Academy is stagnant – dead,' he proclaimed.

Two years later, Llewellyn having left, he accepted re-election to become what Lewis described as 'the most distinguished Royal Academician ... of a sleeping-partner order'. In 1944 he almost woke up to find himself President. Once again the honour attracted him, but common sense counselled refusal : once again he prevaricated. 'I would of course like to do my best for the R.A.,' he confided to Philip Connard, 'and would be fully conscious of the honour of such a position but am only doubtful of my ability to cope with the duties, official and social, it would entail. Here's the snag. Apart from this, as P.R.A. is only an extension of R.A. I would have no logical reason to refuse.'[63] This snag was successful enough to stave off his election, and by 17 votes to 24 he eventually beat Alfred Munnings for second place.

To match this new eminence, John had allowed himself to be overtaken by several major changes in the gallery world. Once the war was over, Knewstub, slightly bombed, emerged to dream again. From his upstairs room at the Chenil he gazed across Chelsea and saw in his mind a great art centre with him-

For Knewstub this was a bitter blow. For years he had modelled himself on John, drinking beer, producing litters of children, training his wife to resemble Dorelia: and now John had deserted him. He retired to Hastings, to the singing of the birds and of his kettle. 'A well-fitted cellar of the best would certainly rejuvenate me,' he suggested. But in vain. He fell back pitiably on tea. 'Possibly', he estimated, 'the outstanding comfort I have is being able to make good hot tea *very easily* in the morning ... It is an almost indispensable stimulant and restorative.' It stimulated him to do no work and to luxuriate in the 'humiliation' of National Assistance – which showed, he insisted, how far 'on the downward path' he had travelled. John had not helped him – and no one else should without a struggle. He threatened to 'sell my few possessions', even his 'worn out lot of rubbish and rags'; he threatened to live to a hundred so that he might receive a Royal Telegram for his 'dear ones the generations ahead'; he threatened, in the most embarrassing way, to start again : 'I think I must somehow refit myself with Evening Dress,' he calculated. Refitted thus, he proposed to write doggerel for charity, in particular the Women's Voluntary Service. Or else: 'A lavatory attendant would not be too great an effort,' he told one of his sisters, 'and would allow me ample time for quiet meditation.' But when the family, responding to this blitzkrieg, implored him to visit them, he shook his head. 'I have had nearly half-a-gallon of my blood drawn from my arm by way of donation to the Blood Transfusion Service,' he explained, refusing the invitation. '... I am by far and away the oldest in the whole of this South-East Area Service. The true "Blue Blood" is graded "O" – as mine is – and is the most suitable for a child, or even the most delicate of patients. So you will understand, my dear, that I cannot abandon my interests in this town – only a fortnight ago I was called upon for another pint ... Courage as always, until the final peace comes to us.'

So this Augustus Moddle of the South-East area lived on, making his relations scale Himalayas of reluctance on their way to Hastings. And what a welcome they received when they got there! Holding them with glittering eye and an endless monologue, he would contrast his dreams of the past – 'something beautiful in Chelsea' – with his present degradation – an old

self at its summit.[64] The idea was irresistible. Although he had no head for business, he was possessed of a genius for advertisement. He whispered into the ears of the wealthy; he wrote letters of indignation and enthusiasm; he interviewed reporters. News of his dreams travelled to Boston and Calcutta.[65] Then, towards the end of 1923, vast advertisements began to spread themselves across the press.[66] His arguments were simple. The galleries of London were closing. The old Grosvenor Gallery had long ago collapsed and its successor, the New Gallery, been converted into a cinema. The Grafton Gallery, until recently the home of the International Society of Sculptors, Painters and Gravers, was now a dancing arena. The Doré Gallery and Messrs Dowdeswell's in Bond Street, the Dudley Gallery in the Egyptian Hall: all had disappeared. The National Portrait Society and the New English Art Club had no galleries of their own. The Royal Society of British Artists and the Royal Society of Painters in Water Colours, in Suffolk Street and Pall Mall East respectively, were threatened with demolition. In such conditions the living artist had almost nowhere to exhibit his pictures. 'The root of the difficulty is obvious,' Knewstub proclaimed, 'as is the remedy.' The difficulty was rates and rents; the remedy decentralization. 'A new and commodious Art Institution, *untrammelled by the impossible burden of West End expenses*, has become an urgent need of the day.' Chelsea, with its literary and artistic traditions, was 'unquestionably the alternative'.

The New Chenil Galleries was an enlargement of old 'Chenil's' on a Napoleonic scale. The adjoining premises were taken over and, with the aid of George Kennedy, the Bloomsburgian architect, and the co-operation of the Cadogan Estate, robust plans were planted for a 'temple of the muses'. 'Under three spacious new roofs,' explained Knewstub, 'are to be large and small galleries for paintings, drawings, prints and sculpture; a musical society; a literary club or institution, a school of art, a large block of private studios, a first-class restaurant, a café or lounge, a library, and a hall that may be let for lectures, concerts, dancing, and other social gatherings.'[67]

In a letter (30 January 1924) written for publication, John applauded Knewstub: 'I consider you deserve great credit for showing the imagination to conceive and the business ability to

bring to fruition so ambitious an undertaking.' With the significant exception of *The Economist*,[68] congratulations flowed in
from every quarter. Knewstub was beside himself. He published
a Prospectus; he held meetings; he offered large quantities of
shares for subscription; he invented several 'honorary advisory
councils' on which John's name was prominent; and he appointed directors including (besides himself) an editor of *The Queen*,
the proprietor of a defunct rival gallery, an eminent conductor
of music and a catering expert. On Saturday, 25 October the
foundation stone was laid. After a few words from John Ireland
representing orchestras, John entered the ring amid cheers,
smoking a cigarette and with marks of deep concentration on
his brow. Baring his head, he spoke. Though inexperienced in
laying stones, he had read that it was customary on these
occasions to slay a man and lay his corpse in the foundation of
the building, so that his spirit would guard the place from
malevolent influences : he now appealed for volunteers whom
(raising a mason's mallet) he could offer an expeditious exit and
any amount of posthumous glory. His large uneasy eyes contemplated a crowd that numbered Augustine Birrell very
leonine, the Sitwell brothers in plain clothes, and James Pryde
wearing a blue Count d'Orsay coat and soft travelling hat. No
one coming forward, John (hoping this would 'do the trick')
placed a George V half-crown on the lower stone and energetically applied the mortar, bespattering the noblemen and artist's
models in the front row. Suddenly a choir, conjured up by
Knewstub, broke into a rendering of 'Let us now praise famous
men', while John and the other famous men stiffened to attention. 'In Paris', commented the *Manchester Guardian Weekly*,
'such a figure would be continuously before us on the revue
stage and the comic press.'[69]

A year later the building was ready. Much impressed by its
'solidity and elegance', John assured Will Rothenstein that
'Knewstub with all his faults deserves considerable credit'.
Knewstub not only deserved it, he needed it. By the end of
1926 he was bankrupt, and had resigned his managing director-
ship. 'Knewstub was the curse of the place,' John explained to
Mitchell Kennerley.[70] The débâcle had been caused, Knewstub
told everyone, by the General Strike, the slump, and by John's

disloyalty. 'I've known John for twenty-five year
you'd known him for half that time you'd realise
was.' To long service, honour is due. But Knewstub
that John abandoned him in this year of need and
resentment against John as the one friend who never
to his retirement fund are more complicated matters.

On 22 October 1925 John had received a letter from
Tooth explaining that his gallery in Bruton Street was n
to be exclusively associated 'with the academic work
ceased masters of the British School,' but intended to
the best modern art of to-day'. The letter, asking John to
gallery handle all his future work, apparently went unansw
Then, in 1926, John held a joint exhibition with his sister
at Knewstub's New Chenil Gallery. When Dudley Tooth w
again, on 9 February 1928, Mrs Fleming, acting as go-betwe
gave him little chance of success. But by that time Knewst
had already collapsed and John, who had tried unsuccessfully
find someone to take over his Chelsea art emporium, finally de
cided to invade the West End. At a meeting on 12 March 1928,
Tooth proposed setting up an agency to deal with all John's
pictures (excluding portraits painted to private commission) and
holding a one-man show to identify the gallery as John's sole
agents. To these proposals John agreed, his first exhibition at
Tooth's being held in April 1929.

All this postdated Knewstub's period of utmost need. But it is
true that after 1927 his friendship with John had ceased. When
J. B. Manson appealed for a fund to assist him, he received from
John a categorical reply : 'I shall certainly not help Knewstub
or any other crooked swine.'[71] To many this smelt of rank ingratitude. But from John's letters to Manson and others it appears that there were two causes for this vindictiveness. He believed that Knewstub had taken advantage of Gwen John's financial innocence to cheat her of fifty pounds; and that, by his suspect dealings, he had been a hole in John's own pocket over a
number of years. Yet he did help Knewstub's wife and at least
one of her children 'on the understanding that K[newstub] is to
know nothing,' he instructed Manson. 'I gather that K's family
see nothing of him and don't particularly want to.'[72]

After Knewstub's fall, John refused to see or write to him.

man 'making my own bed; blacking my own grate; washing my own shirt; darning my own socks; and doctoring myself'. Upon his family, bowed in boredom, he took revenge for the bitterness of his life, lecturing them in tones of unctuous self-praise, smiling with steadfast self-pity, bragging of his modesty, rubbing his poverty into their faces like an enormous scab: repeating himself. Had he mentioned the time, he often wondered, Augustus John 'said to me nearly forty years ago that in his opinion your tactfulness was the greatest of your many charms'? He would have liked to remind John of that now, face to face, here in Hastings.

But John, with his nose for boredom, had escaped, and was moving beyond his reach into new territories.

5. UNDISCOVERED COUNTRIES

'Whenever I see a bottle of Chateauneuf du Pape I am reminded of him,' wrote the painter A. R. Thomson. Most years, 'to refresh myself', John would ease his way down to Provence, taking to the inevitable wine 'with great gusto'.[73] One day he would announce that they were off, and everything else was dropped. These journeys were great adventures. Cats, daughters, perhaps a son or a governess – all filed into the train and by night meandered through the charging carriages, while John sat peacefully asleep in the corridor.

But Martigues was no longer the place it had been before the war. More cafés were opening up on the Cours de la République, more motor cars herded under the plane trees. A new bascule bridge was put up, useful but unbeautiful. Creeping industrialism was beginning to mar that air of innocence which had first attracted John to this little community of fishermen. Progress did not stampede through Martigues: it infiltrated. For ten years he and his family continued to come and then, submitting to the advance of commercialism, left for ever.

Bazin, that essayist of the air, was now dead, and his daughter 'rather mad'[74] and, once intended as mistress for the mighty Quinn, was recast as Poppet and Vivien's governess. The two girls loved the Villa St Anne. 'It seems to me', wrote Poppet,[75] 'that life went by very smoothly on these visits to Martigues.

There were great expeditions round the country and picnics as many as we could wish for ... Saturday nights were very gay', dining 'chez Pascal', then descending to the *Cercle Cupidon* and dancing to their heart's content while John, a glass of marc-cassis at his elbow, sat watching them. Like the village girls, Poppet and Vivien danced together until, tiring of this, Poppet took to lipstick. 'After that we hardly missed a dance with the young men.' They would present themselves at John's table to ask for his permission then, after the dance was over, escort the girls back to him. 'Augustus seemed to enjoy watching us and sometimes would whirl us round the floor himself,' Poppet remembered. 'Then suddenly one Saturday night at dinner he looked at me with a glaring eye and growled: "Wipe that muck off your face!" Whereupon Vivien piped up with: "But she won't get asked to dance without it – they'll think she's too young." Augustus was furious. "Wipe it off!" he shouted, "and stop ogling the boys!" Then I lost my temper (always a good thing to do I later found) and I flew at him, telling him it was he who ogled all the time and that I must have picked up the habit from him – also that I noticed the girls he ogled used lipstick and I was jolly well going to do so too! This made him laugh, the whole thing passed off and I continued to dance with le joli garçon every Saturday night ... So life went on.'[76]

For John, life depended upon weather, flowers, girls. If the sun shone he was happy. Though 'there was a brothel near John's villa I always found him playing draughts,' protested A. R. Thomson. '... He liked to wander in back streets of old France, smell of wine-and-garlic or wine-and-cheese in his nostrils.' Then, if he spotted an unusual-looking woman he would rise and, with swollen eyes, pursue her. But more often he found the models he needed from among his family, posing them in a setting of olive or pine trees, the speckled aromatic hills beyond and, further off, bordering the blue Etang, distant amethyst cliffs.

But there were other days when the sun refused to shine and he would energetically tinker with plans to be off elsewhere. 'The weather is cold and grey,' he wrote to Dorelia. '... There's nothing much in the way of flowers here and I have no models. I might as well be dead.' He would decide to leave, to return to

London, paint portraits; he would decide that Martigues was 'revolting' – then the clouds dispersed and he was suddenly negotiating to buy another house there. 'Martigues is like some rustic mistress one is always on the point of leaving,' he confided to Mitchell Kennerley, 'but who looks so lovely at the last moment that one falls back into her arms.'[77]

John's scheme, 'quite wise for once',[78] was to pass his winters in Provence painting intermittently out-of-doors, and then, in the spring or summer, explore new regions. In May 1922 he found himself in Spain. His son Robin, then in Granada studying Castilian affairs with the tutor, seems to have been a less magnetic motive for travel than the faulty English weather. 'I don't know if I can get painting materials in Spain,' he had hesitated; and then : 'Spanish people, I imagine, are hideous.'[79] But he went.

He went first to Paris for a hectic week with Tommy Earp, then descended south. 'Down here in the wilds life is much calmer,' he assured Viva Booth, 'indeed there are perhaps too many vacant moments and unoccupied gaps.' Like other of his random travels, there was no plot or continuity. Spain was a series of impressions : in Madrid the sight of Granero, the famous matador, limping from the ring where, the following Sunday, he would be killed; at the Café Inglés the bull-fighters, in Andalusian hats and pigtails 'looking rather like bulls themselves',[80] vibrating with energy; the blind, hideously deformed beggars crouching in the gutters and appealing for alms; and, at evening, the ladies of the *bourgeoisie* collecting in the pastry-shops to 'pass an hour or two before dinner in the consumption of deleterious tarts and liqueurs'.[81] Then, in the Alhambra, two friends : Pepita d'Albaicin, an elegant Gitana dancer, and Augustine Birrell, until recently Chief Secretary for Ireland – 'a surprising combination'; and at Ugijar the spectacle of Robin full of silent Spanish and the tutor taking photographs – 'very bad ones, and he's very slow about it, changing his spectacles, losing bits of his machine and tripping over the tripod continually'.[82]

By mid-June his white paint had 'just about come to an end'[83] and he started back, crossing the Sierra and descending on the north to Guadix, where he was to catch a train. 'The ascent was long. Snow lay upon the heights. At last we reached the Pass and, surmounting it, struck the downward trail. A thick fog veiled the land. This suddenly dispersed, disclosing an illimitable plain in which here and there white cities glittered. The distant mountains seemed to hang among the clouds. At our feet blue gentians starred our path, reminding me of Burren in County Clare . . . the country became more and more enchanting. As we rode on, verdurous woods, grassy lawns and gentle streams gladdened our eyes so long accustomed to the stark and sun-baked declivities of the Alpujarras.'[84]

Finally, to Barcelona. Spain, John told Dorelia, was 'very fine in parts, but there are *immense* stretches with nothing'. The spirit of the country had come near, but it had not taken hold of him. 'Art, like life, perpetuates itself by contact,' he wrote. The moment of contact came as he was leaving Barcelona. 'I was walking to the station, when I saw three Gitanas engaged in buying flowers at a booth. Struck numb with astonishment by the flashing beauty and elegance of these young women, I almost missed my train.' He went on to Marseilles, but the vision of these Gitanas persisted: 'I was unable to dismiss it.' In desperation he hired a car and returned all the way to Barcelona. But 'of course I did not find the gypsies again. One never does.'

Spain incubated but never hatched. When he flew back there in December 1932 on his way to Majorca, rain had made the world unpaintable; after which Franco, like a hated bird of prey, kept him off until too late.

'I am sure it will stimulate me,' he had written to Ottoline Morrell, 'and I shall come back fresher and more myself.'[85] In fact he came back as someone else. He had seen many pictures in Spain. 'At the Prado I found Velasquez much greater and more marvellous than I had been in the habit of thinking,' he told Dorelia. 'There is nobody to touch him.' He went to the Academy of S. Fernando and the shabby little church of S. Antonio de la Florida to see the Goya frescoes of the cupola: 'My passion for Goya was boundless.' The streets of Madrid seemed to throb and pulse with Goyaesque characters afterwards, bringing the place alive for him. There were other paintings too that 'bowled me over': Rubens's 'The Three Graces' and 'a dream of noble luxury', Titian's 'Venus'. Only El Greco, at the Prado, disappointed him. Yet, mysteriously, it was El Greco who, in the cock-pit of John's imagination, planted a seed. John's 'Symphonie Espagnole' of 1923 is a self-confessed essay in the El Greco style, a parody that marshals all the mawkishness and conveys none of his ecstatic rhythm. These weeks in Spain form a parallel to his journey through northern Italy in 1910. From Italy he had discovered a tradition to which he belonged; in Spain he lost himself. 'He is painting very much like El Greco now since his visit to Spain,' Christopher Wood noted in December 1922. This influence of El Greco became a mannerism devitalizing his natural talent. The phallic lengthening of the head worked well for very few of his sitters, and the elongation of the body seemed to draw all life out of it. It was an attempt by John to speak a new language, but he could say little in it that was original.

It was as a Distinguished Guest of the Irish Nation that in the summer of 1924 John went with Mrs Fleming to Dublin. The occasion was a festival of 'fatuous self-glorification' called the Taillteann Games. Oliver St John Gogarty, as commander of the social operations, had billeted him with Lord Dunsany. 'Here I am entrapped,' John wrote desperately from Dunsany Castle. '... Mrs Gogarty has developed into a sort of Duchess. I must get out of this.'[86] As a practical joke, Gogarty had warned Dunsany not to give John any alcohol – which made Dunsany determined to offer his guest as much as he could want. This would have suited John well, had Gogarty not confided to him that Dunsany was a fierce teetotaller and would fly into a rage if anyone in his home accepted a drink. The result was that, in an agony of politeness, John persisted in refusing everything until, according to Compton Mackenzie, 'Dunsany started to explain how to play the great Irish harp ... After they went to bed Augustus climbed over the wall of Dunsany Park and walked the fourteen miles to Dublin.'[87]

The crisis of this festival was a banquet at which the Commander-in-Chief of the Free State Army delivered a long speech in Gaelic. As he stood unintelligibly uttering, the municipal gas and electricity workers decided upon a two minutes' strike. Unperturbed by the blackness, the Commander spoke on. After a

minute, John leant over to Compton Mackenzie, and whispered:
'What's going on?' Mackenzie explained. 'Thank God,' breathed
John. 'I'm only drunk then. I thought I'd gone mad.'

Mrs Fleming also accompanied him to Berlin. For one month
in the spring of 1925 he stayed at the British Embassy and, with
a key to the side entrance, was free to explore this 'strange and
monstrous city' at all hours. His impressions were scattered –
Max Liebermann at eighty painting better than ever; 'some
marvellous wall decorations brought back from Turkistan by a
German digger';[88] beer 'like nectar'; and girls, 'hearty creatures
and sometimes very good looking' who, on a more vital in-
spection, were revealed as being men 'devoted to buggery' and
'furnished by the police with licences to adopt female attire'.[89]
As for embassy life, it was all very swell but 'too strenuous for
me ... there are hours of *intense* boredom'.

Of the three portraits John painted in Berlin, the most important was of Gustav Stresemann, the German Chancellor. It
was Lord D'Abernon who arranged the sittings during which the
Locarno Treaties advanced to the point of signature. In Lord
D'Abernon's diplomatic language, Stresemann's 'lively intelligence and extreme facility of diction' inclined him 'to affect
monologue rather than interchange of ideas'.[90] The British ambassador could not get a word in. By early March, when sittings
began, their negotiations had reached the verge of collapse. It
was then that he had his idea. Since John knew no German,
D'Abernon reasoned, there could be no grounds for not carrying on their discussions while he worked. The advantage was
that Stresemann would be 'compelled to maintain immobility
and comparative silence'. John, by treating the German Chancellor as one of his own family, exercised his rôle strongly. At
the first sitting, after a sentence or two from Lord D'Abernon,
Stresemann broke in and was about to go on at his customary
length when John 'armed with palette and paint-brushes' asserted his artistic authority. 'I was therefore able to labour on
with my own views without interruption,' D'Abernon records.
'... the assistance given by the inhibitive gag of the artist was of
extreme value ... Reduced to abnormal silence ... Stresemann's quickness of apprehension was such that he rapidly

seized and assimilated the further developments to which the Pact proposals might lead.'[91]

The pact was eventually less controversial than the portrait. Stresemann faced it bravely and 'even his wife', John reported, 'admits it's like him at his worst'.[92]* To Dorelia he wrote: 'I like Stresemann. He is considered the strongest man in German politics.' But Lord D'Abernon, who now felt some tenderness for Stresemann, thought the painting 'a clever piece of work' though 'not at all flattering; it makes Stresemann devilishly sly'.[93] This proved an accurate foretaste of popular reaction. Nobody much liked Stresemann, and no party trusted him. When the portrait was shown in New York in 1928, John was much acclaimed for his 'cruelty'. Modestly he rejected this praise. 'I have nothing to do with German politics, but I thought Stresemann an *excellent* fellow, most sympathetic, intelligent and even charming,' he wrote on 13 March 1928 to his American dealer Mitchell Kennerley,† adding with less modesty: 'One must remember that even God chastises those whom he loves.'

Apart from Stresemann's silences, John had not greatly relished Berlin. The perpetual motor-cars and hard-boiled eggs, combined with a lack of handkerchiefs, unnerved him. He felt 'very impatient' to go somewhere new, and paint. 'For God's sake learn up a little Italian,' he urged Dorelia. It was May when he boarded the train for Italy, with Dorelia, Poppet and Vivien. Romilly too was coming. 'In a fit of megalomania',[94] he had decided to cross the Alps on foot, aided by the tutor at the head of fourteen schoolgirls 'on their way to spend a week-end in Paris'.[95] Drifting through Italy, the main party played at being tourists to the extent, in John's case, of losing his wallet with all their money in it. This calamity, credited to the quick fingers of Italian train thieves, may have been attributable to Eileen

---

* 'The sittings for this portrait took place mostly at 3 o'cl. p.m. and already at that time I have asked Sir Augustus to put below the portrait: The German Minister for Foreign Affairs at 3 o'cl. in the afternoon, for I don't think that I am really so sleepy and broken down as I am represented on this picture.' Stresemann to Dr Ruppel, 12 June 1926.

† Publisher, and director of the Anderson Gallery, 489 Park Avenue, New York. The portrait of Stresemann is now in the Albright-Knox Art Gallery, Buffalo, N.Y.

Hawthorne's abortion for which urgent funds had just then been prescribed. For some days they were stranded in acute luxury within the most expensive hotel in Naples (the only one that would accept their credit), and when they finally approached the 'barbarous island' of Ischia, their destination, they were irritated to see Romilly, his feet in ruins, waving to them from the harbour.

Skirting the shores, John sought anxiously for some pictorial motif. They were to stay at the Villa Teheran, a little wooden house with a veranda, that stood by itself on a miniature bay. It belonged to Mrs Nettleship and, being rich only in fleas, proved uninhabitable: 'it was clear this place offered nothing to a painter'.[96] John marched his family off to Forio, the next town along the coast, and quartered them more happily above some vineyards overlooking the sea. The oleander, nespoli, quince, orange, lemon and pepper trees, 'with the addition of a bottle of *Strega*', contributed greatly, John recalled, 'towards our surrender to the spirit of the place. Indeed, at night, when the moon shone, as it generally did ... resistance had been folly.'[97] But it was as a holidaymaker, not primarily a painter, that John surrendered. He would float on his back in the phosphorescent seawater for hours, while Dorelia bathed more grandly in a black silk chemise that billowed about her as she entered the water. There were picnics on the beach, sunbathing on the long flat roof of their new villa, and expeditions through the island behind a strongly smelling horse. It was a pleasant life, but tame. 'Apart from drowning, life on the island presented few risks,' John grumbled.[98] Even the werewolves, reported to range the mountain, remained invisible. So, it was back to portrait painting, 'finding myself very well occupied here with the two superbly fat daughters of the local Contessa'.[99] Another picture he painted, entitled 'Sea, Wine and Onions', was a portrait of Tommy Earp. The cook's little girls also came to sit, side by side in a window, wearing alarmingly white-starched dresses. But a portrait of Mussolini, arranged by an ardent fascist they had met, fell through. In his place Dorelia assembled some exotic blooms: and so began John's first flower pictures.

Unlike Columbus, John was destined to cross the Atlantic six times; and, in one form or another, America visited him several times more. The purpose of all this traffic was the innocent one of 'making a useful bit of money'.[100]

He had first attracted attention in America when, in 1910, his portrait of William Nicholson was shown at the Carnegie Institute's International Exhibition in Pittsburgh. When he first went there thirteen years later it was as the guest of the Carnegie Institute, which had invited him to act as the British representative on its jury. He embarked on 28 March 1923, elated to be on his way at last to the land of his day-dreams as a boy. 'The Americans all wear caps and smoking-suits in the evenings, and smoke very long cigars,' he wrote to Dorelia from the S.S. *Olympic*. 'They are very friendly people.' When his hat flew off into the sea, they rushed up in numbers to offer him their own which, one by one as he accepted them, also flew off. 'There must be a continuous track of caps along our route.' On board he met a number of passengers who petitioned him to paint portraits: Mrs Harry Payne Whitney, 'quite a pleasant woman but infernally lazy'; a 'big fat sententious oil king ... who argues with me'; and Arthur Conan Doyle who told him 'startling things about the spook world. It really seems quite a good place somewhat superior to this one in fact ... Lady Conan Doyle is like people I've met in my youth – all spiritual love and merriment and dowdy clothes.'

Of all contemporary British artists, John was then the best known in America. At the famous Armory Show of 1913 in New York no other modern painter, with the exception of Odilon Redon, had been so well represented.[101] The huge Armory had been packed with the élite of New York 'cheering the different American artists, cheering Augustus John, cheering the French ...'[102] Critics and journalists had soon been dispatched to interview John, and many reports of his 'recent activities' appeared in the American papers. 'Augustus John is now at the height of his fame,' the New York magazine *Vanity Fair* had declared in June 1916. 'Not even the war ... has taken public attention off Britain's most conspicuous native painter.'

On arriving, hatless, in New York harbour he was penned down by a press of journalists who, like pirates, boarded the boat even before it berthed. 'They sought to get a "story" out

of me. I stood them a drink instead.'[103] They were delighted by
his appearance – 'thoroughly consistent in living up to what he
ought to look like'; he thought them 'nice boys'.

That evening, after dinner at the Coffee House, Frank Crown-
inshield whirled him round the city and eventually landed
him back at his hotel 'exhausted and bewildered by an orgy of
colour, noise, smartness and multitudinous legs'.[104]

Of Pittsburgh, where he arrived next day, John remembered
little but the boundless hospitality of its natives and the 'infernal
splendour' of their steelworks. He did not stay long. He had
been invited to Buffalo to paint the elderly mother of a general,
and after four days hurried off there to keep this assignation.

On the platform General Goodyear was surprised to see hovering at John's elbow the assistant director of the Carnegie
Museum, John O'Connor. O'Connor whispered that he had come
to explain away the 'extraordinary capacity' of John's drinking
habits. 'I replied, somewhat haughtily that I thought Buffalo
men could take care of themselves in the drinking line,' Goodyear reported. 'Pittsburgh might have suffered but I had every
confidence in my fellow citizens. I was wrong.'[105]

John was lodged at the Saturn Club, reputedly – in those days
of Prohibition – 'the most bibulous of our social institutions'. He
appreciated the compliment. 'This club is a very good place' he
acknowledged, 'full of determined anti-Prohibitionists ... There
is a little back room with lockers all round the walls in which
the members keep their "hootch". About 6 o'clock this room
gets densely packed with a crowd of vociferating men wildly
mixing cocktails. I have the freedom of Conger Goodyear's
locker.'[106] For part of the first evening, about which he could
recall nothing, the General 'participated lap by lap'. 'The following afternoon and evening I decided to stay aloof and keep
count,' Goodyear wrote. 'Some of my friends formed relay
teams to pace the visitor. The official score showed seventeen
cocktails for our guest without visible effect other than a slight
letting down of British taciturnity. There were a few highballs
during dinner and after and we sat in a respectful silence as the
champion walked a straight path bedwards.'[107]

Work on the portrait sped along intermittently, and sometimes John would escort the old lady politely to the shops. One

morning, as she was emerging from her dressmaker, Mrs Good-year cracked a joke, fell down a flight of stairs and broke her ankle. 'Just my luck!' commented John.[108] That afternoon he left for New York.

Over the next weeks a gradual disenchantment with Ameri-can life may be traced in his letters. He had hoped to ride over the American West, he told a reporter from the *New York Times*, to set up camp along the prairies, push up the Mississippi, mix with the Negroes on the cotton plantations. His plans were greeted with bewilderment. 'The prairies had been ploughed; the backwoods levelled; the Indians mostly tamed or exter-minated; the frontiersmen replaced by "regular fellows".'[109]

In a letter to his ten-year-old daughter Poppet (28 April 1923) he gives his own child's eye view of New York.

This is a strange country. There are railways over your head in the streets and the houses are about a mile high ... The policemen chew gum and hold clubs to knock people down. The people don't say 'yes'. They say instead Yep, yeah, yaw, yawp, yah and some-times yump. Otherwise they simply say 'you bet' or 'bet your life'. They eat clams, fried chicken, chives, slaw soup and waffles with maple syrup. They drink soda-ices all the time. The rich people drink champagne and whisky for dinner and go about with bottles of gin in their pockets. When a policeman catches them they have to pay him about 1,000 dollars after which he drinks their gin and locks them up.

John did not seek publicity in New York : the more publicity the less freedom. So far as possible he kept his whereabouts secret from journalists.[110] He put up temporarily at the Hotel des Artistes at 67th and Central Park, then moved to a studio owned by Harrington Mann. To this studio numbers of Americans trekked, convinced that they were discovering a new Sargent.* Over their portraits John agonized indefinitely. 'It's been a fear-ful grind,' he wrote to Dorelia. Everyone wanted to give parties for him and 'I am employed mainly in accepting invitations and getting out of keeping them. The telephone rings continuously.' There was always something to do, a boxing match, a cocktail party, the theatre, a trip to Philadelphia, another party. His best

---

* 'Since the death of the American Sargent, nobody scarcely looms so tall [as John]'. *The Chicago Evening Post*, 16 February 1926.

hours were in the company of the decorative artist 'Sheriff' Bob
Chanler, 'a Gargantuan creature, as simple as a babe,' with great
flapping arms and hands, at whose house he met 'easy-going
ladies, eccentrics and hangers-on' : it was almost like home. But
John was cautious. 'I walked down Fifth Avenue,' he told
Dorelia,

– there were a number of rather tarty-looking damsels walking
about giving glad or at any rate significant eyes – of course one
mustn't respond, for if you as much as say 'how do you do' to a
woman, you are immediately clapped into gaol for assault or otherwise blackmailed for the rest of your life. The country is chiefly
controlled by a villain named Hearst who owns most of the papers
... This city at night is dominated by a stupendous scintillating sign
advertising Wrigley's chewing gum. The poor bewildered multitude
seethe aimlessly below.

He saw the Americans as 'inconceivably naif' though 'not
unattractive', but it is possible to see John himself as floundering
naïvely within the bowl of this highly artificial society. Despite
all the hectic enjoyment he was never quite at ease, except in
Harlem. It was with great difficulty at first that he could persuade anyone to take him there. After that, to the horror of his
friends, he went alone and sometimes stayed all night. 'The
dancing that took place in these Harlem clubs was brilliant beyond description ... I was immensely pleased.'[111]

Harlem at that time was not known in polite society and
when John spoke of his plans to paint New York's Negroes
there was some high-pitched embarrassment. 'Do you like the
mulattoes, or the brown or black Negroes?' one incredulous
journalist asked. 'I like them all,' he growled. He was questioned on Harlem as if about some far-off planet. 'They seem
to be natural artists,' he told the New York press. 'It seems too
bad that when any of them in this country show talent in the
graphic and plastic arts, or in any line of artistic endeavour, they
are denied an equal chance with other artists.'[112]

John's other area of criticism was Prohibition. 'There's a new
rich class springing up,' he told Dorelia, ' – the *bootleggers*. They
are the strongest advocates of Prohibition and extremely powerful.' In public he aimed his protest at what appeared to him the
most appropriate point. The secretary of the Independent

Society of Artists in New York had been convicted for hanging
a picture by François Kaufman that showed Christ being prevented by some prohibitionist politicians from changing water
into wine, a joke that appealed to John. 'The conviction was an
outrage on liberty and art,' he thundered. 'Your prohibitionists
seem the richest subjects for satire ... Prohibition is more than
a farce – it is a tragedy. I agree with those who say it breeds dis-
respect for all laws. It is unjust to the poor, because one doesn't
have to be in this country long before discovering that anyone
with money can get all the liquor he wants, while it's beyond
the reach of those with little money.'[113]

These were scarcely the tones of a new Sargent. Nevertheless,
New Yorkers were generously disposed to find him very wonderful. Like the Indians, he could be tamed. 'I could get *any
number* of portraits to do if I liked,' he informed Dorelia. The
idea of having done them, swiftly, painlessly, profitably, was
attractive; but the work itself paralysed him. Letters from
Dorelia arrived, describing the flowers in her garden, the girls'
new pony, the dogs, cats and vegetables. Amid the sterile
canyons of New York, all this seemed infinitely green and desirable, and he longed to be back.

Before leaving, he saw for the last time his old patron John
Quinn. Quinn had been dreading this encounter. Having largely
lost interest in John's painting, he was then arranging to sell off
most of his pictures on the open market. To his relief John 'was
very pleasant and did not allude to the episode of my selling
the paintings at all,' he confided to Percy Moore Turner. 'I
took him out riding with a lady ...' By admiring his new collection and his young mistress the beautiful Jeanne Foster, John
so charmed Quinn as to modify his selling programme. The
following year, Quinn was dead. The doctors had given him
up months before, but once again he knew better than any of
them, and simply would not die. They told him he was suffering from a hardening of the liver; he shook his head. Barely
alive, hardly able to move, his body skeletal though swollen
with fluid and (except his teeth) yellow all over, he admitted
to a small glandular disorder. He was 'run down', he believed,
and must be careful not to catch a cold. Once he had picked up,
he would do such things ... He died, on 28 July 1924, of cancer.

'He was a strange man,' Mitchell Kennerley wrote to John (13 Augustus 1924): 'led a strange life: died a strange death. Properly handled his Collections will ensure his fame.'

In the last week of June, John sailed back on the *Berengaria*. 'The first few days he seemed quite low,' noted Conger Good-year, who was with him on the same boat. 'He said he thought he had rather overdone it in New York and that he was glad to be getting back from American Prohibition to England and temperance.'

Though affecting a boastful attitude in the wake of this first trip, he seems to have interpreted it as a reconnaissance to be followed up by an intenser campaign. By April the next year he was back in New York in a big bare studio in the Beaux Arts Building at 80 West 40th Street. This second coming, which has been described as 'an electric event ... that enriched the great saga of John's career,'[114] was largely indistinguishable from the first. 'All the newspapers reproduced photographs of him,' Jeanne Foster wrote to Gwen John. The Mellons and the Wideners queued up for their society portraits; Harlem, all-aglow at night, bewitched him more and more. He was less cautious now. He began painting Negresses 'semi-nude'; and he began quarrelling with American dealers from whose 'unctuous greetings' he protected himself with a 'cold zone'. There was something about New York, he discovered, that for all its speed and activity, deprived him of initiative. All around throbbed a deceptive air of industry: yet it was impossible to work.

'Life', he warned Homer Saint Gaudens, 'is full of pitfalls (and gin).' This time he was in the thick of it, and rapidly growing impatient. At the end of one dinner he broke his silence and, to everyone's amazement, apologized in booming tones for having 'monopolized the conversation'. At a lunch he was seated next to a lady who pressed him continuously about young artists of the day – what pictures could she buy that would multiply in value ten times within five years? 'But is there no one?' she finally asked in desperation, 'is there no one whom *you* are watching?' His reply ended their conversation: 'I am watching myself, madam, with considerable anxiety.'

John's reputation in America, at this time unnaturally high, was built largely on hearsay. The Carroll Gallery and the Photo-

Secession Gallery in New York; the Boston Art Club, the Art Institute of Chicago, the Cleveland Museum of Art and numerous other galleries had been endeavouring over several years to hold John exhibitions. The Carnegie Institute itself had offered to set up a one-man show that would tour the country. All these institutions had the disadvantage of John's active co-operation. He was, as one gallery director put it, always 'cordial ... but persistently indefinite'.[115] When his first one-man show in New York was held early in 1928 at the Anderson Gallery, John inadvertently was in Martigues and never saw it. Stevenson Scott, who had brought him over in 1924 to 'secure commissions for the paintings that commemorate his American period', and had undertaken to show the fruit of this period at Scott and Fowles, did not live to see the exhibition take place. It opened, a quarter of a century later, in the spring of 1949.

Perhaps John's best portraits of Americans were done in Europe: of Tom Mix, the movie actor, who visited Mallord Street with a camera team to film the event; and of the musical McLanahans, plumped up with Philadelphian philanthropics, at their aptly named house in the Côte d'Or, Château de Missery. His portrait of Frances McLanahan,[116] a real beauty, large-eyed and oval-faced, is a Swedish study, blue and yellow, of peach-fed innocence. It was eventually brought to fruition in London where, about the same time, he was failing to finish a portrait of Governor Fuller of Massachusetts.

It was in pursuit of Fuller that he made his last voyage to America in 1928 – a journey he never failed to regret. 'I didn't think it was possible to be so bored,' he complained to Carrington. 'Come over and rescue me!' He had been carried off to the Fullers' country house, 'an appalling place' some fifty miles from Boston, and presented with the task of painting the Governor and his problematic children. 'This sort of work is very ageing,' he grieved. 'I have practically no hair left.' One difficulty was that the Fullers 'do not yet grasp the difference between a hired photographer and an artist. As I am their guest I cannot point out the difference as forcibly as I should like.'[117] The children were devilish – in John's picture the son has no feet because 'that boy drives me crazy, swinging his legs about all the time'; and one of the daughters ('a nice young bitch ... if

one could catch her on the hop') he dismissed altogether because
'neither she nor I could concentrate'. Mrs Fuller, a good soul
brimming over with imbecile cheerfulness, had 'designs on my
virtue', making his position in the house tricky. 'I can't stick
this,' he wrote darkly to Dorelia. 'I *can't* tell you *all*.' The Governor himself, John decided, 'is the best of the lot . . . I could make
Fuller the most ridiculous figure in two hemi-spheres if I wanted
to.'

As the weeks flowed by, his lamentations reached a comic
intensity. 'It's hell and damnation here!' he cried. The prolonged
and dreary meals with mushy food and iced-water; the gramophone grinding out all day its bathetic melodies; the political
guests with their deadly tales of golf and fish; the 'advice' on
painting; the burden of all their labour-saving devices including
a 'ridiculous old ass of a butler' with a pseudo-cockney accent
who, John believed, 'was suffering from a disease of the spine
till I realized his attitude was merely one of deference'; the
gloom, the tears: all these conspired to make the months of
August and September 'the most hideous ordeal of my life'.

In the second week of October they moved, *en masse*, to
Boston. The Fullers expected John to stay at their official residence, or 'mad house', in Beacon Street, but he had been lent a
studio in the Fenway by Charles Woodbury, the marine artist, 'a
perfect old dear . . . I could have embraced him'. Though the
walls were covered with alarming pictures of sharks leaping
from the Caribbean Sea, 'I think I shall recover here,' he assured
Dorelia. 'That stay with the Fullers pulled me down terribly. The
darkest passage of my life undoubtedly.' He had, he added,
devised a 'good method of doing portraits with much use of
toilet-paper'.

This autumn marked a watershed in John's American career.
Offers for portraits poured in – 'there are millions to be made
. . . but I would rather paint vegetables'.[118] He took up his
brushes and produced four cyclamen, two begonias and a
chrysanthemum. It was a long way to have come for such work.
Among his few exciting portraits was one of a coloured elevator
girl who offered to return with him to England. He was determined to penetrate the underworld of Boston but wherever he
went could see nothing but 'masses of full-grown men dismally

guzzling soda-ices'. 'This city is a desert,' he concluded. To the Fullers his behaviour appeared dangerously 'wild'. It was almost as bad for them as the Sacco and Vanzetti trial. No longer did John have to rely on charity for a glass of wine. A coffin-like object in his studio had been filled with drink, and he began to suffer from terrible hangovers. Worse still, he had picked up 'a little actress' with whom he was seen in public. This was Harriet Calloway, the coloured star of *Blackbirds* and famous for her 'Diga Diga Do'. By December the Fullers were as eager as John himself for his departure. 'They seem to think I'm a comic here,' he grumbled. The last laugh was theirs. When the portrait was finished, an official telegram of congratulation was sent from the Governor's residence – to Augustus's father in Tenby.

'How happy I shall be to get on the Ocean,' John had written to Dorelia on 28 November, ' – even if the ship sinks it will be better than staying here, where one sinks only less quickly.' He sailed from New York on 14 December. 'I am a complete wreck,' he warned his family. ' . . . Be ready to meet me at Southampton with a drink.'

John's chief endowment to America was his unfinished work. Over the next thirty years, numbers of ageing Americans continued to throng the Atlantic in vain pursuit of their portraits. One exemplar of this was Mrs Vera Fearing, a niece of Whistler's. John had begun to paint her in October 1928, but not having completed it to his satisfaction by the time he left, he refused to sign it. She promised to come over. The first time she came, he was ill. Later she followed him to Connemara and then back to England. From August to December 1931 she stayed at Fryern, being painted in the tool shed. In the course of these sittings she changed her dress, he changed his studio. She learnt to drink, helped Dorelia with the housework, met Lytton Strachey, Carrington and Lawrence of Arabia, went for death-defying drives to London. Then, in 1935, she tried again – as Mrs Montgomery with a husband and two children. Everyone was extremely kind, John himself offering to give her a child of their own. But one day – 'one of the worst days I've ever been through' – John decided his studio was haunted and disappeared at midnight to London. So it went on. Telegrams and letters flowed between them, and ruses of all dimensions were engineered to lever the picture from John's grasp. He worked on, sometimes using photographs and the clothes of other sitters, grappling with the abominable job of fitting someone else's body onto her head. 'I want to work some more on your extremities,' he pleaded. She waited: was divorced, remarried, became a grandmother. Her father-in-law, who had originally commissioned the portrait, died never having seen it. War came, went. 'Augustus means you to have it,' Reine Pitman assured her on 13 July 1959, 'but is already slightly baulking, and saying he wants to show it before sending it off'. That autumn it had reached 'an electric fire having its signature dried! So it won't be long now ...' Then, in 1960, Vera Stubbs (as she had now become) was repossessed of her picture. But her new husband didn't care for it and it was hung in a disused hut.

There was another curious aftermath to John's American period. Ann and Joan from New York, Doris from Massachusetts, Karin in *Runnin' Wild*, wrote giving times and addresses. Myrtle, a music student 'particularly interested in art', wondered 'if you would like to see me'; Margaret and her friends wished to know whether he would 'consent to stimulate our interest in art'; could he, another correspondent inquired, 'spare a few moments to look at four paintings by my sister, who is in a lunatic asylum?' Some letters, mentioning cocktails, are anonymous; others, providing names and ages of children, affectionate. Others again, containing financial calculations, were torn up. A 'celebrated squawker' offered her services, as vocalist 'at any social function'. Another Vera, who had stopped him in the street one day to demand his 'opinion as to the future of art' wrote to inform him that 'I interrupted my artist's career in order to find out the meaning of things', adding: 'It seems to me that a great figure in the art world like yourself ought to give your contribution to this problem.'

And it was true that, in some manner, John was still 'a great figure in the art world' for the Americans, though they could not see him clearly. It was a mirage: the nearer they approached the more urgently he threatened to vanish. He had come, seen, and turned away. Whenever his name burst into their newspapers – on the cover of *Time* magazine and of *Life*, or as the first artist to wireless a drawing across the Atlantic – curiosity was quickly rekindled. But there was too little of his best work on public view to sustain serious interest, so there remained only a vague impression of his bloodshot personality, some memory of those powerful party manners, a rumour of exploits: then nothing.

On one of his voyages back from America, the ship touching at Cherbourg, John had disembarked. 'I was unable to resist the urge to land first of all on the soil of France,' he explained.[119] 'It was a moving experience after the glitter and turmoil of New York to find myself in the quiet and mellow ambience of a Norman town such as Bayeux and taste again a dish of *moules marinières* with a litre of *rouge* . . .' The gentle aspect of the country, the leisureliness of life, the detachment and intimacy mixed: these were virtues of the Old World that now seemed most appealing to him. In the past, when submerged by spleen or boredom, he had speculated on the existence of a better land to the West. After 1928 he knew it did not exist. When asked whether he would return to America, perhaps to paint Franklin D. Roosevelt, he had answered no: Goethe's dictum 'America is here' was turning out to be literally true, and saved him the journey.

The New World, once it invaded Europe, revealed itself as his enemy. Like a Canute, John held his hand up to halt the tide of history; and such was the force of his personality and the sphere of his influence in style and fashion that, for a moment, he appeared to succeed. The waves held back, there was a frenzied pause – then the sea of modern life flooded past him and he was lost. But in the interval between the Great War and the Great Depression, his values and many that were inimical to them were held in miraculous suspension. To all appearances he was a modern figure, travelling fast.

Travelling downhill. In 1927 began a long process of evacuation. During March that year he moved with his family from Alderney. For a while the strange castellated bungalow, in which they had lived for more than fifteen years, stood empty, a shell behind its broken-down garden wall and the rising screen of rhododendrons. Then it vanished altogether, and in its place stood a brand new housing estate.*

By April the following year, 'in submission to the march of progress as conceived by business men or crooks', they left the Villa St Anne. In their absence, petroleum factories refined the air with their perfume, landscaped the country with their blocks and craters. The fishing village of Martigues grew pock-marked with industrialism: docks and aerodromes besieged it, plastic furniture infested its shops and houses. The Villa St Anne was converted into the Hostelerie St Anne, credited with three knives and forks in the *Guide Michelin*, though still with its 'vue exceptionelle' over the blue Etang de Berre.

In Mallord Street it was the same story. The Chelsea fruit and flower market just opposite their house was obliterated; blocks of flats and a telephone exchange blotted out the sun. In the early 1930s they sold the house to Gracie Fields; the Anrep mosaics were covered up, the basic structure altered, the house and its surroundings made almost unrecognizable.†

Elsewhere too the old world was vanishing, and John was a part of it. Though he might blare his defiance, though he would heave out an announcement from time to time about 'turning a corner', there was only one direction for him to go. The retreat was sounded on all fronts, and everything would depend upon the skill and subtlety with which he conducted it.

---

* The old site, purged of its pagan associations, is now consecrated ground, being occupied by the Alderney Methodist Chapel.

† Much of it has been changed back again, as if 'the intervening years had never been', by Nicola Waymouth in the early 1970s.

IO

The Way They Lived Then

'I got stuck here.' AUGUSTUS JOHN TO BILL DUNCALF
(22 MAY 1959)

I. FRYERN COURT

Fryern Court had originally been a fourteenth-century friary which, in the early nineteenth century, was converted into a farmhouse. Later a Georgian front had been stuck on to the old farm building, and it was transformed into a conventional manor house.

It was a secluded place, in fields, on the edge of the New Forest, a mile from Fordingbridge. A porch 'like a nose'[1] divided the fine long windows that reached almost to the ground; wings and outhouses stretched away into garden and meadow. The sitting-room, dining-room, studies and a fourteenth-century kitchen with carved stone heads (then heavily painted over) protruding from the walls – all had their floors level with the ground. But upstairs there was more the feel of the old farmhouse, the passages rambling crookedly past eight bedrooms.

They moved in early in 1927. Augustus descended from London and 'like the traditional clown'[2] busily did nothing. Everything that could be removed from Alderney was taken. Poppet and Vivien, in great excitement, rode over on their horses; the old vans and carts, soon to be embedded as garden furniture, set out on their last rusty journey; cats, dogs, pigs joined in the stampede past the large copper beeches, magnolias, yellow azaleas up the curving gravel drive to their new home.

The routine and rituals at Fryern were to be arranged as a perfect background for John: but, as with Alderney, it was Dorelia's arrangement. The beauty she conjured up, plenteous and instinctive, gave him no cause for plausible complaint, yet it was far removed from the vast empty scene that stimulated his painter's imagination. He saw all round a beauty he could not use, and he recognized, with despair, the rich orchestration that everywhere supported his external needs. 'Here', exclaimed Cecil Beaton,[3] a frequent visitor, 'is the dwelling place of an artist.' The irony seemed invisible, though the changes that were made to Fryern, in particular a mammoth new studio, on stilts like a child's plaything and 'entirely based on mathematical calculation',[4] were expressions of John's discontent. Year by year his painting deteriorated. In an agony of guilt, disappointment, incomprehension, released in thunderous bursts of temper, he worked on amid these tranquil surroundings.

Meanwhile Dorelia 'busies herself in the garden', John noted. It was a grander garden than at Alderney, and more formal. The old dark yew trees were neatly clipped; the soft mature lawn, with a pond at its centre, was enclosed by hedges; in the orchard, the pear and apple trees were hung with little bags against the wasps. Up the walls of the house roses and clematis twined, the matted stems making a nest for cats; and on the north side, a hazard for drivers, bunched the holly and laurels. There were garden seats, tables of stone and teak, a hammock strung between the Judas and an apple tree. It was a place for animals and children to play in, a place to relax in and read.

But it was also a place to be used, keeping the house replenished with fruit and herbs, bright yellow goats' butter, quince and raspberry jam, grape-juice from the vine in the greenhouse, sweetcorn, lavender, flowers. During the 1930s Dorelia was helped by two gardeners. One, a fine man, strayed into hospital. The other was Mr Cake. He and his wife, Mrs Cake the cook, had been at Alderney and, though often promising to leave, remained with the family for over thirty years. Old Cake was a small man with a limp and a bright button-hole who would go swinging off each evening to the pub over a mile away. He seldom spoke, and his wife, who 'did wonders' especially with fish, could not read. Larger and more voluble than her husband, and always grinning, Mrs Cake appeared (on account of her wall eye) a fearsome creature.* She was immensely proud of her hair, which was long and thick and washed, she would

---

* Mrs Cake's verdict on John was: 'Trouble with 'im is 'e's got too many brains and they've gone to 'is 'ead.'

explain, in juice of rosemary. She spoke with a strong Dorset accent. 'Old Cake was very lucky to get me,' she would say. 'All the boys were after me. It was my hair.' Old Cake, pursued by several goats, said nothing.

There was soon much of Alderney about Fryern Court, the same smells of beeswax, pomanders and lavender, wood- and tobacco-smoke, coffee, cats; and the same amiable disorder, spontaneously thrown together, of vegetables, tubes of paint, nuts from the New Forest, saddles, old canvases, croquet mallets, piles of apples. The furniture was not fine nor the pictures very valuable: it was the opposite of a museum. Alongside those paintings of John's which had eluded fire and finish were some lovely Gwen Johns, a watercolour by Augustus's son Edwin, a small Henry Moore sketch, small Wilson Steers, Conders and other contemporary works, in particular, later on, some Matthew Smiths. An Epstein head of a small child stood on a table, and in the hall, crowned with a cactus, one of the two Modigliani stone heads John had bought in Paris. Then there were paintings by friends: Eve Kirk, Adrian Daintrey and a passing number of gypsy artists.

Though far from being a smart house, it had an unpretentious beauty. The colours were rich, but without any premeditated scheme; the atmosphere lavish yet shabby; it had much of the farm about it. The physical fascination it had for people was difficult to analyse. 'There is no beguiling, ready-made impact of beauty,' wrote Cecil Beaton; 'rather, an atmosphere of beauty is sensed. No intention to decorate the house ever existed. The objects that are there were originally admired and collected for their intrinsic shape. They remain beautiful ... the colours have gratuitously grown side by side. Nothing is hidden; there is an honesty of life which is apparent in every detail – the vast dresser with its blue and white cups, the jars of pickled onions, the skeins of wool, the window sills lined with potted geraniums and cacti ...'[5]

With its squadrons of guests, its explosive parties, Fryern was the most open of houses, a mandatory first stop between London and the west. Many were invited, many more came. But the informality was rigorous and the welcome, at least to strangers, not always decipherable. Hugo Pitman remembered every window of the house lit up (though it was still light outdoors) when he first approached: 'It was like arriving at a stage set. Through the long windows of the refectory-table room, he saw two figures sitting by a blazing fire. On the other side of the front door, some children moved about in the drawing-room. Upstairs, Augustus could be seen in bed ... The bell did not work, so they rattled the front door. Instantly every light in the house went out, except Augustus's – and his blind came down immediately.'[6]

John was emphatic about people enjoying themselves. Up in London, his laugh volleying round the Eiffel Tower; or seen striding about the sunlit gymkhanas where Poppet and Vivien loved to ride; or picnicking with the family on the phallic giant of Cerne; or in the evenings, seated at one end of the long scrubbed oak table opposite Dorelia, with twenty people between them, and candles, bottles of wine, he seemed lit up by joie de vivre. Broad-shouldered, athletic still in his fifties, capable of gestures of great warmth and sympathy, there was yet 'a touch of tragedy in his appearance', Adrian Daintrey noted.[7]

Parties were conspiracies of self-forgetfulness. Fierce fits of depression had made him dependent upon the momentary gaiety of a clamorous, adoring public whom he did not honestly admire but whom he allowed to play him out of his gloom into the false light of their fan-club gala-world. Hating publicity, he had become the object of 'image-making'. But the praise they filled him with was counterfeit: hot air. As numerous letters of apology testify, he could behave very rudely when drunk, but there was some truth in this rudeness. The good things they said about him he did not believe. He could suspend disbelief but never long enough to achieve complacency. For this reason he was never the Impostor of a Wyndham Lewis fantasy, even if from time to time he strove to act that rôle. '*La bonne peinture* is all the praise I want!' he wrote to Will Rothenstein (26 May 1936). This was not vocal approbation, but a sense of right. 'I am painting better than ever before,' he growled one day to Lady Waverley. But when she congratulated him – 'how happy you must be' – he snapped back: 'You have never said anything more silly!'

That it became, with time, more difficult to flatter him stood to his credit. But it did not make him an easier person. False praise, like alcohol, was ultimately a depressant, allowing him briefly to 'take off' while it drilled a deeper cavity into which he must fall back. Among his family who, reflecting only distorted versions of himself, provided no escape, he was often at his most difficult. 'Daddy has returned to the scene so it will be gloom, gloom, gloom,' Vivien wrote in one of her letters from Fryern. Meals could be 'absolute killers' affording all the silence, the strictness and fear that had saturated his father's dining-room at Tenby. When the going was bad, John would sit, a crazed look on his face, his eyes staring out with an insane glare, like a Flaxman horse. Something odd was going on inside him as he sat, silent, watching the gangway of brooding children. Almost anything they did could be a target – the way a knife was held, the expression of a face, a chance sentence. To others he spoke in a mild, cultivated voice, saying something unexceptional, even academic, about the birth of language, the origin of nomads. His speech was exactly calculated. He would chuckle first, as if amused by what was about to come out, then pause, selecting his vocabulary with care, and pronounce the words slowly in old-fashioned English, without short-cuts or slang. Then he would relapse into silence, and again something nameless appeared to be torturing him. But sometimes, when he thought no one could see him, his whole body quivered with silent laughter.

The house was controlled by these moods. Intrigues and hostilities thundered through the rooms, threatening, exploding, blowing over: and all the time something within John was shrinking. His generosity, the largeness of his attitude, these were still communicated. He was a big man: but inside the magnificent shell his real self was diminishing. One sign of this was his handwriting, which had been wild in youth, handsome and expansive in middle-age and, from the 1930s began to contract until, during the last fifteen years of his life, it had become tiny – a trembling crawl across conventional small-scale writing-paper.

Fryern, which would remain their home until they died, was a beautiful cobweb spun by Dorelia round John. Like a fly, suspended, exposed, he buzzed and was silent, buzzed and grew smaller. There was no spider to devour him, no danger, only a gradual diminution towards zero.

And Dorelia was caught too. After the war, Lamb had been invalided back to England 'in a desperate state'.[8] From the General Hospital at Rouen he was sent to a hospital in London where Dorelia went to see him. 'He's not allowed more than one visit a day so it's very maddening,' she had written to Lytton Strachey (11 December 1918). '. . . his heart and nerves are in a very bad state. He's in a very comfortable place [27 Grosvenor Square] which is a blessing, and being looked after properly for the first time.' In so far as she could – though 'it's very difficult for me to get away' – Dorelia helped him back to health. He was often at Alderney, and to be near her set up house in Poole.* To the children he had been a glorified uncle; to Dorelia he was her other artist, the theoretical alternative reconciling her to life. But for John he was merely some nerve-ridden sparrow imitating an eagle. He knew that Lamb was cleverly critical of his painting, and feared that this might affect Dorelia, on whom he still counted for strength.

Though the atmosphere had sometimes been uneasy, and there were too few opportunities for Lamb and Dorelia to escape together, some aspects of Alderney had been 'perfect' – piano duets, moments alone. But always after a few precious hours, 'that old tarantula Augustus' would reappear 'in his customary nimbus of boredom, silence and helpless gloom', Dorelia would step back into the shadows and Lamb retire bitterly alone. A drawing he did of her in 1925, sensitive and tender, hints at the deep feelings she aroused in him, and his letters to Carrington (who was herself very close to Dorelia) proclaim them.[9] She absorbed his waiting life. When she fell ill he felt 'terrified', blaming John for thoughtlessly loading her with work. He tried to extricate her from the 'perfect cataract' of hangers-on in the country, to rescue her when 'bemallorded with the old monster' in London. 'I find her quite inaccessible,' he sighed to Carrington (12 September 1925), 'and of course she makes no effort.' But there were glimpses of her, secret times when she would slip away to him, bringing plants for his garden or going with him to

* At No. 10 Hill Street.

concerts. For years he persisted in his hope that she would finally come to him 'and then perhaps part of the day dream could be realized. After all there is such fair hope of it all coming off some day when that strange woman is less perplexed and all our nerves less raging'.[10] This hope was extinguished only when, starting a fresh chapter of her life with John, Dorelia moved to Fryern. For Lamb, as for John, it was a crisis. 'The worst of it is,' Lamb complained to Carrington, 'that I think Augustus's threatened breakdown is all fiddle-dedee – just some of his melodramatic methods. Though I suppose he is quite plainly, though slowly, breaking up if not down.'

From this time onwards Lamb's attitude changed. 'I think she [Dorelia] is already pretty well bored there,' he wrote sourly to Carrington not long after the move to Fryern. He had managed at last to get divorced from Euphemia, and the next year, 1928, he married Pansy Pakenham, the eldest daughter of the fifth Earl of Longford, springing the news on Dorelia a few days beforehand.

Dorelia's life with John had grown more difficult. She made at least two attempts to leave. Once she got so far as the railway station. A pony and trap was sent off in scalding pursuit, arriving just before the train, and she was persuaded to return. The letters John wrote whenever he was abroad reveal his dependence on her, and it was this need that finally held her back. After which it was too late, too unthinkable that 'Dodo', as everyone called her, should not always be there. She grew more fatalistic, relying on the swing of her pendulum – a ring harnessed to a piece of string – to decide everything from a marriage to the authenticity of a picture. It was impossible to tell to what extent she counted on blind faith or the subconscious workings of common sense. From anything that might cause pain she averted her inner eye, though she might seem to stare at it without emotion. The range of her interests narrowed. She had stopped drawing, now she read less, eventually gave up the piano, perfected her immunity. Nothing got on top of her, nothing came too near. She had turned her attention to the vegetable world, and conducted, with precision, the times of meals. The sounds at Fryern matched this quiet equanimity: no longer the jaunty duets with Lamb, but a softer noise, the purring amid the pots and plants, of the sewing-machine as she sat in front of it, alone, as if for dear life.

2. A LONG LOVE-AFFAIR WITH DRINK

In the first four years at Fryern a great physical change came over John. 'He had aged very much in those years,' Diana Mosley remembered, '... John was fifty-three in 1931, but he seemed old, his hair was grey, his eyes bloodshot, and he already looked almost as he did in the cruelly truthful self-portrait he painted after the war.'[11]

The immediate cause of this change was alcohol. Almost certainly he had drunk more in the 1920s than in any other decade of his life. 'I drink in order to become more myself,' he stated once to Cecil Gray.[12] Drink banished his awkwardness, carried him across the moat of isolation. At Fryern he was king of the castle; but outside this castle he could feel ill-at-ease, and remained loyal to one or two places – Stulik's or the Queen's Restaurant in Sloane Square – he had made homes-from-home.

Drink changed him into a different person. It was the passport enabling him to go anywhere, giving him the gift of tongues. After a glass or two he relaxed, the terrible paralysis lifted, and the warmth that had been locked up within him flowed out. But then there was a third stage, when the geniality and amorousness gave way to senseless actions, such as punching out a cigarette on someone's face: of which, afterwards, he felt bitterly ashamed.

It is impossible to be certain what were the predisposing factors in John's character that forced him across the line dividing the social drinker from the man dependent upon alcohol, but a knowledge of his biography does suggest one cause. He had been aged six when his mother died, and though he nowhere laments her death, his obsessive theme as a painter – a mother with her children in an ideal landscape – illustrates the deep effect this loss had produced. If his father, whom he so disliked, represented the actual world, the deprivation of his mother became the source of that fantasy world, happy and beautiful, he created in its place. It was an example of how art can transmute deprivation into an asset. But actual life was always conflicting with this dream world. Alcohol, by blurring the distinction between them, lessened the tension of this conflict.

But in practice, it was impossible neatly to segregate these two spheres. Whenever he felt submerged by day-to-day realism, his inspiration faded and he grew deeply melancholic; whenever he pursued his visions too far into real life, he spread confusion. It was this that had culminated in Ida's death. About her death, as about his mother's, he was reticent, but she had been a casualty in the warring of these worlds, committing him, if he were to justify it, more deeply to the fantasy of his art. The tension grew. Alcohol, by subduing the light of everyday, seemed to enable the moon to shine out more brilliantly in the firmament of his imagination. This, at the start, was its function. The eruption of the First World War had sent his dream-planet spinning off into the unknown. The rest of John's life was the saga of his search to rediscover it. But it was a twilight search, for drink had dimmed his moon as well as the sun.

From this time on, alcohol fulfilled another function: it screened the truth. It did so in many ways, lightening the fatigue of his search, numbing the disappointment, leading him into moods of self-deception, expanding the ego. But while he looked for another world he lived in this one, painting portraits instead of 'invented' pictures, and seldom converting a sitter into one of his own people. He had lost confidence and the courage to experiment. In their place alcohol gave him false substitutes – a bragging that contradicted his modesty when sober; and an expensive life, ostentatiously generous to others, that required more commissioned portraits to finance it.

John was an actor. Amid the fictitious jollity of the bar, he acted happy and almost felt so; sometimes he even acted drunk. Acting, which had begun as a means to self-discovery, became a method of escaping his sense of exile. It was this remoteness that people sensed about him. 'I'm sure he has no human heart,' noted Hugh Walpole in his diary (3 July 1926), 'but is "fey", a real genius from another planet than ours.'[13] But if he was not of this planet, he did not now belong to any other. 'Sometimes one feels positively the old *horror vacui* overwhelming one,' he admitted to Christabel Aberconway.[14] Although alcohol promoted a temporary sense of well-being, John recognized it as an enemy that could impair his health and competence as an artist. He made many attempts, some of them on paper, to reduce his drinking, or to give it up altogether. 'I feel so restless and agitated I can hardly write,' he told Alice and Will Rothenstein at one point. His withdrawal symptoms seem to have bordered on *delirium tremens*, and he decided to seek medical help. Treatment was made difficult because John never admitted his addiction to alcohol. 'There's nothing the matter with me except occasional "nerves",' he diagnosed in a letter to Ottoline Morrell (8 June 1929). On this matter of nerves he consulted Dr Maurice Wright who was 'very eminent in his own line – psychology, and he is already an old friend of mine'.[15] Discussing his illness, John used a rich supply of euphemisms, inviting the psychologist to treat symptoms which, masking the real complaint, he saw as diseases in themselves. Some of them were so bad, he joked, they could drive a man to drink. 'You are quite right,' he wrote to Dr Gogarty, 'catarrh makes one take far more drink than one would want without it.' Pretending to treat a variety of somatic sicknesses, from lumbago to sinusitis, while achieving a cure for alcoholism was too stern a test for even so eminent a psychologist, and these consultations came to nothing. But by the end of March 1930, on the advice of Ottoline Morrell, John was attending her doctor.

Dr Cameron, 'nerve-specialist', was fairly knowledgeable about alcohol. When drunk one day he ran over a child, and was sent to gaol. But he was a persuasive man, and many of his patients returned to him. Later, after a number of them had died, he went on to commit suicide.

John took to Cameron at once. 'I shall bless you to the end of your days for sending me to Dr Cameron,' he wrote, thanking Ottoline. 'Would that I had seen him years ago. He put his finger on the spot *at once*. Already I feel happy again and ten years younger.' The treatment involved no surrender of pride, and John's relief came from having escaped a long process of humiliation. Both he and Cameron knew that in alcohol lay the real cause of his 'nerves', but they entered a conspiracy to gloss over this truth. 'The defect in my works has been poisoning me for ages,' John reported. 'It explains so much . . .'[16] Cameron's diagnosis was delivered with a vagueness very dear to alcoholics. John had been 'overdrawing his bank account' and should go to a convalescent home where (though expensive in terms of money) he would make a sound investment. Under this guise of tackling the rigours of a rest cure, John allowed himself to be sent to Preston Deanery Hall, a curious private nursing home in Northampton that had opened in 1929 and was to be closed in 1931. Here, as if by accident, he was removed from all alcohol though permitted to equivocate as much as he liked. He was 'travelling in the midlands' he told people, or suffering from a 'liver attack'. In a letter to Will Rothenstein (May 1930) he explained that he was undergoing 'a thorough spring-cleaning' because 'my guts weren't behaving harmoniously'. Expressing her gratitude for Ottoline's 'great brain wave', Dorelia wrote on 5 May 1930: 'Of course J. would be perfectly well without wine or spirits. Many a time I've managed to keep him without any for *weeks* and then some idiot has undone all my good work in one evening. He may be impressed this time. All the other doctors have said the same, Dr Wright included. One can only hope to do one's best ...'

What Dorelia did not appreciate was that the first phase of a successful cure must be the patient's admission that he needs special treatment for alcoholism. This admission John was never required to make. He stayed at the nursing home a month, and his treatment appears to have been largely custodial – abstinence, vitamin supplements and some tranquillizing drugs served on silver platters by footmen. 'They are making a good job of me, I feel,' he broadcast.[17] '... I am a different being and they tell me in a week or two I'll be as strong again as a horse.' He was allowed out with another inmate for a 'debauch of tea and toast', for walks to the church and, more recklessly, drives in his car. In the absence of gypsies, he made friends with 'some nice animals', cows and sheep mostly; while indoors there were erotic glimpses of a remarkable young chambermaid. As always when alone, he read voraciously, but was sometimes 'rather forlorn'. 'If I were not beginning to feel as I haven't felt for years I *might* be bored,' he threatened in a note to Ottoline, who had entered the nursing home herself for a few days, '– as it is – I am smiling to myself, as at some huge joke.'

After having 'had it out with the doctor', John left a week earlier than planned. 'No doubt I'll have to follow a regime for a while,' he wrote to Dorelia. 'They say I'll be marvellously well in about 10 days after leaving.' His after-care came in the form of a diet. 'Unfortunately I have lost that almost ethereal quality which I had so welcomed,' he told Ottoline (23 May 1930). '. . . I blame the cook for giving me unauthorized potatoes and beef steak.'

'You'd be all right if you lived sensibly,' Eve Fleming instructed him. 'You're as strong as twelve lions by nature.' But sense of this sort, careful, programmed, grey, was unavailable to him: 'I who always live from hand to mouth and have so little practical sense'.[18] He was awash with optimism. His strong constitution, with its more than ordinary powers of recovery, quickly misled him. Austerity, he claimed, had made him 'much more like myself' – though he had also bought a new hat which was making him 'a different person and a better'. One way or another he felt like 'a giant refreshed'.[19]

It was not long before he relapsed into drinking, and the deterioration went on. 'John is in ruins,' T. E. Lawrence noted in 1932, 'but a giant of a man. Exciting, honest, uncanny.'[20] He never became a chronic drinker – 'I was never a true alcoholic,' he admitted to Mavis Wheeler – and there were many fluctuating phases in this third period of his drinking. From time to time he went back to doctors who tried to remove him from alcohol altogether. But Dorelia's tactics worked better. She rationed him with lock and key at home, and in restaurants would furtively empty his glass into the potted plants. Without drink he tended to avoid people : 'I find my fellow-creatures very troublesome to contend with without stupéfiant,' he told Christabel Aberconway. He still retreated into the comforting womb of pubs, but 'to get alone for a bit'.[21] A solitary figure in a muffler, booted and corduroyed, he sat quietly in a corner, drinking his beer. Latterly he consumed far less, because his tolerance to alcohol had diminished. Conger Goodyear, who had been so struck by his capacity at the Saturn Club in the 1920s, was regretting by the 1940s that 'his ancient alcoholic prowess had departed', and after a few drinks 'Augustus did not improve'.[22]

The loss of confidence, upsurges of temper, the tremulousness of his hands, his inability to make decisions – all grew more pronounced. He knew the truth, but would not hear it from anyone. But it amused him sometimes to make people connive at his inventions – then, with disconcerting relish, come out with the facts. 'I have heard of a new treatment for my complaint – it consists of total abstention from liquor'.[23] At other times he would innocently complain of Dodo that she smoked too much; or of J. B. Manson (who was dismissed as Director of the Tate Gallery) that 'the fellow drinks', deliberately slurring his words as he spoke.

He had used alcohol at first to help illuminate that visionary world from which his art took its vitality, his painter's moon. But when that dream was eclipsed, he drank to obliterate the concrete world about him. Long before the end, intermittently between bursts of renewed effort, he was drinking to destroy himself. Painting alone mattered. If he could not paint well, and if he could not disguise his inability to do so, then he would be better dead. But Dorelia, who had tolerated so much, could not tolerate this. Her watchfulness, care, relentless programme of meals and early nights, propped him up, pulled him through – the ghost of a man he had once been.

3. ODYSSEUS UNBOUND

The first test came that summer of 1930. He had been invited by Gogarty to assist at the opening of his hotel, Renvyle House, in Connemara. Yeats was also coming, and Gogarty arranged for John to do a 'serious portrait' of him. 'I would think it a great honour,' Yeats had murmured. But standing before the mirror, he began to examine himself with some apprehension, 'noticing certain lines about my mouth and chin marked strongly by shadows', and to wonder 'if John would not select those very lines and lay great emphasis upon them, and, if some friends complain that he has obliterated what good looks I have, insist that those lines show character, and perhaps that there are no good looks but character'.[24]

Yeats, John observed, had made the mistake of growing older. He was 'now a mellow, genial and silver haired old man'.[25] He had put on weight, seemed distrustful and, despite the vastly

poetical manner, presented a diluted version of the poet John
had met twenty-three years earlier. Somehow he looked less
Yeats-like. Studying his own reflection, Yeats had noted 'marks
of recent illness, marks of time, growing irresolution, perhaps
some faults that I have long dreaded; but then my character is
so little myself that all my life it has thwarted me'. This was
a development very close to John's own, explaining why critics
of a different persuasion, such as Robert Graves, could dismiss
them both as poseurs. John himself seems to have been entertained by Yeats up to, and beyond, the frontiers of boredom.
'Lord and Lady Longford had fetched him over to be painted,' he
remembered.

The conversation at dinner consisted of a succession of humorous
anecdotes by Yeats, chiefly on the subject and at the expense of
George Moore, punctuated by the stentorian laughter of his Lordship
and the more discreet whinny of his accomplished wife. I was
familiar with most of these stories before, or variants of them: for
the Irish literary movement nourished itself largely on gossip ... My
difficulties while painting Yeats were not lightened by the obligation
of producing an appreciative guffaw at the right moment, and I
fear my timing was not always correct.[26]

It was Yeats's melancholy that John recognized, and shied
away from. 'The portrait represents the poet in his old age,'
Gogarty records. 'He is seated with a rug round his knees and his
broad hat on his lap. His white hair is round his head like a
nimbus, and behind him the embroidered cloths of heaven are
purple and silver. It is the last portrait of Yeats.'[27]
Once this portrait was finished, John was free to do whatever
he wanted. What he wanted was to go to Galway City, and,
denouncing the Connemara weather and the atmosphere at
Renvyle (too 'new and raw'), he went. From O'Flaherty's bar
and from parties flowing with barmaids on and around Francis
Macnamara's boat *Mary Anne*, he was eventually fished up and
carried back to Renvyle where an admiring entourage had
assembled – painters Adrian Daintrey and George Lambourn,
and any number of painterly girls including 'the ladies Dorothea
and Lettice Ashley-Cooper', and their sister Lady Alington who
'has been posing for him and does not confine it to that'.[28] To
this number a beautiful American, Hope Scott, added herself,

arriving in Dublin straight from Pennsylvania and being rushed across Ireland in a hearse. Her first sight of John, his beard caught by the sun, his eyes gleaming with anticipation, was at a ground-floor window. The hearse door was flung open, and nearly fainting with terror 'I fell out on my head'.[29]

John was then painting most days, Adrian Daintrey and George Lambourn acting as pacemakers. But every evening there were parties, and the effect of these began to infiltrate the day. Sometimes he was not well enough to paint, and at other times it was the girls he chose. Only occasionally, for 'relaxation', did he turn to the empty landscape. His seclusion in Preston Deanery Hall seems to have precipitated two reactions: a greater urgency in his pursuit of girls, and a crippling anxiety over his work. 'Though I was sitting, I did not lack exercise. Most of Augustus's models found themselves doing a good bit of sprinting round the studio,' recalled Mrs Scott, into whose bed John was prevented from blundering by the presence of a bolster he angrily mistook for Adrian Daintrey. But Hope Scott also noticed: 'He was enormously concentrated, at times he seemed actually to suffer over his work.'

Dorelia and Poppet, who had gone with him to Ireland, left early. To them, arranged as a compliment, he confessed his depression: 'J'étais dans un gloom affreux quand tu et Dodo êtes parties. Tu pourrais bien m'avoir embrassé . . .'

To lose this gloom in something new became the theme of this decade. He travelled to the Hebrides, to Jersey, Cornwall and, for short visits, back to Wales. Now that he no longer had the Villa St Anne, he stayed during part of two winters at Cap Ferrat with Sir James Dunn 'the friendly financier'.[30] But, like Sickert, John failed to please Dunn, who destroyed a conversation piece and promoted two portraits above stairs to his attic. 'Dunn's quarrels with John over the various portraits were furious,' Lord Beaverbrook wrote, 'and much tough language was tossed to and fro, without reaching any conclusion . . . John, however, gave as much as he got.'[31] Though the hospitality was lavish, sapping his willpower, these fashionable pleasure grounds, full of self-conscious holiday-makers and millionaire property-owners flying like migratory birds of prey back to Big Business after the season was over, induced a 'period of intense gloom' in John. 'I could find nothing in Cap Ferrat to excite me, and with a violent effort of will we pulled ourselves together and decamped.'

Other journeys were more productive. In October 1930 he set off with Dorelia to see a 'tremendous' Van Gogh exhibition in Amsterdam, and from there went on alone to Paris, where he did some drawings of James Joyce. 'He sits patiently,' John noted in a letter to Dorelia. A photograph of the two of them, in which John appears the more anxious to take part, shows Joyce like a blind prisoner – dark glasses, upright and foursquare, but with his head rigidly tilted back – and John a blind man's protector, gripping him, brandishing his pipe, apparelled in a pugilist's dressing-gown.[32]

All these places – France, which he loved; Wales, where he belonged; Ireland, that had once suggested great pictures to him – inhabited a past he seemed unable to evoke. What he sought now was a fresh scene, without associations. It had been such a wish that persuaded him, in December 1932, to try what he described as a 'health trip'[33] to Majorca. But there had been rain, and heavy air. By nature the island might have been what he was looking for, but 'big operations' were going on 'with screeching rock-drills and a general banging of machinery'. The developers had arrived; he was too late. Feeling 'like death' he returned with the news that Majorca was 'not paintable'.[34]

Back in the mellow atmosphere of Fryern Court, he racked his brains, consulted maps, looked up trains and boats, and, retrieving a plan from the spring of 1912, settled on Venice. His last fortnight in Italy, a tiny trigger movement releasing extraordinary artistic forces, had been nearly twenty-two years ago. Now, entering at a different part, he seems to have tried a similar experiment. With him travelled his daughter Vivien, aged eighteen, 'to keep an eye on the money'.[35] John, 'determined to see all the famous paintings', would go off on expeditions to Ferrara and elsewhere, spending hours in churches and galleries. But though there was much to enchant him, it was the pressure of people once again and not of paintings that predominated. On landing on the steps of his hotel the first day, he had been hailed from a passing gondola by Georgia Sitwell. From that moment, word getting round, he was sucked into a life of Firbankian excess.

The most serious encroachments came from Vivien's admirers, whom he took elaborate steps, on behalf of them both, to avoid. 'We are caught up in the maelstrom of Venetian society,' he wrote to Dorelia (29 August 1933). '... the place is full of bores, buggers and bums of all kinds. Vivien is greatly in request and there are various optimistic members of the local aristocracy on her tracks. Conditions are not favourable for painting and money goes like water, so I think an early return is indicated.' Much of this time Vivien was in tears, and John, though very protective, had sudden fits of anger, passionately complaining that her clothes were *too smart*. 'The air of Venice was getting me down,' he acknowledged. 'I became more and more indolent ... it was the people I tired of most. My God, what a set! ... I was seeing less of Vivien ... but at last even my daughter agreed it was time to depart.'[36]

He had done no painting. The truth that had eluded him lay in his dreams, which no longer had the power to overwhelm the emotional complications of life. The mother-and-child obsession gave way before a father-daughter possessiveness; the simple life evaporated in the heat of social life. Like some new Ulysses, he had unbound himself from the mast, plugged up his ears, and did not know from where the sirens called him, or if they called at all. Now more than ever, since his life was on the wane, since he could no longer brush aside as fanciful the fear of a fading talent, a yearning for new distant scenes, a craving for freedom, the impulse towards flight, filled him. They filled him, but he could not act on them. Like a giant ship, stranded in shallow water, its propellers grating in the air, he stayed.

But one last voyage awaited him – had awaited him, by the time he embarked, for twenty-six years. 'I think Jamaica would be a nice place to go and work,' he had written to Dorelia. That was in September 1911. 'I think of going to Jamaica,' he insisted in a letter to Vera Stubbs on 4 June 1929. By 1936, the effects of renewed drinking had led him to consult an occultist who, responding to the challenge, proposed casting John's horoscope. This exercise led to the prediction that he would turn up soon in one of the British Colonies. 'I would have been sorry to leave the astrologer's forecast unfulfilled and his prophetic gift in dispute,' John wrote. '. . . I decided [on] a visit to Jamaica.'

By this time Dorelia was set on joining the adventure. With them went Vivien, Francis Macnamara's daughter Brigit now 'une grosse blonde . . . très aimable'[37] and Tristan de Vere Cole, also blonde, but aged two-and-a-half, who 'imagines himself to be the Captain of this ship'.[38] The tropics suited John. Though the island was 'altogether too fertile', parts of it reminded him of North Wales. The internal conflict he carried with him wherever he went externalized itself in Jamaica very satisfactorily. The enemy were the bridge-playing colonials, golf club members, and the management of the American United Fruit Company. His allies were the natives, dusky beauties, with complexions as various as their fruits. There were the same risks as in Venice, but he controlled them better. 'We are in some danger of being launched into the beau monde of Jamaica. Nobody believes I am serious when I tell them I am only interested in painting the coloured people,' he wrote to Mavis de Vere Cole (10 March 1938). '. . . I shall have a mass of work done before I am finished.' To gain extra time, Jamaica being so expensive, he dispatched 'the females and Tristan' back to England after a month, and continued working alone until the rains came six weeks later. In *Chiaroscuro*, where he devotes over ten pages to this time,[39] John records that he felt 'anything but satisfied' with his painting. Like gypsies, the natives were difficult of access. In a perfect world he would have built a 'house of mud, mahogany and palms' and lived there as one of them. Instead – the ultimate degradation – he was taken for a visiting politician. Yet, the place 'suits me and stimulates me', he decided. 'I am painting with a renewal of energy quite remarkable and will not cease till I have accomplished much.'[40]

He could have accomplished more. 'With the rain a great gloom descended upon me, almost depriving me of volition.' He returned on a banana boat to Fryern and struggled to pursue these pictures before the dream slid behind the invisible screen of habit and impaired memory. His portraits of 'Aminta', 'Daphne', 'Phyllis' and many others, which had puzzled the subjects themselves on account of their not appearing white, delighted London when they were exhibited at Tooth's Gallery in May and June 1938. The show, Dudley Tooth noted in his diary, 'has been a tremendous success, nearly everything having been sold at prices between £200 and £550. Among the purchasers were J. B. Priestley, Thelma Cazalet, Mrs Syrie Maugham, Vincent Massey, Oswald Birley, Sir Lawrence Phillips and Stafford Cripps, the announcement of whose purchase to his horror was in the *Evening Standard* to-night.'

The most splendid celebration of these Jamaican pictures was sounded by Wyndham Lewis in *The Listener*:

As one passes in review these blistered skins of young African belles, with their mournful doglike orbs, and twisted lips like a heavyweight pugilist, one comes nearer to the tragedy of this branch of the human race than one would in pictures more literary in intention, such as Gauguin would have supplied us with ...

Mr John opens his large blue eyes, and a dusky head bursts into them. His large blue eyes hold fast the dusky object while his brushes stamp out on the canvas a replica of what he sees. But what he sees (since he is a very imaginative man) is all the squalor and beauty of the race – of this race of predestined underdogs, who have never been able to meet on equal terms the crafty white man or even more crafty Arab.

In describing Mr Augustus John's assault upon these Negro belles – his optical assault, as his large blue eyes first fall upon them in Jamaica – I was indicating what is, in fact, a good deal his method of work. Nature is for him like a tremendous carnival, in the midst of which he finds himself. But there is nothing of the spectator about Mr John. He is very much a part of the saturnalia. And it is only because he enjoys it so tremendously that he is moved to report upon it – in a fever of optical emotion, before the object selected passes on and is lost in the crowd.[41]

These Jamaican pictures, constructed rather as a modeller builds up his clay to make shapes, represent the most vigorous body of John's work during the last twenty-five years of his career. There were other fine pictures – the occasional flamboyant flowerpiece, or a portrait of someone he loved or admired – but the general drift was downwards. He sought new subjects to avoid comparison with his past self, and bring about a rebirth of his talent. In 1929 C. B. Cochran had daringly pro-

posed his name for the important second act of Sean O'Casey's*
play *The Silver Tassie*. On Cochran's suggestion, and without her
husband's knowledge, Eileen O'Casey called on John at Mallord
Street like 'an angel rushing in where a devil feared to tread'.⁴²
There was, she noticed, 'a debutante trying to get in, ringing the
bell, appearing at various windows'. John ignored this as they
talked over the project. The play was fine, but he had qualms.
'I have never done one before; I don't really think I could.' He
was, Eileen remembered, 'extremely shy, though as ever
courteous and complimentary, for he liked good-looking women.
This helped me to plead my cause.' At the end of the afternoon,
she asked: 'Have I persuaded you?' 'I'm afraid you have,' he
replied.⁴³

Everything had gone with surprising ease. 'I have the Silver
Tassie with me,' he wrote from Cap Ferrat on 3 February 1929,
'and I don't see much difficulty about the second act'. O'Casey
had described this act in detail: a War Zone, its 'jagged and
lacerated ruin of what was once a monastery', the life-size
crucifix, stained glass window, and great howitzer with 'long
sinister barrel now pointing towards the front at an angle of
forty-five degrees'. In a note he had added: 'Every feature of the
scene seems a little distorted from its original appearance.' All
this approximated closely to what John had wanted to depict as
a war artist and, given this new impetus, he turned to his sketch-
books of France and produced a set that was as overpowering to
the audience as to the scene-shifters.† O'Casey was delighted

---

* John had met O'Casey through William McElroy, a coal merchant,
impresario and part-horse-owner ('the left hind leg, I think it was'). He painted
two portraits of O'Casey in 1926, one now in the Metropolitan Museum of
Art, New York, the other which he gave to O'Casey as a wedding present.
'Blue-green coat, silver-grey sweater, with a gayer note given by an orange
handkerchief flowing from the breast-pocket of the coat,' O'Casey described
it; 'the face set determinedly in contemplation of things seen and heard, the
body shrinking back right to the back of the chair, as if to get further away to
see and hear more clearly; a sensitive and severe countenance with incisive
lines of humour braiding the tightly-closed mouth'. It is now in the collection
of Eileen O'Casey. 'He [John] is evidently intensely interested in what he sees
behind what is understood as my face,' Sean O'Casey wrote on 16 May 1926.

† For whom it was too heavy to move. The set was designed, as an oil painting, on canvas stretchers. 'John's scene was an exterior with a derelict church,
with a fine stained glass window,' Alick Johnstone remembered. 'He designed

by the church window and sinister gun, and Bernard Shaw pronounced 'the second act a complete success for both of you'.[44]

John too felt excited by what seemed a completely new arena in which to exercise his talent. He was already hot with plans for designing the sets of Constant Lambert's 'Pomona' for the Camargo Society, when he succumbed to Preston Deanery Hall. In the following years there were many rumours of his re-entry into the theatre, but all came to nothing until, in 1935, again at the suggestion of Cochran, he agreed to do the scenery and costumes for J. M. Barrie's *The Boy David*.

The changes that had overtaken John in the seven years between the two plays are very clear. On 25 October 1935, coinciding with an announcement in *The Times*, Cochran sent John a letter confirming the details of their arrangement. Less than two months later, on 13 December, he was sending out an S.O.S. for Ernst Stern, who had been the chief designer to Max Reinhardt, and was the most professional artist in the theatre of his day. With the exception of Barrie, everyone in the production had taken to John at once. 'John, in his extraordinary innocence of the theatre, was never too proud to defer to their expertise,' recorded Malcolm Easton. 'On them, and on all Cochran's brilliant band of technicians, he smiled benevolently. From the benevolence, however, proceeded few practical results ... John's efforts to envisage Barrie's characters rarely got further than the upper half of the body. When it was a question of the precise cut of the skirt of a tunic, exact length of a cloak, or clothing of the legs, it seemed that, like Byron, he *never looked so low*.'[45] These tactics had driven the needlewomen to despair, given Barrie a high temperature and aggravated Cochran's arthritis for which, at rehearsals, he wore a splint. It was to everyone's relief, John's included, that Stern took over these costumes.

To Barrie's irritation (he retired to bed shortly afterwards) John had depicted Bethlehem as a Provençal village, decorated with terraces, boulders and cypress trees. The principal set, and

this originally on cartridge paper . . . and I suggested he should do it on a linen panel in thin oils or aniline dye; which he did, and it was an enormous success, and, as it was in scale to the scene, was inserted in the church construction.'
Apollo, October 1965, p. 324 n. 3.

John's main contribution to the play, was the Israelite outpost of Act II scene ii. For this he provided 'a dark and lowering sky, with immense rocks in the foreground, from which descended a slender waterfall, giving rise to the brook from the bed of which David chose the pebbles he was to sling at Goliath'.[46] Although attending a few rehearsals – 'an impressive figure splendidly sprawled across two stalls'[47] – he did not travel up to see the opening night at Edinburgh. The greatest problem that night had been how to force the actors on and off stage. 'Having delivered their exit line,' John Brunskill, the scenery builder, remembered, 'they were forced to clamber over a number of rocks before getting off stage.' By the end of the scene the stage was crowded with these bruised and scrambling actors attempting to reach or retire from their lines. In a desperate move to halt these gymnastics, Cochran again called on Stern, this time to re-design the set. Numbers of rock-units were scrapped, the sky replaced with a white canvas cloth, the inset scenes altered and, worst of all, John's waterfall – 'how charmingly it glittered and fell!' – dried up. Stern, who respected John, describing him as 'the typical painter, and we understand one another', hated this work which went against the 'artists' freemasonry'. Such was the guilt that no one dared to tell John of the alterations. He arrived at His Majesty's Theatre for the London premiere on 12 December 1936 happily ignorant of the fearful mutilations to his work.

The change to Act I had been minimal, and John sat through it undisturbed. But when the curtain rose on Act II, he rose from his seat, hurried from the auditorium, and stayed for the rest of the performance in the bar, pondering this betrayal. 'This play was a complete flop from the start, and I wasn't sorry.' But later, having been handsomely paid by Cochran, he concluded: 'It dawned on me too late that I had neither the technique nor the physical attributes for this sort of work, apart from the question of my artistic ability.' Stern's final comment, which goes wider to achieve unconscious irony, corroborates this: 'How I envy John, as he stands in front of his easel, palette and brushes in hand.'

One advantage of working in collaboration is that it provides people towards whom one may extend the finger of blame.

Alone with his easel, palette and brushes, John could only point
to failures in geography, to weather and viruses. In June 1935
he borrowed Vanessa Bell's studio; by November that year he
had moved into Euphemia's house at 49 Glebe Place (later owned
by Gerald Reitlinger and by Edward Le Bas); then in March
1938 he rented the 'cottage' in Primrose Codrington's estate,
famous for its garden, at Park House in South Kensington. From
these places he came and went, tampering with their lighting
then leaving them for good. In 1940, when bombs began falling
on London, the top windows of Park Studio, fantastically illuminated in the night sky, were smashed, and John moved on to
33 Tite Street* in Chelsea where he rested comfortably throughout the blitz.

'My life seems to get more and more complicated,' he wrote
wonderingly.[48] The multiplicity of studios reflected this confusion. In 1936 Dorelia had rented 'for the large sum' of £12 a
year, the 'Mas de Galeron', a little farmhouse 'au ras des Alpilles'
behind 'les Antiques' at St Rémys-de-Provence.† 'There are 3
large rooms and one smaller one,' Dorelia wrote to him. 'One
would make a good studio for you. It is quite isolated with a
rather rough track ... There are grey rocks on one side, vines
and olives and an immense view from the north ... Why not
come down?'

John went down for the first time in September 1937 and,
against his worst fears (he had imagined Dorelia might be mad)
loved it. The house was built into the hillside, a little grey old
building, its floors uneven, with small surprising rooms turning
up round corners and down steps. Outside a hot aromatic terrace, flanked by pine trees, overlooked a field of stones, olives
and euphorbias. And just above them ran the rocky Alpilles,
dotted with green scrub and the spiky plumes of cypress trees –
'an endless sequence of exquisite landscapes'.[49] Anyone who
knows and likes this landscape will enjoy John's paintings of it,
recognize how well he has observed it. Yet these paintings lack
the inspirational quality of his early landscapes, and he con-

---

* Where Whistler had lived during 1882–5, and Sargent between 1887 and
1915.

† Now re-named 'Mas de la Fé', it has been taken over by Alphonse Daudet's
grand-daughter-in-law.

fessed to his neighbour there, Marie Mauron, that 'ces Alpilles attendent encore *leur* peintre – mais ce n'est pas moi. Regardez! Ces jeux de gris, de bleu, de rose, ces touffes de plantes aromatiques, en boules, taches, traits sur le roc de toutes couleurs insaisissables, me désespèrent'.*[50]

The next year he went again, and once more in July 1939 with Dorelia, Vivien, Zoë and Tristan de Vere Cole, intending to stay there three months. 'Il n'y aura pas de guerre,' Derain scoffed as the two artists sat peacefully drinking on the terrace of the Café des Variétés and watching the soldiers and horses crowd through the streets. 'C'est une blague.' But the clouds of war thickened round them and it became, John suspected, 'necessary to make a decision'. It was eventually Dorelia, responding to urgent telephone calls from Poppet, who decided. At the last moment they set off, John gaining maximum delay with the aid of dictionaries, by sending a very long telegram to England in correct French. 'C'est la guerre! C'est la guerre!' the farmers cried, as they fumed and thundered through the villages in a furious convoy of two cars. At Orléans they put up for one night, and while Dorelia and Tristan slept, John led out Vivien and Zoë to a night club run by two spinsters from Kensington, and full of gay girls. 'And what do you do, sir?' one of them asked John. 'I am a ballet dancer,' he explained quietly.

Le Havre, which they reached on 2 September, was in confusion. There were no porters, the last boat was preparing to leave and passengers were told they must abandon their cars and only take what luggage they could carry. John's car had now run dry of petrol and rested on a rival passenger's baggage. Money changed hands, and somehow the cars were hauled on board. John was the last to embark, tugging a large travelling rug out of which splashed a bottle of Chateauneuf du Pape.

They drove back to Fryern. Next morning it was work as usual. John was painting Zoë in the old studio in the orchard. During a rest, he switched on the radio and they listened to

---

* But, Marie Mauron went on, 'ce désespoir-là éclatait d'un grand rire car, lui, savait qu'il recommencerait une toile le lendemain. Avec la même obstination, le même 'désespoir', le même enthousiasme, le même amour, vif et sans amertume, rancune ou vanité devant, tout de même de magnifiques réussites!'

Chamberlain's speech. Then he turned it off and without a word continued painting until the bell rang for lunch.

4. HIS FIFTIES, THEIR THIRTIES

'The disastrous decade', Cyril Connolly has called the 1930s.[51] For John, if in no other way a thirties figure, it was disastrous – 'the worst spell of my bloody life,' he called it.

The world around him, as it plunged towards war, had become horrific, and in its place he had created little. His artistic philosophy of 'meaninglessness' was not supported, in the abstract sense, by a grasp of form, and his paintings, though skilful, convey a curious emptiness. Once the early lyricism had faded, his flashing eye, searching for something fresh, found nothing on which to focus. The happy accident, travelling through the dark, came to him less often. And beyond this dark, lending it intensity, rose the shadow of Hitler out-topping the more substantial shape of Mussolini. To such sinister circumstances John's pretty girls, wide-eyed and open-legged, his vast unintegrated and unfinished compositions, his vacant landscapes appeared irrelevant.

Yet he worked hard. Reviewing his exhibition at Tooth's in 1938, the *Times* critic had expressed 'admiration for what is achieved and regret, with a touch of resentment, that so great a natural talent for painting, possibly the greatest in Europe, should have been treated so lightly by its possessor ... This is not to accuse Mr John of idleness ... As everybody knows there is a kind of industry which is really a shirking of mental effort ...'[52]

In the opinion of David Jones, who admired John, it was the company he kept that finally ruined him: in particular 'that crashing bore' Horace de Vere Cole. John had known Cole since before the First World War. He was a commanding figure, with needle blue eyes, a mane of white hair, bristling upswept moustaches and the carriage of a regimental sergeant-major. This exterior had been laid on to mask the effects of having only one lung, a shoulder damaged in the war and a considerable deafness. Fighting pomposity was what he claimed to be doing; but his real enemy, like John's, was actuality. What John liked about Cole was his way of repunctuating life with absurdity, so that it no longer read the same. His whoops and antics were often better to hear about, however, than be involved in. When John learnt how Cole, dressed as 'the Anglican Bishop of Madras', had confirmed a body of Etonians, he laughed out loud. But when Cole took some of John's drawings, sat in the street with them all day in front of the National Gallery, and, having collected a few coppers, came back with the explanation that this was their value on the open market, John was less amused. Cole liked to ruffle John's feelings 'for I think he gets too much flattery'. Rivalry and rages interrupted their friendship, sometimes with violence; but the bond between them held. John used Cole as his court jester; while Cole 'seemed to have no friends – except John,' A. R. Thomson noted. 'People who knew him avoided him.'

In the autumn of 1926 they had set out together on a walk through Provence. 'Horace was a famous walker in the heel and toe tradition,' John recorded, 'and, with his unusual arithmetical faculty, was a great breaker of records, especially when alone.'[53] Their expedition quickened into a fierce walking-match and, in the evenings, contests for the attentions of village girls. It was an exhausting programme which they at last agreed to cut short by taking to a fishing-boat. A. R. Thomson, who joined them for part of this competitive tour, remembers, 'in the bright moon, Horace flanked by John and I marched along the bridge over the Rhone – swinging arms, hats tilted, cigars. John's swaggers were natural, not put on. I watched Horace impersonating John. His plenty white hair, busy moustaches, fierce eyes. He was "Super-John".'[54] A caricature that Thomson drew, 'John and Super-John', catches much of their pantomine relationship – John leading, Cole an extravagant shadow behind, mocking, but needing John to parody.

It was a fantasy-friendship they enjoyed, part of a make-believe life; and when it collided with the actual world, it exploded. The course for this collision had been set early in 1928. It was this year, in the Café Royal, that Cole had met Mabel Wright. 'Mavis', as she was always to be called, was nineteen, a strikingly tall girl with big brown eyes, curly blonde hair and a fine and friendly figure. About her background she was secretive, confiding that her mother had been a child stolen by gypsies. In later years she varied this story to the extent of denying, in a manner challenging disbelief, that she was John's daughter by a gypsy. In fact she was the daughter of a grocer's assistant and had been at the age of sixteen a scullery maid. In 1926, clutching a golf club, she arrived in London and, despite her lack of education, took a post as governess to the children of a clergyman in Wimbledon. A year later she had become a waitress at Veeraswamy's, the pioneer Indian restaurant in Swallow Street.

John was one of those that night at the Café Royal who had witnessed Cole break through a circle of men and make an assignation with Mavis. He was not pleased at being out-John'd, but, despite 'our pitched battles',[55] the romance persisted. Two years later, when Cole obtained a divorce from his first wife, they married. It was like a practical joke that misfired, and from that time on everything began to go wrong. But for Mavis it was an extraordinary leap upwards along her altitudinous career. On coming to London she had learnt the astonishing power of sex. This was her talent. Already a winner of beauty contests, she was naturally affectionate and liked to break the polite distance between people by touching them. But sex, she felt, was not enough; for real security she must acquire education, and she selected Cole to play Professor Higgins to her Eliza Doolittle. To have married him was a triumph, for was he not an Old Etonian and a de Vere, a cousin of Neville Chamberlain, rich, cultivated, famous?

Cole, now fifty and a sufferer from what John called 'pretty-girl-itis', was very possessive of his twenty-two-year-old wife; but Mavis had no wish to be restricted, and their marriage was full of plot and tension. Under this strain, Cole's antics grew manic. After a hard day's joking, he would set out late at night with bell, candle and shroud to haunt houses. By an unhappy perversion, he had begun to interpret whatever he misheard to his own disadvantage, and reacted excessively. Then, a last bad joke, he lost almost all his money in an unlikely Canadian venture. Reality, which had been leaking into his life for so long, now overflowed. To struggle free, he left Mavis and fled abroad.

It was at this moment that John stepped forward to help –

himself. 'You must be frightfully lonely I fear,' he sympathized with Mavis. That year, 1934, she became his mistress and on 15 March 1935 she gave birth to a son, Tristan Hilarius John de Vere Cole. 'What a whopper!' John exclaimed in delight. One thing was certain: Horace, disconsolately exiled in France, could not have been Tristan's father. John himself immediately assumed that role. In a letter to Wyndham Lewis, he explained: 'Tristan is not Cole's son, though born in wedlock ... at my last meeting with Cole, before he departed for France, he stung me for £20 which, of course, he never repaid. So when Mavis deserted him after four years of matrimonial bliss, I felt no compunction in taking it out in kind.'[56]

But the initiative was less with John than this suggests. Though Mavis was not intelligent, she was shrewd. Her attractions for him were glaring: she was his 'sweet honey-bird', sexy, eye-catching, easy-going. Round those of whom she was fond she spun a protective aura, from which John specially benefited. She brought a zest to his life, made him feel young and vigorous again. He sent her 'tasty poems' about orgasms, did drawings of her with legs kicked high and wide. 'She is really a good wench,' he urged Dorelia, 'and has a good deal of *gumption*.' But Dorelia saw a different Mavis: someone who was using her sex, like honey, to lure John away from Fryern so that she might marry him. One of the guests at Fryern, Andrea Cowdin, remembers Mavis playing on the floor with Tristan, rolling about and laughing and 'being delightful', but always with an eye on John who sat there gloomily without a word or sign. John's letters to Mavis and Dorelia indicate that, if only for the sake of his 'nerves', he wished them to be friends. But, though outwardly polite, they recognized more clearly than he their opposing interests.

Mavis was not perhaps 'mysterious' but she could be elusive. She would disappear down to her cottage in the West, or suddenly stop answering letters. In her absence John became an old man. Sometimes there were weeks of suspense, and 'I cannot bear it'. He knew she had affairs with other men and would imagine her in bed with all manner of commercial travellers from Birmingham, Manchester and Sheffield. 'Try to hold yourself in till our next,' he would beg. Then she would return to

London, generous, beautiful, irresistible; the sun would shine again and he was young.

Though Mavis pulled hard, and John wobbled a little, she could not pluck him from Dorelia. By 1936 she had switched tactics. Putting Tristan into a children's home, she went down to Cornwall from where she announced her impending marriage to a man she called 'the Tapeworm', six feet seven inches tall who 'looks as if he has come from another planet'.[57] Dorelia's response was an offer to bring up Tristan at Fryern. John was overjoyed.*

Because of Mavis's passionate indecisiveness, John decided legally to adopt her son. 'Are you clear about adopting Tristan?' he asked Dorelia (September 1936). She was. But Mavis's powers of incoherence were such that no legal formula could be devised to contain them, and when Tristan went to Fryern in 1937 it was under a wholly informal arrangement. Mavis herself was now free to cast her eyes on a target even loftier than the tapeworm. In the summer of 1937 she had gone one day to Maiden Castle, where the archaeologist Mortimer Wheeler was working. 'I was wandering about at the eastern end of Maiden Castle when I saw a curious entourage on its way towards me,' Mortimer Wheeler recalled. 'It consisted of Augustus John and his party, in the odd clothes they always wore. Mavis was skipping in front on long legs; very distinctive that skipping walk of hers – I was greatly taken with her straight away. All work stopped as the cavalcade arrived.'[58]

By the following year Mavis had elected to marry Mortimer Wheeler and let him 'run in harness' with John. 'It will be like an amputation to let you go,' John protested. '. . . I felt you were part of *me*.' He did not accept this operation without a fight. Seeing himself *in loco parentis*, he simply declined to give Wheeler his consent: 'You must wait. I haven't finished with her yet.' On one occasion, reduced to 'a mass of nerves and

---

* 'Mavis was somewhat hysterical and required a good deal of calming down. I think she'll probably marry this man who seems very devoted but she won't tell me anything decisive. I think it's very angelic of you to offer to take charge of Tristan. Mavis has several times asked me if you would. I said I wasn't going to ask you to do any such thing. I don't know if she's really prepared to part with the child.' John to Dorelia (undated).

brandy' by Wheeler's 'grinning mask', he most alarmingly lost his temper, writing to apologize next day. 'I was in a wrought-up state and have been for some time ... Do write and say you will be friends again.' In a desperate moment he had challenged his rival to a duel. 'As the challenged party,' Wheeler related, 'I had choice of weapons. Being a field gunner I chose field guns.'* John, declaring this to be 'very ungentlemanly conduct' bowed to the inevitable, and, putting the best face on it, advised Mavis to accept this 'distinguished personality' as her husband. They were married in March 1939,† occasioning a brief interlude in John's relationship with Mavis.

But there was an awkward corollary. In many of his letters to her, John assures Mavis that Tristan is 'full of beans', 'in the pink', 'incredibly beautiful' and 'eating well'. 'Don't disturb yourself,' he urges her. 'Dodo seems absolutely stuck on him.' But Mavis was never reconciled to leaving Tristan at Fryern, and one day in January 1941 she abducted him. John at once sent off an indignant letter protesting at this 'Rape of Tristan' to Mortimer Wheeler who, in his tactful reply (31 January 1941) explained: 'Mavis has always regarded Fryern Court as her real home and you and Dodo as an integral part of her life. This little episode is entirely subordinate to that overwhelming factor ... The fact is, Mavis does not want to feel that T's destinies are completely beyond her control and that she is merely a name in the visitors' book.'

'The Battle of Fordingbridge', as Wheeler called it, was quickly over. John and Dorelia had no legal rights and in any case Tristan continued to spend a number of his holidays at Fryern. 'The incident is closed,' John assured Mavis. Almost at once they were back on friendly terms. But he remembered – this and much else that he tried to drink into oblivion.

'Soon I will be ready to paint you off in *one go*,' John had written to Mavis. 'That is what I live for.' But though he drew

---

* He later attributed this procedure to a speech made in parallel circumstances by Shaw's Captain Bluntschli: '. . . I'm in the artillery; and I have the choice of weapons. If I go, I shall take a machine gun . . .' (*Arms and the Man*, Act III).

† John and A. P. Herbert were witnesses.

plot was confused, a tremendous atmosphere of
built up. Caitlin was on stage for most of the per-
ut when the exigencies of the theatre demanded it,
xit, while the two men made their entrances. The
ughout was remarkable, and there were many
onologues in the high-flown style. To the spectators,
eyes, the outcome appeared uncertain. But a year
spell in the Charing Cross Hospital, Caitlin married
nzance registrar's office; and when their first child
hn and Richard Hughes were godfathers.
then moved, the Thomases, to Laugharne and, as
f Richard Hughes, were said to feel 'nervous' of
there. John too was nervous. Sometimes he put up
e, 'Sea View, for a night or two 'in circumstances of
squalor'.[67] It had been to relieve this austerity that
n some furniture, including 'a wonderful bed'. At
he went up to his room, Mervyn Levy remembered,
o stuff ten-shilling notes and pound notes in his
sort of reddy-brown notes, and hang this vast coat
chair. Then we would creep upstairs and nick a
it was the only way of gaining any money from
Though 'bloated and dumb from his deafness'[69]
elped Dylan in a number of practical ways) was
f these raids. In *Finishing Touches* he gives as his
n the belief that Dylan had once been a Communist,
that attached himself to no other political move-
his propensity for sponging on his better-to-do
s could be dignified by such a name. In any case he
be relied upon as a borrower ...'[70]
help to explain the grudging tone of John's essay.
yns, was 'a genius' – but his shove-ha'penny was
o *Under Milk Wood*, in which 'there is no trace of
omerangs bruised John badly, though they were
tempts at wit, the tone of which misfired. 'There
,' he explained to D. S. MacColl, 'only a little play-
he affection between them, much enlivened by
was on Dylan's side partly filial, and within John
ist behind a prickly barricade of 'unsentimental'
has a split personality of course,' he wrote to Mary

and painted her often, this 'supreme picture ... which I know
would come off at the right time' never did come off. In taxis or
at dinner parties, on almost any occasion, she rejoiced in flinging off her clothes and would strike provocative attitudes towards John who, when severe, restricted his drawing to her face.
In Cornwall or Provence he led her out into the country, posed
her achingly against some expert expanse of rocks and trees,
then painted. But the finished canvases were of landscapes un-
tenanted by any figure. Yet he needed her company: she gave
him the 'authentic thrill'. His feelings for her were intensely
sentimental. Though Mavis could disguise the fact, the pictures
proclaim it: he was losing his sexual drive. At the beginning of
the war he was in his sixty-second year. His age, the psychological uncertainty of his work, and alcohol which 'provokes the
desire and takes away the performance' had left their mark.
His vigorous letters to Mavis, with their characteristic signing
off, 'Yours stiff and strong', urge a degree of potency that only
she could summon up. 'I drink but I am not a "boozer". I have
affairs of the heart but I do not womanize,' he wrote in a letter
to D. S. MacColl (14 January 1945). 'Drinking helps (for a time)
to overcome the horrors of a world into which I rarely seem to
fit; love renews (alas for a time) the divine illusion of beauty. By
which you may perceive that my soul is sick.'[59]

This sickness was a pessimistic sentimentality replacing the
lyrical romanticism of his early years and the 'hectic sexuality'
of the 1920s. His portraits of women between the 1930s and late
1940s are sweet and feeble echoes of eroticism. Far better were
his paintings of exotic flowers to which he responded visually
as if they were girls, but which did not involve his feelings on
such a disastrous scale.

Mavis was the chief mistress-model of these years, but his
agitation over her became the reason 'why I haven't had much
success painting of late'. Other models to whom he escaped
were sometimes less unsettling. Of these, two were daughters
of his old friend Francis Macnamara: Brigit (who was briefly
engaged to Caspar) and Caitlin (who was to marry Dylan
Thomas). Brigit was the better model. Though John depicted her
as a fit companion for Falstaff,[60] she was a sensitive person. She
had an instinctive sympathy with John, independent of words.

'An intonation, a pause, a movement from Brigit's ... hand was answered by Augustus with a smile that started slowly all over his face and faded in his beard ... In this shorthand of long term sympathy, the eaves-dropper might catch a hint or two, yet the depth of the meaning was a secret kept between them.'[61] She saw the terrifying glare, the tremendous male arrogance: but she saw through them to someone more interesting. He would pounce on girls, but work always came first. Even at sixty, she remembered, his body was good – well-shaped hands and feet, narrow hips, small bones.

Caitlin, her sister, remembers something else. She had been in love with one of John's sons, but this first passion was not returned. 'Almost her second,' according to Constantine Fitz-Gibbon, 'which was returned, was for Augustus himself, though he sometimes became confused and thought she was his daughter as well.'[62] Later she denied this passion for John, claiming only one 'luridly vivid memory ... pure revulsion ... and inevitable pouncing ... an indelible impression ... of the basic vileness of men'.[63]

She was, John noted, 'apparently in a perpetual state of disgust with the world in general'.[64]

It was John who introduced Caitlin to Dylan Thomas. In Constantine FitzGibbon's version he had met Dylan at The Fitzroy Tavern and it was at another pub, The Wheatsheaf, that he brought the two of them together: 'Come and meet someone rather amusing.' Caitlin, 'quite mute',[65] nervously approached, Dylan at once proposed and 'within ten minutes'* they were in bed together, spending several days and nights at the Eiffel Tower and charging everything to John's account. But however 'deaf and obtuse' John might be, Caitlin explained, there was a danger he might find out. So they parted, Dylan for Cornwall, she to Hampshire to continue her energetic sittings.

By means of an elaborate plot they met again in the summer of that year, 1936, in Richard Hughes's roofless castle at Laugharne, Dylan in the interval having contracted gonorrhoea.

Caitlin, Hughes remembers, was very pretty and gauche and, though twenty-two years old (she concealed her age from Dylan), impressed him as about 'the equivalent of eleven years

* Dylan's own estimate, cheerfully exaggerated.

---

of age'.[66] She arrived with
there was much giggling
visible evidence, at least to
morning John (possibly at
the Hugheses invite Dylan
ing awfully near Laughar
stayed the night. Dylan an
before.*

John was judging a p
Eisteddfod in Fishguard, a
cylinder Wolseley, 'the P
too; but when John arrive
alone with Caitlin who lo
been fed on cream'. 'Wl
gutter,' drawled John, slu
in. 'What happened?' 'I p
bring a drunk man to a h

It transpired that at C
day John had felt irritate
making. It may also h
gonorrhoea, he felt mora
Carmarthen, Dylan had i
Caitlin to Laugharne. But
raised their fists in the
pleads that 'he and I ne
been literally true only
qualified as blows, and Jo
battle: which seems pro

The following mornin
ping outside into the su
was set for a spectacular
house, and no sooner ha
John, judging it to perfe

* John, however, seems no
letter to Dorelia (20 July 19
Caitlin who wanted to see Dy
the next day by a strange coin
drove them to Fishguard, Cai
of the car.'

Though
melodran
formance
she woul
timing t
rhetorica
wiping th
later, afte
Dylan at
was born.

They h
neighbour
John's vis
at their ho
indescriba
he gave th
night, whe
John 'used
pockets, ri
of his ove
few, becau
Augustus.'
John (who
well aware
interpretati
though 'aft
ment, unle
acquaintan
could alwa

These fac
Dylan, he
superior far
wit'. Such
themselves
is no rancou
ful malice'.
this malice,
could only
jibes. 'Dylan

Keene. 'He can be unbearable and then something else comes out which one loves.'

Of the two oil portraits John did of him in the late 1930s one, now in the National Museum of Wales, is possibly his best painting of this period – a 'diminutive masterpiece', as Wyndham Lewis described it, that perfectly illustrates his pen-portrait in *Finishing Touches*: 'Dylan's face was round and his nose snub. His rather prominent eyes were a little veiled and his curly hair was red, or auburn rather. A pleasant and slightly sardonic smile registered amusement and, I think, satisfaction. If you could have substituted an ice for the glass of beer he held you might have mistaken him for a happy schoolboy out on a spree.'

Both John and Dylan were 'bad Welshmen' whose ruin was precipitated by America, where they broke new records in drinking. There are passages in John's essay that could be applied with equal stringency to himself since, perhaps unconsciously, he identified himself with the younger man. Having passed on some of his own traits in this way, he is enabled to deplore them the more heartily. It was a technique, peculiarly successful in the case of Dylan Thomas, he often used to pep up his writing, and it accounts for the paradox that his sharpest sallies are directed towards those with whom he felt most in common.

5. CHILDREN OF THE GREAT

When walking the streets of Chelsea, so the story goes, John had a habit of patting local children on the head 'in case it is one of mine'.* Calculations over the quantity of these children floated high into the land of fantasy reaching, in James Laver's autobiography, a number of three figures at which, in the opinion of Max Beerbohm, John stopped counting.[71]

John was never quick to deny fathering a child. Improbable rumours, incapable of proof, seethed around him. But the basis

* But Romilly John remembers that 'as a small boy I frequently encountered Augustus striding arrogantly down the King's Road on his way to the Six Bells. He never deigned to notice one on these occasions. Nor did it occur to me to claim any relationship. We passed as perfect strangers.' Romilly John to the author, 25 January 1973.

of this legend was his election by many people he had never met
– in particular chronic readers of newspapers – as an archetypal
father figure. It is not uncommon for children, especially girls
perhaps, as they grow up and away from their parents to
wonder for a while whether they are illegitimate. To the
imagination of these girls, especially if there was a connection
with art or with Wales, the personality of Augustus John came
readily to mind. One middle-aged woman in North Wales has
written in a Welsh magazine the · elaborate story of John's
friendship with her mother, ingeniously tracing her own family
connections with the Johns to show that, in addition to being
her father, John was a cousin. Every detail that can be checked
pushes this narrative further into invention.

Another example is sadder and perhaps still more revealing.
In about 1930, Sheila Nansi Ivor-Jones, a schoolgirl, was sent by
her parents to see a Dr Clifford Scott. Although she was not
unintelligent, Sheila had done no good at school, could not stick
to any routine, and was either annoyed or made lethargic by
school life. Her father, Robert Ivor Jones, headmaster of West
Monmouth School at Pontypool, and his wife Edwina Claudia
Jones (*née* Lewis) were worried. But Sheila did display some
artistic ability and, after going up to an art-school in Tunbridge
Wells, blossomed out. Her troubles seemed over. In October
1937 she transferred to the Slade and by the 1940s had become
an art instructor at the Chelsea School of Art. Then, on 15
February 1948, she again consulted Dr Scott, complaining of
terrible nightmares about horses, fighting and hysterical love-
scenes; and adding that she had discovered herself to be the
illegitimate daughter of Augustus John – to which she attributed
this trouble. The nightmares and delusions persisted throughout
this year, growing worse. She seems to have neglected herself,
lost her job and in February 1949 was admitted to West Park
Mental Hospital, Epsom, where on 28 February she died. The
cause of her death was recorded as bronchial pneumonia and
acute mania.

Sheila Ivor-Jones (she hyphenated her name in London) had
been born at Llanllwchaiarn in Montgomeryshire on 28 September 1912 and, from the evidence that exists, it seems most unlikely that John could have been her father. If then, this was

fantasy, it seems to have taken possession of her after the death of her real father. She may have seen John fairly frequently in Chelsea since she lived round the corner from Mrs Fleming's house (and no distance from John's various studios) at 77 Cheyne Walk above 'the Cheyne Buttery' – tea and supper rooms and a Great House run by a man called Stancourt whose christian names were John Augustus.

Whatever the source of her delusion, it represents, in an extreme form, a tendency that was widespread. The irony was that, as an actual father, John was extraordinarily difficult. 'I have no gifts as a paterfamilias,' he admitted.[72] For all his children self-help was the only salvation – the key for entry into, as to liberation from, the powerful John orbit. Fryern Court 'wasn't my home', wrote Amaryllis Fleming, 'but it was the only place I ever felt utterly at home in'.[73] Another daughter who was not often at Fryern felt her exclusion to be a paralysing deprivation of love. But the magnetic field rejecting her trapped others, Ida's sons and the son and daughters of Dorelia, who needed supreme willpower to escape.

John was partly a Victorian father, in part a caricature of modern liberalism. Children were to be seen and not heard, painted and glared into silence. He was particularly alert to table-manners. An incorrectly pronounced syllable or a swear word uttered in front of the girls would provoke a terrible pedantic wrath. 'I have awful memories of those meals,' Poppet recalled. One morning when she arrived at breakfast wearing her dress the wrong way round, she was picked up by the scruff of the neck, deposited behind some curtains, and left. At another time when Vivien committed a social misdemeanour, John refused to speak to her and all communication had to pass via a third party. 'As a child I can only say I feared him greatly,' Vivien wrote, 'and if spoken to by him would instantly burst into tears.'

But he was more severe with the boys. The tension between them was sometimes agonizing. One of them had a habit of smelling his food before starting to eat, and this infuriated John so much that once he pushed his face hard into the plate. His son retaliated by flinging the plate out of the window, but John made him go out, collect every morsel from the gravel and eat it. It was a battle of wills and John, with all the advantages, won.

John's silences could last thirty hours or more and were echoed back at him by his brooding sons. 'Why don't you say something?' he growled at David, whose silence darkened. But it was the quality of Robin's silence, grimmer than any of the others', seeming to accuse him of something literally unspeakable, that maddened John most. 'He hardly utters a word and radiates *hostility*,' he wrote to Mavis. 'I fear I shall reach a crisis and go for him tooth and nail. That happened once here and I soon floored him on the gravel outside.' He affected to believe that all his sons were slightly mad. Could there be something *glandular?* he wondered. Should he hire strait-jackets? 'Do you think it would be a good idea,' he asked Inez Holden, 'to have the lot of them psycho-analysed?'

'As children,' Romilly acknowledged, 'we made no allowances for, since we had no conception of, the despairs of an artist about his work.' John's glooms, charged with an intense hostility to those near by, cut him off from easy family relationships. 'They may have been a bid for love and reassurance,' wrote Romilly, 'the psychology of this phenomenon is a little obscure! Needless to say they produced dread.' Yet he resented not being confided in, and wanted in a discreet way to be loved by all of them. 'On rare occasions when Augustus and I talked, it was almost invariably about Sanskrit,' remembers Romilly, 'a subject neither of us knew much about.' On more intimate matters they were dumb.* At the end of a letter written to a Dartmouth schoolmaster (a retiring bachelor of thirty-eight) John added a timorous postscript suggesting something might be mentioned to his son Caspar about sex: 'Boys of Caspar's age stand particularly in need of help and enlightenment on certain subjects, don't you agree?' For almost all his life, John used conversation as a neutral territory where he and his sons might guardedly

---

* On one occasion when one of his sons wrote to him in personal distress, John confined his reply to matters of prose style which 'I find overweighted with latinisms', and to the envelope itself upon which 'you have, either by design or carelessness, omitted to place the customary dot after the diminutive *Hants*.. In an old Dane Courtier this seems to me unpardonable but I put it down to your recent bereavement.'

meet without giving anything away. It was a tragedy, Caspar remembered, that, by the time they could talk on easier terms, John was deaf, and everything had to be conducted with a shout.

To this severity John added a bewildering generosity and the attitude of *laissez-aller*. He gave all his sons good allowances well into their twenties when he could not well afford it. If he was open-handed, he was also open-minded, allowing the boys at the ages of ten or twelve to choose their own schools. David had gone to Westminster, Caspar to Osborne, Robin (briefly) to Malvern and then to Le Rosey in Switzerland, Edwin and Romilly separately to an eccentric school near Paris. As for the girls, when asked at the ages of nine and seven whether they would like to go to school, Vivien burst into tears and Poppet said 'No'. A procession of tutors and governesses (one of whom Romilly married) were erratically employed, but the two sisters passed more of their time with ponies than people, and in later years John would pour scorn on their lack of education. He showed real interest only in their art work, though when Vivien went up to the Slade she was under specific orders that there was to be no instruction. 'Little', she remembers, 'came of this.'

The sisters had served almost as stern an art apprenticeship as the boys. 'I had to look at him,' wrote Poppet, 'and if I caught his eye he would ask me very politely to come and pose for him, and this would mean the whole morning gone . . . all our plans for swimming at Bicton or riding in the forest with Vivien . . .' These 'gruellings', as Vivien called them, continued until the girls married, 'then ceased abruptly'. There was an occasional attempt at fancy-dress (Vivien, for example, depicted as a Russian peasant after a visit to Moscow) and a considerable number of nude drawings of them both, which, not identified by name, were mostly hurried off to Australia, Canada, Japan.

As they grew up their relationship with their father became more complicated. When Vivien took up dancing, hoping to go on the London stage, John violently objected on the grounds that it was not art but an entertainment for jaded businessmen. Towards both of them he was jealously possessive. No boy friend was good enough, since to be good enough he would have to prove himself better than John. 'Why should you bother with boy-friends when you have such a magnificent father?' he once asked Mollie O'Rourke, and this appeared to sum up his attitude. After Poppet's wedding to Derek Jackson, he hopped into the car at Fordingbridge beside his daughter and, happily acknowledging the cheers, was driven off with her while Jackson sat disconsolately next to the chauffeur.* 'He was like an old stag,' Poppet's second husband Villiers Bergne observed, 'with his herd of women and children round him. Interlopers were beaten off.'†

If it had been hard for boy friends, it was harder still for husbands. Vivien's husband, a distinguished doctor specializing in research into bone marrow, was known as her 'medical attendant'. At meals, John would sometimes draw caricatures of his in-laws, passing them round for comic appreciation; and his letters to all the family contain many invitations to disloyalty between his sons and daughters, their wives and husbands who, at one time or another, were 'revolting', 'villainous', or 'repulsive little swine' and who would generally learn this through some third party. His daughters-in-law ('no oil-paintings'), who he affected to believe had been chosen for their plainness so that his sons 'need fear no competition from me', had a scarcely easier time of it. A favourite theme of his was the grave exploration of how to do away with all this proliferating family. 'I know little of toxology but I have heard the merits of *ratsbane* well recommended. The only question is:

---

* These, apparently, were John's usual tactics. In a letter to Richard Hughes (29 March 1939), Dylan Thomas wrote that Augustus is 'out and more or less about now, although Mavis's wedding put him back a few weeks. We saw the newsfilm of the departure from the registry office, and Augustus, blowing clouds of smoke, hopped in the first car before bride and groom could get in . . .'

† 'I hope it will be their last visit,' he wrote after Poppet and Bergne had gone to Fryern for the first time. But he made an exception of Wilhelm Pol, the Dutch painter who became Poppet's third husband. 'This time I favour the match,' he told Caspar (1 March 1952). '. . . Poppet, a thorough bourgeoise, provided there is plenty to laugh at, reasonable access of food and drink, and of course the indispensable privileges of matrimony, will stay put.' To others he exclaimed, with an oblique slap at Edwin, Robin, Vivien and perhaps himself: 'Thank God there is a painter in the family at last!' In David Herbert's autobiography, *Second Son* (Peter Owen, 1973), Poppet is described as 'extremely attractive, she had almost as many boy friends as her father had mistresses'. p. 61.

should the whelps be included in the purge? Personally I am all for it.'

Possessive over his daughters, he was fiercely competitive with his sons; and it was with them that the most bitter battles were fought. One developed an eczema that would visibly spread over his skin during a quarrel. 'He is quite insupportable. I shall kill him soon,' John promised Dorelia – and in certain moods this did not seem an exaggeration. He genuinely wanted all of them to succeed and would take pleasure in their achievements; but he could not avoid putting obstacles in their path. He gave them money, he introduced them to useful people; but he could not give them any sense of direction. When David wanted to take up architecture, John recommended that he design a lunatic asylum in which he and his brothers could comfortably lodge. There was only one way for them to please him, and that was to be an unmitigated success, to excel everyone: anything else was rewarded with paralysing sarcasm.

By others, outside the family, the sons were treated like some special branch of the nobility. When they were to arrive at a party, the news was buzzed about. *Augustus John's sons are coming!* They grew anxious to disguise themselves, to avoid this vicarious limelight, play down the possession of the awful name John. David, for example, never referred to 'my father' but always to 'John' as if to underline his detachment.

All of them had talent but, in the shadow of the Great Man, they dwindled. David, who played the oboe for several major orchestras, eventually gave up music and, narrowly missing a career as public lavatory attendant, became a postman, turning in retirement to occasional furniture removals. Romilly, who had joined Francis Macnamara on the river Stour for long philosophical explorations of *Robinson Crusoe* and the Book of Genesis, later became the erratic apprentice to a farmer, then (though despising alcohol) a student innkeeper at John Fothergill's public house The Spread Eagle at Thame, before at last 'commencing author'. Perhaps his finest book was *The Seventh Child*, a minor masterpiece of autobiography, that John tried to dissuade him from publishing. When Romilly pressed for a reason, he looked harassed and, after casting round in his mind some minutes in silent agony, thundered out that Romilly had misspelt the name of a Welsh mountain.

Robin, it was held, achieved the most bizarre reaction against his father. After leaving school he became assistant to Sir Charles Mendel, Press attaché at the British Embassy in Paris. Despite his dislike of the Press, John accepted this as a fairly honourable beginning. When Robin gave it up to study painting, John was still obstinately delighted, believing that his son had a remarkable talent for drawing. Robin, however, concentrated on the study of colour, especially blue, 'from the scientific or purely aesthetic angle'.[74] It was this apparent neglect of natural ability, infuriating to John, that Robin appeared to perfect. He travelled widely, mastered seven languages, and was silent in all of them. Maddened by this misuse, as he saw it, of 'linguistic genius' John struggled to find him employment – with Elizabeth Arden. More appropriately Robin took a job 'in the censorship', being transferred to Bermuda and Jamaica where (care of the Royal Bank of Canada) he did fruit and flower farming in the hills, dabbling on lower levels in real estate. Over the years he wandered invisibly from job to job, from place to place, and in 1965 he married. 'I'm sure he [John] regretted our inability – as I did – to achieve a friendly and easy relationship,' Robin wrote. 'But the main obstacle was that he – fundamentally – was a rebel against established society and most conventions, while I hated Bohemianism and yearned for a normal life – which made me in my turn also a rebel – but in reverse.'[75]

Some variation in this pattern was offered by Edwin. His gift, in John's eyes, was for clowning, and the stage (which had been forbidden Vivien) was recommended. 'I feel strongly you yourself could make a great success on the stage,' John advised. 'You have a good voice and ear and an unusual comedic sense.' After studying art in Paris, Edwin accidentally became a professional boxer, winning, as 'Teddy John of Chelsea', seven of his first nine fights. 'Edwin fought a black man last Monday and beat him,' John wrote proudly to a friend. To these ring-side parties John led his family and friends in great spirits; and on one occasion he entered the ring himself, squared up opposite his son and had his photograph taken, bulging with satisfaction. 'I like him [Edwin] immensely,' he wrote to his son Henry. '... he has be-

come a tall hefty fellow full of confidence, humour and character'. This delight at Edwin's spectacular success was intensified
by his own father's horror. Old Edwin John, he told David, 'is
outraged in all his best feelings that Edwyn has adopted the
brutal and degrading profession of prize-fighter but everybody
else seems pleased except some Tenbyites who, according to
Papa, have decided that *my* little career is at an end in consequence of Edwyn's career in the Ring'. But one other person
disapproved: Gwen John. She told her nephew he was wasting
his time boxing and should become a serious artist. In the pull-
pugilist, pull-painter contest, the painter won and to John's
acute disappointment Edwin threw in the towel. Following
Gwen's death, he and not John was appointed her residuary
legatee, in charge of all her paintings. Often after this, when
father and son inflicted their company on each other, a sense of
impotence threatened John. It seemed better to stay apart. 'Is
your presence really necessary? . . . my advice is, Keep away.'

Caspar, the one who, from earliest days, had kept away, was
the exception. By 1941 he was a naval captain; by 1951 a Rear-
Admiral; by 1960 First Sea Lord and Chief of the Naval Staff.
Of his son's enthusiasm for ships and the sea John understood
nothing: but he understood success. 'My son Caspar hasn't done
too badly,' he remarked once to Stuart Piggott. Of course he
would make fun sometimes of 'the gallant admiral . . . looking
like a Peony in full bloom', but such sallies had no poison in
them. Their relationship seemed a grim enough affair, neither
giving an inch, but the more senior Caspar became the more
John thawed. 'Still in the navy?' he asked when Caspar returned
on leave. But though he took this success lightly, not embarrassing Caspar with encomiums, it afforded him deep satisfaction.

There was another son, Ida's fifth child, Henry: the odd one
out. He had been brought up by a stray cousin, Edith Nettleship, in the village of Sheet, near Petersfield. It was an energetic
upbringing: long walks in the open, long prayers indoors. While
serving as a nurse during the First World War, Edith had been
converted to Catholicism. She sent Henry to school at Stonyhurst College where, a little later, he too suffered conversion to
north-sea Catholicism. Sometimes in the holidays, and after he

had left school, he would come to Alderney and to Fryern, entering for a week or two the amazing world of his brothers and half-sisters, foreign to anything he had known. It was like a dream – the riding and tree-climbing; the invention with Romilly of a machine that *thought*; the urgent swopping of stories, information, books; the pictures; the endless talk of love and philosophy that continued in Henry's illustrated letters and included his poem about Eden in the style of Edward Lear and a complicated theological essay on 'Girls' Bottoms' much criticized for its inaccuracy. He was a strangely attractive figure to the Johns, with striking good looks, a vehement personality, his laugh fierce, his manner harsh and precise. At Stonyhurst he had gained a reputation as a brilliant scholar, actor and orator, and at week-ends would mount a platform at Marble Arch to argue dramatically on behalf of the Catholic Evidence Guild. He was respected, even feared; but he was too unconventional to be a popular boy. The problem was: with all his energy and gifts, what should he do? Father Martin D'Arcy had been sent down to Stonyhurst to meet him and, if he judged him sufficiently remarkable, groom him for the Jesuit priesthood. In his opinion and that of Father Martindale, Henry was outstanding; and so, in 1926, Father D'Arcy carried him off to Rome. Henry's letters from Rome to his father show in what strange way his Catholic training and John-like paganism had become fused into a charming fantasy:

Another thing which is absorbing is how I am going to bring up my children and how I am going to spend my honeymoon (supposing I don't become a p[riest]). I think the most awful thing that could happen to anybody would be to have horrible children ... I should bring them up in some sunny place by the sea, pack their heads with fairy-stories and every conceivable pleasant Catholic custom, be extremely disciplinary when need arose, and make them learn Japanese wrestling, riding, prize-fighting (i.e. not boxing), swimming, dancing, French, Latin, and acting from the cradle. We would have the most glorious caravan expeditions (like you used to do, didn't you?) in Devonshire and France and Wales. The catechism lesson, once a week, given by myself, would be a fête. At Christmas – Xmas tree, stockings, crib, miracle-play, everything. I would take them somewhere where they could play with poor children ... on at least one day of the week they would be allowed to run about naked and vast quantities of mud, soot and straw-berries etc. would be piled up for their disposal. All the apostolic precepts would have to be encouraged ... Tell me ... what amend-ments you suggest. Quick, else I shall be having them on my hands. The first Communion of the ten small Johns will be a magnificent affair; if possible it will be on the sands in the sun, and afterwards the whole family will sit round having great bowls of bread and milk. Then we shall go out in sailing ships and have dances when we come back and a picnic with a terrific stew ending up with Benediction and bed.[76]

Henry had not liked Rome, but everywhere he went, even the zoo, there at his side was Father D'Arcy, 'who is the *paragon*', he told John, '– he sees every conceivable point of view without being the least bit vague or cocksure, and allows himself to be fought and contradicted perhaps more than is good for me'. In an ejaculation of enthusiasm he invited John swiftly to 'come to Rome' so that he could 'cheer up D'Arcy and paint the Pope (green) and the town (red)'.

It was after his return that Henry decided to commit himself to the priesthood. In 1927 he entered as a novice the Jesuit House, Manresa, at Roehampton. He suffered and survived this rigorous training in spiritual exercises, but it altered him. By the time he went up to Heythrop College he had become passion-ately religious, discharging his fervent emotionalism into the-ology. No longer did the worlds of the two fathers, D'Arcy and John, mingle in happy fantasy; they frothed within him in a continuous chemical antipathy. 'You are like Fryern,' he wrote to Vivien. 'Fryern is a sort of enchanted isle – very beautiful and nice and kind and fantastic; but nobody ever *learns* any-thing there.' It was strict Neo-Thomist learning that, like some missionary gospel, he strove to implant there. Summoning up all the resources of Farm Street, he rained on them books and words. With time, and lack of consequence, these proselytizing exercises grew more frantic. 'Acquaint yourself with Romilly,' he ordered Father D'Arcy. 'Write to him. Save him from Be-haviourism ... send him something on psycho-analysis ... Start on immortality.' And then : 'There is no reason why David should travel separately. Therefore *get hold of him on the plat-form* and talk to him all the way. [Christopher] Devlin can go to the W.C. Hint forcibly to him that he should seek companions among the other youths . . .' But for conversion, the Johns seemed very unripe fruit, and the only result was 'our vocabularies have increased'.

Top of this Tree of Ignorance was John himself, a mighty plum. To scale such heights was an impossibility, yet Henry did not hesitate. At times, it even seemed to him he was gaining. 'Daddie says there might be "some small corner" for him in the Church,' he hopefully advised Father D'Arcy. But hope sank eternal. 'I'm afraid though we're at a deadlock. He spurns revelation entirely – says he's just as religious as we are.' John's objection to Catholicism was strong, mainly on political grounds, for he saw the Church as a reactionary power. He retaliated to Henry's sermonizing by endeavouring to undermine his faith. 'What do you believe in?' he asked.

What you're told I suppose. It would be a grand training for you to get out of your church and take your chance with common mortals. When I'm well and sane I detest the anti-naturalism of religiosity and become a good 'Pagan'. Chastity and poverty are horrible ideals – especially the first. Why wear a black uniform and take beastly vows? Why take your orders from a 'provincial', some deplorable decrepit in Poland. Why adopt this queer discredited premedical cosmogony? Why emasculate yourself – you will gradually become a nice old virgin aunt and probably suffer from fits which will doubtless be taken for divine possession. Much better fertilize a few Glasgow girls and send them back to Ireland – full of the Holy Ghost.

In the hope of miracles, Henry persuaded John to paint him in the robes of a Jesuit saint, but neither mystically nor aesthetically was the experiment a success. The struggle between them, for all its ludicrous aspects, was serious. 'I am a person of absolutely feverish activity . . . I am madly impatient and madly irritable and appallingly critical . . . yet I have an immense desire to be exactly the opposite of what I tend to be,' Henry had written. The Jesuit training, he believed, would teach him the secret of self-renunciation, the absolute submission of his rebellious spirit to the Will of God as manifested in Superiors. Yet while his family remained blatant 'bloody fools' basking in 'flashy old paganism', they were an intolerable irritant. He felt exasperated. 'I cannot *stand* the idea of myself as introspective and hesitating when there are things to be done, souls to be saved,' he burst out in a letter to Father D'Arcy. He had sought sublimation of his will, but confronted by the Johns' refusal *en masse* to be saved, he was unendurably frustrated. The philosophy he had elected to read at Campion Hall gave him no outlet for this turmoil. His letters, written in a shuddering hand, relentlessly illegible, are saturated with violence, page after page like a protracted scream. Watching him, Father D'Arcy (who had advised against philosophy) was increasingly worried by what he called 'your periods of heats ... the temperature you rise to, the complications ...'

At the end of his time at Campion Hall, Henry gained Second Class Honours in philosophy; but this was not good enough. That summer he submitted a dispensation of his vows and in August 1934, explaining why 'the Jesuit life is not any longer my cup of tea', he wrote: 'I am not leaving for intellectual reasons but for physical ones i.e. I do not think I meant to lead a *life of books only* ... nor can S.J. Superiors, generous as they are, be expected to cater for a permanent eccentric ... Having had a determined shot, I failed. I don't think the chastity question comes into it very much at all – at any rate disinclination for a life of chastity is not a prominent reason in my mind, though of course it is present ... I should not mind if people said I was funking disobedience – for that's quite plausible.'

This letter, far more controlled than anything he usually wrote, was sent to John via Henry's Provincial 'to make sure things are quite clear'. But other writings, that sit less politely upon the page, affirm a different truth. Henry appears to have been highly-sexed. At school he had had a devastating infatuation for another boy; and during his noviciate he seems to have become painfully involved, though in a more sophisticated way, in another unrequited passion. But he was not homosexual: it was simply that he was always in the society of other men. His correspondence to his Provincial and Superiors was extraordinary preoccupied with birth-control and questions of sexual ethics; while to others, such as his friend Robert McAlmon, it was 'one long wail about carnal desire ... and the searing sin of weakening'.[77] He also did a series of drawings, harshly pornographic, depicting a Jesuit entering heaven by violently explicit sexual means.

One of Henry's reasons for becoming a Jesuit had been 'the absence of any definite and satisfactory alternative'. He had hoped that the discipline, like that imposed on Caspar in the navy, might supply him with a purpose. He had won the high opinion of G. K. Chesterton and of Wyndham Lewis, but to follow them would be once more to 'lead a *life of books only*'. To John, he insisted: 'I have got to make what amounts to a fairly big fresh start, do a lot more "abdicating".' This took the form of plunging into the East End of London among the poor. 'He seems as mad as a hatter,' was John's verdict. 'His highly intensive education seems to have deprived him of any sense of reality – if he ever had any. He is studying dancing – for which he shows no aptitude – and the prices of vegetables.'[78] In the newspapers it was announced that, like Edwin, Henry had become a boxer and would wear the papal colours on his pants. John was not pleased. In the past he had often urged his son to 'quit this stately Mumbo Jumbo'. Yet he had not relished the manner of his quitting: it reeked of failure. Now he poured scorn on Henry for not discovering 'your own Divinity', and for still carrying out to the letter the injunction of Loyola by failing to look 'directly at any female'.[79] Julia Strachey, who saw him in November 1934, confirms this curious obliqueness: 'Henry John to tea . . . Sitting down in the small chair – which he placed sideways on to me – beside the bookcase, he conducted the whole conversation – metaphysical almost entirely – with his face turned away, and looked round at me only three times, I counted, during the whole session, which lasted from 4.30 till 7 . . . He refused both butter, and jam, for his scone.'

His experiments at slipping, or barging, from the metaphysical to the physical world over the next six months were unhappy. His chief girl-friend at this time was Olivia Plunket-Greene, a disconcerting creature with bobbed hair, 'pursed lips and great goo-goo eyes'.[80] She belonged to a generation that had found in the 1920s a new emancipation; but her outrageous, Charleston-crazy party-goings-on overlaid a character that was secretive. She was more fun-loving than loving, more intimate with crowds than single people, and apparently unwilling to make friends save from among those who, so Evelyn Waugh observed, 'were attracted by her and forced their way into her confidence'.[81] Waugh had been one of several who fell in love with her, but she played him off against a formidable rival, the black singer Paul Robeson. The old inhibitions, that social emancipation was lifting, she re-applied through religion. One evening, as she was dressing for a party, the Virgin Mary dropped in with instructions to pursue a life of chastity. This experience, in Waugh's judgement, was to make her 'one third drunk, one third insane, one third genius'.[82] She still seemed the fun-loving, party-going girl; but whenever she took off her clothes she would hear the Virgin Mary's voice, and immediately dress again. It was with her that Henry now sought to make his 'big fresh start'.

They held hands; she wrote poems; they talked; she let him kiss her: and then there were her love-letters. 'You are rather a darling with your long legs, and our jerky sensitive notions and your mind busy with acceptance, I would like to give you breasts and knees and curved embraces ... Wish you hadn't made me think of loving, I need to be loved, charms and skin and embraces soft and strong ... But if I let you hold me in your arms, it is for a variety of reasons ... Your embraces are lessons, but most enjoyable, like lessons in eating ice-cream or treacle.'

They had planned to spend part of June at a bungalow belonging to Henry's aunt, Ethel Nettleship, near Crantock in Cornwall. In the first week of June he received a six-page letter from Olivia explaining some of the reasons why she could not have sexual intercourse with him. 'I never knew how anti-birth control I was before but evidently I am.' He argued abstractedly; she promised to write again. He drove down to Cornwall; she did not come. On the evening of 22 June he bicycled to a desolate stretch of the cliffs, unbroken for miles by any habitation. He was seen walking along, swinging a towel, his aunt's Irish terrier at his heels: then he vanished.

Within forty-eight hours police were methodically searching the cliffs; scouts were lowered down on ropes to explore the caves, aeroplanes circled the region, and motor boats manned by coastguards with binoculars patrolled the seas. John, who had rushed down, joined in the hunt. 'I'm searching for my

blessed son who's gone and fallen in the sea,' he explained to
Mavis. 'I have no hope of finding him alive. His corpse will come
to the surface after nine days. A damn shame you are not here-
abouts ... I suppose I'll be here a few days although corpses
don't interest me.' The description of these few days he gave in
Chiaroscuro has been criticized for its unfeeling tone. Partly
this was the result of press reporters tracking him for a 'story';
and their melodramatic accounts of the artist 'speechless with
grief' and the 'disconsolate terrier' that for days continued to
appear in the newspapers. John never revealed guilt; he buried
it away to reappear as something else. That the son Ida had died
giving birth to should so recklessly have lost his own life tormented him, but he resolved to force the matter from his mind.
For the sake of appearance, he stayed in Cornwall a week exploring every detail of the coast, but directing much of his attention to the cormorants, puffins and seals. There was some cheerful weather for the search, and almost without thinking he took
a pad of paper and began sketching.

On 5 July, thirteen days after his disappearance, Henry's body
was washed up on the beach at Perranporth, dressed only in a
pair of shorts. 'Though it was without a face, from the attention
of birds and crabs, I was able to identify it all the same.'[83]

In the press Father D'Arcy was quoted as saying that there
could be no possibility of Henry's death having been anything
other than an accident. 'In many ways he was a cheerfully
irresponsible young man, and I only wonder that he has not had
a serious accident before. He always took risks and loved adventure.'[84]

John suspected otherwise. In 1943, travelling from London to
Salisbury, the train being held up by an air raid, he suddenly
became very talkative with the young man sharing his compart-
ment about 'the suicide'[85] of his son. Otherwise he showed little.
To the many people who wrote offering their sympathy he
agreed it was a tragedy that, having climbed out of the Society
of Jesus, Henry should have fallen into the sea. Dorelia too was
calm. 'It's perfectly all right,' she assured Lady Hulse. 'Henry
wasn't mine.'

6. BARREN OUR LIVES

'In spite of all,' a friend noted in her diary, 'he wasn't dead yet.' It was the others, family and friends, who kept 'popping off'. 'People seem to be dying off like flies,' he complained.[86] In December 1932 it was Mrs Nettleship. Over the years John and she had reached some sort of understanding – particularly strong when they could unite in disapproval (against, for example, Henry's Catholicism). As she lay dying in Weymouth Street, following a bad stroke, John burst in with two of his sons and a supply of beer. He settled down by the fire in her bedroom, Ursula Nettleship recalled, 'and talked about his life in France, about French literature, what he had read, about the quayside at Marseilles and the people he'd known there, all night replenishing our glasses from the beer bottles, watching mother ... had she been conscious she would have vastly appreciated both his presence and the completely unconventional Russian play atmosphere. And somehow, again in all simplicity, proving a very real support ... a good memory to treasure up.'[87]

The previous year it had been his old crony, the gypsy scholar John Sampson.* 'It's a ghastly blow to me,' John wrote to Margaret Sampson, 'for the Rai was so much part of my life.' He was cremated on 11 November and ten days later his ashes were carried to Wales. In those ten days mysterious messages passed between the gypsies, and the private ceremony was crowded with Woods and Lees, Smiths and Robertses and illustrious enthusiasts from the Gypsy Lore Society, judges, architects, girls, professors and that other great Rai, Scott Macfie, ill but indefatigable, mounted on a Welsh pony. The straggling procession, trailed at a cautious distance by a platoon of pressmen, was slowly overtaken along the way by John in his ulster and flowing scarlet scarf, who had been chosen to act as Master of Ceremonies. He led them panting up the slopes of Foel Goch, a mountain where Sampson had often rallied his crew. Here, eyes fixed in the distance, in his hand a smouldering cigarette, he delivered his eulogium.[88] It was a blue day, his words rang out over the bright green fields, the brown woods below. After this

* In his Will, Sampson left John 'as a small memento of long friendship my Smith and Wesson Revolver No. 239892'.

oration was over, a powerful silence. Michael Sampson, expressionless, scattered handful after handful of the ashes which swept in showers of fine white dust down the mountainside. The sun shone, the wind lifted their hair a little, blew the ashes round to land, like dandruff, on their shoulders. Then John, 'with his right hand out-stretched in a simple gesture as if actually to grasp that of his old friend',[89] spoke a poem in Romany. Everyone murmured the benediction *Te soves misto* (Sleep thou well) and, as the words died away, the music began – first the strings of the harp, then the fiddles, mouth organ, clarinet and dulcimer. Someone lit a match, started a pipe; and 'we each found our own way down the hilly slopes,' Dora Yates remembered, '... I myself saw the tears rolling down Augustus John's cheeks as he tramped in silence back to Llangwm.'[90]

In 1935, Horace Cole died in exile at Ascaigne. 'I went to his funeral,' John wrote, 'which took place near London, but I went in hopes of a miracle – or a joke. As the coffin was slowly lowered into the grave, in dreadful tension I awaited the moment for the lid to be lifted, thrust aside, and a well-known figure to leap out with an ear-splitting yell. But my old friend disappointed me this time. Sobered, I left the churchyard with his widow on my arm.'[91]

But there was one who refused to die, obstinately, year after year: John's father. Often he had given notice of doing so; and, summoning his courage, John would journey down to Wales. He liked on these death-trips to make use of Richard Hughes's castle as an Advance Base, inviting himself to tea, arriving shortly after closing-time and stabling himself there for ten days or so. 'My father,' he would say, 'is on his death-bed, but refuses to get into it.' Every morning he set off for Tenby in his 'saloon' car with a bottle of rum, stopping on the way to sketch and then, after a telephone call, arriving back at Laugharne. Richard Hughes, watching these forays, concluded that he must fear his father. Then, one day he would finally reach Tenby, find old Edwin John, like some Strindberg, miraculously recovered, and at once motor back to Fryern, his duty accomplished. Once, when his father was out for a short walk, he seized the opportunity and rushed back to Hampshire without seeing him.

'My father writes of the uncertainty of life and his Will – so I suppose he is thinking of moving onwards,' John notified Dorelia. That had been in 1925. Shortly afterwards the old man added a postscript: 'He would prefer to wait till Gwen and I have returned.' No obstacle, John considered, should be put in his way. In 1927 he advanced Gwen some money to buy and furnish Yew Tree Cottage* at Burgate Cross, very close to Fryern, so that the old man could take his leave of them together. For six weeks during August and September that year Gwen prepared this cottage, whitewashing its rooms, removing partitions, filling it with cups, curtains, counterpanes. 'My cottage is *lovely*,' she told Ursula Tyrwhitt. '... I don't mind seeing Gus now or the family.' She left England on 19 September, intending to return when 'I have sold 1 or 2 pictures as I don't want to be gêné for money and there is a lot of expense which Gus has paid . . . It is such a beautiful place . . . I sometimes want to be there very much.' She never returned. In her absence, Fanny Fletcher used the cottage, putting, perhaps, mild spells on it that might have jarred on Gwen. Or, it may be, she never allowed herself to sell the few pictures; or, simply, when it came to it, could not leave her barren room at Meudon.

Old Edwin John had also decided not to leave. He kept in remorseless touch with his children, his letters exhibiting a constant devotion to the weather. 'What is the weather like in Paris?' he would ask urgently. News of its behaviour in parts of America or Canada were passed anxiously on to France. 'The climate is very hot,' he instructed Gwen of conditions in Jamaica while Augustus was there, '– but usually tempered by a breeze from the sea.' As for home affairs, he was always finding himself dramatically overtaken by some 'nice breeze', afflicted with 'unbearable heat waves', or 'in the grip of a fierce blizzard'. 'Typical November weather' did not go unobserved, nor the curious fact that 'the cycle of time has brought us to the season of Christmas again'. As he advanced into his young nineties, so the climate hardened, 'the present weather being the worst I think I have ever experienced in my life'. 'How,' he de-

---

* She was by now a woman of property, having bought with part of the proceeds of her Chenil Gallery show a shack on a strip of waste ground in the Rue Babie. She continued also renting her room at Meudon.

manded, 'is it going to end?' However it was to end, it never seemed to. After each winter, with its unexampled frosts and snows, he revived. 'I am making good progress to recovery of health,' he assured Gwen on 28 March 1938. 'I eat and sleep well and take short walks daily . . . How near Easter has become has it not? I must really purchase some Easter cards . . .' On the afternoon of 7 April, while he was resting in bed, his house-keeper heard him call out: 'Good-bye, Miss Davis. Good-bye.' When she went up to see him, he was dead.

They buried him in the cemetery at Gumfreston, a tiny damp grey church two miles from Tenby where, with deliberation, he had played out the hymns on Sundays. After some delay, an inscription, considered to be definitive, was cut upon his grave-stone:

Edwin William John
1847–1938
With Long Life will I satisfy
Him and show Him my Salvation

John and Caspar attended the funeral; Thornton and Winifred were too far off; and Gwen did not come. She seldom went any-where now. Her passion for solitude was exercised, as John and Rodin had feared, at the expense of her health. She had ceased to paint and was allowing herself to die. The end came in September 1939 when, falling ill, she was overcome by a sudden longing for the sea. She caught a train to Dieppe, but collapsed on arriving there and was taken to the 'Hospice de Dieppe', where she died.* It was characteristic that, though she had brought no baggage with her, she had not omitted to provide for her cats. 'Few on meeting this retiring person in black,' wrote John, 'with her tiny hands and feet, a soft, almost inaudible voice, and delicate Pembrokeshire accent, would have guessed that here was the greatest woman artist of her age, or, as I think, of any other.'[92]

* At 8.30 a.m. on 18 September, not, as has previously been thought, 13 September.

II

Things Past

'I keep working away – what else is there to do?'
AUGUSTUS JOHN TO CONGER GOODYEAR
(3 OCTOBER 1943)

'I was always a success, in spite of my many failures'
AUGUSTUS JOHN TO MARY SORRELL
(9 JUNE 1948)

1. BLACK OUT

The hectic drive from St Rémy to Fordingbridge in the late summer of 1939 had been for John a journey into old age. The Second World War cut off his retreat and confined him to a narrower routine. On the surface there seemed little change: it was business as usual. 'I don't see what I can do but go on painting.'[1] But there was a difference to his campaign of work. He had been studying the papers that were coming to light from Gwen's studio. 'Astonishing how she cultivated the scientific method,' he exclaimed in a letter to his daughter Vivien. 'I feel ready to shut up shop.' His own *premier coup* days were long past, and he sought, adopting some of Gwen's patience, to invest more time than ever before in one or two imaginative pictures on the grand scale. 'I want a good 20 years more to do something respectable,' he had told Sir Herbert Barker.[2]

During the 1940s he laboured hesitantly over a cartoon in grisaille twelve feet long called 'The Little Concert'. The picture represents three itinerant musicians entertaining a group of peasants on the fringe of a land-locked bay. 'Though the conception is romantic, it is carried out with a classic authority of form,' wrote T. W. Earp when it was first shown at the Leicester Galleries in 1948, 'and is easily the most important achievement in English painting since the war.'[3] Wyndham Lewis, reviewing the same exhibition, described it as 'as fine an example of

Augustus John's large-scale decorative work as I have ever seen'.[4]
Yet it is difficult not to see such words as partisan. John himself
felt unsatisfied, snatched the picture back and after some revision re-exhibited it at the Royal Academy in 1950, after which
it went to a private collection. Even then he could not think of
it as 'finished', and as late as 1957 was proposing to 'warm up'
the monochrome.

Over the last twenty years of his life there was always one of
these big decorative compositions 'cooking' in his studio.
'Imaginative things occupy me mostly now,' he wrote to Conger Goodyear.[5] He worked on them laboriously, with much
anguish and persistence, continually revising and from time to
time challenging the public to see in them his finest achievement. 'They interest me very much and take up a lot of my
time,' he wrote. 'What will become of them God knows.'[6] This
reabsorption into imaginative work shifted the pattern of John's
life. Commissioned portraits, he told Dudley Tooth, had rarely
paid off and he was tired of making promises he was unable to
keep. The artist's loyalty should be to himself. 'The artist doesn't
consider the "Public" – which is the concern of the theatrical
producer, the journalist, the politician and the whore.'[7] The
First World War had obliterated the visionary world he had
created in his painting; the Second threatened to devastate the
world itself, destroying almost everything from which he might
derive spiritual energy. He resolved therefore to use the opportunity war provided to retire into greater privacy, there, by the
magical operation of his art, to re-illumine that paradise of sea
and mountain, women, children, age and youth, music, dancing
that had faded from his mind. From sixty till he died aged
eighty-three this task overwhelmed everything else.

It overwhelmed but it never eliminated his portrait painting,
for he was still a slave to the visible world. In the war years
portraits belonged to two categories: pretty girls and public
men. Drawing girls he could not resist. They were to be seen –
'living fragments of my heart'[8] – in shows at the Wildenstein,
Redfern and Leicester Galleries: magnified faces, almost identical, large-eyed and honey-lipped.*

* 'My drawing rather large heads appears to synchronize with wearing spectacles which do distinctly magnify . . . It often takes me ½ dozen tries before I

After weeks of refuge 'from contact with a depressing epoch', weeks in his studio spent painting 'huge decorations as remote as possible from the world we precariously live in',[9] a longing to paint portraits again, to be swept back into the world as an artist-biographer, would overcome him. It was an honourable pursuit in wartime, he believed, for an artist to paint those men who were leading the fight for one's country. He accepted a number of such commissions, but a lack of interest in his sitters helped to make this wartime portraiture unsatisfactory.* He did not set out to caricature; he wanted to produce noble painting. But the difficult short sittings and the absence of contact with his be-ribboned subjects would eventually tempt him into ambiguously exaggerated concoctions of paint that pleased no one. The most celebrated of these portraits, mopped-up shortly before the Normandy landing, was of Field-Marshal Lord Montgomery of Alamein. Montgomery would motor in his Rolls Royce each day to Tite Street and sit 'as tense as a hunting dog on a shoot'[10] upon the dais John had positioned for him. 'Monty has been sitting like a brick,' John reported to Mavis, 'and the picture progresses.' But it did not progress well. Montgomery felt downright suspicious of the whole business. It smelt fishy. 'Who is this chap?' he demanded. 'He drinks, he's dirty, and I know there are women in the background!'[11] John painted away in a spirit of deepening gloom. 'It's rather unfortunate the Colonel has to be in the room while I'm working,' he lamented, 'as I feel his presence through the back of my head which interferes with concentration. I seem to be a very sensitive plant.'[12]

---

get anything satisfactory: at any rate one can choose the best.' John to D. S. MacColl, 17 January 1945. 26 February 1940.

* 'He [John] was usually asleep when I arrived at Tite Street,' Lord Portal remembered, 'and loud knocks were required to rouse him. When roused he came noisily to the door, greeted me gruffly and started clearing the space for my chair by kicking away any pieces of furniture that were in the way . . . I did not get the impression that he enjoyed painting me, but he certainly got a wonderful picture after 5 or 6 sittings. He then asked that my wife should come and look at it, which she did and admired it. She told me that while she was actually watching him at work he turned the portrait, in the course of a few minutes, into the "caricature" which she and others think it now is . . . I don't think he ever asked me what I thought . . . A powerful character, but I don't think we attracted each other.'

To improve the atmosphere between the two men, another figure was imported: Bernard Shaw. For an hour Shaw 'talked all over the shop to amuse your sitter and keep his mind off the worries of the present actual fighting'.[13] Then, his hour up, he was driven home by Montgomery's chauffeur (whom he goaded into reaching ninety miles an hour) and sat down to write John two brilliantly nonsensical letters about the portrait.*

According to John, Shaw 'has a wild admiration for Monty';[14] whereas, in Shaw's view, John really was not 'interested' in him. Nevertheless, 'I don't think the result is too bad,' John hazarded after the sittings were over, 'though I haven't got his decorations exact.' Montgomery was appalled when he finally saw the portrait. An unpleasant blue cloud had been suspended over his head, he declared, and it wasn't 'the sort of likeness he would want to leave to his son'. 'I daresay', commented John, 'I stressed the gaunt and boney aspect of his face – the more interesting one I thought.'[15] But he was familiar with dismay from his sitters, accepting it with particular geniality when, as in this instance, it enabled him to sell the picture for more elsewhere.

Though his heart was seldom in such work and it occupied less of his time, he still loomed large in the public mind where even his worst failures were regarded as 'controversial'. The peculiar conditions of war held him in the limelight. He was often asked to open exhibitions, to donate pictures for one or another category of war victims. But it was on behalf of artists he exercised himself most energetically. He had been one of those, along with Eric Gill, Henry Moore and Ben Nicholson, who in 1933, the year of Hitler's ascendancy, had helped to form the Artists' International Association. The aim of this body had been to establish an army of artists opposing the advance of 'philistine barbarism', to repulse which it erupted with periodic exhibitions 'Against Fascism and War'. In one major objective, which (it noted) was 'preventing war', the association had been defeated. But, believing 'all art is propaganda', it persisted in these war years with shows to which John prominently contributed. He also presented several pictures to sales for raising

---

* 'The worst of being 87–88 is that I never can be quite sure whether I am talking sense or old man's drivel.' Shaw to John 27 February 1944. His second letter is dated 29 February 1944.

war funds and used his influence to free a number of German and Austrian refugee artists who had been interned by the British Government.*

Though remote from politics, John was not aloof from the effects of political actions on ordinary people – especially gypsies,† on whose behalf he wrote to newspapers and peti-tioned members of parliament to the end of his life. But the war, itself a political explosion, affected everyone. 'People carry on marvellously through it all I must say,' he wrote to Conger Goodyear on 19 April 1941. '... Life in London goes on much as usual except that people don't go out so much at nights – though I do.' It was an uneventful time, 'punctuated with pin-pricks'. There was less to eat and drink, but they were rich in vegetables at Fryern and from friends and family in America came many parcels of food, whisky, pipes. No longer could he rove and rumble round France, but there was Mousehole in Cornwall where one of his daughters-in-law now lived – 'very pleasant. I go to Penzance for my rum.' Petrol rationing had made travel even in England difficult ('we hardly move a yard'), but the trains still ran between London and Fordingbridge, and since his journeys were 'really necessary' he could admit to being 'moderately gregarious'.

The country, in wartime, was 'like a paddock which one grazes in, like a cow, but less productive'. To enliven the scene at Fryern 'we must get a lot of children,' he announced.[16] He was particularly keen to attract black children – 'darkies' as he called them – and by the spring of 1940 he and Dodo had five evacuees, all white. Dodo herself appeared to take no notice of the war, spending it in the garden; but John's letters are full of

* Among John's papers is a letter from Oscar Kokoschka thanking John for his attempts to help him escape from Prague.

† 'After my election to the House of Commons in 1950,' Montgomery Hyde wrote to the author, '. . . I took up the cause of gypsies. At that time they were being pushed around by the police, particularly in Kent, and Augustus took a lot of trouble in briefing me on the subject of their troubles. He was convinced that their periodic clashes with the police which were reported in a not too favourable press at the time were largely due to a misunderstanding.' His campaign ranged from an article in *Encounter* (1956) to physical intervention in the case of Sven Berlin, whose house the authorities were attempting to convert into a public lavatory.

jibes against 'old Schicklgruber'. In London no one could ignore it. 'London is being badly bombed,' he wrote to his sister Winifred on 18 October 1940. 'I was up there with Vivien the other day and saw a good deal of devastation. Still the people are sticking it out *wonderfully*. Life goes on as usual – in the day time, and the streets are full of people and all very cheerful in spite of loss of sleep. The row at night is hellish.'

He was determined not to allow these disturbances to interrupt his work – a programme that sometimes endangered his sitters. One of them, Constance Graham, remembers posing for him when an air-raid broke out overhead. John 'was utterly unperturbed, and we were seated by the enormous studio window while the bombs buzzed overhead. They might have been blue bottles for all he cared so of course I felt obliged to remain equally unmoved.'

London had become a village. People stopped each other in the streets, swopped stories about last night's raid, drank together, made one another laugh. John, like a great tree in the wind, swaying from one pub to the next, was a cheerfully reassuring sight. 'He is like some great force of nature,' noted Chips Channon, 'so powerful, immense and energetic.'[17] It was out of the question that anything Hitler could do might disturb him. While the 'Doodle-Bug' or 'Buzz-Bombs' were falling, twice 'buggering up' his Tite Street studio, he would sit with Norman Douglas and Nancy Cunard in the Pier Hotel at Battersea Bridge, where the 'drink supply had generously expanded – to steady the clients' nerves'.[18] There was a marvellously enhancing quality about his presence that seemed to come from the earth itself. After an evening here, or at the Gargoyle Club in Dean Street, or the Antelope in Chelsea, he liked to invite his drinking companions, for a last unneeded drink or two, back to Tite Street. At such times there was something undeniably lovable about him; by turns generous then angry, an old gentleman wobbling through the black-out. Back at Tite Street, on one fuddled occasion, he laid himself down vaguely on top of Michael Ayrton, as if, Ayrton recalled, quite shocked, 'I were his daughter'. The third member of the party, Cecil Gray, snatching up his Quaker hat, shouted: 'I'm not going to remain here to watch this', and opening a door, walked into the broom cupboard. 'He's gone into the broom cupboard,' John declared, sitting up. 'By God he has!' Ayrton agreed, also sitting up. They stared at the closed door from which faint scufflings could be heard. Then Cecil Gray knocked, came in and took off his hat: 'I think I'll stay after all.' After which they all went to sleep.

Such stories, revealing an innocence not altogether lost, endeared him to his friends. 'Look at Augustus John!' proclaimed Norman Douglas. 'Take away his beard, close-crop his hair and Augustus would be as impressive as before. Him I admire not only as a fine man but for his way of thinking about life. Alas! I fear *he's* the last of the Titans.' In wartime his stature appeared to grow. He was unafraid, and there seemed to be an external enemy to account for his obscure look of suffering. People now needed parties, drink and the boosting of their morale in much the same way as he had needed these things in peacetime. Homes and buildings were everywhere being destroyed; friends, family, lovers killed. The marks of torture on John's face reflected what everyone was feeling. But his real enemy was invisible. Late one night, when Michael Ayrton was being driven home, his taxi, swerving suddenly to a halt, nearly ran over a pedestrian. It was John. Tears were streaming down his face. At Ayrton's insistence he got into the taxi to be taken back to Tite Street. 'It's not good enough,' he kept murmuring to himself. Disliking histrionics, and believing the old actor to be up to his tricks again, Ayrton tried to tease him out of this mood. 'What girl is that, Augustus? What girl's not good enough?' John gave a dismissive wave. 'My work's not good enough,' he said; and Ayrton suddenly understood that this was a deep grief. Nor would John be comforted: 'My work's not good enough.'

It was seldom he could speak of anything for which he felt deeply. 'The only English thing about me is my horror of showing emotion,' he once confessed to Mary Keene.[19] 'This makes my life a hideous sham.'[20] This 'sham' was a necessary covering against what he called 'the ghastliness of existence'. Only those close to him appreciated how much he hated this war. His five adult sons were in different services; Vivien had become a nurse, Poppet worked in a canteen. Everyone, even the girls, seemed to be in uniform. In such circumstances it was 'not amusing' to remain a civilian. 'I think of joining the Salvation Army,' he joked, 'though I believe the training is severe.'[21] What depressed him was 'this foul and bogus philosophy of violence'.[22] It was a world war to end all worlds he could recognize as his own. 'I can hardly bear to think of France being overrun by those monsters,' he told Will and Alice Rothenstein.[23]

He tried to keep working, but felt that he was missing much and that eventually painting might become 'impossible in England. The future for an artist in particular looks very problematic,' he admitted to Evan Morgan.[24] But this war, which was to transform the entire art world, eroding the influence of figurative painters and setting up an international style of art that would be severely abstract, had at first produced the reverse effect. Owing partly to Britain's isolation and the difficult conditions for young painters, attention was forced back to previous generations of artists, to Whistler, Sickert and John himself. In November 1940, the National Gallery assembled one hundred and twelve Augustus John drawings 'representative of various aspects of my draughtsmanship from student days to the present'. 'It is an astonishing record,' wrote Herbert Read, 'and it is doubtful if any other contemporary artist in Europe could display such virtuousity and skill.'[25] A year later Lillian Browse produced her successful volume *Augustus John Drawings*, and in 1944 John Rothenstein his Phaidon Press *Augustus John* which, despite wartime restrictions, went into three editions in two years.

In June 1942 he was named by George VI to the Order of Merit. Rumours of a knighthood had been blowing about the previous year. The prospect cheered John mightily, but Dorelia would not countenance it. *She* wasn't going to be known as 'Lady John'; it was ridiculous, out of the question. The knighthood receded and for a few moments John was mightily cast down. Then, three months after the death of Wilson Steer, he was offered the O.M. – a far more distinguished award, it was explained: and he brightened at once. 'It is of course a matter both of pride and humility to succeed Steer in this order,' he instructed D. S. MacColl on 25 June 1942.[26] He was engulfed with congratulations: but there were some who deplored the old anarchist accepting recognition from the State. His response to all criticism was that people should be allowed to do whatever they liked, and benefit by whatever gave them pleasure. Of compulsory hereditary titles he disapproved but found in other awards a romantic appeal. He supported Anthony Wedgwood Benn's fight against disqualification as a member of parliament due to peerage.[27] But he defended Herbert Read's 'courageous decision' to take on a knighthood in 1953 when his fellow-anarchists were sharply critical. 'Although we may diverge in some matters, I think you were quite right to accept a knighthood (though I feel it should have been a baronetcy),' John wrote to him. 'If there is one thing certain, it is that there is no such thing as "equality" in human society, and your Order, symbolizing this truth, justifies itself in admitting you.'[28]

As for his own award, though not to be over-valued, it gave him a deal of innocent pleasure. 'Would you believe it?' he exclaimed in a letter to his sister Winifred. 'It is the rarest of all orders.' He treated it in the manner of a private transaction between himself and George VI – and particularly good of the monarch considering how much of his wife's time he had squandered. But he discouraged outsiders from concerning themselves with it. 'I only remember the O.M.,' he reprimanded D. S. MacColl, 'when others forget it.'

2. IN ASKELON

'I am two people instead of one: the one you see before you is the old painter. But another has just cropped up – the young writer.' With these words at a Foyle's Literary Lunch in March 1952, John announced the publication of *Chiaroscuro*, his 'fragments of autobiography'. It had been a lengthy cropping-up – a month or two short of thirty years. 'I think we must all write autobiographies. There would be such side-splitting passages,' he had urged Henry Lamb on 13 June 1907. But it was not for another fifteen years that he was first importuned by a publisher, Hubert Alexander. 'I've been approached by another firm on the subject of my memoirs,' he replied on 21 February 1923. The approaches multiplied, grew bolder; the delay lengthened, became confused. A synopsis – three-and-a-half sides of Eiffel Tower paper in fluent handwriting reaching forward to 1911 –

was probably done before the end of 1923, but sent to no one; and another period of fifteen years slipped by before a contract was signed. The interval was full of rumours: whispering of vast advances* and extraordinary disclosures, almost all of which were unfounded.

'Other people's writing has always interested me,' runs the first sentence of *Chiaroscuro*. He was surprisingly well-read – surprisingly because he was never *seen* with a book. At Alderney and Fryern visitors were made to feel it was somehow reprehensible to be caught in the act of book-reading. John himself read in bed. He devoured books voraciously, reading himself into oblivion, to escape the horrors of being alone. His library, an unselfconscious accumulation, reflected the wide extent of his tastes – occultism, numerology, French novels, Russian classics, anarchical studies, Kaballah – and the ill-discipline with which he pursued them all.

He had long dreamed of writing. Privately he composed verse – ballads, sonnets, limericks – and was immoderately gratified when Dylan Thomas exhorted him to pack in painting for poetry. But he had also written for publication: first, with the encouragement of Scott Macfie, for the *Journal of the Gypsy Lore Society*; then, with the approval of T. E. Lawrence, a preface for a J. D. Innes catalogue; after that, with the help of T. W. Earp, his eight articles on painting for *Vogue*; finally, with Anthony Powell's support, an essay on Ronald Firbank. He needed encouragement, and when Jonathan Cape offered him a contract in 1938 he responded eagerly.

This contract is an engaging work of fantasy. John would deliver his completed manuscript by All Fools' Day 1939 'or before'. The length was to be 'at least 100,000 words' and it should be 'copiously illustrated'. The prospect excited everyone. 'I believe this to be a big book on both sides of the water,' enthused his American publisher.[29] Much correspondence crossed this water over the next twelve months from one publisher to

---

* 'Did I tell you about August[us] John, whom I duly tackled or rather sounded, weeks ago? He said lots of publishers had been at him. One offered him £10,000 in advance for his memoirs. He said, "Oh, that's not enough: I want £20,000." They rose to £13,000.' T. E. Lawrence to Jonathan Cape. See Michael Howard's *Jonathan Cape, Publisher* p. 151.

the other: but from John, nothing. He had equipped himself with a literary agent* to whom, on 2 May 1939, he expressed his appreciation of their dismay. Nevertheless 'the idea of the book has developed and interests me more and more,' he maintained '... when I am quite myself again it will unroll itself without much difficulty and turn out a success'. This game continued for another year. To each fast service he would return the same slow lob. The war, interpreted by his publishers as a cause for acceleration, he re-interpreted as a fresh reason for delay. Yet he continued patiently to play the optimist. Already by January 1940 he had made 'an important step forward in destroying what I have already written'. he promised Cape. In vain his agent would expound John's method of allowing 'his work to accumulate until everybody loses patience and subsequently complete it in an incredibly short time'. It was a case of 'this year, next year, sometime –' growled Cape.[30] 'Each time I have seen him [John], he has told me how busy he is, painting portraits.'[31] The publishers formally conceded defeat in the autumn of 1940, the fabulous contract expired and this first stage of negotiations was at an end.

But Jonathan Cape himself had not surrendered. 'I have the strong conviction that John is a natural writer,' he had told the American publisher. The book had been conceived; what it now needed was a team of midwives to nurse it into the world. First of these *aides-mémoire* was Cyril Connolly, who had recently launched his monthly review of literature and art, *Horizon*. In conversation with Connolly one day, John volunteered to write something for the review, and this led to an arrangement whereby Cape allowed Connolly to have, without fee, what amounted to serial rights in John's autobiography. Between February 1941 and April 1949, when he relapsed with nervous exhaustion, John contributed eighteen instalments to *Horizon*.[32] He liked writing in short sections and, every time he had a few pages ready, he would organize an evening with Connolly in London. Without this constant support, it is unlikely that the book would ever have been written.[33] John's letters are full of author-complaints. 'Writing costs me great pain and labour,' he pointed out to Leonard Russell, 'besides taking up much time.'[34] He seized

* M. S. Wilde of the British and International Press.

upon air-raids, black-outs, apple-tree accidents, electricity cuts, bouts of 'Mongolian 'Flu', broken ribs, operations, thunderstorms – any narrow squeak or Act of God that made painting impracticable – to turn to 'my literary responsibilities'. The guaranteed publication in *Horizon* helped to give him impetus, but his contributions there have a stranded look – unconnected with anything happening in the world or with much else in the review.

At the beginning of 1949 Jonathan Cape tiptoed back into the arena, and John was persuaded to reorganize his *Horizon* pieces into a book. He made heavy weather of this 'colossal task'.[35] Secretaries were provided; he changed his agent; joined the Society of Authors: but the written word was still recalcitrant. In place of Cyril Connolly, Jonathan Cape dispatched John Davenport as literary philosopher and friend, and the two of them 'spent many pleasant days together at odd intervals'.[36]

Back in London, Cape foamed with impatience. He began to petition some of John's friends and, a bad blunder, girl-friends. Learning this, John fell into a passion. His publisher was excavating for 'scurrility and scandal which I'm not able or willing to provide'. To John Davenport he pointed out the terrible lesson this had taught him against over-familiarity with tradespeople. 'I regret having been inveigled into getting on friendly terms with this business man ... He had incidentally an eye on Mavis.'

In 1950 Cape sent his last ambassador to Fryern, Daniel George. 'My function was merely that of the tactful prodder, the reminder of promises, the suggester of subjects, the gentle persuader,' Daniel George wrote.[37] John's writing technique, similar to his method of painting, depended upon timeless revision. 'From time to time I would receive from him two or three quarto sheets of small beautifully formed and regular script,' Daniel George remembered. '... On one such sheet now before me are twenty-five lines, only seven of which are without some emendation. One line reads: "I am a devil for revision. I cannot write the simplest sentence without very soon thinking of a better one." Here the words "very soon" have been changed to "at once".'

John called it 'putting my stuff in order'. Once a few pages had been typed, they were sent back to him, and after further copious corrections he would submit them for re-typing. They were then returned to him and he would set about 'improving certain recent additions and making a few new ones'.[38] This process would jog on until, somewhere on its peregrinations, the typescript was mislaid. 'I am most unmethodical,' John admitted, 'and have been troubled too by a poltergeist which seizes sheets of writing from under my nose and hides them, often never to reappear.'[39] It was Daniel George who released him from this deadlock by inventing a conspiracy of forgetfulness. He 'forgot' to send the revised revisions back to John who forgot never having received them. It worked perfectly. After this John's area for revision was restricted to the title, which he altered a dozen times before uniting everyone in opposition to his final choice, *Chiaroscuro*.*

The book was reviewed widely and favourably. Lawrence Hayward in the *Guardian* called John 'a writer of genius', and other distinguished authors, including Desmond MacCarthy, Sacheverell Sitwell and Henry Williamson all specially praised the quality of his prose.[40] 'Augustus John is an exceptionally good writer; and upon this most reviewers have dilated, with a tendency to compare him with other painters who have written books,' criticized Wyndham Lewis in *The Listener*. 'This is the obvious reaction, it would seem, when a painter takes to the pen: to see a man of that calling engaged in literary composition, affects people as if they had surprised a kangaroo, fountain-pen in hand, dashing off a note. The truth is that Augustus John is doubly endowed: he is a born writer, as he is a born painter ...'[41]

These reviews were an accurate measurement of the great affection in which John was held – an affection that ignored the unhappy complications of his character. 'What a pleasure it is to read this robust autobiography of a man who has achieved all he has desired from life,' exclaimed Harold Nicolson in the *Observer*. To the devastating irony of such a conclusion many were blind. Only Tom Hopkinson, in *Tribune*, attacked the book

---

* *Painter in Masquerade, A Painter's Life, Painter's Pastime, Painter's Pantomime, Painter's Paradise, Painter's Patchwork, Painter in Patchwork, Many Coloured Life, Episodes and Reticences* and *Who Am I?* were some of them.

in print; otherwise criticisms were voiced in private. One of the most severe critics was the man who, perhaps more than any other, had helped to get it written: Cyril Connolly. In Connolly's view, despite the long years of preparation, John had not gone through enough agony. 'For someone who was such a brilliant conversationalist he was terribly inhibited when he wrote ... He would fill his writing with the most elaborate clichés. He couldn't say "she was a pretty girl and I pinched her behind". He would say: "The young lady's looks were extremely personable and I had a strong temptation to register my satisfaction at her appearance by a slight pressure on the *derrière.*" '[42]

Only in the opening pages, recalling his boyhood in Pembrokeshire, did John achieve a sustained and imaginative narrative. The rest of the autobiography arranges itself into a scrapbook, broken up into brief, haphazardly plotted incidents without reference to dates or chronological sequence. The absence of any discussion of his work, or any self-revelation, disappointed some readers.* Increasingly he relied on a procession of famous names and a chain of indistinct anecdotes relating, with much relish, the misfortunes of his friends and the loss of their women to him – traits that were to be amusingly parodied by J. Maclaren-Ross.[43]

John's preference for a combination of long reverberating syllables to a single short word greatly encumbers his prose, but does not conceal his genuine enjoyment of language. There are many passages of sudden beauty, of wit and penetrating irony: but being unattached to anything they do not contribute to a cumulative effect. He had laboured long at these fragments, but never to connect them, and the result, he concluded, was 'a bit crude and unatmospheric'. Contrasting Caitlin Thomas's *Left-*

---

* In a passage which the editor J. R. Ackerley removed from Wyndham Lewis's review in *The Listener* (20 March 1952) Lewis had written: 'There is one more thing I would like to say about a future book by John: namely why should there not be something in the way of a "Confession"? He informs us at the end of "Chiaroscuro" that he does not lay bare his heart, which, he adds, concerns no one but himself. I think he is wrong there, everyone would be delighted to look into his heart; and so great a heart as his is surely the concern of everybody.' John persisted in his reticence, not wishing, he claimed, to 'spoil other people's fun' later on.

over Life to Kill with *Chiaroscuro*, he wrote to Daniel George:
'As a self-portrait it's an absolute knock-out. Unlike me she cannot avoid the truth even at its ghastliest.'

There is an obvious parallel between John's writing and his
later pictures. In both the many accomplished parts do not add
up to an accomplished whole. His talent had been for turning
what was visual into something imaginative – the women,
children and landscapes had been real. But two wars and the
industrial changes that had taken over France and England
made much of the visible world horrific to him. Latterly he did
not attempt to transform reality but to establish a fantasy
world in opposition to it. This involved working against the
grain of his natural talent, which was for intense observation
rather than invention. He was one of those for whom, however
long he might shut himself away in his studio, the visible world
existed. The intermittent portraits he painted were one sign of
this; his continued writing was another.

As soon as *Chiaroscuro* was published he started 'writing on
the sly'[44] a second series of fragments. John Lehmann, editor of
the *London Magazine*, and Leonard Russell of the *Sunday Times*
assisted one section or another into print, and 'Book-lined Dan',
as he now called Daniel George, continued with him to the end.
As with *Chiaroscuro*, there are good pages.[45] But generally this
second volume is scrappier than its predecessor. The fragments
are often abrupt and composed with such a wealth of hintings
and obscurities that it is difficult to quarry out any meaning.
John had become so 'literary' that he could not achieve an innocent style. Against the background of his paintings, simple and
primitive at their best, the deviousness of this writing is extraordinary. Like a cataract, it had spread over his eyes, obscuring
his painting too. In the book he focused his mind retrospectively
on the actual world which, in these last years, held for him a
lessening interest. His dream world, an anthology of past sights
and sensations, lay elsewhere serenading his imagination. In
almost ten years he completed a hundred-and-ten pages – and
his passion for postponement seemed to extend even beyond
the grave. Not until three years after his death and four years
following the death of Jonathan Cape was it published, in 1964.

There could be no amendments this time to the title which,

unintentionally, summarized all that had plagued him most: *Finishing Touches.*

3. THE MORNING AFTER

Our late Victory has left us with a headache, and the Peace we are enjoying is too much like the morning after a debauch.[46]

For John, the war had been a winter, long, dark, 'immobilizing me for a devil of a time'. Six years: then all at once 'a whiff of spring in the air, a gleam of blue sky . . . renewal of hope and a promise of resurrection'.[47] It was impossible not to feel some tremor of optimism. Though the world had been spoilt 'there must be some nice spots left'.[48] He was still able-bodied – it was time to be on the move again. But moving had somehow become more difficult. 'We sometimes refer to St Rémy,' John wrote to his son Edwin, 'and, in monosyllables, wonder if we might venture there with car.' It was not until the late summer of 1946 that he came again to the little *mas* 'au ras des Alpilles'.

He had left, in 1939, after much anguish and delay. His neighbour Marie Mauron remembered that day: 'Il regarda au mur les toiles qu'il laissait inachevées, les meubles qui avaient charmé sa vie provençale de leur simplicité de bon aloi, les beaux fruits de sa table et de ses "natures mortes", ses joies et ses regrets . . . Sur quoi, Dorelia et lui, émus et tristes mais le cachant sous un pâle sourire, nous laissèrent les clés de leur mas pour d'éventuels réfugiés, amis ou non, qui ne manquèrent pas, et de l'argent pour payer le loger, chaque année, jusqu'à leur retour.'[49]

Seven years later they collected their keys. St Rémy had been a place of no military importance and the damage was not spectacular. Yet the war had left its shadow. 'Everything and everybody looked shabbier than usual,' John noted.[50] The *mas* had been broken into and a number of his canvases carried off: one of a local girl – 'a woman at St Rémy I simply can't forget' – he missed keenly. French feeding wasn't what it had been once and the wine seemed to have gone off. But in the evening, at the Café des Variétés, he could still obtain that peculiar equilibrium of his spirit he described as 'detachment-in-intimacy'. The conversation thundered around him, the accordion played, and sometimes he was rewarded 'by the apparition of a face or part of a face, a gesture or conjunction of forms which I recognize as belonging to a more real and harmonious world than that to which we are accustomed'.[51]

To fit together these gestures and faces so that they reflected the harmony that played beneath the discord of our lives – that was still John's aim. 'I began a landscape to-day which seemed impossible,' he wrote to Wyndham Lewis in October. 'At any rate I will avoid the *violence* of the usual meridional painter. In reality the pays est très doux.' For two months he continued painting out-of-doors, and the next year he painted in Cornwall. Then in the summer of 1950 he returned to St Rémy, tried again, 'and I despair of landscape painting'.[52] That summer, as an act symbolizing this surrender, they gave up the lease of the Mas de Galeron. After this there was little point in travelling far. Each summer they would prepare for some journey west or south; the suitcases stood ready but the way was barred by unfinished pictures; autumn came, the air grew chill, and the unpacking began.

There seemed so little time. John could seldom bear to leave the illusory lands he was striving to discover in his studio; for the actual world had little to give him now. He moved about it like a ghost. William Empson recalls a last meeting with him in the 1950s.

I came alone into a pub just south of Charlotte St, very near the Fitzroy Tavern but never so famous, and found it empty except for John looking magnificent but like a ghost, white faced and white haired ... it was very long after he had made the district famous, and I had not expected to see anyone I knew. 'Why do you come here?' I said, after ordering myself a drink. 'Why do you?' he said with equal surliness, and there the matter dropped. I had realized at once that he was haunting the place, but not that I was behaving like a ghost too. It felt like promotion ...[53]

For John, as for Norman Mailer, the fifties was 'one of the worst decades in the history of man'. The corrosive blight of the Industrial Age seemed to have attacked everything in which he once took pleasure. Even the public houses were being made hideous by 'manifestations of modern domestic technology' –

dreadful wallpapers and monotonous contemporary furniture. Young girls walked about looking like the Queen Mother. The drab clothes, the rationing and restrictions all contributed to 'the sense of futility and boredom which, together with general restlessness and unease, marks the end of an epoch'.[54]

The future looked worse. 'My outlook on life or rather death ... [assumes] a Jeremy Bentham-like gloom,' John told Tommy Earp.[55] 'We shall have little to do with the New World that approaches and, by the look of it, it is just as well.' He saw a special danger in the effect of architecture upon the philosophy of our lives. Government programmes ran on statistics, their success depending upon numbers. Millions of pre-fabricated bungalows, their concrete uniformity corresponding in no way to variations of local character and environment, threatened to iron all individuality out of their inhabitants. Already 'Paris at night has the aspect of a vast garage'; and as for London 'either it or I or both have ... deteriorated greatly since our earlier associations which I so much loved'. There seemed nowhere, and he was 'reconciled', he told Mrs Cazalet, 'to a change of planet in the near future. If we are due to be blown to Kingdom Come, it may be our only chance of getting there after all.'

The end of austerity had inaugurated the age of Admass – an unprecedented vulgarity that John identified as another symptom of decadence. But this was also a time of fear. The hydrogen bomb seemed like a giant stride in the march towards self-destruction. The anxiety people felt about their future was something to which John was acutely sensitive. 'The bombs improve,' he wrote to his son Robin, 'the politics grow worse'. He had never been interested in the ephemera of politics. 'I've got a clean slate,' he swore to Felix Hope-Nicholson. 'I've never voted in my life.' The endless macaroni of depressing news from the radio made him despair. His mounting dislike of politicians – all politicians ought to be 'liquidated' he concluded[56] – marked a late-flowering and unorthodox political creed. He had brought it into focus with one eye on the Utopia of the socialist philosopher Charles Fourier – a phalanstery where the community, based on natural groups instead of family units, ruled itself on a shareholder basis. The other eye, since the 1930s, had been on the man John saw as arch-villain of modern politics: Franco. In

1942 he had joined the Social Credit Party, 'our only certainty',[57] and in 1945, with Benjamin Britten, E. M. Forster, George Orwell, Herbert Read and Osbert Sitwell, he helped to establish the Freedom Defence Committee 'to uphold the essential liberty of individuals and organizations and to defend those who are persecuted for exercising their rights to freedom of speech, writing and action'.[58]

But John was not a man for committees and political parties. The best elucidation of his beliefs appeared in *The Delphic Review*,[59] a magazine edited in Fordingbridge. 'We are not very happy' – this was his starting-point. Looking round for the cause of this unhappiness, he sees the threat of catastrophe: 'the extinction not only of ourselves, but of our children; the annihilation of society itself'. Left to themselves, he believed, 'people of different provenance' would not 'instinctively leap at each other's throats'. The atmosphere of political propaganda which we constantly breathed in from our newspapers, radios and television sets had promoted a reversal of our instincts. 'Propaganda in the service of ideology is the now perfected science of *lying* as a means to power.' For someone passionately neutral like himself and 'no great Democrat either', the best course had been silence. But silence was no longer a sufficient safeguard to neutrality. So 'I have decided that a practice of ceaseless ... loquacity should be cultivated'.

By the end of the 1940s he began using words. National Sovereign States, he argued, were by definition bound to fall foul of one another. All nationalities are composed of a haphazard conglomeration of tribes. But the State, originating in violence, must rely on force to impose its artificial uniform on this conglomeration, transmitting its laws and class-privileges like a hereditary disease. 'The State', he warned, 'must not be judged by human standards nor ever be personified as representing the quintessence of the soul of the people it manipulates. The State is immoral and accountable to nobody.' The real quintessence of all people lay in their 'needs and in their dreams' – their need 'to gain their living; freedom to use their native tongue; to preserve their customs; to practise any form of religion they choose; to honour their ancestors (if any); to conserve and transmit their cultural traditions, and, in general, to

mind their own business without interference'. Their need also
to get back to the land: though many would not know what to
do when they got there. 'The vast Common Lands of England,
held by them from time immemorial ... [were] completely enclosed by Act of Parliament, and only in the last century we
have lost our Commons but kept the *House of Commons*, which
played this trick and still give our votes to the suppliants
who periodically come begging for a seat in the best club in
London.'

Greed versus immortality: that was our moral quandary.
John's alternative to 'the collective suicide pact' of the 1950s
was for a breaking down of communities into smaller groups –
the opposite of what has taken place in the last twenty years.
He began with hedges. The modern hedge, with which the
country had been parcelled out by financial land-grabbers, must
be dug up:

Hedges are miniature frontiers when serving as bulkheads, not
wind-screens. Hedges as bulkheads dividing up the Common Land
should come down, for they represent and enclose stolen property.
Frontiers are extended hedges, and divide the whole world into compartments as a result of aggression and legalized robbery. They too
should disappear. There is nothing sacred about them, for they are
often shifted, as they have been erected, by force and fraud. They
stand for no ethnological distinctions, for all races are inextricably
mixed, and, in any case, should not be divided but joined. Frontiers
serve no useful purpose for, costly as they are to guard, they have
never stopped a conqueror yet, or checked the scramble for
Lebensraum. They are obsolete militarily though still an incentive to
aggression. They give rise to the morbid form of Patriotism known
as Chauvinism or Jingoism. Frontiers besides are a great hindrance
to trade and travel with their customs barriers, tariffs and
douanes ...

Without frontiers, John reasoned, the State would wither and
the whole pattern of society change from a heavy pyramid to
the fluid form of the amoeba 'which alone among living organ-
isms possesses the secret of immortality'. Our monstrous industrial towns, our congested capital cities with their moats of
oxygen-excluding suburbs would melt away, and a multiplicity
of small communities appear, dotted over the green country,

autonomous, self-supporting, federated, reciprocally free. 'Gigantism is a disease,' he warned. '... Classical Athens was hardly bigger than Fordingbridge.'

Such beliefs, later commonplace among those advocating an alternative society to capitalism and communism, sounded strange in the late 1940s. During the last dozen years of his life John found himself part of a gathering minority. What joined him to others was the atomic bomb. Progress by massacre, historically so respectable, was no longer possible. Even the last war had shown this. The bomb had been hatched in a climate of self-destruction. 'With only a limited capacity for emotion, a surfeit of excitement and horror induces numbness, or a desire for sleep : even Death is seen to offer advantages.' The malignant glooms against which John had partly anaesthetized himself, the urgent uncertainty, ill-thoughts of death – these that he had lived with so long he now saw reflected in the faces of young people. 'It is impossible not to be worried about world conditions,' he wrote to Cyril Clemens. 'We are on the edge of a volcano.'

It was not just his own future now but everyone's that was in jeopardy :

Since a competition in armaments can only end in collision, we may as well face realities and decide what to do about it : for we are all responsible. In the practice of some primitive 'savages', warfare is a kind of ritual : should a casualty occur through the blunder of an inexperienced warrior, a fine of a pig or two will settle the business and everybody goes home, (except one). Modern warfare is different. We'll all be in it, the helpless as well as the armed, the women, the children and the aged. There will be no quarter given, for the new Crusaders have no use for 'Chivalry'. War will be waged impersonally from the power-house and the laboratory. Science, once our servant, is now our master. Civilization is doomed, our Planet itself in danger, and mankind will survive, if at all, as brute beasts ravening on a desert island.

By the late 1950s even words were not enough. John's beliefs had brought him in contact with Bertrand Russell whose antinuclear movement of mass civil disobedience, called the Committee of 100, he joined. 'You may count on me to follow your lead,' he assured Russell on 26 September 1960, '... it is up to all those of us above the idiot line to protest as vigorously as possible.'[60] He had planned to participate in the demonstrations against governmental nuclear policy held on 18 February 1961 and on 6 August 1961, 'Hiroshima Day', but early in February suffered an attack of thrombosis that 'forbids this form of exercise'.[61] 'As you see,' he scribbled almost illegibly, 'I cannot write; still less can I speak in public, but if my name is of any use, you have it to dispose of.' Later he made a partial recovery, and came quietly up to London for the great sit-down in Trafalgar Square on Sunday 17 September. 'I have quite lost my hearing and am becoming a nuisance to myself and everybody,' he had told Russell. He loathed crowds, feared policemen, 'didn't want to parade my physical disabilities'; but he would 'go to prison if necessary'. The public assembly began at five o'clock, and until that time John hid. Unprecedented numbers took part in this demonstration. 'Some of them were making what was individually an heroic gesture,' Russell wrote. 'For instance, Augustus John, an old man, who had been, and was, very ill ... emerged from the National Gallery, walked into the Square and sat down. No one knew of his plan to do so and few recognized him. I learned of his action only much later, but I record it with admiration.'[62]

The following month John was dead.

4. A WAY OUT

He had shrunk into old age. Over his lifetime the changes had been remarkable. Emerging from the little renaissance of the 'nineties, a romantic Welshman in a Guy Fawkes hat, he had imposed a new physical type, almost a new way of life, on British Bohemia. 'Under his influence', wrote Anthony Powell, 'painters became, almost overnight, a bearded, silent, unapproachable caste ... Huge families, deep potations were the order of the day. A new race of models came immediately into being, strapping, angular nymphs with square-cut hair and billowing smocks. The gipsies, too, were taken over wholesale, so that even today it is hard to see a caravan by the roadside without recalling an early John.'[63]

Then, in his middle years, he had moved from the roadside

into the town, a commanding personality in shaggy well-cut suits, embracing whole parties at the Eiffel Tower or in Mallord Street. He had swelled into a national figure, 'the demi-god round which the post-war carnival was danced'.

After the Second World War there had been no carnival, and he retired to a quieter country life. The caravans had halted; the fierce nights in Chelsea and Fitzrovia drifted into dreams; the national figure itself whitewashed and converted into a monument to be photographed on birthdays. To art-students he was now irrelevant. One of them, visiting Fryern in 1948, found him 'old and very deaf ... It was rather like visiting Rubens ... I noticed various goats and people dotted about in the sun. I noticed too, as we stepped into his surprisingly small and cluttered studio at the end of the garden, that he came alive, his rambling memory returned and he moved about the canvases with the agility of.youth.'[64]

Most of his days were passed in this little studio. He painted there each morning, and in winter Dodo would send in to him a little milk-and-whisky. After lunch he slept for an hour, then returned to the studio until tea time when he would come stumping across to the house for two cups of punctual cold tea. His mood depended upon his work, which was never good enough. He would sit with his hands round the cup, growling complaints. In summer he often went back to the studio again and continued painting until half-past six or so. Then out would come the wine bottles from the telephone cupboard, perhaps a visitor or two would call, and he relaxed.

Dodo, who he claimed was becoming more 'tyrannical', treated him as a child. He was sent to bed at about eight and would have his dinner brought to him on a tray. He listened to the radio a lot at night, growing frantic with knobs and the wilful obscurities of the *Radio Times*. In bed he would wear his beret at a revolutionary angle or, when it was mislaid, a straw hat, and often fell asleep in it, his pyjamas smouldering gently from his pipe, the radio blaring around him with competing programmes.

In these last years John and Dodo have been represented as Darby and Joan. The 'resentments had faded away with the years', Nicolette Devas has written.[65] They were 'enviable in the peace between them'. There were days like this, and there are photographs that catch these moments of tranquillity. But difficulties persisted almost to the end. Outrage was never far below the surface of John's melancholia. The fanatical stare put some people in mind of Evelyn Waugh. 'Shocked by a bad bottle of wine, an impertinent stranger, or a fault in syntax, his mind like a cinema camera trucked furiously forward to confront the offending object close-up with glaring lens'; Waugh's description of himself is closely tailored to John.

He found it difficult to accept the limitations of old age. The world closed in on him. 'Age in my case brings no alleviation of life's discomforts,' he told Sylvia Hay, 'and the way to the grave is beset with pot-holes.'[66] He was often breaking fingers, ribs, legs. 'I am too old for these shocks,' he admitted.[67] But it was less accidents that tormented him than galling disabilities. He hated having to rely on spectacles to see, a hearing-aid to understand. He would borrow other people's spectacles – 'I say, these are rather good. Where did you get them from?' But his hearing-aid infuriated him and he would hurl it across the room into a corner where it lay feverishly ticking. The trouble, he explained to friends, was that Dodo grudged spending the money on batteries: it had come to that. He had reached the age 'when one is far too much at the mercy of other people. I shall never get used to it – nor will they.'[68]

Old age had become his schoolmaster but he was always playing truant by darting up to London. 'Augustus, when he comes to town, seems to set a terrific pace,' Mavis wrote in the 1950s. 'I wonder how the old boy doesn't drop dead in his tracks.' Almost always he would demand her presence for 'an hour or two's sitting and a sweet embrace'. 'Must get hold of the old cow,' he would gruffly tell other people. She could still – 'how was it possible?' – make him forget his age, and their battles at the bar of the Royal Court Hotel, or at the Queen's Restaurant in Sloane Square, were precious to both of them.

He had given up Tite Street in the autumn of 1950 'and am on the pavement till I find another studio'.[69] The new studio he found was in Charlotte Street, the very one he had shared with Orpen and Albert Rutherston after leaving the Slade. It belonged now to his daughter Gwyneth, who lent him a room there. For an easel he turned a chair upside down, but the light was not good and he did very little work in town.

He came to London to escape the 'decrepit' household at Fryern and, by implication, his own decrepitude, and would put up at 14 Percy Street, where Poppet kept a flat. He never gave warning of these trips, but expected everyone to fit in with him the moment he arrived. Otherwise he would grow depressed and begin dialling girl friends and old cronies – anyone who might be free to lead him astray for a few hours. Robert and Cynthia Kee, who had a room next to his at Percy Street, could sometimes hear the stentorian blast of his snores, mixed with powerful swearing, through the dark. At night, it seemed, he fought again the old campaigns, vanquished long-dead rivals. But during the day his manner was guardedly courteous, sinking periodically to alarming troughs of modesty.

He was still, even to the age of eighty, apparently in the thick of life. 'He could outdrink most of his companions and engage in amorous – if that is the word – relations that would have debilitated constitutions generally held robust,' remembered John Rothenstein.[70] The two of them would go off into Chelsea and be joined by others. 'After a longish visit to a bar he would apprehend that his guests might be inclined to eat. "I want to stay here for a bit longer. There's a girl who's going to join us. Sturdy little thing ..." We would wait. Sometimes she would turn up and sometimes not. Augustus did not seem to mind, assured that before the evening was finished there would be others.'

He still distributed love-poems – only now it was the same poem he handed out to everyone; he was still given to sudden lunges at women, but took no offence at their rebuffs. 'May I fig-and-date you?'* he politely inquired of Sonia Brownell. These days he felt relief at being spared such duties, but he was seldom so discourteous as to forget them. Nor were they always refused. Late one night at Percy Street a young girl with long fair hair came beating on the door, shouting that she loved him and must be let in. The Kees cowered beneath their bedclothes, the old man's snoring halted and he eventually heaved himself downstairs. There followed a series of substantial sounds, then silence.

* i.e. fecundate.

Next day several of the bannister supports were missing, there was blood on the floor and, more mysteriously, sugar. John looked sheepish. ' 'Fraid there was rather a rumpus last night,' he muttered. Later that day he visited the girl in hospital and came back elated. 'Said she still loved me,' he declared wonderingly.

There is no greater misfortune, Disraeli once said, than to have a heart that will not grow old. This was John's misfortune. To everyone's consternation he had fallen in love in 1950 with a young art-student. To separate them, Poppet dragged him and Dodo down France to her house at Opio. John arrived very depressed. For days he was abominably rude to Dodo who sat silently absorbing his insults. Eventually Poppet flared up into a red-hot temper. 'Didn't know you had it in you,' John exclaimed, beaming. He seemed delighted, and quickly regained his spirits. 'Not going to lose your temper again, are you?' he would ask hopefully from time to time during the rest of their holiday.

From the prison of old age, he saw his family as gaolers. Dodo, he complained, barred all visitors, never spoke, was 'practically illiterate' and had made Fryern into a tomb. The place was 'infested with relatives'. On good days he took most delight in his grandchildren and liked to league with them against their 'respectable' fathers. On bad days it was often Dodo he attacked, because she was there. 'I begin to think it's about time,' he wrote to Robin on 3 September 1961, 'that I put an end to our relationship. She comes from a stinking cockney breed.' Gwen, he recalled, had felt the same. When the two girls had 'walked to Rome', John had offered Dodo a pistol, but she had preferred to take a passport. It proved what 'a fishy lot' the McNeills were. 'I'm glad you at least are a true-bred Nettleship,' he congratulated David (27 October 1956). This querulousness, which was sometimes violent, masked his real agony: his vanished talent and the irreversible change of life. It was Dodo who had kept him alive and helped, therefore, to make him older. By identifying her as an enemy and deliberately making his complaints absurd, he tried to diminish the pain. As a device it acted like a drug, numbing the truth. But the side-effects were powerful: strong personalities make hypocrites of us all. Then the effects would ebb away and he was confronted by the full horror of his condition. 'Hell seems nearer every day. I have never felt so near it as at Fryern Court. There must be a bricked-up passage leading straight to it from here. I see no way of escape. Meanwhile I have to pretend to work away gaily and enjoy my world-wide renown . . .'

The pretence, though still accepted by the world, had become very brittle. It took little to crack it. Cyril Connolly remembers him having lost his temper with a taxi-driver, bursting out of the taxi and measuring up to fight him in the road.[71] 'I'm sorry, but it's the right fare,' insisted the driver. 'Why, so it is,' hesitated John, lowering his fists. 'I apologize.' In a moment he had changed from an angry giant to a gentle, Lear-like old man, confessing his error and touchingly polite to the driver, who was himself overwhelmed with remorse.

In 1951, though warned by mutual friends against it, Alan Moorehead suggested to John that he write his biography. 'I was captivated by John at that time,' Moorehead records, '. . . and I believed that my genuine admiration for him would smooth over any difficulties that arose between us.' At John's suggestion they met in the saloon bar of the Royal Court Hotel, a quiet spot, he described it, where they could chat undisturbed. 'Directly he walked in . . . all conversation among the other customers ceased while they gazed at the great man and listened with interest to the remarks I shouted into his hearing-aid.'

John was inclined to think a biography not possible. He had no head for dates and many of his friends were dead 'usually through having committed suicide'. Yet the past for him was not a different country. 'He appeared to look back on his life as he might have looked at a broad large painting spread out before him, all of it visible to the eye at once, and having no connection with time or progression', Moorehead noticed. 'It was the sum of his experiences that counted, the pattern they presented . . . Once one grew accustomed to this approach it had a certain coherence and I believed that with persistence I could enter, in terms of writing, into that close relationship that presumably exists between a painter and his sitter.' It was agreed he should start work at once, calling on those friends who had so far failed to commit suicide and meeting with John from time to time to check his notes. After several months Moorehead ventured fifteen thousand words on paper 'as a sort of sample or blue-print' of the projected book, and sent them to John. 'This typescript,' he records, 'came back heavily scored with a pen, whole pages crossed out and annotated with such comments as "Wrong" and "Liar".' It was accompanied by a letter : '*All* your statements of fact are wrong. I prefer the truth. Your own observations I find quite incredibly out of place. I must refuse to authorize this effort at biography.'[72]

'I can remember,' wrote Moorehead, 'feeling appalled and humiliated – indeed after all these years the rebuff is still fresh and it remains in some ways the worst set-back I have ever experienced in my attempts to write.'

The two of them were due to meet that month at a Foyle's lunch. Moorehead was 'determined to go to this lunch and to have it out with him'. As soon as the speeches were over John made for the door with Tommy Earp, growling out at Moorehead as he passed : 'Come on.' The three of them went by taxi to a Soho wine shop, and there Moorehead tackled him. 'I thought for a moment he was going to strike me. Where, he demanded, had I obtained the information about his father's Will? I had gone to Somerset House, I replied, and had got a copy. What business had I going to Somerset House? That was spying ...'

The argument went on long, reaching nowhere, until Moorehead revealed that he had abandoned the biography and was sailing to Australia next week. John then grew calmer, the blue eyes glared less loudly, and when they said good-bye he was gruffly amiable. A week later Moorehead's ship reached Colombo. There was a cable waiting for him from John : '*For heavens sake lets be friends.*' 'I remember now the feelings of intense relief, contrition and happiness with which I read those few words,' he wrote. 'In an instant all was well again ... After all these years I am left admiring him as much as I ever did. If there was pettiness in his life and much ruthlessness, he was also a mighty life-enhancer and a giant in his day ... Reflecting, long after our contretemps, about his really passionate anger at my mentioning such matters as his father's Will, I saw that in a way he hated his own wealth and his notoriety. These things diminished his true purpose which was to paint to the final extent of his powers.'

Difficulties, like watch-dogs, lay about his work and it was almost impossible not to stir them up whenever anyone approached him professionally. Over a book of fifty-five drawings that George Rainbird published in 1957, no one escaped censure, because no one was 'able to tell the difference between a drawing and a cow-pat'.[73] Lord David Cecil, who contributed a long introduction, came from a good family but clearly knew nothing about art; Rainbird was a philistine businessman; and from the expert advice of Brinsley Ford, John sought relief through referring to him by his initials. 'I prefer,' he told Joe Hone, 'to make my own mistakes.'[74] To other people's eyes these mistakes arose from his preference for his current work. 'References to my early efforts sometimes make me sick,' he grumbled to D. S. MacColl, '– as if I had done nothing since.'[75]

The contrast between the old and new was often painfully marked, particularly when, in 1954, four hundred and sixty exhibits from all periods of his career were shown together in the four rooms of the Diploma Gallery in Burlington House. This great honour John treated as an affliction. For months he worked feverishly in order to have as many of his recent pictures as possible ready for 'this threatening show', which he had successfully postponed for two years. 'I am trying to live down my adolescent past,' he pointed out to John Davenport, 'but I cannot bury it altogether. I have sweet hopes of my maturity though.' For much of the time he was at loggerheads with the hanging committee, especially the President, Sir Gerald Kelly. Shortly before the official opening he was invited privately to go round the gallery and took advantage of this invitation to 'eliminate' about a dozen early canvases ('by no means enough') modestly claiming some of them to be forgeries – a charge that, as soon as it was too late to re-introduce them, he withdrew.

Though he had continued to be ogled by Fleet Street and by the public as the Grand Old Man of Bohemia, he had not received much serious critical attention since the 1930s. This vast Diploma show gave an opportunity for critics to estimate his work again. Apart from a few miscellaneous pictures, the exhibition could be divided into three parts : a dazzling display of early drawings; a compact group of small panels executed between 1910 and 1914; and the portraits. Perhaps the fairest summary of his career appeared in *The Times*.[76] The display at Burlington House, this critic wrote, made his 'neglect seem outrageous, but at the same time explains it'.

The effect of the drawings, when seen in such abundance, is overwhelming. They do more than explain why Mr John's contemporaries were convinced that here at last was a great modern artist in England; they suggest even now that a genius of that order had really appeared ... His power of draughtsmanship would have fitted him to work in Raphael's studio, but in 1900 there was no way in which it could be used directly and with conviction.

With the panels came John's poetry. Their colour was

radiant and clear, and the paint, which has aged very beautifully on almost all the small panels of this time, is laid with a sweet and sensitive touch. At the same time Mr John now found expression for the vein of true poetry that runs through the best of his work. In part the sentiment of these pictures is Celtic, other-worldly, and ideal, but never for a moment did he paint in a Celtic twilight. To these blue distances and golden suns Mr John transferred, not some wraith of the literary imagination, but quite simply and in literal fact his family and friends.

Finally there was his gift for catching a likeness – at its best not just a superficial resemblance but a physical identity imprinted upon the features from childhood to old age. As a portrait painter he had chosen an art that was guided by fewer standards than formerly. In consequence he was thrown back on his own judgement 'and quite clearly Mr John is not a good critic; the unevenness of his later work is really startling, and this even in the simplest technical matters'. Even so, the *Times* critic concluded, 'he remains a force and a power and every now and then there is a picture, a landscape or a portrait of one of his sons, in which all has gone brilliantly well. But though it is impossible not to see that here is a great man, this is too great a man, one sometimes feels, to practise the painter's slow and nine-tenths mechanical art.'

Ironically, in this last decade, John was applying himself to these mechanical matters as never before. He lacked only the one-tenth of inspiration. However long he waited in his studio, it did not visit him. The only remedy he understood was time; to stay by his easel endless hours hoping for a miracle. But the hit-or-miss stage was over – it was all miss now. He was barricaded in by unfinished canvases. 'I fear I shan't accomplish as much as I intended,' he confessed to Tommy Earp. 'Life is definitely too short.' He had begun to learn something of physical exhaustion, of multiplying illnesses that consumed days and weeks. In November 1954, after two years' medically-supervised delay, he entered Guy's Hospital for a double operation. 'My bloody old prostate might need attending to and also a stone in my bladder,' he told Hugo Pitman. 'Together they are responsible for my condition which has become very troublesome.'[77] He lay in a modest room where 'there is no room for modesty',[78] surrounded by flowers, and sending out in vain for bottles of wine. 'I have instructed ... [the surgeon] not to make a new man of me but to do what he could to restore the old one to working order,' he informed John Davenport. 'The worst is to stick in this horrible place, attended not by one but by at least a dozen vague females in uniform. I have considered getting away but it's difficult now.' To meet this crisis he inflated himself with optimism : the vague girls blossomed, the invisible future glowed. But after the operation, his relief flowed out unchecked. 'I had a most successful op, and am still considered the prize boy of the hospital,' he boasted to Dorothy Head.[79] 'The only snag is it seems to have increased my concupiscence about 100%! What makes my situation almost untenable is the arrival of a pure-blooded African nurse from Sierra Leone ... you may imagine the difficulties with which I am constantly confronted ...'

Though he had made a 'wonderful' recovery, he was still very weak. Dodo, too, needed a long convalescence. While grappling with some garden creature, a goat or lawn mower, she had broken her arm. They decided to go away and, on the advice of Gerald Brenan, submitted to Spain. It was a victory of climate over politics, and therefore partly a defeat. 'I would love to visit Spain again,' John had written many years earlier to Sir Herbert Barker, 'but not during the horible regime of General Franco.'

Like many artists he had backed the Republican cause, but his
hatred of Franco was personal and recurs obsessionally through
his correspondence over twenty years. He believed that Britain's
failure to come out against the insurgents had led to the Second
World War. 'With our backing the Spanish people would rise
and throw Franco and the Fascists into the sea and chase the
Germans out of the country,' he had written to Maud Cazalet
on 4 December 1940. '... Spain is the key country and our
potential friend. Meanwhile Franco continues to murder good
men ... Remember the Spanish War was the preliminary to this
one and our benighted Government backed the wrong horse.
We are now expiating that crime.' With rare passion, too, he
spoke of Vichy's handing over to Germany of Republican refugees in France. 'What is he [President Roosevelt] or what are we
doing for Franco's million prisoners, imprisoned and enslaved
by that foul renegade and his Axis allies?'[80] After the liberation
of France ('a real re-birth') and the defeat of Germany, he looked
for the freeing of Spain. 'When we have dealt with Franco in
his turn Europe will be a hopeful continent again and fit to
travel in.'[81] He attended anti-Franco meetings and contributed
pictures for the relief of prisoners (though 'I cannot approach
anything like the munificence of Picasso or any other millionaire'[82]) up to the end of his life. But for four months, between
December 1954 and April 1955, he rested there. Though the outpouring of criticism continued – 'Franco is beneath contempt,
he "knows nothing of nothing" I think is the general view'[83] – it
dwindled into petty complaints against the postal system.

Romilly had bought their tickets and driven them to Heath-
row. 'Almost the last time I saw this remarkable couple together,' he remembered, 'they were standing arm in arm, at the
entrance to the airport, quite clearly petrified by the mon-
strosities that, unknown to them, had sprung up since the days
of their youth. Augustus was glaring angrily at me for having
got them into this fearful situation, while Dodo, thinking I was
about to desert them, cried out in anguish, "Don't leave us,
don't leave us!" '

They had flown to Madrid, travelled by train to Torremolinos
where they took rooms at a hotel, the Castello Santa Clara, belonging to Fred Saunders, a castrated cockney who had served

with T. E. Lawrence. 'This is a Paradise of convalescents, full of
elderly English rentiers,' John recommended on his arrival.
'... The Bar is hideous.'[84] Gerald Brenan, of whom they saw
much, noted that 'Augustus had become very genial in his old
age'.[85] But much of this mildness was attributable to post-
operative fatigue – 'weaker than any cat and hardly able to eat
a thing'.[86] After a single debauch amid rear-admirals in Gibraltar,
he collapsed. The sun shone every day, he cast lustful eyes at
the 'superb landscape back of here',[87] but contented himself
with Edie, Fred Saunders's wife – though 'my bedroom proved
unsatisfactory as a studio'.[88] Vowing to return to his unfinished
canvases in Spain, he left with some relief for Fryern.

'I get anchored down here,' he had told Matthew Smith, 'with
some endless work.'[89] It was to Matthew Smith that he cast off
for his last journey abroad in 1956. Tickets were bought for him,
money of various denominations placed in his pockets, his
clothes in a suitcase, and reminders of all breeds flapped about his
ears. For days the atmosphere at Fryern was saturated with time-
tables, taxis, trains. A network of old girl-friends along the route
was alerted. Most of this planning was conducted in whispers,
for John would vastly have objected. In Paris, where he was
obliged to change trains, it had been arranged that William de
Belleroche would chaperone him as if by accident from one
station to the other. John blandly accepted the coincidence.
'Extraordinary! When I stepped out of the train, there was
Belleroche who happened to be passing.' Even so, John lost his
tickets. After a few nights with Matthew Smith and his friends
John and Vera Russell at Villeneuve-lès-Avignon, he pressed on
to Aix to see Poppet, but failed to turn up at the agreed meeting-
point. They found him, not far off, grazing over lunch, and took
him for a few days to their house near Ramatuelle. But he felt
physically ill away from his paints and insisted on being driven
to St Raphael so as to catch a train direct to Calais. 'I would
have liked to have stayed in Provence,' he told William de Belleroche, 'but felt still more drawn to my work here. I find I cannot stop working ...'[90] Yet it had been a good expedition because of the Cézanne exhibition at Aix. 'The Cézanne show
was overwhelming,' he wrote to Matthew Smith on his return
to Fryern, 'and painting seems more mysterious than ever if not

utterly impossible. Only the appearance of a young woman out-side, with very little on, restored me more or less to normality and hope. But she belonged to an earlier and more fabulous age than ours.'[91]

Most fellow-creatures from that age were dead. Among the artists and writers, Will Rothenstein had died in 1945, 'a severe loss'; Dylan Thomas in 1953, which 'greatly saddened me';[92] Brangwyn in 1956, though 'he was a courageous man who made the best use of his talents and could have nothing to regret'.[93] Gogarty had long before gone to America, a fate worse than death. Among the women, the Rani had rushed off, in which direction no one could tell; Alick Schepeler had disappeared with all her illusory charm, something she had always been threatening to do; and Edie faded virginally away as Francis Macnamara's neglected wife.

One of those whose company John missed most was Tommy Earp, who pursued his solitary recreation, silence, to its ultimate lair in 1958. He was buried at Selborne. 'John came with Dorelia – a quiet little elderly lady by then,' William Gaunt remem-bers.[94] He wore a black-varnished straw hat, headgear venerable enough for a Dean, yet as he sported it taking on a rakish elegance. 'Painted it myself,' he boasted. 'Best thing you've done for years,' a friend retorted. William Gaunt murmured something about its being a sad occasion. 'Oh, awful!' John thundered enthusiastically. 'I noticed at the same time,' Gaunt records,

how the artist's eye professionally functioning in a separate dimen-sion was observing the architectural and natural details of the scene: and when all the mourners were assembled in Selborne Church and all was hushed, suddenly a roar reverberated along the nave. It was Augustus with a superb disregard of devout silence. 'A fine church', he roared. There was ... a shocked rustling through the interior. With perfect sang-froid he went on with his meditations aloud. 'Norman!' the word pealed to the rafters. There were some who seemed to scurry out into the open with relief at no longer being subjected to this flouting of convention.

Of the survivors, those who had strayed prehistorically into the bland 1950s, he saw something of Wyndham Lewis. The jousting between these two artists-in-arms continued to the end.

Passages of complimentary abuse were interrupted by sudden acts of kindness. When Lewis went blind in 1951, John bragged that he had sent him a telegram expressing the hope that it would not interfere with his real work : *art-criticism*. When pressed to account for this message, he declared that he wasn't, through sentimentality, going to lay himself open to some crushing rejoinder. In fact his letter had not been unsympathetic. 'I hope you find a cure as did Aldous Huxley,' he wrote. 'Anyhow indiscriminate vision is a curse. Although without the aid of a couple of daughters like Milton, I don't really see why you should discontinue your art criticism – you can't go far wrong even if you do it in bed. You can always turn on your private lamp of aggressive voltage along with your dictaphone to discover fresh talent and demolish stale.' At other times he treats this blindness as a gift of which Lewis has taken full advantage. Lewis received these 'impertinent' congratulations with an appreciative silence. Never once did he allude to his blindness, preferring to make any accusation obliquely : 'Dear John, I'm told you've mellowed.' John hotly denied the charge, but Tristan de Vere Cole remembers him taking Lewis out to dinner shortly before his death, seeing that his food was properly cut up, deferring to him in their talk and exerting all his charm for Lewis's entertainment.

Wyndham Lewis died in 1957; Matthew Smith two years later. The war had devastated him. Evacuated from France, he had abandoned many canvases and later lost his two sons on active service. In 1944 he came to Fryern for some months, and in October that year the two artists painted each other. Smith's portraits of John are wild-eyed and florid; John's of Smith full of quietness and sympathy – perhaps his last great portrait.

They were often seen about Chelsea in these years after the war : a curious couple – Smith 'whose canvases suggest that a stout model has first been flogged alive, then left to bleed to death, slowly and luxuriously, on a pile of satin cushions'[95] looking timid and myopic, a pale, spindly specimen like some bankrupt financial expert; John, with his late-flowering addiction to anaemic prettiness, like an ageing lion full of sound. 'It is always an amusing experience to see them together,' Peter Quennell observed, Matthew Smith 'shrinking into his chair and glancing nervously about the room, John looking too large for the table and ordering the wine in a voice of rusty thunder'.

They went, regularly, to the Queen's Restaurant in Sloane Square, where the atmosphere – a little French, a little Edwardian – suited them well. The menu was always the same and so were the waiters, the tired flowers on the tables, the potted palm at the foot of the staircase. Having a large but dispersed clientele, it was haunted by the past – old friends you could have sworn were long dead appearing there from time to time like ghosts. 'They were easily distinguishable,' Lucy Norton remembered:

John with his lion-coloured hair, the wisps drawn thinly over the top of his head, and the numerous mufflers that he never seemed to take off ... the cavalier-puritan hat on the antlers of the old hat stand, and the black coat below, could have prepared anyone for the sight of him. Matthew Smith was always in the best place, against the wall, facing the room, looking very old now, but serene and gentle, seeming to say very little but a very bright smile unexpectedly lighting up his face ... What struck me was John's attitude, his care for the other old man, the way he turned his attention upon him, leaning forwards towards him over the table, encouraging him to talk and listening to everything he said ... I used to join them a moment before I left ... and I remember talk about Sickert and his odd clothes (no odder than Augustus's), of Paul Nash's illness and death ... It was a totally different side to all that I had ever known of John. He had always been the focus of attention whenever I had seen him. In the very distant past, with a circle of people round him, women particularly, trying to flatter him; in later years, when he was growing old, sitting against a wall muzzy and fuddled with drink, waiting to be rescued, to be taken safely home. To see him thus sober, in command, so wrapped up in someone who took all his interest, was extraordinarily moving.[96]

The Royal Academy, that 'asylum for the aged',[97] put on a memorial show after Matthew Smith's death. 'Bloody marvel,' John grunted. Some days it seemed he really wanted to die himself but did not know how to go about it. On other days his work kept him alive: it was not good enough yet. During a television interview with Malcolm Muggeridge in 1957 he demanded 'another hundred years' to become a good painter.[98] It was a dog's life, an agony from start to finish. If he had it all over again he would probably do exactly the same.

Early in the 1950s, in an effort to break new ground, he had taken to sculpture 'like duck to water'. He had met in 1952 the Italian sculptress Fiore de Henriques and 'a new phase in my history opened up'.[99] She was a young woman 'of robust physique', he noted, savagely-featured, with coal-black hair, stalwart legs and a grip of iron. She came to Fryern late that year and 'has done a very successful bust of me'.[100] He could not keep his hands, while she worked, off the clay, and eventually she gave him some with which to experiment. The result was 'a prognathous vision of the young Yeats',[101] followed by busts of some of his family, friends and a model. 'Getting the hang of this medium', as he called it, was as exciting for John as a birth from the womb. 'I visited the Foundry where my busts are being cast,' he told Mary Anna Marten, 'and I saw yours partly emerging from its covering of sand. I feel all the excitement of a Renaissance artist who had happened on a head of Venus of the Periclean age while digging in his back garden.'[102]

It may have been that John hoped to overcome in sculpture some of those muscular vagaries that were so affecting his draughtsmanship and painting. In the opinion of Epstein it was 'the sculpture of a painter; it's sensitive, but you could stick your finger through it. It's interesting, but it's not real sculpture.'[103] John had many mighty plans, in particular for a colossal statue of the mature Yeats to confront all Dublin – 'Would you advise trousers,' he questioned Joe Hone, 'or a more classic nudity?'[104] But within eighteen months this 'new phase' was over, and he was free to pursue with fewer interruptions the big composition upon which the reputation of these post-war years would depend.

The only other interruption was portraiture – often drawings of famous men such as Thomas Beecham, Frank Brangwyn, Walter de la Mare, Charles Morgan, Gilbert Murray, Albert Schweitzer ('sat like a brick he did'). These drawings provided John with 'outings', moments of adventure and respite from his main work. His studies of old men are probably the best. Of the original talent nothing remains: yet a certain ingenuity has developed, the skill of using a very limited vocabulary. The

trembling contours, the blurred and fading lines convey very
poignantly the frailty of old age. Some, who guarded their
public image scrupulously and would have given much for a
John portrait before the war, now refused his requests: among
them J. B. Priestley and A. L. Rowse. But one who welcomed him
enthusiastically was John Cowper Powys. 'Here *is* Augustus
John Himself with his daughter [Vivien] as his driver,' he wrote
to Phyllis Playter (26 November 1955). 'Hurrah!- Hurrah!
Hurrah! – He himself is a splendid picture.' In an hour and a
quarter John polished off two drawings, retired for the night to
the Pengwern Hotel, then 'like Merlin' returned next morning
for another session. When he rose to depart, Powys told Louis
Wilkinson, 'I leapt at him exactly as a devoted Dog of considerable size leaps up at a person he likes, and kissed his Jovian
forehead which is certainly the most noble forehead I have ever
seen. I kissed it again and again as if it had been marble, holding
the godlike old gent so violently in my arms that he couldn't
move till the monumental and marmoreal granite of that forehead cooled my feverish devotion. His final drawing was simply
of my very soul – I can only say it just *awed* me.'[105]

Almost his last 'outing', in October 1959, was to Tenby, which
had conferred on him the Freedom of the Borough, its highest
honour. Dodo, 'under the impression that it rains perpetually
in Wales', did not go, and he was accompanied by his daughter-
in-law, 'Simon' John who 'was very much admired'.[106] The two
of them lingered over dinner with the Mayor while a large
audience, waiting impatiently for them in the Town Hall, was
assailed by Mussorgsky's 'Pictures from an Exhibition'. At last,
to the sound of cheers, the diners clambered on to the flower-
camouflaged platform with, the *Tenby Observer and County
News* reported, 'an air of deep sincerity and of historic significance'. John, though 'the piercing eyes still flashed', seemed enveloped by a cocoon of benevolence. Sandwiched between the
Mayor and Town Clerk, flanked by aldermen, councillors and
burgesses, buffeted by sonorous compliments, he looked 'deeply
moved and at times somewhat overcome by . . . an emotion that
he did not try to conceal'.[107] As he rose to sign the Freeman's
Roll, the audience rose too, singing 'For he's a jolly good fellow!'
In a speech of stumbling thanks, he spoke of his walks as a boy

over the beaches and burrows: 'I could take those walks again now and I don't think I would get lost,' he declared defiantly. 'I can find my way about still.'

But to many, in these last years, he looked pitifully lost, the beard stained with nicotine, the deaf eyes glaring, the actions slurred, menacing the traffic. He was shepherded back by Simon 'my eldest son's wife', he explained to his sister Winifred, 'or rather ex-wife for I think they are now divorced'. Simon had come to live at Fryern in 1956 'and to my astonishment is quite a success'.[108] He relied on her as a model (his voluptuous portrait of her, very dashing *en déshabille*, was shown at the Royal Academy in 1959); she was devoted to him, though there was a number of what he lightly called 'fracas' or 'scenes' – matters of words and tablets, after which they would all return to 'friendly terms' again.

John's face – 'one of the most remarkable faces I have ever seen' Maurice Collis called it[109] – appeared on television, was often splendidly photographed for the newspapers, and was occasionally seen at galleries being 'assaulted' by some dear old lady 'whose summer costume quite concealed her identity till a warm embrace on parting brought me to my senses'.[110] He had little to say. Every birthday the journalists telephoned and every time they reported his words: 'Work as usual'. No one seemed interested in this work – it was the past for which he was famous. From time to time phantoms from that past would overtake him, dragging his name into the headlines: Mavis, shooting her lover Lord Vivian in the stomach and being charged at the Assize Court in Salisbury with attempted murder; and Mrs Fleming, aged over seventy, fighting a succession of tough legal battles against the daughter of a Parsee high priest for the affections of Lord Winchester, the sixteenth Marquess, then in his youthful nineties.

But it was to a remoter past that he felt himself tied. The subject of his gigantic triptych, *Les Saintes-Maries de la Mer with Sainte Sara, l'Egyptienne*, had first fired his imagination when, in 1910, he became involved with the pilgrim-mystery of the gypsies. In the years between the wars, the dreams symbolized for John by this legend had paled. Then, with the Second World War, he had turned back to the land of his dreams. His first major attempt to re-illumine this land had been 'The Little Concert' which, he told William de Belleroche on 1 April 1948, 'will never be really finished as I want to alter it every time I see it'. He could resign himself to its inconclusive state only by becoming more interested in something else. It was then, in the late 1940s, that his long-slumbering vision of Sainte Sara awoke. It was as if, on opening her eyes, she mesmerized him. 'I am astonished at my own industry,' he declared. She became his reason for not travelling and for not taking on much profitable portrait work. For over a dozen years, with few pauses, she held him, like some siren, calling him back to his studio day after day, and making his nights sleepless. She enchanted, tortured him; she was to be his resurrection or his death.

The saga of this vast mural and John's 'dreadful expenditure of time and effort' over it can be assembled from his letters. 'There will soon not be an inch of wall-space left for me to disfigure,' he had joked to Doris Phillips on 24 July 1951. The triptych was too big for anybody to accommodate and represented 'a world only remotely connected with our own' : yet 'I have never worked so hard or long'.[111] By 1952 the three compositions appeared to be combining harmoniously. 'So much depends on them,' he confessed to Daniel George. 'They wax and wane like the moon.'[112]

The spirit in which he met this challenge is well conveyed in a letter to Alfred Hayward : 'It seems to me one wasted most of one's time when young. At last I feel myself interested only in work and feel always on the brink of discovery. That surely is excitement enough. We are left very much in the dark and have to find a way out for ourselves. One thing becomes clear – nothing worth doing is easy – though it may and should look so, after ages of effort and god knows what failures!'[113]

The months moved on and 'I work from morning to night on the big panels which are developing well but seem to need *years* of work'.[114] In May 1954 he reported that they were showing 'signs of "coming out" like a game of Patience'.[115] But four years later he was still labouring at them and admitting : 'Unfinished things are often the best.' But there was no chance this time of supplanting his obsession with another. For this was love and must give birth to beauty. 'My wall decorations keep changing

and evolving like life itself,' he had told Cecil Beaton. But 'the
sureness of hand and mind', Sir Charles Wheeler records,
'... was waning and more than ever he scraped, altered and
hesitated ... I was charmed by the design which had all the
Celtic poetry so characteristic of his figure work. Each time I
saw it, it became less and less resolved ...'[116]

At Fryern he could sometimes be heard alone in his studio,
roaring in distress. 'What the hell do I know about art?' Hugo
Pitman came across him once in tears contemplating an early
canvas of Dorelia: 'I can't paint like that now – just can't do
it.' His right hand was partly crippled with arthritis and, as he
smoked, it trembled. Canvases lay everywhere, hanging on the
walls, stacked in cupboards and on ledges, propped up or lying
on the floor. People scurried in and out taking what they
wanted. John stood, a skull cap on his head, wearing a woollen
sweater and denims, scraping and hesitating before the triptych,
caring for nothing else. Sometimes he drew in chalk on top of
the paint; sometimes he splashed on gold and silver paint, or
pasted it over and over again with dozens of pieces of paper to
try out modifications; sometimes it seemed to him that even
now, after all these years, he was about to pull it back from the
precipice and have a 'triumph of a sort'.[117]

He was impatient with sympathy, but longed for the expert
encouragement of another artist. Over the last two or three
years he relied increasingly on the President of the Royal
Academy, Charles Wheeler. 'I think he needed someone to lean
on,' Wheeler wrote, 'so that I received many letters begging me
to visit him at Fryern Court.'[118] They would lunch together with
Dodo, then pass most of the afternoon in John's studio discussing the composition. 'When it was time to leave Augustus would
hug us and, standing side by side with Dorelia at the tall
Georgian windows, wave us good-bye.' He had undertaken to
show his triptych at the Royal Academy Summer Exhibition of
1960. The sending-in day was 22 March. On 10 February 'a
strange thing happened', he told Philip Dunn. 'I rapidly made
some bold changes and the results have delighted me beyond
measure!'[119] A month later he was writing to Charles Wheeler:
'I think it *impossible* to finish the triptych in time ... I shall
have to keep the big panels for another time.'[120]

Early in 1961, on the evidence of some photographs[121] of the cartoon, the Abbey Trust offered to purchase the central panel for £5,000 and present it for the decoration of Burlington House. It was hoped that this 'magnificent proposal'[122] would give John the stimulus he needed. In fact it engendered a feeling that had been vaguely pregnant within him a long time. After five agonizing days, he could not keep back the truth any longer: *the triptych was not good enough and never would be.* Before, locked up with his fantasies, he could pretend and try to conjure something from this pretence. But studying the panel with the objectivity that the Abbey Trust's offer now compelled, he could see only the truth. The letter he wrote 'in great distress' to Wheeler on 9 March 1961 bows to this truth:

I have some bad news for you. After working *harder than ever* I have come to the conclusion that I cannot continue without ruining whatever merit these large pictures may have had, nor can I expect to recover such qualities as have already been lost. I want to ask you to release me from my promise to have these things ready for the coming show while there is still time to replace them. *I cannot work against time.* That is now quite obvious: it will be a disappointment for you, and perhaps a disaster for me ... I will not again make unnecessary promises but will return to the work I love with renewed zest and confidence ...

Wheeler at once replied with a wire, following this up with a letter accepting John's reasons and absolving him from his promise: 'They saved me and I am almost myself again,' John answered.

But nothing could be the same. The pretence was threadbare and truth clearly visible through it. In a real sense it had been *against time* he sought to work: to reach out and reassemble the past – a legendary past that had never existed otherwise than in man's imagination. 'This working from the imagination is killing me,' he had written to Tim Phillips on 5 May 1960. 'I find myself so variable that sometimes I lose all sense of identity and even forget my name.' So, at the end, he had been brought back to the central predicament of his life: 'Who *am* I in the first place?' In the early visual lyrics, he had revealed a Paradise composed in the image of his desire which, though mysterious in its origin, was real. But his desire, arising perhaps from the loss of his mother, had been overlaid by other more superficial desires. What had been killed could not now be re-kindled. In his triptych the dream paled into dreaminess and the Paradise that had once been earthly became ethereal – nebulous shadows miming the sensuous beauty, stately gestures of earlier days. With the disappearance of the mystery, his identity itself had vanished.

John never abandoned the triptych, but was freer in this final year to turn to 'lesser and handier things'. Almost his last portrait was of Cecil Beaton. It had been begun in June 1960, but much to John's fury Beaton left shortly afterwards for America. John felt mollified, however, on being introduced to Greta Garbo. 'I fell for her of course,' he assured Beaton. '... Quel oiseau! ... I really must try to capture that divine smile but to follow it to the U.S.A. would kill me. I wouldn't mind so much dying *afterwards* ...'[123] The sittings started up again after Beaton's return, and became increasingly painful for them both. John seemed at his last gasp. The portrait would change, change, and change again. John daubed it with green paint like a cricket pavilion, then with pillar-box red. He stumped about, lunging at the canvas to add a pupil to one eye or, it might turn out, a button. His hands shook fearfully, his beret fell off, he glared; and Beaton, exquisitely posed, watched him suffer. 'I think,' John puffed, '... that this is going to be ... the best portrait ... I have ever ... painted.'

Sex had been one medicine that, in the past, could lift him clear of melancholia. In the summer of 1961, Simon John having left to marry a neighbour, John's daughter Zoë came to stay at Fryern. John, then in his eighty-fourth year, was sleeping on the ground floor. One night, carrying a torch and still wearing his beret, he fumbled his way upstairs to Zoë's room, and came heaving in. 'Thought you might be cold,' he gasped, and ripped off her bedclothes. He was panting dreadfully, waving the torch about. He lay down on the bed; she put her arms round him; and he grew calmer. 'Can't seem to do it now,' he muttered. 'I don't know.' After a little time she took him down to his own bed-room, tucked him up, and returned to her room. It was probably his last midnight adventure.

There was no escape now from the tyranny of the present,

no land of hope in his studio, no forgetfulness elsewhere. 'I have been struck deaf and dumb,' he told Poppet, 'so that the silence here is almost more than I can bear.' Old age had become a nightmare. 'I feel like a lost soul at Fryern!' he cried out to Vivien. Honours, now that he cared little for them, came to him from America, Belgium, France.* 'I'd like to quit and get away from it all,' he told a friend. 'But where is there to go?'

The end, when it came, was simple. He caught a chill; it affected his lungs; and after a short illness he died of heart failure, his heart having been greatly weakened by previous illnesses.

During the last weeks, his abrupt exterior largely fell away and he revealed his feelings more directly. He was agitated at being a nuisance to Dodo and Vivien, worried lest they were not getting enough rest. The night he died, they left him alone for a minute and he at once got up and sat in an armchair complaining that he could not sleep. 'You try it,' he suggested, indicating the bed. They got him back and, when David arrived later that evening, he was 'breathing very quickly and with difficulty but just about conscious'. Vivien told him that David had come, and he spoke his name. In his sleep he rambled about a picture of an ideal town which he claimed to have finished, but which in fact did not exist. The doctor came and John lay very quiet, rousing himself suddenly to remind the women 'to give the doctor a drink'.

Dodo, Vivien and David took turns sitting up with him that night. At 5.30 a.m. on Tuesday 31 October, with Dodo beside him, he died. 'His face looked very fine,' David wrote, 'calm and smoothed out, in death'.[124]

The funeral service was at Fordingbridge Parish Church. Apart from the many members of John's family, there were few people – Charles Wheeler and Humphrey Brooke from the Royal Academy; one or two students who had 'footed it' from Southampton. Afterwards, at Fryern, they had a party. Dodo, tiny

* He had been elected an honorary member of the American National Institute of Arts and Letters in 1943; in 1946 he became an associate of the Académie Royale de Belgique; and in 1960 he was invited to join the Institut de France.

but regal, seemed to have taken it wonderfully well, as if she could not believe yet that John was dead.

He had been buried in an annexe of Fordingbridge cemetery, an allotment for the dead up one of the lanes away from the town. To this rough field, in the months that followed, odd groups of hard-cheek-boned people, with faces like potatoes, silent, furtive-looking, made their pilgrimage. Sven Berlin, man of the road, took Cliff Lee of Maghull. Under the great expanse of sky they stood before the grave-stone. 'He rested with councillors and tradesmen of the area,' Sven Berlin wrote. '. . . His name was carved in simple Roman letters. Cliff Lee was moved to grief, as he stood holding a rose he had torn from the hedge on the way.

' "The first time I've seen you take a back seat, old *Rai*," he said, speaking to Augustus with tears falling from his eyes. "Here is a wild rose from a wild man." He threw the rose on the grave and turned away; perhaps to hide from me the grief in his dark face though he was not ashamed.'[125]

The newspapers were full of obituaries, photographs, reproductions of pictures that would soon be hurried back to their dark repositories. 'A man in the 50 megaton range,' wrote Richard Hughes.[126] 'We lose in him a great man,' declared Anthony Powell.[127] He had personified 'a form of life-enhancing exhibitionism,' said Osbert Lancaster, 'which grew up and flourished before the Age of Anxiety'.[128] His death was treated as a landmark. 'In a very real sense it marks the close of an era,' recorded the leader-writer of the *Daily Telegraph*.[129] More remarkable, perhaps, was the affection and admiration he had engendered in artists whose work and manner of life were entirely different from his own : men such as Bernard Leach and David Jones.

On 12 January 1962 a memorial service was held at St Martin-in-the-Fields. Among the large crowd were many who seemed gifted with a similar physiognomy. Caspar read the lesson; Amaryllis Fleming played Bach's Prelude and Fugue from Suite No. 5 in C Minor for unaccompanied 'cello. In his address, Lord David Cecil spoke of the heroic scale of John's personality ('a natural king among men'), of the strength and sensibility of his imagination, and the pictures in which it found perfect expression. 'A visionary gleam pervades these rocky shores, these wind-blown skies; through the eyes of the majestic figures, the soul gazes out lost in reverie. This blend of the earthy and the spiritual in his art expresses the essence of the man who created it ... it was sacramental; that is to say, it was rooted in the sense that the spiritual is incarnate in the physical, that the body is the image of the soul.'

In questioning how future generations would assess his work, many agreed that it was essential to discount most of what he had done during the last twenty-five years. Public estimation even of his earlier pictures had changed, but would change again. The extreme puritanism that had descended on modern art criticism could not discover in his drawings or paintings the quality of intellectual deliberation it found interesting, could not in a sense 'see' what he had done. But one day his pictures would be brought out again – 'Caravan at Dusk', 'Dorelia Standing Before a Fence', 'Ida in a Tent', 'The Smiling Woman', 'The Red Feather', 'The Red Skirt', 'The Blue Shawl', 'The Mumper's Child', 'Lyric Fantasy' – passing moods and moments of beauty that he had made permanent.

John's reputation, already low in art circles, was sent into a further decline by the many sales and exhibitions that took place just before and following his death.[130] The market was flooded with his pictures, often very inferior work that he had never intended to be shown, and it has taken over a dozen years to absorb this deluge.

Romilly and his wife Kathie came to Fryern, and Dodo lived on. She still wore the same style of clothes, radiated the same grace, sitting as if posing for, walking as though out of, another John painting. At work in the garden, or seated at the long refectory table over tea – Gwen John's 'Dorelia by Lamplight at Toulouse' behind her – she appeared more like the mythical Dorelia than might be thought possible. 'Her white hair,' noted Mary Taubman, doyenne of Gwen John scholars, '– strange and unexpected but accentuating the unchanged features ... very kind and smiled quickly ... – her whole face quick and intelligent. Self-contained, rather frightening, though charming. Conversation conducted very much on her terms.'

This was how she remained to the end. Brigid McEwen, who

visited Fryern in December 1963, noted her 'long dress of saffron cotton patterned in black, a neckerchief, long cardigan, long earrings, pierced ears, rings on wedding finger, white stockings & no shoes. She kept playing with her spectacles rather like an old man. Her asymmetrically done hair – a long plait & a white comb. Very young voice . . . and young expressions "Jolly difficult" (to write life of John so soon) . . .'

For years she had been pliant, undemanding. But following John's death she flexed the muscles of her personality and rather enjoyed being 'difficult'. Though she travelled more to France, staying with Poppet, most of this time she remained at Fryern.

Fryern was ageing. Dry rot burrowed through the house; the large studio stood deserted, like an empty warehouse; brambles and nettles made the path to the old studio impenetrable. Vandals had broken in and covered the vast triptych of Sainte Sara with graffiti and explosions of paint. Under Dodo's orders, Romilly laboured heroically in the garden among the wilderness of giant weeds. Yet even in disarray, a magic, like some sultry atmosphere, clung to the place. Kittens still nested in the matted stems of the clematis; the magnolias and yellow azaleas flowered with the same colours John had painted; the hammock still swung between the apple and the Judas tree; the faded brick, the long windows leading to cool dark rooms, the crazy paving inaccurately sprayed with weed-killer, the roses, the huge yew tree and, outgrowing everything, the mountainous rubbish dump: all were part of this magic.

On 19 December 1968 Dodo was eighty-seven. She had been getting visibly weaker and, to her consternation, able to do less. On the evening of 23 July 1969, Romilly found her fallen on the dining-room floor. He and Kathie got her to bed, and she slept. Next morning when they went in she lay in the same position. She had died in her sleep.

DESECRATION OF SAINT PAUL'S

To the Art-Students of London

Since the so-called decorations of Saint Paul's have been encroaching actually on the substructure of the mighty Dome itself, a great feeling of indignation has arisen. The atrocities of the design, the meanness of the patterns, the crudity of the colour, and the vulgarity of the whole is too evident to those who have inspected the results of Sir William Richmond's scheme of decoration. Even *good* decoration would be out of place, superfluous, and utterly contrary to the expressed wish of Wren.

But what are we to say to the treatment in Romanesque Style of a Renaissance building, the Petroleum Stencilled Frieze (already condemned), the false accentuation of architectural features nullifying the Master's intended effect, but, above all, the audacious demolishing of the stonework of the structure itself to provide a bed for these detestable Mosaics?

We feel assured none who have at heart the preservation of the Masterpiece can submit to see the glorious memory of its illustrious Author thus insulted, or can do less than their utmost to avert what can only be regarded as a National Calamity.

The initiators of this movement call upon the Students of the various Art Schools in London to send their representatives to join with them in determining the most effective means of making their protest.

A Meeting will be held to that end at Mr A. Rothenstein's Rooms, No. 20, Fitzroy Street, Fitzroy Square, W., on Saturday, May 6. from 5. P.M. till —

Secretary, MAX WEST,
Slade School, Gower Street.

THE CHELSEA ART SCHOOL
ROSSETTI STUDIOS
FLOOD STREET, CHELSEA EMBANKMENT

PRINCIPALS:
AUGUSTUS JOHN
WILLIAM ORPEN

YEAR 1904
FIRST TERM: MONDAY, JANUARY 11TH TO FRIDAY, MARCH 25TH.
SECOND TERM: MONDAY, APRIL 11TH TO FRIDAY, JUNE 24TH.
THIRD TERM: MONDAY, OCTOBER 3RD TO FRIDAY, DECEMBER 18TH.

THE STUDIOS SEPARATE TO EACH SEX WILL BE OPEN ON WEEK DAYS (SATURDAYS EXCEPTED) FROM 10 TO 5. AND MODELS WILL BE POSED DAILY. A LADY SUPERINTENDENT WILL BE PRESENT. SEATS AND EASELS WILL BE FOUND, BUT SUCH OTHER MATERIALS AND APPLIANCES AS MAY BE NECESSARY MUST BE PROVIDED BY THE STUDENTS.

FEES
FOR FIVE DAYS PER WEEK. SEVEN GUINEAS PER TERM, OR NINETEEN GUINEAS PER YEAR.
FOR THREE DAYS PER WEEK. FOUR GUINEAS PER TERM, OR ELEVEN GUINEAS PER YEAR.
ALL FEES MUST BE PAID IN ADVANCE. CHEQUES SHOULD BE DRAWN IN FAVOR OF THE SECRETARY AND CROSSED.

COMMUNICATIONS SHOULD BE SENT TO THE SECRETARY.
J. KNEWSTUB,
18 FITZROY STREET, W.

IT IS TO BE UNDERSTOOD THAT MR JOHN AND MR ORPEN WILL FIND THEIR PART IN STIMULATING, BY ADVICE AND SUGGESTION, THE MOST PERSONAL ARTISTIC AIMS, AND THEY ARE BOLD TO HOPE THAT BY SYSTEMATIC DISCOURAGEMENT

OF THE CHEAP AND MERETRICIOUS AND HEARTY PROMOTION
OF THE MOST REAL AND SINGLE-MINDED VIEW OF LIFE,
NATURE AND ART, THEIR EFFORTS WILL NOT TEND OTHER-
WISE THAN TO THE BEST PROGRESS OF THEIR STUDENTS IN
ART, IN NATURE AND IN LIFE

Mr AUG. E. JOHN and Mr WILLIAM ORPEN desire to bring to your notice the ART COURSES to which they propose to give their assistance during the forthcoming year.

The CLASSES will consist of Drawing and Painting from Life (figure, portrait, and costume), Painting from Still Life, Figure Composition, Landscape and Decorative Painting, together with the usual Elementary Subjects where required.

The STUDIOS will be situated in Chelsea; classes will be held for ladies and gentlemen, and every arrangement will be made to meet the convenience of individual students. A Lady Superintendent will be present daily.

The SPRING TERM of Session 1904 commences on the 11th January, and intending students should give prompt notification as the numbers are strictly limited, and no application can be considered later than the 31st December.

The FEES are moderate, and particulars and all other information can be obtained by writing to

THE SECRETARY,
18 *Fitzroy Street,*
London, W.

To Iris [Tree]. A poem in parody of Arthur Symons

To her foul breathing maw I hold
The guttering candle of my lust,
That smoketh like burnt offerings
Upon the altars of that old
Intoxicate goddess of the bust,
Multiple and indeterminate,
The fume whereof waxes and wanes
As spew upon the floor of Hell,
That bubbles with the heat of it;
Red lips that smack of carrion
And the faint penetrating smell
That comes of eating onions
That grow beside the lake of Sin;
And eager cloven tongue that laps
The froth from off the jaws of Shame;
(Ah God, ah God, the Joy thereof!)
Beneath the fulsome beaded paps,
Her devastated belly quakes
With the unmentionable aches
And agonies without a name,
As used to ravage and lay waste,
The carcase of Lucrezia,
When she lay panting with the Pope.
And thro' her burning violet veins,
The corpuscles of passion chased
The Molecules of virtue out;
Her heavy eyes quite glazed with Dope
And fume of the abominable wine,
That sinners serve to sinners, shine
With the extraordinary desire for trout
Caught by lost souls in Acheron;
The issue of her riven loins,
As evil monsters pullulate
About the shadow of her groin's
Unholy sanctuary; ululate
Like Hell's spawn unredeemable,
Brought forth to torment, damnably
And writhe and twist and turn again.

SIMPLE SYMON

'Augustus John'

Sung by Mrs GRUNDY and the JOHN BEAUTY CHORUS.

Music by H. FRASER-SIMSON

Words by HARRY GRAHAM

Some people will squander
   Their savings away
      On paintings by Rankin or Steer;
For Brangwyn or Conder
   Huge sums they will pay,
      And they buy all the Prydes that appear!
But if you'd be smart,
   As patrons of Art,
      It's almost a *sine qua non*
To prove your discretion
   By gaining possession
      Of works by the wonderful John!
                    Augustus John!

Refrain   John! John!
   How he's got on!
      He owes it, he knows it, to me!
Brass earrings I wear,
And I don't do my hair,
   And my feet are as bare as can be;
When I walk down the street,
All the people I meet
   They stare at the things I have on!
When Battersea-Parking
You'll hear folks remarking:
   'There goes an Augustus John!'

Chorus   John! John!
   If you'd get on,
      The quaintest of clothes you must don!
      When out for an airing,

You'll hear folks declaring:
'There goes an Augustus John!

Good people acquainted
   With Sargent or Strang
     Will sit to them week after week!
It's nice being painted
   By Nicholson's gang,
     And McEvoy's touch is unique!
But if 'in the know,'
   You'll hasten to go
     Where all the best people have gone:
His portraits don't flatter
But that doesn't matter,
     So long as you're painted by John!
                     Augustus John!

Refrain   John! John!
                If you'd get on,
                   Just sit for a bit, and you'll see!
                Your curious shape
                He will cunningly drape
                With an Inverness cape to the knee!
                   What a wealth of design!
                   And what colour and line!
                       He turns ev'ry goose to a swan!
                   And though you're not handsome,
                   You're worth a king's ransom,
                     If you're an 'Augustus John!'

Chorus   John! John!
                How he's got on!
                   He turns ev'ry goose to a swan!
                You needn't be pretty,
                Or wealthy or witty,
                   If you're an 'Augustus John!'

Our ancestors freely
   Expressed their dislike
     Of all unconventional styles;
They raved about Lely,
   They worshipped Vandyke,
     And Leighton they greeted with smiles!

To-day if one owns
A Watts or Burne-Jones,
   Its subject seems bloodless and wan!
One misses the vigour,
The matronly figure,
   That marks all the drawings of John!
                    Augustus John!

Refrain

John! John!
How he's got on!
   He's quite at the top of the tree!
From Cotman to Corot,
From Tonks to George Morrow,
   There's no-one as famous as he!
On the scrap-heap we'll cast
All those works of the past,
   By stars that once splendidly shone!
Send Hoppners and Knellers
To attics and cellars,
   And stick to Augustus John!

Chorus

John! John!
How he's got on!
   No light half so brightly has shone!
The verdict of Chelsea's
That nobody else is
   A patch on Augustus John!

Chorus

Miss SILVIA FAUSSETT BAKER.
Miss FAITH CELLI.
Miss VERA BERINGER.
Miss BERYL FREEMAN.
Miss WINIFRED BATEMAN.
Miss MANORA THEW.
Miss ELLEN O'MALLEY.
Miss ELSIE McNAUGHT.
Mrs CAMPBELL.
Miss ETHEL MACKAY.
Mdme VANDERVELDE.
Mrs GORDON CRAIG.
Miss SYLVIA MEYER.

Miss MARGARET GUINNESS.
Miss MARJORIE ELVERY.
Miss EVE BALFOUR.
Miss STELLA STOREY.
Miss DOROTHY GOODDAY.
Miss JANET ROSS.
Miss OLGA WARD.
Miss BARBARA HILES.
Miss PHYLLIS DICKSEE.
The Hon. SYLVIA BRETT.
Miss IRENE RUSSELL.
Miss NORTH.
Mrs HENDERSON.
Mrs FRENCH.
Miss EMILY LOWES.
Miss DOROTHY CHRISTINE.
Miss D'ERLANGER.
Miss HONOR WIGGLESWORTH.
Mrs HANNEY.
Mrs NIGEL PLAYFAIR.
Masters GILES and LYON PLAYFAIR.
Mrs DODGSON.
Miss FAUSSETT.
          and
CARRINGTON.

Select Bibliography

Aberconway, Christabel. *A Wiser Woman? A Book of Memories.*
Hutchinson: London 1966.

Allinson, Adrian. 'Painter's Portrait: An Autobiography' (unpublished).

Amory, Mark. *Lord Dunsany.* Collins: London 1972.

Anonymous (Hesketh Pearson). *The Whispering Gallery: Being
Leaves from a Diplomat's Diary.* John Lane & The Bodley Head:
London 1926.

Asquith, Lady Cynthia. *Haply I May Remember.* James Barrie:
London 1950.

Portrait of Barrie. James Barrie: London 1950.

Diaries 1915–18; with a foreword by L. P. Hartley. Hutchinson:
London 1968.

Bankhead, Tallulah. *Tallulah: My Autobiography.* Gollancz: London
1952.

Bantock, Myrrha. *Granville Bantock: A Personal Portrait.* Dent:
London 1972.

Barker, Sir Herbert A. *Leaves from My Life.* Hutchinson: London
1927.

Barnes, James Strachey. *Half a Life*; with portraits of the author by
Max Beerbohm, Augustus John, and Antonio Maraini. Eyre &
Spottiswoode: London 1933.

Beaton, Cecil. *The Glass of Fashion.* Weidenfeld & Nicolson: London
1954.

The Years Between: Diaries 1939–44. Weidenfeld & Nicolson:
London 1965.

Beaverbrook, Lord. *Courage: The Story of Sir James Dunn.* Collins:
London 1961.

Benkovitz, Miriam J. *Ronald Firbank: A Biography.* Weidenfeld &
Nicolson: London 1970.

Berlin, Sven. *Dromengro: Man of the Road.* Collins: London
1971.

Bertram, Anthony. *A Century of British Painting 1851–1951.* Studio
Publications: London/New York 1951.

Bisson, R. F. *The Sandon Studios Society and the Arts.* Parry Books:
Liverpool 1965.

Boyle, Andrew. *Montagu Norman: A Biography*. Cassell: London 1967.

Brenan, Gerald. *A Life of One's Own: Childhood and Youth*. Hamish Hamilton: London 1962.

A Personal Record. Jonathan Cape: London 1974.

Brett, Hon. Dorothy. 'Autobiography' (unpublished).

Brinnin, John Malcolm (ed.). *A Casebook on Dylan Thomas*. Thomas Y. Crowell Company: New York 1960.

Brown, Milton W. *The Story of the Armory Show*. Joseph H. Hirshhorn Foundation: Greenwich, Conn. 1963.

Brown, Oliver. *Exhibition: The Memoirs of Oliver Brown*. Evelyn, Adams & Mackay: London 1968.

Browse, Lillian (ed.). *Augustus John: Drawings*; with 'A Note on Drawing' by Augustus John and a preface by T. W. Earp. Faber & Faber: London 1941.

Bury, Adrian. *Just a Moment, Time. Some Recollections of a Versatile Life in Art, Literature and Journalism*. Charles Skilton: London 1967.

Campbell, Roy. *Light on a Dark Horse: An Autobiography (1901–1935)*. Hollis & Carter: London 1951.

Cazalet-Keir, Thelma. *From the Wings: An Autobiography*. The Bodley Head: London 1967.

Cecil, Lord David. *Max: A Biography*. Constable: London 1964.

Cecil, Lord David (ed.). *Augustus John: Fifty-two drawings*. George Rainbird: London 1957.

Chamot, Mary. *Modern Painting in England*. Country Life Ltd: London 1937.

Chamot, Mary, Dennis Farr & Martin Butlin. *Tate Gallery Catalogues: The modern British paintings, drawings and sculpture*. 2 vols. Oldbourne Press: London 1964–65.

Clemens, Cyril. *My Chat with Thomas Hardy*; with an Introduction by Carl J. Weber. International Mark Twain Society: Webster Groves, Mo./T. Werner Laurie: London, Eng. 1944.

Cochran, C. B. *Cock-a-Doodle-Do*. Dent: London 1941.

Cooper, Lady Diana. *The Rainbow Comes and Goes*. Hart-Davis: London 1958.

Cunard, Nancy. *Grand Man: Memories of Norman Douglas*; with Extracts from His Letters, and Appreciations by Kenneth Macpherson, Harold Acton, Arthur Johnson, Charles Duff, and Victor Cunard; and a Bibliographical Note by Cecil Woolf. Secker & Warburg: London 1954.

D'Abernon, Viscount. *An Ambassador of Peace; Volume III: The*

Years of Recovery, January 1924–October 1926. Hodder & Stoughton: London 1930.

Portraits and Appreciations. Hodder & Stoughton: London 1931.

Daintrey, Adrian. *I Must Say.* Chatto & Windus: London 1963.

Davies, W. H. *Later Days.* Jonathan Cape: London 1925.

Dean, Basil. *Seven Ages: An Autobiography 1888–1927.* Hutchinson: London 1970.

Mind's Eye: An Autobiography 1927–1972; the second volume of *Seven Ages.* Hutchinson: London 1973.

Deghy, Guy, and Keith Waterhouse. *Café Royal: Ninety Years of Bohemia.* Hutchinson: London 1955.

Dent, Alan (ed.). *Bernard Shaw and Mrs. Patrick Campbell: Their Correspondence.* Gollancz: London 1952.

Devas, Nicolette. *Two Flamboyant Fathers.* Collins: London 1966.

Dodgson, Campbell. *A Catalogue of Etchings by Augustus John 1901–1914.* Chenil: London 1920.

Dunlop, Ian. *The Shock of the New: Seven Historic Exhibitions of Modern Art.* Weidenfeld & Nicolson: London 1972.

Earp, T. W. *Augustus John.* Nelson: Edinburgh/T.C. & E.C. Jack: London 1934.

Easton, Malcolm, and Michael Holroyd. *The Art of Augustus John.* Secker & Warburg: London 1974.

Epstein, Jacob. *Let There Be Sculpture: An Autobiography.* Michael Joseph: London 1940.

Everett, John. 'Diaries' (unpublished).

Everett, Katherine. *Bricks and Flowers: Memoirs.* Constable: London 1949.

Fielding, Daphne. *Mercury Presides.* Eyre & Spottiswoode: London 1954.

Emerald and Nancy: Lady Cunard and her Daughter. Eyre & Spottiswoode: London 1968.

The Rainbow Picnic: A Portrait of Iris Tree. Eyre Methuen: London 1974.

FitzGibbon, Constantine. *The Life of Dylan Thomas.* Dent: London 1965.

Fletcher, Ifan Kyrle. *Ronald Firbank: A Memoir;* with personal reminiscences by Lord Berners, V. B. Holland, Augustus John, R.A., and Osbert Sitwell; with portraits by Alvaro Guevara, Augustus John, R.A., Wyndham Lewis and Charles Shannon, R.A. Duckworth: London 1930.

Forge, Andrew. *The Slade 1871–1960.* Privately printed 1961.

Fothergill, John. *James Dickson Innes: Llanelly 1887–Swanley 1914;*

with an Introduction by John Fothergill to the reproductions collected and edited by Lillian Browse. Faber & Faber (Ariel Books): London 1946.

Fox Pitt, Elspeth. 'From Stomacher to Stomach: the Meanderings of a Dressmaker' (unpublished).

Garnett, David (ed.). *The Letters of T. E. Lawrence*. Jonathan Cape: London 1938.

Carrington: Letters and Extracts from her Diaries. Jonathan Cape: London 1970.

Gathorne-Hardy, Robert (ed.). *Ottoline: The Early Memoirs of Lady Ottoline Morrell*. Faber & Faber: London 1963.

Gertler, Mark. *Selected Letters*; edited by Noel Carrington, with an Introduction on his work as an artist by Quentin Bell. Hart-Davis: London 1965.

Gill, Brendan. *Tallulah: Biography of Tallulah Bankhead*. Michael Joseph: London 1973.

Glenavy, Lady Beatrice. *'Today We Will Only Gossip'*. Constable: London 1964.

Gogarty, Oliver St John. *As I Was Going Down Sackville Street: A Phantasy in Fact*. Rich & Cowan: London 1937.

Collected Poems. Constable: London 1951.

It isn't This time of Year at All!: An Unpremeditated Auto-biography. MacGibbon & Kee: London 1954.

Start from Somewhere Else: An Exposition of Wit and Humour Polite and Perilous. Doubleday: Garden City, N. Y., 1955.

Goldring, Douglas. *The Nineteen Twenties: A General Survey and Some Personal Memories*. Nicholson & Watson: London 1945.

Goodyear, Conger. *Augustus John*. Privately printed.

Gray, Cecil. *Peter Warlock: A Memoir of Philip Heseltine*. Jonathan Cape: London 1934.

Musical Chairs, or, Between Two Stools. Home & Van Thal: London 1948.

Green, Kensal (Colin Hurry). *Premature Epitaphs: Mostly Written in Malice*. Cecil Palmer: London 1927.

Gregory, Anne. *Me and Nu: Childhood at Coole*; illustrated by Joyce Dennis, with a prefatory note by Maurice Collis. Colin Smythe: Gerrards Cross 1970.

Gregory, Lady. *Coole*; completed from the manuscript and edited by Colin Smythe, with a foreword by Edward Malins. Colin Smythe: Gerrards Cross 1971.

Gwynne-Jones, Allan. *Portrait Painters: European Portraits to the End of the Nineteenth Century and English Twentieth-Century Portraits*. Phoenix House: London 1950.

Hammersley, Doreen. 'Augustus John' (unpublished).

Hamnett, Nina. *Laughing Torso: Reminiscences.* Constable: London 1932.

Is She a Lady? A Problem in Autobiography. Allan Wingate: London 1955.

Harris, Frank. *Contemporary Portraits.* Methuen: London 1915; Second Series: 57 Fifth Avenue, New York 1919; Third Series: 40 Seventh Avenue, New York 1920; Fourth Series: Grant Richards: London 1924.

Hart-Davis, Rupert. *Hugh Walpole: A Biography.* Macmillan: London 1952.

Hart-Davis, Rupert (ed.). *The Letters of Oscar Wilde.* Hart-Davis: London 1962.

Hassall, Christopher. *Edward Marsh: Patron of the Arts.* Longmans: London 1959.

Rupert Brooke: A Biography. Faber & Faber: London 1964.

Holroyd, Michael. *Lytton Strachey: A Biography.* Heinemann: London 1973.

Hone, Joseph. *The Life of Henry Tonks.* Heinemann: London 1939.

Howard, Michael S. *Jonathan Cape, Publisher: Herbert Jonathan Cape, G. Wren Howard.* Jonathan Cape: London 1971.

Hubbard, Hesketh. *A Hundred Years of British Painting 1851–1951.* Longmans: London 1951.

Hudson, Derek. *James Pryde 1866–1941.* Constable: London 1949.

Huncker, James. *Ivory Apes and Peacocks.* T. Werner Laurie: London 1915.

Hunt, Violet. *The Flurried Years.* Hurst and Blackett: London 1926.

Hutchison, Sidney C. *The History of the Royal Academy 1786–1968.* Chapman & Hall: London 1968.

Huxley, Aldous. *Point Counter Point.* Chatto & Windus: London 1928.

Israel, Lee. *Miss Tallulah Bankhead.* W. H. Allen: London 1972.

James, Robert Rhodes (ed.). *'Chips': The Diaries of Sir Henry Channon.* Weidenfeld & Nicolson: London 1967.

Jepson, Edgar. *Memoirs of an Edwardian.* Martin Secker: London 1937.

John, Augustus. *Chiaroscuro: Fragments of Autobiography: First Series.* Jonathan Cape: London 1952.

Finishing Touches; edited and introduced by Daniel George. Jonathan Cape: London 1964.

The Drawings of Augustus John: with an Introduction by Stephen Longstreet. Borden: Borden Publishing Co., California, America 1967.

John, Romilly. *The Seventh Child: A Retrospect.* Heinemann: London 1932.

Jones, Jo. *Paintings and Drawings of the Gypsies of Granada.* Text by Augustus John, Laurie Lee, Sir Sacheverell Sitwell, Walter Starkie, Marguerite Steen. Athelnay Books: London 1969.

Joyce, James. *Letters, Volume III;* edited by Richard Ellmann. Faber & Faber: London 1966.

Kennedy, Margaret. *The Constant Nymph.* Heinemann: London 1924.

Keynes, Geoffrey (ed.). *The Letters of Rupert Brooke.* Faber & Faber: London 1968.

King, Viva. 'Autobiography' (unpublished).

Kingsmill, Hugh (ed.). *The English Genius.* Eyre and Spottiswoode: London 1938.

Lago, Mary M. (ed.). *Imperfect Encounter: Letters of William Rothenstein and Rabindranath Tagore 1911–1941.* Harvard University Press: Cambridge, Mass. 1972.

Laver, James. *Portraits in Oil and Vinegar.* John Castle: London 1925.

Museum Piece, or, The Education of an Iconographer. André Deutsch: London 1963.

Lawrence, A. W. (ed.). *Letters to T. E. Lawrence.* Jonathan Cape: London 1962.

Lawrence, T. E. *Letters;* edited by David Garnett. Jonathan Cape: London 1938.

To His Biographer, Liddell Hart: Information about himself, in the form of letters, notes, answers to questions and conversations. Faber & Faber: London 1938.

To His Biographer, Robert Graves: Information about himself, in the form of letters, notes and answers to questions, edited with a critical commentary. Faber & Faber: London 1938.

Lehmann, John. *I Am My Brother: Autobiography II.* Longmans: London 1960.

Leslie, Seymour. *The Silent Queen;* with drawings by Nina Hamnett. Jonathan Cape: London 1927.

The Jerome Connexion. John Murray: London 1964.

Lewis, Percy Wyndham. *Blasting & Bombardiering.* Eyre & Spottiswoode: London 1937; revised edition with additional material. Calder & Boyars: London 1967.

Rude Assignment: A Narrative of My Career Up To Date. Hutchinson: London 1950.

Lhombreaud, Roger. *Arthur Symons: A Critical Biography.* Unicorn Press: London 1963.

Lipke, William. *David Bomberg. A Critical Study of his Life and Work*. Evelyn, Adams & Mackay : London 1967.

Lloyd George, Frances. *The Years That Are Past*. Hutchinson : London 1967.

Lloyd George: A Diary; edited by A. J. P. Taylor. Hutchinson : London 1971.

Lockhart, Robert Bruce. See Young, Kenneth.

McAlmon, Robert. *Being Geniuses Together 1920–1930;* revised and with supplementary chapters by Kay Boyle. Michael Joseph : London 1970.

MacColl, D. S. *Life Work and Setting of Philip Wilson Steer*. Faber & Faber : London 1945.

Mackenzie, Compton. *My Life and Times: Octave Three 1900–1907; Octave Five 1915–1923; Octave Six 1923–1930*. Chatto & Windus: London 1964, 1966, 1967.

Maclaren-Ross, J. *The Funny Bone*. Elek Books : London 1956.

Maritain, Jacques. *Carnet de Notes*. Desclée de Brouwer : Paris 1965.

Marriot, Charles. *Augustus John* (Masters of Modern Art). Colour Ltd : London 1918.

Meynell, Viola (ed.). *Friends of a Lifetime: Letters to Sydney Carlyle Cockerell*. Jonathan Cape : London 1940.

Michel, Walter, and C. J. Fox (eds.). *Wyndham Lewis on Art: Collected Writings 1913–1956*. Thames & Hudson : London 1969.

Montagu, George, Earl of Sandwich. 'Reminiscences' (unpublished).

Moorehead, Alan. *Montgomery: A Biography*. Hamish Hamilton : London 1967. 'Augustus John' (unpublished).

Morphet, Richard. *British Painting 1910–1945*. Tate Gallery : London 1967.

Murry, John Middleton (ed.). *The Letters of Katherine Mansfield*. 2 vols. Constable : London 1928.

Nash, Paul. *Outline: an autobiography and other writings;* with a preface by Herbert Read. Faber & Faber : London 1949.

Nehls, Edward (ed.). *D. H. Lawrence: A Composite Biography. Volume One: 1885–1919; Volume Two: 1919–1925; Volume Three: 1925–1930*. University of Wisconsin Press: Madison, Wis. 1957, 1958, 1959.

Nevinson, C. R. W. *Paint and Prejudice*. Methuen : London 1937.

O'Casey, Eileen. *Sean;* edited with an Introduction by J. C. Trewin. Macmillan : London 1971.

O'Casey, Sean. *Autobiographies I: I Knock at the Door; Pictures in the Hallway; Drums under the Windows*. Macmillan : London 1963.

Autobiographies II: Inishfallen, Fare Thee Well; Rose and Crown; Sunset and Evening Star. Macmillan: London 1963.

O'Connor, Ulick. *Oliver St John Gogarty: A Poet and his Times.* Jonathan Cape: London 1964.

Owen, Roderic, with Tristan de Vere Cole. *Beautiful and Beloved: The Life of Mavis de Vere Cole.* Hutchinson: London 1974.

Paige, D. D. (ed.). *The Letters of Ezra Pound 1907–1941.* Faber & Faber: London 1951.

Pearson, Hesketh. *Extraordinary People.* Heinemann: London 1965.

Pearson, John. *The Life of Ian Fleming.* Jonathan Cape: London 1966.

Pocock, Tom. *Chelsea Reach: The Brutal Friendship of Whistler and Walter Greaves.* Hodder & Stoughton: London 1970.

Pound, Reginald. *Running Commentary.* Rockliff: London 1946.

A Maypole in The Strand. Ernest Benn: London 1948.

The Englishman: A Biography of Sir Alfred Munnings. Heinemann: London 1962.

Harley Street. Michael Joseph: London 1967.

Pullar, Philippa. *Frank Harris.* Hamish Hamilton: London 1975.

Raleigh, Lady (ed.). *The Letters of Sir Walter Raleigh (1879–1922);* with a Preface by David Nichol Smith. Volume II. Methuen: London 1926.

Reeve, Dominic. *No Place Like Home.* Foreword by Augustus John, O. M. Phoenix House: London 1960.

Reid, B. L. *The Man from New York: John Quinn and His Friends.* Oxford University Press: New York 1968.

Reilly, C. H. *Scaffolding in the Sky: A semi-architectural autobiography.* Routledge: London 1938.

Roberts, Cecil. *Sunshine and Shadow: being the fourth book of an Autobiography 1930–1946.* Hodder & Stoughton: London 1972.

Rose, W. K. (ed.). *The Letters of Wyndham Lewis.* Methuen: London 1963.

Ross, Margery (ed.). *Robert Ross, Friend of Friends: Letters to Robert Ross, Art Critic and Writer, together with extracts from his published articles.* Jonathan Cape: London 1952.

Rothenstein, John. *Summer's Lease: Autobiography 1901–1938.* Hamish Hamilton: London 1965.

Brave Day, Hideous Night: Autobiography 1939–1965. Hamish Hamilton: London 1966.

Time's Thievish Progress: Autobiography III. Cassell: London 1970.

Rothenstein, John (ed.). *Augustus John* (British Artists No. 2). Allen

& Unwin: London 1944/Oxford University Press: New York 1944.

Modern English Painters. Volumes 1 & 2. Eyre & Spottiswoode: London 1952, 1956. Volume 3. Macdonald & Jane's: London 1974.

Augustus John 1878–1961 (British Painters). Beaverbrook Newspapers: London 1962.

British Art since 1900: An Anthology. Phaidon Press: London 1962.

Augustus John (The Masters No. 79). Purnell: London 1967.

Rothenstein, William. *Men and Memories: Recollections 1872–1900*. Faber & Faber: London 1931.

Men and Memories: Recollections 1900–1922. Faber & Faber: London 1932.

Since Fifty: Men and Memories, 1922–1938: Recollection. Faber & Faber: London 1939.

Russell, Bertrand. *Autobiography. Volume 3: 1944–1967*. Allen & Unwin: London 1969.

Rutherston, A. D. (ed.). *Augustus John*. Ernest Benn: London 1923.

Rutter, Frank. *Evolution in Modern Art: A Study of Modern Painting 1870–1925*. Harrap: London 1926.

Since I was Twenty-five. Constable: London 1927.

Art in My Time. Rich & Cowan: London 1933.

Savage, Henry. *The Receding Shore: Leaves from the Somewhat Unconventional Life of Henry Savage*. Grayson & Grayson: London 1933.

'Autobiography' (unpublished).

Shaw, Martin. *Up to Now*. Oxford University Press: London 1929.

Sitwell, Osbert. *Noble Essences, or, Courteous Revelations; being a Book of Characters and the Fifth and Last Volume of Left Hand, Right Hand!* Macmillan: London 1950.

Sitwell, Osbert (ed.). *A Free House! or, The Artist as Craftsman; being the Writings of Walter Richard Sickert*. Macmillan: London 1947.

Speaight, Robert. *William Rothenstein: The Portrait of an Artist in his Time*. Eyre and Spottiswoode: London 1962.

Spender, Stephen. *World within World: Autobiography*. Hamish Hamilton: London 1951.

Starkie, Walter. *Scholars and Gypsies: An Autobiography*. John Murray: London 1963.

Steen, Marguerite. *William Nicholson*. Collins: London 1943.

Stewart, Jessie. *Jane Ellen Harrison: A Portrait from Letters*. Merlin Press: London 1959.

Stonesifer, Richard J. *W. H. Davies: A Critical Biography.* Jonathan Cape: London 1963.

Sutton, Denys (ed.). *Letters of Roger Fry.* 2 vols. Chatto & Windus: London 1972.

Symons, Arthur. *The Fool of the World & Other Poems.* Heinemann: London 1906.

Tedlock, E. W. (ed.). *Dylan Thomas: The Legend and the Poet,* A Collection of Biographical and Critical Essays. Heinemann: London 1960.

Thomas, Dylan. *Selected Letters;* edited by Constantine Fitz-Gibbon. Dent: London 1966.

Thomas, R. S. *The Stones of the Field.* Druid Press: Carmarthen 1946.

Thornton, Alfred. *Fifty Years of the New English Art Club.* Curwen Press: London 1935.

The Diary of an Art Student. Pitman & Sons: London 1938.

Titterton, W. R. *A Candle to the Stars.* Grayson & Grayson: London 1932.

Tree, Iris 'In Praise of ——' (uncompleted and unpublished autobiography).

Vandon, George. *Return Ticket.* Heinemann: London 1940.

Wade, Allan (ed.). *The Letters of W. B. Yeats.* Hart-Davis: London 1954.

Waugh, Evelyn. *A Little Learning: The First Volume of an Autobiography.* Chapman & Hall: London 1964.

Wheeler, Charles. *High Relief: The Autobiography of Sir Charles Wheeler, Sculptor.* Country Life Books: Feltham, Mx. 1968.

Wilkinson, Louis ('Louis Marlow') (ed.). *Letters of John Cowper Powys to Louis Wilkinson 1935–1956.* Macdonald: London 1958.

Willett, John. *Art in a City.* Methuen: London 1967.

Williamson, Henry. *The Golden Virgin.* Macdonald: London 1957.

The Innocent Moon. Macdonald 1961.

Winsten, S. *Days with Bernard Shaw.* Hutchinson: London 1948.

Wood, Christopher. 'Letters to My Mother.' 3 vols. (unpublished).

Woodeson, John. *Mark Gertler: Biography of a Painter, 1891–1939.* Sidgwick & Jackson: London 1972.

Woolf, Virginia. *Roger Fry: A Biography.* Hogarth Press: London 1940.

Yates, Dora E. *My Gypsy Days: Recollections of a Romani Rawnie.* Phoenix House: London 1953.

Yeats, W. B. *Autobiographies: Reveries over Childhood and Youth and The Trembling of the Veil.* Macmillan: London 1926.

Memoirs: Autobiography—First Draft; Journal; transcribed and edited by Denis Donoghue. Macmillan: London 1972.

Young, Kenneth (ed.). *The Diaries of Sir Robert Bruce Lockhart. Volume One: 1915–1938.* Macmillan: London 1973.

Yoxall, H. W. *A Fashion of Life.* Heinemann: London 1966.

Notes

CHAPTER 1: LITTLE ENGLAND BEYOND WALES

1. *Horizon*, Vol III, No. 14, February 1941, pp. 98–9.
2. *Chiaroscuro*, p. 28. All page numbers are taken from the first Jonathan Cape edition of *Chiaroscuro* and *Finishing Touches*.
3. Letter to the author, 18 October 1968.
4. *Chiaroscuro*, p. 25.
5. *Chiaroscuro*, p. 36.
6. Letter to the author, 18 October 1968.
7. *Chiaroscuro*, p. 37.
8. *Chiaroscuro*, p. 19.
9. *Chiaroscuro*, pp. 31–2.
10. Letter to the author from Darsie Japp, 13 December 1968.
11. *Chiaroscuro*, p. 12.
12. Gwen John to Jeanne Foster, 11 August 1924.
13. William Rothenstein to Max Beerbohm, 24 July 1941. Quoted in Robert Speaight's *William Rothenstein*, p. 402.
14. *Evening Standard*, 19 January 1929.
15. *Horizon*, Vol. XIX, No. 112, April 1949, p. 295.
16. op. cit.
17. *Chiaroscuro*, p. 35.
18. *Evening Standard*, 19 January 1929.

CHAPTER 2: 'SLADE SCHOOL INGENIOUS'

1. B.B.C. talk first transmitted on 17 November 1967.
2. 'The Slade School of Fine Art' by George Charlton, *The Studio*, October 1946.
3. See Randolph Schwabe, *The Burlington Magazine*, June 1943.
4. *Men and Memories*, Vol. I, pp. 22–5.
5. 'The Slade School of Fine Art' by George Charlton, *The Studio*, October 1946.
6. *Horizon*, Vol. III, No. 18, June 1941, p. 394.
7. *Chiaroscuro*, p. 41.
8. *Chiaroscuro*, p. 42.
9. *Chiaroscuro*, p. 44.
10. *Finishing Touches*, p. 29.

11. Letter to the author, 1969.
12. Letter to Ursula Tyrwhitt.
13. Famous People, No. 31 of a series of 50. Illustrated by Angus McBride and described by Virginia Shankland.
14. *Evening Standard*, Saturday, 19 January 1929, p. 18.
15. 'Face to Face' television interview, B.B.C., 15 May 1960.
16. *Finishing Touches*, p. 30.
17. *Rude Assignment*, pp. 118–19.
18. *Chiaroscuro*, p. 49.
19. *Chiaroscuro*, p. 249.
20. See catalogue of the Gwen John exhibition 1968. The Arts Council. Introduction by Mary Taubman.
21. Gwen John to Ursula Tyrwhitt, 4 April 1928.
22. Gwen John to Ursula Tyrwhitt, 22 July 1936.
23. Undated letter from Gwen John to Ursula Tyrwhitt.
24. Gwen John to Ursula Tyrwhitt, July 1927.
25. Gwen John to Ursula Tyrwhitt, 6 June 1925.
26. *Modern English Painters*, Vol. I, 'Gwen John', pp. 160–61.
27. *Modern English Painters*, Vol. I, 'William Orpen', p. 227.
28. *Men and Memories*, Vol I, p. 334.
29. See *The Listener*, 23 November 1967.
30. *Men and Memories*, Vol. I, p. 333.
31. See John's Introduction to the Catalogue of Drawings by Ulrica Forbes, Walker's Galleries, 118 New Bond Street, London, 17 October 1952.
32. 'A Note on Drawing', p. 10. From *Augustus John: Drawings* edited by Lillian Browse (Faber and Faber, October 1941).
33. *Chiaroscuro*, p. 46.
34. *Chiaroscuro*, p. 48.
35. *Rude Assignment*, p. 119.
36. *Men and Memories*, Vol. I, p. 333.
37. See John Russell's obituary in *The Sunday Times*, 5 November 1961.
38. *Chiaroscuro*, p. 36.
39. *Chiaroscuro*, p. 27.
40. At the Cornell University Library.
41. Ethel Nettleship to Caspar John, 29 June 1951.
42. *Autobiographies* by W. B. Yeats, p. 271.
43. *Autobiographies* by W. B. Yeats, p. 193.
44. ibid., loc. cit.
45. *Chiaroscuro*, p. 48.
46. op. cit.
47. *Finishing Touches*, p. 40.

48. *Chiaroscuro*, p. 147.
49. Undated letter from Ida Nettleship to her mother.
50. *Chiaroscuro*, p. 250.
51. Introduction to the William Rothenstein Memorial Exhibition Catalogue, Tate Gallery (May–June 1950).
52. *Men and Memories*, Vol. I, p. 348.
53. *Horizon*, Vol. III, No. 18, June 1941, p. 400.
54. Oscar Wilde to William Rothenstein, 4 October 1899. See *The Letters of Oscar Wilde* edited by Sir Rupert Hart-Davis.
55. *Men and Memories*, Vol. I, p. 352.
56. ibid., loc. cit.
57. John to Michel Salaman, February 1900.
58. *Horizon*, Vol. III, No. 18, June 1941, p. 401.
59. Undated letter from John to Michel Salaman.
60. *Horizon*, Vol. III, No. 18, June 1941, p. 401.
61. *Chiaroscuro*, p. 38.
62. *Men and Memories*, Vol I, p. 358.
63. *Chiaroscuro*, p. 49.
64. *From Stomacher to Stomach*, the unpublished autobiography of E. Fox Pitt.
65. *Men and Memories*, Vol. II, p. 1.

CHAPTER 3: LOVE FOR ART'S SAKE

1. From an essay Osbert Sitwell did not include in *A Free House*. It will be found in André Theuriet, *Jules Bastien-Lepage & his Art* (1892) pp. 139–40. See also Malcolm Easton, *Augustus John* (The University of Hull, 1970).
2. *Fifty Years of the New English Art Club* by Alfred Thornton.
3. *Cambridge Review*, March 1922.
4. *Victorian Artists* by Quentin Bell, p. 91.
5. *The English Review*, January 1912.
6. *Burlington Magazine*, February 1916.
7. *New Age*, 28 May 1914.
8. Letter from Augustus John to Lady Ottoline Morrell, 5 August 1910. This correspondence is now at the University of Texas, Austin.
9. This and other unpublished Orpen letters are owned by Miss Miriam Benkovitz, the biographer of Ronald Firbank.
10. *My Gipsy Days* by Dora E. Yates, p. 74.
11. Most of John's letters to Will Rothenstein are at the Houghton Library, at Harvard, Cambridge, Mass.
12. *Chiaroscuro*, p. 60.
13. *Letters of Sir Walter Raleigh*, Vol. II, p. 333.

14. John to Will Rothenstein. See *Men and Memories*, Vol. II, p. 9.

15. C.D. 14.

16. One of his subjects, for instance, was 'A Rabbi Studying', from a drawing by Rembrandt. C.D. 73.

17. Lord David Cecil, *52 Drawings*, p. 12.

18. To Will Rothenstein, 9 March 1902.

19. To Will Rothenstein, undated.

20. In his preliminary synopsis for an autobiography, 1923.

21. One impression, at least, is dated 1902. C.D. 47.

22. Unpublished diaries of Arthur Symons.

23. Ethel Nettleship to Sir Caspar John, 27 June 1951.

24. Unpublished diary of L. A. G. Strong, in the possession of Mr B. L. Reid, biographer of John Quinn.

25. *Men and Memories*, Vol. II, p. 4.

26. 'I Speak for Myself', B.B.C. recording. Far Eastern Service, 10 September 1949.

27. ibid.

28. Walter Pater, *The Renaissance*.

29. *Finishing Touches*, p. 26.

30. The painting was bought by Charles Rutherston and now hangs in the Manchester Art Gallery.

31. *Modern English Painters*, Vol. I, p. 179. The picture is in the Manchester City Art Gallery.

32. Called simply 'Esther'. C.D. 1903.

33. Tate Gallery, London, 3171.

34. Reproduced in *Augustus John*, British Painters series (1962) by John Rothenstein. Plate No. 8. Owned by the Pitman family.

35. *Journal of the Gypsy Lore Society*, Vol. XLIX, 3rd Series, parts 1–2.

36. 'Miss McNeil', Manchester City Art Gallery.

37. Now in the Manchester City Art Gallery.

38. *Augustus John* by Malcolm Easton (1970), p. 43.

39. *Bohemia in London* by Arthur Ransome (1907) 2nd edn., 1912, p. 89. See also *Augustus John* by Malcolm Easton (1970).

40. *The Burlington Magazine*, No. 475, October 1942, p. 237.

41. Gwen John, Retrospective Exhibition Catalogue (Arts Council, 1968). Introduction by Mary Taubman.

42. In an undated letter to Mrs Hugh Hammersley.

43. Dorelia to John Rothenstein (19 January 1951). See *Modern English Painters* (1962 edn), 'Sickert to Grant', p. 187.

44. 'Dorelia by lamplight, at Toulouse' (in the collection of Romilly John); 'The Student' (City of Manchester Art Gallery); and 'Dorelia in a Black Dress' (Tate Gallery, 5910).

45. Dorelia's actual words, spoken to the author, while describing this time.
46. Dorelia to the author, 3 July 1969.
47. 19 January 1926.

CHAPTER 4: MEN MUST PLAY AND WOMEN WEEP

1. John to Ottoline Morrell, 30 November 1908.
2. See *Imperfect Encounter* by Mary Lago (1972), p. 207.
3. *Men and Memories*, Vol. 2, p. 166.
4. *Athenaeum*, 19 November 1904, p. 700.
5. In an undated letter to the Rani.
6. Letter to the author, 23 November 1968.
7. Undated letter from Ida to the Rani.
8. In an undated letter to Mrs Sampson.
9. Extract from an undated letter from Ida to Augustus.
10. John to Ulick O'Connor. See *Spectator*, 10 November 1961.
11. *The Letters of Wyndham Lewis* edited by W. K. Rose, p. 39, where this letter is wrongly guessed as *ca*. 1908.
12. John to Alick Schepeler, undated (1907).
13. Now in the National Portrait Gallery, London, No. 4119.
14. *The Evening Standard and St James's Gazette*, 19 June 1908.
15. Letter (undated, *ca*. autumn 1906) to Alick Schepeler.
16. Undated letter to Alick Schepeler.
17. *Chiaroscuro*, p. 68.
18. Undated letter to Alick Schepeler.
19. *Chiaroscuro*, p. 26.
20. *Horizon*, Vol. V, No. 26, February 1942, p. 125.
21. Anne Stuart Lewis, his mother. See *The Letters of Wyndham Lewis*, p. 12.
22. Letter from Ida to Mrs Sampson.
23. Letter from Ida to Alice Rothenstein.
24. Undated letter to Alick Schepeler.
25. *The Letters of Wyndham Lewis*, p. 31.
26. Dorelia John to the author, July 1969.
27. To Alick Schepeler.
28. Undated letter to Alick Schepeler.
29. Letter from Ida John to the Rani, December 1906.
30. *Finishing Touches*, p. 45.
31. Letter from Augustus to the Rani, March 1907.
32. *Finishing Touches*, p. 46.
33. Letter from Augustus to Mrs Sampson, March 1907.
34. *The Letters of Wyndham Lewis*, p. 36.

35. See *Men and Memories*, Vol. II, p. 90.
36. Letter from Augustus to William Rothenstein, 20 March 1907.
37. Letter from Augustus to the Rani, March 1907.
38. *The Letters of Wyndham Lewis*, p. 36.
39. Information from 'Augustus John', an unpublished typescript by Alan Moorehead, whose source was Henry Lamb.
40. Unpublished diaries of Arthur Symons: 'Gwen and Doulia' (*sic*).

CHAPTER 5: BUFFETED BY FATE

1. John to Alice Rothenstein.
2. John to Chaloner Dowdall.
3. John to Will Rothenstein.
4. Delacroix to Félix Guillemardet, 1 December 1823.
5. John to Will Rothenstein, April 1907.
6. John to Alick Schepeler from Equihen.
7. *Horizon*, Vol. IV, No. 22, October 1941, p. 289.
8. W. B. Yeats to John Quinn, 4 October 1907.
9. John to Henry Lamb, 21 August 1907.
10. John to Henry Lamb.
11. John to Henry Lamb, 25 June 1907.
12. Letter (undated, but probably September 1907) from Dorelia to Augustus.
13. ibid.
14. *Chiaroscuro*, p. 69.
15. *Ottoline: The Early Memoirs of Lady Ottoline Morrell* edited by Robert Gathorne-Hardy, p. 141.
16. *Ottoline*, p. 157.
17. ibid.
18. ibid., p. 158.
19. Augustus to Ottoline Morrell, 10 March 1909.
20. *Ottoline*, p. 159.
21. *Ottoline*, p. 163.
22. Augustus to Dorelia.
23. John to Wyndham Lewis, 28 June 1908.
24. John to Ottoline Morrell, 7 July 1908.
25. John to Ottoline Morrell, 11 November 1908.
26. Letter to the author, 25 November 1968.
27. John to Lamb, September 1908.
28. ibid.
29. From 'The Wanderers' by Arthur Symons. *Amoris Victima*, 1897.
30. See *Augustus John* by Malcolm Easton (1970).

31. *Edward Marsh* by Christopher Hassall (1959), pp. 145, 148.
32. *Letters from Edward Thomas to Gordon Bottomley* edited and introduced by R. George Thomas (1968), p. 144.
33. John's contributions to the J.G.L.S. are: *New Series*, Vol. 2, 'Wandering Sinte' (frontispiece), pp. 197–9; *Russian Gypsy Songs*, Vol. 3, pp. 251–3; *French Romani Vocabulary*, Vol. 4, pp. 217–35; *Russian Gypsies at Marseilles and Milan*, Vol. 5, pp. 135–8; *The Songs of Fabian de Castro*, pp. 204–18; *O Bovedantuna*, 'Calderari Gypsies from the Caucasus' (frontispiece). *Third Series*, Vol. 7, 'Portrait of Dr. Sampson' (opp. p. 97); Vol. 17, 'Self-Portrait' (frontispiece), p. 136; *Le Château de Lourmarin*, Vol. 23, pp. 120–22; *Portrait of a Russian Gypsy*, Vol. 27, pp. 155–6; *Keyserling on Hungarian Gypsy Music*, Vol. 36, pp. 81–2; *Miss Jo Jones's Frontispiece*, Vol. 39, 'Les Saintes Maries de la Mer, with Sainte Sara, l'Egyptienne, and a Child' (opp. p. 3), pp. 3–4, *Dora E. Yates*.
34. John to Ottoline Morrell, 8 April 1909.
35. Ottoline's daughter.
36. John to Ottoline Morrell, 9 July 1909.
37. John to Ottoline Morrell, 22 July 1909.
38. 'Augustus John – the pattern of the painter's career', B.B.C. Radio 3 (15 April 1954).
39. *Jane Ellen Harrison: A Portrait from Letters*, pp. 129–30.
40. Jane Harrison to D. S. MacColl, 15 August 1909.
41. John to Jessie G. Stewart, October 1957.
42. *Chiaroscuro*, pp. 64–5.
43. John to Ottoline Morrell, 22 July 1909.
44. *Ottoline*, pp. 181–2.
45. Chaloner Dowdall to Vere Egerton Cotton, 6 November 1945.
46. ibid.
47. Augustus to Dorelia.
48. *Chiaroscuro*, p. 154.
49. *My Gypsy Days* by Dora E. Yates, p. 71.
50. John to the Rani.
51. *Daily Dispatch*, 4 October 1909.
52. *Scotsman*, September 1909.
53. Albert Fleming in a letter to Dowdall, 16 December 1911. Liverpool Public Library.
54. See *Augustus John* by Malcolm Easton, p. 52.
55. *The Fool of the World* (1906) by Arthur Symons, p. 69.
56. Arthur Symons to Rhoda Bowser, 6 May 1900. See *Arthur Symons: A Critical Biography* by Roger Lhombreaud, p. 175.
57. Symons to Quinn, 5 April 1915.

58. See *Agnes Tobin: Letters, Translations, Poems. With some account of her life*. Grabhorn Press for John Howell. San Francisco 1958, p. xii.
59. Quinn to Joseph Conrad, 12 April 1916.
60. By Alice B. Saarinen, *The Proud Possessors* (1959), p. 206.
61. Quinn to Josephine Huneker, 10 April 1909 and 14 July 1909.
62. Quinn to John, 31 January 1910.
63. B. L. Reid, p. 73.
64. B. L. Reid, p. 76.
65. B. L. Reid, p. 77.
66. *Horizon*, Vol. IV, No. 20, August 1941, p. 125. This description and comment were omitted from *Chiaroscuro* twelve years later.
67. This letter is not in the Quinn Collection at the New York Public Library, but belongs to the author.
68. John to Quinn, 18 December 1909.
69. From, in fact, Lord Grimthorpe's villa at Ravello.
70. *Chiaroscuro*, pp. 104–5.
71. Interview with Marie Mauron, September 1971.
72. John to Dorelia.
73. John to Ottoline Morrell, 11 February 1910.
74. John to Dorelia.
75. *Horizon*, Vol. VI, No. 36, December 1942, p. 422.
76. Helen Maitland to Henry Lamb, 23 February 1910.
77. Dorelia to Ottoline Morrell, February 1910.
78. *The Seventh Child* by Romilly John, p. 8.
79. John to Scott Macfie, 2 May 1910.
80. John to Arthur Symons.
81. John to Scott Macfie.
82. *Ottoline*, p. 199.
83. *Ottoline*, p. 200.
84. John to Chaloner Dowdall.
85. *Horizon*, Vol. VI, No. 32, August 1942, pp. 135–8.
86. *Contemporary Portraits: Third Series*.
87. *Chiaroscuro*, p. 128.
88. *Extraordinary People* by Hesketh Pearson, p. 212. Also private information.
89. The Gertz papers are in the Library of Congress, Washington, D.C.
90. *Frank Harris* (1931) by Elmer Gertz and A. I. Tobin, a dentist.
91. John to Quinn, 25 May 1910.
92. To Quinn, 25 August 1910.
93. John to Quinn.

94. John to Ottoline Morrell.
95. John to Quinn, 25 May 1910.

CHAPTER 6: REVOLUTION 1910

1. In her lecture 'Mr Bennett and Mrs Brown' delivered on 18 May 1924 at Cambridge.
2. *The Times*, 7 November 1910, p. 12.
3. *Morning Post*, 1 November 1910, p. 3.
4. *Morning Post*, 16 November 1910, p. 3.
5. In a letter dated March 1909 to Florence Beerbohm. David Cecil Transcripts, Merton College, Oxford.
6. 22 May 1909.
7. *Outline* by Paul Nash, p. 7.
8. *Paint and Prejudice* by C. R. W. Nevinson, p. 189.
9. *The Saturday Review*, 7 December 1907, pp. 694–5.
10. *Magazine of Fine Arts*, May–August 1906.
11. 'Augustus John – the pattern of the painter's career' by David Piper, B.B.C. Radio 3 (15 April 1954).
12. See 'Mark Gertler. A Survey' by John Woodeson, 1971.
13. 'The Academy in Totalitaria', *Art News Annual*, 1967.
14. *Burlington Magazine*, Vol. XV, No. 73, April 1909, p. 17.
15. *Modern English Painters* by John Rothenstein (rev. edn 1962), Vol. I, 'Sickert to Grant', p. 207.
16. 'Augustus John – the pattern of the painter's career', B.B.C. Radio 3 (15 April 1954).
17. *The Saturday Review*, 10 December 1910, p. 747.
18. *Pall Mall Gazette*, 11 December 1910.
19. *The Queen*, 10 December 1910.
20. *Daily Graphic*, 10 December 1910.
21. *Burlington Magazine*, February 1910, p. 267.
22. The Tate Gallery (T. 656).
23. *Vogue*, 11 January 1928, 'The Paintings of Evan Walters'; 7 March, 'The Unknown Artist'; 18 April, 'The Woman Artist'; 27 June, 'Paris and the Painter'; 25 July, 'Three English Artists'; 22 August, 'Some Contemporary French Painters'; 3 September, 'Five Modern Artists'; 31 October, 'Interior Decoration'. The series was originally intended to comprise twelve articles but, even with the encouragement of T. W. Earp, Augustus could not get beyond eight.
24. *Since I was Twenty-five* (1927) by Frank Rutter, pp. 191–2.
25. Roger Fry to Will Rothenstein, 28 March 1911. *Letters of Roger Fry* edited by Denys Sutton, Vol. I, p. 344.
26. 27 July 1920. See *Letters of Roger Fry*, Vol. II, p. 486.

27. See *Imperfect Encounter*, pp. 10–13.

28. The Library, King's College, Cambridge.

29. 'J. Dickson Innes', an unpublished essay by Augustus John in the possession of Mr William Gaunt.

30. Information from Mr Charles Hampton, to whom I am indebted for many facts concerning Innes's career.

31. 'Fragment of an Autobiography' by Augustus John, *Horizon*, Vol. XI, No. 64, April 1945, p. 25.

32. *James Dickson Innes* by John Fothergill, 1946.

33. 'Reminiscences of Fellow Students' by Randolph Schwabe, *The Burlington Magazine*, January 1943, p. 6.

34. *Modern English Painters*, Vol. II, 'Innes to Moore', p. 25.

35. Augustus John to John Quinn, 10 February 1911. This letter was in answer to one of Quinn's agreeing to buy some Innes watercolours.

36. Rough draft for his Introduction to the Innes exhibition of 1923 at the Chenil Gallery.

37. *Horizon*, Vol. XV, No. 64, April 1945, p. 255.

38. William Gaunt holograph.

39. 'The Late J. D. Innes. A Short Appreciation' by Augustus John A.R.A.

40. For a Derwent Lees 'John' see 'The Round Tree' at the Aberdeen Art Gallery, which may be compared with John's own 'Gipsy in the Sandpit' at the same gallery.

41. John to Dorelia, from the Hotel Corneille. Probably January 1911.

42. John to Quinn, 5 January 1911.

43. John to Quinn, 11 January 1911.

44. *Bricks and Flowers* by Katherine Everett, p. 232.

45. ibid., pp. 232–3.

46. 15 June 1911. 'It's an excellent place for the boys and I think we are pretty lucky to have got it. The towns near by are perfectly awful, being horrible conglomerations of red brick hutches.'

47. *Bricks and Flowers*, p. 232.

48. John to Quinn, 16 August 1911.

49. John to Dorelia, July 1911.

50. Henry Lamb to Lytton Strachey, 18 October 1911.

CHAPTER 7: BEFORE THE DELUGE

1. *The Seventh Child*, p. 21.

2. Gilbert Spencer to the author, 3 November 1968.

3. *The Seventh Child*, p. 25.

4. ibid., p. 109.

5. ibid., pp. 116–18.

6. *A Life of One's Own*, pp. 241–2.

7. *The Seventh Child*, p. 134.

8. ibid. p. 58.

9. Tate Gallery, 3730.

10. Aberdeen Art Gallery.

11. Collection Robert Byng.

12. Pittsburgh Art Gallery.

13. This composition, bought in advance by Quinn, 'after undergoing continual alterations became gradually unrecognizable and finally disappeared altogether.' *Horizon*, December, Vol. VI, No. 36, 1942, p. 430.

14. Detroit Art Gallery. 'So that's what became of "the Mumpers",' John wrote to Homer St. Gaudens. 'They will feel more than ever out of place in that hot bed of Ford's.' The picture had been bought at the Quinn sale of 10 February 1927 by René Gimpel. See his *Journal d'un Collectionneur*, p. 327.

15. Bequeathed by Hugo Pitman to the Tate Gallery. See *Two Flamboyant Fathers* by Nicolette Devas, pp. 103–7.

16. *The Seventh Child*, p. 54.

17. Oliver St John Gogarty. See *It Isn't This Time of Year at All!*, p. 152.

18. John to Alick Schepeler undated.

19. Michaela Pooley to the author 1969.

20. *Chiaroscuro*, p. 103.

21. The source for this is Quinn's diary – John having told him. In John's published account he relates that 'my caller, though uninvited, entered the house and with great good-nature made herself at home.'

22. *Horizon*, February, Vol. V, No. 26, 1942, p. 127.

23. *Marriage and Genius* by John Stewart Collis (Cassell 1963), pp. 117–18.

24. ibid., p. 64.

25. *Chiaroscuro*, p. 116.

26. *Marriage with Genius* by Frida Strindberg (Jonathan Cape 1937), p. 20.

27. John Quinn to Jacob Epstein 7 August 1915. Quinn Collection. New York Public Library.

28. Quinn's unpublished diary page 16.

29. *Horizon*, August, Vol. VI, No. 32, 1942, p. 131.

30. ibid., loc. cit.

31. *The Man from New York* by B. L. Reid, p. 105.

32. John to Ottoline Morrell, 27 September 1911. University of Texas.
33. John to Dorelia, undated.
34. Quinn to James Gibbons Huneker, 15 November 1911.
35. John to Ottoline Morrell, 27 September 1911.
36. Quinn to Huneker, 15 November 1911.
37. Quinn to Conrad, 17 November 1912.
38. *Chiaroscuro*, p. 122.
39. *Horizon*, August, Vol. VI, No. 32, 1942, p. 133.
40. John to Quinn, 23 May 1910.
41. On 27 September 1911.
42. *The Seventh Child*, p. 38.
43. *A Life of One's Own*, p. 147.
44. Romilly John to the author, 9 December 1972.
45. In a letter to the author, January 1969.
46. *The Seventh Child*, p. 62.
47. 'A Name to Live Up to' by Tom Pocock. *Evening Standard*, 5 June 1967.
48. B.B.C. interview, 16 November 1962.
49. Vivien White to the author, 1971.
50. John to Ottoline Morrell, 28 February 1912.
51. John to Quinn, 9 May 1912.
52. John to Ottoline Morrell, 10 March 1912.
53. John to Quinn, 9 May 1912.
54. John to Quinn, 8 May 1913.
55. *It Isn't This Time of Year at All!*, p. 151.
56. 'To Augustus John' by Oliver St John Gogarty. *Collected Poems*, pp. 27–30.
57. *Horizon*, October, Vol. IV, No. 22, 1941, p. 289.
58. *It Isn't This Time of Year at All!*, pp. 150, 151.
59. *As I Was Going Down Sackville Street*, p. 246.
60. *Oliver St John Gogarty* by Ulick O'Connor, p. 149. See also 'Blue Eyes and Yellow Beard' by Ulick O'Connor, *Spectator*, 10 November 1961.
61. *As I Was Going Down Sackville Street*, p. 247.
62. *It Isn't This Time of Year at All!*, pp. 153–4.
63. *Horizon*, October, Vol. IV, No. 22, 1941, p. 286.
64. *Two Flamboyant Fathers*, p. 21. There is a reproduction of this portrait facing page 32.
65. *Horizon*, October, Vol. IV, No. 22, 1941, p. 286.
66. In *Two Flamboyant Fathers*, p. 28.
67. ibid. p. 25.
68. *Horizon*, October, Vol. IV, No. 22, 1941, p. 287.

69. John to Quinn, 6 August 1912.
70. *Chiaroscuro*, p. 93.
71. John to Quinn, 11 October 1911. It is an impression of Holbrooke quite different from Beatrice Dunsany's description of 'a pathetic, good-natured deaf child' who played the piano beautifully. See *Lord Dunsany*: a biography by Mark Amory, pp. 104–6.
72. John to Mrs Nettleship, 8 January 1913.
73. Epstein to Quinn, 11 January 1913.
74. John to Dorelia, undated. Written from Hôtel du Nord, Cours Belsance, Marseilles.
75. John to John Hope-Johnstone, undated.
76. John to Ottoline Morrell, July 1914.
77. In a letter to his brother James Strachey.
78. John to Hope-Johnstone, 1916.
79. *Horizon*, August, Vol. VIII, No. 44, 1943, p. 140.
80. See *Lord Dunsany*: a biography by Mark Amory, pp. 73–4.
81. John to Hope-Johnstone, 20 February 1914.
82. John to Quinn, 19 February 1914.
83. Interview with the author, 1969. See also 'Dame Laura Knight' by Margaret Laing. *Evening Standard*, 5 November 1968, p. 12.
84. Dame Laura Knight to the author. She recalled that they were living in three cottages knocked into one, which made a room thirty feet in length.
85. *Horizon*, April, Vol. XI, No. 64, 1945, p. 258. In *Chiaroscuro*, p. 205, 'our excitement' has been changed to 'the general excitement'.

CHAPTER 8: HOW HE GOT ON

1. John to Dorelia, October 1914.
2. John to Quinn, 12 October 1914.
3. John to Quinn, 13 August 1915.
4. John to Ottoline Morrell, 1 January 1915.
5. John to Quinn, 15 February 1915.
6. Undated, but October 1915. Written from the Railway Hotel, Galway.
7. John to Quinn, 15 November 1915.
8. John to Shaw, 18 December 1915, from Mallord Street. British Museum, Add. 50539.
9. John to Quinn, 10 October 1914.
10. John to Quinn, 12 October 1914.
11. John to Dorelia, undated.
12. Albert Rutherston to William Rothenstein, 8 December 1916.

13. *The Times*, 3 March 1920.
14. John to Quinn, 19 January 1916.
15. John to Ottoline Morrell, undated.
16. *The Years That Are Past* by Frances Lloyd George, p. 84.
17. *Lloyd George. A Diary* by Frances Stevenson. Edited by A. J. P. Taylor, 12 March 1916, pp. 83, 103–4.
18. It is now in the Aberdeen Art Gallery.
19. Quinn to Kuno Meyer, 10 May 1916.
20. See *Later Days* by W. H. Davies, pp. 177–84.
21. Berg Collection. New York Public Library.
22. John to Dorelia, undated, from Coole Park.
23. *Me and Nu: Childhood at Coole* by Anne Gregory, p. 47.
24. Lady Gregory to W. B. Yeats, undated.
25. *Days with Bernard Shaw* by S. Winsten, p. 164.
26. *Bernard Shaw and Mrs Patrick Campbell: Their Correspondence* edited by Alan Dent, p. 175.
27. John to Dorelia, undated.
28. *Chiaroscuro*, pp. 96–9.
29. John to Quinn, 15 November 1915.
30. Shaw to John, 6 August 1915.
31. John to Shaw, 31 October 1916.
32. Shaw to John, 6 August 1915. From the Hydro, Torquay.
33. Dorelia to Lytton Strachey, 16 March 1915.
34. Lytton Strachey to Carrington, 8 March 1917. 'At first she [Vivien] completely ignored me. She then would say nothing but "Oh no!" whenever I addressed her. But eventually she gave me a chocolate – "Man! Have a chockle." – which I consider a triumph.'
35. *Vivien John*. Malaysia: its People and its Jungle. Upper Grosvenor Galleries, 19 January–6 February 1971.
36. See *Two Flamboyant Fathers*, pp. 36–49.
37. John to Dorelia, 7 January 1918.
38. John to Quinn, 13 August 1915.
39. According to Ezra Pound, this verse sprang from 'the Castalian fount of the Chenil'. In a letter to Wyndham Lewis (13 January 1918) Pound noted: '(Authorship unrecognised, I first heard it in 1909). It is emphatically NOT my own, I believe it to have come from an elder generation'.
40. Dorelia to Lytton Strachey, 13 September 1916.
41. Dorelia to Lytton Strachey, 10 May 1916.
42. John to Quinn, 26 January 1914. See also John's Foreword to *Peter Warlock, A Memoir of Philip Heseltine* by Cecil Gray, pp. 11–12.

43. John to Evan Morgan (Lord Tredegar), undated.
44. See *Finishing Touches*, pp. 84–5.
45. 'To the Eiffel Tower Restaurant', *Sublunary* pp. 93–5.
46. *The Life of Dylan Thomas* by Constantine FitzGibbon (Sphere Books 1968, p. 163).
47. ibid., loc. cit.
48. *High Relief* by Charles Wheeler, p. 31.
49. Letter from Dorothy Brett to the author, 7 August 1968.
50. See *Carrington. Letters and Extracts from her Diaries*, pp. 74–5, where this letter is incorrectly dated 25 July 1917.
51. And repeated on 29 July at the Lyric Theatre. It had been organized in conjunction with the Ladies Auxiliaries Committee of the Young Men's Christian Association. See the Enthoven Theatre Collection at the Victoria and Albert Museum.
52. See Appendix Four.
53. Epstein to Quinn, 12 August 1914.
54. Epstein to Quinn, 4 September 1914.
55. Epstein to Quinn, 20 July 1917.
56. See, for example, the *Sunday Herald*, 10 June 1917.
57. *Chiaroscuro*, p. 125.
58. *Leaves from My Life* (1927) by Sir Herbert A. Barker, pp. 263–5.
59. The phrase is Dr Malcolm Easton's. See *The Art of Augustus John* (Secker and Warburg 1974).
60. *The Times*, 27 November 1917.
61. *Great Morning* by Osbert Sitwell (St Martin's Library edn, p. 248).
62. In the *Burlington Magazine*, April 1916. See also his article for February 1916 on the New English Art Club.
63. John to Evan Morgan, December 1914.
64. December 1914.
65. John's letters to Grant Richards are in the University of Illinois Library, Urbana.
66. John to Campbell Dodgson, 11 September 1917. Imperial War Museum, London.
67. Arthur Symons to Quinn, 22 November 1917.
68. Lytton Strachey to Clive Bell, 4 December 1917.
69. William Orpen to William Rothenstein, 23 February 1918.
70. John to Tonks, 21 February 1918. The library, the University of Texas at Austin.
71. John to Lady Cynthia Asquith, 5 October 1917.
72. John to Alick Schepeler, 2 February 1918.
73. John to Evan Morgan, 27 October (1915).
74. John to Dorelia, undated.

75. John to Dorelia, undated.
76. *The Letters of Katherine Mansfield* edited by John Middleton Murry (1928), p. 77. John is not identified by name in this published version of the letter.
77. From the Dorothy Brett papers, Dept of English, University of Cincinnati, Ohio.
78. John to Quinn, 13 December 1918.
79. John to Evan Morgan, 1 March 1918.
80. John to Arthur Symons, 22 February 1918.
81. *Blasting and Bombardiering. An Autobiography 1914–26*, London 1937, p. 198.
82. John to Dorelia, 3 February 1918.
83. 'Lord Beaverbrook Entertains' was intended to occupy pages 79–81 of *Finishing Touches* but, for reasons of libel, was dropped at proof stage and the chapter 'Gwendolen John' was substituted. This was done by Daniel George, of Jonathan Cape, after John's death.
84. John to Gogarty, 24 July 1918. At the time of writing this correspondence is being bought by Bucknell University.
85. John to Cynthia Asquith (April) 1918.
86. *The Times*, 4 January 1919. 'War Story in Pictures – Canadian Exhibition at the Royal Academy'.
87. John to Cynthia Asquith, 24 July (1919).
88. Now in the Imperial War Museum, London. Oil on canvas, 93½ × 57 inches.
89. *To-day We will Only Gossip* by Beatrice Lady Glenavy, p. 111.
90. In a letter to Cynthia Asquith.
91. Lady Asquith, *Diaries, 1915–18*, p. 471.
92. John to Frances Stevenson, 13 February 1919.
93. John to Cynthia Asquith.
94. *Horizon*, December, Vol. VIII, No. 48, 1943, p. 406.
95. John to Cynthia Asquith, 1 February 1919.
96. John to Cynthia Asquith.
97. John to Cynthia Asquith, 17 September 1919.
98. John to Gwen John, September 1919.
99. John to Ottoline Morrell, 14 March 1920.
100. John to Eric Sutton, 6 April 1920. Written from the hospital, 12 Beaumont Street, London W.1.
101. John to Cynthia Asquith, April 1920.

CHAPTER 9: ARTIST OF THE PORTRAITS

1. In Aldous Huxley's *Point Counter Point*, for example, where he appears as John Bidlake, at forty-seven 'at the height of his

powers and reputation as a painter; handsome, huge, exuberant, careless; a great laugher, a great worker, a great eater, drinker, and taker of virginities'. Professor Grover Smith, editor of *Letters of Aldous Huxley*, writes (22 February 1970) that 'it is said that John was indeed the prototype of the artist John Bidlake in *Point Counter Point*. Aldous nowhere wrote that this was the case; but he was extremely cautious and tactful where his literary models were concerned'.

John is said to be the prototype of characters in several novels – the artist in Margery Allingham's *Death of a Ghost*; Struthers in D. H. Lawrence's *Aaron's Rod*; Tenby Jones, the 'lion of Chelsea', in Henry Williamson's *The Golden Virgin* and *The Innocent Moon*; the sculptor Owen in Aleister Crowley's *The Diary of a Drug Fiend* (Crowley noted this in his own copy of the novel); the musician Albert Sanger in Margaret Kennedy's *The Constant Nymph* (though in part this may be based on Henry Lamb), Gulley Jimson in Joyce Cary's *The Horse's Mouth*, though popularly supposed to be based on Stanley Spencer, may also contain some aspects of John – in particular the urge to paint large murals. Cary and John knew each other a little in Paris, when Cary was studying art there. Cary mentions John in his letters and diary of 1909–10; and in the autumn of 1956, writing to Ruari Maclean, he suggested John might do illustrations for the Rainbird edition of *The Horse's Mouth*. Nothing came of this, though John greatly admired the novel.

Of Somerset Maugham's *The Moon and Sixpence* John Quinn wrote (9 September 1919): 'The description of the artist, red beard and all, and his words and manner and the first part of the book up to the time he leaves France, is obviously based upon a superficial study of Augustus John. The second part of the book, the Tahiti part, is obviously based upon the life of Gauguin.'

2. See 'Cat's Whiskers'. Philip Oakes talks to Kathleen Hale, *Sunday Times*, 19 March 1972.
3. Christopher Wood to his mother, September 1925.
4. John to Ottoline Morrell, 29 September 1911.
5. *The Seventh Child*, pp. 165–6.
6. ibid., p. 167.
7. *Musical Chairs* by Cecil Gray, p. 228.
8. *The Seventh Child*, p. 167.
9. Lucy Norton to the author (undated).
10. Montgomery Hyde to the author, 17 November 1969.

11. Poppet Pol to the author, 27 February 1970.
12. *Musical Chairs*, pp. 228–9. Another description of this incident is given in Adrian Daintrey's autobiography *I Must Say*, p. 126.
13. *The Seventh Child*, p. 168.
14. John to Quinn, 20 April 1917.
15. John to Dorelia undated.
16. John to William Rothenstein, 29 September 1921.
17. *The Seventh Child*, p. 169.
18. John's essay on Firbank was written for Ifan Kyrle Fletcher's *Ronald Firbank*. See pp. 113–15. 'In his life as in his books he left out the dull bits and concentrated on the irrelevant.'
19. See John's tribute to A. R. Orage in the *New English Weekly*, 15 November 1934.
20. T. E. Lawrence to William Rothenstein, 25 April 1925.
21. *D'Annunzio* by Philippe Jullian, p. 182.
22. *Horizon*, December, Vol. VIII, No. 48, 1943, p. 413.
23. Of the two versions of this picture, one was bought by Lord Alington and is now in the collection of his daughter, the Hon. Mrs George Marten. The other, which is misdated April 1918, was acquired in 1934 by the Art Gallery of Ontario from Sir Evan Charteris, through Lord Duveen, for £1,500. In a letter (26 February 1934) to the gallery, Duveen wrote: 'I consider it to be an outstanding masterpiece of our time. It is no exaggeration to say that this will live forever, which is true of very few pictures of modern times. You have bought a masterpiece for practically nothing ... Such painting of the head, for instance, I have never seen surpassed by any artist, and you can safely place it for comparison alongside the greatest Velasquez, Giorgione or even Titian! That is what I think about this picture.'
24. *The Life of Ian Fleming*, by John Pearson, p. 15.
25. Chiquita to the author (undated).
26. Chiquita to the author (undated).
27. Mrs Val Fleming to Seymour Leslie, 16 May 1923.
28. John to Reine and Hugo Pitman (undated).
29. John to Viva King (undated).
30. *Since Fifty, Men and Memories*, 1922–38, p. 19.
31. John to William Rothenstein, 6 May 1929.
32. The picture (73½ × 65 inches) now belongs to the Tate Gallery (4043) which also owns a charcoal study (4448).
33. 'Sitting for Augustus John' by Mme Suggia. *Weekly Dispatch*, 8 April 1928.
34. *Modern Painting in England*, p. 58.
35. *Horizon*, December, Vol. VII, No. 36, 1942, p. 424.

36. See *My Chat with Thomas Hardy* by Cyril Clemens (T. Werner Laurie 1944), Introduction by Carl J. Weber. See also, for a strange corollary to this portrait, *The Times Literary Supplement*, 16 June 1972, p. 688. The picture was presented by H. T. Riches (for £3,000) to the Fitzwilliam Museum, Cambridge, after J. M. Barrie had refused Sydney Cockerell's petition to present it ('I don't think they ought to ask me to do these things'. See *Seven Ages* by Basil Dean, pp. 212–13). According to Florence Hardy, Hardy himself said that he would rather have the painting bought for the Fitzwilliam 'than receive the Nobel Prize – and he meant it'. See *Friends of a Lifetime: Letters to Sydney Carlyle Cockerell* edited by Viola Meynell, p. 310. The Fitzwilliam also has a drawing of Hardy by John.

37. John to Hardy, 20 November 1923. Thomas Hardy Memorial Collection, Dorset County Museum, Dorchester.

38. *Chiaroscuro*, pp. 148–9.

39. *Montagu Norman*, by Andrew Boyle, pp. 218–20. See also p. 252.

40. *Horizon*, August, Vol. X, No. 56, 1944, pp. 132–3.

41. ibid., p. 132.

42. Lord D'Abernon Papers. British Museum 48932.

43. ibid., 48936.

44. Lord Leverhulme to A. Wilson Barrett, editor of *Colour* Ltd. Blumenfeld Papers. Beaverbrook Library.

45. *Daily Express*, 15 October 1920. See also the editions of 8 and 9 October. Also *The Literary Digest*, 27 November 1920, and *American Art News*, 13 November 1920.

46. *Chiaroscuro*, pp. 150–51. See also *Horizon*, August, Vol. X, No. 56, 1944, pp. 134–5.

47. ibid.

48. *Sunday Dispatch*, 28 September 1930. See also *News-Chronicle*, 29 September 1930; *Daily Mail*, 29 September 1930, and *The Scotsman*, 30 September 1930.

49. *Chiaroscuro*, p. 147. See also *Horizon*, August, Vol. X, No. 56, 1944, p. 131.

50. *Tallulah, My Autobiography*, by Tallulah Bankhead, p. 156.

51. ibid., p. 154.

52. See *Miss Tallulah Bankhead* by Lee Israel, p. 127. Also Brendan Gill's *Tallulah* in which a letter and photo of John are reproduced on page 130, and a drawing on page 131. After Tallulah Bankhead's death, both her John pictures were sold at the Parke-Barnet Galleries, New York. Her own portrait, appraised at $15,000 was sold for $19,500 and is now in the National Gallery in Washington D.C. The portrait of Gerald du Maurier, appraised

between $9,000 and $12,000, fetched only $5,000 and is now in the collection of Gerald du Maurier's daughter, Miss Jeanne du Maurier.

53. T. E. Lawrence to John, 14 April 1930.
54. 'Face to Face', B.B.C. Television interview, 15 May 1960.
55. John to Maud Cazalet, 3 March 1939.
56. John to Maud Cazalet, 23 September 1959.
57. Letter from A. Penn, the Queen's private secretary, to John, 1 November 1939. Clarence House.
58. John to H.M. the Queen, 20 January 1940.
59. *The Times*, 31 March 1920. 'Mr Augustus John and the Royal Academy.'
60. *Horizon*, August, Vol. X, No. 56, 1944, p. 146.
61. John to Sean O'Casey (undated, winter 1928/9).
62. John to Laura Knight, 9 April 1938.
63. John to Philip Connard, 18 January 1944.
64. See *Daily Graphic*, 14 June 1924.
65. *The Christian Science Monitor*, Boston, 17 December 1923. *The Statesman*, Calcutta, 12 October 1924.
66. See, for example, *Colour*, November–December 1923, and January 1924.
67. *Daily Express*, 19 July 1924. 'Culture in Music' by Eugene Goossens.
68. *Economist*, 15 March 1924, p. 592.
69. *The Manchester Guardian Weekly*, 3 October 1924.
70. John to Mitchell Kennerley, 22 November 1926. New York Public Library.
71. John to J. B. Manson, 2 July 1927.
72. John to J. B. Manson, 4 July 1927.
73. John to Wyndham Lewis, 9 December 1927.
74. John to Dorelia (undated).
75. Poppet Pol to the author, March 1970.
76. ibid.
77. John to Mitchell Kennerley, 22 November 1926.
78. John to Mitchell Kennerley, 22 November 1922.
79. John to Viva Booth, 14 May 1922.
80. John to Dorelia, 13 May 1922.
81. *Horizon*, January, Vol. VII, No. 37, 1943, p. 60. Cf. *Chiaroscuro*, p. 181.
82. John to Dorelia, 20 May 1922.
83. John to Dorelia, 13 June 1922.
84. *Horizon*, January, Vol. VII, No. 37, 1943, pp. 63–4.
85. John to Ottoline Morrell, 1 February 1922.

86. John to Dorelia (undated, July 1924).
87. *My Life and Times*, Octave 6, pp. 39–40, and *Oliver St John Gogarty* by Ulick O'Connor, p. 212. But for an amended version of this story see *Lord Dunsany: A Biography* by Mark Amory.
88. John to Dorelia (undated, March 1925).
89. *Horizon*, August, Vol. X, No. 56, 1944, p. 129.
90. *An Ambassador of Peace*. Lord D'Abernon's Diary. Vol. III (January 1924–October 1926), p. 15.
91. ibid., p. 16.
92. John to Dorelia undated (March 1925).
93. Lord D'Abernon, op. cit., p. 152.
94. *Horizon*, April, Vol. XI, No. 64, 1945, p. 242.
95. *The Seventh Child*, p. 218.
96. *Chiaroscuro*, p. 190.
97. *Horizon*, April, Vol. XI, No. 64, 1945, p. 244.
98. ibid., p. 244.
99. John to Oliver St John Gogarty, 22 May 1925. The two girls, Cleves and Pita, were the daughters of Countess Stead.
100. John to Dorelia, undated.
101. For a list of John's works shown at this exhibition, see *The Story of the Armory Show*, by Milton W. Brown, pp. 253–5.
102. *The Man from New York*, by B. L. Reid, p. 152.
103. *Horizon*, August, Vol. X, No. 56, 1944, p. 141.
104. *Chiaroscuro*, p. 160.
105. *Augustus John*, by Conger Goodyear, p. 29 (privately printed).
106. John to Dorelia (undated).
107. Goodyear, op. cit., p. 29.
108. John to Dorelia (undated).
109. *Horizon*, August, Vol. X, No. 56, 1944, pp. 141–2.
110. See, for example, his letter of 16 February 1923 to Homer Saint-Gaudens (American Archives of Art). Most of the articles written about him show little evidence of his co-operation – see *New York Times Magazine* (24 June 1923) 'A Much-Talked of Painter'.
111. *Horizon*, December, Vol. XII, No. 72, 1945, p. 418.
112. *Art News* (New York), 16 June 1923, p. 1, p. 4.
113. ibid., p. 4.
114. Introduction by E. J. Rousuck to 'Augustus John', Scott and Fowles catalogue, 21 March–12 April 1949: 'an electric event which produced not only a new group of paintings, but countless anecdotes, legends, friendships that enriched the great saga of John's career.'
115. Homer Saint-Gaudens to Martin Birnbaum, 23 June 1924. American Archives of Art.

116. Now in the National Gallery, Washington, D.C.
117. John to Mitchell Kennerley (undated).
118. John to Christabel Aberconway, 29 September 1928. This correspondence is in the British Museum. See also the correspondence with Nina Hamnett at the University of Texas.
119. *Horizon*, December, Vol. XII, No. 72, 1945, pp. 419–20.

CHAPTER 10: THE WAY THEY LIVED THEN

1. *Two Flamboyant Fathers*, p. 65.
2. John to Christabel Aberconway. British Museum Add. 52556.
3. *The Glass of Fashion*, p. 156.
4. For a full analysis of this studio, which was designed by Christopher Nicholson, see *Architectural Review*, February 1935, Vol. LXXVII, pp. 65–8.
5. *The Glass of Fashion*, p. 158.
6. *Two Flamboyant Fathers*, p. 66.
7. *I Must Say*, p. 75.
8. Dorelia to Lytton Strachey, 4 December 1918.
9. Henry Lamb's letters to Carrington are in the University of Texas Library, Austin, Texas.
10. Lamb to Carrington (undated).
11. Diana Mosley to the author, 5 January 1970.
12. *Musical Chairs*, by Cecil Gray, p. 278.
13. *Hugh Walpole*. A Biography by Rupert Hart-Davis, p. 272. John's portrait of Walpole is reproduced opposite this page, and a chalk drawing as frontispiece.
14. John to Christabel Aberconway, 3 November 1928. See also *A Wiser Woman*: A Book of Memories by Christabel Aberconway.
15. John to Ottoline Morrell (undated).
16. John to Ottoline Morrell (undated).
17. John to Ottoline Morrell (undated).
18. John to Ottoline Morrell, 20 July 1932.
19. John to Tallulah Bankhead, 12 May 1930.
20. T. E. Lawrence to G. W. M. Dunn, 9 November 1932. *The Letters of T. E. Lawrence*, edited by David Garnett, p. 752.
21. John to Al Wright, 13 August 1946. *Time* magazine 'Morgue' (8 June 1948).
22. 'Augustus John' by Conger Goodyear, p. 35.
23. John to Viva King (undated).
24. 'Pages from a Diary Written in Nineteen Hundred and Thirty' by William Butler Yeats. The Cuala Press (September 1944).

25. *Horizon*, October, Vol. IV, No. 22, 1941, p. 291. For a variant description see *Chiaroscuro*, p. 101.
26. *Horizon*, October, Vol. IV, No. 22, 1941, p. 291.
27. *It Isn't This Time of Year at All!*, p. 242. The portrait is now in Glasgow Art Gallery and Museum, Scotland.
28. Hope Scott to her mother (undated). ·
29. Hope Scott to the author, 29 November 1968.
30. *Horizon*, December, Vol. XII, No. 72, 1945, p. 428.
31. *Courage. The Story of Sir James Dunn*, pp. 247–8. See also *The Bruce Lockhart Diaries 1915–38*, edited by Kenneth Young, 25 January 1931, p. 149.
32. For Joyce's reaction to these drawings, see *The Art of Augustus John*.
33. *Daily Telegraph*, 1 December 1932.
34. *Daily Telegraph*, 20 December 1932.
35. Vivien White to the author, June 1973.
36. *Horizon*, January, Vol. XIII, No. 73, 1946, pp. 51–2.
37. John to Casati (undated).
38. John to Mavis de Vere Cole (undated; January 1937).
39. *Chiaroscuro*, pp. 264–74.
40. John to Mavis de Vere Cole, 21 February 1937.
41. *The Listener*, 25 May 1938, pp. 1105–7.
42. Sean O'Casey to John, 15 January 1929.
43. *Sean* by Eileen O'Casey, edited with an introduction by J. C. Trewin. Pan edition (1973), p. 77.
44. Shaw to John, 31 October 1929.
45. 'The Boy David: Augustus John and Ernst Stern' by Malcolm Easton, *Apollo*, October 1965, pp. 318–25, to which my narrative owes most of its facts.
46. *Finishing Touches*, p. 89.
47. *Portrait of Barrie*, by Lady Cynthia Asquith, p. 206.
48. John to John Davenport undated.
49. *Chiaroscuro*, p. 257.
50. Marie Mauron to the author, 1969.
51. *The Modern Movement*, p. 67.
52. *The Times*, 21 May 1938.
53. *Horizon*, August, Vol. VIII, No. 44, 1943, p. 136.
54. A. R. Thomson to the author, undated.
55. Cole to John, 17 July 1930.
56. John to Wyndham Lewis, 15 August 1954.
57. John to Dorelia (undated; 1936).
58. See *Beautiful and Beloved* by Roderic Owen with Tristan de Vere Cole, pp. 89–90.

59. John's letters to D. S. MacColl are in the Special Collections Library at the University of Glasgow.

60. See, for example, John's portrait of her, at the Southampton Art Gallery, clasping a tankard of ale.

61. *Two Flamboyant Fathers*, by Nicolette Devas, pp. 269–70.

62. *The Life of Dylan Thomas*, by Constantine FitzGibbon (Sphere Books), p. 191.

63. Caitlin Thomas to the author, 16 September 1968. 'It was merely a question of a brief dutiful performance for him to keep up his reputation as a Casanova ogre,' Mrs Thomas hazarded. '... Not the best introduction to the carnal delights of the marriage bed. I may add that this lofty favour was not reserved for me alone, but one and all of his models, of whatever age and social category, suffered the identical treatment. I hope I have been able to add a drop of at least truthful spice, no doubt unprintable, to enliven your cleaned-up eminently respectable book, plodding in the heavy-going dark (God help you and your public).'

64. *Finishing Touches*, p. 114.

65. 'Aquarius', I.T.V., 3 March 1972.

66. In an interview with the author.

67. John to Vivien John, August 1938.

68. *The Listener*, 5 October 1972, pp. 433–4.

69. Dylan Thomas to Henry Treece, 1 September 1938. *Selected Letters of Dylan Thomas* edited by Constantine FitzGibbon, p. 212.

70. *Finishing Touches*, p. 111.

71. *Museum Piece or The Education of an Iconographer*. In the 1960s James Laver did some preliminary work for a biography of John.

72. John to Amaryllis Fleming, 27 November 1953.

73. Amaryllis Fleming to the author, 25 July 1969.

74. Robin John to the author, 13 January 1969. See also *Horizon*, January, Vol. VII, No. 37, 1943, pp. 64–5: 'Robin displayed also, or rather attempted to conceal, a remarkable talent for drawing; but in the course of his studies lost himself in abstraction, which he pushed finally to the point of invisibility. Thus his later efforts, hung on the walls of his studio, presented no clear image to the physical eye. Refinement carried to such a pitch ceases to amuse. Art, like life, perpetuates itself by contact.'

75. Robin John to the author, 13 January 1969.

76. Henry John to Augustus John, 11 March 1926.

77. *Being Geniuses Together* by Robert McAlmon and Kay Boyle. rev. edn. 1970, p. 26.
78. John to Father D'Arcy (undated).
79. *Chiaroscuro*, p. 212.
80. *Memoirs of an Aesthete*, by Harold Acton, p. 146.
81. *A Little Learning*, by Evelyn Waugh (Chapman and Hall), p. 218.
82. 'The Private Diaries of. Evelyn Waugh' edited by Michael Davie. *Observer*, magazine, 6 May 1973, p. 28.
83. *Chiaroscuro*, p. 213.
84. *Daily Mail*, 24 June 1935.
85. The Rev. Canon K. J. Woolcombe to the author, 24 December 1968.
86. John to Dorelia (undated).
87. In an unrecorded B.B.C. script.
88. The words of this eulogium are given in *My Gypsy Days* by Dora E. Yates, pp. 119–20; also, in a slightly different form, in *The Daily Mirror*, 23 November 1931.
89. *My Gypsy Days*, p. 120.
90. ibid., p. 121.
91. *Chiaroscuro*, pp. 89–90.
92. *The Burlington Magazine*, Vol. lxxxi No. 475 (October 1942), pp. 237–8. Reprinted in *Gwen John*, a retrospective exhibition by the Arts Council, pp. 10–11, and in *Finishing Touches*, pp. 79–81 where, after page proof stage it replaced the potentially libellous 'Lord Beaverbrook Entertains'.

CHAPTER 11: THINGS PAST

1. John to Mrs W. M. Cazalet, September 1939.
2. John to Herbert Barker, 4 February 1938.
3. *Daily Telegraph*, 5 May 1948.
4. *The Listener*, 13 May 1948, p. 794.
5. John to Conger Goodyear, 10 January 1948.
6. John to Conger Goodyear, 8 August 1949.
7. John to T. W. Earp, 6 June 1944.
8. John to Mrs W. M. Cazalet, 10 May 1943.
9. John to Kit Adeane (undated).
10. 'Augustus John', unpublished monograph by Alan Moorehead.
11. *Sunday Times*, 22 July 1973, p. 34.
12. John to Mavis Wheeler (undated).
13. Shaw to John, 26 February 1944. See *Montgomery. A Biography* by Alan Moorehead, pp. 187–90.

14. John to Simon John, 15 April 1944.-
15. John to Simon John, 14 September 1944.
16. John to Mrs W. M. Cazalet, 16 June 1941 and 26 September 1941.
17. *Chips. The Diaries of Sir Henry Channon*, edited by Robert Rhodes James, p. 389.
18. *Grand Man*, by Nancy Cunard, p. 195.
19. John to Mary Keene, 26 January 1948.
20. John to Vivien John (undated).
21. John to Winifred Shute, 21 June 1942.
22. John to Winifred Shute, 18 October 1940.
23. John to Will and Alice Rothenstein, 15 June 1940.
24. John to Evan Morgan, 19 October 1940.
25. *The Burlington Magazine*, December 1940, p. 28.
26. John to Dorelia, 21 May 1942.
27. 'I am thoroughly in sympathy with your determination to remain a commoner in spite of antique conventions. May you win the battle!' John to Anthony Wedgwood Benn, 16 March 1961.
28. John to Sir Herbert Read, 18 January 1953. This letter is in the Collections Division of the University of Victoria, British Columbia. Some of the matters in which they diverged are given in a review Read wrote in *The Burlington Magazine* (December 1940, p. 28) where he criticized John's tendency to idealize his types. 'We must say "idealize" in preference to "romanticize" because one has only to compare such drawings with the superficially similar drawings of Picasso's "blue" period to see that, while Picasso has a particular brand of romanticism (a Baudelairean romanticism), he never palliates the underlying drabness and horror. John's gypsies are too coy, and they share this quality with his religious and allegorical figures ... "Le dessin, c'est la probité de l'art" – Mr John quotes this saying of Ingres' at the head of his catalogue, but it is a maxim with a double edge. In the sense that draughtsmanship is an index to the sensibility and skill of the artist, these drawings are a triumphant vindication; but the maxim might also mean that an artist's drawings betray his limitations – the limitation of his interests no less than the degree of his skill. John is a typical studio artist, and there is little in his work to show that he has lived through one of the most momentous epochs of history. An artist creates his own epoch, it will perhaps be said, his own world of reality; and this is true enough. But surely that world, if it is to com-

pete in interest with the external world, must be inhabited by figures somewhat more substantial than John's appealing sylphs'.

About John's portraits, however, Read admitted 'there is no denying his superb mastery of this form ... the pencil already prepares us for that balance out of psychological insight and formal harmony which his brush secures with such instinctive facility'.

29. Alfred McIntyre of Little, Brown and Company to Jonathan Cape, 27 June 1938. The contract with Little, Brown, dated 26 July 1938, gave John an advance on royalties of five thousand dollars and provided for delivery of the manuscript by 1 January 1940. The Jonathan Cape contract, dated 2 May 1938, allowed John an advance of two thousand pounds. Both advances were payable on the day of publication, and both contracts lapsed in 1940.

30. Jonathan Cape to Alfred McIntyre, 24 January 1940.

31. Jonathan Cape to Alfred McIntyre, 15 August 1940.

32. February, Vol. III, No. 14, 1941, pp. 97–103; April, Vol. III, No. 16, 1941, pp. 242–52; June, Vol. III, No. 18, 1941, pp. 394–402; August, Vol. IV, No. 20, 1941, pp. 121–30; October, Vol. IV, No. 22, 1941, pp. 285–92; February, Vol. V, No. 26, 1942, pp. 125–37; August, Vol. VI, No. 32, 1942, pp. 128–40; December, Vol. VI, No. 36, 1942, pp. 421–35; January, Vol. VII, No. 37, 1943, pp. 59–66; August, Vol. VIII, No. 44, 1943, pp. 136–43; December, Vol. VIII, No. 48, 1943, pp. 405–19; August, Vol. X, No. 56, 1944, 128–46; April, Vol. XI, No. 64, 1945, pp. 242–61; December, Vol. XII, No. 72, 1945, pp. 417–30; January, Vol. XIII, No. 73, 1948, pp. 49–61; October, Vol. XIV, No. 82, 1946, pp. 224–31; June, Vol. XVII, No. 102, 1948, pp. 430–41; April, Vol. XIX, No. 112, 1949, pp. 292–303.

33. John's letters to Cyril Connolly are at the University of Texas, Austin.

34. John to Leonard Russell, 20 January 1947.

35. John to T. W. Earp, 20 March 1947.

36. Introduction by Daniel George to *Finishing Touches*, p. 9.

37. ibid., p. 11.

38. John to Daniel George, 19 October 1950.

39. John to Clare Crossley, 9 May 1952.

40. 'Augustus John' by Sir Desmond MacCarthy, *Sunday Times*, 2 March 1952; 'Memories of a Great Artist' by Sacheverell Sitwell, *The Spectator*, 7 March 1953, p. 302; 'Augustus John's Self-Portrait' by Henry Williamson, *John O' London*, March

1952, pp. 296–7. See also 'Self-Portrait' by Harold Nicolson, *The Observer*, 2 March 1952; 'Augustus John: A Self-Portrait' by Denys Sutton, *Daily Telegraph*, 8 March 1952; *The Times*, 5 March 1952; 'Painting with a Pen' *The Times Literary Supplement*, 21 March 1952. The book was also well received in America where it was published by Pellegrini and Cudahy. See, for example, 'Magic-Lantern Show' by Joseph Wood Krutch, *The Nation*, pp. 277–8.

41. *The Listener*, 20 March 1952, p. 476.
42. Harlech Television, 18 July 1968.
43. 'Sfumato', *The Funny Bone*, by J. Maclaren-Ross, pp. 25–9.
44. John to Daniel George, 11 August 1954.
45. 'The piece called "The Girl with the Flaming Hair" – a young woman picked up in Tottenham Court Road – might very reasonably be allowed a place in Villiers de L'Isle-Adam's "Contes Cruels" ' wrote Anthony Powell in the *Daily Telegraph*, 3 December 1964.
46. 'Frontiers', by Augustus John. *The Delphic Review*, Winter, 1946, p. 6.
47. John to Pamela Grove, 25 February 1945.
48. John to Sylvia Hay, 5 June 1959.
49. Marie Mauron to the author, 1969.
50. *Chiaroscuro*, p. 261. See also *Horizon*, June, Vol. XVII, No. 102, 1948, p. 438.
51. *Chiaroscuro*, p. 262.
52. *Horizon*, June, Vol. XVII, No. 102, 1948, p. 440. In a letter to Matthew Smith (5 December 1946) he wrote: 'I thought the country as good as ever but didn't do anything with it.'
53. William Empson to the author, 6 December 1968.
54. *Chiaroscuro*, p. 264.
55. John to T. W. Earp, 20 March 1947.
56. John to Viva King, 16 December 1959.
57. John to David John, 22 June 1942.
58. *Socialist Leader*, 18 September 1948. See also *The Collected Essays, Journalism and Letters of George Orwell*, Vol. 4, *In Front of Your Nose*, 1945–50 (Penguin edn., pp. 505–6).
59. There were only two issues of *The Delphic Review*, Winter 1949 and Spring 1950. John's article 'Frontiers' occupies pages 6–11 of the first issue.
60. John's letters to Bertrand Russell are part of the Russell Archive at the Mills Memorial Library, McMaster University, Hamilton, Ontario, Canada.
61. John to Russell, 6 February 1961.

62. *The Autobiography of Bertrand Russell*, Vol. III, 1944-67, p. 118. See also p. 146.
63. 'The Great Bohemian', *Time and Tide*, 9 November 1961.
64. Breon O'Casey to the author, 7 September 1969.
65. *Two Flamboyant Fathers*, p. 277.
66. John to Sylvia Hay, 7 September 1956. In the collection of Professor Norman H. Pearson, Yale University, New Haven.
67. John to Cyril Clemens, December 1955.
68. John to Sylvia Hay, 7 January 1959.
69. John to Hope Scott, 3 October 1950.
70. *Time's Thievish Progress*, pp. 24-5.
71. Harlech Television, 18 July 1968.
72. John to Alan Moorehead, 31 March 1952.
73. John to John Davenport, 11 March 1956.
74. John to Joe Hone, 4 February 1956.
75. John to D. S. MacColl (undated).
76. *The Times*, 13 March 1954.
77. John to Hugo Pitman, 27 December 1952.
78. John to Hugo Pitman, 10 November 1954.
79. John to Dorothy Head, 16 November 1954.
80. John to Mrs W. M. Cazalet, 16 June 1941.
81. John to Simon John, 14 September 1944.
82. John to Michael Ayrton, February 1961.
83. John to Sir Caspar John, 7 January 1955.
84. John to Edwin John (undated).
85. *A Personal Record* by Gerald Brenan, p. 356.
86. John to Sir Caspar John, 7 January 1955.
87. John to Clare Crossley, 12 January 1955.
88. John to Sylvia Hay (undated).
89. John to Matthew Smith, 22 December 1948.
90. John to Count William de Belleroche, 5 September 1956.
91. John to Matthew Smith, 5 September 1956.
92. John to Matthew Smith, 24 December 1953. In a letter to Sir Caspar John of about the same date, John wrote: 'I have been much distressed by the death of Dylan Thomas and have managed to write a note about it for a paper called *Adam* in an edition wholly devoted to the Poet.' John's essay, 'The Monogamous Bohemian', appeared in the January 1954 issue of *Adam Literary Magazine*, and was reprinted in E. W. Tedlock's *Dylan Thomas – the legend and the poet* (1960). Another essay by John, originally appearing in the *Sunday Times* (28 September 1958), was reprinted in J. M. Brinnin's *A Casebook on Dylan Thomas* (1960) and in *Finishing Touches*.

93. John to Count William de Belleroche, 21 June 1956.

94. William Gaunt to the author, 16 October 1971.

95. 'Augustus John' by Peter Quennell, *Harper's Bazaar*, February 1952, p. 45. Photographs by Cartier Bresson.

96. Lucy Norton to the author, 1973.

97. John to Matthew Smith, 1 July 1959.

98. B.B.C. Panorama, 4 November 1957.

99. *The Sunday Times*, 18 January 1953.

100. John to Eric Phillips, 9 December 1952.

101. John to Joe Hone, 9 February 1956. It was purchased by a number of subscribers, headed by Hugo Pitman and Lennox Robinson, and unveiled at the Abbey Theatre, Dublin, in November 1955.

102. John to Mary Anna Marten, 31 January 1953.

103. *Time's Thievish Progress* by Sir John Rothenstein, p. 15.

104. John to Joe Hone, 9 February 1956.

105. *Letters of John Cowper Powys to Louis Wilkinson*, 8 December 1955.

106. John to Winifred Shute, November 1959.

107. *The Tenby Observer and County News*, 30 October 1959.

108. John to Tristan de Vere Cole, 5 February 1956.

109. Maurice Collis's diary, 9 September 1953. 'His face in old age was very expressive ... and like an actor's. Affection, intimacy, indignation, sadness flitted across his features. There was emotion of some kind showing all the time ... not intellectual, not kind, not even very intuitive or sympathetic for others but human and greatly experienced in life.'

110. John to Sir Charles Wheeler, 11 April 1960.

111: John to Mrs W. M. Cazalet.

112. John to Daniel George, 28 September 1952.

113. John to Alfred Hayward, 13 June 1952.

114. John to Doris Phillips, 9 December 1952.

115. John to Edwin John, 30 May 1954.

116. *High Relief*, p. 116.

117. John to Edwin John, 1 December 1960.

118. *High Relief*, p. 116.

119. John to Sir Philip Dunn, 11 February 1960.

120. John to Sir Charles Wheeler, 8 March 1960.

121. Now in the Royal Academy Library.

122. John to Sir Charles Wheeler, 4 March 1961.

123. John to Cecil Beaton (undated).

124. David John to Robin John, 20 November 1971.

125. *Dromengro: Man of the Road*, by Sven Berlin, pp. 196–7.

126. 'Last Words from Augustus' by Richard Hughes. *Sunday Telegraph*, 5 November 1961.
127. 'The Great Bohemian', by Anthony Powell. *Time and Tide*, 9 November 1961.
128. 'Last of the great Unbeats' by Osbert Lancaster. *Daily Express*, 1 November 1961.
129. *Daily Telegraph*, 1 November 1961, p. 12.
130. Tooth's Gallery, 15–30 March 1961, 'Paintings and Drawings not previously exhibited'. Christie's, First Studio Sale, 20 July 1962 (115 drawings, 70 paintings) £99,645. Christie's, Second Studio Sale, 21 June 1963 (103 drawings, 62 paintings) £33,405. Both studio sales were held primarily to pay off death duties, John's estate having been valued at approximately £90,000. A considerable number of other works came up for auction at Christie's and Sotheby's in these years. Among the exhibitions were 'Drawings and Murals by Augustus John', Upper Grosvenor Galleries, 1–30 April 1965; and 'Drawings by Augustus John', 2–18 December 1971 at the Lefevre Gallery. The first finely-selected loan exhibition that marked the beginning of a revival in John's work was 'Portraits of the Artist's Family' compiled and edited by Dr Malcolm Easton, 24 October–14 November 1970, The University of Hull, and at the National Museum of Wales, 21 November–13 December 1970.

Acknowledgements

This biography, which was first authorized by Dorelia John, has been made possible by her son and daughters, and by the children of Ida John. From them I received very many letters, photographs and other documents; and much information. Admiral of the Fleet Sir Caspar John and Mr Romilly John, as Dorelia's executors and representatives of the family, have checked my book for facts; but neither of them is responsible for its presentation or opinions. I would like to exonerate and express my thanks to them and to all the family. I also owe much to the generous cooperation of Dr Malcolm Easton (with whom I collaborated on *The Art of Augustus John*) and to Mrs Mary Taubman who is working on the authorized biography of Gwen John.

I must also record my indebtedness to many people who in one way or another have helped me: Sir Robert Abdy, the Late Lady Aberconway, Sir Harold Acton, Mr Reginald A. Addyer-Scott, the late Lady Adeane, Mr Noel Adeney, Mr Hubert Alexander, Mrs Marcia Allentuck, Mr Antony Alpers, Mr Gordon Anderson, Lord Annan, the late Boris Anrep, Lord Antrim, the late Simon Asquith, Mrs M. V. Atkinson, Dr Ronald Ayling, the late Michael and Mrs Ayrton, Mrs Nora Back, Mrs Barbara Bagenal, Mr Raymond Bantock, Dr Wendy Baron, Mr Douglas Bartrum, Miss Diana Batchelor, Mr Howard Batchelor, Mr Ernest Bateman, Mr David Batterham, Mr Adrian Beach, Sir Cecil Beaton, Mr F. N. Beaufort-Palmer, Professor Karl Beckson, Professor Quentin Bell, the late Count William de Belleroche, Miss Miriam J. Benkovitz, Mr Anthony Wedgwood Benn, Mr Villiers Bergne, Mr Sven Berlin, Mrs Martin Birkbeck, Mrs Deirdre Bland, Miss Philippa Bone, Miss E. J. Boyte, Mr Laurence Bradbury, Mr Gerald Brenan, the Hon. Miss Dorothy Brett, Mrs Robin Brook, Mr Humphrey Brooke, Miss Lillian Browse, Mr Thomas B. Brumbaugh, Mr Russell Bryant, Mr Richard Buckle, Mr John M. Bunting, Mr Tom Burns, Miss Lynn Bushell, Mr Arthur Byron, Mr Arthur Calder-Marshall, Mr David Campbell, Mrs Roy Campbell, Mr Richard Carline, Mr Noel Carrington, Miss Juanita Casey, Mrs Thelma Cazalet-Keir, Lord David Cecil, Mr George Charlton, Miss Josephine Cheeseman, Lord Clark, Mrs Deirdre Clarke, Lady Clarke Hall, Mr Cyril Clemens, Mrs Madeline Clifton, Mrs Betty Cobb, Commander Kenneth Cohen, Mr and Mrs Tristan de

Vere Cole, the late Maurice Collis, the late Tony Commerford, Mrs Jane Connard, the late Cyril Connolly, Mrs Thomas F. Conroy, Mrs Hope Consett, Mrs Diana Cooke, Mrs Sally Cooke-Smith, Mr Egerton Cooper, Lord Cottesloe, Mrs Andrea Cowdin, Mr John Craigie, Lord Croft, Mrs Anthony Crossley, Mrs Violet Crowther, Sir Michael Culme-Seymour, Mr Adrian Daintrey, Mr and Mrs Theo Dampney, Father Martin D'Arcy S. J., Mr Rhys Davies, Mr Terence Davis, Mr Guy Deghy, Miss Nicolette Devas, Mr Anthony d'Offay, Mr C. W. K. Donaldson, Mrs James Dowdall, Lord and Lady Drogheda, Mrs Honor Drysdale, Miss Janet Dunbar, Sir Philip and Lady Mary Dunn, Mrs Mary Edwards, Mrs Bettina Ehrlich, Mr Malcolm Elwin, Professor William Empson, Lady Kathleen Epstein, Mrs Rosemary Everett, Mr Dennis Farr, Mrs Margaret Morris Fergusson, Mrs Xan Fielding, Mr and Mrs Harry Fisher, Lady Fisher, Mr Constantine FitzGibbon, Miss Amaryllis Fleming, Mr Richard Fleming, Mr Brinsley Ford, Mr Malcolm Foster, the late Mrs Jeanne Robert Foster, Mrs Jane P. Fothergill, Mr Thomas Fox Pitt, the Rt Hon. John Freeman, Mr Peter Fullar, Dr George Furlong, the late Tony Gandarillas, Mr David Garnett, Mr Jonathan Gathorne-Hardy, Mr William Gaunt, Mr Elmer Gertz, Mr Peter Gibson, Mr Brendan Gill, Mr Douglas Glass, Mr Mark Glazebrook, Senator Oliver D. Gogarty, Mr J. W. Goodison, Lord Adam Gordon, Mrs Constance Graham, Mr Duncan Grant, Mr Robert Graves, Miss Mair Griffiths, Mrs Pamela Grove, Mrs Suzanne Guinness, Mr Peter Gunn, Mr Philip Guy, Mr Allan Gwynne-Jones, Mrs Joan Haig, Miss Kathleen Hale, Mrs Cynthia Hall, Mrs Karin Hall, Mr Robert Halsband, Mrs Doreen Hammersley, Mr Charles Hampton, Mr James Hanley, Mr Peter Harris, the late Sir Basil Liddell Hart, Mrs Maria Harrison, Mr Wilfred Harrison, Mr Duff Hart-Davis, Mr Edward Harvane, the late Ethel Hatch, the late Alfred Hayward, Lady Dorothea Head, Miss Fiore de Henriques, Mrs Vivien Henriques, Mr Norman Hepple, Miss Zoë Hicks, Mr Brian Hill, Mr Bevis Hillier, the late Inez Holden, Mrs Didy Holland-Martin, Mr and Mrs Ensor Holliday, Mr Mark Holloway, Miss Diana Holman-Hunt, Mrs Nicandra Hood, Lieutenant-Colonel W. V. Hope-Johnstone, Mr Felix Hope-Nicholson, Mrs Jean Hornack, Mrs Cecily Hornby, Lady Howard de Walden, the late Irene Huddleston, Mr Derek Hudson, Mr Richard Hughes, Mrs Patricia Huskinson, Mr Ferdinand G. Huth, Mrs St John Hutchinson, Mr Sidney C. Hutchison, Mr Daniel Huws, Mr H. Montgomery Hyde, Professor Samuel Hynes, Mr Derek Jackson, Mr G. Douglas James, Mr Darsie Japp, Mr I. E. Tregarthen Jenkin, Mrs Margaret Jennings, Mrs Betty Jewson, Miss Sandra Jobson, Mrs Betty John, Miss Rebecca John, Miss Sara John, Miss Gwyneth Johnstone, Dr R. Brinley Jones, the late David Jones, Mr J. E. Jones, Miss Josette Jones, Mr O. Jones-Lloyd, Mr E. D. Kamm, Mrs Mary Keene, the late Paul Keiffer, the late Sir Gerald Kelly, Mr John Kelly, Mr Jascha Kessler, Mrs Anita Leslie King, Mrs William King, the late Eve Kirk, the late Dame Laura Knight, Mrs Oscar Kokoschka, Mr Henry R. Labouisse, Mrs Mary M. Lago, Lady Pansy Lamb, Mr George Lambourn, Mr Dan H. Laurence, Mrs Julia Chanler Laurin, Mr James Laver, Professor A. W. Lawrence, Mr Bernard Leach, Miss Kate Lechmere, Mr Cliff Lee, Miss Rosamond Lehmann, Mr Robert Lescher, Mr Seymour Leslie, Mrs Juliette de Baivacli Levy, Mr Paul Levy, Mrs Margaret Lewthwaite, Mr Dwight N. Lindley, the late Countess Lloyd-George, Mr Stanley Loomis, Mrs Violet Lort-Phillips, Mr John Lumley, Miss Moira Lynd, Mr David Machin, Mrs René MacColl, the late Compton Mackenzie, the late Yvonne Macnamara, Mrs Mary Mailes, Mrs Mary Manson, Miss Penny Marcus, Miss Miriam Margolyes, Mrs Brigit Marnier, Mrs Dorothy Marston, the Hon. Mrs Marten, Mr George Matthews, Mrs Muriel Matthews, the late Lady Mayer, the late F. H. Mayor, Mr Alastair McAlpine, Mr Alexander K. McLanahan, the late Frances McLanahan, Mr Ruari McLean, Mr Tony Measham, Gwen Lady Melchett, Mrs Yvonne Meo, Miss Alice Methfessel, Mr Walter Michel, Mr Dillwyn Miles, Miss Mollie Mitchell-Smith, Mrs Curtis Moffat, Mr and Mrs Alan Moorehead, Mrs Peggy Morgan, Mr A. M. Morley, Mr Richard Morphet, Lady Diana Mosley, Lord Moyne, Mr Rodrigo Moyniham, Mr Malcolm Muggeridge, Mr Frank Muir, Dr A. N. L. Munby, Miss Winifred A. Myers, Mrs Ulla Nares, Mr John Nash, Mr Benedict Nicholson, Miss Lucy Norton, Mr Breon O'Casey, Mrs Sean O'Casey, Mr Ulick O'Connor, Mrs S. J. Olivier, Mr Stanley Olson, Miss Iris Origo, Mr Roderic Owen, the late Arnold Palmer, Mrs Ralph Partridge, Miss M. Patch, Mr Michael Orr Paterson, Professor Norman Holmes Pearson, Mr Anthony Penny, Mr Bernard Penrose, Mrs Jesse Petrie, Mr Wogan Philipps, Mrs Eric Phillips, Professor Stuart Piggott, the late Reine Pitman, Miss Phyllis Playter, Mr Tom Pocock, Lady Polwarth, the late Hugh Pooley, the late Michaela Pooley, the late Lord Portal, Mr Reginald Pound, Mr Anthony Powell, Mrs Christopher Powell, Mrs Philippa Pullar, Miss Diana Pullein-Thompson, Mr Peter Quennell, Mr George Rainbird, Mrs Monica Rawlings, Mr Herbert Rees, Mr Dominic Reeve, Professor Ben L. Reid, Sir Paul Reilly, Mr Kenneth Rendall, Mr Peter Rhodes, Mr William Rider-Rider, Mr Vivian Ridler, Mr Ivor Roberts-Jones, Mrs Primrose Roper, Professor Pat Rosenbaum, Mr Anthony Rota, Sir John Rothenstein, the late E. J. Rousuck, Mr Eric Rowan, Dr A. L. Rowse, Mr Hilary Rubinstein, Mrs J. J. Rudder, the late Leonard

Russell, the late Lord Russell, Mr David Rutherston, the late Louise Salaman, Mr Michael Salaman, the late Michel Salaman, Mr Raphael Salaman, Mr Anthony Sampson, Mr Guy Rayne Savage, Mr Arnold T. Schwab, Mrs Randolphe Schwabe, Dr Clifford Scott, Mrs Martin Shaw, Mr Dale Shute, Sir Sacheverell Sitwell, Mr Adrian Slade, Mr Christopher Slade, Mr F. W. Slade, Mrs Lilian M. Slade, Mr Richard H. W. Smart, Professor Grover Smith, Mr W. Roger Smith, Mr Ben Sonnenburg Snr, Mr Robert Speaight, Mr Gilbert Spencer, Mr Stephen Spender, Professor Walter Starkie, Mrs Sally Stephen, Mr James Stern, Miss Julia Strachey, Mrs Jenny Stratford, Mrs Valerie Stewart, Viscount Stuart of Findhorn, Mrs John O. Stubbs, the late Gerald Summers, Mrs Holman Sutcliffe, Mr John Symonds, Professor A. J. P. Taylor, the late Mrs Teltsch, Sir Charles Tennyson, Mrs Dylan Thomas, the late J. F. Thomas, Mr Lately Thomas, Mr W. A. Thomas, Mr A. R. Thomson, Mr Ruthven Todd, the late Dudley Tooth, Mr Felix Topolski, Mrs Theodosia Townshend, Mr Christopher Turton, the late Jean Varda, Mrs Ithiel Vaughan-Poppy, Miss Gillian Vincent, Mrs Igor Vinogradoff, Miss Pauline Vogelpoel, Mr R. V. Walling, Mr G. A. Walters, Mrs Rachel Ward, Mrs Sheilah Wardrop, Mr Nicholas Watkins, the Viscountess Waverly, Mr W. J. Weatherby, Mr James M. Wells, Lady Wharton, the late Sir Charles Wheeler, Sir Mortimer Wheeler, Mr Henry Williamson, Mr John Wilson, Mr Clough Williams-Ellis, Miss Jane With, Mr John Woodeson, Mrs Oliver Wood, Mr J. H. Woods, the Rt. Rev. K. J. Woollcombe, Mr John Worsley, the late Dora E. Yates, Mr Michael Yeats, Mr H. W. Yoxall.

I have also received help from the Allbright-Knox Art Gallery, American Archives of Art, *Apollo Magazine*, Arts Council of Great Britain, Beaverbrook Library, Bodleian Library (Department of Western Manuscripts), British Broadcasting Corporation, the British Museum, Buffalo and Erie County Historical Society, *Burlington Magazine*, the University of California, Jonathan Cape Ltd, the Carnegie Institute, P. and D. Colnaghi and Co., Ltd, Contemporary Art Society, Cornell University Library, Dalhousie University Art Gallery, Dorset Natural History and Archeological Society, Fitzwilliam Museum Cambridge, the University of Glasgow, Gypsy Lore Society, Harlech Television, David Higham Associates Ltd, Historical Manuscripts Commission, the Houghton Library, Cambridge, Mass., the Henry E. Huntington Library, University of Illinois, the Imperial War Museum, Kensington and Chelsea Public Libraries, King's College Cambridge, Kingston Galleries Inc., the Law Society Services Ltd, Liverpool City Libraries, Lloyds Bank Ltd, Martins Bank Trust Company Ltd, McMaster University, Ministère de la

Défense Nationale, Canada, the Morris Library Southern Illinois, National Book League, National Gallery London, National Portrait Gallery London, the Newberry Library, the New York Public Library (Manuscript Division; Berg Collection), New York University Libraries, the Pembrokeshire Countryside Unit, Pembrokeshire Local History Society, Pembrokeshire Record Office, Public Record Office, General Register Office, Musée Rodin, Royal Academy of Arts, Royal College of Surgeons, Slade School of Fine Art, Sterling Memorial Library Yale University, the Strachey Trust, Tate Gallery, Texas University Library, State Library of Victoria, National Library of Wales, National Museum of Wales, University of Wales, Widener Library Cambridge Mass., R. T. P. Williams and Sons, Haverfordwest.

I am grateful to Mr Rex De C. Nan Kivell for permission to quote from the unpublished letters of Christopher Wood; and to Mrs Igor Vinogradoff for allowing me to quote from *Ottoline: The Early Memoirs of Lady Ottoline Morrell* edited by Robert Gathorne-Hardy.

A Winston Churchill Fellowship made it possible for me to go to Europe; and a grant from the Phoenix Trust helped me to complete my researches in America. I record both with gratitude.

Index

Castello Santa Clara, Torremolinos, 708

Catholic Evidence Guild, 666

Catholicism, Roman: Rosina and Leah Smith's dislike of, 17; Gwen John's adoption of, 80; Edith Nettleship's and Henry John's conversion, 665; Augustus's objections to, 668

Caveau des Innocents, 273 n.

Cave of the Golden Calf, 533

Cavendish Hotel, Jermyn Street, 535

Cazalet, Maud, 590, 593, 694, 708

Cazalet, Thelma, 641

Cecil, Lord David: description of Augustus's models, 93; visits to Alderney Manor, 470; Augustus's portrait, 584; introduction to Rainbird's book of Augustus's drawings, 705; address at Augustus's memorial service, 721

Cercle Cupidon, Martigues, 604

Cézanne, Paul, 434, 596–7, 709

Chagall, Marc, admired by Augustus, 440

Chamberlain, Neville, 647, 649

Chamot, Mary, 582

Chanler, 'Sheriff' Bob, 614

Channon, Chips, 682

Charles, R. L., 505 n.

Charlotte Street, 535, 693

Charlotte Street, No. 76: Augustus and McEvoy sharing a studio, 106; Augustus's expulsion from, 122–4

Charlotte Street, No. 101, Mrs Everett's 'Sunday School', 85

Charlton, Randall, 60 n.

Charteris, Sir Evan, 555 n., 573 n.

Château de Missery, Côte d'Or, 617

Château de Polignac, 129 n.

Chatham Street, No. 146, 151

Chelsea Art School: opening, 195; absorption of Augustus's energy, 200; Epstein's visits to, 270; its future, 310; decline, 321; Sheila Ivor-Jones an art instructor, 658; prospectus, 726–7

Chelsea Palace Theatre, Monster Matinée performance, 539–40

Chenil Gallery: Orpen's persuasion of Knewstub to open, 262; exhibition of Augustus's etchings, 262; exhibitions of Augustus's pictures, 311, 332, 419, 431, 453,

511, 526, 544–5; 'Provençal Studies and Other Works', 419; Innes Memorial Exhibition, 456; Augustus's studio, 457, 477; exhibition of Anrep's drawings, 458 n. *See also* New Chenil Gallery

Chesterton, G. K., admiration for Henry John, 670

'Cheyne Buttery', 659

Cheyne Walk, Epstein's studio, 267

Cheyne Walk, No. 77, 659

Cheyne Walk, No. 118, 577

Chiaroscuro: reference to Aunts Lily and Rose, 16 n.; reference to Allen Evans's death, 42; amusing description of Edwin John, 421; reference to Augustus and Gwen sharing rooms in London, 77; reference to Alick Schepeler, 274; acknowledgement of Lady Ottoline Morrell, 337; the comedy of Mrs Strindberg's attempted suicides, 484; description of Shaw, 525; Augustus's record of his Jamaican trip, 640; description of the search for Henry, 672; publication, and a Foyle's Literary Lunch, 685; favourable reviews, 689

Chicago Art Institute, 617

Chicago Evening Post, discovery that Augustus was a new Sargent, 613 n.

Chiquita: arrival at Mallord Street with Hope-Johnstone, 577; a frightful sitter, 578; pregnant by Augustus and refusal of an abortion, 578; life at Alderney, 578–9; birth of Zöe, 579; the row with Mrs Fleming, 579; outings with Zöe, 579; contract to live with Seymour Leslie as his mistress, 580; marriage to Michael Birkbeck, 580

Chirk Castle, 505

Chowne, Mrs, prospective foster parent for one of Augustus's children, 309–10

Church Street, No. 153: 'a house with a big studio', 354; arrival of Augustus and a troop of cronies from Paris, 459; outbreak of fire, 459

Churchill, Winston Spencer, Augustus's portrait, 523 n.

Clausen, George, 137

joining Innes at Nant-Ddu, 489;
infuriated by Trelawney Dayrell
Reed's refinement, 491; the hiring
of a tutor for the children, 491;
deriving more benefit from Hope-
Johnstone than the children, 493;
tiring of Hope-Johnstone, 494;
complaints about the boys' new
School, Dane Court, 495; attraction to Michaela Pooley, 496;
against Caspar making the navy his
career, 497–8; love of babies, 498;
ruling his sons with 'a rod of iron'
and 'not a great deal of sympathy',
498, inhibitions from expressions
of tenderness, 498; Pyramus's
death, 499; preference to visit his
family rather than live with them,
500; friendship with Gogarty,
500–503; portrait of Gogarty,
502–3; addition of Francis Macnamara to his adornment of friends,
503; introduction to Ireland by
Macnamara, 504; arrival at Doolin,
504; impatience to return to
Doolin to paint, 505; return to
Wales with Innes, and the return
of his family to Alderney, 505;
invitation to paint Lady Howard de
Walden, 505; portrait of Ida when
she was pregnant, 505 n.; suggestion of himself as artist-in-residence
at Chirk Castle, 506; his death as a
brilliant symbolist painter, 506;
rising opinion of Lees's work, 506;
admiration of the simple life,
despite complications to his own,
507; prospect of Lord Howard de
Walden becoming a new patron,
507; wild motor rides round Wales
with Holbrooke and Sime, 507; to
France with the intention of
working out of doors, 508; complaints about Innes's behaviour in
Marseilles, 508–9; painting in
Wales and exhibiting at the Goupil
Gallery, 509; painting in tempera,
509; exhibitions at the New
English Art Club, 509, 511, 526;
'Forza e Amore' at the New English
Art Club, 509; Hugh Lane's big
picture, 510; epidemic of long
unfinished pictures, 510; prodigious output, 511; elected President

of the National Portrait Society,
511; commissioning a Dutch
architect to build him a new house
and studio, 511; a fortnight round
Cardiganshire, 512; baptism of his
new studio by a fancy dress party,
512–13; feeling of incarceration
in his new house, 513; rid of his
two Welsh cottages, 513; sketching
with Munnings, 514 n.; beanos at
Lamorna Cove, 514; Cornwall a
most sympathetic county, 515;
Dorelia and one of his models both
pregnant, 515; indifference to the
outbreak of war, 515; drilling for
home defence, 516; fallen victim to
war propaganda, 516; tendency to
claustrophobia, 517; attempt to
persuade Gwen to return to
England for the duration of the
war, 517; visits to Ireland, 518;
plans to execute a big dramatization of Galway, 518; a bearded
spy, 518; sketching in Galway
City, 518; hard at work on his
return to Alderney, 519; painting
commissioned portraits to earn
money, 520; portrait of Admiral
Lord Fisher, 520; portraits of Lloyd
George, 521–2; public admiration
for Lloyd George, 521; Frances
Stevenson's fascination, 522; portraits of Winston Churchill, Ramsay
MacDonald and A. J. Balfour, 523
n.; relish of meeting the famous, 523;
three portraits of George Bernard
Shaw, 524–5; sittings for Shaw's
portraits, 524; Shaw's purchase of
one of the portraits, 525; 'house
without children isn't worth living
in', 527; presiding at the birth of
Vivien, 527; Nicolette Macnamara's adoption of him as a second
father, 527; a race of demi-Johns
at Alderney, ˉ528; Nora Brownsword's pregnancy, 528; sense of
deadness tempting him to rush
into new love-making, 529; extri-
cation from the affair with Nora
Brownsword, 529; Hope-Johnstone's offer of marriage to her,
530; parties at Mallord Street, 531,
550, 565–6; roll-call of women,
531; celebrated in the 'Virgin's

FOR THE BEST IN PAPERBACKS, LOOK FOR THE

In every corner of the world, on every subject under the sun, Penguins represent quality and variety – the very best in publishing today.

For complete information about books available from Penguin and how to order them, write to us at the appropriate address below. Please note that for copyright reasons the selection of books varies from country to country.

In the United Kingdom: For a complete list of books available from Penguin in the U.K., please write to *Dept EP, Penguin Books Ltd, Harmondsworth, Middlesex, UB7 0DA*

In the United States: For a complete list of books available from Penguin in the U.S., please write to *Dept BA, Viking Penguin, 299 Murray Hill Parkway, East Rutherford, New Jersey 07073*

In Canada: For a complete list of books available from Penguin in Canada, please write to *Penguin Books Canada Limited, 2801 John Street, Markham, Ontario L3R 1B4*

In Australia: For a complete list of books available from Penguin in Australia, please write to the *Marketing Department, Penguin Books Australia Ltd, P.O. Box 257, Ringwood, Victoria 3134*

In New Zealand: For a complete list of books available from Penguin in New Zealand, please write to the *Marketing Department, Penguin Books (N.Z.) Ltd, Private Bag, Takapuna, Auckland 9*

In India: For a complete list of books available from Penguin in India, please write to *Penguin Overseas Ltd, 706 Eros Apartments, 56 Nehru Place, New Delhi 110019*

LYTTON STRACHEY:

A BIOGRAPHY

Michael Holroyd

'I am certain that this is one of the great biographies of our time
. . . The last pages read with the inevitability, the sadness and
perhaps the affirmation of a great novel' – C. P. Snow in *Book
Week*

'*Lytton Strachey* makes absorbing reading. This is because it is
written with vivacity and scrupulousness . . . (Michael Holroyd)
has a great novelist's sense of the obstinate mystery of the human
person; he knows that through sheer intensity of perception a
terrible beauty can be born of trivia' – George Steiner in *New
Yorker*

'He brings to life the galaxy of strange men and women . . .
whose amatory gyrations produced one of the most fantastic
tragic comedies that any biographer has had the good fortune to
discover' – Leonard Woolf in the *New Statesman*

'A triumphant success . . . His prose is confident, clear and occa-
sionally perfect. His workmanship is beyond reproach . . . Mr
Holroyd achieves superb moments, genuine literature' – Dennis
Potter in *The Times*

'It is impossible to suppose that this "Life" will ever be super-
seded . . . the best literary biography to appear for many years.
It may well prove revolutionary' – John Rothenstein in *The
New York Times*

PENGUIN LITERARY BIOGRAPHIES